Xanth: The Quest for Magic

Xanth: The Quest for Magic

Piers Anthony

BALLANTINE BOOKS • NEW YORK

A Del Rey® Book
Published by The Ballantine Publishing Group

Introduction copyright © 2002 by Piers Anthony Jacob

The omnibus was originally published by The Ballantine
Publishing Group, a division of Random House, Inc., in
separate volumes under the titles:

A Spell for Chameleon, copyright © 1977 by Piers Anthony Jacob
The Source of Magic, copyright © 1979 by Piers Anthony Jacob
Castle Roogna, copyright © 1979 by Piers Anthony Jacob

www.delreydigital.com

Library of Congress Cataloging-in-Publication Data
is available upon request from the publisher.

ISBN 0-345-45328-X

Manufactured in the United States of America

First Ballantine Books Edition: November 2002

10 9 8 7 6 5 4 3 2 1

Contents

Introduction

None of us saw it coming, though I think Judy-Lynn del Rey hoped for it. But let me, in classic narrative technique, use a flashback to set the scene.

Back in the late 1940s and early 1950s, science fiction and fantasy were the stepsister genres, given little respect. But for those few isolated oddballs who related to it, it was the ultimate universe of escape. I did not much like the dreary mundane world; the realms of fantastic imagination were much better. I avidly tracked several science fiction and fantasy magazines. My favorite was *Space Science Fiction*, edited by Lester del Rey, although it soon folded in one of the periodic boom/bust cycles the genre suffered, diminishing my joy of life. But I remembered the editor, and believed that if I ever succeeded in becoming a writer myself, he was one I could work with.

Well, a decade later I did become a writer, and Lester was there, at *If* magazine with his assistant Judy-Lynn Benjamin. Then Judy-Lynn married Lester and became a book editor, and installed Lester as the fantasy editor at Del Rey Books. They sent me an invitation to submit material there, and I pondered, and decided to write a fantasy novel so I could work with Lester. As it happened, I had saved two weeks so I could catch up on the chore of cleaning up my house and yard, which had gone to cluttered pot. The thought of all that drudgery really turned me on to an alternative: outlining the fantasy novel. So I never did get to the cleanup work, and my premises remained cluttered and messy, but I had a viable fantasy novel notion.

This was *A Spell for Chameleon*, set in the realm of Xanth, where every person had a magic talent of greater or lesser degree, and dragons, griffins, centaurs, and assorted monsters roamed the landscape.

My wife and I were then buying property in central Florida, making ready to move from the city to the backwoods, literally. I like forest and field and wildlife, and wanted my children to have the same sort of exposure to it that I had as a child. It's a sad commentary on today's world that a child can safely walk alone through a forest, but not along a city street. So Xanth became like backwoods Florida, only made magic. The huge live oak trees with their dangling shrouds of Spanish moss became tangle trees with tentacles; the heart-of-pine the locals called lighter knot because it burned so ferociously became reverse wood—dangerous to toy with. The shape of Xanth matched the outline of Florida, with place names as magic puns. There was a railroad cut through the hill near our property, a sudden fifty-foot cleft with tracks at the bottom that astonished my daughters and me when we first came across it. That, somewhat enlarged, became the mile-deep Gap Chasm across Xanth, roughly where Interstate Highway 4 crosses Florida. The train that might run along the tracks became—what else?—a long steaming dragon confined to the canyon.

Lester accepted the novel, though he was afraid it would be taken for juvenile, so I upgraded the language to make it fully adult. As it happened, the children read it anyway. Later, Lester asked for another. I pondered, and realized that I had more to say about the Land of Xanth, so the singleton became a trilogy. That was where we planned to leave it. But a funny thing happened on the way to Xanth's retirement: We started receiving reactions from readers. I had plans for more serious projects, but publishers kept turning them down, so I filled in by writing a couple more Xanth novels. As I had been called an ogre at fan conventions, when at that time I had never even been to one, I decided to make an ogre the hero, and now am known as the ogre. Ogres aren't bad fellows once you understand them. *Ogre, Ogre*, my fifth Xanth novel, broke onto the national bestseller lists. After that, Xanth was impossible to stop. It became a magic trilogy, which is three cubed, and continues to this day.

But as I said, none of us saw it coming, except possibly Judy-Lynn. She believed that fantasy could find a larger market, and she gave it a good try. She was an innovative and determined marketer, and succeeded in putting half a raft of fantasy writers onto the bestseller lists, before her untimely death. I call her a giant, because of what she accomplished—transforming fantasy from a fading flower to a vigorous genre. There is a hint of humor there, because Judy-Lynn was about three-and-a-half feet tall, a literal dwarf. But her spirit was that of a giant, and her imprint on publishing was enormous. I did not set out to do this, but some of my characters came to resemble, in an emotional way, some real people. Thus Lester del Rey was the Good Magician Humfrey, often difficult to deal with but a magician nonetheless; and Judy-Lynn was the Gorgon, whose direct stare could turn folk to stone. Judy-Lynn even sent in suggestions for the Gorgon, like Gorgonzola cheese, which I used, and credited her in an Author's Note. Readers, I told her, would take her for a young fan. She retorted, "I *am* a young fan." And when Humfrey and the Gorgon married in Xanth, I made the date the same as Lester and Judy-Lynn's wedding day. I came to the publisher for

Lester, but it is Judy-Lynn who I really miss. I don't think fantasy or publishing have seen her like since.

The first Xanth novel won the August Derleth Fantasy Award for the best novel of 1977. But when the series got successful, the critics trashed it, claiming that the following novels weren't worth anything. This is what critics do; they seem to hate success. Remember their lie about the ogre. Actually Xanth was never intended as great literature, but as entertainment. Yet there are aspects that should be considered. I have received letters from readers telling me how when times were hard, Xanth was their salvation. They were able to escape to it for a time, forgetting the unpleasantness of their dreary lives—and I don't mean mere boredom. Folk on chemotherapy for cancer wrote, and those who suffered severe abuse. There are times when escape is not mere pleasure, but necessity, and Xanth gave them that. I also received letters from the parents of young readers, thanking me for in effect teaching their children to read. They had not been interested in the kinds of books on school reading lists—you know, expurgated Shakespeare or ponderous classics—but when they tried Xanth, suddenly they discovered that reading could be fun. By the time they caught up with the Xanth novels, their reading had improved from the practice, and their school grades improved too. In some sections of our world, it seems that things are considered valuable only if they are unpleasant. Thus medicine tastes bad, and sports competition injures children, and reading becomes a deadly chore. But I feel that diversion has its place, and entertainment too, and humor; and perhaps the best literature is not what is hardest to read, but what most effectively transports the reader into its realm. On that basis, Xanth competes.

As time passed, I refined elements of Xanth, eliminating real-world units of measurement and embroidering the Adult Conspiracy to Keep Interesting Things from Children, such as exactly how folk signal the stork to deliver a baby. It's really a parody of conventional attitudes about sex. New characters came in, and old ones faded gracefully to the background. There are puns galore, because readers keep sending them in. But the essence of Xanth is unchanged: It remains like a forested Florida, each person has a magic talent, and someone generally has to forge his way into the Good Magician's castle to ask a question. Monsters are not necessarily stupid, and what is obvious is not always true. These first three novels show the way of it. If you like it, you know where to find more of it.

A Spell for Chameleon

Contents

Chapter 1

Xanth

A small lizard perched on a brown stone. Feeling threatened by the approach of human beings along the path, it metamorphosed into a stingray beetle, then into a stench-puffer, then into a fiery salamander.

Bink smiled. These conversions weren't real. It had assumed the forms of obnoxious little monsters, but not their essence. It could not sting, stink, or burn. It was a chameleon, using its magic to mimic creatures of genuine threat.

Yet as it shifted into the form of a basilisk it glared at him with such ferocity that Bink's mirth abated. If its malice could strike him, he would be horribly dead.

Then abruptly a silent moth hawk swooped down from the sky and caught the chameleon in its beak. There was a thin scream of anguish as the lizard convulsed; then it dangled limply as the hawk ascended. The chameleon, despite all its pretensions, was dead. Even while trying to threaten Bink, it had been destroyed by another agency.

This realization continued to percolate through Bink's emotion. The chameleon was harmless—but most of untamed Xanth was not. Was this some twisted omen, a small suggestion of a dire fate awaiting him? Omens were serious business; they always came true, but usually were misinterpreted until too late. Was Bink fated to die brutally—or was some enemy of his?

He had, so far as he knew, no enemies.

The golden sun of Xanth shone through the magic Shield, striking sparkles from the trees. All plants had their enchantments, but no spell could eliminate the need for light, water, and healthy soil. Instead, magic was used to make these necessities of the vegetable kingdom more available, and to protect the plants from destruction, unless they were overpowered by stronger magic or simple bad luck, like the chameleon.

Bink looked at the girl beside him as she stepped through a slanting sunbeam. He was no plant, but he too had needs, and even the most casual inspection of her made him aware of this. Sabrina was absolutely beautiful—and her beauty was completely natural. Other girls managed to enhance their appearance by cosmetics or padding or specialized spells, but beside Sabrina all other females looked somewhat artificial. She was no enemy!

They came to Lookout Rock. This was not a particularly lofty promontory, but its situational magic made it seem more elevated than it was, so that they could look down on a quarter slice of Xanth. This was a land of multicolored vegetation, small pretty lakes, and deceptively quiet fields of flowers, ferns, and crops. Even as Bink watched, one of the lakes expanded slightly, making itself seem cooler and deeper, a better place for a swim.

Bink wondered briefly about this, as he often did. He had an unruly mind, which constantly pestered him with questions for which there were no ready answers. As a child he had driven parents and friends almost to distraction with his "Why is the sun yellow?" "Why do ogres crunch bones?" "Why can't sea monsters cast spells?" and similarly infantile prattle. No wonder he had soon been hustled away to centaur school. Now he had learned to control his mouth, but not his brain, and so he let it run on in silence.

Animate spells he could understand, such as those of the unfortunate chameleon; they facilitated comfort, survival, or image for living creatures. But why should inanimate things have magic? Did a lake care who swam in it? Well, maybe so; a lake was an ecological unit, and the community of living things within it might have a mutual interest in promoting it. Or a freshwater dragon might be responsible, luring in prey. Dragons were the most varied and dangerous life forms of Xanth; species occupied air, earth, and water, and a number breathed fire. One thing they all had in common: good appetite. Pure chance might not bring in enough fresh meat.

But what about Lookout Rock? It was bare, without even lichen, and hardly beautiful. Why should it want company? And if it did, why not make itself more handsome, instead of remaining gray and drab? People did not come here to admire the rock, but to admire the rest of Xanth. Such a spell seemed self-defeating.

Then Bink stubbed his toe on a sharp fragment of stone. He was standing on a cracked-rock terrace, formed generations ago by the breaking up of a pretty-colored boulder and—

There it was! That other boulder, which must have been close to Lookout Rock and of similar size, had been fragmented to make this path and terrace, losing its identity. Lookout Rock had survived. Nobody would break it up, because it would make an ugly path, and its unselfish magic made it useful as it stood. One minor mystery solved.

Still, there were philosophical considerations, his insatiable mind insisted. How could an inanimate thing think or have feelings? What was survival to a rock? A boulder was merely the fragment of a prior layer of rock; why should it have a personal identity if the bedrock didn't? Still, the same question could be asked of a man: he had been formed from the tissues of the plants and animals he consumed, yet he had a separate—

"What did you wish to talk to me about, Bink?" Sabrina inquired demurely.

As if she didn't know. But as his mind formed the necessary words, his mouth balked. He knew what her answer had to be. No one could remain in Xanth after his twenty-fifth birthday unless he demonstrated a magic talent. Bink's own critical birthday was barely a month away. He was no child now. How could she marry a man who was so soon to be exiled?

Why hadn't he thought of that before bringing her out here? He could only embarrass himself! Now he had to say something to her, or suffer further embarrassment, making it awkward for her as well. "I just wanted to see your—your—"

"See my *what?*" she inquired with an arch lift of eyebrow.

He felt the heat starting up his neck. "Your holograph," he blurted. There was much more of her he longed to see, and to touch, but that could come only after marriage. She was that sort of girl, and it was part of her appeal. The girls who had it didn't need to put it on casual display.

Well, not quite true. He thought of Aurora, who certainly had it, yet who—

"Bink, there *is* a way," Sabrina said.

He glanced sidelong at her, then quickly away, confused. She couldn't be suggesting—

"The Good Magician Humfrey," she continued blithely.

"What?" He had been on quite a different track, no credit to his willful mind. "Humfrey knows a hundred spells. Maybe one of them—I'm sure he could find out what your talent is. Then everything would be all right."

Oh. "But he charges a year's service for a single spell," Bink protested. "I have only a month." But that was not quite accurate; if the Magician identified a talent for Bink, then he would not be exiled, and he would have a year available. He was deeply touched by Sabrina's faith in him. She did not say what others said: that he had no magic. She did him the immense courtesy of choosing to believe that his magic merely remained undiscovered.

Perhaps it was that faith that had first attracted him to her. Certainly she was beautiful and intelligent and talented, a prize by any definition. But she could have been much less in all categories and still been his—

"A year is not so long," Sabrina murmured. "I would wait."

Bink stared down at his hands, pondering. His right hand was normal, but he had lost the middle finger of his left hand in a childhood accident. It had not even been the result of inimical magic; he had been playing with a cleaver, holding down a stalk of coilgrass while he chopped, pretending it was the tail of a dragon. After all, a boy could not start to practice too early for the serious side of life. The grass had twitched out of his grip as he swung, and he had grabbed for it, and the cleaver had come down hard on his extended finger.

It had hurt, but the worst of it was that because he was not supposed to play with the cleaver, he had not dared scream or tell of his injury. He had controlled himself with extreme effort and suffered in silence. He had buried the finger, and managed to hide his mutilation by keeping his hand closed for several days. When the truth finally came out, it was too late for a restorative spell; the finger was rotted and could not be reattached. A strong-enough spell could have attached it—but it would have remained a zombie finger.

He had not been punished. His mother, Bianca, believed he had learned his lesson—and he had, he had! Next time he played with a cleaver on the sly he would watch where his fingers were. His father seemed privately pleased that Bink had shown so much courage and tenacity in adversity, even in his wrong-doing. "The lad's got nerve," Roland had said. "Now if only he had magic—"

Bink jerked his eyes away from the hand. That had been fifteen years ago. Suddenly a year seemed short indeed. One year of service—in exchange for a lifetime with Sabrina. It was a bargain.

Yet—suppose he had no magic? Was he to pay a year of his life to verify the certainty of being thrust into the drear realm of the null-talented? Or would it be better to accept exile, preserving the useless hope that he did have a latent talent?

Sabrina, respecting his flurry of contemplation, began her holograph. A haze of blue appeared before her, hanging over the slope. It expanded, thinning at the edges, intensifying in the center, until it was two feet in diameter. It looked like thick smoke, but did not dissipate or drift.

Now she began to hum. She had a good voice—not a great one, but right for her magic. At the sound, the blue cloud quivered and solidified, becoming roughly spherical. Then she changed her pitch, and the outer rim turned yellow. She opened her mouth, singing the word "girl," and the colors assumed the shape of a young lass in a blue dress with yellow frills. The figure was three-dimensional, visible from all sides with differing perspective.

It was a fine talent. Sabrina could sculpt anything—but the images vanished the moment her concentration stopped, and never had any physical substance. So this was, strictly speaking, useless magic. It did not improve her life in any material fashion.

Yet how many talents really did help their people? One person could make a leaf of a tree wither and die as he looked at it. Another could create the odor of sour milk. Another could make insane laughter bubble up from the ground. These were all magic, no question about it—but what use were they? Why should such people qualify as citizens of Xanth while Bink, who was smart, strong, and handsome, was disqualified? Yet that was the absolute rule: no nonmagical person could remain beyond his quarter-century mark.

Sabrina was right: he had to identify his talent. He had never been able to find it on his own, so he should pay the Good Magician's price. Not only would this preserve him from exile—which really might be a fate worse than death, since what was the point in life without magic?—and win him Sabrina, a fate considerably better than death. It would also redeem his battered self-respect. He had no choice.

"Oh!" Sabrina exclaimed, clapping her hands to her pert derriere. The holograph dissolved, the blue-dressed girl distorting grotesquely before she vanished. "I'm on fire!"

Bink stepped toward her, alarmed. But even as he moved, there was loud juvenile laughter. Sabrina whirled furiously. "Numbo, you stop that!" she cried. She was one of those girls who was as appealing in anger as in joy. "It's not funny."

It was, of course, Numbo who had given her a magical hotseat, a fiery pain in the posterior. Talk about a useless talent! Bink, his fists clenched so tightly that his thumb jammed into the stub of his missing finger, strode toward the grinning youth standing behind Lookout Rock. Numbo was fifteen, cocky and annoying; he needed a lesson.

But Bink's foot struck a loose rock, which turned his ankle long enough to cost him his balance. It didn't hurt, but it interrupted his forward progress. His hand swung forward—and his fingers touched an invisible wall.

There was another shout of laughter. Bink hadn't crashed headlong into the wall, thanks to the providential stone under his foot, but evidently someone thought he had.

"You too, Chilk," Sabrina said. That was Chilk's talent: the wall. It was a kind of complement to Sabrina's talent; instead of being visible without substance, it had substance without visibility. It was only six feet square; and, like so many talents, it was strictly temporary—but it was hard as steel in the first few moments.

Bink could dodge around it and run the kid down—but he was sure to get caught several times by that remanifesting wall, and suffer more damage than he could do to the boy. It wasn't worth it. If only he had a talent of his own, such as Numbo's hotseat, he could make the joker sorry regardless of the wall. But he didn't, and Chilk knew it. Everyone knew it. That was Bink's big problem. He was fair game for all the pranksters, because he couldn't strike back—not magically, and it was deemed crass to do it physically. Right now he was quite ready to be crass, however.

"Let's get out of here, Bink," Sabrina said. There was disgust in her voice, nominally directed at the intruders, but Bink suspected part of it applied to him. An impotent kind of rage began building up—one he had felt many times before, and had never gotten used to. He had been balked from proposing to her by the lack of a talent, and he could not stay here, for the same reason. Not here at Lookout Rock or here in Xanth. Because he didn't fit.

They walked back down the path. The jokers, getting no further rise from their prey, went in search of other mischief. The landscape no longer seemed so lovely. Maybe he'd be better off away from here. Maybe he should take off now, not waiting to be officially exiled. If Sabrina really loved him, she'd come with him—even Outside, into Mundania.

No, he knew better than that. Sabrina loved him—but she loved Xanth, too. She had such a sweet shape, such kissable lips, that she could find another man much more easily than she could adjust to the rigors of life among the unmagical. For that matter, he could find another girl more easily than . . . what he faced. So probably, objectively, he'd be better off going alone.

So why didn't his heart agree?

They passed the brown stone where the chameleon had perched, and he shuddered.

"Why don't you ask Justin" Sabrina suggested as they approached the village. It was dusk, closing in faster here than up at Lookout Rock. The village lamps were coming on.

Bink glanced across at the unique tree she indicated. There were many kinds of trees in Xanth, a number of them vital to the economy. Beerbarrel trees were tapped for drink, and oilbarrel trees for fuel, and Bink's own footwear came from a mature shoe tree east of the village. But Justin Tree was something special, a species never sprouted from seed. Its leaves were shaped like flat hands, and its trunk was the hue of tanned human flesh. This was scarcely surprising, since it had once been human.

In an instant that history flashed across Bink's mind—part of the dynamic folklore of Xanth. Twenty years ago there had been one of the greatest of the Evil Magicians: a young man named Trent. He had possessed the power of transformation—the ability to change any living thing into any other living thing, instantly. Not satisfied with his status of Magician, granted in recognition of the awesome strength of his magic, Trent had sought to use his power to preempt the throne of Xanth. His procedure had been simple and most direct: he transformed anyone who opposed him into something that could not oppose him. The worst threats he converted to fish—on dry land, allowing them to flop until they died. The mere nuisances he changed to animals or plants. Thus several intelligent animals owed their status to him; though they were dragons, two-headed wolves, and land-octopi, they retained the intelligence and perspective of their human origins.

Trent was gone now—but his works remained, for there was no other transformer to change them back. Holographs, hotseats, and invisible walls were qualifying talents, but transformation was of a different order. Only once in a generation did such power manifest in an individual, and it seldom manifested twice in the same form. Justin had been one of Magician Trent's annoyances— no one remembered exactly what he had done—so Justin was a tree. No one had the ability to change him back into a man.

Justin's own talent had been voice projection—not the parlor trick that was ventriloquism, or the trivial talent of insane laughter, but genuine comprehensible utterance at a distance without the use of vocal cords. He retained this talent as a tree, and as he had a great deal of time for thought, villagers often came to this tree for advice. Often it was good advice. Justin was no genius, but a tree had greater objectivity about human problems.

It occurred to Bink that Justin might actually be better off as a tree than he had been as a man. He liked people, but it was said that in his human form he had not been handsome. As a tree he was quite stately, and no threat to anyone.

They veered to approach Justin. Suddenly a voice spoke directly in front of them: "Do not approach, friends; ruffians are lurking."

Bink and Sabrina drew up short. "Is that you, Justin?" she asked. "Who is lurking?"

But the tree could not hear as well as it could speak, and did not answer. Wood did not seem to make the best ears.

Bink, angry, took a step toward it. "Justin is public scenery," he muttered. "Nobody has a right to—"

"Please, Bink!" Sabrina urged, pulling back on his arm. "We don't want any trouble."

No, she never wanted any trouble. He would not go so far as to call this a fault in her, but at times it became annoyingly inconvenient. Bink himself never let trouble bar him from a matter of principle. Still, Sabrina was beautiful, and he had caused her trouble enough already tonight. He turned to accompany her away from the tree.

"Hey, no fair!" a voice exclaimed. "They're going away."

"Justin must've tattled," another cried.

"Then let's chop down Justin."

Bink halted again. "They wouldn't!" he said.

"Of course they wouldn't," Sabrina agreed. "Justin is a village monument. Ignore them."

But the voice of the tree came again, a bit misplaced in relation to Bink and Sabrina—evidence of poor concentration. "Friends, please fetch the King quickly. These ruffians have an axe or something, and they've been eating locoberries."

"An axe!" Sabrina exclaimed in sheer horror.

"The King is out of town," Bink muttered. "Anyway, he's senile."

"And he hasn't summoned more than a summer shower in years," Sabrina agreed. "Kids didn't dare make so much mischief when he had his full magic."

"*We* certainly didn't," Bink said. "Remember the hurricane flanked by six tornadoes he summoned to put down the last wiggle spawning? He was a real Storm King then. He—"

There was the ringing sound of metal biting into wood. A scream of sheer agony erupted from the air. Bink and Sabrina jumped.

"That's Justin!" she said. "They're doing it."

"No time for the King anyway," Bink said. He charged toward the tree.

"Bink, you *can't!*" Sabrina cried after him. "You don't have any magic."

So the truth came out, in this moment of crisis. She didn't really believe he had a talent. "I've got muscle, though!" he yelled back. "You go for help."

Justin screamed again as the blade struck a second time. It was an eerie wooden noise. There was laughter—the merry mirth of kids out on a lark, having no care at all what consequences their actions might have. Loco? This was mere insensitivity.

Then Bink was there. And—he was alone. Just when he was in the mood for a good fight. The malicious pranksters had scattered.

He could guess their identities—but he didn't have to. "Jama, Zink, and Potipher," Justin Tree said. "Oooo, my foot!"

Bink squatted to inspect the cut. The white wood-wound was clearly visible in contrast to the shoelike bark of the base of the tree trunk. Driblets of reddish sap were forming, very much like blood. Not too serious for a tree this size, but surely extremely uncomfortable.

"I'll get some compresses for that," Bink said. "There's some coral sponge in the forest near here. Yell if anyone bothers you while I'm gone."

"I will," Justin said. "Hurry." Then, as an afterthought: "You're a great guy, Bink. Much better than some who—uh—"

"Than some who have magic," Bink finished for him. "Thanks for trying to spare my feelings." Justin meant well, but sometimes spoke before he thought. It came from having a wooden brain.

"It isn't fair that louts like Jama are called citizens, while you—"

"Thanks," Bink said gruffly, moving off. He agreed completely, but what was the use talking about it? He watched out for anyone lurking in the bushes, waiting to bother Justin when the tree was unprotected, but saw nobody. They were really gone.

Jama, Zink, and Potipher, he thought darkly—the village troublemakers. Jama's talent was the manifestation of a sword, and that was what had chopped Justin's trunk. Anyone who could imagine that such vandalism was funny—

Bink remembered one of his own bitter experiences with that bunch, not so many years ago. Intoxicated by locoberries, the three had lurked in ambush along one of the paths beyond the village, just looking for mischief. Bink and a friend had walked into that trap, and been backed up against the cloud of poison gas that was Potipher's magic talent, while Zink made mirage-holes near their feet and Jama materialized flying swords for them to duck. Some sport!

Bink's friend had used his magic to escape, animating a golem from a stick of wood that took his place. The golem had resembled him exactly, so that it fooled the pranksters. Bink had known the difference, of course, but he had covered for his friend. Unfortunately, though the golem was immune to poison gas, Bink was not. He had inhaled some of it, and lost consciousness even as help arrived. His friend had brought Bink's mother and father—

Bink had found himself holding his breath again as the poison cloud enveloped him. He saw his mother tugging at his father's arm, pointing Bink's way. Bianca's talent was replay: she could jump time back five seconds in a small area. This was very limited but deviously powerful magic, for it enabled her to correct a just-made mistake. Such as Bink's breath of poison gas.

Then his breath had whooshed out again, making Bianca's magic useless. She could keep replaying the scene indefinitely, but *everything* was replayed, including his breath. But Roland looked, piercingly—and Bink had frozen.

Roland's talent was the stun gaze: one special glance and what he looked at was frozen in place, alive but immobile until released. In this manner Bink had been prevented from breathing the gas a second time, until his rigid body had been carried out.

As the stun abated, he had found himself in his mother's arms. "Oh my baby!' she cried, cradling his head against her bosom. "Did they hurt you?"

Bink came to an abrupt stop by the bed of sponge, his face flushing even now with the keen embarrassment of the memory. Had she had to do that? Certainly she had saved him from an early death—but he had been the laughingstock of the village for an interminable time thereafter. Everywhere he went, kids exclaimed "My baby!" in falsetto, and sniggered. He had his life—at the expense of his pride. Yet he knew he could not blame his parents.

He had blamed Jama and Zink and Potipher. Bink had no magic, but, perhaps for that reason, he was the huskiest boy in the village. He had had to fight as long as he could remember. He was not especially well coordinated, but he had a lot of raw power. He had gone after Jama privately and demonstrated convincingly that the fist was swifter than the magic sword. Then Zink, and finally Potipher; Bink had hurled him into his own gas cloud, forcing him to dissolve it very suddenly. Those three had not sniggered at Bink thereafter; in fact, they tended to avoid him—which was why they had scattered when he charged the tree. Together they could have overcome him, but they had been well conditioned by those separate encounters.

Bink smiled, his embarrassment replaced by grim pleasure. Perhaps his manner of dealing with the situation had been immature, but there had been a lot of satisfaction in it. Down underneath he knew it had been his irritation at his mother that motivated him, displaced to people like Jama—but he did not regret it. He did love his mother, after all.

But in the end his only chance to redeem himself had been to find his own magic talent, a good strong one like that of his father, Roland. So no one would dare to tease him or laugh at him or baby him, ever again. So that pure shame would not drive him from Xanth. And that had never happened. He was known contemptuously as the "Spell-less Wonder."

He stooped to gather several good, strong sponges. These would abate Justin Tree's discomfort, for that was their magic: they absorbed agony and spread a healing comfort. A number of plants and animals—he was not quite sure in which category the sponges fit—had similar properties. The advantage of the sponges was that they were mobile; plucking them would not kill them. They were tough; they had migrated from the water when the corals did, and now thrived on land. Probably their magic healing properties had been developed to facilitate their lives in the new medium. Or maybe before the migration, since coral was cutting stuff.

Talents tended to run in schools, with one overlapping another; thus many variants of each type of magic showed up in the plant and animal kingdoms. But among people, magic varied extremely widely. It seemed that individual personality had more to do with it than heredity, though the strongest magic tended to turn up in particular family lines. As if strength of magic was hereditary, while type of magic was environmental. Yet there were other factors—

Bink could fit a lot of reflection into a passing moment. If reflection were magic, he'd be a Magician. But right now he'd better concentrate on what he was doing, or he'd be in trouble.

Dusk was intensifying. Dismal shapes were rising out of the forest, hovering as if seeking prey. Eyeless and formless, they nevertheless conducted themselves with a disquieting awareness, orienting on Bink—or seeming to. More magic was unexplained than was safely catalogued. A will-o'-the-wisp caught Bink's nervous eye. He started to follow the half-glimpsed light, then abruptly caught himself. The lure of the wisp was sheer mischief. It would lead him into the wilderness and lose him there, prey to the hostile magic of the unknown. One of Bink's childhood friends had followed the wisp and never returned. Warning enough!

Night transformed Xanth. Regions like this one that were innocent by day became horrors as the sun sneaked down. Specters and shades came out, questing for their ghastly satisfactions, and occasionally a zombie ripped free of its grave and marched clumsily about. No sensible person slept outdoors, and every house in the village had repulsion spells against the supernatural. Bink did not dare use the shortcut back to Justin Tree; he would have to go the long way, following the looping but magically protected trails. This was not timidity but necessity.

He ran—not from fear, for there was no real danger on this charmed route, and he knew the paths too well to stray accidentally from them, but in order to reach Justin more swiftly. Justin's flesh was wood, but it hurt every bit as much as normal flesh. How anyone could be so crass as to chop at Justin Tree . . .

Bink passed a field of sea oats, hearing the pleasant swish and gurgle of their oceanic tides. When harvested, they made excellent foamy broth, except that it tended to be rather salty. The bowls could only be filled halfway; otherwise the broth's continuing sea waves slopped over.

He remembered the wild oats he had planted as an adolescent. Sea oats were restless, but their cousins the wild oats were hyperactive. They had fought him savagely, their stems slashing across his wrists as he tried to harvest a ripe ear. He had gotten it, but had been uncomfortably scratched and abraded before getting clear of the patch.

He had planted those few wild seeds in a secret plot behind his house, and watered them every day, the natural way. He had guarded the bad-tempered shoots from all harm, his anticipation growing. What an adventure for a teenaged male! Until his mother, Bianca, had discovered the plot. Alas, she had recognized the species instantly.

There had been a prompt family hassle. "How could you?" Bianca demanded, her face flaming. But Roland had labored to suppress his admiring smile. "Sowing wild oats!" he murmured. "The lad's growing up."

"Now, Roland, you know that—"

"Dear, it isn't as if there's any real harm in it."

"No harm!" she exclaimed indignantly.

"It is a perfectly natural urge for a young man—" But her furious expression had halted Bink's father, who feared nothing in Xanth but was normally a peaceable man. Roland sighed and turned to Bink. "I gather you *do* know what you were doing, son?"

Bink felt excruciatingly defensive. "Well—yes. The nymph of the oats—"

"Bink!" Bianca snapped warningly. He had never seen her so angry before.

Roland held up his hands, making peace. "Dear—why don't you let us work this out, man-to-man? The boy's got a right."

And so Roland had betrayed his own bias; when his man-to-man chat was with Bink, it was with a *boy*.

Without another word, Bianca had stalked out of the house.

Roland turned to Bink, shaking his head in a gesture that was only nominally negative. Roland was a powerful, handsome man, and he had a special way with gestures. "Genuine wild oats, culled thrashing from the stem, sown by the full moon, watered with your own urine?" he inquired frankly, and Bink nodded, his face at half heat. "So that when the plants mature, and the oat nymph manifests, she will be bound to you, the fertilizer figure?"

Bink nodded grimly.

"Son, believe me, I comprehend the attraction; I sowed wild oats myself when I was your age. Got me a nymph, too, with flowing green hair and a body like the great outdoors—but I had forgotten about the special watering, and so she escaped me. I never saw anything so lovely in my life—except your mother, of course."

Roland had sown wild oats? Bink had never imagined such a thing. He remained silent, afraid of what was coming.

"I made the mistake of confessing about the oats to Bianca," Roland continued. "I fear she became somewhat sensitized on the subject, and you caught the brunt. These things happen."

So his mother was jealous of something that had happened in his father's life before he married her. What a pitful of concepts Bink had stumbled into, unwittingly.

Roland's face became serious. "To a young man, inexperienced, the notion of a lovely, nude, captive nymph may be phenomenally tempting," he continued. "All the physical attributes of a real woman, and none of the mental ones. But, son, this is a juvenile dream, like finding a candy tree. The reality really would not be all you anticipated. One quickly becomes surfeited, tired of unlimited candy, and so it also is with—with a mindless female body. A man can not love a nymph. She might as well be air. His ardor rapidly turns to boredom, and to disgust."

Still Bink dared not comment. He would not have become bored, he was sure.

Roland understood him, too well. "Son, what you need is a real live girl," he concluded. "A figure with a personality, who will talk back to you. It is far more challenging to develop a relationship with a complete woman, and often extremely frustrating." He glanced meaningfully at the door through which Bianca had departed. "But in the long run it is also far more rewarding. What you sought in the wild oats was a shortcut—but in life there are no shortcuts." He smiled. "Though if it had been up to me, I'd have let you try the shortcut. No harm in it; no harm at all. But your mother—well, we have a conservative culture here, and the ladies tend to be the most conservative—especially the pretty ones. It's a small village—smaller than it used to be—so everybody knows his neighbor's business. So we are circumscribed. Know what I mean?"

Bink nodded uncertainly. When his father laid down the law, however circumspectly, that was final. "No more oats."

"Your mother—well, she was caught by surprise by your growing up. The oats are out—she's probably rooting them up right this instant—but you still have a lot of good experience ahead of you. Bianca might like to think of you as a little boy forever, but even she can't balk nature. Not for more than five seconds! So she'll simply have to go along with it."

Roland paused, but Bink was silent again, unsure of what his father was leading up to.

"There's a girl due to move here from one of the lesser villages," Roland continued. "Theoretically this is for proper schooling, since we have the best centaur schoolmaster in Xanth. But I suspect the underlying reason is that there simply aren't many eligible boys in her village. I understand she has not yet discovered her magic talent, and she's about your age—" He paused to glance meaningfully at Bink. "I think she could use a handsome, healthy young man to show her around and warn her of local hazards. I understand she is extremely smart and pretty, and soft-spoken—a rare combination."

Then Bink began to understand. A girl—a real girl—for him to get to know. One who would not be prejudiced by his lack of magic. And Bianca would not be able to disapprove, though privately she might dislike the fact of Bink's newly masculine drives. His father had given him a viable option. Suddenly he realized he could do without wild oats.

"Her name is Sabrina," Roland said.

A light ahead brought Bink back to the present. Someone was standing by Justin Tree, holding a magic lamp. "It is all right, Bink," Justin's voice said in the air beside him. "Sabrina brought help, but it wasn't needed. Did you get the sponge?"

"I got it," Bink said.

So his little adventure had been no adventure at all. Just like his life. As Sabrina helped him pack the sponge around Justin's wound, Bink realized that he had decided. He could not go on this way, a nonentity; he would go to see the Good Magician Humfrey and learn what his own magic talent was.

He glanced up. His eyes caught those of Sabrina, glowing by the light of the lamp. She smiled. She was even more lovely now than she had been when he first met her, so many years ago, when they had both been adolescents, and she had always been true to him. There was no question: Bink's father had been correct about the advantages—and frustrations—of a real live girl. Now it was up to Bink to do what he had to do—to become a real live man.

Chapter 2

Centaur

Bink set off on foot, wearing a stuffed knapsack and bearing a good hunting knife and a home-cut staff. His mother had urged him to let them hire a guide for him, but Bink had had to refuse; the "guide" would really be a guard to keep him safe. How would he ever live that down? Yet the wilderness beyond the village had its hazards for the traveler unfamiliar with it; few people hiked it alone. He really would have been better off with a guide.

He could have had transport on a winged steed, but that would have been expensive, and risky in its own fashion. Griffins were often surly creatures. He preferred to make his own way on the secure ground, if only to prove that he could, despite the fancied snickers of the village youths. Jama wasn't snickering much at the moment—he was laboring under the mortification spell the village

Elders had put on him for his attack on Justin Tree—but there were other snickerers.

At least Roland had understood. "One day you'll discover that the opinions of worthless people are worthless," he had murmured to Bink. "You have to do it your own way. I comprehend that, and wish you well—on your own."

Bink had a map, and knew which path led to the castle of the Good Magician Humfrey. Rather, which path *had* led there; the truth was that Humfrey was a crotchety old man who preferred isolation in the wilderness. Periodically he moved his castle, or changed the approaches to it by magical means, so that one never could be sure of finding it. Regardless, Bink intended to track the Magician to his lair.

The first leg of his journey was familiar. He had spent his whole life in the North Village and explored most of its surrounding bypaths. Hardly any dangerous flora or fauna remained in the immediate vicinity, and those that were potential threats were well known.

He stopped to drink at a water hole near a huge needle cactus. As he approached, the plant quivered, making ready to fire on him. "Hold, friend," Bink said commandingly. "I am of the North Village." The cactus, restrained by the pacification formula, withheld its deadly barrage. The key word was "friend"; the thing certainly was not a friend, but it had to obey the geis laid on it. No genuine stranger would know this, so the cactus was an effective guard against intruders. Animals below a certain size it ignored. Since most creatures had to have water sooner or later, this was a convenient compromise. Some areas had been ravaged occasionally by wild griffins and other large beasts, but not the North Village. One experience with an irate needler more than sufficed as a lesson for the animal lucky enough to survive it.

Another hour's swift march brought him to less-familiar territory, by definition less safe. What did the people of this area use to guard their water holes? Unicorns trained to impale strangers? Well, he would find out soon enough.

The rolling hills and small lakes gave way to rougher terrain, and strange plants appeared. Some had tall antennas that swiveled to orient on him from a distance; others emitted subtly attractive crooning noises, but had branches bearing powerful pincers. Bink walked at a safe distance around them, taking no unnecessary risks. Once he thought he spied an animal about the size of a man, but it had eight spiderlike legs. He moved on rapidly and silently.

He saw a number of birds, but these were of little concern. Since they could fly, they had little need for defensive magic against man, so he had no cause to be wary of them—unless he saw any big birds; those might consider him prey. Once he spied the monstrous form of a roc in the distance, and cowered down, letting it wing on without seeing him. So long as the birds were small, he actually preferred their company, for the insects and bugs were at times aggressive.

In fact, a cloud of gnats formed around his head, casting a mass sweat spell that made him even more uncomfortable. Insects had an uncanny ability to discern those with no magic for defense. Maybe they merely used trial and error, getting away with whatever they could. Bink looked about for bug-repellent weeds, but found none. Weeds were never where one wanted them. His temper was getting short as the sweat streamed down his nose and into his eyes and mouth. Then two little sucker-saps swooped in, sucking up the gnats, and he had relief. Yes, he liked little birds!

He made about ten miles in three hours, and was tiring. He was in good condition generally, but was not used to sustained marching with a heavy pack. Every so often he got a twinge from the ankle he had turned at Lookout Rock. Not a bad twinge, for it turned out to be a minor hurt; just enough to keep him cautious.

He sat on a hillock, first making sure it contained no itch ants, though it did have a needle cactus. He approached this very cautiously, uncertain as to whether it had been tamed by the spell. "Friend," he said, and just to make sure he spilled a few drops of water from his canteen onto the soil for its roots to taste. Apparently it was all right; it did not let fly at him. Even wild things often responded to common courtesy and respect.

He broke out the lunch lovingly packed by his mother. He had food for two days—enough to get him to the Magician's castle under ordinary circumstances. Not that things in Xanth were usually ordinary! He hoped to extend that by staying overnight with some friendly farmer. He would need food for the return trip, too, and in any event did not relish the notion of sleeping outdoors. Night brought out special magic, and it could be ugly. He did not want to find himself arguing cases with a ghoul or ogre, since the case would most likely be the proper disposition of his human bones: whether they should be consumed live, while the marrow was fresh and sweet, or crunched after being allowed to age for a week after death. Different predators had different tastes.

He bit into the cressmato sandwich. Something crunched, startling him, but it was not a bone, just a flavorstem. Bianca certainly knew how to make a sandwich. Roland always teased her about that, claiming she had mastered the art under the tutelage of an old sandwitch. Yet is was unfunny to Bink, for it meant he was still dependent on her—until he finished what she had prepared and foraged for himself.

A crumb dropped—and vanished. Bink looked around and spied a chipmouse chewing busily. It had conjured the crumb ten feet, avoiding the risk of close approach. Bink smiled. "I wouldn't hurt you, chip."

Then he heard something: the pounding of hooves. Some big animal was charging, or a mounted man approached. Either could mean trouble. Bink stuffed a chunk of wingcow cheese into his mouth, suffering a brief vision of the cow flying up to graze on the treetops after being relieved of her load of milk. He closed up his pack and shrugged his arms into the straps. He took his long staff in both hands. He might have to fight or run.

The creature came into sight. It was a centaur, the body of a horse with the upper torso of a man. He was naked, in the manner of his kind, with muscular flanks, broad shoulders, and an ornery visage.

Bink held his staff before him, ready for defense but not aggressively so. He had little confidence in his ability to outfight the massive creature, and no hope of outrunning him. But maybe the centaur was not unfriendly, despite appearances—or did not know that Bink had no magic.

The centaur pulled up close. He held his bow ready, an arrow nocked. He looked formidable indeed. Bink had developed a lot of respect for centaurs in school. This was obviously no elder sage, however, but a youthful brute. "You are trespassing," the centaur said. "Move off this range."

"Now wait," Bink said reasonably. "I'm a traveler, following the established path. It's a public right-of-way."

"Move off," the centaur repeated, his bow swinging around menacingly.

Bink was normally a good-natured fellow, but he had a certain ornery streak that manifested in times of stress. This journey was vitally important to him. This was a public path, and he had had his fill of deferring to magical menaces. The centaur was a magical creature, having no existence in the Mundane world beyond Xanth, by all accounts. Thus Bink's aggravation against magic was stirred up again, and he did something foolish.

"Go soak your tail!" he snapped.

The centaur blinked. Now he looked even huskier, his shoulders broader, his chest deeper, and his equine body even more dynamic than before. Obviously he was not accustomed to such language, at least not directed at him, and the experience startled him. In due course, however, he made the requisite mental and emotional adjustments, signaled by an awe-inspiring knotting of oversized muscles. A deep red, almost purple wash of color ascended from the hairy horse base up through the bare stomach and scarred chest, accelerating and brightening as it funneled into the narrower neck and finally dying the head and ugly face explosively. As that inexorable tide of red rage ignited his ears and penetrated to his brain, the centaur acted.

His bow swung about, the nocked arrow drawing back. As it bore on Bink, the arrow let fly.

Naturally, Bink wasn't there. He had had ample opportunity to read the storm signals. As the bow moved, he ducked under. Then he straightened up right under the centaur's nose and brought his staff around in a hard swing. It fetched the creature a smart rap on the shoulder, doing no actual harm. But it had to sting severely.

The centaur emitted a bellow of sheer impassioned rage. He whipped his bow around with his left hand while his right hand dived for the quiver of arrows hanging on his equine shoulder. But now Bink's staff was tangled in his bow.

The creature threw down the bow. The action ripped the staff out of Bink's hands. The centaur made a huge fist. Bink scurried around to the rear as that fist swung at him. But the rear of the centaur was no safer than the front; one leg licked back violently. Through a freak of timing, it missed Bink and clubbed into the trunk of the needle cactus.

The cactus responded with a barrage of flying needles. Even as the hoof struck, Bink threw himself flat on the ground. The needles overshot him and plunked into the handsome posterior of the centaur. Once more Bink had lucked out: he was miraculously untouched by either hoof or needles.

The centaur neighed with truly amazing volume. Those needles *hurt;* each one was two inches long, and barbed, and a hundred of them decorated the glistening surface, tacking the tail to the donkey, as it were. Had the creature been facing the cactus, he could have been blinded or killed as the barbs punctured his face and neck; he was lucky, too, though he hardly seemed to appreciate his fortune at the moment.

Now there were no bounds to the centaur's anger. An unholy contortion of utter rage ravaged his homely face. He did a massive prance, his hindquarters rising and descending in an arc, bringing his front part abruptly adjacent to Bink. Two crushingly powerful arms shot out, and two horny hands closed about Bink's relatively puny neck. Slowly they tightened, with viselike deliberation. Bink, lifted off the ground so that his feet dangled, was helpless. He knew he was about to be strangled; he could not even plead for mercy, for his air and much of his blood were cut off.

"Chester!" a female voice cried.

The centaur stiffened. This did Bink no good.

"Chester, you put that man down this instant!" the voice said peremptorily. "Do you want an interspecies incident?"

"But, Cherie," Chester protested, his color abating several shades. "He's an intruder, and he asked for it."

"He's on the King's path," Cherie said. "Travelers are immune to molestation; you know that. Now let him go!"

The lady centaur hardly seemed to be in a position to enforce her demand, but Chester slowly bowed to her authority. "Can't I just squeeze him a little?" he begged, squeezing a little. Bink's eyeballs almost popped out of their sockets.

"If you do, I'll never run with you again. Down!"

"Aaaww . . ." Reluctantly Chester eased off. Bink slid to the ground, reeling. What a fool he had been to tangle with this brute!

The female centaur caught him as he swayed. "Poor thing!" she exclaimed, cushioning his head against a plush pillow. "Are you all right?"

Bink opened his mouth, gagged, and tried again. It seemed that his crushed throat would never unkink. "Yes," he croaked.

"Who are you? What happened to your hand? Did Chester—"

"No," Bink said hastily. "He didn't bite off my finger. That's a childhood injury. See, it's long since healed over."

She inspected it carefully, running her surprisingly delicate fingers over it. "Yes, I see. Still . . ."

"I—I am Bink of the North Village," he said. He turned his head to face her —and discovered the nature of the pillow he rested against. *Oh no, not again!* he thought. *Will I always be babied by women?* Centaur females were smaller than the males, but still stood somewhat taller than human beings. Their humanoid portions were somewhat better endowed. He jerked his head away from her bare front. It was bad enough being babied by his mother, let alone a lady centaur. "I am traveling south to see the Magician Humfrey."

Cherie nodded. She was a beautiful creature, both as horse and as human, with glossy flanks and a remarkable human forefigure. Her face was attractive, only very slightly long of nose in the equine manner. Her brown human hair trailed all the way down to her saddle region, balancing her similarly flowing tail. "And this ass waylaid you?"

"Well—" Bink looked at Chester, again noting the rippling muscle beneath the deadly glower. What would happen when the filly departed? "It was—it was a misunderstanding."

"I'll bet," Cherie said. But Chester relaxed a trifle. Evidently he did not want to tangle with his girlfriend. Bink could readily appreciate why. If Cherie was not the loveliest and spunkiest centaur of the herd, she was surely close to it.

"I'll just be moving on now," Bink said. He could have done this at the outset, allowing Chester to run him off in a southerly direction. He had been as much to blame for the altercation as the centaur. "Sorry about the problem." He held out his hand to Chester.

Chester showed his teeth, which were more like horse's teeth than human ones. He made a big fist.

"Chester!" Cherie snapped. Then, as the centaur guiltily relaxed his fist: "What happened to your flank?"

The male's complexion darkened again, but not precisely with rage this time. He trotted his damaged posterior around to avoid the inquiring gaze of the female. Bink had almost forgotten about the needles. They must still be hurting —and it would hurt more to yank them all out. What a pain in the tail! A most awkward locale to discuss in mixed company. He almost felt sympathy for the surly creature.

Chester suppressed his assorted reactions and with fine discipline took Bink's hand. "I hope everything comes out all right in the end," Bink said, with a smile that became a bit broader than intended. In fact, he feared it resembled a smirk. And abruptly he knew he shouldn't have chosen those particular words or that particular expression on this particular occasion.

Something homicidal reddened the whites of the centaur's eyes. "Quite all right," he gritted through the grinding of clenched teeth. His hand began to squeeze—but his eyes were not yet so bloodshot as to miss the filly's glare. The fingers relaxed unwillingly. Another close call. Bink could have had his fingerbones pulped in that grip.

"I'll give you a lift," Cherie decided. "Chester, put him on my back."

Chester put his hands under Bink's elbows and hoisted him like a feather. For a moment Bink feared he would be thrown fifty feet . . . but Cherie's fair eye was still on them, and so he landed safely and gently on the lady's back.

"Is that your staff?" she inquired, glancing at the tangled staff and bow. And Chester, without even being directed, lifted the staff and returned it to Bink, who tucked it slantwise between his back and his pack for easy transport.

"Put your arms around my waist, so you won't fall off when I move," Cherie said.

Good advice. Bink was inexperienced at riding, and there was no saddle. Very few honest horses remained in Xanth. Unicorns were very touchy about being mounted, and the winged horses were almost impossible to catch or tame. Once, when Bink was a child, a horsefly had been singed by a dragon, losing its flight feathers, and had had to prostitute itself so far as to give the villagers short rides in exchange for food and protection. The moment it had recovered, it had flown away. That had been Bink's only prior riding experience.

He leaned forward. The staff interfered, preventing him from bending his back sufficiently. He reached back to draw it out—and it fell out of his hands to the ground. There was a snort from Chester that sounded suspiciously like humor. But the centaur picked it up and returned it to him. Bink tucked it under his arm this time, leaned forward again, and hugged Cherie's slender waist, heedless of Chester's renewed glower. Some things were worth the risk—such as getting out of here in a hurry.

"You go to the vet and get those needles out of your—" Cherie began, speaking over her shoulder to the male.

"Right away!" Chester interrupted. He waited for her to start, then turned and cantered off in the direction he had come from, a little awkwardly. Probably each motion inflamed his hindquarters more.

Cherie trotted down the path. "Chester is really a good creature at heart," she said apologetically. "But he does tend to be a bit arrogant, and he gets his tail all knotted up when balked. We've had some trouble with outlaws recently, and—"

"Human outlaws?" Bink asked.

"Yes. Kids from the north, doing mischief magic, gassing our livestock, shooting swords into trees, making dangerous pits seem to appear under our feet, that sort of thing. So naturally Chester assumed—"

"I know the culprits," Bink said. "I had a scrape with them myself. They've been grounded now. If I had known they were coming down here—"

"There just doesn't seem to be much discipline on the range these days," she said. "According to the Covenant, your King is supposed to keep order. But recently—"

"Our King is getting old," Bink explained. "He's losing his power, and there's a lot of trouble cropping up. He used to be a major Magician, a storm brewer."

"We know," she agreed. "When the fireflies infested our oatfields, he generated a storm that rained five days and drowned them all. Of course, it also ruined our crops—but the flies were doing that already. Every day new fires! At least we were able to replant without further molestation. We are not forgetting the help he rendered. So we don't want to make an issue of it—but I don't know how much longer stallions like Chester are going to put up with these annoyances. That's why I wanted to talk with you—maybe when you go home, if you could call things to the attention of the King—"

"I don't think that would work. I'm sure the King wants to keep order; he just doesn't have the power any more."

"Then perhaps it is time for a new King."

"He's getting senile. That means he hasn't got the sense to step down, and won't admit there's any problem."

"Yes, but problems don't go away by being ignored!" She made a delicate feminine snort. "Something has to be done."

"Maybe I can get some advice from Magician Humfrey," Bink said. "It's a serious business, deposing a King; I don't think the Elders would go for it. He did do good work in his prime. And there's really nobody to replace him. You know that only a great Magician can be King."

"Yes, of course. We centaurs are all scholars, you know."

"Sorry, I forgot. Our village school is run by a centaur. I just wasn't thinking of that, in the wilderness."

"Understandable—though I'd call this range, not wilderness. I specialize in humanoid history, and Chester studies horsepower applications. Others are legal scholars, experts in natural sciences, philosophers—" She broke off. "Now hang on. There's a trench up ahead I've got to hurdle."

Bink had been relaxing, but now he leaned forward again and clasped his hands tightly around her waist. She had a sleek, comfortable back, but it was too easy to slide off. However, if she weren't a centaur, he would never have had the nerve to assume such a position!

Cherie picked up speed, galloping down the hill, and the motion made him bounce alarmingly. Peering ahead under her arm, he saw the trench. Trench? It was a gorge, some ten feet across, rushing up at them. Now he was more than alarmed; he was frightened. His hands became sweaty, and he began to slide off the side. Then she leaped with a single mighty spasm of her haunches and sailed up and across.

Bink slipped further. He had a glimpse of the stony bottom of the trench; then they landed. The jolt caused him to slide around even more. His arms scrambled desperately for a more secure hold—and wandered into distinctly awkward territory. Yet if he let go—

Cherie caught him around the waist and set him on the ground. "Easy," she said. "We made it."

Bink blushed. "I—I'm sorry. I started to fall, and just grabbed—"

"I know. I felt your weight shift as I leaped. If you had done it on purpose, I'd have dropped you into the trench." And in that instant she looked uncomfortably like Chester. He believed her: she could drop a man into a trench if she had reason to. Centaurs were tough creatures!

"Maybe I'd better walk now."

"No—there's another trench. They've been opening up recently."

"Well, I could climb down one side and up the other, carefully. It would take longer, but—"

"No—there are nickelpedes at the bottom."

Bink quailed. Nickelpedes were like centipedes, but about five times as large and considerably more deadly. Their myriad legs could cling to vertical rock faces, and their pincers could gouge out disks of flesh an inch across. They inhabited shadowed crevices, not liking direct sunlight. Even dragons hesitated to walk through ditches known to be infested by nickelpedes, and for good reason.

"The cracks have been opening up recently," Cherie continued as she kneeled to permit Bink to mount her again. He picked up his dropped staff and used it to help him climb. "I'm afraid there's big magic brewing somewhere, spreading throughout Xanth, causing discord in animal, vegetable, and mineral. I'll get you across that next trench; then it's beyond centaur territory."

It hadn't occurred to him that there would be such barriers. They didn't show on his map. The trail was supposed to be clear and reasonably safe throughout. But the map had been made years ago, and these cracks in the ground were new, Cherie said. Nothing in Xanth was permanent, and travel was always somewhat risky. He was lucky he had obtained the lady centaur's help.

The landscape changed, as if the trench separated one type of place from another. Before it had been rolling hills and fields; now it was forest. The path became narrower, crowded by huge mock-pine trees, and the forest floor was a red-brown carpet of mock needles. Here and there were patches of light green ferns, which seemed to thrive where weeds could not, and regions of dark green moss. A cold wind gusted through, tousling Cherie's hair and mane, carrying strands back against Bink. It was quiet here, and there was a pleasant piney smell. He felt like dismounting and lying down in a bed of moss, just appreciating this peaceful spot.

"Don't do it," Cherie warned.

Bink jumped. "I didn't know centaurs practiced magic!"

"Magic?" she inquired, and he knew she was frowning.

"You read my mind."

She laughed. "Hardly. We do no magic. But we do know the effect these woods have on humans. It's the peace spell the trees make to protect themselves from getting chopped."

"Nothing wrong in that," Bink said. "I wasn't going to chop them anyway."

"They don't trust in your good intentions. I'll show you." She stepped carefully off the beaten trail, her hooves sinking into the soft pine-needle floor. She threaded her way between several dagger-spoked buckspruce trees, passed a thin snake palm, which didn't even bother to hiss at her, and stopped near a tangle willow. Not too near; everyone knew better than that. "There," she murmured.

Bink looked where her hand pointed. A human skeleton lay on the ground. "Murder?" he asked, shivering.

"No, just sleep. He came to rest here, as you wished to do just now, and never got up the gumption to depart. Complete peace is an insidious thing."

"Yes . . ." he breathed. No violence, no distress—just loss of initiative. Why bother to work and eat when it was so much easier merely to relax? If a person wanted to commit suicide, this would be the ideal manner. But he had reason to live—so far.

"That's part of why I like Chester," Cherie said. "He'll never succumb to anything like this."

That was a certainty. There was no peace in Chester. Cherie herself would never succumb, Bink thought, though she was considerably more gentle. Bink felt the lassitude, despite the sight of the skeleton, but she was evidently able to resist the spell. Maybe the biology of the centaurs differed enough—or maybe she had savagery in her soul that her angelic form and pleasant words masked. Most likely a bit of both. "Let's get out of here."

She laughed. "Don't worry. I'll see you safely through it. But don't come back this way alone. Travel with an enemy, if you can find one; that's best."

"Better than a friend?"

"Friends are peaceful," she explained.

Oh. That did make sense. He'd never relax under a pine tree if he were with someone like Jama; he'd be too afraid of getting a sword in his gut. But what an ironic necessity: to locate an enemy to accompany one to walk through a peaceful forest! "Magic makes strange companions," he murmured.

This peace spell also explained why there was so little other magic here. The plants did not need individual defensive spells; no one was going to attack. Even the tangle tree had seemed quiescent, though he was sure it would make a grab when it had the chance, since that was the way it fed. Interesting how quickly magic faded when the immediate imperative of survival abated. No—there was magic, strong magic; it was the communal magic of the entire forest, with each plant contributing its modicum. If a person could figure out a way to nullify the effect in himself, perhaps with a countercharm, he could live here in absolute safety. That was worth remembering.

They threaded their way back to the path and resumed travel. Bink almost slid off his perch twice, falling asleep, each time awakening with a shock. He would never have made it out of here alone. He was glad to see the pine forest thin, shifting into hardwoods. He felt more alert, more violent, and that was good. Harder wood, harder feelings.

"I wonder who that was back there," Bink mused.

"Oh, I know," Cherie answered. "He was one of the Last Wave, who got lost, wandered in here, and decided to rest. Forever!"

"But the Lastwavers were savage!" Bink said. "They slaughtered indiscriminately."

"All Waves were savage, when they came, with one exception," she said. "We centaurs know; we were here before the First Wave. We had to fight all of you—until the Covenant. You didn't have magic, but you had weapons and numbers and vicious cunning. Many of us died."

"My ancestors were First Wave," Bink said with a certain pride. "We always had magic, and we never fought the centaurs."

"Now don't get aggressive, human, just because I took you out of the peace pines," she cautioned. "You do not have our knowledge of history."

Bink realized that he'd better moderate his tone if he wanted to continue the ride. And he did want to continue; Cherie was pleasant company, and she obviously knew all the local magic, so that she was able to avoid all threats. Last and most, she was giving his tired legs a good rest while bearing him forward rapidly. Already she had taken him a good ten miles. "I'm sorry. It was a matter of family pride."

"Well, that's no bad thing," she said, mollified. She made her way delicately across a wooden trestle over a bubbling brook.

Suddenly Bink was thirsty. "May we stop for a drink?" he asked.

She snorted again, a very horselike sound. "Not here! Anyone who drinks from that water becomes a fish."

"A fish?" Suddenly Bink was twice as glad to have this guide. He surely would have drunk otherwise. Unless she was merely telling him that to tease him, or trying to scare him away from this area. "Why?"

"The river is trying to restock itself. It was cleaned out by the Evil Magician Trent twenty-one years ago."

Bink remained a bit skeptical about inanimate magic, especially of that potency. How could a river desire anything? Still, he remembered how Lookout Rock had saved itself from being broken up. Better to play it safe and assume that some features of the landscape could cast spells.

Meanwhile, the reference to Trent preempted his attention. "The Evil Magician was here? I thought he was a phenomenon of our own village."

"Trent was everywhere," she said. "He wanted us centaurs to support him, and when we balked—because of the Covenant, you know, not to interfere in human business—he showed us his power by changing every fish in this river into a lightning bug. Then he departed. I think he figured that those shocking buggers would force us to change our minds."

"Why didn't he change the fish into a human army, and try to conquer you that way?"

"No good, Bink. They might have had the bodies of men, but their minds would have remained fish. They would have made very wishy-washy soldiers, and even if they had been good soldiers, they would hardly have served the man who had put them under that enchantment. They would have attacked Trent."

"Um, yes. I wasn't thinking. So he transformed them into lightning bugs and got well away from there so they couldn't shock him. So they went for the next best thing."

"Yes. It was a bad time for us. Oh, those bugs were a pain! They pestered us in clouds, scorching us with their little lightning bolts. I've still got scars on my—" She paused, grimacing. "On my tail." It was obviously a euphemism.

"What did you do?" Bink inquired, fascinated, glancing back to see whether he could locate the scars. What he could see seemed flawless.

"Trent was exiled soon after that, and we got Humfrey to abate the spell."

"But the Good Magician isn't a transformer."

"No, but he told us where to find repellent magic to drive off the flies. Denied our electrocooked flesh, the scourge soon died out. Good information is as good as good action, and the Good Magician certainly had the information."

"That's why I'm going to him," Bink agreed. "But he charges a year's service for a spell."

"You're telling us? Three hundred head of centaur—one year each. What a job!"

"All of you had to pay? What did you have to do?"

"We are not permitted to tell," she said diffidently.

Now Bink was doubly curious, but he knew better than to ask again. A centaur's given word was inviolate. But what could Humfrey have needed done that he could not do himself via one of his hundred spells? Or at least by means of his good information? Humfrey was basically a divinator; anything he didn't know, he could find out, and that gave him enormous power. Probably the reason the village Elders had not asked the Good Magician what to do about their senile King was that they knew what he would answer: depose the King and install a new, young, fresh Magician instead. That they obviously weren't ready to do. Even if they could find such a young Magician to serve.

Well, there were many mysteries and many problems in Xanth, and it was hardly given to Bink to know of them all or to solve any. He had learned long ago to bow, however ungraciously, to the inevitable.

They were past the river now, and climbing. The trees were closing in more thickly, their great round roots ridging across the path. No hostile magic threatened; either the centaurs had cleaned out the area, the way the villagers had cleaned out Bink's home region, or Cherie knew this path so well that she avoided spells automatically, without seeming to. Probably some of both.

Life itself, he thought, involved many alternate explanations for perplexing questions, and was generally "some of both." Few things were hard and fast in Xanth.

"What was that history you know that I don't?" Bink inquired, becoming bored by the trail.

"About the Waves of human colonization? We have records of them all. Since the Shield and the Covenant, things have quieted down; the Waves were terrors."

"Not the Firstwavers!" Bink said loyally. "We were peaceful."

"That's what I mean. You are peaceful now, except for a few of your young hoodlums, so you assume your ancestors were peaceful then. But my ancestors found it otherwise. They would have been happier had man never discovered Xanth."

"My teacher was a centaur," Bink said. "He never said anything about—"

"He'd have been fired if he had told you the truth."

Bink felt uneasy. "You're not teasing me, are you? I'm not looking for any trouble. I have a very curious mind, but I've already had more trouble than I care for."

She turned her head around to fix him with a gentle stare. Her torso twisted from the human waist to facilitate the motion. The torque was impressive; her midsection was more limber than that of a human girl, perhaps because it was harder for a centaur to turn her whole body around. But if she had a human lower section to match the upper section, what a creature she would be!

"Your teacher didn't lie to you. A centaur never lies. He merely edited his information, on orders from the King, so as not to force on the impressionable minds of children things their parents did not want them to hear. Education has ever been thus."

"Oh, I wasn't implying any slight on his integrity," Bink said quickly. "I liked him, as a matter of fact; he was the only one who didn't get fed up with all my questions. I learned a lot from him. But I guess I didn't ask about history much. I was more preoccupied with something he couldn't tell me—but at least he did tell me about the Magician Humfrey."

"What is your question for Humfrey, if I may ask?"

What difference did it make? "I have no magic," he confessed. "At least, I seem to have none. All through my childhood I was at a disadvantage because I couldn't use magic to compete. I could run faster than anybody else, but the kid who could levitate still won the race. Stuff like that."

"Centaurs get along perfectly well without magic," she pointed out. "We wouldn't take magic if it were offered."

Bink did not believe that, but did not make an issue of it. "Humans have a different attitude, I guess. When I got older, it got worse. Now I will be exiled if I don't show some magic talent. I'm hoping Magician Humfrey can—well, if I do have magic, it means I can stay and marry my girl and have some pride. Finally."

Cherie nodded. "I suspected it was something like that. I suppose if I were in your situation I could choke down the necessity of having magic, though I really think your culture's values are distorted. You should base your citizenship on superior qualities of personality and achievement, not on—"

"Exactly," Bink agreed fervently.

She smiled. "You really should have been a centaur." She shook her head so that her hair flung out prettily. "You have undertaken a hazardous journey."

"Not more hazardous than the one to the Mundane world that will otherwise be forced on me."

She nodded again. "Very well. You have satisfied my curiosity; I'll satisfy yours. I'll tell you the whole truth about the human intrusion into Xanth. But I don't expect you to like it much."

"I don't expect to like the truth about myself much," Bink said ruefully. "I might as well know whatever there is to know."

"For thousands of years Xanth was a comparatively peaceful land," she said, assuming the somewhat pedantic tone he remembered from his school days. Probably every centaur was at heart a teacher. "There was magic, very strong magic—but no unnecessary viciousness. We centaurs were the dominant species, but, as you know, we have absolutely no magic. We *are* magic. I suppose we migrated here from Mundania originally—but that was so long ago it is lost even to our records."

Something tripped over in Bink's mind. "I wonder if that really is true—about magic creatures not being able to work spells? I saw a chipmouse conjure a crumb of bread—"

"Oh? Are you sure it wasn't a chip*munk*? That is a natural creature, according to our taxonomy, so it might work magic."

"You tax animals?" Bink asked, amazed.

"Taxonomy," she repeated with an indulgent smile. "The classification of living things, another centaur specialty."

Oh. Bink considered, embarrassed. "I thought it was a chipmouse, but I'm not quite certain now."

"Actually, we're not quite certain either," she admitted. "It may be that some magical creatures can work magic. But, as a general rule, a creature either *does* magic or *is* magic, not both. Which is just as well—think of the havoc a dragon Magician could make!"

Bink thought of it. He shuddered. "Let's get back to the history lesson," he suggested.

"About a thousand years ago the first human tribe discovered Xanth. They thought it was just another peninsula. They moved in and cut down the trees and slaughtered the animals. There was more than enough magic here to repulse them, but Xanth had never been subjected to such callous, systematic ravage before, and we did not quite believe it. We thought the humans would leave soon.

"But then they realized that Xanth was magic. They saw the animals levitating and the trees moving their branches. They hunted the unicorns and griffins. If you wonder why those big animals hate people, let me assure you they have good reason: their ancestors would not have survived if they'd tried to be friendly. The Firstwavers were nonmagical creatures in a land of spells, and after they got over the initial shock they liked it."

"Now that's wrong!" Bink exclaimed. "Humans have the very strongest magic. Look at all the great Magicians. You yourself told me just now how Evil Magician Trent changed all the fish—"

"Pipe down before I buck you off!" Cherie snapped. Her tail swished menacingly past Bink's ear. "You don't know the quarter of it. Of course humans have magic now. That's part of their problem. But not at the start."

Bink backed down again. It was increasingly easy to do; he liked this centaur lady very well. She was answering questions he hadn't even thought to ask yet. "Sorry. This is new to me."

"You remind me of Chester. I'll bet you're awful stubborn, too."

"Yes," Bink said contritely.

She laughed, and it sounded a bit like neighing. "I do like you, human. I hope you find your"—she pursed her lips distastefully—"magic." Then she flashed a sunny smile, and as quickly sobered. "Those Firstwavers had no magic, and when they found out what magic could do they were fascinated but a bit afraid of it. A number of them perished in a lake that had a drown spell, and some ran afoul of dragons, and when they met the first basilisk—"

"Are there still basilisks?" Bink inquired worriedly, abruptly remembering the omen of the chameleon. It had stared at him in the guise of a basilisk just before it died, as if its spell had backfired. He had yet to be sure of the meaning of that sequence.

"Yes, there are—but not many," she answered. "Both humans and centaurs labored to stamp them out. Their glance is fatal to us too, you know. Now they hide, because they know that the first intelligent creature killed that way will bring an avenging army of mirror-masked warriors down on them. A basilisk is no match for a forewarned man or centaur; it's just a small winged lizard, you know, with the head and claws of a chicken. Not very intelligent. Not that it usually needs to be."

"Say!" Bink exclaimed. "Maybe that's the missing factor—intelligence. A creature can do magic or be magic or be smart—or any two of the three, but never all three. So a chipmouse might conjure, but not a smart dragon."

She turned her head about again to face him. "That's a novel idea. You're pretty smart yourself. I'll have to think about it. But until we verify it, don't go into the central wilderness unprotected; there just might be a smart spell-throwing monster in there."

"I won't go into the wilderness," Bink promised. "At least, I won't stray from the cleared path through it, until I get to the Magician's castle. I don't want any lizards looking death at me."

"Your ancestors were more aggressive," Cherie remarked. "That's why so many of them died. But they conquered Xanth, and formed an enclave where magic was banned. They liked the country and the uses of magic, you see, but they didn't want it too close to home. So they burned the forest there, killed all magical animals and plants, and built a great stone wall."

"The ruins!" Bink exclaimed. "I thought those old stones were from an enemy camp."

"They are from the First Wave," she insisted.

"But I am descended from—"

"I said you wouldn't like this."

"I don't," he agreed. "But I want to hear it. How can my ancestors have—"

"They settled in their walled village and planted Mundane crops and herded Mundane cattle. You know—beans and wingless cows. They married the women they had brought along or that they could raid from the closest Mundane settlements, and had children. Xanth was a good land, even in that region expunged of magic. But then something amazing happened."

Cherie turned to face him again, glancing obliquely in a manner that would have been most fetching in a human girl. In fact, it was fetching in a centaur girl, especially if he squinted so as to see only her human portion: splendidly fetching, despite his knowledge that centaurs lived longer than humans, so that she was probably fifty years old. She looked twenty—a twenty that few humans ever achieved. No halter would hold this filly!

"What happened?" he asked, catering to her evident desire for an intellectual response. Centaurs were good storytellers, and they did like a good audience.

"Their children came up magic," she said.

Aha! "So the Firstwavers *were* magic!"

"No, they were not. The land of Xanth is magic. It's an environmental effect. But it works much better with children, who are more formative, and it works best with babies conceived and birthed here. Adults, even of long residence, tend to suppress the talents they have, because they 'know better.' But children accept what is. So not only do they have more natural talent, they use it with more enthusiasm."

"I never knew that," he said. "My folks have much more magic than I do. Some of my ancestors were Magicians. But me—" He sobered. "I'm afraid I was a terrible disappointment to my parents. By rights I should have had very strong magic, maybe even have been a Magician myself. Instead . . ."

Cherie discreetly did not comment. "At first the humans were shocked. But soon they accepted it, and even encouraged the development of special talents. One of the youngsters had the ability to transform lead into gold. They ravaged the hills, searching for lead, and finally had to send a mission to obtain it from Mundania. It was almost as if lead had become more valuable than gold."

"But Xanth has no dealings with the Mundane world."

"You keep forgetting: this is ancient history."

"Sorry again. I wouldn't interrupt so much if I weren't so interested."

"You are an excellent audience," she said, and he felt pleased. "Most humans would refuse to listen at all, because it is not a complimentary history. Not to your kind."

"I'd probably be less open-minded if I didn't face exile myself," he admitted. "About all I have to work with is my brain and body, so I'd better not fool myself."

"A commendable philosophy. You are, incidentally, getting a longer ride than I planned, because you pay such good, responsive attention. At any rate, they got the lead out—but paid a hideous price. Because the Mundanes of Mundania learned about the magic. They were true to their type: greedy and rapacious.

The notion of cheap gold sent them into a frenzy. They invaded, stormed the wall, and killed all the First Wave men and children."

"But—" Bink protested, horrified.

"These were the Secondwavers," Cherie said gently. "They saved the Firstwaver women, you see. Because the Second Wave was an all-male army. They thought there was a machine to convert the lead into gold, or an alchemical process organized by a secret formula. They didn't really believe in magic; that was just a convenient term to describe the unknown. So they didn't realize that the lead was converted into gold by the magic of a child—until too late. They had destroyed what they had come for."

"Horrible!" Bink said. "You mean I am descended from—"

"From the rape of a First Wave mother. Yes—there is no other way you can authenticate your lineage. We centaurs had never liked the Firstwavers, but we were sorry for them then. The Secondwavers were worse. They were literal pirates, rapacious. Had we known, we would have helped the Firstwavers fight them off. Our archers could have ambushed them—" She shrugged. Centaur archery was legendary; no need to belabor the point.

"Now the invaders settled," she continued after a pause. "They sent their own archers all over Xanth, killing—" She broke off, and Bink knew how keenly she felt the irony of her kind being prey to the inferior archery of human beings. She gave a little shudder that almost dislodged him, and forced herself to continue. "Killing centaurs for meat. Not until we organized and ambushed their camp, putting shafts through half of them, did they agree to let us alone. Even after that, they did not honor their agreement very well, for they had precious little sense of honor."

"And their children had magic," Bink continued, seeing it now. "And so the Thirdwavers invaded and killed off the Secondwavers—"

"Yes, this happened after several generations, though it was every bit as vicious when it came. The Secondwavers had become tolerably good neighbors, all things considered, by then. Again, only the women were saved—and not many of them. Because they had been in Xanth all their lives, their magic was strong. They used it to eliminate their rapist husbands one by one in ways that could not be directly traced to the women. But their victory was their defeat, for now they had no families at all. So they had to invite in more Mundanes—"

"This is ghastly!" Bink said. "I am descended from a thousand years of ignominy."

"Not entirely. The history of man in Xanth is brutal, but not without redeeming values, even greatness. The Second Wave women organized, and brought in only the finest men they could locate. Strong, just, kind, intelligent men, who understood the background but came more from principle than from greed.

They promised to keep the secret and to uphold the values of Xanth. They were Mundanes, but they were noble ones."

"The Fourthwavers!" Bink exclaimed. "The finest of them all."

"Yes. The Xanth women were widows and victims of rape and finally murderesses. Some were old, or scarred physically and emotionally by the campaign. But they all had strong magic and iron determination; they were the survivors of the cruel upheaval that had wiped out all other humans in Xanth. These qualities were quite evident. When the new men learned the whole truth, some turned about and returned to Mundania. But others liked marrying witches. They wanted to have children with potent magic, and they thought it might be hereditary, so they regarded youth and beauty as secondary. They made excellent husbands. Others wanted the potentials of the unique land of Xanth developed and protected; they were the environmentalists, and magic was the most precious part of the environment. And not all the Fourthwavers were men; some were carefully selected young women, brought in to marry the children, so that there would not be too much inbreeding. So it was a settlement, not an invasion, and it was not rooted in murder but based on sound commercial and biological principles."

"I know," Bink said. "That was the Wave of the first great Magicians."

"So it was. Of course, there were other Waves, but none so critical. The effective dominance of human beings in Xanth dates from that Fourth Wave. Other invasions killed many and drove more into the backwoods, but the continuity was never broken. Just about every truly intelligent or magical person traces his ancestry to the Fourth Wave; I'm sure you do too."

"Yes," Bink agreed. "I have ancestors from the first six Waves, but I always thought the First Wave lineage was the most important."

"The institution of the Magic Shield finally stopped the Waves. It kept all Mundane creatures out and all Xanth creatures in. It was hailed as the salvation of Xanth, the guarantor of utopia. But somehow things didn't improve much. It is as if the people exchanged one problem for another—a visible threat for an invisible one. In the past century Xanth has been entirely free from invasion—but other threats have developed."

"Like the fireflies and the wiggles and Bad Magician Trent," Bink agreed. "Magical hazards."

"Trent was not a *bad* Magician," Cherie corrected him. "He was an *Evil* Magician. There's a distinction—a crucial one."

"Um, yes. He was a good Evil Magician. Lucky they got rid of him before he took over Xanth."

"Certainly. But suppose another Evil Magician appears? Or the wiggles manifest again? Who will save Xanth this time?"

"I don't known," Bink admitted.

"Sometimes I wonder whether the Shield was really a good idea. It has the net effect of intensifying the magic in Xanth, preventing dilution from outside. As if that magic were building up toward an explosion point. Yet I certainly wouldn't want to return to the days of the Waves!"

Bink had never thought of it that way. "Somehow I find it hard to appreciate the problems of the concentration of magic in Xanth," he said. "I keep wishing there were just a little more. Enough for me, for my talent."

"You might be better off without it," she suggested. "If you could just obtain a dispensation from the King—"

"Ha!" Bink said. "I'd be better off living like a hermit in the wilderness. My village won't tolerate a man without a talent."

"Strange inversion," she murmured.

"What?"

"Oh, nothing. I was just thinking of Herman the Hermit. He was exiled from our herd some years back for obscenity."

Bink laughed. "What could be obscene to a centaur? What did he do?"

Cherie drew up abruptly at the edge of a pretty field of flowers. "This is as far as I go," she said tersely.

Bink realized that he had said the wrong thing. "I didn't mean to offend—I apologize for whatever—"

Cherie relaxed. "You couldn't know. The odor of these flowers makes centaurs do crazy things; I have to stay clear except in real emergencies. I believe Magician Humfrey's castle is about five miles south. Keep alert for hostile magic, and I hope you find your talent."

"Thanks," Bink said gratefully. He slid off her back. His legs were a bit stiff from the long ride, but he knew she had gained him a day's travel time. He walked around to face her and held out his hand.

Cherie accepted it, then leaned forward to kiss him—a motherly kiss on his forehead. Bink wished she had not done that, but he smiled mechanically and started walking. He heard her hooves cantering back through the forest, and suddenly he felt lonely. Fortunately, his journey was nearly over.

But still he wondered: what had Herman the Hermit done that the centaurs considered obscene?

C h a p t e r   3

Chasm

Bink stood at the brink, appalled. The path had been sundered
by another trench—no, not a trench, but a mighty chasm, half
a mile across and seemingly of bottomless depth. Cherie the centaur could not
have known of it, or she would have warned him. So it must be of very recent
formation—perhaps within the past month.

Only an earthquake or cataclysmic magic could have formed such a canyon so
rapidly. Since there had been no earthquakes that he knew of, it had to be
magic. And that implied a Magician—of phenomenal power.

Who could it be? The King in his heyday might have been able to fashion
such a chasm by using a rigidly controlled storm, a channeled hurricane—but he
had no reason to, and his powers had faded too much to manage anything like
this now. Evil Magician Trent had been a transformer, not an earthmover. Good

Magician Humfrey's magic was divided into a hundred assorted divinatory spells; some of those might tell him how to create such a gross channel, but it was hardly conceivable that Humfrey would bother to do it. Humfrey never did anything unless there was a fee to be earned from it. Was there another great Magician in Xanth?

Wait—he had heard rumors of a master of illusion. It was far easier to make an apparent chasm than a genuine one. That could be an amplification of Zink's pretend-hole talent. Zink was no Magician, but if a real Magician had this type of talent, this was the kind of effect he might create. Maybe if Bink simply walked out into this chasm, his feet would find the path continuing on . . .

He looked down. He saw a small cloud floating blithely along, about five hundred feet down. A gust of cool dank wind came up to brush him back. He shivered; that was extraordinarily realistic for an illusion!

He shouted: "Hallooo!"

He heard the echo following about five seconds after: "Allooo!"

He picked up a pebble and flipped it into the seeming chasm. It disappeared into the depths, and no sound of its landing came back.

At last he kneeled and poked his finger into the air beyond the brim. It met no resistance. He touched the edge, and found it material and vertical.

He was convinced, unwillingly. The chasm was real.

There was nothing to do but go around it. Which meant he was not within five miles of his destination, but within fifty—or a hundred, depending on the extent of this amazing crevice.

Should he turn back? The villagers certainly should be advised of this manifestation. On the other hand, it might be gone by the time he brought anyone else back here to see it, and he would be labeled a fool as well as a spell-less wonder. Worse, he would be called a coward, who had invented a story to explain his fear of visiting the Magician and gaining absolute proof of his talentlessness. What had been created magically could be abolished magically. So he had better try to get around it.

Bink looked somewhat wearily at the sky. The sun was low in the west. He had an hour or so of diminishing daylight left. He'd better spend it trying to locate a house in which to spend the night. The last thing he wanted was to sleep outside in unfamiliar territory, at the mercy of strange magic. He had had a very easy trip so far, thanks to Cherie, but with this emergency detour it would become much more difficult.

Which way to turn—east or west? The chasm seemed to run interminably in both directions. But the lay of the land was slightly less rugged to the east, making a gradual descent; maybe it would approach the bottom of the chasm, enabling him to cross it. Farmers tended to build in valleys rather than on mountains, so as to have ready sources of water and be free of the hostile magic of high places. He would go east.

But this region was sparsely settled. He had seen no human habitations along the path so far. He walked increasingly swiftly through the forest. As dusk came, he saw great black shapes rising out of the chasm: vastly spreading leathery wings, cruelly bent beaks, glinting small eyes. Vultures perhaps, or worse. He felt horribly uneasy.

It was now necessary to conserve his rations, for he had no way of knowing how far they would have to stretch. He spotted a breadfruit tree and cut a loaf from it, but discovered the bread was not yet ripe. He would get indigestion eating it. He had to find a farmhouse.

The trees became larger and more gnarled of trunk. They seemed menacing in the shadows. A wind was rising, causing the stiff, twisted branches to sigh. Nothing ominous about that; these effects weren't even magical. But Bink found his heart beating more rapidly, and he kept glancing back over his shoulder. He was no longer on the established trail, so his comparative security was gone. He was going deeper into the hinterland, where anything could happen. Night was the time of sinister magic, and there were diverse and potent kinds. The peace spell of the pines was only an example; there were surely fear spells and worse. If only he could find a house!

Some adventurer he was! The moment he had to go a little out of his way, the instant it got dark, he started reacting to his own too-creative imagination. The fact was, this was not the deep wilderness; there would be few real threats to a careful man. The true wilds were beyond the Good Magician's castle, on the other side of the chasm.

He forced himself to slow down and keep his gaze forward. Just keep walking, swinging the staff over to touch anything suspicious, no foolish—

The end of the staff touched an innocuous black rock. The rock burst upward with a loud whirring noise. Bink scrambled back, falling on the ground, arms thrown up protectively before his face.

The rock spread wings and flapped away. "Koo!" it protested reproachfully. It had been only a stone dove, folded into its rock shape for camouflage and insulation during the night. Naturally, it had reacted when poked—but it was quite harmless.

If stone doves nested here, it was bound to be safe for him. All he had to do was stretch out anywhere and sleep. Why didn't he do just that?

Because he was foolishly terrified of being alone at night, he answered himself. If only he had some magic, then he would feel more secure. Even a simple confidence spell would serve.

He spied a light ahead. Relief! It was a yellow square, nearly certain indication of human habitation. He was almost tearfully pleased. He was no child, no adolescent, but he might as well be, here in the forest and off the bounds of his map. He needed the comfort of human companionship. He hurried toward the light, hoping it would not turn out to be some illusion or trap sponsored by an inimical being.

It was real. It was a farm at the edge of a small village; now he could see other squares of light farther down the valley. Almost joyfully, he knocked on the door.

It opened grudgingly to show a homely woman in a soiled apron. She peered at him suspiciously. "I don't know you," she grumped, edging the door closed again.

"I am Bink of the North Village," he said quickly. "I have traveled all day, and was balked by the chasm. Now I need lodging for the night. I will perform some reasonable service for the favor. I'm strong; I can chop wood or load hay or move rocks—"

"You don't need magic to do those things," she said.

"Not with magic! With my hands. I—"

"How do I know you're not a wraith?" she demanded.

Bink held out his left hand, wincing. "Prick me; I bleed." It was a standard test, for most nocturnal supernatural creatures had no blood, unless they had recently fed on some living creature. Even then they had none that would flow.

"Oh, come on, Martha," a man's gruff voice called from inside. "There hasn't been a wraith in these parts for a decade, and they don't do no harm anyway. Let him in; if he eats, he's human."

"Ogres eat," she muttered. But she cracked the door open far enough for Bink to squeeze through.

Now Bink saw the farm's guardian animal: a small werewolf, probably one of their children. There were no true werewolves or other weres that he knew of; all were humans who had developed the talent. Such changelings were increasingly frequent, it seemed. This one had the large head and flattish face typical of the type. A real werewolf would have been indistinguishable from a canine until it changed; then it would have been a wolfish man. Bink put out his hand as it slunk up to sniff him, then patted it on the head.

The creature metamorphosed into a boy about eight years old. "Did I scare you, huh?" he begged.

"Terrified," Bink agreed.

The lad turned toward the man. "He's clean, Paw," he announced. "No smell of magic on him."

"That's the trouble," Bink murmured. "If I had magic, I wouldn't be traveling. But I meant what I said. I can do good physical work."

"No magic?" the man inquired as the woman poured Bink a steaming bowl of stew. The farmer was in his mid-thirties, as homely as his wife, but possessed of a few deep smile-lines around his mouth and eyes. He was thin, but obviously sturdy; hard physical labor made for tough men. He flexed purple as he talked, then green, his whole body changing color smoothly: his talent. "How'd you make it all the way from North Village in one day, then?"

"A lady centaur gave me a lift."

"A filly! I'll *bet* she did! Where'd you hang on to when she jumped?"

Bink smiled ruefully. "Well, she said she'd drop me in a trench if I did it again," he admitted.

"Haw! Haw! Haw!" the man brayed. Farmers, being relatively uneducated, tended to have an earthy sense of humor. Bink noticed that the homely wife wasn't laughing, and the boy merely stared uncomprehendingly.

Now the farmer got down to business. "Listen, I don't need no hand labor nowsabout. But I've got a part in a hearing coming up, and I don't want to go. Upsets the missus, you know."

Bink nodded, though he did not understand. He saw the wife nod grim agreement. What sort of thing was this?

"So if you want to work off your lodging, you can stand in for me," the farmer continued. "Won't only take 'bout an hour, no work to it 'cept to agree to anything the bailiff says. Softest job you can find, and easy for you, too, 'cause you're a stranger. Playing opposite a cute young thing—" He caught the grim look of his wife and aborted that line. "How 'bout it?"

"Anything I can do," Bink said uncertainly. What was this about playing opposite a cute young thing? He'd never find out while the wife was present. Would Sabrina object?

"Fine! There's hay in the loft, and a bucket so you won't have to go outside. Just don't snore too loud—the missus don't like it."

The missus didn't like a lot of things, it seemed. How did a man ever come to marry a woman like that? Would Sabrina turn shrewish after marriage? The idea made him uneasy. "I won't," Bink agreed. The stew was not very tasty, but it was filling. Good stuff to travel on.

He slept comfortably in the hay, with the wolf curled up beside him. He did have to use the pot, and it stank all night, having no cover—but that was much better than going into the magic night. After that initial expression of objection to the stew, his innards settled down. Bink really had no complaint.

He had gruel for breakfast, heated without fire. That was the wife's talent, a useful one for a farmstead. Then he reported to the neighbor's house a mile on down along the chasm for the hearing.

The bailiff was a big, bluff man, above whose head a small cloud formed when he concentrated on anything too intently. "Know anything about it?" he inquired after Bink explained.

"Nothing," Bink admitted. "You'll have to tell me what to do."

"Good! It's just a sort of little playlet, to settle a problem without ruining anybody's reputation. We call it surrogate magic. Mind you, don't use any actual magic."

"I won't," Bink said.

"You just agree to whatever I ask you. That's all."

Bink began to get nervous. "I don't believe in lying, sir."

"This ain't exactly lying, boy. It's in a good cause. You'll see. I'm s'prised you folk don't practice it in North Village."

Bink was uneasily silent. He hoped he had not gotten himself into something ugly.

The others arrived: two men and three young women. The men were ordinary, bearded farmers, one young, one middle-aged; the girls ranged from indifferent to ravishing. Bink forced his eyes away from the prettiest one lest he stare. She was the most voluptuous, striking black-haired beauty he had ever seen, a diamond in the mud of this region.

"Now the six of you sit down acrost from each other at this table," the bailiff said in his official voice. "I'll do the talking when the judge comes. Mind you, this is a play—but it's secret. When I swear you in, it's for keeps—absolutely no blabbing about the details after you get out, understand?"

They all nodded. Bink was becoming more perplexed. He now understood about playing opposite a sweet young thing—but what kind of play was this, with an audience of one, that no one was permitted to report on later? Well, so be it; maybe it *was* a kind of magic.

The three men sat in a row on one side of the table, and the three girls faced them. Bink was opposite the beautiful one; her knees touched his, for the table was narrow. They were silky smooth, sending a shiver of appreciation up his legs. *Remember Sabrina!* he told himself. He was not ordinarily swayed by a pretty face, but this was an extraordinary face. It didn't help that she wore a tight sweater. What a figure!

The judge entered—a portly man with impressive paunch and sideburns. "All stand," the bailiff said.

They all stood respectfully.

The judge took a seat at the end of the table and the bailiff moved to the far side. They all sat down.

"Do you three ladies swear to tell no truth other than that presented in this hearing, any time, anywhere, and to shut up about that?" the bailiff demanded.

"We do," the girls chorused.

"And do you three louts swear the same?"

"We do," Bink said with the others. If he was supposed to lie here, but never to talk about it outside, did that mean it wasn't really a lie? The bailiff knew what was true and what was false, presumably, so in effect—

"Now this is the hearing for an alleged rape," the bailiff announced. Bink, shocked, tried to conceal his dismay. Were they supposed to act out a rape?

"Among these present," the bailiff continued, "is the girl who says she was raped—and the man she charges. He says it happened but it was voluntary. That right, men?"

Bink nodded vigorously along with the others. Brother! He would rather have chopped wood for his night's lodging. Here he was, possibly lying about a rape he never committed.

"This is done anonymously to protect the reputations of those involved," the bailiff said. "So's to have an advisory opinion, in the presence of the first parties, without advertising it to the whole community."

Bink was beginning to understand. A girl who had been raped could be ruined, though it was no fault of her own; many men would refuse to marry her for that reason alone. Thus she could win her case but lose her future. A man guilty of rape could be exiled, and a man accused of rape would be viewed with suspicion, complicating his own future. It was almost, he thought grimly, as serious a crime as having no magic. Getting at the truth could be a very delicate matter, not something either party would want to advertise in a public trial. Win or lose, reputations would suffer grievously. Yet how could justice be done if it never came to trial? Thus this private, semianonymous hearing. Would it suffice?

"She says she was walking down by the Gap," the bailiff said, glancing at his notes. "He came up behind her, grabbed her, and raped her. Right, girls?"

The three girls nodded, each looking hurt and angry. The vigorous head motion caused the knee of the girl facing Bink to shake, and another ripple of suggestion traveled up his leg. What an opposite lady, in what a play!

"He says he was standing there and she came up and made a suggestion and he took her up on it. Right, men?"

Bink nodded with the others. He hoped his side won; this was nervous business.

Now the judge spoke. "Was it close to a house?"

" 'Bout a hundred feet," the bailiff said.

"Then why did she not scream?"

"He said he'd push her off the brink if she made a sound," the bailiff replied. "She was frozen in terror. Right, girls?"

They nodded—and each looked momentarily terrified. Bink wondered which of the three had actually been raped. Then he corrected his thought hastily: which one had made the accusation? He hoped it wasn't the one opposite him.

"Were the two known to each other prior to the occasion?"

"Yes, Your Honor."

"Then I presume she would have fled him at the outset, had she disliked him

—and that he would not have forced her if she trusted him. In a small community like this, people get to know each other very well, and there are few actual surprises. This is not conclusive, but it strongly suggests she had no strong aversion to contact with him, and may have tempted him with consequence she later regretted. I would probably, were this case to come up in formal court, find the man not guilty of the charge, by virtue of reasonable doubt."

The three men relaxed. Bink became aware of a trickle of sweat on his forehead, generated while he listened to the judge's potential decision.

"Okay, you have the judge's ifso," said the bailiff. "You girls still want to bring it to open trial?"

Grim-faced, looking betrayed, the three girls shook their heads, no. Bink felt sorry for his opposite. How could she avoid being seductive? She was a creature constructed for no other visible purpose than ra—than love.

"Then take off," the bailiff said. "Remember—no talking outside, or we'll have a *real* trial, for contempt of court." The warning seemed superfluous; the girls would hardly be talking about this one. The guilty—uh, innocent—man would also shut up, and Bink himself just wanted to get clear of this village. That left only one man who might want to talk—but if he breathed a word, all the others would know who had blabbed. There would be silence.

So it was over. Bink stood and filed out with the others. The whole thing had taken less than the promised hour, so he was well off. He'd had a night's lodging and was well rested. All he needed now was to find a route past the chasm to the Good Magician's castle.

The bailiff emerged, and Bink approached him. "Could you tell me if there is any way south from here?"

"Boy, you don't want to cross the Gap," the bailiff said firmly, the little cloud forming over his head. "Not unless you can fly."

"I'm on foot."

"There's a route, but the Gap dragon . . . You're a nice boy, young, handsome. You did a good job in the hearing. Don't risk it."

Everybody thought he was so damned young! Only good, strong, personal magic would give him real manhood in the eyes of Xanth. "I *have* to risk it."

The bailiff sighed. "Well, I can't tell you no then, son. I'm not your father." He sucked in his paunch, which was almost as impressive as that of the judge, and contemplated the cloud over his head momentarily. The cloud seemed about to shed a tear or two. Again Bink winced inwardly. Now he was getting fathered as well as mothered. "But it's complicated. Better have Wynne show you."

"Wynne?"

"Your opposite. The one you almost raped." The bailiff smiled, making a signal with one hand, and his cloud dissipated. "Not that I blame you."

The girl approached, apparently in answer to the signal.

"Wynne, honey, show this man to the southern slope of the Gap. Mind you keep clear of the dragon."

"Sure," she said, smiling. The smile did not add to her splendor, because that was impossible, but it tried.

Bink had mixed emotions. After this hearing, suppose she accused him of . . . ?

The bailiff glanced at him understandingly. "Don't worry about it, son. Wynne don't lie, and she don't change her mind. You behave yourself, difficult as that may be, and there'll be no trouble."

Embarrassed, Bink accepted the girl's company. If she could show him a quick, safe route past the chasm, he would be well ahead.

They walked east, the sun beating into their faces. "Is it far?" Bink asked, still feeling awkward for assorted reasons. If Sabrina could see him now!

"Not far," she said. Her voice was soft, somehow sending an involuntary thrill through him. Maybe it was magic; he hoped so, because he didn't like to think that he could be so easily subverted by mere beauty. He didn't know this girl!

They continued in silence for a while. Bink tried again: "What is your talent?"

She looked at him blankly.

Uh-oh. After the hearing, she could not be blamed for taking that the wrong way. "Your magic talent," he clarified. "The thing you can do. A spell, or . . ."

She shrugged noncommittally.

What was with this girl? She was beautiful, but she seemed somewhat vacuous.

"Do you like it here?" he asked.

She shrugged again.

Now he was almost certain: Wynne was lovely but stupid. Too bad; she could have made some farmer a marvelous showpiece. No wonder the bailiff had not been concerned about her; she was not much use.

They walked in silence again. As they rounded a bend, they almost stumbled over a rabbit nibbling a mushroom in the path. Startled, the creature jumped straight into the air and hung there, levitating, its pink nose quivering.

Bink laughed. "We won't hurt you, magic bunny," he said. And Wynne smiled.

They passed on under it. But the episode, minor as it was, bothered Bink in retrospect, and for a familiar reason. Why should a common, garden-variety rabbit possess the magic power of floating, while Bink himself had nothing? It simply wasn't fair.

Now he heard the strains of a lovely melody, seeming to punctuate his thoughts. He looked about and saw a lyrebird playing its strings. The music carried through the forest, filling it with a pseudo joy. Ha!

He felt the need to talk, so he did. "When I was a kid they always teased me because I had no magic," he said, not caring whether she understood. "I lost footraces to others who could fly, or put walls in my way, or pass through trees, or who could pop out in one place and in at another place." He had said as much to Cherie the centaur; he was sorry to be stuck in this groove, but some unreasonable part of his mind seemed to believe that if he repeated it often enough he would find some way to alleviate it. "Or who could cast a spell on the path ahead of them, making it all downhill, while I had to cover the honest lay of the land." Remembering all those indignities, he began to feel choked up.

"Can I go with you?" Wynne asked abruptly.

Uh-oh. Maybe she figured he could regale her with more stories indefinitely. The other rigors of travel did not occur to her. In a few miles her shapely body, obviously not constructed for brute work, would tire, and he'd have to carry her. "Wynne, I'm going a long way, to see the Magician Humfrey. You don't want to come along."

"No?" Her marvelous face clouded up.

Still conscious of the rape hearing, and wary of any possible misunderstanding, he phrased it carefully. They were now descending a tortuous path into a low section of the chasm, winding around tufts of clatterweed and clutchroot saplings. He had taken the lead, bracing with his staff, so as to be able to catch her if she lost her footing and fell; when he glanced up at her he caught distracting glimpses of her exquisite thighs. There seemed to be no part of her body that was not perfectly molded. Only her brain had been neglected. "It is dangerous. Much bad magic. I go alone."

"Alone?" She was still confused, though she was handling the path very well. Nothing wrong with her coordination! Bink found himself a bit surprised that those legs could actually be used for climbing and walking. "I need help. Magic."

"The Magician charges a year's service. You—would not want to pay." The Good Magician was male, and Wynne had only one obvious coin. No one would be interested in her mind.

She looked at him in perplexity. Then she brightened, standing upright on the path above him. "You want payment?" She put one hand to the front of her dress.

"No!" Bink yelled, almost dislodging himself from the steep slope. He already visualized a reenactment of the hearing, and a different verdict. Who would believe he had not taken advantage of the lovely idiot? If she showed him any more of her body— "No!" he repeated, more to himself than to her.

"But—" she said, clouding up again.

He was rescued by another distraction. They were near the bottom now, and

Bink could see across the base to the more gentle rise of the south slope. No problem about climbing that. He was about to tell Wynne she could go home when there was an uncomfortable sound, a kind of slide-bump. It was repeated —very loud and shuddersome, without being precisely definable.

"What's that?" he asked nervously.

Wynne cupped her ear, listening, though the noise was plainly audible. With the shift in her balance, her feet lost purchase, and she began to slide down. He jumped to catch her, and eased her to the chasm floor. What an armful she was, all softness and resilience and slenderness in miraculous proportions!

She turned her face to him, brushing back her slightly disarrayed hair, as he stood her back on her feet. "The Gap dragon," she said.

For a moment he was confused. Then he remembered that he had asked her a question; now she was answering it, with the single-mindedness of the meager intellect she had.

"Is it dangerous?"

"Yes."

She had been too stupid to tell him before he asked. And he had not thought to ask before he heard it. Maybe if he hadn't been looking at her so much—yet what man would not have looked?

Already he saw the monster coming from the west—a smoking reptilian head, low to the ground, but large. Very large. "Run!" he bawled.

She started to run—straight ahead, into the chasm.

"No!" he yelled, sprinting after her. He caught her by one arm and spun her about. Her hair swirled winsomely, a black cloud about her face.

"You want payment?" she asked.

Brother! "Run *that* way!" he cried, shoving her back toward the northern slope, since it was the closest escape. He hoped the dragon was not a good climber.

She obeyed, moving fleetly over the ground.

But the glaring eyes of the Gap dragon followed her, orienting on the motion. The creature swerved to intercept her. Bink saw she could not reach the path in time. The monster was whomping along at galloping-centaur velocity.

Bink sprinted after her again, caught her, and half hurled her back toward the south. Even in this desperate moment, her body had a limber, appealing quality that threatened to distract his mind. "That way!" he cried. "It's catching up!" He was acting as foolishly as she, changing his mind while doom closed in.

He had to divert the monster somehow. "Hey, steamsnoot!" he bawled, waving his arms wildly. "Look at me!"

The dragon looked. So did Wynne.

"Not you!" Bink yelled at her. "Get on across. Get out of the Gap."

She ran again. No one could be so stupid as not to understand the danger here.

Now the dragon's attention was on Bink. It swerved again, bearing down on him. It had a long, sinuous body and three sets of stubby legs. The legs lifted the torso and whomped it forward, causing it to slide several feet. The process looked clumsy—but the thing was traveling disconcertingly fast.

Time for him to run! Bink took off down the chasm, toward the east. The dragon had already cut him off from the north slope, and he didn't want to lead it in the direction Wynne was going. For all its awkward mode of propulsion, it could run faster than he; no doubt its speed was enhanced by magic. It was, after all, a magical creature.

But what of his theory about no creature having magic and intelligence if it was magical in itself? If that was valid, this thing would not be very smart. Bink hoped so; he'd rather try to outwit a dumb dragon than a smart one. Especially when his life depended on it.

So he ran—but already he knew this course was hopeless. This was the dragon's hunting ground, the factor that stopped people from crossing the chasm on foot. He should have known that a magically constructed chasm would not be left unattended. Someone or something did not want, people crossing freely from north Xanth to south Xanth. Especially nonmagical people like him.

Bink was puffing now, out of breath, and a pain was developing in his side. He had underestimated the speed of the dragon. It was not a little faster than he was, it was substantially faster. The huge head snapped forward, and steam gushed around him.

Bink inhaled the stuff. It wasn't as hot as he had feared, and it smelled faintly of burning wood. But it was still uncomfortable. He choked, gasped—tripped on a stone and fell flat. His staff flew out of his hands. That fatal moment of distraction!

The dragon whomped right over him, unable to stop so rapidly. It was so long and low that it couldn't fall. The metallic body shot past, inertia carrying the head beyond range. If magic enhanced the thing's speed, then there was no magic to help it brake, for what that small blessing was worth.

Bink's breath was momentarily knocked out of him by the fall. He was already desperately short of air. He gasped for more, unable to concentrate on anything else at the moment, not even on escape. While he lay, effectively paralyzed, the middle set of legs came down—right at him. They came together as though yoked, ready to heave the heavy body up and forward again. He couldn't even roll aside in time. He would be crushed!

But the massive claws of the right foot landed squarely on the rock that had tripped him. It was a big rock, bigger than it looked, and he had fallen on the lower side after stumbling on its built-up upper side. He was sprawled in a kind of erosion gully. The three claws were splayed by the rock, so that one missed him to the left, another to the right, and the middle one arched right over him, hardly touching the ground. Perhaps a ton of dragonweight on that one foot, none of it touching him. A lucky placement that could never have happened by design!

Now he had some of his breath back, and the foot was gone, already lifted for the next whomp. Had Bink been able to roll aside, he would have been caught squarely by one of the claws, and squished.

But one freak break did not mean he was out of trouble. The dragon was curling around to find him again, steaming back along its own long torso. It was marvelously supple, able to bend in a tight U-turn. Bink would have admired this quality more from a safe distance. Snakelike, the monster could convolute into knots if it had to, reaching him wherever he tried to hide. No wonder it whomped; it had no rigid backbone.

Knowing it was futile, Bink still found himself trying to escape. He dashed under the tree-trunk-thick tail. The head followed him, the nostrils pursuing his scent as accurately as the eyes traced his motion.

Bink reversed course and leaped up over the tail, scrambling for handholds on the scales. He was in luck; some dragons had scales with serrated edges that sliced the flesh of anything that touched them; this one's scales were innocuously rounded. It was probably a survival trait in a chasm like this, though Bink wasn't sure why. Did sharp scales tend to snag on things, slowing the velocity of a low-to-the-ground monster?

He tumbled over the tail—and the dragon's head followed smoothly. No steam now; maybe the monster didn't want to heat up its own flesh. It was already savoring its conquest and repast, playing cat and mouse with him, though he'd never seen a werecat do that; possibly real cats did play that way, though there weren't many of those—or mice—around these days, for some reason.

But he was letting his mind run away with his attention again, and he couldn't afford it. Could he lead the dragon's head such a merry chase around its own body that it actually did tie itself in a knot? He doubted it, but might have to give it a try anyway. It was better than just getting swallowed.

He was back at the rock he had stumbled over. Now its position was changed; the moving weight of the dragon had dislodged it. There was a crack in the ground where it had been: a deep, dark hole.

Bink didn't like holes in the ground; no telling what might lurk in there: nickelpedes, stinglice, hoopworms, lepermud—ugh! But he had no chance at all here amid the coils of the Gap dragon. He jumped feet first into the hole.

The earth crumbled beneath his weight, but not quite enough. He sank in up to his thighs, and stuck.

The dragon, seeing him about to escape, blasted a torrent of steam. But again it was warm vapor, not burning hot, actually little more than coalesced breath. This was not after all a fire dragon, but a pseudo fire dragon. Few people were likely to get close enough to know the difference. The mist bathed Bink, soaking him down thoroughly, and turned the dirt around him to mud. Thus lubricated, he began to move again. Down.

The dragon snatched at him—but Bink popped through the constriction with a sucking sound that complemented the futile clicking of the dragon's teeth. He dropped about two feet, to solid rock. His feet stung, especially the ankle that had been turned, but he was unhurt. He ducked his head down and felt about him in the darkness. He was in a cave.

What luck! But he still wasn't safe. The dragon was clawing at the ground, gouging out huge chunks of dirt and rock, steaming the remainder into rivulets of mud. Gooey chunks splatted against the cave floor. The opening was widening, letting in more light. Soon it would be big enough for the dragon's head. Bink's doom had only been postponed.

This was no occasion for caution. Bink strode ahead, hands touching each other before him, arms bowed in a horizontal circle. If he hit a wall, he would only bruise his forearms. Better a bruise than the crunch of dragon's teeth.

He did not hit a wall. He struck a mud slick instead. His foot shot out from under, and he took a bellyflop. There was water here—real water, not dragon's breath—a trickle wending down.

Down? Down *where*? Surely to an underground river! That could account for the sudden canyon. The river could have been tunneling for centuries, and suddenly the ground above collapsed, forming the chasm. One phenomenal sinkhole. Now the river was working again—and he would surely drown if he splashed into it, for there was no guarantee that its current was slow or that there was air in its passage. Even if he swam well, he could be consumed by river monsters, the especially vicious kind that frequented dark, cold waters.

Bink clawed his way back up the slope. He found a branching passage leading up, and followed it as rapidly as possible. Soon he saw a shaft of light from above. Safe!

Safe? Not while the dragon still lurked. Bink dared not dig his way out until it left. He would have to wait, hoping the predator didn't dig this far. He hunkered down, trying not to get any more mud on him.

The sounds of the dragon's digging diminished, then ceased altogether. There was silence—but Bink wasn't fooled. Dragons were of the hide-and-pounce variety, generally. At least the landbound ones were. They could move fast when they moved, but could not keep it up long. A dragon would never successfully run down a deer, for example, even if the deer lacked escapist magic. But dragons were very good at waiting. Bink would have to stay low until he actually heard it move off.

It was a long wait, complicated by the cold discomfort of the mud and dark and his prior wetting by the dragon's breath. Plus the fact that he could not be quite sure the dragon was there. This might all be for nothing, and the dragon could be emitting steamy chuckles as it retreated silently—they could be very quiet when they wanted to—and hunted elsewhere.

No! That was what the predator wanted him to think. He dared not emerge, or even move, lest the thing hear him. That was why it was so quiet now; it was listening. Dragons had excellent senses; perhaps that was why they were so common in the wilderness regions, and so feared. They were a survival type. Apparently his scent had suffused the area, issuing from stray vents, so that it did not give away his precise location. The dragon was not about to wear itself out digging up the entire cave system. But sound or sight would do him in.

Now that he was absolutely still, he was cold. This was summer in Xanth, and it really did not get very cold even in winter, for many plants had heat magic, local weather control, or other mechanisms for comfort. But the chasm was sparsely vegetated, and sheltered from much of the sun, and the cool air tended to settle and be trapped. It had taken awhile for the heat of his exertions to dissipate, but now he was shivering. He could not afford to shiver too violently! His legs and feet hurt, becoming cramped. To top it off, he felt a scratchiness in his throat. He was coming down with a cold. This present discomfort would hardly help him to throw that off, and he could not go to the village doctor for a medicinal spell.

He tried to distract himself by thinking of other things, but he did not care to rehearse yet again the assorted indignities of his bitter childhood, or the frustration of having but not being able to hold a lovely girl like Sabrina because of his lack of magic. The notion of lovely girls reminded him of Wynne; he would not be human if he didn't react to her fantastic face and body! But she was so abysmally stupid; and anyway, he was engaged already, so he had no business thinking of her. His efforts at self-distraction came to nothing; it was better to suffer in mental silence.

Then he became aware of something more insidious. It had been in evidence for some time, but he had not been consciously aware of it because of his other concerns. Even unsuccessful distractions did some good.

It was a peripheral, almost subliminal thing. A kind of flickering, which vanished when he looked directly at it, but became insistent at the fringe of his vision. What was it? Something natural—or something magic? Innocent or sinister?

Then he recognized it. A shade! A half-real spirit, ghost, or some unquiet dead, doomed to skulk in shadow and night until its wrongs were righted or its evil exonerated. Because the shades could not go abroad by day, or enter light, or intrude in populous places, they represented no threat to ordinary folk in ordinary circumstances. Most were bound to the place of their demise. As Roland had advised Bink, long ago: "If a shade bothers you, walk away from it." They were easy to escape; this was called "pulling the shade."

Only if an unwary person foolishly slept near the abode of a shade was he in trouble. It took a shade about an hour to infiltrate a living body, and a person could move away at any time and be free of it. Once Roland, in a fit of uncharacteristic ire, had threatened to stun an annoying trespasser and leave him in the nearest shade barrow. The man had quickly departed.

Now Bink was neither stunned nor asleep—but if he moved, the Gap dragon would pounce. If he did not move, the shade would infiltrate his body. That could be a fate worse than death—really!

All because he had tried to rescue a beautiful, vacuous girl from a dragon. In folklore, such a hero always received a most intriguing reward. In reality, the hero was as likely as not to find himself in need of rescue, as now. Well, such was real-life justice in Xanth.

The shade grew bolder, thinking him helpless or inattentive. It did not glow; it was merely a lesser darkness than that of the cave. He could see it fairly well now, by not looking at it: a vague, mannish outline, very sad.

Bink wanted to leap away, but he found the dank wall close behind him, and in any event he could not afford to take a step. No matter how silently he did it, the dragon would hear. He could walk forward, right through the shade, and all he would feel would be a momentary chill, like that of the grave. It had happened on occasion to him before; unpleasant but hardly critical. But this time the dragon would be on him.

Maybe he could run, being fully rested, and get a head start before the dragon woke. The dragon must surely be sleeping, getting its rest, while its keen ears were attuned to the quarry.

The shade touched him. Bink jerked his arm away—and the dragon stirred above. It was there, all right! Bink froze—and the dragon lost him again. The mere jerk had not been quite enough.

The dragon circled, trying to sniff him out. Its huge nose passed over the upper crack; steam jetted down. The shade retreated in alarm. Then the dragon settled in place, giving up the chase for the moment. It knew its prey would give itself away sooner or later. When it came to waiting, the dragon was much better equipped than the human.

One more reptilian twitch—and the end of the tail dropped through the crack, dangling almost to the floor. In order to escape, Bink would have to brush past it. Now what were his chances?

Suddenly Bink had an idea. The dragon was a living, if magical, animal. Why shouldn't the shade take over *its* body? A shade-dominated dragon would probably have other things on its mind than eating a hiding person. If he could just move over so as to place the dangling tail between him and the shade—

He tried, shifting his balance with tedious slowness, trying to lift one foot so as to put it forward. Silently. But the moment it lifted, it hurt, and he flinched. The dragon's tail twitched, and Bink had to freeze. This was extremely awkward, because his balance in this semisquatting position was at best tenuous, and now both feet and ankles felt as if they were on fire.

The shade advanced again.

Bink tried to ease his foot farther forward, so as to achieve a more comfortable balance without falling over. Away from the shade! Again agony shot through him, and again the tail twitched; once more he froze, in even more discomfort. And yet again the shade moved in. He could not go on this way.

The shade touched his shoulder. This time Bink steeled himself not to flinch; he would certainly have lost his balance, and then his life. The touch was hideously cool, not cold; it made his skin crawl. What was he to do?

He controlled himself, with continuing effort. It would take an hour or so for the shade to take over his body; he could break the spell at any time before it was complete. The dragon would gobble him down in seconds. Appalling as the notion was, the shade was the better risk; at least it was slow. Maybe in half an hour the dragon would have gone away . . .

Maybe the moon would fall out of the sky and squish the dragon under green cheese, too! Why wish for the impossible? If the dragon did not go, then what? Bink just didn't know. But so far he didn't see much choice.

The shade moved in inexorably, cooling his shoulder through to chest and back. Bink felt the intrusion with barely suppressed loathing. How would it be possible to submit to this invasion of the dead? Yet he had to do it, at least for a while, lest the dragon quickly convert him to a shade himself. Or would that be preferable? At least he would die a man.

The ghastly cool essence impinged slowly on his head. Now Bink was terrified, yet frozen; he could not lean his head away any farther. The horror crept through, and he felt himself sinking, slipping, being blotted up by . . . and then he was eerily calm.

Peace, the shade said in his mind.

The peace of the pine forest, where the sleepers never woke? Bink could not protest aloud, because of the dragon's ears. But he gathered himself for a final effort, to leap away from this dread possession. He would crash past the dragon's tail before the monster could react, and take his chance with the subterranean river.

No! Friend, I can help you! the shade cried, louder but still silently.

Somehow, insidiously, Bink began to believe. The spirit actually seemed sincere. Perhaps it was just in contrast to the alternatives: consumption by dragon or drowning in river.

Fair exchange, the shade persisted. *Permit me, for one hour. I will save your life, then dissipate, my onus abated.*

It had the ring of conviction. Bink faced death anyway; if the shade could somehow save him, it would certainly be worth an hour of possession. It was true that shades dissipated once their burden was lifted.

But not all shades were honest. The criminal ones sometimes were recalcitrant, choosing not to atone for their crimes in life. Instead, they added to them in death, under cover of the new identity, ruining the reputation of the unlucky person they controlled. After all, the shade had little to lose; he was already dead. Absolution would merely consign him to oblivion or to his place in the infernal regions, depending on his faith. Small wonder some chose never to die completely.

My wife, my child! the shade pleaded. *They go hungry, they sorrow, ignorant of my status. I must tell them where the silver tree grows that I died to locate.*

The silver tree! Bink had heard of the like. A tree with leaves of pure silver, incredibly valuable—for silver was a magic metal. It tended to repel evil magic, and armor made from it resisted magic weapons. And, of course, it could even be used as money.

No, it is for my family! the shade cried. *That they may never again dwell in poverty. Do not take it for yourself!*

That convinced Bink. A dishonest shade would have promised him everything; this one promised only life, not riches. *Agreed,* Bink thought, hoping he was not making a dreadful mistake. Trust unwisely given—

Wait until merging is complete, the shade said gratefully. *I cannot help you until I become you.*

Bink hoped it was no deception. But what, really, did he have to lose? And what did the shade have to gain by a lie? If it did not save Bink, it would only share the sensation of being eaten by the dragon. Then they would both be shades—and Bink would be an angry one. He wondered what one shade could do to another. Meanwhile, he waited.

At last it was done. He was Donald, the prospector. A man whose talent was flying.

"We go!" Donald cried through Bink's lips exultantly. He put his arms up as if diving and rose straight up through the crack in the ceiling, with such power that the edges of rock and dirt were flung aside.

The sheer brightness of day blinded them as they emerged. The Gap dragon took a moment to orient on this strange occurrence, then pounced. But Donald made another effort, and shot up so swiftly that the huge teeth snapped on air.

He kicked the monster on the snout, hard. "Ha, gaptooth!" he yelled. "Chew on this." And he stomped on the tender portion of the dragon's nose.

The jaws gaped open, and a cloud of steam shot out. But Donald was already zooming out of reach. The dragon had no chance to catch them before they were too high.

Up, up they sailed, straight out of the canyon, above the trees and slopes. There was no effort other than mental, for this was magic flight. They leveled off, proceeding north across Xanth.

In delayed reaction, Bink realized that he had a magic talent. By proxy, certainly—but for the first time in his life he was experiencing what every other citizen of Xanth experienced. He was performing. Now he knew how it felt.

It felt wonderful.

The sun bore down from almost straight overhead, for it was now midday. They were up amid the clouds. Bink felt discomfort in his ears, but an automatic reaction by his other self popped them, making the pain abate before it intensified. He didn't know why flying should hurt his ears; maybe it was because there wasn't enough to hear up here.

For the first time, too, he saw the full upper contours of the clouds. From beneath they were generally flat, but from above they were elegantly if randomly sculptured. What seemed like tiny puffballs from the ground were big masses of fog in person. Donald flew through them with equanimity, but Bink didn't like the loss of vision. He was nervous about banging into something.

"Why so high?" he inquired. "I can hardly see the ground." This was an exaggeration; what he meant was that he could not make out the details he was accustomed to. Also, it would have been nice to have some of the people see him flying. He could buzz around the North Village, astounding the scoffers, qualifying for his citizenship . . . no, that would not be honest. Too bad the most tempting things were not right to do.

"I don't want to advertise," Donald said. "It could complicate things if people thought I was alive again."

Oh. Perhaps so. There could be renewed expectations, maybe debts to be paid, ones that mere silver would not abate. The shade's business was necessarily anonymous, at least so far as the community was concerned.

"See that glint?" Donald inquired, pointing down between two clouds. "That's the silver oak tree. It's so well hidden it can be spotted only from above. But I can tell my boy exactly where to find it. Then I can rest."

"I wish you could tell me where to find a magic talent," Bink said wistfully.

"You don't have one? Every citizen of Xanth has magic."

"That's why I'm not a citizen," Bink said glumly. They both spoke through the same mouth. "I'm going to the Good Magician. If he can't help me, I'll be exiled."

"I know the feeling. I spent two years exiled in that cave."

"What happened to you?"

"I was flying home, after discovering the silver tree, and a storm came up. I was so excited by the thought of riches that I couldn't wait. I risked the trip in high winds—and got blown into the Gap. The impact was so great I landed in the cave—but I was already dead."

"I didn't see any bones."

"You didn't see any hole in the ground, either. The dirt filled in over me, and then my body got washed away by the river."

"But—"

"Don't you know anything? It's the place of death that anchors the shade, not the place of the corpse."

"Oh. Sorry."

"I hung on, though I knew it was hopeless. Then you came." Donald paused. "Look, you've done me such a favor—I'll share the silver with you. There's enough on that tree for both my family and you. Only promise not to tell anyone else where it is."

Bink was tempted, but a moment's reflection changed his mind. "I need magic, not silver. Without magic, I'll be exiled from Xanth, so I won't be able to share the silver. With magic—I don't care about wealth. So if you want to share it, share it with the tree; don't take all its leaves, but just a few at a time, and some of the silver acorns that drop, so the tree can go on living in health and perhaps reproduce itself. In the long run that will be more productive anyway."

"It was a fortunate day for me when you dropped into my cave," Donald said. He banked into a curve, going down.

Bink's ears popped again as they descended. They dropped into a forest glade, then walked half a mile to an isolated, run-down farm. It took that much motion to completely eliminate the lingering cramps in Bink's legs. "Isn't it beautiful?" Donald inquired.

Bink looked at the rickety wooden fence and sagging roof. A few chickens scratched among the weeds. But to a man who had love invested here, love enough to sustain him two years after violent death, it must be the fairest of ranches. "Um," he said.

"I know it isn't much—but after that cave, it is like heaven itself," Donald continued. "My wife and boy have magic, of course, but it isn't enough. She cures feather fade in chickens, and he makes little dust devils. She brings in barely enough to feed them. But she's a good wife, and lovely beyond belief."

Now they entered the yard. A seven-year-old boy looked up from the picture he was making in the dirt. He reminded Bink briefly of the werewolf boy he had left—was it only six hours ago? But that impression was destroyed when this boy opened his mouth. "Go 'way!" he yelled.

"Better I don't tell him," Donald said slowly, a bit taken aback. "Two years—that's a long time for that age. He doesn't recognize this body. But see how he's grown."

They knocked on the door. A woman answered: plain, in a dingy dress, her hair swept back under a soiled kerchief. In her heyday she might have been ordinary; now hard work had made her old before her time.

She hasn't changed a bit, Donald thought admiringly. Then, aloud: "Sally!"

The woman stared at him with uncomprehending hostility.

"Sally—don't you know me? I'm back from the dead to wrap up my affairs."

"Don!" she exclaimed, her pale eyes lighting at last.

Then Bink's arms enfolded her, and his lips kissed hers. He saw her through Donald's overwhelming emotion—and she was good and lovely beyond belief.

Donald drew back, staring into the splendor of her love as he spoke. "Mark this, darling: thirteen miles north-northeast of the small millpond, beside a sharp east-west ridge, there is a silver tree. Go harvest it—a few leaves at a time, so as not to damage it. Market the metal as far away as you can, or get a friend to do it for you. Tell no one the source of your wealth. Remarry—it will make a fine dowry, and I want you to be happy, and the boy to have a father."

"Don," she repeated, tears of grief and joy in her eyes. "I don't care about silver, now that you're back."

"I'm not back! I'm dead, returning only as a shade to tell you of the tree. Take it, use it, or my struggle has been for nothing. Promise!"

"But—" she started, then saw the look on his face. "All right, Don, I promise. But I'll never love any other man!"

"My onus is abated, my deed is done," Donald said. "One more time, beloved." He bent to kiss her again—and dissipated. Bink found himself kissing another man's wife.

She knew it immediately, and jerked her face away. "Uh, sorry," Bink said, mortified. "I have to go now."

She stared at him, suddenly hard-eyed. What little joy remained in her had been wrung out by the brief manifestation of her husband. "What do we owe you, stranger?"

"Nothing. Donald saved my life by flying us away from the Gap dragon in the chasm. The silver is all yours. I will never see you again."

She softened, comprehending that he was not going to take away the silver. "Thank you, stranger." Then, on obvious impulse: "You could share the silver, if you wanted. He told me to remarry—"

Marry her? "I have no magic," Bink said. "I am to be exiled." It was the kindest way he could think of to decline. Not all the silver of Xanth could make this situation attractive to him, on any level.

"Will you stay for a meal?"

He was hungry, but not that hungry. "I must be on my way. Do not tell your son about Donald; he felt it would only hurt the boy. Farewell."

"Farewell," she said. Momentarily he saw a hint of the beauty Donald had seen in her; then that too was lost.

Bink turned and left. On the way out of the farm he saw a whirling dust devil coming toward him, product of the boy's minor malice toward strangers. Bink dodged it and hurried away. He was glad he had done this favor for the prospector, but also relieved that it was done. He had not properly appreciated before what poverty and death could mean to a family.

Chapter 4

Illusion

Bink resumed his journey—on the wrong side of the chasm. If only Donald's farm had been to the south!

Strange, how everyone here knew about the chasm and took it for granted—yet nobody in the North Village did. Could it be a conspiracy of silence? That seemed unlikely, because the centaurs didn't seem to know about it either, and they were normally extremely well informed. It had been present for at least two years, since the shade had been there that long, and probably much longer, since the Gap dragon must have spent its whole life there.

It must be a spell—an ignorance spell, so that only those people in the immediate vicinity of the chasm were aware of it. Those who departed—forgot. Obviously there had never been a clear path from the north to the south of Xanth—not in recent years.

Well, that was not his concern. He just had to get around it. He was not going to attempt to cross it again; only a phenomenal series of coincidences had saved his skin. Bink knew that coincidence was an untrustworthy ally.

The land here was green and hilly, with head-high candy-stripe ferns sprouting so thickly that it was impossible to see very far ahead. He had no beaten trail now. He got lost once, apparently thrown off by an aversion spell. Some trees protected themselves from molestation by causing the traveler to veer aside, so as to pass some distance from them. Maybe that was how the silver oak had remained undiscovered so long. If someone got into a patch of such trees, he could be bounced far afield, or even routed in a perpetual circle. It could be difficult indeed to break out of that sort of trap, because it was not at all obvious; the traveler thought he was going where he wanted to go.

Another time he encountered a very fine path going right his way, so fine that natural caution made him avoid it. There were a number of wilderness cannibal plants that made access very attractive, right up until the moment their traps sprung.

Thus it was three days before he made significant progress—but he remained in good form, apart from his cold. He found a few nosegays that helped clear his nose, and a pillbox bush with headache pills. At irregular intervals there were colorfruit trees, bearing greens, yellows, oranges, and blues. He had fair luck finding lodging each night, for he was obviously a fairly harmless type, but he also had to spend some hours in labor, earning his board. The people of this hinterland were minimally talented; their magic was of the "spot on a wall" variety. So they lived basically Mundane lives, and always needed chores done.

At last the land wound down to the sea. Xanth was a peninsula that had never adequately been mapped—obviously! the unmarked chasm proved that! —so its precise dimensions were unknown, perhaps unknowable. In general, it was an oval or oblong stretching north-south, connected to Mundania by a narrow bridge of land on the northwest. Probably it had been an island at one time, and so evolved its distinct type of existence free from the interference of the outside world. Now the Shield had restored that isolation, cutting off the land bridge by its curtain of death and wiping out the personnel of invading ships. If that weren't enough, there was said to be a number of ferocious sea monsters. Offshore. No, Mundania did not intrude any more.

Bink hoped the sea would permit him to get around the chasm. The Gap dragon probably could not swim, and the sea monsters should not come too close to land. There should be a narrow section where neither dragon nor sea monster prevailed. Maybe a beach he could walk across, plunging into the water if the terror of the chasm charged, and onto land if magic threatened from the sea.

There it was: a beautiful thread of white sand stretching from one side of the chasm to the other. No monsters were in sight. He could hardly believe his luck —but he acted before it could change.

Bink hit the beach running. For ten paces everything was fine. Then his foot came down on water, and he fell into the brine.

The beach was illusion. He had fallen for a most elementary trap. What better way for a sea monster to catch its prey than a vanishing beach converting to deep water?

Bink stroked for the real shoreline, which he now saw was a rocky waste upon which the waves broke and spumed. Not a safe landing at all, but his only choice. He could not go back on the "beach" he had come along; it no longer seemed to exist even in illusion. Either he had somehow been borne across the water or he had been swimming without knowing it. Either way, it was not magic he cared to get tangled up in again. Better to know exactly where he was.

Something cold and flat and immensely powerful coiled around one ankle. Bink had lost his staff when the Gap dragon ran him down, and had not yet cut a new one; all he had was his hunting knife. It was a puny resource against a sea monster, but he had to try.

He drew the knife from its sheath, held his breath, and lashed in the vicinity of his ankle. What held him felt like leather; he had to saw at it to sever it. These monsters were tough all over

Something huge and murky loomed at him under the water, reeling in the tongue he sawed at. Yard-long teeth flashed as the giant jaws opened.

Bink lost what little nerve he had left. He screamed.

His head was underwater. The scream was a disaster. Water rushed into his mouth, his throat.

Firm hands were pressing his back rhythmically, forcing the water out, the air in. Bink choked and hacked and coughed. He had been rescued! "I—I'm okay!" he gasped.

The hands eased off. Bink sat up, blinking.

He was on a small yacht. The sails were of brightly colored silk, the deck of polished mahogany. The mast was gold.

Gold? Gold plate, maybe. Solid gold would have been so heavy as to overbalance the ship.

Belatedly, he looked at his rescuer, and was amazed again. She was a Queen.

At least, she looked like a Queen. She wore a platinum crownlet and a richly embroidered robe, and she was beautiful. Not as lovely as Wynne, perhaps; this woman was older, with more poise. Precise dress and manner made up for the sheer voluptuous innocence of youth that Wynne had. The Queen's hair was the richest red he had ever seen—and so were the pupils of her eyes. It was hard to imagine what a woman like this would be doing boating in monster-infested surf.

"I am the Sorceress Iris," she said.

"Uh, Bink," he said awkwardly. "From the North Village." He had never met a Sorceress before, and hardly felt garbed for the occasion.

"Fortunate I happened by," Iris remarked. "You might have had difficulties."

The understatement of the year! Bink had been finished, and she had given him back his life. "I was drowning. I never saw you. Just a monster," he said, feeling inane. How could he thank this royal creature for sullying her delicate hands on something like him?

"You were hardly in a position to see anything," she said, straightening so that her excellent figure showed to advantage. He had been mistaken; she was in no way inferior to Wynne, just different, and certainly more intelligent. More on a par with Sabrina. The manifest mind of a woman, he realized, made a great deal of difference in her appeal. Lesson for the day.

There were sailors and servants aboard the yacht, but they remained unobtrusively in the background, and Iris adjusted the sails herself. No idle female, she!

The yacht moved out to sea. Soon it bore upon an island—and what an island it was! Lush vegetation grew all around it, flowers of all colors and sizes: polka-dot daisies the size of dishes, orchids of exquisite splendor, tiger lilies that yawned and purred as the boat approached. Neat paths led from the golden pier up toward a palace of solid crystal, which gleamed like a diamond in the sun.

Like a diamond? Bink suspected it was a diamond, from the way the light refracted through its myriad faces. The largest, most perfect diamond that ever was.

"I guess I owe you my life," Bink said, uncertain as to how to handle the situation. It seemed ridiculous to offer to chop wood or pitch animal manure to earn his keep for the night; there was nothing so crude as firewood or animal refuse on this fair island! Probably the best favor he could do her was to remove his soaking, bedraggled presence as rapidly as possible.

"I guess you do," she agreed, speaking with a surprising normality. He had somehow expected her to be more aloof, as befitted pseudo-royalty.

"But my life may not be worth much. I don't have any magic; I am to be exiled from Xanth."

She guided the yacht to the pier, flinging a fine silver chain to its mooring post and tying it tight.

Bink had thought his confession would disturb her; he had made it at the outset so as not to proceed under false pretenses. She might have mistaken him for someone of consequence. But her reaction was a surprise. "Bink, I'm glad you said that. It shows you are a fine, honest lad. Most magic talents aren't worthwhile anyway. What use is it to make a pink spot appear on a wall? It may be magic, but it doesn't accomplish anything. You, with your strength and intelligence, have more to offer than the great majority of citizens."

Amazed and pleased by this gratuitous and probably unjustified praise, Bink could make no answer. She was correct about the uselessness of spot-on-wall magic, certainly; he had often thought the same thing himself. Of course, it was a standard remark of disparagement, meaning that a given person had picayune magic. So this really was not a sophisticated observation. Still, it certainly made him feel at ease.

"Come," Iris said, taking him by the hand. She guided him across the gangplank to the pier, then on along the main path to the palace.

The smell of flowers was almost overwhelming. Roses abounded in all colors, exhaling their perfumes. Plants with sword-shaped leaves were even more common; their flowers were like simplified orchids, also of all colors. "What are those?" he inquired.

"Irises, of course," she said.

He had to laugh. "Of course!" Too bad there was no flower named "Bink."

The path passed through a flowering hedge and looped around a pool and fountain to the elaborate front portico of the crystal palace. Not a true diamond after all. "Come into my parlor," the Sorceress said, smiling.

Bink's feet balked, before the significance penetrated to his brain. He had heard about spiders and flies! Had she saved his life merely to—

"Oh, for God's sake!" she exclaimed. "Are you superstitious? Nothing will hurt you."

His recalcitrance seemed foolish. Why should she revive him, then betray him? She could have let him choke to death instead of pumping the water out of him; the meat would have been as fresh. Or she could have tied him up and had the sailors bring him ashore. She had no need to deceive him. He was already in her power—if that was the way it was. Still . . .

"I see you distrust me," Iris said. "What can I do to reassure you?"

This direct approach to the problem did not reassure him very much. Yet he had better face it—or trust to fate. "You—you are a Sorceress," he said. "You seem to have everything you need. I—what do you want with me?"

She laughed. "Not to eat you, I assure you!"

But Bink was unable to laugh. "Some magic—some people do get eaten." He suffered a vision of a monstrous spider luring him into its web. Once he entered the palace—

"Very well, sit out there in the garden," Iris said. "Or wherever you feel safe. If I can't convince you of my sincerity, you can take my boat and go. Fair enough?"

It was too fair; it made him feel like an ungrateful lout. Now it occurred to Bink that the whole island was a trap. He could not swim to the mainland—not with the sea monsters there—and the yacht's crew might grab him and tie him up if he tried to sail across.

Well, it wouldn't hurt to listen. "All right."

"Now, Bink," she said persuasively—and she was so lovely in her intensity that she was very persuasive indeed. "You know that though every citizen of Xanth has magic, that magic is severely limited. Some people have more magic than others, but their talents still tend to be confined to one particular type or another. Even Magicians obey this law of nature."

"Yes." She was making sense—but what was the point?

"The King of Xanth is a Magician—but his power is limited to weather effects. He can brew a dust devil or a tornado or a hurricane, or make a drought or a ten-day downpour—but he can't fly or transmute wood into silver or light a fire magically. He's an atmospheric specialist."

"Yes," Bink agreed again. He remembered Donald the shade's son, who could make dust devils, those evanescent swirls of dust. The boy had an ordinary talent; the King had a major one—yet they differed in degree, not type.

Of course, the King's talent had faded with age; perhaps all he could conjure now would be a dust devil. It was a good thing the Shield protected Xanth!

"So if you know a citizen's talent, you know his limitations," Iris continued. "If you see a man make a storm, you don't have to worry about him forming a magical pit under you or changing you into a cockroach. Nobody has multiple *fields* of talent."

"Except maybe Magician Humfrey," Bink said.

"He is a powerful Magician," she agreed. "But even he is restricted. His talent is divination, or information; I don't believe he actually looks into the future, just the present. All his so-called hundred spells relate to that. None of them are performance magic."

Bink did not know enough about Humfrey to refute that, but it sounded correct. He was impressed with how the Sorceress kept up with the magic of her counterpart. Was there professional rivalry among those of strong magic? "Yes—talents run in schools. But—"

"My talent is illusion," she said smoothly. "This rose—" She plucked a handsome red one and held it under his nose. What a sweet smell! "This rose, in reality, is . . ."

The rose faded. In her hand was a stalk of grass. It even smelled grassy.

Bink looked around, chagrined. "All of this is illusion?"

"Most of it. I could show you the whole garden as it is, but it would not be nearly as pretty." The grass in her hand shimmered and became an iris flower. "This should convince you. I am a powerful Sorceress. Therefore I can make an entire region seem like something it is not, and every detail will be authentic. My roses smell like roses, my apple pies taste like apple pies. My body—" she paused with half a smile. "My body feels like a body. All seems real—but it is illusion. That is, each thing has a basis in fact, but my magic enhances it, modifies it. This is my complex of talents. Therefore I have no other talent— and you can trust me to that extent."

Bink was uncertain about that last point. A Sorceress of illusion was the last type of person to be trusted, to any extent! Yet he comprehended her point now. She had shown him her magic, and it was unlikely that she would practice any other magic on him. He had never thought of it this way before, but it was certainly true that no one in Xanth mixed types of magic talents.

Unless she were an ogre, using illusion to change her own appearance, too . . . No. An ogre was a magical creature, and magical creatures did not have magical talents. Probably. Their talents *were* their existence. So centaurs, dragons, and ogres always seemed like what they were, unless some natural person, animal, or plant changed them. He had to believe that! It was possible that Iris was in collusion with an ogre—but unlikely, for ogres were notoriously impatient, and tended to consume whatever they could get hold of, regardless of the consequence. Iris herself would have been eaten by this time.

"Okay, I trust you," Bink agreed dubiously.

"Good. Come into my palace, and I will tend to all your needs."

That was unlikely. No one could give him a magic talent of his own. Humfrey might discover his talent for him—at the price of a year's service!—but that would be merely revealing what was there, not creating it.

He suffered himself to be led into the palace. It was exquisite inside, too. Rainbow-hued beams of light dropped down from the prismatic roof formations, and the crystal walls formed mirrors. These might be illusion—but he saw his own reflection in them, and he looked somehow healthier and more manly than he felt. He was hardly bedraggled at all. More illusion?

Soft pretty pillows were piled in the corners in lieu of chairs or couches. Suddenly Bink felt very tired; he needed to lie down for a while! But then the image of the skeleton in the pine forest returned to him. He didn't know what to feel.

"Let's get you out of those wet clothes," Iris said solicitously.

"Uh, I'll dry," Bink said, not wanting to expose his body before a woman.

"Do you think I want my cushions ruined?" she demanded with housewifely concern. "You were floundering in salt water; you've got to rinse the salt off before you start itching. Go into the bathroom and change; there is a dry uniform awaiting you."

A uniform awaiting him? As though she had been expecting him. What could that mean?

Reluctantly, Bink went. The bathroom was, appropriately, palatial. The tub was like a small swimming pool, and the commode was an elegant affair of the type the Mundanes were said to employ. He watched the water circle around the bowl and drain out into a pipe below, disappearing as if by magic. He was fascinated.

There was also a shower; a spray of water, like rain, emerged from an elevated nozzle, rinsing him off. That was sort of fun, though he was not sure he would want it as a regular thing. There must be a big tank of water upstairs somewhere, to provide the pressure for such devices.

He dried with a plush towel embroidered with images of irises.

The clothing was hung on a rack behind the door: a princely robe, and knickers. Knickers? Ah, well—they were dry, and no one would see him here in the palace. He donned the uniform, and stepped into the ornate sandals awaiting him. He strapped his hunting knife on, concealing it beneath the overhang of the robe.

Now he felt better—but his cold was developing apace. His sore throat had given way to a runny nose; he had thought this was merely aggravation by the salt water he had taken in, but now he was dry and it was apparent that his nose needed no external supply of fluid. He didn't want to sniff overtly, but he had no handkerchief.

"Are you hungry?" Iris asked solicitously as he emerged. "I will fetch you a banquet."

Bink certainly was hungry, for he had eaten only sparingly from his pack since starting along the chasm, depending on foraging along the way. Now his pack was soaked with salt water; that would complicate future meals.

He lay half buried in cushions, his nose tilted back so that it wouldn't dribble forward, surreptitiously mopping it with the corner of a pillow when he had to. He snoozed a bit while she puttered in the kitchen. Now that he knew this was all illusion, he realized why she did so much menial work herself. The sailors and gardeners were part of the illusion; Iris lived alone. So she had to do her own cooking. Illusion might make for fine appearance, texture, and taste, but it would not prevent her from starving.

Why didn't Iris marry, or exchange her services for competent help? Much magic was useless for practical matters, but her magic was extraordinary. Anyone could live in a crystal palace if he lived with this Sorceress. Bink was sure many people would like that; appearance was often more important than substance anyway. And if she could make ordinary potatoes taste like a banquet, and medicine taste like candy—oh yes, it was a marketable talent!

Iris returned, bearing a steaming platter. She had changed into a housewifely apron, and her crownlet was gone. She looked less regal and a good deal more female. She set things up on a low table, and they sat cross-legged on cushions, facing each other.

"What would you like?" she inquired.

Again Bink felt nervous. "What are you serving?"

"Whatever you like."

"I mean—really?"

She made a moue. "If you must know, boiled rice. I have a hundred-pound bag of the stuff I have to use up before the rats catch on to the illusory cat I have guarding it and chew into it. I could make rat droppings taste like caviar, of course, but I'd rather not have to. But you can have anything you want— anything at all." She took a deep breath.

So it seemed—and it occurred to Bink that she was not restricting it to food. No doubt she got pretty lonely here on her island, and welcomed company. The local farmers probably shunned her—their wives would see to that!—and monsters weren't very sociable.

"Dragon steak," he said. "With hot sauce."

"The man is bold," she murmured, lifting the silver cover. The rich aroma wafted out, and there lay two broiled dragon steaks steeped in hot sauce. She served one expertly onto Bink's plate, and the other onto her own.

Dubiously, Bink cut off a piece and put it to his mouth. It was the finest dragon steak he had ever tasted—which was not saying much, since dragons were very difficult prey; he had eaten it only twice before. It was a truism that more people were eaten by dragons than dragons eaten by people. And the sauce —he had to grab for the glass of wine she had poured for him, to quench the heat. But it was a delicious burn, converting to flavor.

Still, he doubted. "Uh—would you mind . . . ?"

She grimaced. "Only for a moment," she said.

The steak dissolved into dull boiled rice, then back into dragon meat.

"Thanks," Bink said. "It's still a bit hard to believe."

"More wine?"

"Uh, is it intoxicating?"

"No, unfortunately. You could drink it all day and never feel it, unless your own imagination made you dizzy."

"Glad to hear it." He accepted the elegant glass of sparkling fluid as she refilled it, and sipped. He had gulped down the first too fast to taste it. Maybe it was actually water, but it seemed to be perfect blue wine, the kind specified for dragon meat, full-bodied and delicately flavored. Much like the Sorceress herself.

For dessert they had home-baked chocolate-chip cookies, slightly burned. That last touch made it so realistic that he was hard put to it to preserve his disbelief. She obviously knew something about cooking and baking, even in illusion.

She cleared away the dishes and returned to join him on the cushions. Now she was in a low-cut evening gown, and he saw in more than adequate detail exactly how well-formed she was. Of course, that too could be illusion—but if it felt the same as it looked, who would protest?

Then his nose almost dripped onto the inviting gown, and he jerked his head up. He had been looking a mite *too* closely.

"Are you unhappy?" Iris inquired sympathetically.

"Uh, no. My nose—it—"

"Have a handkerchief," she said, proffering a lovely lace affair.

Bink hated to use such a work of art to honk his nose into, but it was better than using the pillows.

"Uh, is there any work I can do before I go?" he inquired uneasily.

"You are thinking too small," Iris said, leaning forward earnestly and inhaling deeply. Bink felt the flush rising along his neck. Sabrina seemed very far away— and she would never have dressed like this, anyway.

"I told you—I have to go to the Good Magician Humfrey to find my magic— or be exiled. I don't really think I have any magic, so—"

"I could arrange for you to stay, regardless," she said, nudging closer.

She was definitely making a play for him. But why would such an intelligent, talented woman be interested in a nobody like him? Bink mopped his nose again. A nobody with a cold. Her appearance might be greatly enhanced by illusion, but mind and talent were obviously genuine. She should have no need of him—for anything.

"You could perform magic that everyone would see," she continued in that dismayingly persuasive way of hers, nudging up against him. She certainly felt real—most provocatively so. "I could fashion an illusion of performance that no one could penetrate." He wished she hadn't said that while touching him so intimately. "I can do my magic from a distance, too, so there would be no way to tell I was involved. But that is the least of it. I can bring you wealth and power and comfort—all genuine, nonillusive. I can give you beauty and love. All that you might desire as a citizen of Xanth—"

Bink grew more suspicious. What was she leading up to? "I have a fiancée—"

"Even that," Iris agreed. "I am not a jealous woman. You could have her as a concubine, provided you were circumspect."

"As a concubine!" Bink exploded.

She was unshaken. "Because you would be married to me."

Bink stared at her, aghast. "Why should you want to marry a man with no magic?"

"So I could be Queen of Xanth," she said evenly.

"Queen of Xanth! You'd have to marry the King."

"Precisely."

"But—"

"One of the quaint, archaic laws and customs of Xanth is that the nominal ruler must be male. Thus some perfectly capable magical females have been eliminated from consideration. Now the present King is old, senile, and without heir; it is time for a Queen. But first there must be a new King. That King could be you."

"Me! I have no knowledge of governing."

"Yes. You would naturally leave the dull details of government to me."

Now at last it was coming clear. Iris wanted power. All she needed was a suitable figurehead, to get herself installed. One sufficiently talentless and naive to be readily managed. So he would never get delusions of actually being King. If he cooperated with her, he would be dependent on her. But it was a fair offer. It provided a viable alternative to exile, regardless of the state of his own magic.

This was the first time he had seen his magic infirmity as a potential asset. Iris did not want an independent man or legitimate citizen; she would have no lasting hold on that kind of person. She needed a magic cripple like him— because without her he would be nothing, not even a citizen.

That diminished the romantic aspect considerably. Reality always did seem to be less enticing than illusion. Yet his alternative was to plunge back into the wilderness on a mission he suspected was futile. His luck was already considerably overextended; his chances of even making it as far as the castle of the Magician Humfrey were not ideal, since he now had to trek through the fringe of the central wilderness. He would be a fool not to accept the offer of the Sorceress.

Iris was watching him intently. As he looked back at her, her gown flickered, becoming transparent. Illusion or not, it was a breathtaking sight. And what difference did it make if the flesh only seemed real? He had no doubt now of what she was offering on the immediate, personal level. She would be glad to prove how good she could make it, as she had with the meal. Because she needed his willing cooperation.

Really, it made sense. He could have citizenship and Sabrina, since obviously the Sorceress Queen would never betray that aspect . . .

Sabrina. How would she feel about the arrangement?

He knew. She would not buy it. Not for anything, not for an instant. Sabrina was very straitlaced about certain things, very proper in the forms.

"No," he said aloud.

Iris's gown snapped opaque. "No?" Suddenly she sounded like Wynne, when he had told that idiot girl she could not accompany him.

"I don't want to be King."

Now Iris's voice was controlled, soft. "You don't think I can do it?"

"I rather think you can. But it's not my sort of thing."

"What *is* your sort of thing, Bink?"

"I just want to be on my way."

"You want to be on your way," she repeated, with great control. "Why?"

"My fiancée wouldn't like it if I—"

"She wouldn't like it!" Iris was working up a substantial head of steam, like the Gap dragon. "What does she offer you that I cannot better a hundredfold?"

"Well, self-respect, for one thing," Bink said. "She wants me for myself, not to use me."

"Nonsense. All women are the same inside. They differ only in appearance and talent. They all use men."

"Maybe so. I'm sure you know more about that sort of thing than I do. But I have to be going now."

Iris reached out a soft hand to restrain him. Her gown disappeared entirely. "Why not stay the night? See what I can do for you? If you still want to go in the morning—"

Bink shook his head. "I'm sure you could convince me overnight. So I have to go now."

"Such candor!" she exclaimed ruefully. "I could give you an experience like none you have imagined."

In her artful nudity, she already stimulated his imagination far more than was comfortable. But he steeled himself. "You could never give me back my integrity."

"You idiot!" she screamed, with a startling shift of attitude. "I should have left you to the sea monsters."

"They were illusions too," he said. "You set up the whole thing, to make me beholden to you. The illusion beach, the illusion threat, all. That was your leather strap that wrapped around my ankle. My rescue was no coincidence, because I never was in danger."

"You are in danger now," she gritted. Her lovely bare torso became covered by the military dress of an Amazon.

Bink shrugged and stood up. He blew his nose. "Good-bye, Sorceress."

She studied him appraisingly. "I underestimated your intelligence, Bink. I'm sure I can improve my offer, if you will only let me know what you want."

"I want to see the Good Magician."

Now her rage burst out anew. "I'll destroy you!"

Bink walked away from her.

The crystal ceiling of the palace cracked. Fragments of glass broke off and dropped toward him. Bink ignored them, knowing they were unreal. He kept walking. He was quite nervous, but was determined not to show it.

There was a loud, ominous crunching sound, as of stone collapsing. He forced himself not to look up.

The walls shattered and fell inward. The remaining mass of the roof tumbled down. The noise was deafening. Bink was buried in rubble—and pushed on through it, feeling nothing. Despite the choking smell of dust and plaster, and the continued rumble of shifting debris, the palace was not really collapsing. Iris was a marvelous mistress of illusion, though! Sight, sound, smell, taste—everything but touch. Because there had to be something to touch, before she could convert it to feel like something else. Thus there was no solidity to this collapse.

He banged face first into a wall. Jarred more than physically, he rubbed his cheek and squinted. It was a wooden panel, with flaking paint. The real wall, of the real house. The illusion had concealed it, but now reality was emerging. Doubtless she could have made it feel like gold or crystal or even like slimy slugs, but the illusion was breaking down. He could find his way out.

Bink felt his way along the wall, tuning out the terrifying sights and sounds of the collapse, hoping she did not change the feel of the wall so that he would be deceived by that and led astray. Suppose it became a row of mousetraps or thistles, forcing his hand away?

He found the door and pulled it invisibly open. He had made it! He turned and for a moment looked back. There was Iris, standing in the splendor of her female fury. She was a middle-aged woman running slightly to fat, wearing a worn housecoat and sloppy hair net. She had the physical qualities she had shown him via her peek-a-boo outfit, but they were much less seductive at age forty than at the illusion of age twenty.

He stepped outside. Lightning flared and thunder cracked, making him jump. But he reminded himself that Iris was mistress of illusion, not weather, and walked out into it.

Rain pelted him, and hailstones. He felt the cold splats of water on his skin, and the stones stung—but they had no substance, and he was neither wet nor bruised after the initial sensation. Iris's magic was in its prime, but there were limits to illusion, and his own disbelief in what he saw tended to reduce the impact.

Suddenly there was the bellow of a dragon. Bink jumped again. A fire-belching winged beast was bearing down on him, not a mere steamer like the Gap dragon, but a genuine flamer. Seemingly genuine; was it real or illusion? Surely the latter—but he could not take the chance. He dived for cover.

The dragon swooped low, passing him. He felt the wash of air from its motion, the blast of heat. He still didn't know for sure, but he might be able to tell from its action; real fire-belchers were very stupid, as dragons went, because the heat shriveled their own brains. If this one reacted intelligently—

It looped about almost immediately, coming at him for a second run. Bink made a feint to the right, then scooted left. The dragon was not fooled; it zeroed right in on him. That was the intellect of the Sorceress, not the animal.

Bink's heart was thudding, but he forced himself to stand upright and still, facing the menace as it came. He lifted one finger in an obscene gesture at it.

The dragon opened its jaws, blowing out a tremendous cloud of fire and smoke that enveloped Bink, singeing the hair of his body—and leaving him untouched.

He had gambled and won. He had been almost certain, but his body still trembled in reaction, for none of his senses had doubted the illusion. Only his brain had defended him, preventing him from being reduced to quivering acquiescence to the will of the Sorceress, or from being herded into some genuine hazard. Illusions could kill—if one heeded them.

Bink moved out again, with more confidence. If there were a real dragon in the vicinity, there would have been no need for an illusory one; therefore all dragons here were illusion.

He stumbled. Illusion could hurt him another way, though—by covering up dangerous breaks in the terrain, forcing him to misstep or fall or drop into a well. He would have to watch his step—literally.

As he concentrated on the region near his feet, he was able to penetrate the illusion with greater facility. Iris's talent was phenomenal, but in covering the entire island it was necessarily thinly spread. His will could oppose hers in a localized area while her attention was distracted. Behind the façade of the flower gardens was the weedy wilderness of the island. The palace was a rickety shack, first cousin to the farmhouses he had met along the way. Why build a good house when illusion could do it so much easier?

His borrowed clothing, too, had changed. Now he wore a crude feminine shawl and—he verified with dismay—panties. Lacy silk girl-style panties. His fancy handkerchief was exactly what it appeared to be. Apparently the Sorceress did indulge herself in some reality, and lace hankies were what she could afford. And panties.

He hesitated. Should he go back for his own clothing? He didn't want to encounter Iris again, but to travel in the wilderness or meet people in *this* outfit—

He had a vision of walking up to the Good Magician Humfrey to ask for his boon of information.

BINK: Sir, I have come across Xanth at great peril to ask—

MAGICIAN: For a new dress? A bra? Ho, ho, ho!

Bink sighed, feeling his face redden again. He turned back.

Iris spotted him as soon as he reentered the shack. A flicker of hope lighted her face—and that briefly honest expression had more compulsion than all her illusion. Human values moved Bink. He felt like the supreme heel.

"You changed your mind?" she asked. Suddenly her voluptuous youth was back, and a section of the glittering palace formed around her.

That dashed it. She was a creature of artifice, and he preferred reality—even the reality of a shack among weeds. Most of the farmers of Xanth had nothing better, after all. When illusion became an essential crutch to life, that life lost value. "Just want my own clothes," Bink said. Though his decision was firm, he still felt like a heel for interfering with her splendid aspirations.

He proceeded to the bathroom—which he now saw was an attached outhouse. The fabulous toilet was merely the usual board with a hole sawed in it, and flies buzzed merrily below it. The bathtub was a converted horse-watering trough. How had he taken a shower? He saw a bucket; had he dumped water on his own head, not knowing it? His clothing and pack were in a pile on the floor.

He started to change—but found that the facility was really only an opening in the back wall of the shack. Iris stood watching him. Had she watched him change before? If so, he had to take it as a compliment; her approach had become much more direct and physical thereafter.

His eye fell on the bucket again. *Someone* had dumped water on him, and he was sure now that he had not done it himself. The only other person who could have done it—ouch!

But he was not about to display himself so freely to her again, though it was obvious that he had no physical secrets remaining! He picked up his things and headed for the door.

"Bink—"

He paused. The rest of the house was dull wood, with flaking paint, straw on the floor, and light showing through the cracks. But the Sorceress herself was lovely. She wore very little, and she looked a lush eighteen.

"What do you want in a woman?" she asked him. "Voluptuousness?" She became extremely well endowed, with an exaggerated hourglass figure. "Youth?" Suddenly she looked fourteen, very slender, lineless and innocent. "Maturity?" She was herself again, but better dressed. "Competence?" Now she was conservatively dressed, about twenty-five, quite shapely but of a businesslike mien. "Violence?" The Amazon again, robust but still lovely.

"I don't know," Bink said. "I'd really hate to choose. Sometimes I want one thing, sometimes another."

"It can all be yours," she said. The alluring fourteen-year-old reappeared. "No other woman can make this promise."

Bink was suddenly, forcefully tempted. There were times when he wanted this, though he had never dared admit it openly. The Sorceress's magic was potent indeed—the strongest he had ever experienced. So it was illusion—yet in Xanth illusion abounded, and was quite legitimate; it was never possible to know precisely what was real. In fact, illusion was part of Xanth reality, an important part. Iris really could bring him wealth and power and citizenship, and she could be, for him, any kind of woman he wanted. Or all kinds.

Furthermore, through her illusions, applied politically, she could in time create an identical reality. She could build an actual crystal palace with all the trappings; the powers of the Queenship would make this possible. In that light, it was reality she offered, with her magic simply a means to that end.

But what was actually in her scheming mind? The reality of her inner thoughts might not be sweet at all. He could never be sure he understood her completely, and therefore could never trust her completely. He was not at all sure she would make a good Queen; she was too interested in the trappings of power, instead of the welfare of the land of Xanth as a whole.

"I'm sorry," he said, and turned away.

She let him go. No more palace, no more storm. She had accepted his decision—and that, perversely, tempted him again. He could not call her evil; she was merely a woman with a need, and she had offered a deal, and was mature enough to accede to necessity, once her temper cooled. But he forced himself to keep going, trusting his logic more than his meandering feeling.

He picked his way down to the sagging wharf, where the rowboat was tied. The craft looked insecure, but it had brought him here, so it could take him away.

He got into it—and stepped into a puddle. The boat leaked. He grabbed a rusty pail and bailed it out somewhat, then sat and took the oars.

Iris must have performed quite a maneuver, to row this boat while seeming to be an idle Queen. She had a lot of plain old-fashioned practical talent to supplement her magic. She probably *could* make a good ruler of Xanth—if she ever found a man who would go along with her.

Why hadn't he cooperated? As he rowed, he considered the matter more carefully, looking back at the isle of illusion. His superficial reasons were sufficient for the moment, but not for an enduring decision. He must have some underlying rationale to which he was true, even though he gave himself some more-presentable justification. It could not just be his memory of Sabrina, evocative as that was, for Iris was as much of a woman as Sabrina, and much more magical. There had to be something else, diffuse but immense—ah, he had it! It was his love of Xanth.

He could not allow himself to become the instrument of his homeland's corruption. Though the present King was ineffective, and many problems were developing, still Bink was loyal to the established order. The days of anarchy, or of brute might making right, were over; there were set procedures for the transfer of authority, and these had to be honored. Bink would do anything to stay in Xanth—except to betray it.

The ocean was calm. The devastating rocks of the shore had also been illusion; there was after all a small beach—but it was not where it had seemed to be, either when he thought he ran along it or after he was in the brine. A long narrow pier angled out from the side of the chasm; that was what he had run along at the beginning. Until he had simply run off the end, splashing abruptly into deep water. In more than one sense.

He beached his boat on the south shore. Now—how was he to return the boat to the Sorceress?

No way. If she didn't have another boat, she would simply have to swim for it. He regretted that, but he was not going back to that isle of illusion again. With her powers, she could probably scare away any sea creatures that threatened, and he was sure she was an adequate swimmer.

He changed into his original clothes, salty though they might be, shrugged into his knapsack, and turned his face to the west.

Chapter 5

Spring

The landscape south of the chasm was rougher than that to the north. It was not hilly, but mountainous. The tallest peaks were enchanted with white snow. The narrow passes were choked with almost impenetrable growth, forcing Bink to detour again and again. Ordinary nettles and itch bushes would have been bad, but there was no telling what magic these strange plants had. A lone tangle tree was well worth avoiding, and there were whole groves of related species. He could not risk it.

So whenever an aspect of the jungle balked him, Bink turned back and tried again farther along. He avoided the most obvious paths also; they were suspect. Thus he tramped through intermediate vegetation—the borderline between jungle and field, often in the roughest terrain of all: barren, burning rock faces; steep rocky slopes; high windswept plateaus. What even magic plants disdained was hardly worth any person's trouble—except for the traveler who wanted to stay out of trouble. One cleared area turned out to be the landing strip for a very large flying dragon; no wonder there were no other predators in that region. Bink's progress was so slow that he knew it would take him many days to reach the Good Magician's castle.

He fashioned himself a burrow in the ground, with a pile of stones for a windshield and dead brush for a blanket, and slept uncomfortably. He wondered now why he hadn't at least accepted the Sorceress's offer to stay the night; it would surely have been much more comfortable than this.

No, he knew why he had to go. He might never have left the island after that night. Not as his own man. And if he had, Sabrina would never have forgiven him. The very fact that such a night tempted him in retrospect—and not merely for the comfort of sleep—meant that it was not a night he could have afforded.

He reminded himself of that several times before he shivered himself to sleep. Then he dreamed of a diamond-crystal palace, woke with mixed emotions, and had to shiver his way to sleep again. Turning down temptation certainly wasn't much pleasure when alone on the open trail. Tomorrow he would search diligently for a blanket tree and some hotsoup gourds.

On the third morning of his south-chasm leg, he trekked along a ridge, his only feasible route westward. He had cut himself a new staff, after several tries; the first saplings he went for magicked him off by using aversion spells of assorted types. He had no doubt there were many suitable trees he never saw at all, because of their passive "do not notice me" spells. One used a physical repulsion charm directed at cutting objects; every time he slashed at it, his knife veered away.

About an hour on the way with his new staff, he was still pondering the natural selectivity of magic. The plants with the most effective spells survived best, so became more common, but how many times did stray travelers come by here with knives? Then he realized that he might make good use of that repulsion spell. If he succeeded in cutting a staff from such a tree, would it repel all attacks against him? Obviously this magic was for defense against the depredations of dragons, beavers, and such, not actual knives, and he would certainly feel safer with an anti-dragon staff. No; cutting the tree would kill it, and its magic would abate. But maybe a seed from it—

No sense consuming time going back; he should be able to locate another such tree. All he had to do was attempt to cut a new staff and note which tree repulsed his knife. He might be able to dig up a small one and take it entire, keeping it alive and effective.

He moved down the side of the ridge, testing trees. This proved to be more hazardous than anticipated; the knife's approach toward their tender bark brought out the worst in them. One dropped hard fruit on him, barely missing his head; another exhaled sleep perfume that almost stopped his journey right there. But no cutting-aversion spells, now.

One large tree had a dryad, an inhabiting wood nymph, who looked very fetching, about like Iris at fourteen, but who cursed Bink roundly in most unladylike language. "If you want to carve defenseless things, go carve your own kind!" she screamed. "Go carve the wounded soldier in the ditch, you son of a—" Fortunately she balked at completing the rhyme. Dryads were not supposed to know such language.

Wounded soldier? Bink located the ditch and explored it carefully. Sure enough, there lay a man in military apparel, blood crusted on his back, groaning piteously.

"Peace," Bink said. "I will help you, if you permit." Xanth had once needed a real army, but now the soldiers were mostly messengers for the King. Still, their costumes and pride remained.

"Help me!" the man exclaimed weakly. "I will reward you—somehow."

Now Bink felt it safe to approach. The soldier was severely wounded and had lost much blood. He was burning with the fever of infection. "I can't do anything for you myself; I'm no doctor, and if I even move you, you may expire. I will return with medication," Bink said. "I must borrow your sword." If the soldier gave up his sword, he was really sick.

"Return soon—or not at all," the man gasped, raising the hilt.

Bink took the heavy weapon and climbed out of the ditch. He approached the tree of the dryad. "I need magic," he told her. "Blood restoration, wound healing, fever abatement—that sort of thing. Tell me where I can get them, quickly, or I will chop your tree down."

"You wouldn't!" she cried, horrified.

Bink hefted the sword menacingly. At this moment he reminded himself of Jama, the village sword conjurer; the image disgusted him.

"I'll tell! I'll tell!" she screamed.

"Okay. Tell." He was relieved; he doubted that he could actually have made himself chop down her tree. That would have killed her, and to no real purpose. Dryads were harmless creatures, pretty to look at; there was no point in molesting them or their cherished tree homes.

"Three miles to the west. The Spring of Life. Its water will cure anything."

Bink hesitated. "There is something you're not telling me," he said, hefting the sword again. "What's the catch?"

"I may not reveal it," she cried. "Anyone who tells—the curse—"

Bink made as if to chop at the trunk of the tree. The dryad screamed with such utter misery that he abated the effort. He had fought to protect Justin Tree back at home; he could not ravage this one. "All right. I'll risk the curse," he said. He set off westward.

He found a path leading his way. It was not an inviting one, merely an animal run, so he felt justified in using it with caution. It seemed others knew the route to the Spring. Yet as he approached, he became increasingly nervous. What was the catch, and what was the curse? He really ought to know before he either risked himself or gave the water to the ailing soldier.

Xanth was the land of magic—but magic had its rules, and its qualifications. It was dangerous to play with magic unless the precise nature of the spell was understood. If this water really could heal the soldier, it was a most strongly enchanted Spring. For that sort of aid, there had to be a price.

He found the Spring. It was in a depression, under a giant spreading acorn tree. The tree's health augured well for the water; it could hardly be poisoned. But there could be some other menace associated with it. Suppose a river monster were hiding in it, using the water as a lure for the unwary? Injured or dying creatures would be easy prey. A false reputation for healing would attract them from many miles around.

Bink didn't have time to wait and watch. He had to help the soldier now or it would be too late. So this was a risk he simply had to take.

He moved cautiously to the Spring. It looked cool and clear. He dipped his canteen into it, keeping his other hand on the sword. But nothing happened; no grim tentacle rose from the depths to challenge him.

Viewing the filled canteen, he had another thought. Even if the water were not poisoned, it was not necessarily curative. What use to take it to the soldier, if it wouldn't do the job?

There was one way to find out. He was thirsty anyway. Bink put the canteen to his mouth and sipped.

The water was chill and good. He drank more deeply, and found it supremely refreshing. It certainly wasn't poisoned.

He dipped the canteen again and watched the bubbles rise. They distorted the view of his left hand under the water, making it seem as if he had all his fingers. He did not think much about the digit he had lost in childhood, but such a view of a supposedly complete hand teased him unpleasantly.

He lifted out the canteen—and almost dropped it. *His finger was whole!* It really was! The childhood injury had been eliminated.

He flexed it and touched it, amazed. He pinched it and it hurt. No question: his finger was real.

The Spring really *was* magic. If it could heal a fifteen-year-old amputation so cleanly and painlessly and instantly, it could heal anything!

How about a cold? Bink sniffed—and discovered that his nose was clear. It had cured his sniffles, too.

No question about it: he could recommend this Spring of Life. A true description for a potent magic. If this Spring were a person, it would be a full Magician.

Again Bink's natural caution came into play. He still did not know the nature of the catch—or of the curse. Why could no one tell the secret of this Spring? What was the secret? Obviously not the fact of its healing properties; the dryad had told him that, and he could tell it to others. The curse could not be a river monster, for none had struck. Now that Bink was whole and well, he would be much better able to defend himself. Scratch one theory.

But this did not mean there was no danger. It merely meant the threat was more subtle than he had thought. A subtle danger was the worst of all. The man who fled from the obvious menace of a flaming dragon could succumb to the hidden menace of the peace spell of the pines.

The soldier was dying. Moments were precious, yet Bink delayed. He had to ferret this out, lest he put both the soldier and himself in greater peril than before. It was said that a person should not look a gift unicorn in the mouth, lest it prove to be enchanted, but Bink always looked.

He kneeled before the Spring and stared deep into it. Looking it in the mouth, as it were. "O Spring of Life," he murmured. "I come on a mission of mercy, seeking no profit for myself, though I have indeed benefited. I conjure you to reveal your rationale, lest I inadvertently trespass." He had little confidence in this formal invocation, since he had no magic with which to enforce it, but it was all he could think of. He just couldn't accept such a wonderful gift without trying to ascertain the payment to be exacted. There was always a price.

Something swirled deep in the Spring. Bink felt the potent magic of it. It was as if he peered through a hole into another world. Oh, yes—this Spring had its own consciousness and pride! The field of its animus rose up to encompass him, and his consciousness plunged through the depths, bringing comprehension. *Who imbibes of me may not act against my interest, on pain of forfeiture of all that I bring him.*

Uh-oh. This was a self-preservation spell, plain and simple. But enormously complicated in its execution. Who defined what was or was not contrary to the interests of the Spring? Who but the Spring itself? There would obviously be no lumbering in this region, for cutting trees could damage the environment and change the climate, affecting rainfall. No mining, for that could lower the water table and pollute the Spring. Even the prohibition against revealing the rationale made sense, for people with minor injuries and complaints might not use the magic water if they knew the price in advance. The loggers and miners certainly wouldn't. But any action had extending if diminishing consequences, like the ripples of a stone dropped in a pool. In time such ripples could cover the whole ocean. Or the whole of Xanth, in this case.

Suppose the Spring decided that its interest was threatened indirectly by some action of the distant King of Xanth, such as levying a tax on lumber that caused the lumbermen to cut more wood in order to pay it. Would the Spring force all its users to oppose the King, perhaps assassinating him? A person who owed his life to the Spring might very well do it.

It was theoretically possible for this magic Spring to change the whole society of Xanth—even to become its *de facto* ruler. But the interests of one isolated Spring were not necessarily the interests of the human society. Probably the magic of the Spring could not extend to such extremes, for it would have to be as strong as the massed powers of all the other entities of Xanth. But slowly, given time, it would have its effect. Which made this an ethical question.

"I cannot accept your covenant," Bink said into the deep swirl. "I hold no animosity toward you, but I cannot pledge to act only in your interest. The interest of the whole of Xanth is paramount. Take back your benefits; I go my own way."

Now there was anger in the Spring. The unfathomable depths of it roiled. The field of magic rose up again, enveloping him. He would suffer the consequence of his temerity.

But it faded like a dissipating storm, leaving him . . . whole. His finger remained healed, and his cold was still cured. He had called the Spring's bluff—and won.

Or had he? Maybe his benefits would not be revoked until he acted specifically against the interest of the Spring. Well, his benefits were minor; he could afford the penalty. He certainly would not be deterred from doing what he felt was right by fear of that consequence.

Bink stood, keeping the sword in his hand as he slung the strap of the canteen over his shoulder. He turned.

A chimera was crawling toward him.

Bink whipped his sword around, though he was hardly expert in its use. Chimeras were dangerous!

But in a moment he saw that the creature was in dire straits. The tongue was hanging out of its lion's head, its goat's head was unconscious, and the snake's head at the end of the tail was dragging on the ground. The creature was scraping along on its stomach toward the Spring, trailing blood.

Bink stood aside and let it pass. He held no malice even for a chimera in this state. He had never before seen a living creature suffering like this. Except the soldier.

The chimera reached the water and plunged its lion head in, drinking desperately.

The change was immediate. The goat's head snapped erect and awake, swiveling from its neck in the middle of the back to glare at Bink. The snake head hissed.

No doubt about it: the chimera was healthy again. But now it was dangerous, for this class of monster hated all things human. It took a step toward Bink, who held his sword tightly before him with both hands, knowing that flight would be futile. If he wounded it, he might escape before it dragged itself back to the Spring for a second restoration.

But abruptly the thing turned away, without attacking. Bink sighed with relief; he had put up a front, but the last thing he wanted to do was to engage in combat with such a monster, in the presence of an unfriendly Spring.

There must be a general truce in this vicinity, Bink realized. It was contrary to the interest of the Spring to have predators lurk here, so no hunting or fighting was permitted. Lucky for him!

He scrambled up the slope and headed east. He hoped the soldier had survived.

The soldier had. He was tough, as soldiers tended to be; he refused to gasp out his last until nature ripped it from him. Bink dribbled some magic water into his mouth, then poured some over the wound. Suddenly the man was well.

"What did you do?" he cried. "It is as if I never got stabbed in the back."

They walked up the hill together. "I fetched water from a magic Spring," Bink explained. He paused at the dryad's tree. "This accommodating nymph very kindly directed me to it."

"Why, thank you, nymph," the soldier said. "Any favor I can do in return—"

"Just move on," she said tightly, eyeing the sword in Bink's hands.

They moved on. "You can't act contrary to the interest of that Spring," Bink said. "Or tell anyone about the price you paid for its help. If you do, you'll be right back where you started. I figured the price was worth it, for you."

"I'll say! I was doing patrol duty, guarding a patch of the King's eyeball ferns, when somebody—hey, one drink of this elixir and the King's eyes would be perfect without those ferns, wouldn't they? I should take—" He broke off.

"I can show you where the Spring is," Bink offered. "Anybody can use it, as far as I know."

"No, it's not that. I just suddenly got the feeling—I don't think the King ought to have this water."

This simple comment had a profound impact on Bink. Did it confirm his reasoning, that the Spring's influence extended widely and selfishly? Revived health of the King might not be in the interest of the Spring, so—

But, on the other hand, if the King were cured by Spring water, then the King himself would serve the Spring's interest. Why should the Spring object to that?

Also, why had Bink himself not suffered the loss of his finger and restoration of his cold when he told the secret to the soldier? He had defied the Spring, yet paid no penalty. Was the curse a mere bluff?

The soldier extended his hand. "I'm Crombie. Corporal Crombie. You saved my life. How can I repay you?"

"Oh, I just did what was right," Bink said. "I couldn't just let you die. I'm on my way to the Magician Humfrey, to see if I have any magic talent."

Crombie put his hand to his beard, pondering. He was rather handsome in that pose. "I can tell you the direction." He closed his eyes, put out his right hand, and slowly rotated. When his pointing finger stabilized, he opened his eyes. "Magician's that way. That's my talent—direction. I can tell you where anything is."

"I already know the direction," Bink said. "West. My main problem is getting through all this jungle. There's so much hostile magic—"

"You said it," Crombie agreed heartily. "Almost as much hostile magic as there is in civilized regions. The raiders must have magicked me here, figuring I'd never get out alive and my body would never be found. My shade couldn't avenge me in the deep jungle."

"Oh, I don't know about that," Bink said, thinking of the shade Donald in the chasm.

"But now I've recovered, thanks to you. Tell you what: I'll be your bodyguard until you reach the Magician. Is that a fair return?"

"You really don't need to—"

"Oh, but I do! Soldier's honor. You did me a good turn, I'll do you a good turn. I insist. I can help a lot. I'll show you." He closed his eyes again, extended his hand, and rotated. When he stopped, he continued: "That's the direction of the greatest threat to your welfare. Want to verify it?"

"No," Bink said.

"Well, I do. Danger never went away by being ignored. You have to go out and conquer it. Give me back my sword."

Bink gave it back, and Crombie proceeded in the direction he had pointed: north.

Bink followed, disgruntled. He did not want to seek out danger, but he knew it was not right to let the soldier walk into it in his stead. Maybe it was something obvious, like the Gap dragon. But that was no immediate threat, so long as Bink stayed out of the chasm. He fully intended to stay out.

When Crombie found himself balked by thick brush, he simply slashed it away with his sword. Bink noticed that some of the vegetation gave way before the blade actually struck; if providing a path was the best route to survival, these plants took it. But suppose the soldier hacked into a tangle tree? That could be the danger he had pointed out.

No—a tangler was deadly to the unwary, but it did not move from the place it had rooted. Since Bink had been going west, not north, no stationary thing was much of a threat to him unless it was west.

There was a scream. Bink jumped, and Crombie held his sword at the ready. But it was only a woman, cringing and frightened.

"Speak, girl!" Crombie roared, flourishing his wicked blade. "What mischief do you intend?"

"Don't hurt me!" she cried. "I am only Dee, lost and alone. I thought you came to rescue me."

"You lie!" Crombie exclaimed. "You mean harm to this man, my friend who saved my life. Confess!" And he lifted his sword again.

"For God's sake—let her be!" Bink yelled. "You made a mistake. She's obviously harmless."

"My talent's never been wrong before," Crombie said. "This is where it pointed your greatest threat."

"Maybe the threat is behind her, beyond," Bink said. "She was merely in the line of sight."

Crombie paused. "Could be. I never thought of that." He was evidently a reasonable man, under the violence. "Wait, I'll verify."

The soldier withdrew somewhat, stationing himself to the east of the girl. He shut his eyes and rotated. His pointing finger came to bear squarely on Dee.

The girl burst into tears. "I mean you no harm—I swear it. Don't hurt me!"

She was a plain girl, of strictly average face and figure, no beauty. This was in contrast to the several females Bink had encountered recently. Yet there was something vaguely familiar about her, and Bink was always unnerved by feminine distress. "Maybe it's not physical danger," he said. "Does your talent differentiate?"

"No, it doesn't," Crombie admitted, a bit defensively. "It can be any kind of threat, and she may not actually mean you harm—but sure as hell, there's something."

Bink studied the girl, whose sniffles were drying up. That familiarity—where had he seen her before? She was not from the North Village, and he really had not encountered many girls elsewhere. Somewhere on his current journey?

Slowly the notion dawned on him: a Sorceress of illusion did not have to make herself beautiful. If she wanted to keep track of him, she could adopt a completely different appearance, thinking he would never suspect. Yet the illusion would be easiest to maintain if it corresponded somewhat to her natural contours. Take off a few pounds here and there, modify the voice—could be. If he fell for the ruse, he could be in dire danger of being led into corruption. Only the soldier's special magic gave it away.

But how could he be sure? Even if Dee represented some critical threat to him, he had to be sure he had identified the right danger. A man who stepped around a venom mouse could be overlooking a harpy on the other side. Snap judgments about magic were suspect.

A brilliant notion came to him. "Dee, you must be thirsty," he said. "Have a drink of water." And he proffered his canteen.

"Oh, thank you," she said, taking it gladly.

The water cured all ills. An enchantment was an ill, wasn't it? So if she drank, it might show her—at least momentarily—in her true guise. Then he would know.

Dee drank deeply.

There was no change.

"Oh, this is very good," she said. "I feel so much better."

The two men exchanged glances. Scratch one bright notion. Either Dee was not Iris, or the Sorceress had better control than he had supposed. He had no way of knowing.

"Now be on your way, girl," Crombie said curtly.

"I am going to see the Magician Humfrey," she said contritely. "I need a spell to make me well."

Again Bink and Crombie exchanged glances. Dee had drunk the magic water; she was well. Therefore she had no need to see the Good Magician on that score. She had to be lying. And if she were lying, what was she concealing from them?

She must have picked this particular destination because she knew Bink was going there. Yet this was still conjecture. It could be pure coincidence—or she could be an ogre in female form—a healthy ogre!—waiting for the expedient moment to strike.

Crombie, seeing Bink's indecision, made a decision of his own. "If you let her go with you, then I'm coming too. With my hand ever on my sword. Watching her—all the time."

"Maybe that's best," Bink agreed reluctantly.

"I bear you no malice," Dee protested. "I would do nothing to hurt you, even were I able. Why don't you believe me?"

Bink found it too complicated to explain. "You can travel with us if you want to," he said.

Dee smiled gratefully, but Crombie shook his head grimly and fingered the hilt of his sword.

Crombie remained suspicious, but Bink soon discovered he enjoyed Dee's company. She had no trace of the personality of the Sorceress. She was such an average girl that he identified with her to a considerable extent. She seemed to have no magic; at least, she evaded that subject. Perhaps she was going to the Magician in the hope of finding her talent; maybe that was what she had meant by needing a spell to make her well. Who was in good shape in Xanth without magic?

However, if she were the Sorceress Iris, her ruse would quickly be exposed by the divination of the Magician. So the truth would be known.

They stopped at the Spring of Life to refill their canteens, traveled half a day, then got caught by a technicolor hailstorm. It was magic, of course, or magic-augmented. The colors gave it away. Which meant that there would not be any great melting or runoff. All they had to do was take shelter from it until it passed.

But they happened to be on a barren ridge: no trees for miles around, no caves, no houses. The land went up and down, cut away by erosion gullies, strewn with boulders—but there was nothing to shield them effectively from the storm.

Pelted by increasingly large hailstones, the three scurried in the direction Crombie's magic pointed: the route to safe shelter. It came into view behind a boulder: a monstrously spreading tentacular tree.

"That's a tangler!" Bink exclaimed in horror. "We can't go there."

Crombie was brought up short, peering through the hail. "So it is. My talent never pointed wrong before."

Except when it accused Dee, Bink thought. He wondered just how reliable the soldier's magic really was. For one thing, why hadn't it pointed out the soldier's danger to himself, before he got stabbed in the back and left to die? But Bink did not say that out loud. There were often complexities and confusions in magic, and he was sure Crombie meant well.

"There's a hephalumph there," Dee cried. "Half eaten."

Sure enough, the huge carcass lay near the trunk orifice of the tree. Its posterior was gone, but the front end was untouched. The tree had evidently caught it and consumed as much as it could—but a hephalumph was so big that even a tangle tree could not polish it off in one meal. Now the tree was sated, its tentacles dangling listlessly.

"So it's safe after all," Bink said, wincing as an egg-sized red hailstone just missed his head. The hail was puffy and light, but it still could hurt. "It will be hours before the tree revives enough to become aggressive. Maybe even days—and even then, it'll start on the lumph first."

Still Crombie balked, understandably. "Could be an illusion, that carcass," he warned. "Be suspicious of all things—that's the soldier's motto. A trap to make us think the tree's docile. How do you think it tempted the hephalumph in there?"

Telling point. Periodic hailstorms on the ridge to drive prey to cover, and seemingly ideal cover waiting—beautiful system. "But we'll be knocked silly by hail if we don't get to cover soon," Bink said.

"I'll go," Dee said. Before Bink could protest, she plunged into the territory of the tree.

The tentacles quivered, twitching toward her—but lacked the imperative to make a real effort. She dashed up and kicked the hephalumph in the trunk—and it was solid. "No mirage," she cried. "Come on in."

"Unless she's a shill," Crombie muttered. "I tell you, she's a threat to you, Bink. If she shilled for the tangler, she could trick dozens of people into its clutches—"

The man was paranoid. Perhaps this was another useful quality for soldiers—though again, it didn't seem to have kept him out of trouble before. "I don't believe it," Bink said. "But I do believe this hailstorm! I'm going in." And he went.

He passed the outer fringe of tentacles nervously, but they remained quiescent. A hungry tangler was not a subtle plant; it normally grabbed the moment its prey was grabable.

Finally Crombie followed. The tree shuddered slightly, as if irritated by its inability to consume them, and that was all. "Well, I knew my talent told the truth. It always does," he said, somewhat weakly.

It was actually very nice here. The hailstones had grown to the size of clenched fists, but they bounced off the tree's upper foliage and piled up in a circle around it, caught by a slight depression. Predator trees tended to sit in such depressions, formed by the action of their tentacles while cleaning brush and rocks out of the way in order to have an attractive lawn for passing creatures. The refuse was tossed beyond in a great circle, so that in the course of years the land surface rose. The tangle was a highly successful type of tree, and some of them formed wells whose rims were fashioned from buried bones of past prey. They had been cleaned out near the North Village, but all children were instructed in this menace. Theoretically, a man pursued by a dragon could skirt a tangler, leading the dragon within range of the tentacles—if he had both courage and skill.

Within the shielded area there was a fine greensward rising in soft hillocks, rather like the torso of a woman. Sweet perfume odors wafted through, and the air was pleasantly warm. In short, this was a seemingly ideal place to seek shelter —and that was by design. It had certainly fooled the hephalumph. Obviously this was a good location, for the tangler had grown to enormous girth. But right now they were here rent-free.

"Well, my magic was right all the time," Crombie said. "I should have trusted it. But by the same token . . ." He glanced meaningfully at Dee.

Bink wondered about that. He believed in the soldier's sincerity, and the location magic was obviously functional. Had it malfunctioned in Dee's case, or was she really a bad if obscure threat? If so, what kind? He could not believe she meant him harm. He had suspected her of being Iris the Sorceress, but now he didn't believe that; she showed no sign of the temperament of the mistress of illusion, and personality was not something that magic could conceal for very long.

"Why didn't your magic warn you of the stab in the back?" Bink asked the soldier, making another attempt to ascertain what was reliable and what was not.

"I didn't ask it," Crombie said. "I was a damned fool. But once I see you safely to your Magician, I'll sure as hell ask it who stabbed me, and then . . ." He fingered the blade of his sword meaningfully.

A fair answer. The talent was not a warning signal; it merely performed on demand. Crombie had obviously had no reason to suspect danger, any more than Bink had reason to feel threatened now. Where was the distinction between natural caution and paranoia?

The storm continued. None of them were willing to sleep, because they did not trust the tree to that extent, so they sat and talked. Crombie told a tough story of ancient battle and heroism in the days of Xanth's Fourth Wave. Bink was no military man, but he found himself caught up in the gallantry of it, and almost wished he had lived in those adventurous times, when men of no magic were considered *men*.

By the end of that story, the storm had eased off, but the hail was piled so high that it didn't seem worthwhile to go out yet. Usually the meltoff from a magic storm was quite rapid once the sun came out again, so it was worth waiting for.

"Where do you live?" Bink asked Dee.

"Oh, I'm just a country girl, you know," she said. "No one else was going to travel through the wilderness."

"That's no answer," Crombie snapped suspiciously.

She shrugged. "It's the only answer I have. I can't change what I am, much as I might like to."

"It's the same answer I have, too," Bink said. "I'm just a villager, nothing special. I hope the Magician will be able to make me into something special, by finding out that I have some good magic talent no one ever suspected, and I'm willing to work for him for a year for that."

"Yes," she said, smiling appreciatively at him. Suddenly he felt himself liking her. She was ordinary—like him. She was motivated—like him. They had something in common.

"You're going for magic so your girl back home will marry you?" Crombie asked, sounding cynical.

"Yes," Bink agreed, remembering Sabrina with sudden poignancy. Dee turned away. "And so I can stay in Xanth."

"You're a fool, a civilian fool," the soldier said kindly.

"Well, it's the only chance I have," Bink replied. "Any gamble is worthwhile when the alternative—"

"I don't mean the magic. That's useful. And staying in Xanth makes sense. I mean marriage."

"Marriage?"

"Women are the curse of mankind," Crombie said vehemently. "They trap men into marriage, the way this tangle tree traps prey, and they torment them the rest of their lives."

"Now that's unfair," Dee said. "Didn't you have a mother?"

"She drove my worthy father to drink and loco," Crombie asserted. "Made his life hell on earth—and mine too. She could read our minds—that was her talent."

A woman who could read men's minds: hell indeed for a man! If any woman had been able to read Bink's mind—ugh!

"Must have been hell for her, too," Dee observed.

Bink suppressed a smile, but Crombie scowled. "I ran off and joined the army two years before I was of age. Never regretted it."

Dee frowned. "You don't sound like God's gift to women, either. We can all be thankful you never touched any."

"Oh, I touch them," Crombie said with a coarse laugh. "I just don't marry them. No one of them's going to get her hooks into me."

"You're disgusting," she snapped.

"I'm smart. And if Bink's smart, he'll not let you start tempting him, either."

"I wasn't!" she exclaimed angrily.

Crombie turned away in evident repugnance. "Ah, you're all the same. Why do I waste my time talking with the likes of you? Might as well argue ethics with the devil."

"Well, if you feel that way, I'll go!" Dee said. She jumped to her feet and stalked to the edge.

Bink thought she was bluffing, for the storm, though abating, was still in force with occasional flurries. Colored hailstones were mounded up two feet high, and the sun was not yet out.

But Dee plunged out into it.

"Hey, wait!" Bink cried. He ran after her.

Dee had disappeared, hidden by the storm. "Let her go, good riddance," Crombie said. "She had designs on you; I know how they work. I knew she was trouble from the start."

Bink put his arms up over his head and face against the hail and stepped out. His feet slid out from under, skidding on hailstones, and he fell headlong into the pile. Hailstones closed in over his head. Now he knew what had happened to Dee. She was buried somewhere out here.

He had to close his eyes, for powder from crushed stones was getting into them. This was not true ice, but coalesced vapor, magic; the stones were dry and not really cold. But they were slippery.

Something caught his foot. Bink kicked violently, remembering the sea monster near the island of the Sorceress, forgetting that it had been an illusion and that there could hardly be a sea monster here. But its grip was tight; it dragged him into an enclosure.

He scrambled to his feet as it let go. He leaped on the troll shape he saw through the film of dust.

Bink found himself flying through the air. He landed hard on his back, the creature drawing on his arm. Trolls were tough! He squirmed around and tried to grab its legs—but the thing dropped on top of him and pinned him firmly to the ground. "Ease up, Bink," it said. "It's me—Crombie."

Bink did as much of a double-take as he was able to, considering his position, and recognized the soldier.

Crombie let him up. "I knew you'd never find your way out of that mess, so I hauled you out by the one part I could reach, your foot. You had magic dust in your eyes, so you couldn't recognize me. Sorry I had to put you down."

Magic dust—of course. It distorted the vision, making men seem like trolls, ogres, or worse—and vice versa. It was an additional hazard of such storms, so that people could not see their way out of them. Probably many victims had seen the tangle tree as an innocent blanket tree. "That's okay," Bink said. "You soldiers sure know how to fight."

"All part of the business. Never charge a man who knows how to throw." Crombie raised one finger near his ear, signifying an idea. "I'll show you how to do it; it's a nonmagical talent you can use."

"Dee!" Bink cried. "She's still out there!"

Crombie grimaced. "Okay. I made her walk out; if it means so much to you, I'll help you find her."

So the man did have some decency, even with regard to women. "Do you really hate them all?" Bink asked as he girded himself to wrestle with the hail again. "Even the ones who don't read minds?"

"They all read minds," Crombie asserted. "Most of them do it without magic, is all. But I won't swear as there's no girl in the whole of Xanth for me. If I found a pretty one who wasn't mean or nagging or deceitful . . ." He shook his head. "But if any like that exist, they sure as hell wouldn't marry me."

So the soldier rejected all women because he felt they rejected him. Well, it was a good enough rationale.

Now the storm had stopped. They went out into the piled hailstones, stepping carefully so as not to take any more spills. The colored storm clouds cleared, dissipating rapidly now that their magic imperative was spent.

What caused such storms? Bink wondered. They had to be inanimate—but the course of this journey had convinced him that dead objects did indeed have magic, often very strong magic. Maybe it was in the very substance of Xanth, and it diffused slowly into the living and nonliving things that occupied the land. The living things controlled their shares of magic, channelizing it, focusing it, making it manifest at will. The inanimate things released it haphazardly, as in this storm. There had to be a lot of magic here, gathered from a large area. All wasted in a pointless mass of hailstones.

Yet not all pointless. Obviously the tangle tree benefited from such storms, and probably there were other ways in which they contributed to the local ecology. Maybe the hail culled out the weaker creatures, animals less fit to survive, facilitating wilderness evolution. And other inanimate magic was quite pointed, such as that of Lookout Rock and the Spring of Life—its magic distilled from water percolating through the entire region, intensifying its potency? Perhaps it was the magic itself that made these things conscious of their individuality. Every aspect of Xanth was affected by magic, and governed by it. Without magic, Xanth would be—the very notion filled him with horror—Xanth would be Mundane.

The sun broke through the clouds. Where the beams struck, the hailstones puffed into colored vapor. Their fabric of magic could not withstand the beat of direct sunlight. That made Bink wonder again: was the sun antipathetic to magic? If the magic emanated from the depths, the surface of the land was the mere fringe of it. If someone ever delved down deep, he might approach the actual source of power. Intriguing notion!

In fact, Bink wished that he could set aside his quest for his own personal magic and make that search for the ultimate nature of reality in Xanth. Surely, way down deep, there was the answer to all his questions.

But he could not. For one thing, he had to locate Dee.

In a few minutes all the hail was gone. But so was the girl. "She must have slid down the slope into the forest," Crombie said. "She knows where we are; she can find us if she wants to."

"Unless she's in trouble," Bink said worriedly. "Use your talent; point her out."

Crombie sighed. "All right." He closed his eyes, rotated, and pointed down the south side of the ridge.

They trotted down—and found her tracks in the soft earth at the fringe of the jungle. They followed them and soon caught up.

"Dee!" Bink cried gladly. "We're sorry. Don't risk the jungle alone."

She marched on determinedly. "Leave me alone," Dee said. "I don't want to go with you."

"But Crombie didn't really mean—" Bink said.

"He meant. You don't trust me. So keep away from me. I'd rather make it on my own."

And that was that. She was adamant. Bink certainly wasn't going to force her. "Well, if you need help or anything, call—or something—"

She went on without answering.

"She couldn't have been very much of a threat," Bink said forlornly.

"She's a threat, all right," Crombie insisted. "But no threat's as much of a threat when it's somewhere else."

They ascended the ridge again and traveled on. In another day they came in sight of the Magician's castle, thanks to the soldier's unerring magic directional sense and ability to avoid the dangers of the wilderness. He had been a big help.

"Well, that's it," Crombie said. "I have seen you to this point safely, and I think that about squares us. I have business of my own elsewhere before I report to the King for reassignment. I hope you find your magic."

"I hope so too," Bink said. "Thanks for the throws you taught me."

"It was little enough. You'll have to practice them a lot more before they'll really serve. Sorry I got the girl mad at you. Maybe my talent was wrong about her after all."

Bink didn't care to discuss that aspect, so he just shook hands and headed for the castle of the Good Magician.

Chapter 6

Magician

The castle was impressive. It was not large, but it was tall and well designed. It had a deep moat, a stout outer wall, and a high inner tower girt with parapets and embrasures. It must have been built by magic, because it would have taken an army of skilled craftsmen a year to build it by hand.

Yet Humfrey was supposed to be a Magician of information, not of construction or illusion. How could he have magicked such an edifice?

No matter; the castle was here. Bink walked down to the moat. He heard a horrible kind of galloping splash, and around from behind the castle came a horse, running on the water. No, not a horse—a hippocampus, or seahorse, with the head and forefeet of a horse and the tail of a dolphin. Bink knew the dolphin only from old pictures; it was a kind of magic fish that breathed air instead of water.

Bink stepped back. The thing looked dangerous. It could not follow him out onto land, but it could pulverize him in water. How was he to cross the moat? There did not seem to be any drawbridge.

Then he noted that the hippocampus wore a saddle. Oh, no! Ride the water monster?

Yet it obviously was the way to go. The Magician did not want his time wasted by anyone who wasn't serious. If he lacked the nerve to ride the seahorse, he didn't deserve to see Humfrey. It made perverse sense.

Did Bink really want the answer to his question? At the price of a year's service?

The picture of beautiful Sabrina came to his mind, so real, so evocative that all else became meaningless. He walked up to the hippocampus, waiting at the edge of the moat expectantly, and climbed onto its saddle.

The creature took off. It neighed as it sped around the moat, instead of across it. The steed was jubilant, using the water as a veritable race track, while Bink clung desperately to the saddle horn. The powerful front legs of the hippocampus terminated in flippers rather than hooves, scooping gouts of water back on either side, drenching him with the spray. The tail, curled in a muscular loop when the creature was stationary, uncoiled and threshed the water with such vigor that the saddle whipped back and forth, threatening to dislodge the rider momentarily.

"Neigh! Ne-ei-igh!" the monster sounded gleefully. It had him where it wanted him: right in the saddle, ripe for bucking off. The moment he hit the water, it would turn and devour him. What a fool he had been!

Wait—so long as he remained in the saddle, it could not get at him. All he had to do was hang on, and in time it would tire.

Easier thought than done. The hippocampus bucked and plunged, first lifting him above the moat, then immersing him in the frothing water. It curled its tail into a spiral and rolled, dunking him again and again. Bink was afraid it would stop with him on the bottom, forcing him to let go or drown. But the saddle was firmly fixed on its backside, and its horse's head projected the same direction Bink's head did, so it had to hold its breath when he held his. The monster was exercising, while Bink was merely hanging on; it was using more energy than he, and so it had to breathe sooner. Hence it could not drown him—once he had figured this out.

In fact, all he needed to do was keep his head and he would win, for whatever that was worth.

Finally the creature gave up. It flopped to the inner gate and lay still while Bink dismounted. He had conquered the first hurdle.

"Thank you, Hip," he said, making a little bow to the seahorse. It snorted and splashed quickly out of reach.

Now Bink faced a giant wooden door. It was closed, and he pounded on it with one fist. It was so solid that his hand hurt, and the sound was minimized: *dink—dink—dink!*

He drew his knife and rapped with the handle, since he had lost his new staff in the moat—with no better result. If a hollow partition made the most noise, this was indubitably solid. There was no way to force it.

Maybe the Magician was out? There should still be servants attending to the castle.

Bink was getting angry. He had made a long, hazardous journey to get here, and he was ready to pay the exorbitant price for one piddling bit of information —and the damned Good Magician lacked the courtesy even to answer the door.

Well, he would get in despite the Magician. Somehow. He would *demand* his audience.

He studied the door. It was a good ten feet tall and five feet wide; it seemed to have been made of handhewn eight-by-eight posts. The thing must weigh a ton —literally. It had no hinges, which meant it had to open by sliding to one side —no, the portals were solid stone. Lifted out of the way? There were no connecting ropes to haul it up, no pulleys that he could see. There might be hidden screws set into the wood, but that seemed a lot of trouble and somewhat risky. Screws sometimes let go at inopportune moments. Maybe the whole door dropped into the floor? But that, too, was stone. So it seemed the whole mass simply had to be removed every time someone wanted access.

Ridiculous! It had to be a phony, a dummy. There would be a more sensible aperture for routine use, either magical or physical. All he had to do was find it.

In the stone? No, that would be unmanageably heavy; if it were not, it would represent a weakened place where an enemy could force entry. No point in building a substantial castle with such a liability. Where, then?

Bink ran his fingers over the surface of the huge mock-door. He found a crack. He traced it around in a square. Yes. He placed both hands against the center and shoved.

The square moved. It slid inward, and finally dropped inside, leaving a hole just big enough for a man to crawl through. Here was his entry.

Bink wasted no time. He climbed through the hole.

Inside was a dimly illuminated hall. And another monster.

It was a manticora—a creature the size of a horse, with the head of a man, body of a lion, wings of a dragon, and tail of a scorpion. One of the most ferocious magical monsters known.

"Welcome to lunch, little morsel," the manticora said, arching its segmented tail up over its back. Its mouth was strange, with three rows of teeth, one inside another—but its voice was stranger. It was something like a flute, and something like a trumpet, beautiful in its fashion but difficult to comprehend.

Bink whipped out his knife. "I am not your lunch," he said, with a good deal more conviction than he felt.

The manticora laughed, and now its tones were the sour notes of irony. "You are not anyone else's lunch, mortal. You have climbed nimbly into my trap."

He had indeed. But Bink was fed up with these pointless obstacles, and also suspected that they were not pointless, paradoxical as that might seem. If the Magician's monsters consumed all callers, Humfrey would never have any business, never obtain any fees. And by all accounts the Good Magician was a grasping man who existed principally to profit himself; he needed those exorbitant fees to increase his wealth. So probably this was another test, like those of the seahorse and the door; all Bink had to do was figure out the solution.

"I can walk back out of this cage any time I want to," Bink said boldly. He willed his knees not to knock together with his shivering. "It isn't made to hold people my size; it holds in monsters your size. You're the prisoner, molar-face."

"*Molar*-face!" the manticora repeated incredulously, showing about sixty molars in the process. "Why, you pipsqueak mortal, I'll sting you into a billion-year suffering sleep!"

Bink made for the square portal. The monster pounced, its tail stabbing forward over its head. It was horribly fast.

But Bink had only feinted; he was already ducking forward, directly at the lion's claws. It was the opposite direction from that which the monster had expected, and the thing could not reverse in midair. Its deadly tail stabbed into the wood of the door, and its head popped through the square hole. Its lion's shoulders wedged tightly against it, unable to fit through the hole, and its wings fluttered helplessly.

Bink could not resist. He straightened up, turned, and yelled: "You didn't think I came all the way here just to back out again, did you, you half-reared monster?" Then he planted a swift hard kick on the creature's posterior, just under the lifted tail.

There was a fluted howl of rage and anguish from the door. Then Bink was away, running down the hall, hoping that there was a man-sized exit. Otherwise—

The door seemed to explode. There was a thump behind as the manticora fell free and rolled back to its feet. It was really angry now! If there were no way out—

There was. The challenge had been to get around the monster, not to kill it; no man could kill such a creature with a knife. Bink scrambled through the barred gate as the manticora charged down the hall too late, splinters of wood falling from its tail.

Now Bink was in the castle proper. It was a fairly dark, dank place, with little evidence of human habitation. Where was the Good Magician?

Surely there would be some way to announce his presence, assuming that the ruckus with the manticora had not sufficed. Bink looked around and spied a dangling cord. He gave it one good yank and stepped back lest something drop on him. He did not quite trust this adorable castle.

A bell sounded. DONG-DONG, DONG-DONG.

A gnarled old elf trotted up. "Who shall I say is calling?"

"Bink of the North Village."

"Drink of what?"

"Bink! B-I-N-K."

The elf studied him. "What shall I say is the business of your master Bink?"

"*I* am Bink! My business is the quest for a magical talent."

"And what recompense do you offer for the invaluable time of the Good Magician?"

"The usual scale: one year's service." Then, in a lower tone: "It's robbery, but I'm stuck for it. Your master gouges the public horrendously."

The elf considered. "The Magician is occupied at the moment; can you come back tomorrow?"

"Come back tomorrow!" Bink exploded, thinking of what the hippocampus and manticora would do to him if they got a second chance. "Does the old bugger want my business or doesn't he?"

The elf frowned. "Well, if you're going to be that way about it, come on upstairs."

Bink followed the little man up a winding staircase. The interior of the castle lightened with elevation and became more ornate, more residential.

Finally the elf showed the way into a paper-filled study. The elf seated himself at a big wooden desk. "Very well, Bink of the North Village. You have won your way through the defenses of this castle. What makes you think your service is worth the old gouging bugger's while?"

Bink started to make an angry exclamation—but cut himself off as he realized that this was the Good Magician Humfrey. He was sunk!

All he could do now was give a straight answer before he got kicked out. "I am strong and I can work. It is for you to decide whether that is worth your while."

"You are oink-headed and doubtless have a grotesque appetite. You'd no doubt cost me more in board than I'd ever get from you."

Bink shrugged, knowing it would be futile to debate such points. He could only antagonize the Magician further. He had really walked into the last trap: the trap of arrogance.

"Perhaps you could carry books and turn pages for me. Can you read?"

"Some," Bink said. He had been a reasonably apt pupil of the centaur instructor, but that had been years ago.

"You seem to be a fair hand at insult, too; maybe you could talk intruders out of intruding with their petty problems."

"Maybe," Bink agreed grimly. Obviously, he had really done it this time—and after coming so close to success.

"Well, come on; we don't have all day," Humfrey snapped, bouncing out of his chair. Bink saw now that he was not a true elf, but a very small human being. An elf, of course, being a magical creature, could not be a Magician. That was part of what had put him off at first—though increasingly he wondered about the accuracy of that conjecture. Xanth continued to show him ramifications of magic he had not thought of before.

Apparently the Magician had accepted the case. Bink followed him to the next room. It was a laboratory, with magical devices cluttering the shelves and piled on the floor, except for one cleared area.

"Stand aside," Humfrey said brusquely, though Bink hardly had room to move. The Magician did not have an endearing personality. It would be a real chore to work for him a year. But it just might be worth it, if Bink learned he had a magic talent, and it was a good one.

Humfrey took a tiny bottle from the shelf, shook it, and set it on the floor in the middle of a pentagram—a five-sided figure. Then he made a gesture with both hands and intoned something in an arcane tongue.

The lid of the bottle popped off. Smoke issued forth. It expanded into a sizable cloud, then coalesced into the shape of a demon. Not a particularly ferocious demon; this one's horns were vestigial, and his tail had a soft tuft instead of a cutting barb. Furthermore, he wore glasses, which must have been imported from Mundania, where such artifacts were commonly used to shore up the weak eyes of the denizens there. Or so the myths had it. Bink almost laughed. Imagine a near-sighted demon!

"O Beauregard," Humfrey intoned. "I conjure thee by the authority vested in me by the Compact, tell us what magic talent this lad, Bink of the North Village of Xanth, possesses."

So that was the Magician's secret: he was a demon-summoner. The pentagram was for containing the demons released from their magic bottles; even a studious demon was a creature of hell.

Beauregard focused his lenscovered eyes on Bink. "Step into my demesnes, that I may inspect you properly," he said.

"Nuh-*uh!*" Bink exclaimed.

"You're a tough nut," the demon said.

"I didn't ask you for his personality profile," Humfrey snapped. "What's his magic?"

The demon concentrated. "He has magic—strong magic—but—"

Strong magic! Bink's hopes soared.

"But I am unable to fathom it," Beauregard said. He grimaced at the Good Magician. "Sorry, fathead; I'll have to renege on this one."

"Then get ye gone, incompetent," Humfrey snarled, clapping his hands together with a remarkably sharp report. Evidently he was used to being insulted; it was part of his life style. Maybe Bink had lucked out again.

The demon dissolved into smoke and drained back into his bottle. Bink stared at the bottle, trying to determine what was visible within it. Was there a tiny figure, hunched over a miniature book, reading?

Now the Magician contemplated Bink. "So you have strong magic that cannot be fathomed. Were you aware of this? Did you come here to waste my time?"

"No," Bink said. "I never was sure I had magic at all. There's never been any evidence of it. I hoped—but I feared I had none."

"Is there anything you know of that could account for this opacity? A counterspell, perhaps?"

Evidently Humfrey was far from omnipotent. But now that Bink knew he was a demon-conjurer, that explained it. Nobody summoned a demon without good reason. The Magician charged heavily for his service because he took a heavy risk.

"I don't know of anything," Bink said. "Except maybe the drink of magic healing water I took."

"Beauregard should not have been deceived by that. He's a pretty savvy demon, a real scholar of magic. Do you have any of that water with you?"

Bink held out his canteen. "I saved some. Never can tell when it might be needed."

Humfrey took it, poured out a drop on his palm, touched his tongue to it, and grimaced thoughtfully. "Standard formula," he said. "It doesn't bollix up informational or divinatory magic. I've got a keg of similar stuff in my cellar. Brewed it myself. Mine is free of the Spring's self-interest geis, of course. But keep this; it can be useful."

The Magician set up a pointer attached to a string, beside a wall chart with pictures of a smiling cherub and a frowning devil. "Let's play Twenty Questions."

He moved his hands, casting a spell, and Bink realized that his prior realization had been premature. Humfrey did do more than demon-summoning—but he still specialized in information. "Bink of the North Village," he intoned. "Have you oriented on him?"

The pointer swung around to indicate the cherub.

"Does he have magic?"

The cherub again.

"Strong magic?"

Cherub.

"Can you identify it?"

Cherub.

"Will you tell me its nature?"

The pointer moved to cover the devil.

"What is this?" Humfrey demanded irritably. "No, that's not a question, idiot! It's an exclamation. I can't figure why you spirits are balking." Angrily he cast the release spell and turned to Bink. "There's something mighty funny here. But it's become a challenge. I'm going to use a truth spell on you. We'll get to the heart of this."

The Magician waved his stubby arms again, muttered a vile-sounding incantation—and suddenly Bink felt strange. He had never experienced this odd type of magic before, with its gestures, words, and assorted apparatus; he was used to inherent talents that worked when they were willed to work. The Good Magician seemed to be something of a scientist—though Bink hardly understood that Mundane term, either.

"What is your identity?" Humfrey demanded.

"Bink of the North Village." It was the truth—but this time Bink said it because the spell compelled him to, not because he wanted to.

"Why did you come here?"

"To find out whether I have magic, and what it might be, so I shall not be exiled from Xanth and can marry—"

"Enough. I don't care about the sordid details." The Magician shook his head. "So you were telling the truth all along. The mystery deepens, the plot thickens. Now—what is your talent?"

Bink opened his mouth, compelled to speak—and there was an animal roar.

Humfrey blinked. "Oh—the manticora is hungry. Spell abate; wait here while I feed him." He departed.

An inconvenient time for the manticora to get hungry! But Bink could hardly blame the Magician for hastening to the feeding chore. If the monster should break out of its cage—

Bink was left to his own devices. He walked around the room, stepping carefully to avoid the litter, not touching anything. He came to a mirror. "Mirror, mirror on the wall," he said playfully. "Who is the fairest one of all?"

The mirror clouded, then cleared. A gross fat warty toad peered out. Bink jumped. Then he realized: this was a magic mirror; it had shown him the fairest one of all—the fairest toad.

"I mean, the fairest female human being," he clarified.

Now Sabrina looked out at him. Bink had been joking at first, but he should have realized that the mirror would take him seriously. Was Sabrina really the fairest girl of all? Probably not, objectively. The mirror showed her because, to Bink's prejudiced eye, she was the one. To some other man—

The picture changed. Now the girl Wynne looked out. Yes, she was pretty too, though too stupid to be worthwhile. Some men would like that very well, however. On the other hand—

Now the Sorceress Iris looked out, in her most beguiling illusion. "Well, it's about time you got around to me, Bink," she said. "I can still enable you to—"

"No!" Bink cried. And the mirror went blank.

He calmed himself, then faced the mirror again. "Can you answer informational questions too?" Of course it could; otherwise it wouldn't be here.

The mirror clouded and cleared. A picture of the cherub appeared, meaning yes.

"Why are we having so much trouble discovering my talent?"

The picture that formed this time was that of a foot, a paw—a monkey's paw.

Bink looked at it for some time, trying to figure out its meaning, but it eluded him. The mirror must have gotten confused and thrown in an irrelevant image.

"What is my talent?" he asked at last.

And the mirror cracked.

"What are you doing?" Humfrey demanded behind him.

Bink jumped guiltily. "I—seem to have broken your mirror," he said. "I was just—"

"You were just asking stupidly direct questions of an instrument designed for subtlety," Humfrey said angrily. "Did you actually think the mirror could reveal what the demon Beauregard balked at?"

"I'm sorry," Bink said lamely.

"You're a lot more trouble than you're worth. But you are also a challenge. Let's get on with it." The Magician made his gesture and incantation again, restoring the truth spell. "What is your—"

There was a crash. The glass had fallen out of the cracked mirror. "I wasn't asking you!" Humfrey yelled at it. He returned to Bink. "What—"

There was a shudder. The castle shook. "Earthquake!" the Magician exclaimed. "Everything happens at once."

He crossed the room and peered out an embrasure. "No, it's only the invisible giant passing by."

Humfrey returned once more to Bink. This time he squinted at him, hard. "It's not coincidence. Something is preventing you—or anything else—from giving that answer. Some very powerful, unidentified magic. Magician-caliber enchantment. I had thought there were only three persons of that rank alive today, but it seems there is a fourth."

"Three?"

"Humfrey, Iris, Trent. But none of these have magic of this type."

"Trent! The Evil Magician?"

"Perhaps you call him evil. I never found him so. We were friends, in our fashion. There is a kind of camaraderie at our level—"

"But he was exiled twenty years ago."

Humfrey looked slantwise at Bink. "You equate exile with death? He resides in Mundania. My information does not extend beyond the Shield, but I am sure he survives. He is an exceptional man. But without magic now."

"Oh." Bink had equated exile with death, emotionally. This was a good reminder; there was life beyond the Shield. He still did not want to go there, but at least it diminished the specter.

"Though it galls me exceedingly, I dare not push the question further. I am not properly protected against interference magic."

"But why would anyone try to prevent me from knowing my own talent?" Bink asked, bewildered.

"Oh, you know it. You just can't tell it—even to yourself. The knowledge is buried deep inside you. And there, it seems, it is going to remain. I simply am not prepared to take the risk involved for a mere one-year service; I'd almost certainly take a loss on that contract."

"But why would a Magician—I mean, I'm nobody! How could it benefit anybody else to stop me from—"

"It might not be a person at all, but a thing placing a geis on you. A geis of ignorance."

"But why?"

Humfrey grimaced. "Lad, you grow repetitive. Your talent could represent some threat to some powerful special interest. As a silver sword is a threat to a dragon, even though it may not be near that dragon. So that entity protects itself by blocking off your knowledge of your talent."

"But—"

"If we knew that, we'd know your talent," Humfrey snapped, answering the unformed question.

Still Bink persisted. "How can I demonstrate my talent, then, so I can stay in Xanth?"

"You do seem to have a problem," Humfrey remarked, as if it were of only academic importance. He shrugged. "I'd answer if I could, but I can't. There is of course no charge for my service, since I was unable to complete it. I will send a note with you. Perhaps the King will allow you to remain after all. I believe the bylaws specify that each citizen shall be possessed of magic, not that he actually has to demonstrate it in public. On occasion the demonstration is suspended. I remember one young man who was able to change the color of his urine at will, for example. An affidavit was accepted in lieu of public display."

Failure seemed to have mellowed the Magician considerably. He served Bink a pleasant meal of brown bread and milk—from his private breadfruit orchard and deerfly stable, respectively—and chatted almost sociably. "So many people come here and waste their questions," he confided. "The trick is not necessarily to find the answer, but to find the correct question. Yours is the first real challenge I've had in years. The last one was—let me think—the amaranth. This farmer wanted to know how to develop a really superior plant for greens and grain, so he could feed his family better, and bring in a little income for the comforts of life. I located the magic amaranth for him, and now its use has spread all over Xanth, and beyond it too, for all I know. It is possible to make bread from it that is almost indistinguishable from the real thing." The Magician pulled out a drawer and brought out a special loaf. "See, this has no stem; it was baked, not budded." He broke off a chunk for Bink, who was glad to accept it. "Now that was the kind of question to ask. The answer benefited the whole country of Xanth as well as the individual. Too many desires are of the monkey's-paw variety, in contrast."

"The monkey's paw!" Bink exclaimed. "When I asked the magic mirror, it showed me—"

"It would. The image derives from a Mundane story. They thought it was fiction. But here in Xanth there is magic like that."

"But what . . . ?"

"Do you want to invest a year's service after all?"

"Uh, no, not for that." Bink concentrated on chewing the new bread. It was tougher than true bread.

"Then have it free. It simply means a type of magic that brings you more grief than good, though it grants what you technically ask. Magic you are better off without."

Was Bink better off not knowing his talent? That was what the mirror had seemed to tell him. Yet how could exile, which would deprive him of it entirely, be better than knowledge? "Do many people come with questions, stupid or otherwise?"

"Not so many now that I built this castle and hid it. Only the really determined find their way here now. Like you."

"How did you build it?" So long as the Magician was talking . . .

"The centaurs built it. I told them how to rid themselves of a local pest, and they served me for a year. They are very skilled craftscreatures, and did a fine job. Periodically I foul up the routes here, applying spells of misdirection, so as not to be pestered by casual querists; it's a good location."

"The monsters!" Bink exclaimed. "The hippocampus, the manticora—they're serving their year's service, discouraging idle questioners?"

"Of course. Do you think they'd stay here for the mere pleasure of it?"

Bink wondered. He remembered the unholy glee with which the seahorse had flung itself about. Still, it would naturally prefer the open sea to a mere moat.

He had finished the bread. It *had* been almost as good as real bread. "With your powers of information, you could—why, you could be King."

Humfrey laughed, and there was nothing whining or bitter about it. "Who in his right mind would want to be King? It's a tedious, strenuous job. I am not a disciplinarian, but a scholar. Most of my labor is in making my magic safe and specific, refining it for greater applicability. Much remains to be done, and I am getting old. I can't waste time with diversions. Let those who wish the crown take it."

Disconcerted, Bink cast about for someone who wanted to rule Xanth. "The Sorceress Iris—"

"The trouble with dealing in illusion," Humfrey said seriously, "is that one begins to be deluded oneself. Iris doesn't need power half so much as she needs a good man."

Even Bink could see the truth in that. "But why doesn't she marry?"

"She's a Sorceress, a good one. She has powers you have not yet glimpsed. She requires a man she can respect—one who has stronger magic than she does. In all Xanth, only I have more magic than she—and I'm of another generation, really too old for her, even if I had any interest in marriage. And of course we would be a mismatch, for our talents are opposite. I deal in truth, she in illusion. I know too much, she imagines too much. So she conspires with lesser talents, convincing herself that it can somehow work out." He shook his head. "It is too bad, really. With the King fading, and no Heir Apparent, and this alternate requirement that the crown go only to a full Magician, it is entirely possible that the throne will be subject to her machinations. Not every young man has your integrity or loyalty to Xanth."

Bink felt a chill. Humfrey knew about Iris's offer, about their encounter. The Magician did not merely answer questions for a fee, he kept track of what was going on in Xanth. But he did not, it seemed, bother to interfere. He just watched. Maybe he investigated the background of specific seekers while the seahorse, wall, and manticora delayed them, so that by the time one won through, Humfrey was ready. Maybe he saved the information, in case someone came to ask "What is the greatest danger facing Xanth?", whereupon he could collect his fee for answering.

"If the King dies, will you take the crown?" Bink asked. "As you said, it will have to go to a powerful Magician, and for the good of Xanth—"

"You pose a question almost as awkward as the one that brought you here," the Good Magician said ruefully. "I do have a certain modicum of patriotism, but I also have a policy against interfering with the natural scheme of things. There is some substance to the concept of the monkey's paw; magic does have its price. I suppose if there were absolutely no alternative I would accept the crown—but first I would search most diligently for some superior Magician to assume the chore. We have not had a top talent appear in a generation; one is overdue." He gazed speculatively at Bink. "There seems to be magic of that caliber associated with you—but we cannot harness it if we cannot define it. So I doubt you are the heir to the throne."

Bink exploded with incredulous, embarrassed laughter. "Me? You insult the throne."

"No, there are qualities in you that would honor the throne—if you only had identified, controllable magic. The Sorceress may have chosen better than she knew, or intended. But evidently there is countermagic that balks you—though I am not sure the source of that countermagic would make a good King either. It is a strange matter, most intriguing."

Bink was tempted by the notion of being a potent Magician, becoming King, and ruling Xanth. Oddly, it quickly turned him off. He knew, deep inside, that he lacked the qualities required, despite Humfrey's remarks. This was not merely a matter of magic, but of basic life style and ambition. He could never sentence a man to death or exile, however justified that sentence might be, or lead an army into battle, or spend all day deciding the altercations of citizens. The sheer responsibility would soon weigh him down. "You're right. No sensible person would want to be King. All I want is to marry Sabrina and settle down."

"You are a most sensible lad. Stay the night, and on the morrow I will show you a direct route home, with protections against the hazards on the way."

"Nickelpede repellent?" Bink asked hopefully, remembering the trenches Cherie the centaur had hurdled.

"Precisely. You will still have to keep your wits about you; no route is safe for a stupid man. But two days' travel on foot will suffice."

Bink stayed the night. He found he rather liked the castle and its denizens; even the manticora was affable now that the Magician had given the word. "I would not really have eaten you, though I admit to being tempted for a moment or three when you booted me in the . . . tail," it told Bink. "It is my job to scare off those who are not serious. See, I am not confined." It pushed against the bars, and the inner gate swung open. "My year is almost up, anyway; I'll almost be sorry to have it end."

"What question did you bring?" Bink inquired somewhat nervously, trying not to brace himself too obviously for flight. In an open space, he was no possible match for the manticora.

"I asked whether I have a soul," the monster said seriously.

Again Bink had to control his reaction. A year's service for a philosophical question? "What did he tell you?"

"That only those who possess souls are concerned about them."

"But—but then you never needed to ask. You paid a year for nothing."

"No. I paid a year for everything. Possession of a soul means that I can never truly die. My body may slough away, but I shall be reborn, or if not, my shade will linger to settle unfinished accounts, or I shall reside forever in heaven or hell. My future is assured; I shall never suffer oblivion. There is no more vital question or answer. Yet that answer had to be in the proper form. A simple yes or no answer would not have satisfied me; it could be a blind guess, or merely the Magician's off-hand opinion. A detailed technical treatise would merely have obfuscated the matter. Humfrey phrased it in such a way that its truth was self-evident. Now I need never doubt again."

Bink was moved. Considered that way, it did make sense. Humfrey had delivered good value. He was an honest Magician. He had shown the manticora— and Bink himself—something vital about the nature of life in Xanth. If the fiercest conglomerate monsters had souls, with all that implied, who could condemn them as evil?

Chapter 7

Exile

The path was broad and clear, with no impinging magic. Only one thing chilled Bink: a region with small wormlike holes in the trunks of trees and surrounding rocks. Holes that wiggled straight through from one side to another. The wiggles had been here!

But he calmed himself. The wiggles had not passed recently, of course; that menace had been abolished. But where they had infested, it was horrible, for the little flying worms had drilled magically through anything that got in their way, including animals and people. A tree could survive a few neat holes, but a person could bleed to death, assuming he did not die outright from the holing of some vital organ. The mere thought made Bink wince. He hoped the wiggles never spawned again in Xanth—but there was no certainty about that. There was no certainty about anything where magic was involved.

He walked faster, made nervous by the old wiggle scars. In half an hour Bink reached the chasm—and there, sure enough, was the impossible bridge the Good Magician had told him of. He verified its existence by tossing a handful of dirt and observing the pattern of its fall into the depths; it guided around one section. Had he known of this on the way over—but of course that was the thing about information. Without it, a person suffered enormous complications. Who would have thought there was an invisible bridge all the way across?

Yet his long detour had not been an entire loss. He had participated in the rape hearing, and helped the shade, and witnessed some fantastic illusions, and rescued Crombie the soldier, and generally learned a lot more about the land of Xanth. He wouldn't care to do it all over again, but the experience had made him grow.

He stepped out onto the bridge. There was one thing about it, the Magician had warned him: once he started across, he could not turn back, or it would dematerialize, dropping him into the chasm. It was a one-way ramp, existing only ahead of him. So he walked across boldly, though the gulf opened out awesomely beneath him. Only his hand on the invisible rail reassured him.

He did risk a look down. Here the base of the chasm was extremely narrow— a virtual crack rather than a valley. The Gap dragon could not run here. But there seemed to be no way to climb down the steep cliff-slope; if the fall did not kill a person, starvation and exposure would. Unless he managed to straddle the narrowest part of the crack and walk east or west to a better section—where the dragon could then catch him.

Bink made it across. All it took was knowledge and confidence. His feet safely on land, he looked back. There was no sign of the bridge, of course, and no obvious approach to it. He was not about to risk another crossing.

The nervous release left him thirsty. He saw a spring to one side of the path. The path? There had been none a moment ago. He looked back toward the chasm, and there was no path. Oh—it led away from the bridge, not toward it. Routine one-way magic. He proceeded to the spring. He had water in his canteen, but it was Spring of Life water, which he avoided drinking, saving it for some future emergency.

A driblet of water emerged from the spring to flow along a winding channel and finally trickle down into the chasm. The channel was richly overgrown with strange plants, species that Bink had never observed before: a strawberry runner bearing beechnuts, and ferns with deciduous leaves. Odd, but no threat to his welfare. Bink looked around carefully for predator beasts that might lurk near a water hole, then lay down to put his mouth to the waiting pool.

As he lowered his head, he heard a fluting cry above him. "You'll be sooorry!" it seemed to say.

He glanced up into the trees. A birdlike thing perched there, possibly a variety of harpy. She had full woman-breasts and a coiled snake tail. Nothing to concern him, so long as she kept her distance.

He bent his head again—and heard a rustle, too close. He jumped up, drew his knife, moved a few paces, and through the trees sighted an incredible thing. Two creatures were locked in combat: a griffin and a unicorn. One was male, the other female, and they were—they were not fighting, they—

Bink retreated, profoundly embarrassed. They were two different species! How *could* they!

Disgusted, he returned to the spring. Now he noted the recent tracks of the creatures: both unicorn and griffin had come to drink here, probably within the hour. Maybe they had crossed the invisible bridge, as he had, and seen the spring, so conveniently located. So the water could hardly be poisoned—

Suddenly he caught on. This was a love spring. Anyone who drank of this water would become compellingly enamored of the first creature he encountered thereafter, and—

He glanced over at the griffin and unicorn. They were still at it, insatiably.

Bink backed away from the spring. If he had drunk from it—

He shuddered. He was no longer remotely thirsty.

"Aw, go take a drink," the harpy fluted.

Bink swept up a rock and hurled it at her. She squawked and fluttered higher, laughing coarsely. One of her droppings just missed him. There was nothing more hateful than a harpy.

Well, the Good Magician had warned him that the path home was not entirely free of problems. This spring must be one of the details Humfrey hadn't thought important enough for specific mention. Once Bink was back on the trail along which he had originally come, the hazards would be familiar, such as the peace pines—

How would he get through them? He needed an enemy to travel with, and he had none.

Then he had a bright idea. "Hey you—birdbrain!" he called up into the foliage. "Stay away from me, or I'll stuff your tail down your filthy throat!"

The harpy responded with a withering torrent of abuse. What a vocabulary she had! Bink threw another rock at her. "I'm warning you—don't follow me," he cried.

"I'll follow you to the edge of the Shield itself," she screeched. "You'll *never* get rid of me."

Bink smiled privately. Now he had a suitable companion.

He hiked on, dodging the occasional droppings the harpy hurled at him, hoping her fury would carry her through the pines. After that—well, first things first.

Soon the path merged with the one he had taken south. Curious, he sighted along the main path both ways; it was visible north and south. He looked back the way he had just come—and there was only deep forest. He took a step back along where he knew he had passed—and found himself knee-deep in glow-briers. The weeds sparkled as they snagged on his legs, and only by maneuvering with extreme caution did he manage to extricate himself without getting scratched. The harpy laughed so hard she almost fell from her perch.

There was simply no path here, this direction. But the moment he faced about again, there it was, leading cleanly through the briers to join the main route. Ah, well—why did he even bother to question such things? Magic was magic; it had no rationale except its own. Everyone knew that. Everyone except himself, at times.

He hiked all day, passing the brook where to drink was to become a fish—"Have a drink, harpy!"—but she already knew of the enchantment, and reviled him with double fury; the peace pines— "Have a nap, harpy!"; and the trench with the nickelpedes—"I'll fetch you something to eat, harpy!"—but actually he used the repellent the Good Magician had provided, and never even saw a nickelpede.

At last he stopped at a farmhouse in the centaur territory for the night. The harpy finally gave up her chase; she dared not come within range of a centaur bow. These were older centaurs, unaggressive, interested in the news of the day. They listened avidly to the narration of his experiences across the chasm and considered this to suffice for his room and board. Their grandchild colt was staying with them, a happy-go-lucky prancing tyke of barely twenty-five years—Bink's age, but equivalent to a quarter that in human terms. Bink played with him and did handstands for him; that was a trick no centaur could do, and the colt was fascinated.

Next day he traveled north again, and there was no sign of the harpy. What a relief; he would almost have preferred to risk the peace pines alone. His ears felt indelibly soiled after the day of her expletives. He passed through the remainder of the centaur area without encountering anyone. As evening approached, he reached the North Village.

"Hey! The Spell-less Wonder is back," Zink cried. A hole appeared at Bink's feet, causing him to stumble involuntarily. Zink would have made a wonderful companion for the pines. Bink ignored the other holes and proceeded toward his house. He was back, all right. Why had he bothered to hurry?

The examination was held next morning, in the outdoor amphitheater. The royal palms formed colonnades setting off the stage area. The benches were formed from the projecting convoluted knees of a giant dryland cypress tree. The back was braced by four huge honey-maple trees. Bink had always liked this formation—but now it was a place of discomfort. His place of trial.

The old King presided, since this was one of his royal offices. He wore his jewel-encrusted royal robe and his handsome gold crown and carried the ornate scepter, symbols of his power. All citizens bowed as the fanfare sounded. Bink could not help feeling a shiver of awe as the panoply of royalty manifested.

The King had an impressive white mane and a long beard, but his eyes tended to drift aimlessly. Periodically a servitor would nudge him to prevent him from falling asleep, and to remind him of the ritual.

At the start, the King performed his ceremonial magic by generating a storm. He held his palsied hands high and mumbled his invocation. At first there was silence; then, just as it seemed the magic had failed entirely, a ghostly gust of wind passed through the glade, stirring up a handful of leaves.

No one said anything, though it was evident that this manifestation could have been mere coincidence. It was certainly a far cry from a storm. But several of the ladies dutifully put up umbrellas, and the master of ceremonies quickly proceeded to the business at hand.

Bink's parents, Roland and Bianca, were in the front row, and so was Sabrina, fully as lovely as he had remembered her. Roland caught Bink's eye and nodded encouragingly, and Bianca's gaze was moist, but Sabrina's eyes were downcast. They were all afraid for him. With reason, he thought.

"What talent do you proffer to justify your citizenship?" the master of ceremonies asked Bink. He was Munly, a friend of Roland's; Bink knew the man would do everything he could to help, but he was duty-bound to follow the forms.

Now it was upon him. "I—I can't show it," Bink said. "But I have the Good Magician Humfrey's note that I do have magic." He held out the note with a trembling hand.

The man took it, glanced at it, and passed it to the King. The King squinted, but his eyes were so watery that he evidently could not read it.

"As Your Majesty can see," Munly murmured discreetly, "it is a message from Magician Humfrey, bearing his magic seal." This was a picture of a flippered creature balancing a ball on its snout. "It states that this person possesses an undefined magical talent."

Something like fire lighted the old monarch's ashy eye momentarily. "This counts for naught," he mumbled. "Humfrey is not King; I am!" He let the paper drop to the ground.

"But—" Bink protested.

The master of ceremonies glanced at him warningly, and Bink knew it was hopeless. The King was foolishly jealous of the Magician Humfrey, whose power was still strong, and would not heed the message. But, for whatever reason, the King had spoken. Argument would only complicate things.

Then he had an idea. "I have brought the King a present," Bink said. "Water from a healing Spring."

Munly's eyes lighted. "You have magic water?" He was alert to the possibilities of a fully functional King.

"In my canteen," Bink said. "I saved it—see, it healed my lost finger." He held up his left hand. "It also cured my cold, and I saw it help other people. It heals anything, instantly." He decided not to mention the attached obligation.

Munly's talent was the conjuration of small objects. "With your permission—"

"Granted," Bink said quickly.

The canteen appeared in the man's hand. "This is it?"

"Yes." For the first time, Bink had real hope.

Munly approached the King again. "Bink has brought a gift for Your Majesty," he announced. "Magic water."

The King took the canteen. "Magic water?" he repeated, hardly seeming to comprehend.

"It heals all ills," Munly assured him.

The King looked at it. One swallow, and he would be able to read the Magician's message, to brew decent storms again—and to make sensible judgments. This could reverse the course of Bink's demonstration.

"You imply I am sick?" the King demanded. "I need no healing! I am as fit as I ever was." And he turned the canteen upside down, letting the precious fluid pour out on the ground.

It was as if Bink's life blood were spilling out, not mere water. He saw his last chance ruined, by the very senility he had thought to alleviate. On top of that, now he had no healing water for his own emergencies; he could not be cured again.

Was this the retribution of the Spring of Life for his defiance of it? To tempt him with incipient victory, then withdraw it at the critical moment? Regardless, he was lost.

Munly knew it too. He stooped to pick up the canteen, and it vanished from his hand, returned to Bink's house. "I am sorry," he murmured under his breath. Then, loudly: "Demonstrate your talent."

Bink tried. He concentrated, willing his magic, whatever it might be, to break its geis and manifest. Somehow. But nothing happened.

He heard a sob. Sabrina? No, it was his mother, Bianca. Roland sat with stony face, refusing by his code of honor to let personal interest interfere. Sabrina still would not look at him. But there were those who did: Zink, Jama, and Potipher were all smirking. Now they had reason to feel superior; none of them were spell-less wonders.

"I cannot," Bink whispered. It was over.

* * *

Again he hiked. This time he headed westward, toward the isthmus. He carried a new staff and a hatchet and his knife; and his canteen had been refilled with conventional water. Bianca had provided more excellent sandwiches, flavored by her tears. He had nothing from Sabrina; he had not seen her at all since the decision. Xanth law did not permit an exile to take more than he could conveniently carry, and no valuables, for fear of attracting unwanted attention from the Mundanes. Though the Shield protected Xanth, it was impossible to be too safe.

Bink's life was essentially over, for he had been exiled from all that he had known. He was in effect an orphan. Never again would he experience the marvels of magic. He would be forever bound, as it were, to the ground, the colorless society of Mundania.

Should he have accepted the offer of the Sorceress Iris? At least he could have remained in Xanth. Had he but known . . . He would not have changed his mind. What was right was right, and wrong was wrong.

The strangest thing was that he did not feel entirely despondent. He had lost citizenship, family, and fiancée, and faced the great unknown of the Outside— yet there was a certain quixotic spring to his step. Was it a counterreaction buoying his spirit so that he would not suicide—or was he in fact relieved that the decision had at last been made? He had been a freak among the magic people; now he would be among his own kind.

No—that wasn't it. He had magic. He was no freak. Strong magic, Magician-caliber. Humfrey had told him so, and he believed it. He merely was unable to utilize it. Like a man who could make a colored spot on the wall—when there was no wall handy. Why he should be magically mute he did not know—but it meant that he was right, the decision of the King wrong. Those who had not stood by him were better off apart from him.

No—not that either. His parents had refused to compromise the law of Xanth. They were good, honest people, and Bink shared their values. He had refused a similar compromise when tempted by the Sorceress. Roland and Bianca could not help him by accompanying him into an exile they did not deserve—or by trying to help him stay by cheating the system. They had done what they felt was right, at great personal sacrifice, and he was proud of them. He knew they loved him, but had let him go his own way without interference. That was part of his buried joy.

And Sabrina—what then of her? She too had refused to cheat. Yet he felt she lacked the commitment of his parents to principle. She would have cheated, had she had sufficient reason. Her surface integrity was because she had not been moved strongly by Bink's misfortune. Her love had not been deep enough. She had loved him for the magic talent she had been convinced he had, as the son of strongly talented parents. The loss of that potential talent had undercut that love. She had not really wanted him as a person.

And his love for her was now revealed as similarly shallow. Sure, she was beautiful—but she had less actual personality than, say, the girl Dee. Dee had walked off because she had been insulted, and stuck by her decision. Sabrina would do the same, but for a different reason. Dee had not been posturing; she had really been angry. With Sabrina it would have been more contrived, with more art and less emotion—because she had less emotion. She cared more about appearances than the reality.

Which reminded Bink of the Sorceress Iris again—the ultimate creature of appearances. What a temper she had! Bink respected temper; it was a window to the truth at times when little else offered. But Iris was too violent. That palace-destruction scene, complete with storm and dragon . . .

Even stupid whatshername—the lovely girl of the rape hearing—Wynne, that was her name—she had feelings. He had, he hoped, enabled her to escape from the Gap dragon. There had not been much artifice in her. But Sabrina was the perfect actress, and so he had never really been sure of her love. She had been a picture in his mind, to be summoned in time of need, just to look at. He had not actually wanted to marry her.

It had taken exile to show him his own motives. Whatever it was that he wanted in a girl, ultimately, Sabrina lacked. She had beauty, which he liked, and personality—which was not the same as character—and attractive magic. All these things were good—very good—and he had thought he loved her. But when the crisis came, Sabrina's eyes had been averted. That said it all. Crombie the soldier had spoken truly: Bink would have been a fool to marry Sabrina.

Bink smiled. How would Crombie and Sabrina have gotten along together? The ultimately demanding and suspicious male, the ultimately artful and protean female. Would the soldier's inherent ferocity constitute a challenge to the girl's powers of accommodation? Would they, after all, have fashioned an enduring relationship? It almost seemed they might. They would either have an immediate and violent falling out or a similarly spectacular falling in. Too bad they couldn't meet, and that he could not be present to observe such a meeting.

The whole of his Xanth experience was passing glibly through his mind now that he was through with it. For the first time in his life, Bink was free. He no longer needed magic. He no longer needed romance. He no longer needed Xanth.

His aimlessly roving eye spotted a tiny dark spot on a tree. He experienced a sudden shudder. Was it a wiggle wound? No, just a discoloration. He felt relief—and realized that he had been fooling himself, at least to this extent. If he no longer needed Xanth, he would not care about things like the wiggles. He *did* need Xanth. It was his youth. But—he could not have it.

Then he approached the station of the Shield man, and his uncertainty increased. Once he passed through the Shield, Xanth and all its works would be forever behind him.

"What are you up to?" the Shield man asked him. He was a big, fat youth with pale features. But he was part of the vital net of magic that formed the barrier to outside penetration of Xanth. No living creature could pass the Shield, either way—but since no inhabitant of Xanth wanted to depart, its net effect was to stop all Mundane intrusions. The touch of the Shield meant death —instant, painless, final. Bink didn't know how it worked—but he didn't know how any magic worked, really. It just was.

"I have been exiled," Bink said. "You have to let me through the Shield." He would not, of course, attempt to cheat; he would leave as directed. Had he been inclined to try to avoid exile, it would not have worked; one villager's talent was spot location of individuals, and he was now tuned to Bink. He would know if Bink remained on this side of the Shield today.

The youth sighed. "Why do all the complications have to come in my shift? Do you know how difficult it is to open up a man-sized hole without bollixing the whole damn Shield?"

"I don't know anything about the Shield," Bink admitted. "But I was exiled by the King, so—"

"Oh, very well. Now look—I can't go with you to the Shield; I have to stay here at my station. But I can make an opening spell that will cancel out one section for five seconds. You be there, and you step through on schedule, because if it closes on you, you're dead."

Bink gulped. For all his thoughts about death and exile, now that it had come to the test, he did want to live. "I know."

"Right. The magic stone doesn't care who dies." Meaningfully the youth tapped the boulder he leaned against.

"You mean that dingy old stone is it?" Bink asked.

"Shieldstone. Sure. The Magician Ebnez located it nearly a century ago, and turned it to form the Shield. Without it, we'd still be subject to invasion by the Mundanes."

Bink had heard of the Magician Ebnez, one of the great historical figures. In fact, Ebnez was in Bink's family tree. He had been able to adapt things magically. In his hands a hammer could become a sledgehammer, or a piece of wood could become a section of windowframe. Whatever existed became whatever was needed—within certain limits. He could not adapt air into food, for example, or make a suit of clothing out of water. But it had been amazing what he could do. So he had adapted a potent deathstone into the Shieldstone, killing at a set distance instead of up close, and thereby he had fashioned the salvation of Xanth. What a proud achievement!

"Okay, now," the youth said. "Here's a timestone." He tapped it against the larger rock, and the small piece fractured into two segments, each fading from the original red to white. He handed one fragment to Bink. "When this goes red, you step across; they're synched. The opening will be right in front of the big beechnut tree—and for only five seconds. So you be ready, and move—on red."

"Move on red," Bink agreed.

"Right. Now *move*; sometimes these timestones heal fast. I'll be watching mine, so as to time the spell; you watch yours."

Bink moved. He ran along the path to the west. Usually a fractured timestone took half an hour or so to heal—but it varied somewhat with the quality of the stone, the surrounding temperature, and assorted unknown factors. Maybe it was inherent in the original piece, because the two fragments always changed color together, precisely, even if one were in the sunshine and the other buried in a well. But, again, what use to seek a rationale for magic? What was, was.

And would be no more—for him. None of this had meaning in Mundania.

He hove in sight of the Shield—or rather, its effect. The Shield itself was invisible, but there was a line of dead vegetation where it touched the ground, and the corpses of animals that had been so foolish as to try to cross that line. Sometimes jumpdeer got confused and sprang through to the safe ground on the other side—but they were already dead. The Shield was invisibly thin, but absolute.

Occasional Mundane creatures blundered into it. A detail walked the line each day on the Xanth side, checking for corpses, hauling them out of the Shield when they were partway across, giving them safe burial. It was possible to handle something that lay across the Shield, so long as the living person did not touch it himself. Nevertheless, it was a grisly chore, sometimes assigned as punishment. There were never any human Mundanes, but there was always the fear that there might one day be some, with all the complications that would entail.

Ahead was the spreading beechnut tree. One branch reached out toward the Shield—and the tip of that branch was dead. Wind must have made it sway across. It helped identify the spot where he should cross.

There was an odor associated with this line of death, too. Probably it was the decay of many tiny creatures: worms in the earth, bugs flying through the Shield, rotting where they fell. This was the region of death.

Bink glanced down at the stone he held—and sucked in his breath in shock. *It was red!*

Had it just now changed—or was he already too late? His life depended on the answer.

Bink launched himself at the Shield. He knew the sensible thing to do was return to the Shield tender and explain why he had balked—but he wanted this done with. Maybe it had been the actual change of the stone's color that had attracted his attention, in which case he did have time. So he took the foolish course, and tried for it.

One second. Two. Three. He'd better have the whole five, because he wasn't there yet. The Shield seemed close, but it took time to make the supposedly instant decision and abolish inertia and get up speed. He was passing the beech-nut tree at a dead run—maybe literally dead—going too fast to stop. Four seconds—he was crossing the line of death. If it closed on his trailing leg, would all of him die, or just the leg? Five—he felt a tingle. Six—no, time was up, stop counting, start panting. He was through; was he alive?

He rolled in the dirt, kicking up dry leaves and small bones. Of course he was alive! How could he worry about it otherwise? As with the manticora, con-cerned about his soul: if he had none, he wouldn't—

Bink sat up, shaking something dead out of his hair. So he had made it. That tingle must have been an effect of the turned-off Shield, since it hadn't hurt him.

Now it was done. He was free of Xanth forever. Free to make his own life, without being ridiculed or mothered or tempted. Free to be himself.

Bink put his face in his hands and cried.

Chapter 8

Trent

After a time he got up and walked on, into the dread world of the Mundanes. It really did not look much different: the trees were similar, the rocks unchanged, and the ocean shore he paralleled was exactly like an ocean shore. Yet an intense nostalgia gripped him. His prior euphoria had been but the swing of the pendulum, providing a false buoyancy. Better if he had died in the crossing.

Well, he could still go back. Just step across the line. Death would be painless, and he could be buried in Xanth. Was that what other exiles had done?

He revolted against the notion. He had called his own bluff. He loved Xanth, and missed it terribly already—but he did not want to die. He would simply have to make his way among the Mundanes. Others had surely done it before him. Maybe he would even be happy there.

The isthmus was mountainous. Bink sweated as he climbed the steep pass. Was this the counterpart to the chasm, a ridge that rose as high above the land as the chasm sank beneath it? Did a ridge dragon run along the heights? No, not in Mundania. But possibly such geography did have something to do with the magic. If the magic quality washed down from the height, concentrating in the depth—no, that didn't seem to make much sense. Most of it would have washed into the ocean and been hopelessly diluted.

For the first time he wondered what Mundania was really like. Was it actually possible to survive without magic? It would not be nearly as nice as Xanth, but the absence of spells should represent a formidable challenge, and there should be some decent places in it. The people should not be evil; after all, his ancestors had come from Mundane stock. Indications were that language and many customs were the same.

He heaved himself over the rise of the pass, braced for his first real glimpse of the new world—and suddenly he was surrounded by men. An ambush!

Bink whirled to run. Maybe he could trick them into plunging into the Shield, and be rid of them the easy way—not that he wanted to be responsible for their death. Anyhow, he had to try to escape them.

But as he turned, his body responding somewhat slower than his thoughts, he found a man behind him, blocking the way with drawn sword.

The sensible thing to do was to give up. They had him outnumbered and surrounded, and they could have put an arrow into his back if they had wanted to kill him outright. If all they wanted to do was rob him, he had almost nothing to lose.

But being sensible had never been Bink's strong point. Not when he was under pressure, or surprised. Reflecting after the fact, he was very sensible and intelligent, but that wasn't much use at this stage. If only he'd had a talent like that of his mother, only stronger, so that he could turn time back a couple of hours and replay all his crises to better advantage—

Bink charged the man with the sword, swinging his staff to block the blade. But someone tackled him, bringing him down hard before he took two steps. Bink's face struck the dirt, and he took a mouthful. Still he fought, twisting about to get at the man who held him.

Then they were all on him, bearing him down. Bink had no chance; in moments he was tied and gagged.

A man thrust his tough face close to Bink's eyes as two others held him erect. "Now get this, Xanth—if you try any magic, we'll knock you out and carry you."

Magic? They didn't know that Bink had none he could use—or that if he had, it would be no good out here beyond the Shield. But he nodded, showing he understood. Maybe they would treat him better if they thought he could somehow strike back.

They marched him down the other side of the pass and to a military camp on the mainland beyond the isthmus.

What was an army doing here? If it were an invasion of Xanth, it could not succeed; the Shield would kill a thousand men as readily as one.

They brought him to the main tent. Here, in a screened enclosure, sat a handsome man in his forties, wearing some sort of green Mundane uniform, a sword, a neat mustache, and an emblem of command. "Here is the spy, General," the sergeant said respectfully.

The General glanced at Bink, appraising him. There was dismaying intelligence in that cool study. This was no bandit thug. "Release him," he said quietly. "He is obviously harmless."

"Yes, sir," the sergeant said respectfully. He untied Bink and removed his gag.

"Dismissed," the General murmured, and without a word the soldiers were gone. They were certainly disciplined.

Bink chafed at his wrists, trying to rub the pain out, amazed at the General's confidence. The man was well formed, but not large; Bink was younger and taller and surely stronger. If he acted quickly, he might escape.

Bink crouched, ready to jump at the man and knock him down. Suddenly the General's sword was in his hand, pointing at Bink. The man's draw had been a blur; the weapon had jumped to his hand as if by magic, but that obviously could not be the case here. "I would not advise it, young man," the General said, as if warning him not to step on a thorn.

Bink staggered, trying to brake without falling on the point of the sword. He did not succeed. But as his chest bore on that blade, the sword retreated, returning to its scabbard. The General, now on his feet, caught Bink by his elbows and stood him back upright. There was such precision and power in the action that Bink knew he had grossly underestimated this man; he had no chance to overcome him, with or without the sword.

"Be seated," the General said mildly.

Cowed, Bink moved awkwardly to the wooden chair and sat on it. Now he was conscious of his own dirty face and hands, the disorganization of his apparel, in contrast to the impeccable neatness of the General.

"Your name?"

"Bink." He did not give his village, since he was no longer affiliated with it. What was the purpose of this question, anyway? He was a nonentity regardless of his name.

"I am the Magician Trent. Perhaps you know of me."

It took a moment for the import to register. Then Bink didn't believe it. "Trent? He's gone. He was—"

"Exiled. Twenty years ago. Precisely."

"But Trent was—"

"Ugly? A monster? Crazy?" The Magician smiled, showing none of these traits. "What stories do they tell of me today in Xanth?"

Bink thought of Justin Tree. The fish of the stream, turned to lightning bugs to harass the centaurs. The opponents who had been transformed to water forms and left to die on land. "You—he was a power-hungry spell-caster who tried to usurp the throne of Xanth when I was but a child. An evil man whose evil still lives after him."

Trent nodded. "This is a kinder repute than is normally accorded the loser in a political contest. I was about your present age when I was banished. Perhaps our cases are similar."

"No. I never killed anyone."

"They accuse me of that too? I transformed many, but I did that instead of killing. I have no need to kill, since I can render an enemy harmless by other means."

"A fish on land still dies!"

"Oh, so that is how they put it. That would indeed be murder. I did transform enemies to fish—but always in water. On land I utilized only land forms. Possibly some subsequently died, but that was the doing of predators in the normal course of nature. I never—"

"I don't care. You abused your magic. I am not at all like you. I—had no magic."

The fair eyebrow lifted expressively. "No magic? Everybody in Xanth has magic."

"Because they exile those who don't have it," Bink said, with a flash of bitterness.

Trent smiled, and it was a surprisingly winning expression. "Nevertheless, our interests may be parallel, Bink. How would you like to return with me to Xanth?"

For an instant wild hope flared in his breast. Return! But immediately he quashed it. "There is no return."

"Oh, I wouldn't say that. To every act of magic there is a countermagic. It is merely a matter of invoking it. You see, I have developed a counter to the Shield."

Again Bink had to take stock of his reactions. "If you had that, you could have gone into Xanth already."

"Well, there is a certain small problem of application. You see, what I have is an elixir distilled from a plant that grows on the very fringe of the magical zone. The magic extends somewhat beyond the Shield, you understand—otherwise the Shield itself wouldn't work, for it is magic and cannot operate beyond the magic demesnes. This plant, which seems to be of basically Mundane stock, competes at the fringe with the magical plants of Xanth. It is very difficult to compete with magic, so it evolved a very special property: it suppresses magic. Do you appreciate the significance?"

"Suppresses magic? Maybe that's what happened to me."

Trent studied him with that disquieting calculation. "So you feel you were wronged by the present administration? We do have something in common."

Bink wanted no common ground with the Evil Magician, however winning the man's aspect might be. He knew that Evil could put on an extremely fair face; otherwise how would Evil ever have survived in the world so long? "What are you getting at?"

"The Shield is magic. Therefore the elixir should nullify it. But it does not, because the source of the Shield is not touched. It is necessary to reach the Shieldstone itself. Unfortunately, we do not know precisely where that stone is now, and there is not enough elixir to blanket the entire peninsula of Xanth, or even a significant fraction of it."

"Makes no difference," Bink said. "Your knowing where the Shieldstone is would not bring it within your reach."

"Ah, but it would. You see, we have a catapult, with a sufficient range to drop a bomb anywhere in nearby Xanth. We have it mounted on a ship that can sail right around Xanth. So it is very likely that we could drop a container of elixir on the Shieldstone—if we only had the precise coordinates."

Now Bink understood. "The Shield would collapse!"

"And my army would overrun Xanth. Of course, the magic-damping effect would be temporary, for the elixir dissipates readily—but a mere ten minutes would suffice to get the bulk of my army across the line. I have been drilling the men in swift short-range maneuvers. After that it would be merely a matter of time until the throne was mine."

"You would return us to the days of conquest and ravage," Bink said, horrified. "The Thirteenth Wave, worse than all the rest."

"By no means. My army is disciplined. We shall exert precisely that force that is necessary, no more. My magic will probably eliminate most resistance anyway, so there need be very little violence. I do not wish to ruin the kingdom I am to rule."

"So you haven't changed," Bink said. "You're still hungry for illicit power."

"Oh, I have changed," Trent assured him. "I have become less naive, more educated and sophisticated. The Mundanes have excellent educational facilities and a broader world view, and they are ruthless politicians. I will not this time underestimate the determination of my opposition or leave myself foolishly vulnerable. I have no doubt I will make a better King than I would have twenty years ago."

"Well, count me out."

"But I must count you in, Bink. You know where the Shieldstone is located."

The Evil Magician leaned forward persuasively. "It is important that the shot be precise; we have only a quarter pound of elixir, and that is the labor of two years' work. We have virtually denuded the fringe region of the source plants; our supply is irreplaceable. We dare not guess at the location of the Shieldstone. We require a precise map—a map that only you can draw."

So there it was. Trent had posted his men to ambush any travelers from Xanth, so that they could update him on the precise position of the Shieldstone. That was the only piece of information the Evil Magician needed to initiate his wave of conquest. Bink had merely happened to be the first exile to walk into the trap. "No, I won't tell you. I won't help overthrow the legitimate government of Xanth."

"Legitimacy is commonly defined after the fact," Trent remarked. "Had I been successful twenty years ago, I would now be the legitimate King, and the present monarch would be a reviled outcast noted for drowning people irresponsibly. I presume the Storm King still governs?"

"Yes," Bink said shortly. The Evil Magician might try to convince him that it all was merely palace politics, but he knew better.

"I am prepared to make you a very handsome offer, Bink. Virtually anything you might desire in Xanth. Wealth, authority, women—"

He had said the wrong thing. Bink turned away. He would not want Sabrina on that basis anyway, and he had already turned down what amounted to a similar offer by the Sorceress Iris.

Trent steepled his fingers. Even in that minor mannerism there was implied power and ruthlessness. The Magician's plans were too finely meshed to be balked by a willful exile. "You may wonder why I choose to return to Xanth, after two decades and evident success in Mundania. I have spent some time analyzing that myself."

"No," Bink said.

But the man only smiled, refusing to be ruffled, and again Bink had the uneasy feeling that he was being skillfully maneuvered, that he was about to play into the hands of the Magician no matter how he tried to fight it. "You should wonder, lest you allow your outlook to be unconscionably narrow—as mine was when I emerged from Xanth. Every young man should go abroad into the Mundane world for a period of a year or two at least; it would make him a better citizen of Xanth. Travel of any type tends to broaden one." Bink could not argue with that; he had learned a great deal in his two-week tour of Xanth. How much more would a year in Mundania teach him? "In fact," the Magician continued, "when I assume power I shall institute such a policy. Xanth cannot prosper cut off from the real world; in isolation is only stagnation."

Bink could not restrain his morbid curiosity. The Magician had intelligence and experience that appealed insidiously to Bink's own intellect. "What is it like out there?"

"Do not speak with such distaste, young man. Mundania is not the evil place you may imagine. That is part of the reason the citizens of Xanth need more exposure to it; the ignorance of isolation breeds unwarranted hostility. Mundania is in many respects more advancèd, more civilized than Xanth. Deprived of the benefits of magic, the Mundanes have had to compensate in ingenious ways. They have turned to philosophy, medicine, and science. They now have weapons called guns that can kill more readily than an arrow or even a deadly spell; I have trained my troops in other weapons, because I do not wish to introduce guns into Xanth. They have carriages that carry them across the land as fast as a unicorn can run, and boats that row across the sea as swiftly as a sea serpent can swim, and balloons that take them as high in the air as a dragon can fly. They have people called doctors who heal the sick and wounded without the use of a single spell, and a device consisting of little beads on columns that multiplies figures with marvelous speed and accuracy."

"Ludicrous!" Bink said. "Even magic can't do figures for a person, unless it is a golem, and then it has really become a person."

"This is what I mean, Bink. Magic is marvelous, but it is also limited. In the long run, the instruments of the Mundanes may have greater potential. Probably the basic life style of the Mundanes is more comfortable than that of many Xanths."

"There probably aren't as many of them," Bink muttered. "So they have no competition for good land."

"On the contrary. There are many millions of people there."

"You're never going to convince me of anything, telling such tall stories," Bink pointed out. "The North Village of Xanth has about five hundred people, counting all the children, and that's the largest one. There can't be more than two thousand people in the whole kingdom. You talk of thousands of thousands of people, but I know the Mundane world can't be much larger than Xanth!"

The Evil Magician shook his head in mock sadness. "Bink, Bink! None so blind as those who will not see."

"And if they really have balloons flying through the air, carrying people, why haven't they flown them over Xanth?" Bink demanded hotly, knowing he had the Magician on the run.

"Because they don't know where Xanth is—don't even believe it exists. They don't believe in magic, so—"

"Don't believe in magic!" The humor had never been very funny, and it was getting worse.

"The Mundanes never did know very much about magic," Trent said seriously. "It appears a great deal in their literature, but never in their daily lives.

The Shield has closed off the border, as it were, so no truly magic animal has been seen in Mundania in about a century. And it may be to our interest to keep them ignorant," he continued, frowning. "If they ever get the notion Xanth is a threat to them, they might use a giant catapult to lob in firebombs—" He broke off, shaking his head as though at some horrible thought. Bink had to admire the perfection of the mannerism, which was as apt as any his father, Roland, employed. He could almost believe there was some fantastic threat lurking. "No," the Magician concluded, "the location of Xanth must remain secret—for now."

"It won't remain secret if you send all Xanth youths out into Mundania for two years."

"Oh, we would put an amnesia spell on them first, and revoke it only after they returned. Or at least a geis of silence, so no Mundane could learn from them about Xanth. Thus they would acquire Mundane experience to augment their Xanth magic. Some trusted ones would be permitted to retain their memories and freedom of speech Outside, so they could act as liaisons, recruiting qualified colonists and keeping us informed. For our own safety and progress. But overall—"

"The Fourth Wave again," Bink said. "Controlled colonization."

Trent smiled. "You are an apt pupil. Many citizens choose not to comprehend the true nature of the original colonizations of Xanth. Actually, Xanth never was very easy to locate from Mundania, because it seems to have no fixed geographic location. Historically, people have colonized Xanth from all over the world, always walking across the land bridge directly from their own countries—and all would have sworn that they migrated only a few miles. Furthermore, all comprehended one another's speech in Xanth, though their original languages were entirely different. So it would appear that there is something magical about the approach to Xanth. Had I not kept meticulous notes of my route, I would never have found my way back this far. The Mundane legends of the animals that departed from Xanth in bygone centuries show that they appeared all over the world, rather than at any specific site. So it seems to work in reverse, too." He shook his head as if it were a great mystery—and Bink was hard put to it not to become hopelessly intrigued by the concept. How could Xanth be everywhere at once? Did its magic extend, after all, beyond the peninsula, in some peculiar fashion? It would be easy to get hooked by the problem!

"If you like Mundania so well, why are you trying to get back into Xanth?" Bink demanded, trying to distract himself from temptation by focusing on the Magician's contradictions.

"I don't like Mundania," Trent said, frowning. "I merely point out that it is not evil, and that it has considerable potential and must be reckoned with. If we do not keep aware of it, it may become aware of us—and that could destroy us.

Right along with itself. Xanth represents a haven, like none other known to man. A provincial, backward haven, to be sure—but there is no other place quite like it. And I—I am a Magician. I belong in my land, with my people, protecting them from the horrors arising, which you are not equipped even to imagine. . . ." He lapsed into silence.

"Well, no Mundane tales are going to make me tell you how to get into Xanth," Bink said firmly.

The Magician's eyes focused on Bink as if only now was he becoming aware of his presence. "I would prefer not to have to employ coercion," Trent said softly. "You know my talent."

Bink felt a shiver of extremely ugly apprehension. Trent was the transformer —the one who changed men into trees—or worse. The most potent Magician of the past generation—too dangerous to be allowed to remain in Xanth.

Then he felt relief. "You're bluffing," he said. "Your magic can't work outside Xanth—and I'm not going to let you into Xanth."

"It is not very much of a bluff," Trent said evenly. "The magic, as I mentioned, extends slightly beyond the Shield. I can take you to that border and transform you into a toad. And I shall do it—if I have to."

Bink's relief tightened back into a knot in his stomach. Transformation—the notion of losing his lifelong body without actually dying had an insidious horror. It terrified him.

But he still could not betray his homeland. "No," he said, his tongue feeling thick in his mouth.

"I don't understand, Bink. You surely did not leave Xanth voluntarily. I offer you the chance to get your own back."

"Not that way."

Trent sighed, with seemingly genuine regret. "You are loyal to your principles, and I cannot fault you for that. I had hoped it would not come to this."

Bink had hoped so too. But he seemed to have no choice. Except to watch his chance to make a break for it, risking his life to escape. Better a clean death in combat than to become a toad.

A soldier entered, reminding Bink faintly of Crombie—mainly a matter of bearing, not appearance—and stood at attention. "What is it, Hastings?" Trent inquired mildly.

"Sir, there is another person through the Shield."

Trent hardly showed his elation. "Really? It seems we have another source of information."

Bink felt a new emotion—but hardly a comfortable one. If there were another exile from Xanth, the Magician could get his information without Bink's help. Would he let Bink go—or turn him into a toad anyway, as an object lesson? Remembering Trent's reputation of past times, Bink had little confidence that he would be freed. Anyone who balked thé Evil Magician, in whatever trifling manner, was in for it.

Unless Bink gave him the information now, redeeming himself. Should he? Since it could make no difference to the future of Xanth . . .

He saw Trent pausing, looking at him expectantly. Suddenly Bink caught on. This was a setup, a fake announcement, to make him talk. And he had almost fallen for it.

"Well, you won't be needing me, then," Bink said. One thing about being turned into a toad—he couldn't tell the Magician anything at all in that form. He imagined a potential dialogue between man and toad:

MAGICIAN: Where is the Shieldstone?

TOAD: *Croak!*

Bink almost smiled. Trent would transform him only as a last resort.

Now Trent returned to the messenger. "Bring the other one here; I will question him immediately."

"Sir—it is a woman."

A woman! Trent seemed mildly surprised, but Bink was amazed. This was not what he expected in a bluff. There was certainly no woman being exiled—and no man either. What was Trent trying to do?

Unless—oh, no!—unless Sabrina had after all followed him out.

Dismay tore at him. If the Evil Magician had her in his power—

No! It could not be. Sabrina did not really love him; the exile and her reaction to it had proved that. She would not give up all she had to follow him out. It simply was not in her nature. And he didn't really love her; he had already decided that. So this had to be a complex ruse on the part of the Magician.

"Very well," Trent said. "Bring her in."

It couldn't be a bluff, then. Not if they actually brought her in. And if it were Sabrina—it couldn't be, he was quite absolutely positively certain of that—or was he projecting, attributing his own attitudes to her? How could he really know what was in her heart? If she had followed him, he couldn't let her be changed into a toad. Yet with all of Xanth at stake—

Bink threw up his hands, mentally. He would just have to play it as it came. If they had Sabrina, he was lost; if it were an ingenious bluff, he had won. Except that he would be a toad.

Perhaps being a toad would not be so bad. No doubt flies would taste very good, and the lady toads would look as good as human girls did now. Maybe the great love of his life was waiting in the grass, warts and all . . .

The ambush detail arrived, half carrying a struggling woman. Bink saw with relief that it was not Sabrina, but a marvelously ugly female he had never seen before. Her hair was wild, her teeth gnarled, her body sexually shapeless.

"Stand," Trent said mildly, and she stood, responsive to his easy air of command. "Your name?"

"Fanchon," she said rebelliously. "Yours?"

"The Magician Trent."

"Never heard of you."

Bink, caught by surprise, had to cough to conceal his snort of laughter. But Trent was unperturbed. "This puts us on an even footing, Fanchon. I regret the inconvenience my men have caused you. If you will kindly inform me of the location of the Shieldstone, I shall pay you well and send you on your way."

"Don't tell him!" Bink cried. "He means to invade Xanth."

She wrinkled her bulbous nose. "What do I care about Xanth?" She squinted at Trent. "I could tell you—but how do I know I can trust you? You might kill me as soon as you had your information."

Trent tapped his long, aristocratic fingers together. "This is a legitimate concern. You have no way of knowing whether my given word is good. Yet it should be obvious that I should bear no malice to those who assist me in the pursuit of my objectives."

"All right," she said. "Makes sense. The Shieldstone is at—"

"Traitor!" Bink screamed.

"Remove him," Trent snapped.

Soldiers entered and grabbed him and hustled him out. He had accomplished nothing except to make it harder for himself.

But then he thought of another aspect. What were the chances of another exile coming from Xanth within an hour after him? There couldn't be more than one or two exiles a year; it was big news when anyone left Xanth. He had heard nothing about it, and no second trial had been scheduled.

So—Fanchon was not an exile. She was probably not from Xanth at all. She was an agent, planted by Trent, just as Bink had first suspected. Her purpose was to convince Bink that she was telling Trent the location of the Shieldstone, tricking him into confirming it.

Well, he had figured out the scheme—and so he had won. Do what he might, Trent would not get into Xanth.

Yet there was a nagging uncertainty . . .

Chapter 9

Transformer

ink was thrown into a pit. A pile of hay broke his fall, and a wooden roof set on four tall posts shaded him from the sun. Other than that, his prison was barren and bleak indeed. The walls were of some stonelike substance, too hard to dig into with his bare hands, too sheer to climb; the floor was packed earth.

He walked around it. The wall was solid all around, and too high for him to surmount. He could almost touch the top when he jumped and reached up—but a lattice of metal bars across the top sealed him in. He might, with special effort, get high enough to catch hold of one of those bars—but then all he would be able to do would be to hang there. It might represent exercise, but it wouldn't get him out. So the cage was tight.

He had hardly come to this conclusion before soldiers came to stand at the grate, shaking rust onto him. They stood in the shade of the roof while one of them squatted down to unlock the little door set in that grate and swing it up and open. Then they dropped a person through. It was the woman Fanchon.

Bink jumped across, wrapping his arms around her before she hit the straw, breaking her fall. They both sprawled in the hay. The door slammed shut, and the lock clicked.

"Now, I know my beauty didn't overwhelm you," she remarked as they disentangled.

"I was afraid you'd break a leg," Bink said defensively. "I almost did, when they threw me in here."

She glanced down at her knobby knees, showing beneath her dull skirt. "A break couldn't hurt the appearance of either leg."

Not far off the mark. Bink had never seen a more homely girl than this one.

But what was she doing here? Why should the Evil Magician throw his stooge in the den with his prisoner? This was no way to trick the captive into talking. The proper procedure would be to tell Bink she had talked, and offer him his freedom for confirming the information. Even if she were genuine, she still should not have been confined with him; she could have been imprisoned separately. Then the guards would tell each one that the other had talked.

Now, if she had been beautiful, they might have thought she could vamp him into telling. But as she was, not a chance. It just didn't seem to make sense.

"Why didn't you tell him about the Shieldstone?" Bink inquired, not certain with what irony he intended it. If she were a fake, she could not have told—but she also should not have been dumped in here. If she were genuine, she must be loyal to Xanth. But then, why had she said she would tell Trent where the Shieldstone was?

"I told him," she said.

She had told him? Now Bink hoped she was phony.

"Yes," she said, looking him straight in the eye. "I told him how it was set under the throne in the King's palace in the North Village."

Bink tried to assess the ramifications of this statement. It was the wrong location—but did she know this? Or was she trying to trick him into a reaction, a revelation of its real location—while the guards listened? Or was she a true exile, who knew the location and had lied about it? That would account for Trent's reaction. Because if Trent's catapult lobbed an elixir bomb on the palace of Xanth, not only would it fail to disrupt the Shield, it would alert the King— or at least the more alert ministers, who were not fools—to the nature of the threat. The damping out of magic in that vicinity would quickly give it away.

Had Trent actually lobbed his bomb—and had he now lost all hope of penetrating Xanth? The moment the threat was known, they would move the Shieldstone to a new, secret location, so that no information from exiles would be valid. No—if that had happened, Trent would have turned Fanchon into a toad and stepped on her—and he would not have bothered to keep Bink prisoner. Bink might have been killed or released, but not simply kept. So nothing that drastic had happened. Anyway, there had not been time for all that.

"I see you don't trust me," Fanchon said.

A fair analysis. "I can't afford to," he admitted. "I don't want anything to happen to Xanth."

"Why should you care, since you got kicked out?"

"I knew the rule; I was given a fair hearing."

"Fair hearing!" she exclaimed indignantly. "The King didn't even read Humfrey's note or taste the water from the Spring of Life."

Bink paused again. How would she know that?

"Oh, come on," she said. "I passed through your village only hours after your trial. It was the talk of the town. How the Magician Humfrey had authenticated your magic, but the King—"

"Okay, okay," Bink said. Obviously she had come from Xanth, but he still wasn't sure how far he could trust her. Yet she must know the Shieldstone's location—and hadn't told it. Unless she had told it—and Trent didn't believe her, so was waiting for corroboration from Bink? But she had announced the wrong location; no purpose in that, regardless. Bink could challenge her on it, but that would still not give away the right location; there were a thousand potential spots. So probably she meant what she said: she had tried to fool Trent, and had not succeeded.

So the balance in Bink's mind shifted; now he believed she was from Xanth and she had not betrayed it. That was what the available evidence suggested. How complex could Trent's machinations become? Maybe he had a Mundane machine that could somehow pick up news from inside the Shield. Or—more likely!—he had a magic mirror set up in the magic zone just outside the Shield, so he could learn interior news. No—in that case he could have ascertained the location of the Shieldstone directly.

Bink felt dizzy. He didn't know what to think—but he certainly wasn't going to mention the key location.

"I wasn't exiled, if that's what you're thinking," Fanchon said. "They don't yet ban people for being ugly. I emigrated voluntarily."

"Voluntarily? Why?"

"Well, I had two reasons."

"What two reasons?"

She looked at him. "I'm afraid you would not believe either one."

"Try me and see."

"First, the Magician Humfrey told me it was the simplest solution to my problem."

"What problem?" Bink was hardly in a good mood.

She gave him another straight look that amounted to a stare. "Must I spell it out?"

Bink found himself reddening. Obviously her problem was her appearance. Fanchon was a young woman, but she was not plain, not homely, but ugly—the living proof that youth and health were not necessarily beauty. No clothing, no makeup could help her nearly enough; only magic could do it. Which seemed to make her departure from Xanth nonsensical. Was her judgment as warped as her body?

Faced with the social necessity of changing the subject, he fixed on another objection, an aspect of his thought: "But there's no magic in Mundania."

"Precisely."

Again his logic stumbled. Fanchon was as difficult to talk with as to look at. "You mean—magic makes you—what you are?" What a marvel of tact he demonstrated!

But she did not chide him for his lack of social grace. "Yes, more or less."

"Why didn't Humfrey charge you—his fee?"

"He couldn't stand the sight of me."

Worse and worse. "Uh—what was your other reason for leaving Xanth?"

"That I shall not tell you at this time."

It figured. She had said he wouldn't believe her reasons, and he had believed the first one, so she wouldn't tell him the other. Typically female logic.

"Well, we seem to be prisoners together," Bink said, glancing around the pit again. It remained as dismal as ever. "Do you think they're going to feed us?"

"Certainly," Fanchon said. "Trent will come around and dangle bread and water at us, and ask which one would like to give him the information. That one will be fed. It will become increasingly difficult to turn him down as time passes."

"You have a gruesomely quick comprehension."

"I am gruesomely smart," she said. "In fact, it is fair to say I am as smart as I am ugly."

Yes indeed. "Are you smart enough to figure out how to get out of here?"

"No, I don't think escape is possible," she said, shaking her head in a definite yes.

"Oh," Bink said, taken aback. Her words said no, her gesture said yes. Was she crazy? No—she knew the guards were listening, though they were out of sight. So she sent them one message while sending Bink another. Which meant she had figured out an escape already.

It was now afternoon. A shaft of sunlight spilled through the grate, finding its route past the edge of the roof. Just as well, Bink thought; it would get unbearably dank in here if the sun never reached the bottom.

Trent came to the grate. "I trust you two have made your acquaintance?" he said pleasantly. "Are you hungry?"

"Now it comes," Fanchon muttered.

"I apologize for the inconvenience of your quarters," Trent said, squatting down with perfect aplomb. It was as if he were meeting them in a clean office. "If you both will give me your word not to depart these premises or interfere with our activities in any way, I shall arrange a comfortable tent for you."

"Therein lies subversion," Fanchon said to Bink. "Once you start accepting favors, you become obligated. Don't do it."

She was making extraordinary sense. "No deal," Bink said.

"You see," Trent continued smoothly, "if you were in a tent and you tried to escape, my guards would have to put arrows in you—and I don't want that to happen. It would be most uncomfortable for you, and would imperil my source of information. So it is vital that I have you confined by one means or another. By word or bond, as it were. This pit has the sole virtue of being secure."

"You could always let us go," Bink said. "Since you aren't going to get the information anyway."

If that ruffled the Evil Magician, he did not show it. "Here is some cake and wine," Trent said, lowering a package on a cord.

Neither Bink nor Fanchon reached for it, though Bink suddenly felt hungry and thirsty. The odors of spice wafted through the pit temptingly; obviously the package contained fresh, good things.

"Please take it," Trent said. "I assure you it is neither poisoned nor drugged. I want you both in good health."

"For when you change us into toads?" Bink asked loudly. What did he have to lose, really?

"No, I am afraid you have called my bluff on that. Toads do not speak intelligibly—and it is important to me that you speak."

Could the Evil Magician have lost his talent in the course of his long Mundane exile? Bink began to feel better.

The package touched the straw. Fanchon shrugged and squatted, untying it. Sure enough—cake and wine. "Maybe one of us better eat now," she said. "If nothing happens in a few hours, the other eats."

"Ladies first," Bink said. If the food were drugged and she were a spy, she wouldn't touch it.

"Thank you." She broke the cake in half. "Pick a piece," she said.

"You eat that one," Bink said, pointing.

"Very nice," Trent said from above. "You trust neither me nor each other. So you are working out conventions to safeguard your interests. But it really is unnecessary; if I wanted to poison either of you, I would merely pour it on your heads."

Fanchon took a bite of cake. "This is very good," she said. She uncorked the wine and took a swig. "This too."

But Bink remained suspicious. He would wait.

"I have been considering your cases," Trent said. "Fanchon, I will be direct. I can transform you into any other life form—even another human being." He squinted down at her. "How would you like to be beautiful?"

Uh-oh. If Fanchon were not a spy, this would be a compelling offer. The ugly one converted to beauty—

"Go away," Fanchon said to Trent, "before I throw a mudball at you." But then she thought of something else. "If you're really going to leave us here, at least give us some sanitary facilities. A bucket and a curtain. If I had a lovely posterior I might not mind the lack of privacy, but as it is I prefer to be modest."

"Aptly expressed," Trent said. He gestured, and the guards brought the items and lowered them through the hole in the grate. Fanchon set the pot in one corner and removed pins from her straggly hair to tack the cloth to the two walls, forming a triangular chamber. Bink wasn't sure why a girl of her appearance should affect such modesty; surely no one would gawk at her exposed flesh regardless of its rondure. Unless she really was extremely sensitive, with her remarks making light of what remained a serious preoccupation. In that case it did make sense. A pretty girl could express shock and distress if someone saw her bare torso, but privately she would be pleased if the reaction were favorable. Fanchon had no such pretense.

Bink was sorry for her, and for himself; it would have made the confinement much more interesting if his companion had been scenic. But actually he was grateful for the privacy, too. Natural functions would otherwise have been awkward. So he was full circle; she had defined the problem before he ever started thinking it out. She obviously did have a quicker mind.

"He's not fooling about making you beautiful," Bink said. "He can—"

"It wouldn't work."

"No, Trent's talent—"

"I know his talent. But it would only aggravate my problem—even if I were willing to betray Xanth."

This was strange. She did not want beauty? Then why her extraordinary sensitivity about her appearance? Or was this some other ploy to get him to tell the location of the Shieldstone? He doubted it. She obviously was from Xanth; no Outsider could have guessed about his experience with the water of the Spring of Life and the senile King.

Time passed. Evening came. Fanchon suffered no ill effects, so Bink ate and drank his share of the meal.

At dusk it rained. The water poured through the lattice; the roof provided some shelter, but enough slanted in to wet them down thoroughly anyway. But Fanchon smiled. "Good," she whispered. "The fates are with us tonight."

Good? Bink shivered in his wet clothing, and watched her wonderingly. She scraped with her fingers in the softening floor of the pit. Bink walked over to see what she was up to, but she waved him away. "Make sure the guards don't see," she whispered.

Small danger of that; the guards weren't interested. They had taken shelter from the rain, and were not in sight. Even if they had been close, it was getting too dark to see.

What was so important about this business? She was scooping out mud from the floor and mixing it with the hay, heedless of the rain. Bink couldn't make any sense of it. Was this her way of relaxing?

"Did you know any girls in Xanth?" Fanchon inquired. The rain was slacking off, but the darkness protected her secret work—from Bink's comprehension as well as that of the guards.

It was a subject Bink would have preferred to avoid. "I don't see what—"

She moved over to him. "I'm making bricks, idiot!" she whispered fiercely. "Keep talking—and watch for any lights. If you see anyone coming, say the word 'chameleon.' I'll hide the evidence in a hurry." She glided back to her corner.

Chameleon. There was something about that word—now he had it. The chameleon lizard he had seen just before starting on his quest to the Good Magician—his omen of the future. The chameleon had died abruptly. Did this mean his time was come?

"Talk!" Fanchon urged. "Cover my sounds!" Then, in conversational tone: "You did know some girls?"

"Uh, some," Bink said. Bricks? What for?

"Were they pretty?" Her hands were blurred by the night, but he could hear the little slaps of mud and rustle of hay. She could be using the hay to contribute fiber to the mud brick. But the whole thing was crazy. Did she intend to build a brick privy?

"Or not so pretty?" she prompted him.

"Oh. Pretty," he said. It seemed he was stuck with this topic. If the guards were listening, they would pay more attention to him talking about pretty girls than to her slapping mud. Well, if that was what she wanted—"My fiancée, Sabrina, was beautiful—is beautiful—and the Sorceress Iris seemed beautiful, but I met others who weren't. Once they get old or married, they—"

The rain had abated. Bink saw a light approaching. "Chameleon," he murmured, again experiencing inner tension. Omens always were accurate—if understood correctly.

"Women don't have to get ugly when they marry," Fanchon said. The sounds had changed; now she was concealing the evidence. "Some start out that way."

She certainly was conscious of her condition. This made him wonder again why she had turned down Trent's offer of beauty. "I met a lady centaur on my way to the Magician Humfrey," Bink said, finding it difficult to concentrate even on so natural a subject as this in the face of the oddities of his situation. Imprisoned in a pit with an ugly girl who wanted to make bricks! "She was beautiful, in a statuesque kind of way. Of course she was basically a horse—" Bad terminology. "I mean, from the rear she—well, I rode her back—" Conscious of what the guards might think he was saying—not that he should even care what they thought—he eyed the approaching light. He saw it mainly by reflections from the bars. "You know, she was half equine. She gave me a ride through centaur country."

The light diminished. It must be a guard on routine patrol. "False alarm," he whispered. Then, in conversational tone: "But there was one really lovely girl on the way to the Magician. She was—her name was . . ." He paused to concentrate. "Wynne. But she was abysmally stupid. I hope the Gap dragon didn't catch her."

"You were in the Gap?"

"For a while. Until the dragon chased me off. I had to go around it. I'm surprised you know of it; I had thought there was a forget spell associated with it, because it was not on my map and I never heard of it until I encountered it. Though how it is that I remember it, in that case—"

"I lived near the Gap," she said.

"You lived there? When was it made? What is its secret?"

"It was always there. There is a forget spell—I think the Magician Humfrey put it there. But if your associations are really strong, you remember. At least for a while. Magic only goes so far."

"Maybe that's it. I'll never forget my experience with the dragon and the shade."

Fanchon was making bricks again. "Any other girls?"

Bink had the impression she had more than casual interest in the matter. Was it because she knew the people of the chasm region? "Let's see—there was one other I met. An ordinary girl. Dee. She had an argument with the soldier I was with, Crombie. He was a woman-hater, or at least professed to be, and she walked out. Too bad; I rather liked her."

"Oh? I thought you preferred pretty girls."

"Look—don't be so damned sensitive!" he snapped. "You brought up the subject. I liked Dee better than—oh, never mind. I'd have been happier talking about plans to escape."

"Sorry," she said. "I—I knew about your journey around the chasm. Wynne and Dee are—friends of mine. So naturally I'm concerned."

"Friends of yours? Both of them?" Pieces of a puzzle began to fit together. "What is your association with the Sorceress Iris?"

Fanchon laughed. "None at all. If I were the Sorceress, do you think I would look like this?"

"Yes," Bink said. "If you tried beauty and it didn't work, and you still wanted power and figured you could somehow get it through an ignorant traveler—that would explain why Trent couldn't tempt you with the promise of beauty. That would only ruin your cover—and you could be beautiful any time you wanted to be. So you might follow me out in a disguise nobody would suspect, and of course you would not help another Magician take over Xanth—"

"So I'd come right out here into Mundania, where there is no magic," she finished. "Therefore no illusion."

That gutted his case. Or did it? "Maybe this is the way you actually look; I may never have seen the real Iris, there on her island."

"And how would I get back into Xanth?"

For that Bink had no answer. He responded with bluster. "Well, why did you come here? Obviously the nonmagic aspect has not solved your problem."

"Well, it takes time—"

"Time to cancel out magic?"

"Certainly. When dragons used to fly out over Mundania, before the Shield was set up, it would take them days or weeks to fade. Maybe even longer. Magician Humfrey says there are many pictures and descriptions of dragons and other magic beasts in Mundane texts. The Mundanes don't see dragons any more, so they think the old texts are fantasy—but this proves that it takes a while for the magic in a creature or person to dissipate."

"So a Sorceress could retain her illusion for a few days after all," Bink said.

She sighed. "Maybe so. But I'm not Iris, though I certainly wouldn't mind being her. I had entirely different and compelling reasons to leave Xanth."

"Yes, I remember. One was to lose your magic, whatever it was, and the other you wouldn't tell me."

"I suppose you deserve to know. You're going to have it out of me one way or another. I learned from Wynne and Dee what sort of a person you were, and—"

"So Wynne did get away from the dragon?"

"Yes, thanks to you. She—"

A light was coming. "Chameleon," Bink said.

Fanchon scrambled to hide her bricks. This time the light came all the way to the pit. "I trust you have not been flooded out down there?" Trent's voice inquired.

"If we were, we'd swim away from here," Bink said. "Listen, Magician—the more uncomfortable you make us, the less we want to help you."

"I am keenly aware of that, Bink. I would much prefer to provide you with a comfortable tent—"

"No."

"Bink, I find it difficult to comprehend why you should be so loyal to a government that treated you so shabbily."

"What do you know about that?"

"My spies have of course been monitoring your dialogues. But I could have guessed it readily enough, knowing how old and stubborn the Storm King must be by now. Magic manifests in divers forms, and when the definitions become too narrow—"

"Well, it doesn't make any difference here."

The Magician persisted, sounding quite reasonable in contrast to Bink's unreason. "It may be that you do lack magic, Bink, though I hardly think Humfrey would be wrong about a thing like that. But you have other qualities to recommend you, and you would make an excellent citizen."

"He's right, you know," Fanchon said. "You do deserve better than you were given."

"Which side are you on?" Bink demanded.

She sighed in the dark. She sounded very human; it was easier to appreciate that quality when he couldn't see her. "I'm on your side, Bink. I admire your loyalty; I'm just not sure it's deserved."

"Why don't you tell him where the Shieldstone is, then—if you know it?"

"Because, with all its faults, Xanth remains a nice place. The senile King won't live forever; when he dies they'll have to put in the Magician Humfrey, and he'll make things much better, even if he does complain about the time it's wasting him. Maybe some new or young Magician is being born right now, to take over after that. It'll work out somehow. It always has before. The last thing Xanth needs is to be taken over by a cruel, Evil Magician who would turn all his opposition into turnips."

Trent's chuckle came down from above. "My dear, you have a keen mind and a sharp tongue. Actually, I prefer to turn my opponents into trees; they are more durable than turnips. I don't suppose you could concede, merely for the sake of argument, that I might make a better ruler than the present King?"

"He's got a point, you know," Bink said, smiling cynically in the dark.

"Which side are you on?" Fanchon demanded, mimicking the tone Bink had used before.

But it was Trent who laughed. "I like you two," he said. "I really do. You have good minds and good loyalty. If you would only give that loyalty to me, I would be prepared to make substantial concessions. For example, I might grant you veto power over any transformations I made. You could thus choose the turnips."

"So we'd be responsible for your crimes," Fanchon said. "That sort of power would be bound to corrupt us very soon, until we were no different from you."

"Only if your basic fiber were not superior to mine," Trent pointed out. "And if it were not, then you would never have been any different from me. You merely have not yet been subjected to my situation. It would be best if you discovered this, so as not to be unconscious hypocrites."

Bink hesitated. He was wet and cold, and he did not relish spending the night in this hole. Had Trent been one to keep his word, twenty years ago? No, he hadn't; he had broken his word freely in his pursuit of power. That was part of what had defeated him; no one could afford to trust him, not even his friends.

The Magician's promises were valueless. His logic was a tissue of rationalization, designed only to get one of the prisoners to divulge the location of the Shieldstone. Veto power over transformations? Bink and Fanchon would be the first to be transformed, once the Evil one had no further need of them.

Bink did not reply. Fanchon remained silent. After a moment Trent departed.

"And so we weather temptation number two," Fanchon remarked. "But he's a clever and unscrupulous man; it will get harder."

Bink was afraid she was right.

Next morning the slanting sunlight baked the crude bricks. They were hardly hard yet, but at least it was a start. Fanchon placed the items in the privacy cubicle so that they could not be seen from above. She would set them out again for the afternoon sun, if all went well.

Trent came by with more food: fresh fruit and milk. "I dislike putting it on this footing," he said, "but my patience is wearing thin. At any time they might move the Shieldstone routinely, rendering your information valueless. If one of you does not give me the information I need today, tomorrow I shall transform you both. You, Bink, will be a cockatrice; you, Fanchon, a basilisk. You will be confined in the same cage."

Bink and Fanchon looked at each other with complete dismay. Cockatrice and basilisk—two names for the same thing: a winged reptile hatched from a yolkless egg laid by a rooster and hatched by a toad in the warmth of a dungheap. The stench of its breath was so bad that it wilted vegetation and shattered stone, and the very sight of its face would cause other creatures to keel over dead. Basilisk—the little king of the reptiles.

The chameleon of his omen had metamorphosed into the likeness of a basilisk—just before it died. Now he had been reminded of the chameleon by a person who could not have known about that omen, and threatened with transformation into— Surely death was drawing nigh.

"It's a bluff," Fanchon said at last. "He can't really do it. He's just trying to scare us."

"He's succeeding," Bink muttered.

"Perhaps a demonstration would be in order," Trent said. "I ask no person to take my magic on faith, when it is so readily demonstrable. It is necessary for me to perform regularly, to restore my full talent after the long layoff in Mundania, so the demonstration is quite convenient for me." He snapped his fingers. "Allow the prisoners to finish their meal," he said to the guard who reported. "Then remove them from the cell." He left.

Now Fanchon was glum for another reason. "He may be bluffing—but if they come down in here, they'll find the bricks. That will finish us anyway."

"Not if we move right out, giving them no trouble," Bink said. "They won't come down here unless they have to."

"Let's hope so," she said.

When the guards came, Bink and Fanchon scrambled up the rope ladder the moment it was dropped. "We're calling the Magician's bluff," Bink said. There was no reaction from the soldiers. The party marched eastward across the isthmus, toward Xanth.

Within sight of the Shield, Trent stood beside a wire cage. Soldiers stood in a ring around him, arrows nocked to bows. They all wore smoked glasses. It looked very grim.

"Now I caution you," Trent said as they arrived. "Do not look directly at each other's faces after the transformation. I can not restore the dead to life."

If this were another scare tactic, it was effective. Fanchon might doubt, but Bink believed. He remembered Justin Tree, legacy of Trent's ire of twenty years ago. The omen loomed large in his mind. First to be a basilisk, then to die . . .

Trent caught Bink's look of apprehension. "Have you anything to say to me?" he inquired, as if routinely.

"Yes. How did they manage to exile you without getting turned into toads or turnips or worse?"

Trent frowned. "That was not precisely what I meant, Bink. But, in the interest of harmony, I will answer. An aide I trusted was bribed to put a sleep spell on me. While I slept, they carried me across the Shield."

"How do you know it won't happen again? You can't stay awake all the time, you know."

"I spent much time pondering that whole problem in the long early years of my exile. I concluded that I had brought the deception upon myself. I had been faithless to others, and so others were faithless to me. I was not entirely without honor; I breached my given word only for what I deemed to be sufficient cause, yet—"

"That's the same as lying," Bink said.

"I did not think so at the time. But I dare say my reputation in that respect did not improve in my absence; it is ever the privilege of the victor to present the loser as completely corrupt, thus justifying the victory. Nevertheless, my word was not my absolute bond, and in time I realized that this was the fundamental flaw in my character that had been my undoing. The only way to prevent repetition was to change my own mode of operation. And so I no longer deceive—ever. And no one deceives me."

It was a fair answer. The Evil Magician was, in many respects, the opposite of the popular image; instead of being ugly, weak, and mean—Humfrey fitted that description better—he was handsome, strong, and urbane. Yet he was the villain, and Bink knew better than to let fair words deceive him.

"Fanchon, stand forth," Trent said.

Fanchon stepped toward him, open cynicism on her face. Trent did not gesture or chant. He merely glanced at her with concentration.

She vanished.

A soldier swooped in with a butterfly net, slamming it down on something. In a moment he held it up—a struggling, baleful, lizardlike thing with wings.

It really was a basilisk! Bink quickly averted his eyes, lest he look directly at its horrible face and meet its deadly gaze.

The soldier dumped the thing into the cage, and another smoke-glass-protected soldier shoved on the lid. The remaining soldiers relaxed visibly. The basilisk scrambled around, seeking some escape, but there was none. It glared at the wire confinement, but its gaze had no effect on the metal. A third soldier dropped a cloth over the cage, cutting off the view of the little monster. Now Bink himself relaxed. The whole thing had obviously been carefully prepared and rehearsed; the soldiers knew exactly what to do.

"Bink, stand forth," Trent said, exactly as before.

Bink was terrified. But a corner of his mind protested: *It's still a bluff. She's in on it. They have rigged it to make me think she was transformed, and that I'm to be next. All her arguments against Trent were merely to make her seem legitimate, preparing for this moment.*

Still, he only half believed that. The omen lent it a special, awful conviction. Death hovered, as it were, on the silent wings of a moth hawk, close . . .

Yet he could not betray his homeland. Weak-kneed, he stepped forth.

Trent focused on him—and the world jumped. Confused and frightened, Bink scrambled for the safety of a nearby bush. The green leaves withered as he approached; then the net came down, trapping him. Remembering his escape from the Gap dragon, he dodged at the last moment, backtracking, and the net just missed him. He glared up at the soldier, who, startled, had allowed his smoked glasses to fall askew. Their gazes met—and the man tumbled backward, stricken.

The butterfly net flew wide, but another soldier grabbed it. Bink scooted for the withered bush again, but this time the net caught him. He was scooped inside, wings flapping helplessly, tail thrashing and getting its barb caught in the fabric, claws snarled, beak snapping at nothing.

Then he was dumped out. Two shakes, three, and his claws and tail were dislodged. He landed on his back, wings outspread. An anguished squawk escaped him.

As he righted himself, the light dimmed. He was in the cage, and it had just been covered, so that no one outside could see his face. He was a cockatrice.

Some demonstration! Not only had he seen Fanchon transformed, he had experienced it himself—and killed a soldier merely by looking at him. If there had been any skeptics in Trent's army, there would be none now.

He saw the curling, barbed tail of another of his kind. A female. But her back was to him. His cockatrice nature took over. He didn't want company.

Angrily he pounced on her, biting, digging in with his talons. She twisted around instantly, the muscular serpent's tail providing leverage. For a moment they were face to face.

She was hideous, frightful, loathsome, ghastly, and revolting. He had never before experienced anything so repulsive. Yet she was female, and therefore possessed of a certain fundamental attraction. The paradoxical repulsion and attraction overwhelmed him and he lost consciousness.

When he woke, he had a headache. He lay on the hay in the pit. It was late afternoon.

"It seems the stare of the basilisk is overrated," Fanchon said. "Neither of us died."

So it had really happened. "Not quite," Bink agreed. "But I feel a bit dead." As he spoke he realized something that had not quite surfaced before: the basilisk was a magical creature that could do magic. He had been an intelligent cockatrice who had magically stricken an enemy. What did that do to his theory of magic?

"Well, you put up a good fight," Fanchon was saying. "They've already buried that soldier. It is quiet like death in this camp now."

Like death—had that been the meaning of his omen? He had not died, but he had killed—without meaning to, in a manner completely foreign to his normal state. Had the omen been fulfilled?

Bink sat up, another realization coming. "Trent's talent is genuine. We were transformed. We really were."

"It is genuine. We really were," she agreed somberly. "I admit I doubted—but now I believe."

"He must have changed us back while we were unconscious."

"Yes. He was only making a demonstration."

"It was an effective one."

"It was." She shuddered. "Bink—I—I don't know whether I can take that again. It wasn't just the change. It was—"

"I know. You made a hell of an ugly basilisk."

"I would make a hell of an ugly anything. But the sheer malignancy, stupidity, and awfulness—those things are foul! To spend the rest of my life like that—"

"I can't blame you," Bink said. But still something nagged at his mind. The experience had been so momentous that he knew it would take a long time for his mind to sift through all its aspects.

"I didn't think anyone could make me go against my conscience. But this—this—" She put her face into her hands.

Bink nodded silently. After a moment he shifted the subject. "Did you notice —those creatures were male and female."

"Of course," she said, gaining control of herself now that she had something to orient on. "We are male and female. The Magician can change our forms but not our sexes."

"But the basilisks should be neuter. Hatched of eggs laid by roosters—there are no parent basilisks, only roosters."

She nodded thoughtfully, catching hold of the problem. "You're right. If there are males and females, they should mate and reproduce their own kind. Which means, by definition, they aren't basilisks. A paradox."

"There must be something wrong with the definition," Bink said. "Either there's a lot of superstition about the origins of monsters, or we were not genuine basilisks."

"We were genuine," she said, grimacing with renewed horror. "I'm sure now. For the first time in my life, I'm glad for my human form." Which was quite an admission, for her.

"That means Trent's magic is all-the-way real," Bink said. "He doesn't just change the form, he really converts things into other things, if you see what I mean." Then the thing that had nagged at his mind before came clear. "But if magic fades outside Xanth, beyond the narrow magic band beyond the Shield, all we would have to do—"

"Would be to go into Mundania!" she exclaimed, catching on. "In time, we would revert to our proper forms. So it would not be permanent."

"So his transformation ability is a bluff, even though it is real," he said. "He would have to keep us caged right there, or we'd escape and get out of his power. He has to get all the way into Xanth or he really has very little power. No more power than he already has as General of his army—the power to kill."

"All he can get now is the tantalizing taste of real power," she said. "I'll *bet* he wants to get into Xanth!"

"But meanwhile, we're still in his power."

She set out the bricks, catching the limited sunlight. "What are you going to do?" she asked.

"If he lets me go, I'll travel on into Mundania. That's where I was headed before I was ambushed. One thing Trent has shown me—it is possible to survive out there. But I'll make sure to note my route carefully; it seems Xanth is hard to find from the other direction."

"I meant about the Shieldstone."

"Nothing."

"You won't tell him?"

"No, of course not," he said. "Now we know his magic can't really hurt us worse than his soldiers can, some of the terror is gone. Not that it matters. I don't blame you for telling him."

She looked at him. Her face was still ugly, but there was something special in it now. "You know, you're quite a man, Bink."

"No, I'm nothing much. I have no magic."

"You have magic. You just don't know what it is."

"Same thing."

"I followed you out here, you know."

Her meaning was coming clear. She had heard about him in Xanth, the traveler with no spell. She had known that would be no liability in Mundania. What better match—the man with no magic, the woman with no beauty. Similar liabilities. Perhaps he could get used to her appearance in time; her other qualities were certainly commendable. Except for one thing.

"I understand your position," he said. "But if you cooperate with the Evil Magician, I won't have anything to do with you, even if he makes you beautiful. Not that it matters—you can get your reward in Xanth when he takes over, if he honors his given word this time."

"You restore my courage," she said. "Let's make a break for it."

"How?"

"The bricks, dummy. They're hard now. As soon as it's dark, we'll make a pile—"

"The grate keeps us in; its door is still locked. A step won't make any difference. If just getting up there were the only problem, I could lift you—"

"There is a difference," she murmured. "We pile the bricks, stand on them, and push the whole grate up. It's not anchored; I checked that when they brought us in here. Gravity holds it down. It's heavy, but you're strong—"

Bink looked up with sudden hope. "You could prop it up after I heave. Step by step, until—"

"Not so loud!" she whispered fiercely. "They may still be eavesdropping." But she nodded. "You've got the idea. It's not a sure thing, but it's worth a try. And we'll have to make a raid on the store of elixir, so he can't use it even if someone else comes out to tell him where the Shieldstone is. I've been working it all out."

Bink smiled. He was beginning to like her.

Chapter 10

Chase

At night they piled up the bricks. Some crumbled, for the scant sunlight had not been sufficient to bake them properly, but on the whole they were surprisingly sturdy. Bink listened carefully for the guards, waiting until they took what they called a "break." Then he stepped to the top of the brick pile, braced his hands against the edge of the grate, and shoved.

As his muscles tightened, he suddenly realized that this was Fanchon's real reason for demanding the privacy curtain of the privy. It had not been to hide her unsightly anatomy, but to hide the bricks—so they would be preserved for this moment, this effort to escape. And he had never caught on.

The revelation gave him strength. He shoved hard—and the grate rose with surprising ease. Fanchon scrambled up beside him and jammed the privy pot under the lifted edge.

Ugh! Maybe some year someone would develop a pot that smelled of roses! But it did the job. It supported the grate as he eased off. Now there was room to scramble out. Bink gave her a boost, then hauled himself up. No guards saw them. They were free.

"The elixir is on that ship," Fanchon whispered, pointing into the darkness.

"How do you know that?" Bink asked.

"We passed it on our way to the—transformation. It's the only thing that would be guarded so carefully. And you can see the catapult aboard it."

She had certainly kept her eyes open. Ugly she might be, but she was smart. He hadn't thought to survey the premises with such an analytic eye!

"Now, getting that elixir will be a problem," she continued. "I think we'd better take the whole ship. Can you sail?"

"I've never been on anything bigger than a rowboat in my life, except maybe Iris's yacht, and that wasn't real. I'd probably get seasick."

"Me too," she agreed. "We're landlubbers. So they'll never look for us there. Come on."

Well, it was better than being changed into a cockatrice.

They crept down to the beach and entered the water. Bink looked back nervously—and saw a light moving toward the pit. "Hurry!" he whispered. "We forgot to put the grate back down; they'll know we're gone right away."

At least they were both reasonably good swimmers. They shed their clothing —what had happened to it during the transformations? again, no explaining the details of magic—and stroked silently for the sailboat moored a quarter mile out. Bink was alarmed by the dark depths of the water beneath him; what type of monsters dwelled in Mundane seas?

The water was not cold, and the exertion of swimming helped warm him, but gradually Bink tired and felt chilled. Fanchon suffered similarly. The ship had not seemed far, viewed from land—but that had been walking distance. Swimming distance was quite another matter.

Then the hue and cry commenced back at the prison pit. Lights flared everywhere, moving around like fireflies—but setting no fires. Bink had an infusion of new strength. "We've got to get there fast," he gasped.

Fanchon didn't answer. She was too busy swimming.

The swim was interminable. It drained strength from Bink, making him become more pessimistic. But at last they came up to the ship. A sailor was standing on the deck, a silhouette in the light of the moon, peering at the shore.

Fanchon drew close to Bink. "You go—other side," she gasped. "I—distract."

She had guts. The sailor might put an arrow in her. But Bink stroked laboriously around the keel, moving to the far side. The ship was about forty feet long, large by Xanth standards. But if any part of what Trent had said about Mundania was true, there were much larger ships there.

He reached up and put his fingers on the edge of the hull. He tried to think of the name of this portion of a ship's anatomy, but could not. He hoped there weren't other sailors watching. He had to haul himself up slowly over the gunwale—that was the name—so as not to rock the boat.

Now Fanchon, with superlative timing, made a clamor, as of someone drowning. The sailors went to the rail—four of them in all—and Bink heaved himself up as silently as he could. He scraped, for his muscles felt leaden, unresponsive. His wet body slapped against the deck, and the ship tilted back a bit under his weight—but the sailors stood riveted to the other side, watching the show.

Bink got to his feet and slunk up to the mast. The sails were furled, so that it offered scant concealment; they would see him when they turned with their lamps.

Well, he would have to act first. He felt ill equipped to indulge in combat, his arms and feet cold and heavy, but it was necessary. He walked silently up behind the four, his heart pounding. They were leaning over the rail, trying to see Fanchon, who was still making a considerable commotion. Bink put his left hand against the back of the nearest sailor and caught the man's trouser with his right hand. He heaved, hard and suddenly—and the sailor went up and over with a cry of alarm.

Bink swung immediately to the next, grabbing and shoving. The man had started to turn toward his companion's exclamation—but too late. Bink heaved, and the sailor went over. Almost over—one hand caught the rail. The sailor clung, twisting around to face inward. Bink knocked at his fingers and finally pried them loose, and the man dropped into the water.

But the loss of time and momentum had been crucial. Now the other two were upon Bink. One wrapped an arm around Bink's shoulder, trying to choke him, while the other hovered behind.

What had Crombie said to do in a situation like this? Bink concentrated and remembered. He grabbed the man, bent his knees, leaned forward, and heaved. It worked beautifully. The sailor sailed over Bink's shoulder and crashed on his back on the deck.

But the last one was stepping in, fists swinging. He caught Bink on the side of the head with glancing but numbing force. Bink fell to the deck himself, and the man dove on top of him. To make things worse, Bink saw one of the others climbing back aboard. He put up his feet to hold off his opponent, but this was only partially effective. The burly sailor was pushing him down, pinning him—and the other was about to join in.

The standing figure lifted a foot. Bink could not even flinch; his arms were tangled, his body held down. The foot swung—and struck the head of Bink's antagonist.

The man rolled off Bink with a groan. It was not fun, being kicked in the head. But how had the kicker missed the proper target, at such close range? The lamps had all gone into the water along with their owners; maybe in the dark a mistake—

"Help me get him over the edge," Fanchon said. "We've got to secure this ship."

And he had mistaken her for a sailor, though she was naked! Well, blame the inadequate light again. Moonlight was pretty, but in a situation like this—

But the remaining two sailors were already rising over the gunwale. Acting on a common impulse, Bink grabbed his erstwhile opponent's shoulders, and Fanchon grabbed his feet. "One—two—three—heave!" she gasped.

They heaved almost together. The man swung up and into his two companions. All three went over the edge to splash in the sea. Bink hoped they were all lively enough to swim. The fourth one lay on the deck, apparently unconscious.

"Pull up the anchor!" Fanchon ordered. "I'll get a pole." She ran to the ship's cabin, a lean figure in the moonlight.

Bink found the anchor chain and hauled on it. The thing snagged infuriatingly, because he did not know how to make it let go, but finally he got it up.

"What did you do to this guy?" Fanchon demanded, kneeling beside the fallen sailor.

"I threw him. Crombie showed me how."

"Crombie? I don't remember—"

"A soldier I met in Xanth. We got caught in a hailstorm, and I was going back after Dee, but—well, it's complicated."

"Oh yes—you did mention the soldier." She paused. "Dee? You went after her? Why?"

"She had run out into the storm and—well, I liked her." Then, to cover up what might have been taken as a slight to his present company, who had shown extreme sensitivity about such things before, he said: "What happened to the other sailors? Did they drown?"

"I showed them this," she said, pointing to a wicked-looking boathook. "They swam for shore instead."

"We'd better get moving. If we can figure out the sail."

"No. The current is carrying us out. Wind's the wrong way. We'd just mess it up, trying to handle the sails when we don't know what we're doing."

Bink looked across at the other ship. Lights were on it. "Those sailors didn't swim ashore," he said. "They went next door. They'll be coming after us—under sail."

"They can't," she said. "I told you—the wind."

But now it was unmistakable. The other sail was being spread. They *were* using the wind.

"We'd better find that elixir," she said.

"Yes." He had forgotten about it. But for that, they could have run across the land and been lost in Mundania. But could he have lived with himself, buying his own freedom while leaving Xanth subject to the siege of the Evil Magician? "We'll dump it overboard—"

"No!"

"But I thought—"

"We'll use it as hostage. As long as we have it, they won't close on us. We'll take turns standing on the deck and holding the vial over the sea so they can see us. If anything happens to—"

"Beautiful!" he exclaimed. "I never would have thought of that."

"First we have to find our hostage. If we guessed wrong about the ship, if they put the catapult on this one and the elixir on the other—"

"Then they wouldn't be chasing us," he said.

"Yes they would. They need the catapult too. And most of all, they need us."

They searched the ship. In the cabin was a chained monster of a type Bink had never seen before. It was not large, but quite horrible in other respects. Its body was completely covered with hair, white with black spots, and it had a thin tail, floppy black ears, a small black nose, and gleaming white teeth. Its four feet had stubby claws. It snarled viciously as Bink approached—but it was chained by the neck to the wall, its mad leaps cut brutally short by that tether.

"What is it?" Bink asked, horrified.

Fanchon considered. "I think it's a werewolf."

Now the creature looked halfway familiar. It did resemble a werewolf, fixed in its animal stage.

"Out here in Mundania?"

"Well, it must be related. If it had more heads, it would be like a cerberus. With only one head, I think it's a dog."

Bink gaped. "A dog! I think you're right. I've never actually seen a dog before. Not in the flesh. Just pictures."

"I don't think there are any in Xanth today. There used to be, but they must have migrated out."

"Through the Shield?" Bink demanded.

"Before the Shield was set up, of course—though I'd thought there were references to dogs and cats and horses within the past century. I must have misremembered the dates."

"Well, it seems we have one here now. It looks vicious. It must be guarding the elixir."

"Trained to attack strangers," she agreed. "I suppose we'll have to kill it."

"But it's a rare creature. Maybe the only one left alive today."

"We don't know that. Dogs might be common in Mundania. But it is rather pretty, once you get used to it."

The dog had quieted down, though it still watched them warily. A small dragon might watch a person that way, Bink thought, if the person were just outside its striking range. With the proper break, the person might come within range . . .

"Maybe we could revive the sailor and have him tame it," Bink said. "The animal must be responsive to members of this ship's crew. Otherwise they could never get at the elixir."

"Good idea," she agreed.

The sailor had finally recovered consciousness, but he was in no condition to resume the fight. "We'll let you go," Fanchon told him, "if you tell us how to tame that dog. We don't want to have to kill it, you see."

"Who, Jennifer?" the man asked dazedly. "Just speak her name, pat her on the head, and feed her." He lay back. "I think my collarbone's broke."

Fanchon looked at Bink. "Can't make him swim, then. Trent may be a monster, but we aren't." She turned back to the sailor. "If you will give your word not to interfere with us in any way, we'll help you recover as well as we can. Deal?"

The sailor didn't hesitate. "I can't interfere with you. I can't get up. Deal."

This bothered Bink. He and Fanchon sounded just like Trent, offering better terms to a captive enemy in return for his cooperation. Were they any different from the Evil Magician?

Fanchon checked the sailor's body around the shoulders. "Yow!" he cried.

"I'm no doctor," she said, "but I think you're right. You have a broken bone. Are there any pillows aboard?"

"Listen," the sailor said as she worked on him. He was obviously trying to divert his attention from the pain. "Trent's no monster. You called him that, but you're wrong. He's a good leader."

"He's promised you all the spoils of Xanth?" Fanchon asked, with an edge to her voice.

"No, just farms or jobs for all of us," he said.

"No killing, no rapine, no loot?" Her disbelief was evident.

"None of that. This ain't the old days, you know? We just protect him and keep order in the territory we occupy, and he'll give us small land grants where nobody's settled yet. He says Xanth's underpopulated. And there'll be—he'll encourage the local gals to marry us, so we can have families. If there aren't enough, he'll bring in gals from the real world. And meanwhile, he'll transform some smart animals into gals. I thought that was a joke, but after what I hear about those cocks—" He grimaced. "I mean those basks—" He shook his head and grimaced again, in pain.

"Keep your head still," Fanchon told him, too late. "It's true about the cockatrice and basilisk; *we* were them. But animal brides—"

"Oh, it wouldn't be so bad, miss. Just temporary, until real gals arrived. If she looks like a gal and feels like a gal, I wouldn't blame her for being a bitch before. I mean, some gals are bitches—"

"What's a bitch?" Bink asked.

"A bitch? You don't know that?" The sailor grimaced again; either he was in considerable pain or it was a natural expression. "A female dog. Like Jennifer. Hell, if Jennifer had human form—"

"Enough," Fanchon muttered.

"Well, anyway, we'll get homesteads and settle in. And our kids will be magic. I tell you, it's that last that recruited me. I don't believe in magic, understand— or I didn't then—but I remember the fairy tales from when I was a little tyke, about the princess and the frog, and the mountain of glass, and the three wishes —well, look, I was a metalworker for a crooked shop, know what I mean? And I really wanted out of the rat race."

Bink shook his head silently. He understood only part of what the sailor was saying, but it did not make Mundania look very good. Stores that were built off balance, crooked? Rats that raced? Bink would want to get out of that culture, too.

"A chance to have a decent life in the country," the sailor continued, and there was no question about his dedication to his vision. "Owning my own land, making good things grow, you know? And my kids knowing magic, real magic— I guess I still don't really believe that part, but even if it's a lie, you know, it's sure nice to think about."

"But to invade a foreign land, to take what doesn't belong to you—" Fanchon said. She broke off, evidently certain that it was pointless to debate that sort of thing with a sailor. "He'll betray you the moment he doesn't need you. He's an Evil Magician, exiled from Xanth."

"You mean he really can do magic?" the man asked with happy disbelief. "I figured all this stuff was sleight of hand, you know, when I really thought about it. I mean, I believed some of the time, but—"

"He sure as hell *can* do magic," Bink put in, becoming acclimatized to the sailor's language. "We told you how he changed us—"

"Never mind about that," Fanchon said.

"Well, he's still a good leader," the sailor insisted. "He told us how he was kicked out twenty years ago because he tried to be King, and how he lost his magic, and married a gal from here and had a little boy—"

"Trent has a family in Mundania?" Bink asked, amazed.

"We don't call our country that," the sailor said. "But yes—he had a family. Until this mystery bug went around—some kind of flu, I think, or maybe food poisoning—and they both got it and died. He said science hadn't been able to save them, but magic could have, so he was going back to magicland. Xanth, you call it. But they'd kill him if he just walked in alone, even if he got by the thing he called a Shield. So he needed an army—oooh!" Fanchon had finished her work and heaved his shoulder up onto a pillow.

So they had the sailor as comfortable as was feasible, his shoulder bound up in stray cloths. Bink would have liked to hear more of the man's unique viewpoint. But time had passed, and it was apparent that the other ship was gaining on them. They traced its progress by its sail, which moved laterally, back and forth, zigzagging against the wind—and with each pass it was closer. They had been wrong about the capabilities of ships in adverse wind. How much else were they wrong about?

Bink went into the cabin. He was feeling a bit seasick now, but he held it down. "Jennifer," he said hesitantly, proffering some of the dog food they had found. The small spotted monster wagged her tail. Just like that, they were friends. Bink screwed up his courage and patted her on the head, and she did not bite him. Then, while she ate, he opened the chest she had guarded so ferociously and lifted out the vial of greenish fluid he found therein, in a carefully padded box. Victory!

"Miss," the sailor called as Bink emerged with the vial. "The Shield—"

Fanchon looked about nervously. "Is the current carrying us into *that?*"

"Yes, miss. I wouldn't interfere, but if you don't turn this boat soon, we'll all be dead. I *know* that Shield works; I've seen animals try to go through it and get fried."

"How can we tell where it is?" she asked.

"There's a glimmer. See?" He pointed with difficulty.

Bink peered and saw it. They were drifting toward a curtain of faint luminescence, ghostly white. The Shield!

The ship progressed inexorably. "We can't stop it," Fanchon cried. "We're going right through."

"Throw down the anchor!" the sailor said.

What else was there to do? The Shield was certain death. Yet to stop meant capture by Trent's forces. Even bluffing them back by means of the vial of elixir would not suffice; the ship remained a kind of prison.

"We can use the lifeboat," Fanchon said. "Give me the vial."

Bink gave it to her, then threw over the anchor. The ship slowly turned as the anchor took hold. The Shield loomed uncomfortably close—but so did the pursuing ship. Now it was clear why it was using the wind instead of the current; it was under control, in no danger of drifting into the Shield.

They lowered the lifeboat. A reflector lamp from the other ship bathed them in its light. Fanchon held the vial aloft. "I'll drop it!" she screamed at the enemy. "Hit me with an arrow—the elixir drowns with me."

"Give it back," Trent's voice called from the other ship. "I pledge to let you both go free."

"Ha!" she muttered. "Bink, can you row this boat yourself? I'm afraid to set this thing down while we're in range of their arrows. I want to be sure that no matter what happens to us, they don't get this stuff."

"I'll try," Bink said. He settled himself, grabbed the oars, and heaved.

One oar cracked into the side of the ship. The other dug into the water. The boat skewed around. "Push off!" Fanchon exclaimed. "You almost dumped me."

Bink tried to put the end of one oar against the ship, to push, but it didn't work because he could not maneuver the oar free of its oarlock. But the current carried the boat along until it passed beyond the end of the ship.

"We're going into the Shield!" Fanchon cried, waving the vial. "Row! Row! Turn the boat!"

Bink put his back into it. The problem with rowing was that he faced backward; he could not see where he was going. Fanchon perched in the stern, holding the vial aloft, peering ahead. He got the feel of the oars and turned the boat, and now the shimmering curtain came into view on the side. It was rather pretty in its fashion, its ghostly glow parting the night—but he recoiled from its horror.

"Go parallel to it," Fanchon directed. "The closer we stay, the harder it'll make it for the other ship. Maybe they'll give up the pursuit."

Bink pulled on the oars. The boat moved ahead. But he was unused to this particular form of exertion, and not recovered from his fatigue of the swim, and he knew he couldn't keep it up long.

"You're going into the Shield!" Fanchon cried.

Bink looked. The Shield loomed closer, yet he was not rowing toward it. "The current," he said. "Carrying us sideways." He had naively thought that once he started rowing, all other vectors ceased.

"Row away from the Shield," she cried. "Quickly!"

He angled the boat—but the Shield did not retreat. The current was bearing them on as fast as he could row. To make it worse, the wind was now changing —and rising. He was holding even at the moment, but he was tiring rapidly. "I can't—keep this—up!" he gasped, staring at the glow.

"There's an island," Fanchon said. "Angle toward it."

Bink looked around. He saw a black something cutting the waves to the side. Island? It was no more than a treacherous rock. But if they could anchor to it—

He put forth a desperate effort—but it was not enough. A storm was developing. They were going to miss the rock. The dread Shield loomed nearer.

"I'll help," Fanchon cried. She set down the vial, crawled forward, and put her hands on the oars, opposite his hands. She pushed, synchronizing her efforts with his.

It helped. But Bink, fatigued, was distracted. In the erratic moonlight, blotted out intermittently by the thickening, fast-moving clouds above, her naked body lost some of its shapelessness and assumed the suggestion of more feminine contours. Shadow and imagination could make her halfway attractive—and that embarrassed him, because he had no right to think of such things. Fanchon could be a good companion, if only—

The boat smashed into the rock. It tilted—rock or craft or both. "Get hold! Get hold!" Fanchon cried as water surged over the side.

Bink reached out and tried to hang on to the stone. It was both abrasive and slippery. A wave broke over him, filling his mouth with its salty spume. Now it was black; the clouds had completed their engulfment of the moon.

"The elixir!" Fanchon cried. "I left it in the—" She dived for the flooded stern of the boat.

Bink, still choking on sea water, could not yell at her. He clung to the rock with his hands, his fingers finding purchase in a crevice, anchoring the boat with his hooked knees. He suffered a foolish vision: if a giant drowning in the ocean grabbed on to the land of Xanth for support, his fingers would catch in the chasm, the Gap. Maybe that was the purpose of the Gap. Did the tiny inhabitants of this isolated rock resent the crevice that Bink's giant fingers had found? Did they have forget spells to remove it from their awareness?

There was a distant flash of lightning. Bink saw the somber mass of ragged stone: no miniature people on it. But there was a glint, as of light reflecting from a knob in the water. He stared at it, but the lightning was long since gone, and he was squinting at the mere memory, trying to make out the surrounding shape. For it had been a highlight from something larger.

Lightning flashed again, closer. Bink saw briefly but clearly.

It was a toothy reptilian creature. The highlight had been from its malignant eye.

"A sea monster!" he cried, terrified.

Fanchon labored at an oar, finally extricating it from its lock. She aimed it at the monster and shoved.

Thunk! The end of the oar struck the armored green snout. The creature backed off.

"We've got to get away from here," Bink cried.

But as he spoke, another wave broke over them. The boat was lifted and wrenched away from his feet. He put one arm about Fanchon's skinny waist and hung on. It seemed the fingers of his other hand would break—but they remained wedged in the crevice, and he held his position.

In the next trough the lightning showed small saillike projections moving in the water. What were they?

Then another monster broke water right beside him; he saw it in the phosphorescence that the complete darkness had attuned his eyes to. It seemed to have a single broad eye across its face, and a round, truncated snout. Huge wattles were at the sides. Bink was transfixed by terror, though he knew that most of the details were really from his imagination. He could only stare at the thing as the lightning permitted.

And the lightning confirmed his imagination. It was a hideous monster!

Bink struggled with his terror to form some plan of defense. One hand clung to the rock; the other held Fanchon. He could not act. But maybe Fanchon could. "Your oar—" he gasped.

The monster acted first. It put its hands to its face—and lifted the face away. Underneath, was the face of Evil Magician Trent. "You fools have caused enough trouble! Give me the elixir, and I'll have the ship throw us a line."

Bink hesitated. He was bone-weary and cold, and knew he could not hold out much longer against storm and current. It was death to stay here.

"There's a crocodile sniffing around," Trent continued. "And several sharks. Those are just as deadly as the mythical monsters you are familiar with. I have repellent—but the current is carrying it away as rapidly as it diffuses into the water, so it's not much help. On top of that, sometimes whirlpools develop around these rocks, especially during storms. We need help now—and I alone can summon it. Give me that vial!"

"Never!" Fanchon cried. She dived into the black waves.

Trent snapped the mask back over his face and dived after her. As he moved, Bink saw that the Magician was naked except for his long sword strapped to a harness. Bink dived after him, not even thinking of what he was doing.

They met in a tangle underwater. In the dark and bubbly swirl, there was nothing but mutual mischief. Bink tried to swim to the surface, uncertain as to what foolishness had prompted him to dive here but sure that he could only drown himself. But someone had a death grip on him. He had to get up, to get his head in air so he could breathe. The water had hold of them all, carrying them around and around.

It was the whirlpool—an inanimate funnel monster. It sucked them down, spinning, into the depth of its maw. For the second time Bink felt himself drowning—and this time he knew no Sorceress would rescue him.

Chapter 11

Wilderness

ink woke with his face in sand. Around him lay the inert
tentacles of a green monster.

He groaned and sat up. "Bink!" Fanchon cried gladly, coming across the
beach to him.

"I thought it was night," he said.

"You've been unconscious. This cave has magic phosphorescence, or maybe
it's Mundane phosphorescence, since there was some on the rock, too. But it's
much brighter here. Trent pumped the water out of you, but I was afraid—"

"What's this?" Bink asked, staring at a green tentacle.

"A kraken seaweed," Trent said. "It pulled us out of the drink, intending to
consume us—but the vial of elixir broke and killed it. That's all that saved our
lives. If the vial had broken earlier, it would have stopped the kraken from

catching us, and we all would have drowned; later, and we would already have been eaten. As fortuitous a coincidence of timing as I have ever experienced."

"A kraken weed!" Bink exclaimed. "But that's magic!"

"We're back in Xanth," Fanchon said.

"But—"

"I conjecture that the whirlpool drew us down below the effective level of the Shield," Trent said. "We passed under it. Perhaps the presence of the elixir helped. A freak accident—and I'm certainly not going to try to reverse that route now. I lost my breathing apparatus on the way in; lucky I got a good dose of oxygen first! We're in Xanth to stay."

"I guess so," Bink said dazedly. He had gradually become accustomed to the notion of spending the rest of his life in Mundania; it was hard to abandon that drear expectation so suddenly. "But why did you save me? Once the elixir was gone—"

"It was the decent thing to do," the Magician said. "I realize you will not appreciate such a notion from my lips, but I can offer no better rationale at the moment. I never had any personal animus against you; in fact, I rather admired your fortitude and personal ethical code. You can go your way now—and I'll go mine."

Bink pondered. He was faced with a new, unfamiliar reality. Back in Xanth, no longer at war with the Evil Magician. The more he reviewed the details, the less sense any of it made. Sucked down by a whirlpool through monster-infested waters, through the invisible but deadly Shield, to be rescued by a man-eating plant, which was coincidentally nullified at precisely the moment required to let them drop safely on this beach? "No," he said. "I don't believe it. Things just don't happen this way."

"It does seem as if we were charmed," Fanchon said. "Though why the Evil Magician should have been included . . ."

Trent smiled. Naked, he was fully as impressive as before. Despite his age, he was a fit and powerful man. "It does seem ironic that the evil should be saved along with the good. Perhaps human definitions are not always honored by nature. But I, like you, am a realist. I don't pretend to understand how we got here—but I do not question that we are here. Getting to land may be more problematical, however. We are hardly out of danger yet."

Bink looked around the cave. Already the air seemed close, though he hoped that was his imagination. There seemed to be no exit except the water through which they had come. In one nook was a pile of clean bones—the refuse of the kraken.

It began to seem less coincidental. What better place for an ocean monster to operate than at the exit to a whirlpool? The sea itself collected the prey, and most of it was killed on the way in by the Shield. The kraken weed had only to sieve the fresh bodies out of the water. And this highly private cave was ideal for leisurely consumption of the largest living animals. They could be deposited here on the beach, and even given food, so that they would remain more or less healthy until the kraken's hunger was sufficient. A pleasant little larder to keep the food fresh and tasty. Any that tried to escape by swimming past the tentacles—ugh! So the kraken could have dropped the human trio here, then been hit by the elixir; instead of split-second timing, it became several-minute timing. Still a coincidence, but a much less extreme one.

Fanchon was squatting by the water, flicking dry leaves into it. The leaves had to be from past seasons of the kraken weed; why it needed them here, with no sunlight, Bink didn't understand. Maybe it had been a regular plant before it turned magic—or its ancestors had been regular—and it still had not entirely adapted. Or maybe the leaves had some other purpose. There was a great deal yet to be understood about nature. At any rate, Fanchon was floating the leaves on the water, and why she wasted her time that way was similarly opaque.

She saw him looking. "I'm tracing surface currents," she said. "See—the water is moving that way. There has to be an exit under that wall."

Bink was impressed again with her intelligence. Every time he caught her doing something stupid, it turned out to be the opposite. She was an ordinary, if ugly, girl, but she had a mind that functioned efficiently. She had plotted their escape from the pit, and their subsequent strategy, and it had nullified Trent's program of conquest. Now she was at it again. Too bad her appearance fell down.

"Of course," Trent agreed. "The kraken can't live in stagnant water; it needs a constant flow. That brings in its food supply and carries away its wastes. We have an exit—if it leads to the surface quickly enough, and does not pass through the Shield again."

Bink didn't like it. "Suppose we dive into that current and it carries us a mile underwater before it comes out? We'd drown."

"My friend," Trent said, "I have been pondering that very dilemma. We can not be rescued by my sailors, because we are obviously beyond the Shield. I do not like to gamble on either the current or what we may discover within it. Yet it seems we must eventually do so, for we can not remain here indefinitely."

Something twitched. Bink looked—and saw one green tentacle writhing. "The kraken's reviving!" he exclaimed. "It isn't dead!"

"Uh-oh," Trent said. "The elixir has thinned out in the current and dissipated. The magic is returning. I had thought that concentration would be fatal to a magic creature, but apparently not."

Fanchon watched the tentacles. Now others were quivering. "I think we'd better get out of here," she said. "Soon."

"But we don't dare plunge into the water without knowing where it goes,"

Bink objected. "We must be well below the surface. I'd rather stay here and fight than drown."

"I propose we declare a truce between us until we get free," Trent said. "The elixir is gone, and we cannot go back the way we came from Mundania. We shall probably have to cooperate to get out of here—and in the present situation, we really have no quarrel."

Fanchon didn't trust him. "So we help you get out—so then the truce ends and you change us into gnats. Since we're inside Xanth, we'll never be able to change back again."

Trent snapped his fingers. "Stupid of me to forget. Thank you for reminding me. I can use my magic now to get us out." He looked at the quivering green tentacles. "Of course, I'll have to wait until all the elixir is gone, for it voids my magic, too. That means the kraken will be fully recovered. I can't transform it, because its main body is too far away."

The tentacles lifted. "Bink, dive for it!" Fanchon cried. "We don't want to be caught between the kraken and the Evil Magician." She plunged into the water.

The issue had been forced. She was right: the kraken would eat them or the Magician would transform them. Right now, while the lingering elixir blunted both threats, was the time to escape. Still, he would have hesitated—if Fanchon had not already taken action. If she drowned, there would be no one on his side.

Bink charged across the sand, tripped over a tentacle, and sprawled. Reacting automatically, the tentacle wrapped itself around his leg. The leaves glued themselves to his flesh with little sucking noises. Trent drew his sword and strode toward him.

Bink grabbed a handful of sand and threw it at the Magician, but it was ineffective. Then Trent's sword slashed down—and severed the tentacle. "You are in no danger from me, Bink," the Magician said. "Swim, if you wish."

Bink scrambled up and dived into the water, taking a deep breath. He saw Fanchon's feet kicking ahead of him as she swam down, and saw the dark tube of the nether exit. It terrified him, and he balked.

His head popped through the surface. There was Trent, standing on the beach, parrying the converging tentacles with his sword. Fighting off the coils of the monster the man was the very picture of heroism. Yet the moment the combat was over, Trent would be a more dangerous monster than the kraken.

Bink decided. He took a new breath and dived again. This time he stroked right into the somber eye, and felt the current take him. Now there was no turning back.

The tunnel opened out almost immediately—into another glowing cavern. Bink had gained on Fanchon, and their heads broke the surface almost together. Probably she had been more cautious about navigating the exit.

Heads turned their way. Human heads, on human torsos—very nice feminine ones. Their faces were elfin, their tresses flowing in magical iridescence over slender bare shoulders and perfectly erect breasts. But the lower quarters merged into fish's tails. These were mermaids.

"What are you doing in our cave?" one of the maids cried indignantly.

"Just passing through," Bink said. Naturally, mermaids spoke the common language of Xanth. He would not have thought anything of it, had Trent not remarked on how Xanth language merged with all Mundane languages. Magic operated in so many ways. "Tell us the shortest way to the surface."

"That way," one said, pointing left. "That way," another said, pointing right. "No, that way!" a third cried, pointing straight up. There was a burst of girlish laughter.

Several mermaids plunged into the water, tails flashing, and swam toward Bink. In a moment he was surrounded. Up close, the creatures were even prettier than from afar. Each one had a perfect complexion, resulting from the natural action of the water, and their breasts floated somewhat, making them seem fuller. Maybe he had been exposed to Fanchon too long; the sight of all this loveliness gave him strange sensations of excitement and nostalgia. If he could grab them all at once—but no, they were mermaids, not his type at all.

They paid no attention to Fanchon. "He's a man!" one cried, meaning Bink was human, not merman. "Look at his split legs. No tail at all."

Suddenly they were diving under to view his legs. Bink, naked, found this distinctly awkward. They began to put their hands on him, kneading the unfamiliar musculature of his legs, a great curiosity to them. Yet why weren't they looking at Fanchon's legs too? There seemed to be more mischief than curiosity here.

Trent's head broke the water behind them. "Mermaids," he commented. "We'll get nothing from them."

So it seemed. It also seemed that the Magician could not be avoided. "I think we'd better make the truce," Bink said to Fanchon. "We have to extend some trust sometime."

She looked at the mermaids, then at Trent. "Very well," she said ungraciously. "For what it's worth—which isn't much."

"A sensible decision," Trent said. "Our long-range objectives may differ, but our short-range one matches: survival. See, here come the tritons."

As he spoke, a group of mermen appeared, swimming in from another passage. This seemed to be a labyrinth of caves and water-filled apertures.

"Ho!" a triton cried, brandishing his trident. "Skewer!"

The mermaids screamed playfully and dived out of sight. Bink avoided Fanchon's gaze; the ladies had been having entirely too much fun with him, and obviously not because of his split legs.

"Too many to fight," Trent said. "The elixir is gone. With your acquiescence, under our truce, I will change you both into fish, or perhaps reptiles, so that you can escape. However—"

"How will we change back?" Fanchon demanded.

"That is the key. I can not change myself. Therefore you will have to rescue me—or remain transformed. So we shall survive together, or suffer apart. Fair enough?"

She looked at the tritons, who were swimming determinedly toward the three, surrounding them, tridents raised. They did not look at all playful. This was obviously a gang of bullies, showing off for the applauding spectators—the mermaids, who had now reappeared on shore—taking time to put on a flashy show. "Why not change them into fish?"

"That would abate the immediate threat, could I get them all in time," Trent agreed. "But it still would not free us from the cave. I suspect we shall have to resort to magic on ourselves at some point, regardless. And we are intruders in their cave; there is a certain proprietary ethic—"

"All right!" she cried, as a triton heaved his three-pointed fork. "Do it your way."

Suddenly she was a monster—one of the worst Bink had seen. She had a huge greenish sheath around her torso, from which arms, legs, head, and tail projected. Her feet were webbed, and her head was like that of a serpent.

The triton's fork struck the Fanchon-monster's shell—and bounced off. Suddenly Bink saw the sense of this transformation. This monster was invulnerable.

"Sea turtle," Trent murmured. "Mundane. Harmless, normally—but the merfolk don't know that. I've made a study of nonmagical creatures, and have developed much respect for them. Oops!" Another trident was flying.

Then Bink was also a sea turtle. Suddenly he was completely comfortable in the water, and he had no fear of the pronged spears. If one came at his face, he would simply pull in his head. It would not retract all the way, but the armor of the shell around it would intercept almost anything.

Something tugged at his carapace. Bink started to dive, trying to dislodge it—then realized, in his reptilian brain, that this was something that had to be tolerated. Not a friend, but an ally—for now. So he dived, but allowed the dragging weight to persist.

Bink stroked slowly but powerfully for the underwater passage. The other turtle had already entered it. Bink didn't worry about air; he knew he could hold his breath for as long as it took.

It did not take long. This passage slanted up to the surface; Bink could see the moon as he broke through. The storm had abated.

Abruptly he was human again—and swimming was harder. "Why did you change me back?" he asked. "We weren't to shore yet."

"When you are a turtle, you have the brain of a turtle, and the instincts of a turtle," Trent explained. "Otherwise you would not be able to survive as a turtle. Too long, and you might forget you ever were a man. If you headed out to sea, I might not be able to catch you, and so would never be able to change you back."

"Justin Tree retained his human mind," Bink pointed out.

"Justin Tree?"

"One of the men you changed into trees, in the North Village. His talent was throwing his voice."

"Oh, I remember now. He was a special case. I made him into a sapient tree— really a man in tree form, not a true tree. I can do that when I put my mind to it. For a tree it can work. But a turtle needs turtle reflexes to deal with the ocean."

Bink didn't follow all that, but he didn't care to debate it. Obviously cases differed. Then Fanchon reappeared in human form. "Well, you honored the truce," she said grudgingly. "I didn't really think you would."

"Reality must intrude sometime," Trent said.

"What do you mean by that?" she demanded.

"I said, we are not out of danger yet. I believe that is a sea serpent on its way."

Bink saw the huge head, and there was no question: the monster had seen them. It was big; the head was a yard across. "Maybe the rocks—" Bink cried, orienting on the outcropping that marked the exit from the tritons' cave.

"That thing's a huge, long snake," Fanchon said. "It could reach right down into the cave, or coil right around the rocks. We can't escape it in this form."

"I could change you into poisonous jellyfish that the serpent would not eat," Trent said. "But you might get lost in the shuffle. It also may not be wise to be transformed more than once a day; I have not been able to verify this during my exile, for obvious reasons, but I am concerned that your systems may suffer a shock each time."

"Besides which, the monster could still eat you," Fanchon said.

"You have a very quick mind," Trent agreed equably. "Therefore, I shall have to do something I dislike—transform the monster."

"You don't want to transform the sea serpent?" Bink asked, surprised. The thing was now quite close, its small red eyes fixed on the prey; saliva dripped from its giant teeth.

"It is merely an innocent creature going about its business," Trent said. "We should not enter its waters if we do not wish to participate in its mode of existence. There is a balance of nature, whether magical or mundane, that we should hesitate to interfere with."

"You have a weird sense of humor," Fanchon said sourly. "But I never claimed to understand the nuances of evil magic. If you really want to protect its life style, transform it into a little fish until we get to shore, then transform it back."

"And *hurry!*" Bink cried. The thing was now looming over them, orienting on its specific targets.

"That would not work," Trent said. "The fish would swim away and be lost. I must be able to identify the particular creature I mean to transform, and it must be within six feet of me. However your suggestion has merit."

"Six feet," Bink said. "We'll be inside it before we get that close." He was not trying to be funny; the monster's mouth was much longer than it was wide, so that as it opened to its full aperture the upper front teeth were a good twelve feet from the lower teeth.

"Nevertheless, I must operate within my limits," Trent said, unperturbed. "The critical region is the head, the seat of identity. When I transform that, the rest naturally follows. If I tried it when only the tail was within range, I would botch the job. So when it tries to take me in its mouth, it comes into my power."

"What if it goes for one of us first?" Fanchon demanded. "Suppose we're more than six feet from you?"

"I suggest you arrange to be within that radius," Trent said dryly.

Hastily Bink and Fanchon splashed closer to the Evil Magician. Bink had the distinct impression that even if Trent had had no magic, they would have been in his power. He was too self-assured, too competent in his tactics; he knew how to manage people.

The sea monster's body convulsed. Its head struck down, teeth leading. Spittle sprayed out from it in obscene little clouds. Fanchon screamed hysterically. Bink felt an instant and pervading terror. That sensation was becoming all too familiar; he simply was no hero.

But as the awful jaws closed on them, the sea serpent vanished. In its place fluttered a glowing, brightly colored insect. Trent caught it neatly in one hand and set it on his own hair, where it perched quiveringly.

"A love bug," Trent explained. "They are not good fliers, and they hate water. This one will stay close until we emerge from the sea."

Now the three swam for shore. It took them some time, for the sea remained choppy and they were tired, but no other creatures bothered them. Apparently no lesser predators intruded on the fishing territory of the sea monster. An understandable attitude—but probably within hours a host of aggressive forms would converge if the sea monster did not return. As Trent had remarked, there was always a balance of nature.

The phosphorescence became stronger in the shallows. Some of it was from glowing fish, flashing in colors to communicate with their respective kinds; most of it was from the water itself. Washes of pale green, yellow, orange—magic, of course, but for what purpose? There was so much Bink saw, wherever he went, that he did not understand. At the bottom he saw shells, some lighted around the fringes, some glowing in patterns. A few vanished as he passed over them; whether they had become truly invisible or merely doused their lights he could not tell. Regardless, they were magic, and that was familiar. Belatedly he realized that he was glad to be back among the familiar threats of Xanth!

Dawn was coming as they reached the beach. The sun pushed up behind the clouds over the jungle and finally burst through to bounce its shafts off the water. It was a thing of marvelous beauty. Bink clung to that concept, because his body was numb with fatigue, his brain locked onto the torture of moving limbs, over and over, on and on.

At last he crawled upon the beach. Fanchon crawled beside him. "Don't stop yet," she said. "We must seek cover, lest other monsters come, from the beach or jungle . . ."

But Trent stood knee-deep in the surf, his sword dangling from his handsome body. He was obviously not as tired as they were. "Return, friend," he said, flicking something into the sea. The sea monster reappeared, its serpentine convolutions much more impressive in the shallow water. Trent had to lift his feet and splash back out of the way, lest he be crushed by a hugely swinging coil.

But the monster was not looking for trouble now. It was extremely disgruntled. It gave a single honk of rage or of anguish or of mere amazement and thrashed its way toward deeper pastures.

Trent walked up the beach. "It is not fun to be a defenseless love bug when you are accustomed to being the king of the sea," he said. "I hope the creature does not suffer a nervous breakdown."

He was not smiling. There was something funny, Bink thought, about a man who liked monsters that well. But of course Trent was *the* Evil Magician of the contemporary scene. The man was strangely handsome, mannerly, and erudite, possessed of strength, skill, and courage—but his affinities were to the monsters more than to the men. It would be disastrous ever to forget that.

Odd that Humfrey, the Good Magician, was an ugly little gnome in a forbidding castle, selfishly using his magic to enrich himself, while Trent was the epitome of hero material. The Sorceress Iris had seemed lovely and sexy, but was in fact nondescript; Humfrey's good qualities were manifest in his actions, once a person really got to know him. But Trent, so far, had seemed good in both appearance and deed, at least on the purely personal level. If Bink had met him for the first time in the kraken's cave and hadn't known the man's evil nature, he would never have guessed it.

Now Trent strode across the beach, seeming hardly tired despite the grueling swim. The nascent sunlight touched his hair, turning it bright yellow. He looked in that instant like a god, all that was perfect in man. Again Bink suffered fatigued confusion, trying to reconcile the man's appearance and recent actions with what he knew to be the man's actual nature, and again finding it so challenging as to be virtually impossible. Some things just had to be taken on faith.

"I've got to rest, to sleep," Bink muttered. "I can't tell evil from good right now."

Fanchon looked toward Trent. "I know what you mean," she said, shaking her head so that her ratty hair shifted its wet tangles. "Evil has an insidious way about it, and there is some evil in all of us that seeks to dominate. We have to fight it, no matter how tempting it becomes."

Trent arrived. "We seem to have made it," he said cheerfully. "It certainly is good to be back in Xanth, by whatever freak of fortune. Ironic that you, who sought so ardently to prevent my access, instead facilitated it!"

"Ironic," Fanchon agreed dully.

"I believe this is the coast of the central wilderness region, bounded on the north by the great Gap. I had not realized we had drifted so far south, but the contour of the land seems definitive. That means we are not yet out of trouble."

"Bink's an exile, you're banished, and I'm ugly," Fanchon muttered. "We'll never be out of trouble."

"Nevertheless, I believe it would be expedient to extend our truce until we are free of the wilderness," the Magician said.

Did Trent know something Bink didn't? Bink had no magic, so he would be prey to all the sinister spells of the deep jungle. Fanchon had no apparent magic —strange, she claimed her exile had been voluntary, not forced, yet if she really had no magic she should have been banished too; anyway, she would have a similar problem. But Trent—with his skills with sword and spell, he should have no reason to fear this region.

Fanchon had similar doubts. "As long as you're with us, we're in constant danger of being transformed into toads. I can't see that the wilderness is worse."

Trent spread his hands. "I realize you do not trust me, and perhaps you have reason. I believe your security and mine would be enhanced if we cooperated a little longer, but I shall not force my company on you." He walked south along the beach.

"He knows something," Bink said. "He must be leaving us to die. So he can be rid of us without breaking his word."

"Why should he care about his word?" Fanchon asked. "That would imply he is a man of honor."

Bink had no answer. He crawled to the shade and concealment of the nearest tree and collapsed in the downy sward. He had been unconscious during part of the last night, but that was not the same as sleep; he needed genuine rest.

When he woke it was high noon—and he was fixed in place. There was no pain, only some itching—but he couldn't lift his head or hands. They were fastened to the ground by myriad threads, as if the very lawn had—

Oh, no! In the numbness of fatigue, he had been so careless as to lie in a bed of carnivorous grass! The root blades had grown up into his body, infiltrating it so slowly and subtly that it had not disturbed his sleep—and now he was caught. Once he had happened on a patch of the stuff near the North Village with an animal skeleton on it. The grass had consumed all the flesh. He had wondered how any creature could have been so stupid as to be trapped by such a thing. Now he knew.

He was still breathing, therefore he could still yell. He did so with a certain gusto. "Help!"

There was no response.

"Fanchon!" he cried. "I'm tied down. The grass is eating me up." Actually that was an exaggeration; he was not hurt, merely bound to the ground. But the tendrils continued to grow into him, and soon they would start to feed, drawing the life proteins from his flesh.

Still nothing. He realized she would not or could not help him. Probably something had put a sleep spell on her. It was obvious, in retrospect, that there were plenty of deadly threats right here at the edge of the beach; she must have fallen into another. She might be dead already.

"Help! Anybody!" he screamed desperately.

That was another mistake. All around him, in the forest and along the beach, things were stirring. He had advertised his helplessness, and now they were coming to take advantage of it. Had he struggled with the grass in silence, he might have managed in time to work his way free; he had awakened before it was ready for the kill, luckily. Maybe he had tried to turn over in his sleep, and his body had objected to the resistance strongly enough to throw off the stasis spell the grass was applying. If he struggled and failed, his demise at least would have been fairly comfortable—just a slow sinking into eternal sleep. Now by his noise he had summoned much less comfortable menaces. He could not see them, but he could hear them.

From the nearby tree came a rustle, as of meat-eating squirrels. From the beach came a scrape, as of hungry acid crabs. From the sea came a horrible kind of splashing, as of a small sea monster who had sneaked into the territory of the big sea monster Trent had transformed. Now this little one struggled to get out of the water and cross to the prey before it was gone. But the most dreadful sound of all was the pound-pound-pound of the footfalls of something deep in the forest, large and far away but moving extremely rapidly.

A shadow fell on him. "Hi!" a shrill voice cried. It was a harpy, cousin to the one he had met on the way back to the North Village. She was every bit as ugly, smelly, and obnoxious—and now she was dangerous. She descended slowly, her talons reaching down, twitching. The other harpy had seen him healthy, so had stayed well out of reach—though she might have descended had he actually drunk from the Spring of Love. Ugh! This one saw him helpless.

She had a human face and human breasts, so was in that sense female, like the mermaids. But in lieu of arms she had great greasy wings, and her body was that of a gross bird. And she was a *dirty* bird; not only were her face and breasts grotesquely shaped, grime was caked on them. It was a wonder she could fly at all. Bink had not had the opportunity—or desire—to appreciate the qualities of the prior harpy at close range; now he had a really excellent nether view. Double ugh! The mermaids had represented much that was lovely in the female form; this harpy was the ugly aspect. She made Fanchon look halfway decent in comparison; at least Fanchon was clean.

She dropped on him, claws clutching and unclutching in air, in anticipation of the glob of entrails they were about to rip out of his exposed gut. Some of the nails were broken and jagged. He caught the odor of her, a stink like none he remembered. "Oooh, you big handsome hunk of meat!" she screeched. "You look good enough to eat. I can hardly choose what to take first." And she burst into maniacal laughter.

Bink, absolutely horrified, put forth the supreme effort of his life and wrenched one arm free of the grass. Little roots trailed from it, and the separation was painful. He was lying partly on his side, one cheek anchored, so he had a very limited field of vision, but his ears continued to bring him the dreadful news of the threats about him. He struck at the harpy, scaring her off for the moment. She was of course a coward; her character matched her appearance.

Her wings fluttered heavily. A soiled feather drifted down. "Oooh, you naughty boy!" she screeched. She seemed to be unable to converse in anything less than a screech; her voice was so harsh as to be almost incomprehensible. "I'll goozle your gizzard for that." And she emitted her horrible cackle again.

But now a shadow fell on Bink, from something he could not see—but the outline was awful. He heard heavy breathing, as of some great animal, and smelled its carrion-coated breath, which for the moment overrode the stench of the harpy. It was the thing from the sea, its feet dragging as it hunched forward. It sniffed him—and the other creatures stopped moving in, afraid to stand up to this predator.

All except the harpy. She was ready to heap vilification on anything, from the safety of the air. "Get away, argus!" she screeched. "He's mine, all mine, especially his gizzard." And she dropped down again, forgetting Bink's free arm. For once Bink didn't mind. He could fight off the dirty bird, but this other thing was too much for him. Let her interfere all she wanted.

The unseen thing snorted and leaped, passing right over Bink's body with amazing agility. Now he saw it: body and tail of a large fish, four stout short legs terminating in flippers, tusked head of a boar, no neck. Three eyes were set along its torso, the middle one set lower than the others. Bink had never seen a monster quite like this before—a land-walking fish.

The harpy flew up out of the way just in time, narrowly missing being gored by the thing's semicircular horns. Another stinking feather fell. She screeched some really disgusting insults in her ire, and let fly with a gooey dropping, but the monster ignored her and turned to concentrate on Bink. It opened its mouth, and Bink made a fist to punch it in the snout—for what little good that might do—when abruptly it paused, gazing balefully over Bink's shoulder.

"Now you'll get it, argus," the harpy screeched gleefully. "Even a fishy lout like you can't ignore catoblepas."

Bink had never heard of either argus or catoblepas, but another quake of deep misgiving went through him. He felt the muzzle of the hidden monster nudge him. It was oddly soft—but such was its power that it ripped him half out of the grass.

Then the pig-snouted argus charged, furious that its meal should be taken away. Bink dropped flat again, letting the slimy flippers pass over him—and their impact dislodged more of his body. He was getting free!

The two brutes collided. "Sic 'em, monsters!" the harpy screeched, hovering overhead. In her excitement over this mischief she let fall another large squishy dropping, which just missed Bink's head. If only he had a rock to throw at her!

He sat up. One leg remained anchored—but now he had anchorage to rip out of the clutch of the demon weed. It didn't even hurt this time. He looked at the battling monsters—and saw the snakelike hair of the catoblepas twined around the head of the argus, gripping it by horns, ears, scales, and eyeballs—anything available. The body of the catoblepas was covered with reptilian scales, from its gorgon head to its cloven hooves, invulnerable to the attack of the argus. In overall shape it was like any quadruped, not all that remarkable; but that deadly writhing prehensile head hair—what a horror!

Had he really wanted to return to magic Xanth? He had so conveniently forgotten its uglier aspect. Magic had as much evil as good. Maybe Mundania would really have been better.

"Fools!" the harpy cried, seeing Bink loose. "He's getting away." But the monsters were now enmeshed in their own struggle, and paid her no attention. No doubt the winner would feast on the loser, and Bink would be superfluous.

She darted down at Bink, forgetting all caution. But he was on his feet now, and able to fight. He reached up and caught her by one wing, trying to get his hands around her scrawny throat. He would gladly have strangled her, in a sense strangling all the meanness of Xanth. But she squawked and fluttered so violently that all he got was a handful of gummy feathers.

Bink took advantage of his luck and ran away from the fray. The harpy fluttered after him for a moment, screeching such hideously foul insults that his ears burned, but soon gave up. She had no chance of overcoming him by herself. Harpies were basically carrion feeders and thieves, not hunters. It was their fashion to snatch food from the mouths of others. There was now no sign of the other creatures that had rustled and scraped toward him; they too were predators only of the helpless.

Where was Fanchon? Why hadn't she come to help him? She surely must have heard his cries for help—if she still lived. There was no way she could have been unaware of the recent fracas. So this must mean—

No! She had to be somewhere. Maybe down by the sea, catching fish, out of hearing. She had been invaluable during the past two days, and unswervingly loyal to the welfare of Xanth. Without her he could never have escaped the power of the Evil Magician. For intelligence and personality she had it all over the other girls he had met. Too bad she wasn't—

He saw her, resting against a tree. "Fanchon!" he cried gladly.

"Hello, Bink," she said.

Now his worry and speculation translated into ire. "Didn't you see me being attacked by those monsters? Didn't you hear?"

"I saw, I heard," she said quietly.

Bink was baffled and resentful. "Why didn't you help me? You could at least have grabbed a stick or thrown rocks. I was almost eaten alive!"

"I'm sorry," she said.

He took another step toward her. "You're sorry! You just rested here doing nothing and—" He cut off, losing the words to continue.

"Maybe if you moved me from the tree," she said.

"I'll dump you in the sea!" he cried. He strode up to her, leaned over to grab her roughly by the arm, and felt a sudden wash of weakness.

Now he understood. The tree had put a lethargy spell on her, and was starting in on him. As with the carnivorous grass, it took time to take full effect; she must have settled here to sleep, as careless in her fatigue as he had been in his, and was now far gone. There was no actual discomfort to alert potential prey, just a slow, insidious draining of vitality, of strength and will, until it all was gone. Very similar to the grass, actually, only this was less tangible.

He fought it off. He squatted beside her, sliding his arms under her back and legs. He really wasn't too weak, yet; if he acted fast—

He started to lift her—and discovered that his squatting posture had given him a false sense of well-being. He could not raise her up; in fact, he wasn't sure he could stand alone. He just wanted to lie down and rest a moment.

No! That would be the end. He dared not yield to it. "Sorry I yelled at you," he said. "I didn't realize what you were in."

"That's all right, Bink. Take it easy." She closed her eyes.

He let go of her and backed away on his hands and knees. "Good-bye," she said listlessly, reopening one eye. She was almost done for.

He took hold of her feet and pulled. Another surge of weakness came, making the job seem impossible. It was as much emotional as physical. There was no way he could haul her weight. He tried anyway, his stubbornness prevailing over even this magic. But he failed. She was too heavy for him here.

He backed farther away—and as he left the environs of the tree his energy and will returned. But now she was beyond his reach. He stood up and took another step toward her—and lost his strength again, so that he fell to the ground. He would never make it this way.

Again he hauled himself back, sweating with the effort of concentration. Were he less stubborn, he would not have gotten this far. "I can't get you out, and I'm only wasting time," he said apologetically. "Maybe I can loop you with a rope."

But there was no rope. He walked along the trees of the edge of the jungle and spied a dangling vine. That would do nicely if he could get it loose.

He grabbed it in one hand—and screamed. The thing writhed in his grasp and looped about his wrist, imprisoning it. More vines dropped from the tree, swinging toward him. This was a land kraken, a variant of the tangle tree! He was still being fatally careless, walking directly into traps that should never have fooled him.

Bink dropped, yanking on the vine with his full weight. It stretched to accommodate him, twining more tightly about his arm. But now he spied a pointed bit of bone on the ground, remnant of prior prey; he swept it up with his free hand and poked at the vine with it, puncturing it.

Thick orange sap welled out. The whole tree shivered. There was a high keening of pain. Reluctantly the vine loosened, and he drew his arm free. Another close call.

He ran on down the beach, searching for whatever would help him. Maybe a sharp-edged stone, to cut off a vine—no, the other vines would get him. Give up that idea. Maybe a long pole? No, similar problem. This peaceful-seeming beach was a morass of danger, really coming alive; anything and everything was suspect.

Then he saw a human body: Trent, sitting cross-legged on the sand, looking at something. It seemed to be a colorful gourd; maybe he was eating it.

Bink paused. Trent could help him; the Magician could change the fatigue tree into a salamander and kill it, or at least render it harmless. But Trent himself was a greater long-term threat than the tree. Which should he choose?

Well, he would try to negotiate. The known evil of the tree might not be as bad as the uncertain evil of the Magician, but it was more immediate.

"Trent," he said hesitantly.

The man paid him no attention. He continued to stare at his gourd. He did not actually seem to be eating it. What, then, was its fascination?

Bink hesitated to provoke the man, but he did not know how long he could afford to wait. Fanchon was slowly dying; at what point would she be too far gone to be revived, even if rescued from the tree? Some risk had to be taken.

"Magician Trent," he said, more firmly. "I think we should extend the truce. Fanchon is caught, and—" He stopped, for the man was still ignoring him.

Bink's fear of the Magician began to change, much as had his attitude toward Fanchon when he thought she was malingering. It was as if the charge of emotion had to be spent one way or another, whatever the cost. "Listen, she's in trouble!" he snapped. "Are you going to help or aren't you?"

Still Trent paid no attention.

Bink, still weary from the rigors of the night and unnerved by his recent experiences, suffered a lapse of sanity. "Damn it, *answer* me!" he cried, knocking the gourd from the Magician's hands. The thing flew six feet, landing in the sand and rolling.

Trent looked up. There was no sign of anger in his countenance, just mild surprise. "Hello, Bink," he said. "What is your concern?"

"My concern!" Bink cried. "I told you three times."

Trent looked at him, puzzled. "I did not hear you." The Magician paused thoughtfully. "In fact, I did not see you arrive. I must have been sleeping, though I had not intended to."

"You were sitting here looking at the gourd," Bink said hotly.

"Now I remember. I saw it lying on the beach, and it looked intriguing—" He broke off, glancing at his shadow. "By the sun, that was an hour ago! Where did the time go?"

Bink realized that something was amiss. He went to pick up the gourd.

"Hold!" Trent barked. "That's hypnotic!"

Bink stopped in place. "What?"

"Hypnotic. That's a Mundane term, meaning it puts you into a trance, a waking sleep. It usually takes some time to do—but of course a magic-spell hypnosis could be instant. Don't look too closely at the gourd. Its pretty colors must be intended to attract the eye; then it has—yes, I remember now—a peephole. A single glance into its fascinating innards becomes eternal. Very nice device."

"But what's the point?" Bink asked, averting his gaze. "I mean, a gourd can't eat a man—"

"But the gourd *vine* might," Trent pointed out. "Or it may be that a quiescent living body might be excellent food for its seeds to grow on. There are wasps in Mundania that sting other creatures, stunning them, and lay their eggs in the bodies. We can be sure it makes some sort of sense."

Still Bink was bemused. "How is it that you, a Magician . . . ?"

"Magicians are human too, Bink. We eat, sleep, love, hate, and err. I am as vulnerable to magic as you are; I merely have a more potent weapon with which to protect myself. If I wanted to be entirely secure, I would lock myself within a stone castle, like my friend Humfrey. My chances of survival in this wilderness would be greatly enhanced by the presence of one or two alert, loyal companions. This is why I proposed the extension of our truce—and I still feel it is a good idea. It is apparent that I need help, even if you don't." He looked at Bink. "Why did you help me, just now?"

"I—" Bink was ashamed to admit the accidental nature of that assistance. "I think we should—extend the truce."

"Excellent. Does Fanchon agree?"

"She needs help now. A—she is in thrall to a lethargy tree."

"Oho! Then I shall repay your favor by rescuing the damsel. Then we shall talk of truce." And Trent jumped up.

On the way up the beach, Bink pointed out the vine tree, and Trent whipped out his sword and neatly lopped off a length of vine. Again Bink was reminded of the skill this man had with his physical weapon; if Trent's magic were taken away entirely, he would still be dangerous. In fact, he had risen to the generalship of an army, in Mundania.

The vine twisted into shuddering convolutions like a dying serpent, oozing orange sap from the end, but it was now harmless. The tree keened again, cowed. Bink almost felt sorry for it.

They took this vine to Fanchon, looped it about her foot, and hauled her unceremoniously away from the tree. So simple with the right equipment!

"Now," Trent said briskly as Fanchon slowly recovered her vital energy. "I propose an extended truce between us, until we three escape the wilderness of Xanth. We seem to have problems separately."

This time Fanchon acquiesced.

Chapter 12

Chameleon

The first thing Fanchon did when she recovered was fetch the magic gourd Bink had told her about. "This could be useful," she said, wrapping it in a great leaf from a blanket plant.

"Now we must plan the best route out of here," Trent said. "I believe we are south of the chasm, so that will balk us if we go north—unless we remain on the coast. I don't think that is wise."

Bink remembered his experience crossing the chasm at the other side. "No, we don't want to stay on the beach," he agreed. The Sorceress Iris had complicated things there—but there could be equivalent menaces here.

"Our alternative is to cut inland," Trent said. "I am not familiar with this specific locale, but I believe Humfrey was building a castle due east of here."

"He completed it," Fanchon said.

"Fine," Bink said. "You can change us into big birds, maybe rocs, and we'll carry you there."

Trent shook his head negatively. "This is not feasible."

"But you changed us before, and we helped you. We made the truce; we wouldn't drop you."

Trent smiled. "It is not a question of trust, Bink. I trust you; I have no question at all about your basic integrity, or Fanchon's. But we are in a peculiar circumstance—"

"Fancy the Evil Magician paying a call on the Good Magician!" Fanchon said. "What a scene that would make."

"No, you would be disappointed," Trent said. "Humfrey and I have always gotten along well. We leave each other alone professionally. I should be happy to meet him again. But he would be obliged to convey the news of my return to Xanth to the King, and once he knew my general whereabouts he would use his magic to keep track of me."

"Yes, I see the problem," she said. "No sense tipping your hand to the enemy. But we could fly somewhere else."

"We can fly nowhere," Trent insisted. "I can not afford to advertise my presence in Xanth—and neither can you."

"That's right," Bink agreed. "We're exiles. And the penalty for violating exile—"

"Is death," Fanchon finished. "I never thought—we're all in trouble."

"If you had forgotten such details two days ago," Trent observed wryly, "we would not be here now."

Fanchon looked unusually sober, as if there were some special significance to the remark. Oddly, the expression made her look less ugly than usual. Probably, Bink thought, he was merely getting used to her.

"What are we going to do?" Bink asked. "The whirlpool brought us in under the Shield; we've already agreed we can't go back that way. We can't stay here on the beach—and we can't let the citizens know we're back, even though we entered only by freak accident."

"We'll have to conceal our identities," Fanchon decided. "There are places in Xanth where we would be unknown."

"That doesn't sound like much of a life," Bink said. "Always in hiding—and if anyone asked Magician Humfrey where we were—"

"Who'd do that?" Fanchon demanded. "One year's service just to check up on someone in exile?"

"That is our only present margin of security," Trent said. "The fact that Humfrey will not bother to check without a potential fee. However, we can worry about such things after we escape the wilderness. Perhaps by then some new avenues will have appeared. I can change you into unrecognizable forms, if necessary, and camouflage myself. It may all prove to be academic."

Because they might never make it through the wilderness, Bink thought.

They traveled along the beach until they found a region of sparse forest and field that seemed less hazardous than the rest. They spaced themselves out somewhat whenever anything dangerous appeared, so that they would not all be caught together. The selection worked well enough; at first the magic they encountered was largely innocuous, as if the concentration were all at the beach. There were spells designed to make passing animals sheer off, or color shows whose purpose was unclear. Bink had been through worse on his trip to the Good Magician's castle. Maybe the wilderness was overrated.

Fanchon spotted a fabric plant and efficiently fashioned togas for them all. The men tolerated this with good humor, having become accustomed to nudity. Had Fanchon been a provocatively proportioned woman there might have been more reason—and less desire—for bodily concealment. Still, Bink remembered how she had professed modesty in the prison pit so as to gain a private section in which to hide the bricks. She probably had her reasons this time, too.

There were several patches of spell-cast coldness, and one of heat; the clothing would have helped protect against these, but they were easy to avoid. The assorted carnivorous trees were readily spotted and bypassed; staying off attractive paths was second nature to them all now.

One region was distinctly awkard, however. It was dry and sandy, with little apparent nutrient in the soil, yet it was covered by luxuriant waist-high broad-leaved plants. The region seemed harmless, so they strode straight through the center. Then all three travelers felt a sudden and almost uncontrollable call of nature. They had to scatter, barely getting separated in time to perform.

These were very practical plants, Bink abruptly realized. Their spells compelled passing animals to deposit nutritious fluids and solids on the soil, greatly promoting plant growth. Fertilizer magic!

Farther along, one animal neither fled their approach nor acted hostile. This was a knee-high, snuffling quadruped with a greatly extended snout. Trent drew his sword as it ambled toward them, but Fanchon stopped him. "I recognize that one," she said. "It's a magic-sniffer."

"It smells by magic?" Bink asked.

"It smells magic," she said. "We used to use one on my folks' farm, to sniff out magic herbs and things. The stronger the magic, the more it reacts. But it's harmless."

"What does it feed on?" Trent asked, keeping his hand on his sword.

"Magic berries. Other magic doesn't seem to affect it one way or the other; it is just curious. It doesn't differentiate by type of spell, just intensity."

They stood and watched. Fanchon was nearest to the sniffer, so it approached her first. It snorted, making a flutelike sound. "See, I have some magic; it likes me," she said.

What magic? Bink wondered. She had never shown any talent, and never actually told him what she could do. There was still too much he did not know about her.

Satisfied, the sniffer moved on to Trent. This time its reaction was much stronger; it danced around, emitting a medley of notes. "Sure enough," Trent said, with a certain justified pride. "It knows a Magician when it smells one."

Then it came to Bink—and frisked almost as much as it had for Trent. "So much for perception," Bink said, laughing with embarrassment.

But Trent did not laugh. "It believes you are almost as strong a magician as I am," he said, his fingers tapping his sword with unconscious significance. Then he caught himself, and seemed to be at ease again.

"I wish I were," Bink said. "But I was banished for lack of magic." Yet the Magician Humfrey had told him he had very strong magic that could not be brought out. Now his curiosity and frustration were increased by this happenstance. What kind of a talent could he have that hid itself so determinedly—or was it hidden by some outside spell?

They trudged on. They cut poles with which to poke the ground ahead for invisible barriers and pitfalls and other suspiciously unsuspect aspects of the wild. This made progress slow—but they dared not hurry. Actually, they had no reason to hurry; their only purposes were concealment and survival.

Food turned out to be no problem. They did not trust the various fruit and candy trees they saw; some might be magic, and serve the interests of their hosts rather than the interests of the consumers, though they looked similar to crop trees. But Trent merely turned a hostile thistle tree into a luxuriant multifruit tree, and they feasted on apples, pears, bananas, blackberries, and tomatoes. It reminded Bink how great was the power of a true Magician, for Trent's talent really embraced that of food conjuration as a mere subtalent. Properly exploited, the reach of his magic was enormous.

But they were still heading into the wilderness, not out of it. Illusions became bolder, more persistent, and harder to penetrate. There were more sounds, louder, more ominous. Now and then the ground shuddered, and there were great not-too-distant bellowings. Trees leaned toward them, leaves twitching.

"I think," Fanchon said, "we have not begun to appreciate the potency of this forest. Its whole innocuous permeability may have been merely to encourage us to get more deeply in."

Bink, looking nervously about, agreed. "We picked the safest-seeming route. Maybe that's where we went wrong. We should have taken the most threatening one."

"And gotten consumed by a tangle tree," Fanchon said.

"Let's try going back," Bink suggested. Seeing their doubt, he added: "Just to test."

They tried it. Almost immediately the forest darkened and tightened. More trees appeared, blocking the way they had come; were they illusions, or had they been invisible before? Bink was reminded of the one-way path he had walked from the Good Magician's castle, but this was more ominous. These were not nice trees; they were gnarled colossi bearing thorns and twitching vines. Branches crisscrossed one another, leaves sprouting to form new barriers even as the trio watched. Thunder rumbled in the distance.

"No doubt about it," Trent said. "We failed to see the forest for the trees. I could transform any in our direct path, but if some started firing thorns at us we would be in trouble regardless."

"Even if we wanted to go that way," Fanchon said, looking west. "We'd never have time to retrace it all through that resistance. Not before night."

Night—that was the worst time for hostile magic. "But the alternative is to go the way it wants us to go," Bink said, alarmed. "That may be easy now, but it surely is not our best choice."

"Perhaps the wilderness does not know us well enough," Trent said with a grim smile. "I do feel competent to handle most threats, so long as someone watches behind me and stands guard as I sleep."

Bink thought of the Magician's powers of magic and swordplay, and had to agree. The forest might be one giant spider web—but that spider might become a gnat, unexpectedly. "Maybe we should gamble that we can handle it," Bink said. "At least we'll find out what it is." For the first time, he was glad to have the Evil Magician along.

"Yes, there is always that," Fanchon agreed sourly.

Now that they had made the decision, progress became easier. The threatenings of the forest remained, but they assumed the aspect of background warnings. As dusk came, the way opened out into a clearing, within which stood an old, run-down stone fortress.

"Oh, no!" Fanchon exclaimed. "Not a haunted castle!"

Thunder cracked behind them. A chill wind came up, cutting through their tunics. Bink shivered. "I think we spend the night there—or in the rain," he said. "Could you transform it into a harmless cottage?"

"My talent applies only to living things," Trent said. "That excludes buildings—and storms."

Glowing eyes appeared in the forest behind them. "If those things rush us," Fanchon said, "you could only transform a couple before they were on us, since you can't zap them from a distance."

"And not at night," Trent said. "Remember—I have to see my subject, too.

All things considered, I think we had better oblige the local powers that be and enter the castle. Carefully—and once inside, we should sleep in shifts. It is likely to be a difficult night."

Bink shuddered. The last place he wanted to spend the night was there—but he realized they had come far too deeply into the trap to extricate themselves readily. There was powerful magic here, the magic of an entire region. Too much to fight directly—now.

So they yielded, goaded by the looming storm. The ramparts were tall, but covered by moss and clinging vines. The drawbridge was down, its once-stout timbers rotting in place. Yet there was an ancient, lingering, rugged magnificence about it. "This castle has style," Trent observed.

They tapped the planks, locating a reasonably solid section on which to cross. The moat was overgrown with weeds, and its water was stagnant. "Shame to see a good castle get run down," Trent said. "It is obviously deserted, and has been for decades."

"Or centuries," Bink added.

"Why would a forest herd us into a derelict edifice?" Fanchon asked. "Even if something really horrible lurks here—what would our deaths profit the forest? We were only passing through—and we would make it much faster if the forest just left us alone. We intend it no harm."

"There is always a rationale," Trent said. "Magic does not focus without purpose."

They approached the front portcullis as the storm broke. That encouraged them to step inside, though the interior was almost black.

"Maybe we can find a torch," Fanchon said. "Feel along the walls. Usually a castle will have something near the entrance—"

Crash! The raised portcullis, which they had assumed was corroded in place, crashed down behind them. The iron bars were far too heavy to lift; the three were trapped inside. "The jaws close," Trent remarked, not seeming perturbed. But Bink could see that his sword was in his hand.

Fanchon made a half-muffled scream, clutching at Bink's arm. He looked ahead and saw a ghost. There was no question about it: the thing was a humped white sheet with dead-black eyeholes. It made a mouthless moan.

Trent's sword whistled as he stepped forward. The blade sliced through the sheet—with no visible effect. The ghost floated away through a wall.

"This castle is haunted, no question," Trent said matter-of-factly.

"If you believed that, you wouldn't be so calm," Fanchon said accusingly.

"On the contrary. It is physical menaces I fear," Trent replied. "The thing to remember about ghosts is that they have no concrete manifestation, and lack also the ability of shades to animate living creatures. Therefore they cannot directly affect ordinary people. They act only through the fear they inspire—so it is merely necessary to have no fear. In addition, this particular ghost was as surprised to see us as we were to see it. It was probably merely investigating the fall of the portcullis. It certainly meant no harm."

It was obvious that Trent was not afraid. He had not used his sword in panic, but to verify that it was a genuine ghost he faced. This was courage of a type Bink had never had; he was shivering with fear and reaction.

Fanchon had better control, now that her initial scream was out. "We could fall into quite physical pits or set off more boobytraps if we tried to explore this place in the dark. We're sheltered from the rain here—why don't we sleep right here in shifts until morning?"

"You have marvelous common sense, my dear," Trent said. "Shall we draw straws for first watch?"

"I'll take it," Bink said. "I'm too scared to sleep anyway."

"So am I," Fanchon said, and Bink felt warm gratitude for her admission. "I have not yet become blasé about ghosts."

"There is not enough evil in you," Trent said, chuckling. "Very well; I shall be first to sleep." He moved, and Bink felt something cool touch his hand. "Do you take my sword, Bink, and run it through whatever manifests. If it has no impact, relax, for it is a true ghost; if it contacts anything material, that threat will no doubt be abated by the thrust. Only take care"—and Bink heard the smile in his voice—"that you do not strike the wrong subject."

Bink found himself holding the heavy sword, amazed. "I—"

"Do not be concerned about your inexperience with the weapon; a straight, bold thrust will have authority regardless," Trent continued reassuringly. "When your watch is done, pass the blade on to the lady. When she is done, I will take my turn, being by then well rested." Bink heard him lie down. "Remember," the Magician's voice came from the floor. "My talent is void in the dark, since I cannot see my subject. So do not wake me unnecessarily. We depend on your alertness and judgment." He said no more.

Fanchon found Bink's free arm. "Let me get behind you," she said. "I don't want you running me through by accident."

Bink was glad for her closeness. He stood peering about, sword in one sweaty hand, staff in the other, unable to penetrate the dark. The sound of the rain outside became loud; then he made out Trent's gentle snoring.

"Bink?" Fanchon said at last.

"Um."

"What kind of a man would give his enemy his sword and go to sleep?"

That question had been bothering Bink. He had no satisfactory answer. "A man with iron nerve," he said at last, knowing that that could only be part of it.

"A man who extends such trust," she said thoughtfully, "must expect to receive it."

"Well, if we're trustworthy and he isn't, he knows he can trust us."

"It doesn't work that way, Bink. It is the untrustworthy man who distrusts others, because he judges them by himself. I don't see how a documented liar and villain and schemer for the throne like the Evil Magician can be this way."

"Maybe he's not the historical Trent, but someone else, an imposter—"

"An imposter would still be a liar. But we've seen his power. Magic is never twice the same; he *has* to be Trent the Transformer."

"Yet something is wrong."

"Yes. Something is right; that's what's wrong. He trusts us, and he shouldn't. You could run him through right now, while he sleeps; even if you didn't kill him with the first thrust, he could not transform you in the dark."

"I wouldn't do that!" Bink exclaimed, horrified.

"Precisely. You have honor. So do I. It is hard to avoid the conclusion that so does he. Yet we know he is the Evil Magician."

"He must have spoken the truth before," Bink decided. "He can't make it through the wilderness alone, and he figures he'll need help to get out of this haunted castle in one piece, and he knows we can't get out alive either, so we're all on the same side and won't hurt each other. So he's serious about the truce."

"But what about when we get out of all this and the truce ends?"

Bink didn't answer. With that they were silent. But his troubled thoughts continued. If they survived the night in this dread castle, they could probably survive the day. In the morning Trent might figure the truce was over. Bink and Fanchon could guard the Magician through the night; then in the morning Trent could slay them both while they slept. If Trent had taken the first watch, he could not have done that, because he would have to slay the people who would protect him for the remainder of the evening. So it made sense to take the last watch.

No. He was not ready to believe that. Bink himself had chosen the first watch. He had to have faith in the sanctity of the truce. If that faith was misplaced, then he was lost—but he would rather lose that way than to win through dishonor. That decision gave him comfort.

Bink saw no more ghosts that night. At last he gave the sword to Fanchon. To his surprise, he managed to sleep.

He woke at dawn. Fanchon was asleep beside him, looking less ugly than he recalled—in fact, not really homely at all. He certainly was acclimatizing. Would it ever come to the point where Trent seemed noble and Fanchon beautiful?

"Good," Trent said. He was wearing his sword again. "Now that you can look out for her, I'll have a look around the premises." He walked on down the dim hall.

They had survived the night. Bink wasn't sure in retrospect whether he had been more worried about the ghosts or the Magician. He still lacked comprehension of the motives of either.

And Fanchon—as the light brightened, he was sure her appearance had improved. She could hardly be called lovely, but she certainly was not the ugly girl he had perceived when he met her four days ago. In fact, she now reminded him of someone—

"Dee!" he exclaimed.

She woke. "Yes?"

Her response amazed him as much as the vague resemblance. He had called her Dee—but Dee was elsewhere in Xanth. Why, then, had she answered to that name as if it were her own? "I—I just thought you—"

She sat up. "You're right, of course, Bink. I knew I couldn't conceal it much longer."

"You mean you actually are . . . ?"

"I am Chameleon," she said.

Now he was totally confused. "That was only a code word we used, to alert—" And an omen . . .

"I am Fanchon-ugly," she said. "And Dee-average. And Wynne-beautiful. I change a little every day, completing the circle in the course of a month. A lunar month. It's the female cycle, you know."

Now he remembered how Dee too had reminded him of someone. "But Wynne was stupid! You—"

"My intelligence varies inversely," she explained. "That is the other facet of my curse. I range from ugly intelligence to lovely idiocy. I've been looking for a spell to turn me normal."

"A spell for Chameleon," he said musingly. What an astonishing enchantment. Yet it had to be true, for he had almost caught the similarity when he met Dee, so close to where he had lost Wynne, and now he had seen Fanchon change day by day. Chameleon—she had no magic talent; she *was* magic, like the centaurs or dragons. "But why did you follow me into exile?"

"Magic doesn't work outside Xanth. Humfrey told me I would gradually center on my normal state if I went to Mundania. I would be Dee, permanently—completely average. That seemed my best choice."

"But you said you followed me."

"I did. You were kind to Wynne. My mind may change, but my memory doesn't. You saved her from the Gap dragon at great peril to yourself, and you didn't take advantage of her when she—you know." Bink remembered the beautiful girl's willingness to disrobe. She had been too stupid to think through the likely consequence of her offer—but Dee and Fanchon, later, would have understood. "And now I know you tried to help Dee, also. She—I shouldn't have cut you off then—but we weren't as smart then as later. And we didn't know you as well. You—" She broke off. "It doesn't matter."

But it did matter! She was not one but three of the girls he had known—and one of those was excruciatingly beautiful. But also stupid. How should he react to this—this chameleon?

The concept of the chameleon, again—the magic lizard that changed its color and shape at will, mimicking other creatures. If only he could forget that omen —or be sure he understood it. He was sure this Chameleon meant him no harm, but she might in fact be the death of him. Her magic was involuntary, but it dominated her life. She had a problem, certainly—and so did he.

So she had learned that he was to be exiled for lack of magic and made her decision. Dee without magic, Bink without magic—two ordinary people with a common memory of the land of magic—perhaps the only thing to sustain them in drear Mundania. No doubt her smart phase had figured that out. What an apt couple they could make, these two demagicked souls. So she had acted—but had had no way of knowing about the ambush set by the Evil Magician.

It had been a good notion. Bink liked Dee. She was not so ugly as to turn him off, and not so lovely as to excite his distrust after his experiences with Sabrina and the Sorceress Iris—what was the matter with beautiful women, that they could not be constant?—but also not so stupid as to make it pointless. Just a reasonable compromise, an average girl he could have loved—especially in Mundania.

But now they were back in Xanth, and her curse was in force. She was not simple Dee, but complex Chameleon, swinging from extreme to extreme, when all he wanted was the average.

"I'm not so stupid yet that I can't figure out what's going through your mind," she said. "I'm better off in Mundania."

Bink could not deny it. Now he almost wished it had worked out that way. To have settled down with Dee, raised a family—that could have been its own special brand of magic.

There was a crash. Both reacted, orienting on the sound. It had come from somewhere above.

"Trent's in trouble!" Bink said. He started down the hall, carrying his staff. "Must be stairs somewhere—" Behind his immediate consciousness he realized that this reaction indicated a fundamental change in his attitude toward the Magician. That night with the sword and the sleeping man—if evil was as evil did, Trent could not be very evil. Trust compelled trust. Maybe the Magician was only trying to manipulate Bink's attitude; regardless, that attitude had suffered a fundamental erosion.

Chameleon followed. Now that it was light, they had no fear of pitfalls, though Bink knew there could be magic ones. There was a grandly curving stone staircase beyond a palatial room. They charged up this.

Suddenly a ghost loomed up. "Ooooo!" it moaned, its great eye holes staring like holes in a dark coffin.

"Get out of my way!" Bink snapped, swinging his pole at it. The ghost, nonplused, phased out. Bink ran through its remnant, feeling the momentary chill of its presence. Trent was right: there was no need to fear the insubstantial.

Every step he took was solid; apparently there were no illusions in this old castle, just its harmless resident spooks. That was a relief after the way they had been herded into it last night.

But now there was silence upstairs. Bink and Chameleon picked their way through surprisingly opulent and well-preserved chambers, searching for their companion. At another time Bink would have admired the arrangements and tapestries of the rooms and halls at leisure, and been glad of the tight roof that had protected them from rain and weathering and rot, but right now his attention was preempted by concern. What had happened to Trent? If there were some monster lurking in this castle, summoning its victims by magic—

Then they found a kind of upstairs library. Fat old books and coiled scrolls were filed on shelves along the walls. In the center, at a polished wood table, sat Trent, poring over an open tome.

"Another peephole spell's got him!" Bink cried.

But Trent lifted his head. "No, merely the thirst for knowledge, Bink. This is fascinating."

A bit abashed, they halted. "But the crash—" Bink started.

Trent smiled. "My fault. That old chair gave way under my weight." He pointed to a tangle of wood. "Much of the furniture here is fragile. I was so interested in this library that I was thoughtless." He rubbed his backside reminiscently. "I paid for it."

"What's so fascinating about the books?" Chameleon asked.

"This one is a history of this castle," Trent explained. "It is not, it seems, just another artifact. This is Castle Roogna."

"Roogna!" Bink exclaimed. "The Magician King of the Fourth Wave?"

"The same. He ruled from here, it seems. When he died and the Fifth Wave conquered Xanth, eight hundred years ago, his castle was deserted, and finally forgotten. But it was a remarkable structure. Much of the King's nature imbued the environs; the castle had an identity of its own."

"I remember," Bink said. "Roogna's talent—"

"Was the conversion of magic to his own purposes," Trent said. "A subtle but powerful asset. He was the ultimate tamer of the forces around him. He cultivated the magic trees around here, and he built this fine castle. During his reign Xanth was in harmony with its populace. It was a kind of Golden Age."

"Yes," Bink agreed. "I never thought I'd see this famous historical place."

"You may see more of it than you want to," Trent said. "Remember how we were guided here?"

"It seems like only yesterday," Bink said wryly.

"Why were we herded here?" Chameleon demanded.

Trent glanced at her, his gaze lingering. "I believe this locale behooves you, Fanchon."

"Never mind that," she said. "I'll be a lot prettier before I'm through, more's the pity."

"She is Chameleon," Bink said. "She shifts from ugly to pretty and back again —and her intelligence varies inversely. She left Xanth to escape that curse."

"I would not regard that as a curse," the Magician commented. "All things to all men—in due course."

"You're not a woman," she snapped. "I asked about this castle."

Trent nodded. "Well, this castle requires a new resident. A Magician. It is very selective, which is one reason it has lain dormant for so many centuries. It wants to restore the years of its glory; therefore it must support a new King of Xanth."

"And you're a Magician!" Bink exclaimed. "So when you came near, everything shoved you this way."

"So it would seem. There was no malign intent, merely an overwhelming need. A need for Castle Roogna, and a need for Xanth—to make this land again what it could be, a truly organized and excellent kingdom."

"But you're not King," Chameleon said.

"Not yet." There was a very positive quality to the statement.

Bink and Chameleon looked at each other in developing comprehension. So the Evil Magician had reverted to form—assuming he had ever changed his form. They had discussed his human qualities, his seeming nobility, and been deceived. He had planned to invade Xanth, and now—

"Not ever!" she flared. "The people would never tolerate a criminal like you. They haven't forgotten—"

"So you do have prior knowledge of my reputation," Trent said mildly. "I had understood you to say you had not heard of me." He shrugged. "However, the good citizens of Xanth may not have much choice, and it would not be the first time a criminal has occupied a throne," he continued calmly. "With the powers of this castle—which are formidable—added to mine, I may not need an army."

"We'll stop you," Chameleon said grimly.

Trent's gaze touched her again, appraisingly. "Are you terminating the truce?"

That gave her pause. The end of the truce would put the two of them directly in Trent's power, if what he said about this castle was true. "No," she said. "But when it does end . . ."

There was no hint of malignancy in Trent's smile. "Yes, it seems there will have to be a settlement. I had thought if I allowed you to go your way, you would extend the same courtesy to me. But when I said the people of Xanth would not necessarily have a choice, I did not mean it precisely the way you seem to have taken it. This castle may not permit us to do other than its will. For centuries it has endured here, hanging on against inevitable deterioration, waiting for a Magician of sufficient strength to qualify. Perhaps the magic-sniffer we encountered in the forest was one of its representatives. Now it has found not one but two Magicians. It will not lightly yield them up. From here we may be bound to glory—or extinction, depending on our decision."

"Two Magicians?" she asked.

"Remember, Bink has almost as much magic as I do. That was the verdict of the sniffer, and I am not certain it was mistaken. That would place him comfortably in the Magician class."

"But I have no talent," Bink protested.

"Correction," Trent said. "To have an unidentified talent is hardly synonymous with having no talent. But even if you are talentless, there is strong magic associated with you. You may *be* magic, as is Fanchon."

"Chameleon," she said. "That's my real name; the others are merely phases."

"I beg your pardon," Trent said, making a little sitting bow to her. "Chameleon."

"You mean I'll change somehow?" Bink asked, half hopeful, half appalled.

"Perhaps. You might metamorphose into some superior form—like a pawn becoming a Queen." He paused. "Sorry—that's another Mundane reference; I don't believe chess is known in Xanth. I have been too long in exile."

"Well, I still won't help you try to steal the crown," Bink said stoutly.

"Naturally not. Our purposes differ. We may even be rivals."

"I'm not trying to take over Xanth!"

"Not consciously. But to prevent an Evil Magician from doing so, would you not consider . . . ?"

"Ridiculous!" Bink said, disgruntled. The notion was preposterous, yet insidious. If the only way to prevent Trent from—no!

"The time may indeed have come for us to part," Trent said. "I have appreciated your company, but the situation seems to be changing. Perhaps you should attempt to leave this castle now. I shall not oppose you. Should we manage to separate, we can consider the truce abated. Fair enough?"

"How nice," Chameleon said. "You can relax over your books while the jungle tears us up."

"I do not think anything here will actually hurt you," Trent said. "The theme of Castle Roogna is harmony with man." He smiled again. "Harmony, not harm. But I rather doubt you will be permitted to depart."

Bink had had enough. "I'll take my chances. Let's go."

"You want me to come along?" Chameleon asked hesitantly.

"Unless you prefer to stay with him. You might make a very pretty Queen in a couple of weeks."

Trent laughed. Chameleon moved with alacrity. They walked to the stairs, leaving the Magician poring over his book again.

Another ghost intercepted them. This one seemed larger than the others, more solid. "Waarrningg," it moaned.

Bink stopped. "You can speak? What is your warning?"

"Dooom beeyonnd. Staay."

"Oh. Well, that's a chance we've already decided to take," Bink said. "Because we are loyal to Xanth."

"Xaaanth!" the spirit repeated with a certain feeling.

"Yes, Xanth. So we must leave."

The ghost seemed nonplused. It faded.

"It almost seems they're on our side," Chameleon commented. "Maybe they're just trying to make us stay in the castle, though."

"We can't afford to trust ghosts," Bink agreed.

They could not exit through the front gate, because the portcullis was firm and they did not understand the mechanism for lifting it. They poked through the downstairs rooms, searching for an alternate exit.

Bink opened one promising door—and slammed it shut as a host of leather-winged, long-toothed creatures stirred; they looked like vampire bats. He cracked the next open more carefully—and a questing rope twined out, more than casually reminiscent of the tree vines.

"Maybe the cellar," Chameleon suggested, spying stairs leading down.

They tried it. But at the foot, huge, baleful rats scurried into place, and they were facing, not fleeing, the intruders. The beasts looked too hungry, too confident; they surely had magic to trap any prey that entered their territory.

Bink poked his staff at the nearest, experimentally. "Scat!" he exclaimed. But the rat leaped onto the pole, climbing up toward Bink's hands. He shook it, but the creature clung, and another jumped to the staff. He thunked it against the stone floor, hard—but still they hung on, and still they climbed. That must be their magic—the ability to cling.

"Bink! Above!" Chameleon cried.

There was a chittering overhead. More rats were crowding the beams, bracing themselves to leap.

Bink threw the staff away and backed hastily up the stairs, holding on to Chameleon for support until he could get turned around. The rats did not follow.

"This castle is really organized," Bink said as they emerged on the main floor.

"I don't think it intends to let us go peacefully. But we've got to try. Maybe a window."

But there were no windows on the ground floor; the outer wall had been built to withstand siege. No point in jumping from an upper turret; someone would surely break a bone. They moved on, and found themselves in the kitchen area. Here there was a back exit, normally used for supplies, garbage, and servants. They slipped out and faced a small bridge across the moat: an ideal escape route.

But there was motion on the bridge already. Snakes were emerging from the rotten planking. Not healthy, normal reptiles, but tattered, discolored things whose bones showed through oozing gaps in the sagging flesh.

"Those are zombie snakes!" Chameleon cried with genuine horror. "Waked from the dead."

"It figures," Bink said grimly. "This whole castle is waked from the dead. Rats can thrive anywhere, but the other creatures died out when the castle died, or maybe they come here to die even now. But zombies aren't as strong as real living things; we can probably handle them with our staffs." But he had lost his own staff in the cellar.

Now he smelled the stench of corruption, worse than that of the harpy. Waves of it rose from the festering snakes and the putrescent moat. Bink's stomach made an exploratory heave. He had seldom encountered genuine, far-advanced decay; usually either creatures were living or their bones were fairly neat and clean. The stages in between, of spoilage and maggot infestation and disintegration, were a part of the cycle of life and death he had chosen not to inspect closely. Hitherto.

"I don't want to try that bridge," Chameleon said. "We'll fall through—and there are zombie crocs in the water."

So there were: big reptiles threshing the slimy surface with leather-covered bones, their worm-eaten eyes gazing up.

"Maybe a boat," Bink said. "Or a raft—"

"Uh-*uh*. Even if it weren't rotten and filled with zombie bugs, it would—well, look across the water."

He looked. Now came the worst of all, walking jerkily along the far bank of the moat: human zombies, some mummified, others hardly more than animate skeletons.

Bink watched the awful things for a long moment, fascinated by their very grotesqueness. Fragments of wrappings and decayed flesh dropped from them. Some dribbled caked dirt left from their over-hasty emergence from their unquiet graves. It was a parade of putrefaction.

He thought of fighting that motley army, hacking apart already-destroyed bodies, feeling their rotting, vermin-riddled flesh on his hands, wrestling with those ghastly animations, saturated with the cloying stink of it all. What loathsome diseases did they bear, what gangrenous embraces would they bestow on him as they fell apart? What possible attack would make these moldering dead lie down again?

The spell-driven things were closing in, coming across the ragged bridge. Surely this was even worse for the zombies, for they could not voluntarily have roused themselves. They could not retire to the pleasant seclusion of the castle interior. To be pressed into service in this state, instead of remaining in the bliss of oblivion—

"I—don't think I'm ready to leave yet," Bink said.

"No," Chameleon agreed, her face somewhat green. "Not this way."

And the zombies halted, giving Bink and Chameleon time to reenter Castle Roogna.

Chapter 13

Rationale

Chameleon was now well through her "normal" phase, which Bink had known before as Dee, and moving into her beauty phase. It was not identical to the prior Wynne; her hair was lighter in color, and her features subtly different. Apparently she varied in her physical details each cycle, never exactly repeating herself, but always proceeding from extreme to extreme. Unfortunately, she was also becoming less intelligent, and was no help on the problem of escaping the castle. She was much more interested now in getting friendly with Bink—and this was a distraction he felt he could not afford at the moment.

First, his priority was to get away from here; second, he was not at all sure he wanted to associate himself in any permanent way with so changeable an entity. If only she were beautiful and bright—but no, that would not work either. He realized now why she had not been tempted by Trent's offer to make her beautiful, when they were first captured outside the Shield. That would merely have changed her phase. If she were beautiful when she was smart, she would be stupid when she was ugly, and that was no improvement. She needed to be free of the curse entirely. And even if she could be fixed permanently at the height of both beauty and brains, he would not trust her, for he had been betrayed by that type too. Sabrina—he choked off that memory. Yet even an ordinary girl could get pretty dull if she had no more than ordinary intelligence or magic . . .

Castle Roogna, now that they were not actively opposing it, was a fairly pleasant residence. It did its best to make itself so. The surrounding gardens provided a rich plenitude of fruits, grains, vegetables, and small game; Trent practiced his archery by bringing down rabbits, shooting from the high embrasures, using one of the fine bows in the castle armory. Some of the creatures were false rabbits, projecting images of themselves a bit apart from their actual locations, causing him to waste arrows, but Trent seemed to enjoy the challenge. One he nabbed was a stinker, whose magic aroma was such that there was nothing to do but bury the carcass in a hurry, very deep. Another was a shrinker; as it died it diminished in size until it was more like a mouse, hardly usable. Magic always had its little surprises. But some were good.

The kitchen did need some attention; otherwise the zombies would come in to do the cooking. Rather than permit that, Chameleon took over. Assisted by advice from the lady ghosts, who were very particular about Castle Roogna cuisine, she made creditable meals. She had no trouble with the dishes, since there was an everlasting magic fountain with aseptic properties; one rinse, and everything sparkled. In fact, having a bath in that water was quite an experience; it effervesced.

The inner partitions of the castle were as solid as the roof; there seemed to be weatherproofing spells in operation. Each person had an opulent private bedroom with costly draperies on the walls, moving rugs on the floors, quivering goose-down pillows and solid-silver chamberpots. They all lived like royalty. Bink discovered that the embroidered tapestry on the wall opposite his bed was actually a magic picture: the little figures moved, playing out their tiny dramas with intriguing detail. Miniature knights slew dragons, tiny ladies sewed, and in the supposed privacy of interior chambers those knights and ladies embraced. At first Bink closed his eyes to those scenes, but soon his natural voyeurism dominated, and he watched it all. And wished that he could—but no, that would not be proper, though he knew that Chameleon was willing.

The ghosts were no problem; they even became familiar. Bink got to know them individually. One was the gatekeeper, who had looked in on them that first night when the portcullis crashed down; another was the chambermaid; a third was the cook's assistant. There were six in all, each of whom had died inappropriately and so lacked proper burial rites. They were shades, really, but without proper volition; only the King of Xanth could absolve them, and they could not leave the castle. So they were doomed to serve here forever, unable to perform their accustomed chores. They were basically nice people who had no control over the castle itself, and constituted only an incidental part of its enchantment. They helped wherever they could, pitifully eager to please, telling Chameleon where to search for the new foods and telling Bink stories of their lives here in the Grand Old Days. They had been surprised and chagrined by the intrusion of living people at first, for they had been in isolation for centuries. But they realized it was part of the imperative of the castle itself, and now they had adjusted.

Trent spent most of his time in the library, as if seeking to master all of its accumulated knowledge. At first Chameleon spent some time there too, interested in intellectual things. But as she lost intelligence, she lost interest. Her researches changed; now she looked avidly for some spell to make her normal. When the library did not provide that, she left it, to poke around the castle and grounds. So long as she was alone, no untoward things manifested: no rats, no carnivorous vines, no zombies. She was no prisoner here, only the men. She searched for sources of magic. She ate things freely, alarming Bink, who knew how poisonous magic could be. But she seemed to lead a charmed existence—charmed by Castle Roogna.

One of her discoveries was serendipitous: a small red fruit growing plentifully on one of the garden trees. Chameleon tried to bite into one, but the rind was tough, so she took it to the kitchen to chop it in half with a cleaver. No ghosts were present; they generally appeared now only when they had business. Thus Chameleon did not have warning about the nature of this fruit. She was careless, and dropped one of the fruits on the floor.

Bink heard the explosion and came running. Chameleon, quite pretty now, was huddling in a corner of the kitchen. "What happened?" Bink demanded, looking about for hostile magic.

"Oh, Bink!" she cried, turning to him with woeful relief. Her homemade dress was in disarray, exposing her finely formed breasts above and her firm round thighs below. What a difference a few days made! She was not at the height of her loveliness, but she was quite adequate to the need.

The need? Bink found her in his arms, aware that she was eager to do any bidding he might make. It was difficult indeed to steel himself against the obvious, for she also had much of Dee in her—the aspect he had liked before he understood her nature. He could take her now, make love to her—and neither her stupid phase nor her smart phase would condemn him.

But he was not a casual lover, and he did not want to make any such commitment at this time, in this situation. He pushed her away gently, the action requiring far more effort than he cared to show. "What happened?" he asked again.

"It—it banged," she said.

He had to remind himself that her diminishing mentality was the other face of her curse. Now it was easier to hold off her lush body. A body without a mind did not appeal to him. "What banged?"

"The cherry."

"The cherry?" This was the first he had heard about the new fruit. But after patient questioning, he elicited the story.

"Those are cherry bombs!" he exclaimed, comprehending. "If you had actually eaten one—"

She was not yet so stupid as to misunderstand that. "Oh, my mouth!"

"Oh, your head! Those things are powerful. Didn't Milly warn you?" Milly was the chambermaid ghost.

"She was busy."

What would a ghost be busy with? Well, this was no time to explore that. "After this, don't eat anything unless a ghost tells you it's okay."

Chameleon nodded dutifully.

Bink picked up a cherry cautiously and considered it. It was just a hard little red ball, marked only where its stem had broken off. "Old Magician Roogna probably used these bombs in warfare. He didn't like war, as I understand it, but he never let his defenses grow soft. Any attackers—why, one man on the ramparts with a slingshot could decimate an army, lobbing these cherry bombs down. No telling what other trees there are in the arsenal. If you don't stop fooling around with strange fruits—"

"I could blow up the castle," she said, watching the dissipating smoke. The floor was scorched, and a table had lost a leg.

"Blow up the castle . . ." Bink echoed, suddenly thinking of something. "Chameleon, why don't you bring in some more cherry bombs? I'd like to experiment with them. But be careful, very careful; don't knock or drop any."

"Sure," she said, as eager to please as any ghost. "Very careful."

"And don't eat any." That was not quite a joke.

Bink gathered cloth and string, and made bags of assorted sizes. Soon he had bag-bombs of varying power. He planted these strategically around the castle. One bag he kept for himself.

"I think we are ready to depart Castle Roogna," he said. "But first I have to talk with Trent. You stand here by the kitchen door, and if you see any zombies, throw cherries at them." He was sure no zombie had the coordination to catch such a bomb and throw it back; wormy eyes and rotting flesh necessarily had poor hand-eye integration. So they would be vulnerable. "And if you see Trent come down, and not me, throw a cherry into that pile. Fast, before he gets within six feet of you." And he pointed to a large bomb he had tied to a major support column. "Do you understand?"

She didn't, but he drilled her on it until she had it straight. She was to throw a cherry at anything she saw—except Bink himself.

Now he was ready. He went up to the library to speak with the Evil Magician. His heart beat loudly within him, now that the moment of confrontation had come, but he knew what he had to do.

A ghost intercepted him. It was Milly, the chambermaid, her white sheet arranged to resemble her working dress, her black-hole eyes somehow having the aspect of once-sultry humanity. The ghosts had become shapeless from sheer neglect and carelessness in the course of the past few centuries of isolation, but now that there was company they were shaping up into their proper forms. Another week would have them back into people outlines and people colors, though of course they would still be ghosts. Bink suspected Milly would turn out to be a rather pretty girl, and he wondered just how she had died. A liaison with a castle guest, then a stabbing by the jealous wife who discovered them?

"What is it, Milly?" he asked, pausing. He had mined the castle, but he bore no malice toward its unfortunate denizens. He hoped his bluff would be effective, so that it would not be necessary to destroy the home of the ghosts, who really were not responsible for its grandiose mischief.

"The King—private conference," she said. Her speech was still somewhat windy, as it was hard for an entity with so little physical substance—hardly any ectoplasm—to enunciate clearly. But he could make it out.

"Conference? There's nobody here but us," he objected. "Or do you mean he's on the pot?"

Milly blushed as well as she was able to. Though as chambermaid she had been accustomed to the chore of collecting and emptying out the chamberpots, she felt that any reference to a person's actual performance on them was uncouth. It was as if the substance were completely divorced from the function. Perhaps she liked to believe that the refuse appeared magically overnight, untouched by human intestine. Magic fertilizer! "No."

"Well, I'm sorry, but I'll have to interrupt him," Bink said. "You see, I don't recognize him as King, and I am about to depart the castle."

"Oh." She put one foggily formed hand to her vague face in feminine misgiving. "But seee."

"Very well." Bink followed her to the little chapel room adjacent to the library. It was actually an offshoot from the master bedroom, with no direct access to the library. But it had, as it turned out, a small window opening onto the library. Since the gloom of the unlit chapel was deeper than that of the other room, it was possible to see without being seen.

Trent was not alone. Before him stood a woman of early middle age, still handsome though the first flush of beauty had faded. Her hair was tied back and up in a functional, fairly severe bun, but there were smile lines around her mouth and eyes. And beside her was a boy, perhaps ten years old, who bore a direct resemblance to the woman, and had to be her son.

Neither person spoke, but their breathing and slight shifts of posture showed that they were alive and solid, not ghosts. How had they come here, and what was their business? Why hadn't Bink or Chameleon seen them enter? It was almost impossible to approach this castle unobserved; it was designed that way, to be readily defensible in case of attack. And the portcullis remained down, blocking off the front entry. Bink had been down by the kitchen entrance, fashioning his bombs.

But, granting that they obviously had come, why didn't they speak? Why didn't Trent speak? They all just looked at each other in eerie silence. This whole scene seemed to make no sense.

Bink studied the odd, silent pair. They were vaguely reminiscent of the widow and son of Donald the shade, the ones he had told about the silver oak so that they would not have to live in poverty any more. The similarity was not in their physical appearance, for these were better-looking people who had obviously not suffered poverty; it was in their atmosphere of quiet loss. Had they lost their man, too? And come to Trent for some kind of help? If so, they had chosen the wrong Magician.

Bink drew away, disliking the feeling of snooping. Even Evil Magicians deserved some privacy. He walked around to the hall and back to the top of the stairs. Milly, her warning completed, vanished. Apparently it required some effort for the ghosts to manifest and speak intelligibly, and they had to recuperate in whatever vacuum they occupied when off duty.

He resumed his march to the library, this time stepping heavily so as to make his approach audible. Trent would have to introduce him to the visitors.

But only the Magician was there as Bink pushed open the door. He was seated at the table, poring over another tome. He looked up as Bink entered. "Come for a good book, Bink?" he inquired.

Bink lost his composure. "The people! What happened to them?"

Trent frowned. "People, Bink?"

"I saw them. A woman and a boy, right here—" Bink faltered. "Look, I didn't mean to peek, but when Milly said you were in conference, I looked in from the chapel."

Trent nodded. "Then you did see. I did not intend to burden you with my private problems."

"Who are they? How did they get here? What did you do to them?"

"They were my wife and son," Trent said gravely. "They died."

Bink remembered the story the sailor had told of the Evil Magician's Mundane family, killed by Mundane illness. "But they were here. I saw them."

"And seeing is believing." Trent sighed. "Bink, they were two roaches, transformed into the likenesses of my loved ones. These were the only two people I ever loved or ever shall love. I miss them, I need them—if only to gaze on their likenesses on occasion. When I lost them, there was nothing left for me in Mundania." He brought an embroidered Castle Roogna handkerchief to his face, and Bink was amazed to see that the Evil Magician's eyes were bright with tears. But Trent retained his control. "However, this is not properly your concern, and I prefer not to discuss it. What is it that brings you here, Bink?"

Oh, yes. He was committed, and had to follow through. Somehow the verve had gone out of it, but he proceeded: "Chameleon and I are leaving Castle Roogna."

The handsome brow wrinkled. "Again?"

"This time for real," Bink said, nettled. "The zombies won't stop us."

"And you find it necessary to inform me? We already have our understanding about this, and I am sure I would become aware of your absence in due course. If you feared I would oppose it, it would have been to your advantage to depart without my knowledge."

Bink did not smile. "No. I feel it behooves me, under our truce, to inform you."

Trent made a little wave of one hand. "Very well. I will not claim I am glad to see you go; I have come to appreciate your qualities, as shown in the precision of your ethic that caused you to notify me of your present action. And Chameleon is a fine girl, of like persuasion, and daily more pretty. I would much prefer to have you both on my side, but since this cannot be, I wish you every fortune elsewhere."

Bink found this increasingly awkward. "This is not exactly a social leave-taking. I'm sorry." He wished now that he hadn't observed Trent's wife and son, or learned their identities; those had obviously been good people, undeserving of their fate, and Bink was wholly in sympathy with the Magician's grief. "The castle won't let us go voluntarily. We have to force it. So we have planted bombs, and—"

"Bombs!" Trent exclaimed. "Those are Mundane artifacts. There are no bombs in Xanth—and shall be none. Never, while I am King."

"It seems there were bombs in the old days," Bink said doggedly. "There's a cherry-bomb tree in the yard. Each cherry explodes on impact, violently."

"Cherry bombs?" Trent repeated. "So. What have you done with the cherries?"

"We have used them to mine the castle supports. If Roogna tries to stop us, we will destroy it. So it is better if it—lets us go in peace. I needed to tell you, so you could disarm the bombs after we're gone."

"Why tell me this? Don't you oppose my designs, and those of Castle Roogna? If Magician and castle were destroyed, you would be the clean victor."

"Not clean. It's not the kind of victory I want," Bink said. "I—look, you could do so much good in Xanth, if you only—" But he knew it was useless. It simply was not the nature of an Evil Magician to devote himself to Good. "Here is a list of the bomb locations," he said, setting a piece of paper on the table. "All you have to do is pick up the packages and bags very carefully and take them outside."

Trent shook his head. "I don't believe your bomb threat will work to effect your escape, Bink. The castle is not intelligent per se. It only reacts to certain stimuli. It might let Chameleon go, but not you. In its perception, you are a Magician, therefore you must remain. You may have out-thought Roogna, but it will not comprehend the full nature of your ploy. Thus the zombies will balk you, as before."

"Then we shall have to bomb it."

"Exactly. You will have to set off the cherries, and all of us will be destroyed together."

"No, we'll get outside first, and heave a cherry back. If the castle cannot be bluffed—"

"It can't be bluffed. It is not a thinking thing. It merely reacts. You will be forced to destroy it—and you know I can't permit that. I need Roogna!"

Now it was getting tough. Bink was ready. "Chameleon will set off the bombs if you transform me," he said, feeling the chill of challenge. He didn't like this sort of power play, but had known it come to this. "If you interfere in any way—"

"Oh, I would not break the truce. But—"

"You can't break the truce. Either I rejoin Chameleon alone or she heaves a cherry into a bomb. She's too stupid to do anything but follow directions."

"Listen to me, Bink! It is my given word that prevents me from breaking the truce, not your tactical preparations. I could transform you into a flea, and then transform a roach into your likeness and send that likeness down to meet Chameleon. Once she set down the cherry—"

Bink's face reflected his chagrin. The Evil Magician *could* void the plan. Chameleon-stupid would not catch on until too late; that nadir of intelligence worked against him as well as for him.

"I am not doing this," Trent said. "I tell you about the possibility merely to demonstrate that I, too, have ethics. The end does not justify the means. I feel that you have allowed yourself to forget this temporarily, and if you will listen a moment you will see your error and correct it. I cannot allow you to destroy this marvelous and historically significant edifice, to no point."

Already Bink was feeling guilty. Was he to be talked out of a course he knew was right?

"Surely you realize," the Evil Magician continued persuasively, "that the entire area would erupt in vengeful wrath if you did this thing. You might be outside the castle, but you would remain in the Roogna environs, and you would die horribly. Chameleon, too."

Chameleon, too—that hurt. That beautiful girl devoured by a tangle tree, ripped apart by zombies . . . "It is a risk I must take," Bink said grimly, though he realized the Magician was correct. The way they had been herded to this castle—there would be no escaping the savagery of the forest. "Maybe you will be able to persuade the castle to let us go, rather than set off that chain of events."

"You are a stubborn one!"

"Yes."

"At least hear me out first. If I cannot persuade you, then what must be must be, though I abhor it."

"Speak briefly." Bink was surprised at his own temerity, but he felt he was doing what he had to. If Trent tried to approach within six feet, Bink would take off, to avoid transformation. He might be able to outrun the Magician. But even so, he could not wait too long; he was afraid that Chameleon would tire of waiting and do something foolish.

"I really don't want to see you or Chameleon die, and of course I value my own survival," Trent said. "While I love nobody alive today, you two have been as close to me as anyone. It is almost as if fate has decreed that like types must be banned from the conventional society of Xanth. We—"

"Like types!" Bink exclaimed indignantly.

"I apologize for an invidious comparison. We have been through a great deal together in a short time, and I think it is fair to say we have saved each other's lives on occasion. Perhaps it was to associate with your like that I really returned to Xanth."

"Maybe so," Bink said stiffly, suppressing the mixed feelings he was experiencing. "But that does not justify your conquering Xanth and probably killing many entire families."

Trent looked pained, but controlled himself. "I do not pretend that it does, Bink. The Mundane tragedy of my family was the stimulus, not the justification, for my return. I had nothing remaining in Mundania worth living for, so naturally my orientation shifted to Xanth, my homeland. I would not try to harm Xanth; I hope to benefit it, by opening it up to the contemporary reality before it is too late. Even if some deaths occur, this is a small price to pay for the eventual salvation of Xanth."

"You think Xanth won't survive unless you conquer it?" Bink tried to put a sneer in his tone, but it didn't register very well. If only he had the verbal control and projection of the Evil Magician!

"Yes, actually, I do. Xanth is overdue for a new Wave of colonization, and such a Wave would benefit it as the prior ones did."

"The Waves were murder and rapine and destruction! The curse of Xanth."

Trent shook his head. "Some were that, yes. But others were highly beneficial, such as the Fourth Wave, from which this castle dates. It was not the fact of the Waves but their mismanagement that made trouble. On the whole they were essential to the progress of Xanth. But I don't expect you to believe that. Right now I'm merely trying to persuade you to spare this castle and yourself; I'm not trying to convert you to my cause."

Something about this interchange was troubling Bink increasingly. The Evil Magician seemed too mature, too reasonable, too knowledgeable, too committed. Trent was wrong—he had to be—yet he spoke with such verisimilitude that Bink had difficulty pinpointing that wrongness. "Try to convert me," he said.

"I'm glad you said that, Bink. I'd like you to know my logical rationale. Perhaps you can offer some positive critique."

That sounded like a sophisticated intellectual ploy. Bink tried to perceive it as sarcasm, but he was sure it was not. He feared the Magician was more intelligent than he, but he also knew what was right. "Maybe I can," he said guardedly. He felt as if he were walking into the wilderness, picking the most likely paths, yet being inevitably guided to the trap at the center. Castle Roogna—on the physical and intellectual levels. Roogna had lacked a voice for eight hundred years, but now it had one. Bink could no more fence with that voice than he could with the Magician's keen sword—yet he had to try.

"My rationale is dual. Part of it relates to Mundania, and part to Xanth. You see, despite certain lapses in ethics and politics, Mundania has progressed remarkably in the past few centuries, thanks to the numbers of people who have made discoveries and spread information; in many respects it is a far more civilized region than Xanth. Unfortunately, the Mundanes' powers of combat have also progressed. This you will have to take on faith, for I have no way to prove it here. Mundania has weapons that are easily capable of eradicating all life in Xanth, regardless of the Shield."

"That's a lie!" Bink exclaimed. "Nothing can penetrate the Shield!"

"Except perhaps the three of us," Trent murmured. "But the main restriction of the Shield is against living things. You could charge through the Shield— your body would penetrate it quite readily—but you would be dead when you got there."

"Same thing."

"Not the same thing, Bink! You see, there are big guns that throw missiles which are dead to begin with, such as powerful bombs, like your cherry bombs but much worse, preset to explode on contact. Xanth is a small area, compared to Mundania. If the Mundanes were determined, they could saturate Xanth. In such an attack, even the Shieldstone would be destroyed. The people of Xanth can no longer afford to ignore the Mundanes. There are too many Mundanians; we can't remain undiscovered forever. They can and will one day wipe us out. Unless we establish relations now."

Bink shook his head in disbelief and incomprehension.

But Trent continued without rancor. "Now, the Xanth internal aspect is quite another matter. It poses no threat to Mundania, since magic is not operative there. But it does pose an insidious but compelling threat to life as we know it in Xanth itself."

"Xanth poses a threat to Xanth? This is nonsense on the face of it."

Now Trent's smile was a bit patronizing. "I can see you would have trouble with the logic of recent Mundanian science." But he sobered before Bink could inquire about that. "No, I am being unfair to you. This internal threat of Xanth is something I learned just in the past few days from my researches in this library, and it is important. This aspect alone justifies the necessity of preserving this castle, for its accumulated ancient lore is vital to Xanth society."

Bink remained dubious. "We've lived without this library for eight centuries; we can live without it now."

"Ah, but the manner of that life!" Trent shook his head as if perceiving something too vast to be expressed. He got up and moved to a shelf behind him. He took down a book and riffled carefully through its creaking old pages. He set it down before Bink, open. "What is that picture?"

"A dragon," Bink said promptly.

Trent flipped a page. "And this?"

"A manticora." What was the point? The pictures were very nice, though they did not coincide precisely with contemporary creatures. The proportions and details were subtly wrong.

"And this?"

It was a picture of a human-headed quadruped, with hoofs, a horse's tail, and catlike forelegs. "A lamia."

"And this?"

"A centaur. Look—we can admire pictures all day, but—"

"What do these creatures have in common?" Trent asked.

"They have human heads or foreparts—except the dragon, though the one in this book has an almost human shortness of snout. Some have human intelligence. But—"

"Exactly! Consider the sequence. Trace a dragon back through similar species, and it becomes increasingly manlike. Does that suggest anything to you?"

"Just that some creatures are more manlike than others. But that's no threat to Xanth. Anyway, most of these pictures are out of date; the actual creatures don't look quite like that any more."

"Did the centaurs teach you the Theory of Evolution?"

"Oh, sure. That today's creatures are evolved from more primitive ones, selected for survival. Go back far enough and you find a common ancestor."

"Right. But in Mundania creatures like the lamia, manticora, and dragon never evolved."

"Of course not. They're magic. They evolve by magic selection. Only in Xanth can—"

"Yet obviously Xanth creatures started from Mundane ancestors. They have so many affinities—"

"All right!" Bink said impatiently. "They descended from Mundanes. What has that got to do with your conquering Xanth?"

"According to conventional centaur history, man has been in Xanth only a thousand years," Trent said. "In that period there have been ten major Waves of immigration from Mundania."

"Twelve," Bink said.

"That depends on how you count them. At any rate, this continued for nine hundred years, until the Shield cut off those migrations. Yet there are many partially human forms that predate the supposed arrival of human beings. Does that seem to be significant?"

Bink was increasingly worried that Chameleon would foul up, or that the castle would figure out a way to neutralize the cherry bombs. He was not certain that Castle Roogna could not think for itself. Was the Evil Magician stalling to make time for this? "I'll give you one more minute to make your case. Then we're going, regardless."

"How could partially human forms have evolved—unless they had human ancestors? Convergent evolution doesn't create the unnatural mishmash monsters we have here. It creates creatures adapted to their ecological niches, and human features fit few niches. There had to have been people in Xanth many thousands of years ago."

"All right," Bink agreed. "Thirty seconds."

"These people must have interbred with animals to form the composites we know—the centaurs, manticoras, merfolk, harpies, and all. And the creatures crossbred among themselves, and the composites interbred with other composites, producing things like the chimera—"

Bink turned to go. "I think your minute is up," he said. Then he froze. "They *what?*"

"The species mated with other species to create hybrids. Man-headed beasts, beast-headed men—"

"Impossible! Men can only mate with men. I mean with women. It would be unnatural to—"

"Xanth is an unnatural land, Bink. Magic makes remarkable things possible."

Bink saw that logic defied emotion. "But even if they did," he said with difficulty, "that still doesn't justify your conquering Xanth. What's past is past; a change of government won't—"

"I think this background does justify my assumption of power, Bink. Because the accelerated evolution and mutation produced by magic and interspecies miscegenation is changing Xanth. If we remain cut off from the Mundane world, there will in time be no human beings left—only crossbreeds. Only the constant influx of pure stock in the last millennium has enabled man to maintain his type —and there really are not too many human beings here now. Our population is diminishing—not through famine, disease, or war, but through the attrition of crossbreeding. When a man mates with a harpy, the result is not a manchild."

"No!" Bink cried, horrified. "No one would—would breed with a filthy harpy."

"Filthy harpy, perhaps not. But how about a clean, pretty harpy?" Trent inquired with a lift of his eyebrow. "They aren't all alike, you know; we see only their outcasts, not their fresh young—"

"No!"

"Suppose he had drunk from a love spring, accidentally—and the next to drink there was a harpy?"

"No. He—" But Bink knew better. A love spell provided an overriding compulsion. He remembered his experience with the love spring by the chasm, from which he had almost drunk, before seeing the griffin and the unicorn in their embrace. There had been a harpy there. He shuddered reminiscently.

"Have you ever been tempted by an attractive mermaid? Or a lady centaur?" Trent persisted.

"No!" But an insidious memory picture of the elegant firm mermaid breasts came to him. And Cherie, the centaur who had given him a lift during the first leg of his journey to see the Magician Humfrey—when he touched her, had it really been accidental? She had threatened to drop him in a trench, but she hadn't been serious. She was a very nice filly. Rather, *person*. Honesty compelled his reluctant correction. "Maybe."

"And surely there were others, less scrupulous than you," Trent continued inexorably. "They might indulge, in certain circumstances, might they not? Just for variety? Don't the boys of your village hang around the centaur grounds on the sly, as they did in my day?"

Boys like Zink and Jama and Potipher, bullies and troublemakers, who had caused ire in the centaur camp. Bink remembered that too. He had missed the significance before. Of course they had gone to see the bare-breasted centaur fillies, and if they caught one alone—

Bink knew his face was red. "What are you getting at?" he demanded, trying to cover his embarrassment.

"Just this: Xanth must have had intercourse with—sorry, bad word!—must have had contact with Mundania long before the date of our earliest records. Before the Waves. Because only in Mundania is the human species pure. From the time a man sets foot in Xanth, he begins to change. He develops magic, and his children develop more magic, until some of them become full-fledged Magicians—and if they remain, they inevitably become magic themselves. Or their descendants do. Either by breaking down the natural barriers between species, or by evolving into imps, elves, goblins, giants, trolls—did you get a good look at Humfrey?"

"He's a gnome," Bink said without thinking. Then: "Oh, no!"

"He's a man, and a good one—but he's well along the route to something else. He's at the height of his magical powers now—but his children, if he ever has any, may be true gnomes. I dare say he knows this, which is why he won't marry. And consider Chameleon—she has no direct magic, because she has become magic. This is the way the entire human populace of Xanth will go, inevitably—unless there is a steady infusion of new blood from Mundania. *The Shield must come down!* The magic creatures of Xanth must be permitted to migrate outside, freely, there to revert slowly and naturally to their original species. New animals must come in."

"But—" Bink found himself fumbling with the horrors of these concepts. "If there was always—always an interchange before, what happened to the people who came thousands of years ago?"

"Probably there was some obstruction for a while, cutting off migration; Xanth could have been a true island for a thousand years or so, trapping the original prehistoric human settlers, so that they merged entirely with the existing forms and gave rise to the centaurs and other sports. It is happening again, under the Shield. Human beings must—"

"Enough," Bink whispered, fundamentally shocked. "I can't listen to any more."

"You will defuse the cherry bombs?"

Like a bolt of lightning, sanity returned. "No! I'm taking Chameleon and leaving—now."

"But you have to understand—"

"No." The Evil Magician was beginning to make sense. If Bink listened any more, he would be subverted—and Xanth would be lost. "What you suggest is an abomination. It can not be true. I can not accept it."

Trent sighed, with seemingly genuine regret. "Well, it was worth a try, though I did fear you would reject it. I still cannot permit you to destroy this castle—"

Bink braced himself to move, to get out of transformation range. Six feet—

Trent shook his head. "No need to flee, Bink; I shall not break the truce. I could have done that when I showed you the pictures, but I value my given word. So I must compromise. If you will not join me, I shall have to join you."

"What?" Bink, whose ears were almost closed to the Evil Magician's beguiling logic, was caught off guard.

"Spare Castle Roogna. Defuse the bombs. I will see you safely clear of these environs."

This was too easy. "Your word?"

"My word," Trent said solemnly.

"You can make the castle let us go?"

"Yes. This is another facet of what I have learned in these archives. I have only to speak the proper words to it, and it will even facilitate our departure."

"Your word," Bink repeated suspiciously. So far Trent had not broken it—yet what guarantee was there? "No tricks, no sudden change of mind."

"My word of honor, Bink."

What could he do? If the Magician wanted to break the truce, he could transform Bink into a tadpole now, then sneak up on Chameleon and transform her. And—Bink was inclined to trust him. "All right."

"Go and defuse your bombs. I will settle with Roogna."

Bink went. Chameleon met him with a glad little cry—and this time he was quite satisfied to accept her embrace. "Trent has agreed to get us out of here," he told her.

"Oh, Bink, I'm so glad!" she exclaimed, kissing him. He had to grab her hand to make sure she didn't drop the cherry bomb she still held.

She was growing lovelier by the hour. Her personality was not changing much, except as her diminishing intelligence caused her to be less complex, less suspicious. He liked that personality—and now, he had to admit, he liked her beauty, too. She was of Xanth, she was magic, she did not try to manipulate him for her private purposes—she was his type of girl.

But he knew that her stupidity would turn him off, just as her ugliness during the other phase had. He could live with neither a lovely moron nor an ugly genius. She was attractive only right now, while her intelligence was fresh in his memory and her beauty was manifest to his sight and touch. To believe otherwise would be folly.

He drew away from her. "We have to remove the bombs. Carefully," he said. But what about the emotional bombs within him?

Chapter 14

Wiggle

The three of them walked out of Castle Roogna without challenge. The portcullis was raised; Trent had found the hoisting winch, oiled it, and cranked it up with the aid of the magic inherent in its mechanism. The ghosts appeared to bid them all fond adieu; Chameleon cried at this parting, and even Bink felt sad. He knew how lonely it would be for the ghosts after these few days of living company, and he even respected the indomitable castle itself. It did what it had to do, much as Bink himself did.

They carried bags of fruits from the garden, and wore functional clothing from the castle closets, stored for eight hundred years without deterioration by means of the potent ancient spells. They looked like royalty, and felt like it too. Castle Roogna had taken good care of them!

The gardens were magnificent. No storm erupted this time. No trees made threatening gestures; instead, they moved their limbs to be touched gently in the gesture of parting friendship. No vicious animals appeared—and no zombies.

In a surprisingly short time, the castle was out of sight. "We are now beyond Roogna's environs," Trent announced. "We must resume full alertness, for there is no truce with the true wilderness."

"We?" Bink asked. "Aren't you going back to the castle?"

"Not at this time," the Magician said.

Bink's suspicion was renewed. "Just exactly what did you say to that castle?"

"I said: 'I shall return—as King. Roogna shall rule Xanth again.'"

"And it believed that?"

Trent's gaze was tranquil. "Why should it doubt the truth? I could hardly win the crown while remaining confined in the wilderness."

Bink did not respond. The Evil Magician had never said he'd given up his plot to conquer Xanth, after all. He had merely agreed to see Bink and Chameleon safely out of the castle. He had done this. So now they were back where they had been—operating under a truce to get them all safely out of the remainder of the wilderness. After that—Bink's mind was blank.

The untamed forest did not take long to make its presence felt. The trio cut through a small glade girt with pretty yellow flowers—and a swarm of bees rose up. Angrily they buzzed the three, not actually touching or stinging, but sheering off abruptly at short range.

Chameleon sneezed. And sneezed again, violently. Then Bink sneezed too, and so did Trent.

"Sneeze bees!" the Magician exclaimed between paroxysms.

"Transform them!" Bink cried.

"I can't—achoo!—focus on them, my eyes are watering so. Achoo! Anyway, they are innocent creatures of the ah, aahh, ACHOOO!"

"Run, you dopes!" Chameleon cried.

They ran. As they cleared the glade, the bees left off and the sneezes stopped. "Good thing they weren't choke bees!" the Magician said, wiping his flowing eyes.

Bink agreed. A sneeze or two was okay, but a dozen piled on top of one another was a serious matter. There had hardly been time to breathe.

Their noise had alerted others in the jungle. That was always the background threat here. There was a bellow, and the sound of big paws striking the ground. All too soon a huge fire-snorting dragon hove into view. It charged right through the sneeze glade, but the bees left it strictly alone. They knew better than to provoke any fire sneezes that would burn up their flowers.

"Change it! Change it!" Chameleon cried as the dragon oriented on her. Dragons seemed to have a special taste for the fairest maidens.

"Can't," Trent muttered. "By the time it gets within six feet, its fire will have scorched us all into roasts. It's got a twenty-foot blowtorch."

"You aren't much help," she complained.

"Transform me!" Bink cried with sudden inspiration.

"Good idea." Abruptly Bink was a sphinx. He retained his own head, but he had the body of a bull, wings of an eagle, and legs of a lion. And he was huge— he towered over the dragon. "I had no idea sphinxes grew this big," he boomed.

"Sorry—I forgot again," Trent said. "I was thinking of the legendary sphinx in Mundania."

"But the Mundanes don't have magic."

"This one must have wandered out from Xanth a long time ago. For thousands of years it has been stone, petrified."

"Petrified? What could scare a sphinx that size?" Chameleon wondered, peering up at Bink's monstrous face.

But there was business to attend to. "Begone, beastie!" Bink thundered.

The dragon was slow to adapt to the situation. It shot a jet of orange flame at Bink, scorching his feathers. The blast didn't hurt, but it was annoying. Bink reached out with one lion's paw and swiped at the dragon. It was a mere ripple of effort, but the creature was thrown sideways into a tree. A shower of rock nuts dropped on it from the angry tree. The dragon gave a single yelp of pain, doused its fire, and fled.

Bink circled around carefully, hoping he hadn't stepped on anyone. "Why didn't we think of this before?" he bellowed. "I can give you a ride, right to the edge of the jungle. No one will recognize us, and no creature will bother us!"

He squatted as low as possible, and Chameleon and Trent climbed up his tail to his back. Bink moved forward with a slow stride that was nevertheless faster than any man could run. They were on their way.

But not for long. Chameleon, bouncing around on the sphinx's horny-skinned back, decided she had to go to the bathroom. There was nothing to do but let her go. Bink hunched down so she could slide safely to the ground.

Trent took advantage of the break to stretch his legs. He walked around to Bink's huge face. "I'd transform you back, but it's really better to stick with the form until finished with it," he said. "I really have no concrete evidence that frequent transformations are harmful to the recipient, but it seems best not to gamble at this time. Since the sphinx is an intelligent life form, you aren't suffering intellectually."

"No, I'm okay," Bink agreed. "Better than ever, in fact. Can you guess this riddle? What walks on four legs in the morning, two legs at noon, and three in the evening?"

"I shall not answer," Trent said, looking startled. "In all the legends I've heard, some sphinxes committed suicide when the correct answers to their riddles were given. Those were the smaller type of sphinx, a different species—but I seem to have muddled the distinctions somewhat, and would not care to gamble on the absence of affinity."

"Uh, no," Bink said, chagrined. "I guess the riddle was from the mind of the sphinx, not me. I'm sure all sphinxes had a common ancestor, though I don't know the difference between one kind and another."

"Odd. Not about your ignorance of Mundane legends. About your riddle memory. You *are* the sphinx. I didn't move your mind into an existing body, for the original creatures have all been dead or petrified for millennia. I transformed you into a similar monster, a Bink-sphinx. But if you actually have sphinx memories, true sphinx memories—"

"There must be ramifications of your magic you don't comprehend," Bink said. "I wish I understood the real nature of magic—any magic."

"Yes, it is a mystery. Magic exists in Xanth, nowhere else. Why? What is its mechanism? Why does Xanth seem to be adjacent to *any* Mundane land, in geography, language, and culture? How is this magic, in all its multiple levels, transmitted from the geographic region to the inhabitants?"

"I have pondered that," Bink said. "I thought perhaps some radiation from the rock, or nutritional value of the soil—"

"When I am King I shall initiate a study program to determine the true story of Xanth's uniqueness."

When Trent was King. The project was certainly worthwhile—in fact, fascinating—but not at that price. For a moment Bink was tempted: with the merest swipe of his mighty forepaw he could squash the Evil Magician flat, ending the threat forever.

No. Even if Trent were not really his friend, Bink could not violate the truce that way. Besides, he didn't want to remain a monster all his life, physically or morally.

"The lady is taking her sweet time," Trent muttered.

Bink moved his ponderous head, searching for Chameleon. "She's usually very quick about that sort of thing. She doesn't like being alone." Then he thought of something else. "Unless she went looking for her spell—you know, to make her normal. She left Xanth in an effort to nullify her magic, and now that she's stuck back in Xanth, she wants some kind of countermagic. She's not very bright right now, and—"

Trent stroked his chin. "This is the jungle. I don't want to violate her privacy, but—"

"Maybe we'd better check for her."

"Umm. Well, I guess you can stand one more transformation," Trent decided. "I'll make you a bloodhound. That's a Mundane animal, a kind of dog, very good at sniffing out a trail. If you run into her doing something private—well, you'll only be an animal, not a human voyeur."

Abruptly Bink was a keen-nosed, floppy-eared, loose-faced creature, smell-oriented. He could pick up the lingering odor of anything—he was sure of that. He had never before realized how overwhelmingly important the sense of smell was. Strange that he had ever depended on any lesser sense.

Trent concealed their supplies in a mock tangle tree and faced about. "Very well, Bink; let's sniff her out." Bink understood him well enough, but could not reply, as this was not a speaking form of animal.

Chameleon's trail was so obvious it was a wonder Trent himself couldn't smell it. Bink put his nose to the ground—how natural that the head be placed so close to the primary source of information, instead of raised foolishly high as in Trent's case—and moved forward competently.

The route led around behind a bush and on into the wilderness. She *had* been lured away; in her present low ebb of intelligence, almost anything would fool her. Yet there was no consistent odor of any animal or plant she might have followed. That suggested magic. Worried, Bink woofed and sniffed on, the Magician following. A magic lure was almost certainly trouble.

But her trace did not lead into a tangle tree or gucktooth swamp or the lair of a wyvern. It wove intricately between these obvious hazards, bearing generally south, into the deepest jungle. Something obviously had led her, guiding her safely past all threats—but what, and where—and why?

Bink knew the essence, if not the detail: some will-o'-the-wisp spell had beckoned her, tempting her ever forward, always just a little out of reach. Perhaps it had seemed to offer some elixir, some enchantment to make her normal —and so she had followed. It would lead her into untracked wilderness, where she would be lost, and leave her there. She would not survive long.

Bink hesitated. He had not lost the trail; that could never happen. There was something else.

"What is it, Bink?" Trent inquired. "I know she was following the *ignis fatuus* —but since we are close on her trail we should be able to—" He broke off, becoming aware of the other thing. It was a shuddering in the ground, as of some massive object striking it. An object weighing many tons.

Trent looked around. "I can't see it, Bink. Can you smell it?"

Bink was silent. The wind was wrong. He could not smell whatever was making that sound from this distance.

"Want me to transform you into something more powerful?" Trent asked. "I'm not sure I like this situation. First the swamp gas, now this strange pursuit."

If Bink changed, he would no longer be able to sniff out Chameleon's trail. He remained silent.

"Very well, Bink. But stay close by me; I can transform you into a creature to meet any emergency, but you have to be within range. I believe we're walking into extreme danger, or having it walk up on us." And he touched his sword.

They moved on—but the shuddering grew bolder, becoming a measured thumping, as of some ponderous animal. Yet they saw nothing. Now it was directly behind them, and gaining.

"I think we'd better hide," Trent said grimly. "Discretion is said to be the better part of valor."

Good idea. They circled a harmless beerbarrel tree and watched silently.

The thumping became loud. Extremely loud. The whole tree shook with the force of the measured vibrations. TRAMP, TRAMP, TRAMP! Small branches fell off the tree, and a leak sprang in the trunk. A thin jet of beer formed, splashing down under Bink's sensitive nose. He recoiled; even in the human state, he had never been partial to that particular beverage. He peered around the trunk—yet there was nothing.

Then at last something became visible. A branch crashed off a spikespire tree, splintering. Bushes waved violently aside. A section of earth subsided. More beer jetted from developing cracks in the trunk of their hiding place, filling the air with its malty fragrance. Still nothing tangible could be seen.

"It's invisible," Trent whispered, wiping beer off one hand. "An invisible giant."

Invisible! That meant Trent couldn't transform it. He had to see what he enchanted.

Together, silently, steeped in intensifying beer fumes, they watched the giant pass. Monstrous human footprints appeared, each ten feet long, sinking inches deep into the forest soil. TRAMP!—and the trees jumped and shuddered and shed their fruits and leaves and branches. TRAMP!—and an icecream bush disappeared, becoming a mere patina of flavored discoloration on the flat surface of the depression. TRAMP!—and a tangle tree hugged its tentacles about itself, frightened. TRAMP!—and a fallen trunk splintered across the five-foot width of the giant's print.

A stench washed outward, suffocatingly, like that of a stench-puffer or an overflowing outhouse in the heat of summer. Bink's keen nose hurt.

"I am not a cowardly man," Trent murmured. "But I begin to feel fear. When neither spell nor sword can touch an enemy . . ." His nose twitched. "His body odor alone is deadly. He must have feasted on rotten blivets for breakfast."

Bink didn't recognize that food. If that was the kind of fruit Mundane trees formed, he didn't want any.

Bink became aware that his own hackles were erect. He had heard of such a monster, but taken it as a joke. An invisible—but not unsmellable—giant!

"If he is in proportion," Trent remarked, "that giant is some sixty feet tall. That would be impossible in Mundania, for purely physical reasons, square-cube law and such. But here—who can say nay to magic? He's looking over much of the forest, not through it." He paused, considering. "He evidently was not following us. Where is he going?"

Wherever Chameleon went, Bink thought. He growled.

"Right, Bink. We'd better track her down quickly, before she gets stepped on!"

They moved on, following what was now a well-trodden trail. Where the huge prints crossed Chameleon's traces, the scent of the giant was overlaid, so heavy that Bink's refined nose rebelled. He skirted the prints and picked up Chameleon's much milder scent on the far side.

Now a whistling descended from right angles to the path they were following. Bink looked up nervously—and saw a griffin angling carefully down between the trees.

Trent whipped out his sword and backed toward the black bole of an oilbarrel tree, facing the monster. Bink, in no condition to fight it, bared his teeth and backed toward the same protection. He was glad it wasn't a dragon; one really good tongue of fire could set off the tree explosively and wipe them all out. As it was, the overhanging branches would interfere with the monster's flight, forcing it to do combat on the ground. Still a chancy business, but it restricted the battle zone to two dimensions, which was a net advantage for Bink and Trent. Maybe if Bink distracted it, Trent could get safely within range to transform it.

The griffin settled to earth, folding its extensive glossy wings. Its coiled lion's tail twitched about, and its great front eagle's talons made streaks in the dirt. Its eagle head oriented on Trent. "Cawp?" it inquired. Bink could almost feel that deadly beak slicing through his flesh. A really healthy griffin could take on a medium-sized dragon in single combat, and this one was healthy. He nudged within transformation range.

"Follow the giant tracks, that way," Trent said to the monster. "Can't miss it."

"Bawp!" the griffin said. It turned about, oriented on the giant tracks, bunched its lion muscles, spread its wings, and launched itself into the air. It flew low-level along the channel the invisible giant had carved through the forest.

Trent and Bink exchanged startled glances. They had had a narrow escape; griffins were very agile in combat, and Trent's magic might not have taken effect in time. "It only wanted directions!" Trent said. "Must be something very strange up ahead. We'd better get there in a hurry. Be unfortunate if some part-human cult was having a ritual sacrifice."

Ritual sacrifice? Bink growled his confusion.

"You know," Trent said grimly. "Bloody altar, beautiful virgin maiden . . ."

"Rrowr!" Bink took off down the trail.

Soon they heard a commotion ahead. It was a medley of thumps, crashes, bellows, squawks, and crashes. "Sounds more like a battle than a party," Trent observed. "I really can't think what—"

At last they came in sight of the happening. They paused, amazed.

It was an astonishing assemblage of creatures, ranged in a large loose circle, facing in: dragons, griffins, manticoras, harpies, land serpents, trolls, goblins, fairies, and too many others to take in all at once. There were even a few human beings. It was not a free-for-all; all were intent on individual exercises, stamping their feet, biting at air, slamming their hooves together, and banging on rocks. In the interior of the circle, a number of creatures were dead or dying, ignored by the others. Bink could see and smell the blood, and hear their groans of agony. This was a battle, certainly—but where was the enemy? It was not the invisible giant; his prints were confined to one quadrant, not overlapping the territory of his neighbors.

"I thought I knew something about magic," Trent said, shaking his head. "But this is beyond my comprehension. These creatures are natural enemies, yet they ignore one another and do not feed on prey. Have they happened on a cache of loco?"

"Woof!" Bink exclaimed. He had spied Chameleon. She had two large flat stones in her hands and was holding them about a foot apart while she stared intently between them. Suddenly she clapped them together, with such force that they both fell out of her hands. She peered at the air above them, smiled enigmatically, picked them up, and repeated the procedure.

Trent followed Bink's gaze. "Loco!" he repeated. But Bink could smell no loco. "Her too. It must be an area spell. We'd better back off before we also fall prey to it."

They started to retreat, though Bink did not want to desert Chameleon. A grizzled old centaur cantered up. "Don't just meander around!" he snapped. "Get around to the north quadrant." He pointed. "We've suffered heavy losses there, and Bigfoot can't do it all. He can't even see the enemy. They'll break through any minute. Get some rocks; don't use your sword, fool!"

"Don't use my sword on what?" Trent demanded, with understandable ire.

"The wiggles, naturally. Cut one in half, all you have is two wiggles. You—"

"The wiggles!" Trent breathed, and Bink growled his own chagrin.

The centaur sniffed. "You been drinking?"

"Bigfoot's passage holed the beerbarrel tree we took refuge behind," Trent explained. "I thought the wiggles had been eradicated!"

"So thought we all," the centaur said. "But there's a healthy colony swarming here. You have to crush them or chew them or burn them or drown them. We can't afford to let a single one escape. Now get moving!"

Trent looked about. "Where are the stones?"

"Here. I've collected a pile." The centaur showed the way. "I knew I couldn't handle it myself, so I sent out will-o'-the-wisps to summon help."

Suddenly Bink recognized the centaur: Herman the Hermit. Exiled from the centaur community for obscenity almost a decade ago. Amazing that he had survived, here in the deepest wilderness—but centaurs were hardy folk.

Trent did not make the connection. The episode had happened after his exile. But he well knew the horror the wiggles represented. He picked up two good rocks from Herman's cache and strode toward the north quadrant.

Bink followed. He had to help too. If even one wiggle got away, there would at some later date be another swarming, perhaps not stopped in time. He caught up to the Magician. "Woof! Woof!" he barked urgently.

Trent looked straight ahead. "Bink, if I transform you here and now, the others will see, and know me for what I am. They may turn against me—and the siege against the wiggles will be broken. I think we can contain the swarm with our present creature-power; the centaur has organized the effort well. Your natural form would not be better equipped to wage this war than your present form. Wait until this is over."

Bink was not satisfied with all the arguments, but he seemed to have no choice. So he determined to make himself useful as he was. Maybe he could smell out the wiggles.

As they came up to their designated quadrant, a griffin gave a loud squawk and keeled over. It resembled the one they had directed here; it must have lost sight of its guiding will-o'-the-wisp. But all griffins looked and smelled pretty much alike to Bink. Not that it mattered, objectively; all creatures here had a common purpose. Still, he felt a certain identification. He ran to it, hoping the injury was not critical.

The creature was bleeding from a mortal wound. A wiggle had holed it through its lion's heart.

Wiggles traveled by sudden rushes along wiggle-sized magic tunnels they created. Then they paused to recuperate, or perhaps merely to contemplate philosophical matters; no one really knew the rationale of a wiggle. Therefore the killer wiggle that had gotten the griffin should be right about here. Bink sniffed and picked up its faint putrid odor. He oriented on it, and saw his first live wiggle.

It was a two-inch-long, loosely spiraled worm, hovering absolutely still in midair. It hardly looked like the menace it was. He barked, pointing his nose at it.

Trent heard him. He strode across with his two rocks. "Good job, Bink," he cried. He smashed the rocks together on the wiggle. As they came apart, the squished, dead hulk of the tiny monster dropped. One down!

Zzapp! "There's another!" Trent cried. "They tunnel through anything—even air—so we hear the collapse of the vacuum behind them. This one should be right about—there!" He smashed his stones together again, crunching the wiggle.

After that it was hectic. The wiggles were zapping determinedly outward, each in its own pattern. There was no way of telling how long they would freeze in place—seconds or minutes—or how far they would zap—inches or feet. But each wiggle went in the precise direction it had started, never shifting even a fraction, so it was possible to trace that line and locate it fairly quickly. If someone stood in front of a wiggle at the wrong time, he got zapped—and if the hole were through a vital organ, he died. But it was not feasible to stand behind a wiggle, for the closer in toward the source of the swarm one went, the more the wiggles were present. There were so many wiggles that a creature smashing one could be simultaneously holed by another. It was necessary to stand at the outer fringe of expansion and nab the leaders first.

The wiggles really seemed to be mindless, or at least indifferent to external things. Their preset wiggle courses holed anything—anything at all—in the way. If a person didn't locate a wiggle fast, it was too late, for the thing had zapped again. Yet it could be tricky to find a still wiggle, for it looked like a twisted stem from the side and a coiled stem from the end. It had to move to attract attention to itself—and then it might be too late to nab it.

"This is like standing in a firing range and catching the bullets as they pass," Trent muttered. That sounded like another Mundane allusion; evidently Mundane wiggles were called bullets.

The invisible giant operated beside Bink on the right, as his nose plainly told him. TRAMP!—and a wiggle was crushed out of existence. Maybe a hundred wiggles at once. But so was anything else that got underfoot. Bink didn't dare point out wiggles for Bigfoot; it would be his own death warrant. For all he knew, the giant was stomping randomly. It was as good a way as any.

On the left side, a unicorn operated. When it located a wiggle, it either crushed it between horn and hoof or closed its mouth over it and ground it to shreds with its equine teeth. This seemed to Bink to be a distasteful and hazardous mode of operation, because if it mistimed a wiggle—

Zzapp! A hole appeared in the unicorn's jaw. Blood dripped out. The creature made a single neigh of anguish—then trotted along the path of the zap. It located the wiggle and chomped down again, using the other side of its jaw.

Bink admired the unicorn's courage. But he had to get on with his own job. Two wiggles had just zapped within range. He pointed out the nearest for Trent, then ran to the other, afraid Trent would not reach it in time. His hound's teeth were made for cutting and tearing, not chewing, but maybe they would do. He bit down on the wiggle.

It squished unpleasantly. Its body was firm but not really hard, and the juices squirted out. The taste was absolutely awful. There was some sort of acid—yecch! But Bink chewed carefully several times, to be sure of crushing it all; he knew that any unsquished fragment would zap away as a tiny wiggle, just as dangerous as the original. He spat out the remains. Surely his mouth would never be the same again.

Zzapp! Zzapp! Two more wiggles nearby. Trent heard one and went after it; Bink sought out the other. But even as they both oriented, a third *zzapp!* sounded between them. The pace was stepping up as the great internal mass of wiggles reached the perimeter. There were too many wiggles to keep up with! The complete swarm might number a million.

There was a deafening bellow from above. "OOAAOUGH!"

Herman the centaur galloped by. Blood trailed from a glancing wiggle-wound in his flank. "Bigfoot's hit!" he cried. "Get out of the way."

"But the wiggles are breaking out," Trent said.

"I know! We're taking heavy losses all around the perimeter. It's a bigger swarm than I thought, more dense in the center. We can't hold them anyway. We'll have to form a new containment circle, and hope that more help arrives in time. Save yourselves before the giant falls."

Good advice. A huge print appeared in Bink's territory as Bigfoot staggered. They got out of there.

"AAOOGAHH!" the giant bawled. Another print appeared, this time in toward the center of the circle. A wash of air passed as he fell, heavy-laden with the giant-aroma. "GOUGH-OOOAAAA-AAHH—" The sound arched down from a fifty-foot elevation toward the center of the wiggle swarm. The crash was like that of a petrified pine felled by magic. WHOOMP!

Herman, who had taken refuge behind the same jellybarrel tree as Trent and Bink, wiped a squirt of jelly out of his eye and shook his head sadly. "There goes a big, big man! Little hope now of containing the menace. We're disorganized and short of personnel, and the strength of the enemy is sweeping outward. Only a hurricane could get them all, and the weather's dry." Then he looked again at Trent. "You seem familiar. Aren't you—yes. Twenty years ago—"

Trent raised his hand. "I regret the necessity—" he began.

"No, wait, Magician," Herman said. "Transform me not. I will not betray your secret. I could have bashed your head in with my foot just now, had I intended you ill. Know you not why I was exiled from my kind?"

Trent paused. "I know not, for I do not know you."

"I am Herman the Hermit, punished for the obscenity of practicing magic. By summoning will-o'-the-wisps. No centaur is supposed to—"

"You mean centaurs can practice magic?"

"They could—if they would. We centaurs have existed so long in Xanth we have become a natural species. But magic is considered—"

"Obscene," Trent finished, voicing Bink's thought. So magic intelligent creatures could do magic; their inability was cultural, not genetic. "So you became a hermit in the wilderness."

"Correct. I share your humiliation of exile. But now we have a need more important than privacy. Use your talent to abolish the wiggle menace!"

"I can't transform all the wiggles. I must focus on one at a time, and there are too many—"

"Not that. We must cauterize them. I had hoped my wisps would lead in a salamander—"

"A salamander," Trent exclaimed. "Of course! But even so, the fire could not spread fast enough to burn out all the wiggles, and if it did, the fire itself would then be unstoppable, a greater menace than the wiggles. We'd merely exchange one devastation for another."

"Not so. There are certain restrictions on salamanders, and with foresight they can be controlled. I was thinking of—"

Zzapp! A hole appeared in the trunk of the tree. Jelly oozed out like purple blood. Bink dashed out to crunch the wiggle, who fortunately had passed between them and injured no one. *Yuch!* That taste!

"They're inside the trees," Trent said. "Some are bound to land within things. Impossible to catch those ones."

Herman trotted over to a nondescript bush. He yanked several vines from it. "Salamander weed," he explained. "I have become a fair naturalist in my years of isolation. This is the one thing a salamander can't burn. It represents a natural barrier to the fire; eventually the flames are stopped by proliferating weeds. If I make a harness of this, I can carry a salamander around in a great circle just beyond the infestation—"

"But how to stop the fire before it destroys most of Xanth?" Trent asked. "We can't wait on the chance of the weeds; half of the wilderness could be ravaged before it burns itself out. We can't possibly clear a firebreak in time." He paused. "You know, that must be why your wisps summoned no salamanders. This thick forest would naturally have a salamander-repulsion spell to keep them away, because such a fire would quickly prejudice this whole environment. Still, if we start a fire—"

Herman held up one strong hand in a halt gesture. He was an old centaur, but still strong; the arm was magnificently muscled. "You know how salamander fire burns only in the direction it starts? If we form a circle of inward-burning magic fire—"

"Suddenly I comprehend!" Trent exclaimed. "It will burn itself out at the center." He looked around. "Bink?"

What else? Bink did not relish being a salamander, but anything was better than yielding Xanth to the wiggles. No person or creature would be safe if the swarms got out of control again. He came up.

Suddenly he was a small, bright amphibian, about five inches from nose to tail. Once more he remembered the omen he had seen back at the outset of this adventure: the chameleon lizard had also become a salamander—before being swallowed up by the moth hawk. Had his time finally come?

The ground he stood on burst into flame. The underlying sand would not burn, but all the material on top of it was fuel. "Climb in here," Herman said, holding a pouch he had cleverly formed of vines. "I will carry you in a great left circle. Be sure you direct your fire inward. To the left." And to make quite sure Bink understood, he pointed with his left hand.

Well, such a limit wouldn't be much fun, but—

Bink climbed into the net. The centaur picked it up and dangled it at arm's length, as well he might, for Bink was *hot*. Only the frustrating salamander-weed vines prevented him from really tearing loose.

Herman galloped. "Clear out! Clear out!" he cried with amazing volume to the straggling, wounded creatures still trying to stop the wiggles. "We're burning them out. Salamander!" And to Bink: "To the left! To the *left!*"

Bink had hoped he'd forgotten about that restriction. Ah, well, half a burn was better than none. From him a sheet of flame erupted. Everything it touched burst up anew, burning savagely. Branches, leaves, whole green trees, even the carcasses of fallen monsters—the flame consumed all. That was the nature of salamander fire—it burned magically, heedless of other conditions. No rainstorm could put it out, for water itself would burn. Everything except rock and earth—and salamander weed. Curse the stuff!

Now a hasty exodus developed. Dragons, griffins, harpies, goblins, and men scrambled out of the path of the terrible fire. Every movable form cleared out—except the wiggles, which proceeded as mindlessly as ever.

The flames spread hungrily up the great trees, consuming them with awesome rapidity. A tangle tree writhed in agony as it was incinerated, and the smell of burning beer and jelly spread. Already a swath of scorched earth was developing, sand and ashes marking the path they had traveled. Glorious!

Zzapp! Bink dropped to the ground. A wiggle, striking with the luck of the mindless, had holed Herman's right hand. Good. Now Bink could get out of the net and really go to work, setting the most magnificent blaze in all salamander history.

But the centaur looped about and grabbed the net with his left hand. The flames touched his fingers momentarily, and the tips shivered into ash, but he hung on with the stubs. Damn the courage of the Hermit! "On!" Herman cried, resuming forward speed. "To the *left.*"

Bink had to obey. Angrily he shot forth an especially intense flame, hoping the Hermit would drop him again, but it didn't work. The centaur galloped on, widening the circle a bit, since the wiggle radius had evidently expanded further. It was useless to burn where the wiggles had been, or where they would be; the flame had to be where they were now. Any that zapped past the sheet of flame and paused in an already burned spot would survive. That made it a tricky calculation. But it was their only chance.

The circle was almost complete; the centaur could really move. They raced up to the broadening swath of their starting point, pausing to let a few trapped monsters get out before being doomed. The last to go was the great land serpent, a hundred feet of slithering torso.

Trent was there, organizing the remaining animals into a cleanup detail to intercept any few wiggles already outside the circle of fire. Now that the great majority of wiggles were being eliminated, it was feasible to go after those few individually. Every last one had to be squished.

The fire closed in on the original wiggle hive. There was a deafening groan. "AAOOGAAH!" Something stirred invisibly.

"Bigfoot!" Trent exclaimed. "He's still alive in there."

"I thought he was dead," Herman said, horrified. "We've already closed the circle; we can't let him out."

"He was riddled through the legs, so he fell—but he wasn't dead," Trent said. "The fall must have knocked him out for a while." He stared into the leaping flames, now outlining the form of a gargantuan man lying prone, stirring at the peripheries. The odor was of roasting garbage. "Too late now."

The doomed giant thrashed about. Flaming branches flew wide. Some landed in the jungle beyond the circle. "Catch those flames!" the centaur cried. "They can start a forest fire."

But no one could quench or move or even contain the flames. No one except Herman himself, with his weed net. He dumped Bink out and galloped toward the nearest, which was dangerously close to an oilbarrel tree.

Trent gestured hastily, and Bink was his human self again. He leaped out of the smoldering ground where his salamander self had touched. What power the Evil Magician had; he could destroy Xanth any time just by making a dozen salamanders.

Bink blinked—and saw Chameleon chasing a wiggle between the prongs of magic fire formed by thrown brands. She was too intent or too stupid to realize the danger!

He ran after her. "Chameleon! Turn back!" She paid no heed, faithful to her chore. He caught up and spun her about. "The fire's getting the wiggles. We have to get out of here."

"Oh," she said faintly. Her once-fancy dress was ragged, and dirt smudged her face, but she was excruciatingly lovely.

"Come on." He took her by the hand and drew her along.

But a determined tongue of fire had crossed behind them. They were trapped in a closing island.

The omen! Now at last it struck—at both Chameleon and him.

Herman leaped over the tongue, a splendid figure of a centaur. "Up on my back," he cried.

Bink wrapped his arms about Chameleon and heaved her up onto the Hermit's back. She was wondrously supple, slender of waist and expansive of thigh. Not that he had any business noticing such things at the moment. But his position behind her as she slid on her belly onto the centaur made the thoughts inevitable. He gave her graceful posterior one last ungraceful shove, getting her balanced, then scrambled up himself.

Herman started walking, then running, ready to hurdle the fire with his double burden.

Zzapp! A wiggle, close by.

The centaur staggered. "I'm hit!" he cried. Then he righted himself, made a convulsion of effort, and leaped.

He fell short. His front legs buckled, and the rear ones were in the flame. Bink and Chameleon were thrown forward, landing on either side of the human torso. Herman grabbed each by an arm, and with a surge of centaur strength shoved both on beyond the danger zone.

Trent charged up. "Hermit, you're burning!" he cried. "I will transform you—"

"No," Herman said. "I am holed through the liver. I am done for. Let the clean fire take me." He grimaced. "Only, to abate the agony quickly—your sword, sir." And he pointed at his neck.

Bink would have temporized, pretending misunderstanding, trying to delay the inevitable. The Evil Magician was more decisive. "As you require," Trent said. Suddenly his blade was in his hand, flashing in an arc—and the centaur's noble head flew off the body, to land upright on the ground just beyond the flame.

Bink stared, aghast. He had never before witnessed such a cold-blooded killing.

"I thank you," the head said. "You abated the agony most efficiently. Your secret dies with me." The centaur's eyes closed.

Herman the Hermit had really wanted it that way. Trent had judged correctly and acted instantly. Bink himself would have bungled it.

"There was a creature I would have been proud to have taken for a friend," Trent said sadly. "I would have saved him had it been within my power."

Little lights danced in close, centering on that dead head. At first Bink supposed they were sparks, but they did not actually burn. "The will-o'-the-wisps," Trent murmured. "Paying their last respects."

The lights dispersed, taking with them their vague impression of wonders barely glimpsed and joys never quite experienced. The fire consumed the body, then the head, and swept on into an already-burned area. Most of the remaining flame was now in the center of the circle, where the invisible giant no longer thrashed.

Trent raised his voice. "All creatures silent, in respect for Herman the Hermit, wronged by his own kind, who has died in defense of Xanth. And for Bigfoot and all the other noble creatures who perished similarly."

A hush fell on the throng. The silence became utter; not even an insect hummed. One minute, two minutes, three—no sound. It was a fantastic assemblage of monsters pausing with bowed heads in deference to the ones who had labored so valiantly against the common enemy. Bink was profoundly moved; never again would he think of the creatures of the magic wild as mere animals.

At last Trent lifted his eyes again. "Xanth is saved, thanks to Herman—and to you all," he announced. "The wiggles are exterminated. Disperse, with our gratitude, and go with pride. There is no more important service you could have performed, and I salute you."

"But some wiggles may have escaped," Bink protested in a whisper.

"No. None escaped. The job was well done."

"How can you be so sure?"

"I heard no zaps during the silence. No wiggle sits still longer than three minutes."

Bink's mouth dropped open. The silence of respect and mourning, sincere as it had been, had also been the verification that the menace had indeed been abated. Bink would never have thought of that himself. How competently Trent had assumed the difficult and demanding chore of leadership, when the centaur died. And without betraying his secret.

The assorted monsters dispersed peaceably, operating under the tacit truce of this effort. Many were wounded, but they bore their pain with the same dignity and courage Herman had, and did not snap at one another. The great land serpent slithered by, and Bink counted half a dozen holes along its length, but it did not pause. The serpent, like the others, had come to do what had to be done —but it would be as dangerous as ever in future encounters.

"Shall we resume our journey?" Trent inquired, glancing for the last time across the flat bare disk of ashes.

"We'd better," Bink said. "I think the fire is dying out now."

Abruptly he was the sphinx again, half as tall as the invisible giant and far more massive. Apparently Trent had decided multiple transformations were safe. Trent and Chameleon boarded, and he retraced the path to their cache of supplies. "And no more comfort breaks," Bink muttered in a boom. Someone chuckled.

A Spell for Chameleon 219

Chapter 15

Duel

They crested a forest ridge—and abruptly the wilderness ended. The blue fields of a bluejean plantation spread out before them: civilization.

Trent and Chameleon dismounted. Bink had trudged all night, tirelessly, sleeping while his great legs worked by themselves. Nothing had bothered the party; even the fiercest things of the wilderness had some caution. Now it was mid-morning, a fine clear day. He felt good.

Suddenly he was a man again—and he still felt good. "I guess this is where we part company at last," he said.

"I'm sorry we could not agree on more things," Trent said, putting out his hand. "But I think separation will abate those differences. It has been a pleasure to know you both."

Bink took the hand and shook it, feeling oddly sad. "I suppose by definition and talent you *are* the Evil Magician—but you helped save Xanth from the wiggles, and in person you have been a friend. I can not approve your designs, but . . ." He shrugged. "Farewell, Magician."

"Same here," Chameleon said, flashing Trent a breathtaking smile that more than made up for the inelegance of her speech.

"Well, isn't this cozy!" a voice said.

All three whirled defensively—but there was nothing to see. Nothing but the ripening jeans on their green vines, and the forbidding fringe of the jungle.

Then a swirl of smoke formed, thickening rapidly. "A genie," Chameleon said.

But now Bink recognized the forming shape. "No such luck," he said. "That's the Sorceress Iris, mistress of illusion."

"Thank you for the elegant introduction, Bink," the now-solid-seeming woman said. She stood among the jeans, ravishing in a low-cut gown—but Bink felt no temptation now. Chameleon, at the full flush of her beauty, had a natural if magical allure that the Sorceress could not duplicate by her artifice.

"So this is Iris," Trent said. "I knew of her before I left Xanth, since she is of my generation, but we never actually met. She is certainly skilled at her talent."

"It happened I had no hankering for transformation," Iris said, giving him an arch glance. "You left quite a trail of toads and trees and bugs and things. I thought you had been exiled."

"Times change, Iris. Didn't you observe us in the wilderness?"

"As a matter of fact, I didn't. That jungle is a dreary place, with quite a number of counter-illusion spells, and I had no idea you were back in Xanth. I don't believe anyone knows, not even Humfrey. It was the huge sphinx that attracted my attention, but I could not be sure you were involved until I saw you transform it into Bink. I knew he had been exiled recently, so something was definitely amiss. How did you pass the Shield?"

"Times change," Trent repeated enigmatically.

"Yes they do," she said, nettled at being put off. She looked at each of them in turn. Bink had not realized she could project her illusions so effectively, so far afield, or perceive things from such distances. The ramifications of the powers of Magicians and Sorceresses were amazing. "Now shall we get down to business?"

"Business?" Bink asked blankly.

"Don't be naive," Trent muttered. "The bitch means blackmail."

So it was strong magic opposing strong magic. Maybe they would cancel each other out, and Xanth would be safe after all. Bink had not anticipated this.

Iris looked at him. "Are you sure you won't reconsider my prior offer, Bink?" she inquired. "I could arrange things so that your exile would be revoked. You could still be King. The time is ripe. And if you really prefer the innocent look in women—" Suddenly another Chameleon stood before him, as beautiful as the real one. "Anything you desire, Bink—and with a mind, too."

That last little dig at the girl's stupid phase annoyed him. "Go jump in the Gap," Bink said.

The figure changed back to Iris-beautiful. It faced Chameleon. "I don't know you, my dear, but it would be a shame to see you fed to a dragon."

"A dragon!" Chameleon cried, frightened.

"That is the customary penalty for violating exile. When I notify the authorities, and they put their magic-spotters on you three and verify your status—"

"Leave her alone!" Bink said sharply.

Iris ignored him. "Now if you could only persuade your friend to cooperate," she continued to Chameleon, "you could escape that horrible fate—those dragons really like to chew on pretty limbs—and be beautiful all the time." Iris had claimed not to know Chameleon, but she had evidently figured things out. "I can make you seem as lovely in your off phase as you are right now."

"You can?" Chameleon asked, excited.

"The deceptions of the Sorceress are apt," Trent murmured to Bink, obviously with double meaning.

"The truth is not in her," Bink murmured back. "Only illusion."

"A woman is as a woman seems," Iris told Chameleon. "If she looks lovely to the eye and feels lovely to the touch, she is lovely. That is all men care about."

"Don't listen to her," Bink said. "The Sorceress just wants to use you."

"Correction," Iris said. "I want to use *you*, Bink. I bear no malice to your girlfriend—so long as you cooperate with me. I am not a jealous woman. All I want is power."

"No!" Bink cried.

Chameleon, following his lead uncertainly, echoed: "No."

"Now you, Magician Trent," Iris said. "I have not been watching you long, but you seem to be a man of your word, at least when it suits your convenience. I could make you a formidable Queen—or I can have the palace guards on the way to kill you in five minutes."

"I would transform the guards," Trent said.

"From longbow range? Perhaps," she said, raising a fair eyebrow skeptically. "But I doubt you could be King after such an incident. The whole land of Xanth would be out to kill you. You might transform a great number—but when would you sleep?"

Telling blow! The Evil Magician had been caught before when he slept. If he were exposed before he could surround himself with loyal troops, he would not be able to survive.

But why should that bother Bink? If the Sorceress betrayed the Evil Magician, Xanth would be secure—through no action of Bink's. His own hands would be clean. He would have betrayed neither his country nor his companion. He should simply stay out of it.

"Well, I might transform animals or people into my own likeness," Trent said. "It would then be very hard for the patriots to know whom to kill."

"Wouldn't work," Iris said. "No imitation will fool a magic-spotter, once it fixes on its subject."

Trent considered. "Yes, it would be very difficult for me to prevail in such circumstance. Considering this, I believe I should accept your offer, Sorceress. There are some details to work out, of course—"

"You can't!" Bink cried, shocked.

Trent gazed at him, affecting mild perplexity. "It seems reasonable to me, Bink. I desire to be King; Iris desires to be Queen. There is power enough to share, that way. Perhaps we could define spheres of influence. It would be a marriage of pure convenience—but I have no present interest in any other kind of liaison."

"Well, now," Iris said, smiling victoriously.

"Well nothing!" Bink cried, conscious that his prior decision to stay clear of this matter was being abrogated. "You're both traitors to Xanth. I won't permit it."

"You won't permit it!" Iris laughed indelicately. "Who the hell do you think you are, you spell-less twerp?"

Obviously, her true attitude toward him had come out now that she had found another avenue for her ambition.

"Do not treat him lightly," Trent told her. "Bink is a Magician, in his fashion."

Bink felt a sudden, well-nigh overwhelming flood of gratitude for this word of support. He fought it off, knowing he could not afford to permit flattery or insult to sway him from what he knew was right. The Evil Magician could spin a web of illusion with mere words that rivaled anything the Sorceress could do with magic. "I'm no Magician; I'm just loyal to Xanth. To the proper King."

"To the senile has-been who exiled you?" Iris demanded. "He can't even raise a dust devil any more. He's sick now; he'll soon be dead anyway. That's why the time to act is now. The throne must go to a Magician."

"To a *good* Magician!" Bink retorted. "Not to an evil transformer, or a power-hungry, sluttish mistress . . ." He paused, tempted to end it there, but knew that wouldn't be entirely honest. "Of illusion."

"You dare address me thus?" Iris screamed, sounding much like a harpy. She was so angry that her image wavered into smoke. "Trent, change him into a stinkbug and step on him."

Trent shook his head, suppressing a smile. He obviously had no emotional attachment to the Sorceress, and shared a masculine appreciation for the insulting pause Bink had made. Iris had, just now, shown them all how ready she was to sell her illusion-enhanced body for power. "We operate under truce."

"Truce? Nonsense!" Her smoke now became a column of fire, signifying her righteous wrath. "You don't need him any more. Get rid of him."

Again, Bink saw how she would have treated him after he had helped her achieve power and she no longer needed him.

Trent was adamant. "If I were to break my word to him, Iris, how could you trust my word to you?"

That sobered her—and impressed Bink. There was a subtle but highly significant difference between these two magic-workers. Trent was a man, in the finest sense of the word.

Iris was hardly pleased. "I thought your truce was only until you got out of the wilderness."

"The wilderness is not defined solely by the jungle," Trent muttered.

"What?" she demanded.

"That truce would be worthless if I abridged its spirit thus suddenly," Trent said. "Bink and Chameleon and I will part company, and with luck we shall not meet again."

The man was being more than fair, and Bink knew he should accept the situation and depart—now. Instead, his stubbornness drove him toward disaster. "No," he said. "I can't just go away while you two plot to conquer Xanth."

"Now, Bink," Trent said reasonably. "I never deceived you about my ultimate objective. We always knew our purposes were divergent. Our truce covered only our interpersonal relation during the period of mutual hazard, not our long-range plans. I have pledges to fulfil, to my Mundane army, to Castle Roogna, and now to the Sorceress Iris. I am sorry you disapprove, for I want your approval very much, but the conquest of Xanth is and always was my mission. Now I ask you to part from me with what grace you can muster, for I have high respect for your motive, even though I feel the larger situation places you in error."

Again Bink felt the devastating allure of Trent's golden tongue. He could find no flaw in the reasoning. He had no chance to overcome the Magician magically, and was probably outclassed intellectually. But morally—he had to be right. "Your respect means nothing if you have no respect for the traditions and laws of Xanth."

"A most telling response, Bink. I do have respect for these things—yet the system seems to have gone astray, and must be corrected, lest disaster overtake us all."

"You talk of disaster from Mundania; I fear the disaster of the perversion of our culture. I must oppose you, in whatever way I can."

Trent seemed perplexed. "I don't believe you can oppose me, Bink. Whatever your strong magic is, it has never manifested tangibly. The moment you acted against me, I should have to transform you. I don't want to do that."

"You have to get within six feet," Bink said. "I could strike you down with a thrown rock."

"See?" Iris said. "He's within range now, Trent. Zap him!"

Yet the Magician desisted. "You actually wish to fight me, Bink? Directly, physically?"

"I don't wish to. I have to."

Trent sighed. "Then the only honorable thing to do is to terminate our truce with a formal duel. I suggest we define the locale of combat and the terms. Do you wish a second?"

"A second, a minute, an hour—whatever it takes," Bink said. He tried to quell the shaking he felt in his legs; he was afraid, and knew he was being a fool, yet he could not back down.

"I meant another person to back you up, to see that the terms are honored. Chameleon, perhaps."

"I'm with Bink!" Chameleon said immediately. She could comprehend only a fraction of the situation, but there was no question of her loyalty.

"Well, perhaps the concept of seconds is foreign here," Trent said. "Suppose we establish an area along the wilderness border, a mile deep into the forest and a mile across. One square mile, approximately, or as far as a man might walk in fifteen minutes. And it shall be until dark today. Neither of us shall leave this area until that time, and if the issue is undecided by then, we shall declare the contest null and separate in peace. Fair enough?"

The Evil Magician seemed so reasonable—and that made Bink unreasonable. "To the death!" he said—and immediately wished he hadn't. He knew the Magician would not kill him unless he were forced to; he would transform Bink into a tree or other harmless form of life and let him be. First there had been Justin Tree; now there would be Bink Tree. Perhaps people would come to rest under his shade, to have picnic lunches, to make love. Except that now it had to be death. He had a vision of a fallen tree.

"To the death," Trent said sadly. "Or surrender." Thus he neatly abated Bink's exaggeration without hurting his pride; he made it seem as if the Magician arranged the loophole for himself, not for Bink. How was it possible for a man so wrong to seem so right?

"All right," Bink said. "You go south, I'll go north, into the forest. In five minutes we'll stop and turn and start."

"Fair enough," the Magician agreed. He held out his hand again, and Bink shook it.

"You should get out of the duel zone," Bink told Chameleon.

"No! I'm with you," she insisted. She might be stupid, but she was loyal. Bink could no more blame her for that than he could blame Trent for pursuing power. Yet he had to dissuade her.

"It wouldn't be fair," he said, realizing that it would be futile to try to scare her by thought of the consequences. "Two against one. You have to go."

She was adamant. "I'm too dumb to go by myself."

Ouch! How true.

"Let her go with you," Trent said. "It really will make no difference."

And that seemed logical.

Bink and Chameleon set out, angling into the jungle to the northwest. Trent angled southwest. In moments the Magician was out of sight. "We'll have to figure out a plan of attack," Bink said. "Trent has been a perfect gentleman, but the truce is over, and he will use his power against us. We have to get him before he gets us."

"Yes."

"We'll have to collect stones and sticks, and maybe dig a pit for a deadfall."

"Yes."

"We have to prevent him from getting close enough to use his power of transformation."

"Yes."

"Don't just say yes!" he snapped. "This is serious business. Our lives are at stake."

"I'm sorry. I know I'm awful dumb right now."

Bink was immediately sorry. Of course she was stupid now—that was her curse. And he might be exaggerating the case; Trent might simply avoid the issue by departing, making no fight at all. Thus Bink would have made his stand, and have a moral victory—and have changed nothing. If so, Bink was the dumb one.

He turned to Chameleon to apologize—and rediscovered the fact that she was radiantly beautiful. She had seemed lovely before, in comparison with Fanchon and Dee, but now she was as he had first met her, as Wynne. Had it really been only a month ago? Now she was no stranger, though. "You're great just the way you are, Chameleon."

"But I can't help you plan. I can't do anything. You don't like stupid people."

"I like beautiful girls," he said. "And I like smart girls. But I don't trust the combination. I'd settle for an ordinary girl, except she'd get dull after a while. Sometimes I want to talk with someone intelligent, and sometimes I want to—" He broke off. Her mind was like that of a child; it really wasn't right to impose such concepts on her.

"What?" she asked, turning her eyes upon him. They had been black in her last beauty phase; now they were dark green. They could have been any color, and she would still be lovely.

Bink knew his chances of surviving the day were less than even, and his chances of saving Xanth worse than that. He was afraid—but he also had a heightened awareness of life right now. And of loyalty. And of beauty. Why hide what was suddenly in his conscious mind, however long it had developed subconsciously? "To make love," he concluded.

"That I can do," she said, her eyes brightening with comprehension. How well she understood, or on what level, Bink hesitated to ponder.

Then he was kissing her. It was wonderful.

"But, Bink," she said, when she had a chance. "I won't stay beautiful."

"That's the point," he said. "I like variety. I would have trouble living with a stupid girl all the time—but you aren't stupid all the time. Ugliness is no good for all the time—but you aren't ugly all the time either. You are—variety. And that is what I crave for the long-term relationship—and what no other girl can provide."

"I need a spell—" she said.

"No! You don't need any spell, Chameleon. You're fine just the way you are. I love you."

"Oh, Bink!" she said.

After that they forgot about the duel.

Reality intruded all too soon. "There you are!" Iris exclaimed, appearing over their makeshift bower. "Tut-tut! What have you two been doing?"

Chameleon hastily adjusted her dress. "Something you wouldn't understand," she said with purely female insight.

"No? It hardly matters. Sex is unimportant." The Sorceress put her hands to her mouth in a megaphone gesture. "Trent! They're over here."

Bink dived for her—and passed through her image cleanly. He took a tumble on the forest floor. "Silly boy," Iris said. "You can't touch me."

Now they heard the Evil Magician coming through the forest. Bink looked frantically for some weapon, but saw only the great boles of the trees. Sharp stones might have been used against these trees—therefore all stones had been magically eliminated. Some other area might have potential weapons, but not this highly competitive wilderness, this fringe near the farms that were always in need of more cleared land.

"I have ruined you!" Chameleon cried. "I knew I shouldn't have—"

Shouldn't have made love? True enough, in one sense. They had wasted vital time, loving instead of warring. Yet there might never be another chance. "It was worth it," Bink said. "We'll have to run."

They started to run. But the image of the Sorceress appeared in front of them. "Here, Trent!" she cried again. "Cut them off before they get away."

Bink realized that they could get nowhere so long as Iris dogged them. There

was no place they could hide, no surprise they could prepare, no strategic placement possible. Inevitably Trent would run them down.

Then his eye fell on an object Chameleon still carried. It was the hypnotic
gourd. If he could get Trent to look into that unwittingly—

Now the Magician came into sight. Bink gently took the gourd from Chameleon. "See if you can distract him until I get close enough to shove this in his
face," he said. He held the gourd behind his back. Iris probably did not realize its
significance, and she would be able to do nothing once Trent was out of commission.

"Iris," the Magician called loudly. "This is supposed to be a fair duel. If you
interfere again, I shall consider our understanding terminated."

The Sorceress started to react with anger, then thought better of it. She
vanished.

Trent stopped a dozen paces from Bink. "I regret this complication. Shall we
start over?" he inquired gravely.

"We'd better," Bink agreed. The man was so damned sure of himself, he could
give away any advantage. Maybe he wanted to wrap it up with a completely
clear conscience—such as it was. But by so doing, Trent had unknowingly saved
himself from possible disaster. Bink doubted he would have another opportunity
to use the gourd.

They separated again. Bink and Chameleon fled deeper into the forest—and
almost into the quivering arms of a tangle tree. "If only we could trick him into
running into that," Bink said—but found he didn't mean it. He had somehow
gotten himself into a duel he really did not want to win—and could not afford
to lose. He was as dumb as Chameleon—only somewhat more complicated
about it.

They spotted a noose-loop bush. The loops were up to eighteen inches in
diameter, but would contract suddenly to a quarter of that when any careless
animal put its head or limb through. Their fibers were so tight that only a knife
or specific counterspell could alleviate the bind. Even when separated from the
bush, the loops retained their potency for several days, gradually hardening in
place. Careless or unlucky animals could lose feet or lives, and no creature ever
bothered a noose-loop plant twice.

Chameleon shied away, but Bink paused. "It is possible to harvest and carry
such loops," he said. "At the North Village we use them to seal packages tight.
The trick is to touch them only on the outside. We can take some of these and
lay them on the ground where Trent has to step. Or we can throw them at him.
I doubt he can transform them once they're detached from the living plant. Can
you throw pretty well?"

"Yes."

He walked toward the bush—and spied another wilderness threat. "Look—a nest of ant lions!" he exclaimed. "If we can put them on his scent . . ."

Chameleon looked at the foot-long, lion-headed ants and shuddered. "Do we have to?"

"I wish we didn't," Bink said. "They wouldn't actually eat him; he'd transform them first. But they might keep him so busy that we could overpower him. If we don't stop him somehow, he's very likely to conquer Xanth."

"Would that be bad?"

It was just one of her stupid questions; in her smart phase, or even her normal phase, she would never have asked it. But it bothered him. Would the Evil Magician really be worse than the present King? He put the question aside. "It is not for us to decide. The Council of Elders will choose the next King. If the crown starts being available by conquest or conspiracy, we'll be back in the days of the Waves, and no one will be secure. The law of Xanth must determine the possession of the crown."

"Yes," she agreed. Bink had surprised himself with an excellent statement of the situation, but of course it was beyond her present understanding.

Still, the notion of throwing Trent to the ant lions bothered him, so he went on searching. In the depths of his mind a parallel search was manifesting, concerning the morality of the present government of Xanth. Suppose Trent were right about the necessity of reopening Xanth to migration from outside? According to the centaurs, the human population had slowly declined during the past century; where had those people gone? Were new part-human monsters being formed even now, by magically enabled interbreeding? The very thought was like being entangled in a noose-loop bush; its ramifications were appalling. Yet it seemed to be so. Trent, as King, would change that situation. Was the evil of the Waves worse than the alternative? Bink was unable to form a conclusion.

They came to a large river. Bink had forded this in his sphinx stage, hardly noticing it, but now it was a deadly barrier. Little ripples betrayed the presence of lurking predators, and eerie mists played about the surface. Bink flipped a clod of mud into the water, and it was intercepted, just before it struck, by a giant crablike claw. The rest of the monster never showed; Bink was unable to determine whether it was a mercrab or a super crayfish or merely a disembodied claw. But he was sure he did not want to swim here.

There were a few round stones at the edge. The river did not have the same reason to be wary of stones that the trees did, but it was best to be careful. Bink poked at them gingerly with his staff to be sure they weren't magic lures; fortunately they weren't. He poked experimentally at a pleasant nearby water lily, and the flower snapped three inches off the tip of his pole. His caution was justified.

"All right," he said when they had a fair reserve of stones. "We'll try to ambush him. We'll arrange noose-loops across his likely path of retreat, and cover them over with leaves, and you can throw your loops at him and I'll throw stones. He'll duck the stones and loops, but he'll have to watch us both to do it, while retreating, so he may step into a hidden loop. It'll bind on his foot, and he'll be vulnerable while he tries to get it off, and maybe we can score. We'll get some material from a blanket tree to throw over his head, so he can't see us and can't transform us, or we can hold the hypno-gourd in front of his face. He'll have to yield then."

"Yes," she said.

They set it up. Their covered loops extended from a hungry tangle tree to the ant-lion nest, and their ambush was in an invisible bush they discovered by sheer accident. That was about the only way such a bush could be discovered. Such plants were harmless, but could be a nuisance when stumbled into. When they hid behind it, they became invisible too, so long as they kept the bush between them and the viewer. They settled down to wait.

But Trent surprised them. While they had been setting up the trap, he had been circling around, orienting on their sounds. Now he came at them from the north. Chameleon, like most girls, had to answer calls of nature frequently, particularly when she was excited. She went behind a harmless mock-tentacle banyan tree, gave one little gasp of alarm, and disappeared. As Bink turned, he saw a lovely young winged deer bound out.

The battle was upon him! Bink charged the tree, stone in one hand, pole in the other. He hoped to knock out the Magician before Trent could throw his spell. But Trent wasn't there.

Had he jumped to a conclusion? Chameleon could have scared out a hiding doe—

"Now!" the Evil Magician cried from above. He was up in the tree. As Bink looked up, Trent gestured, not making a magical gesture, but bringing his hand down within six feet so as to cast the spell effectively. Bink jumped back—too late. He felt the tingle of transformation.

He rolled on the ground. In a moment he got his hands and feet under him—and discovered he was still a man. The spell had failed! He must have made it out of range in time after all, so that only one arm was in range, not his head.

He looked back at the tree—and gasped. The Evil Magician was tangled in the prickles of a candystripe rose bush.

"What happened?" Bink asked, forgetting his own peril for the moment.

"A branch of the tree got in the way," Trent said, shaking his head as if dazed. He must have had a hard fall. "The spell transformed it instead of you."

Bink would have laughed at this freak accident, but now he remembered his own position. So the Magician had tried to turn him into a rose bush. He hefted his rock. "Sorry," he apologized—and hurled it at the handsome head.

But it bounced off the tough shell of a purple tortoise. Trent had converted the rose to the armored animal and was hidden behind it.

Bink acted without thinking. He aimed the pole like a lance, ran halfway around the tortoise, and thrust it at the Magician. But the man dodged, and again Bink felt the tingle of enchantment.

His momentum carried him beyond his enemy. He was still a man. He retreated to the invisible bush, marveling at his escape. The spell had bounced, converting the tortoise to a werehornet. The insect buzzed up angrily, but decided on escape rather than attack.

Now Trent was hot on Bink's trail. The bush became a woman-headed serpent that slithered away with an exclamation of annoyance, and Bink was exposed again. He tried to run—but was caught a third time by the magic.

Beside him a yellow toad appeared. "What is this?" Trent demanded incredulously. "I struck a passing gnat instead of you. Three times my spell has missed you. My aim can't be *that* bad!"

Bink scrambled for his staff. Trent oriented on him again, and Bink knew he could neither get out of range nor bring his weapon to bear in time. He was finished, despite all his strategy.

But the winged deer charged from the side, threatening to bowl over the Magician. Trent heard her coming, and spun to focus on her. As she reached him she became a lovely iridescent butterfly, then a very pretty wyvern. "No problem there," Trent remarked. "She's good-looking in whatever form I put her, but my spells are registering perfectly."

The small winged dragon turned on him, hissing, and suddenly she was the winged doe again. "Scat!" Trent told her, clapping his hands. Startled, the deer bounded away. She was not overly bright.

Meanwhile, Bink had taken advantage of the distraction to retreat. But he had gone toward his own carefully fashioned trap, and now he did not know precisely where the noose loops lay hidden. If he tried to cross that line, he would either trap himself or give away its presence to Trent—assuming the Magician was not already aware of it.

Trent strode toward him. Bink was cornered, victim of his own machinations. He stood unmoving, knowing the Magician would turn on him the moment he tried to act. He cursed himself for not being more decisive, but he simply did not know what to do. He obviously was no duelist; he had been outmaneuvered and outmagicked from the outset of this contest. He should have left the Evil Magician alone—yet he still could not see how he could have stood by and yielded Xanth up without even token protest. This was that token.

"This time, no error," Trent said, stepping boldly toward Bink. "I know I can transform you, for I have done it many times before without difficulty. I must have been overhasty today." He stopped within range, while Bink stood still, not deigning to run again. Trent concentrated—and the magic smote Bink once more, powerfully.

A flock of funnelbirds manifested around Bink. Hooting derisively, they jetted away on their fixed wings.

"The very microbes surrounding you!" Trent exclaimed. "My spell bounced right off you—again. Now I *know* there is something strange."

"Maybe you just don't want to kill me," Bink said.

"I was not trying to kill you—only to transform you into something harmless, so that never again could you oppose me. I never kill without reason." The Magician pondered. "Something very strange here. I don't believe my talent is misfiring; something is opposing it. There has to be some counterspell operating. You have led a rather charmed life, you know; I had thought it was mere coincidence, but now—"

Trent considered, then snapped his fingers ringingly. "Your talent! Your magic talent. That's it. *You cannot be harmed by magic!*"

"But I've been hurt many times," Bink protested.

"Not by magic, I'll warrant. Your talent repels all magical threats."

"But many spells have affected me. You transformed me—"

"Only to help you—or to warn you. You may not have trusted my motives, but your magic knew the truth. I never intended to harm you before, and so my spells were permitted. Now that we are dueling and I am trying to change your status for the worse, my spells bounce. In this respect your magic is more powerful than mine—as certain prior signals have indicated indirectly."

Bink was amazed. "Then—then I have won. You cannot hurt me."

"Not necessarily so, Bink. My magic has brought yours to bay, and forced its unveiling, and thereby rendered it vulnerable." The Evil Magician drew his gleaming sword. "I have other talents than magic. Defend yourself—physically!"

Bink brought up his staff as Trent lunged. He barely parried the blade in time.

He was vulnerable—physically. Suddenly past confusions unraveled. He had never directly been harmed by magic. Embarrassed, humiliated, yes, especially in childhood. But it was evidently physical harm he was protected against. When he had run a race with another boy, and the boy had charged through trees and barriers to win, Bink had not suffered any physical damage, merely chagrin. And when he had chopped off his own finger, nonmagically, nothing had aided him there. Magic had healed that, but magic could not have made the injury. Similarly, he had been threatened by magic many times, and been terrified—but somehow had never had those threats materialize. Even when he had taken a lungful of Potipher's poison gas, he had been saved just in time. He had indeed led a charmed life—literally.

"Fascinating aspects to your magic," Trent said conversationally as he maneuvered for another opening. "Obviously it would be scant protection if its nature were widely known. So it arranges to conceal itself from discovery, by acting in subtle ways. Your escapes so often seemed fortuitous or coincidental." Yes, as when he escaped the Gap dragon. He had also been benefited by countermagic, coincidentally—as when he had been taken over by Donald the shade, enabling him to fly up out of the Gap safely.

"Your pride was never salvaged, merely your body," Trent continued, obviously taking his time about the fight while he worked out all the details, just in case. He was a meticulous man. "Maybe you suffered some discomfort, as in our entry into Xanth, whose purpose was to conceal the fact that nothing serious had happened to you. Rather than reveal itself, your talent allowed you to be exiled—because that was a legal or social matter, not really magical. Yet you were not hurt by the Shield—"

He had felt the tingle of the Shield as he dived through on his way out, and thought he had gotten safely through the opening. Now he knew he had taken the full force of the Shield—and survived. He could have walked through it at any time. But, had he known that, he might have done it—and given away his talent. So it had been concealed—from himself.

Yet now it had been revealed. And there was a flaw. "You were not hurt by the Shield either," Bink cried, striking hard with his staff.

"I was in direct contact with you when we entered," Trent said. "So was Chameleon. You were unconscious, but your talent still operated. To allow the two of us to die while you survived unscathed—that would have given it away. Or possibly a small field surrounds you, enabling you to protect those you touch. Or your talent looked ahead, and knew that if the magic of the Shield eliminated us at that time, you would be cast into the den of the kraken weed alone, and be unable to escape, and die there. You needed me and my power of transformation to survive the magical threats—so I was spared. And Chameleon, because you would not have worked with me if she had not done so. So we all survived, in order to promote your survival, and we never suspected the true cause. Similarly, your magic protected us all during our trek through the wilderness. I thought I needed you to protect me, but it was the other way around. My talent became a mere aspect of yours. When you were threatened by the wiggles and the invisible giant, you drew on my transformation of you to abate that threat, still without revealing . . ."

Trent shook his head, still parrying Bink's clumsy attacks easily. "Suddenly it becomes less amazing—and your talent more impressive. You are a Magician, with not merely the overt complex of talents but the ramifying aspects too. Magicians are not merely more powerfully talented people; our enchantments differ in quality as well as quantity, in ways seldom appreciated by normal citizens. You are on a par with Humfrey and Iris and myself. I'd really like to know your power's full nature and extent."

"So would I," Bink gasped. His efforts were winding him, without effect on the Magician. This was true frustration.

"But alas, it seems I cannot become King while a talent like that opposes me. I sincerely regret the necessity of sacrificing your life, and want you to know this was not my intent at the outset of this encounter. I would have much preferred to transform you harmlessly. But the sword is less versatile than magic; it can only injure or kill."

Bink remembered Herman the centaur, his head flying from his body. When Trent decided that killing was necessary—

Trent made a deft maneuver. Bink flung himself aside. The point of the sword touched his hand. Blood flowed; with a cry of pain, Bink dropped his staff. He could be hurt by Mundane means, obviously. Trent had aimed for that hand, testing, making absolutely sure.

This realization broke the partial paralysis that had limited the imagination of his defense. He was vulnerable—but on a straight man-to-man basis, he did have a chance. The awesome power of the Evil Magician had daunted him, but now, in effect, Trent was merely a man. He could be surprised.

As Trent set up for the finishing thrust, Bink moved with inspired competency. He ducked under the man's arm, caught it with his bloody hand, turned, bent his knees, and heaved. It was the throw that the soldier Crombie had taught him, useful for handling an attacker with a weapon.

But the Magician was alert. As Bink heaved, Trent stepped around, keeping on his feet. He wrenched his sword arm free, threw Bink back, and oriented for the killing thrust. "Very nice maneuver, Bink; unfortunately, they also know such tactics in Mundania."

Trent thrust with instant decision, and with killing force. Bink, off balance, unable to move out of the way, saw the terrible point driving straight at his face. He was done for this time!

The winged doe shot between them. The sword plunged into her torso, the point emerging from the other side, just shy of Bink's quivering nose.

"Bitch!" Trent yelled, though that was not the proper term for a female deer, winged or land-bound. He yanked free the bloody blade. "That strike was not meant for you!"

The doe fell, red blood spurting from her wound. She had been punctured through the belly. "I'll transform you into a jellyfish!" the Evil Magician continued in fury. "You'll smother to death on land."

"She's dying anyway," Bink said, feeling a sympathetic agony in his own gut. Such wounds were not immediately fatal, but they were terribly painful, and the result was the same in the long run. It was death by torture for Chameleon.

The omen! It had finally been completed. The chameleon had died suddenly. Or would die—

Bink launched himself at his enemy again, experiencing a vengeful rage he had never felt before. With his bare hands he would—

Trent stepped nimbly aside, cuffing Bink on the side of the neck with his left hand as he passed. Bink stumbled and fell, half conscious. Blind rage was no substitute for cool skill and experience. He saw Trent step up to him, raising the sword high in both hands for the final body-severing blow.

Bink shut his eyes, no longer able to resist. He had done everything he could, and lost. "Only kill her too—cleanly," he begged. "Do not let her suffer."

He waited with resignation. But the blow did not fall. Bink opened his eyes— and saw Trent putting his terrible sword away.

"I can't do it," the Magician said soberly.

The Sorceress Iris appeared. "What is this?" she demanded. "Have your guts turned to water? Dispatch them both and be done with it. Your kingdom awaits!"

"I don't want my kingdom this way," Trent told her. "Once I would have done it, but I have changed in twenty years, and in the past two weeks. I have learned the true history of Xanth, and I know too well the sorrow of untimely death. My honor came late to my life, but it grows stronger; it will not let me kill a man who has saved my life, and who is so loyal to his unworthy monarch that he sacrifices his life in defense of the one who has exiled him." He looked at the dying doe. "And I would never voluntarily kill the girl who, lacking the intelligence to be cunning, yields up her own welfare for the life of that man. This is true love, of the kind I once knew. I could not save mine, but I would not destroy that of another. The throne simply is not worth this moral price."

"Idiot!" Iris screamed. "It is your own life you are throwing away."

"Yes, I suppose I am," Trent said. "But this was the risk I took at the outset, when I determined to return to Xanth, and this is the way it must be. Better to die with honor than to live in dishonor, though a throne be served up as temptation. Perhaps it was not power I sought, but perfection of self." He kneeled beside the doe and touched her, and she was the human Chameleon again. Blood leaked from the terrible wound in her abdomen. "I cannot save her," he said sadly, "any more than I could cure my wife and child. I am no doctor. Any creature into which I might transform her would suffer similarly. She must have help—magic help."

The Magician looked up. "Iris, you can help. Project your image to the castle of the Good Magician Humfrey. Tell him what has happened here, and ask him for healing water. I believe the authorities of Xanth will help this innocent girl and spare this young man, whom they wrongly exiled."

"I'll do nothing of the sort!" the Sorceress screamed. "Come to your senses, man. You have the kingdom in your grasp."

Trent turned to Bink. "The Sorceress has not suffered the conversion that experience has brought me. She will not help. The lure of power has blinded her to all else—as it almost blinded me. You will have to go for help."

"Yes," Bink agreed. He could not look at the blood coming from Chameleon.

"I will staunch her wound as well as I can," Trent said. "I believe she will live for an hour. Do not take longer than that."

"No . . ." Bink agreed. If she died—

Suddenly Bink was a bird—a fancy-feathered, fire-winged phoenix, sure to be noticed, since it appeared in public only every five hundred years. He spread his pinions and took off into the sky. He rose high and circled, and in the distance to the east he saw the spire of the Good Magician's castle glinting magically. He was on his way.

Chapter 16

King

flying dragon appeared. "Pretty bird, I'm going to eat you up!" it said.

Bink sheered off, but the monster was before him again. "You can't escape!" it said. It opened its toothy mouth.

Was his mission of mercy to end here, so near success? Bink pumped his wings valiantly, climbing higher, hoping the heavier dragon could not achieve the same elevation. But his wounded wing—formerly the hand Trent's sword had cut—robbed him of full lifting power and balance, forcing him to rise with less velocity. The predator paralleled him without effort, staying between him and the far castle. "Give up, dumbo," it said. "You'll never make it."

Suddenly Bink caught on. Dragons did not speak like that. Not flying fire-breathers, anyway; they lacked both the cranial capacity and the coolness of brain to talk at all. They were simply too light and hot to be smart. This was no dragon—it was an illusion spawned by the Sorceress. She was still trying to stop him, hoping that if he disappeared and Chameleon died, Trent would resume his march on the throne. Trent would have done his best, and failed; realistically, he would continue toward his goal. Thus Iris could still achieve her dream of power through him. Naturally, she would never confess her own part in this mischief.

Bink would rather have dealt with a real dragon. The Sorceress's evil plot might work. Because he was a phoenix instead of a talking bird, he could not tell anyone other than the Good Magician what was happening; others would not have the capacity to understand. If he returned to Trent now, too much time would be lost—and in any event, Iris could stop him there, too. This was his own private battle, his duel with the Sorceress; he had to win it himself.

He changed course abruptly and angled directly into the dragon. If he had guessed wrong, he would light a fire in the belly of the fire-breather and lose all. But he passed right through it without resistance. Victory!

Iris shouted something most unladylike at him. What a fishwife she was when balked. But Bink ignored her and winged on.

A cloud formed before him. Uh-oh—a storm? He had to hurry.

But the cloud loomed rapidly larger. Blisters of black vapor boiled out of it, swirling funnels forming below. In moments the sheer mass of it blotted out the castle. Ugly dark satellite clouds scudded about it, menacing as the heads of goblins. A larger rotary pattern developed. The whole thing looked disconcertingly formidable.

There was no hope of rising above it. His injured wing was hurting, and the storm towered into the sky like a giant genie. Bolts of jagged lightning danced about, crackling loudly. There was the odor of metal burning. Deep in the roiling bowels of it were tangled colors and vague shapes of demonic visages. A magic tempest, obviously, girt with colored hail: the most devastating kind.

Bink dropped lower—and the cloud circulation tightened into a single descending gray tube. A super-tornado that would destroy him!

Then Bink almost fell out of the air with the shock of his realization. *He could not be harmed by magic!* This was a magic storm—therefore it could not touch him. He was being balked by a false threat.

Furthermore, there was no actual wind. This was another illusion. All he had to do was fly directly toward the castle, unswayed by optical effects. He shot straight into the cloud.

He was right again. The optical effects had been spectacular, but there was no actual storm, merely opacity and the suggestion of wetness on his feathers. Soon he would be through it, having called its bluff; then nothing could stop him from reaching the castle of the Good Magician.

But the grayness continued. How could he go to the castle when he couldn't see it? Iris couldn't fool him, but she could effectively blind him. Maybe he, personally, could not be harmed by magic—either real or illusory magic—but his talent did not seem to be concerned with the welfare of other people, no matter how Bink himself might feel about them. He would survive if Chameleon died. He might not enjoy that survival, but the technicality would have been honored.

Damn it, talent, he thought fiercely. *You'd better stop being concerned with technicalities and start being concerned with my larger welfare. I'll kill myself, physically, by Mundane means, if I find my life not worth living. I need Chameleon. So you can't save me at all if you let this hostile magic stop me from saving Chameleon. Then where will you be?*

The opacity continued. Apparently his talent was an unreasoning thing. And so, in the end, it was useless. Like a colored spot on a wall, it was magic without purpose.

He peered about, determined to fight it through himself. He had made it this far through life without any talent he had known about; he would have to make it similarly in the future. Somehow.

Had he been headed directly toward the castle? He thought so—but he could not be sure. He had been distracted by the developing cloud, trying to avoid it, and could have lost his bearings. Trent might better have transformed him into an unerring carrier pigeon. But that bird would not have been distinct enough to attract the attention of the Good Magician. Anyway, speculations on what he might have been were useless. He was what he was, and would have to prevail as he was. If he were now aimed wrong, he might never reach the castle —but he would keep trying.

He dropped down, seeking some landmark. But the cloud remained about him. He could not see a thing. If he went too low, he might crash into a tree. Had Iris won after all?

Then he emerged from the cloud floor. There was the castle. He zoomed toward it—and paused, dismayed again. This wasn't the residence of the Good Magician—this was Castle Roogna! He had become completely reversed, and flown across the wilderness to the west instead of eastward to the Good Magician. The Sorceress had surely known this, and kept up the blinding fog so that he would not discover his error until too late. How much precious time had he wasted? If he reversed course and flew straight to the proper castle now—assuming he could find it in the fog—could he possibly get help for Chameleon within the hour? Or would she be dead by the time help arrived, thanks to this delay?

He heard a faint snort. Immediately it was echoed by snorts all around him, coming from every direction. The base of the cloud dropped down to obscure his view again.

Something was funny here! He might not have paid any attention to the sound if there had not been such an obvious effort to mask its direction. Why should the Sorceress try to prevent him from landing at Castle Roogna? Was there healing water there, used to patch up zombies? Doubtful.

So the snort was important in some way. But what had caused it? There was no moat dragon at Roogna; zombies didn't snort very well anyway. Yet obviously something had made that sound—probably something all the way alive. Like a winged horse, or—

He caught on: this was not Castle Roogna but the castle of the Good Magician after all! The Sorceress had only made it look like Roogna, to turn him back. She was mistress of illusion—and he kept being deceived by the ramifications of her power. But the hippocampus of the moat had snorted, giving it away. He had been headed in the right direction after all, perhaps guided by his talent. His talent had always operated subtly; there was no reason for it to change now.

Bink headed for the remembered sound of the first snort, tuning out all others. Abruptly the fog dissipated. Apparently the Sorceress could not maintain her illusions too near the premises of the rival Magician, whose specialty was truth.

"I'll get you yet!" her voice cried from the air behind. Then she and all her effects were gone, and the sky was clear.

Bink circled the castle, which now had its proper aspect. He was shivering with reaction; how close he had come to losing his duel with the Sorceress! If he had turned back—

He found an open portal in an upper turret and angled through it. The phoenix was a powerful flier, with good control; he probably could have outdistanced a real dragon, even with his hurt wing.

It took a moment for his beady eyes to adjust to the gloom of the interior. He flapped from one room to another and finally located the Magician, poring over a massive tome. For an instant the little man reminded Bink of Trent in the Roogna library; both had serious interest in books. Had the two really been friends twenty years ago, or merely associates?

Humfrey looked up. "What are you doing here, Bink?" he inquired, surprised. He didn't seem to notice the form Bink was in.

Bink tried to talk, but could not. The phoenix was silent; its magic related to survival from fire, not to human discourse.

"Come over here by the mirror," Humfrey said, rising.

Bink came. As he approached, the magic mirror showed a scene. Evidently this mirror was a twin to the one he had broken, for he saw no cracks to indicate repair.

The picture was of the wilderness, Chameleon lying nude and lovely and bleeding despite a crude compact of leaves and moss on her abdomen. Before her stood Trent, sword drawn, as a wolf-headed man approached.

"Oh, I see," Humfrey said. "The Evil Magician has returned. Foolish of him; this time he won't be exiled, he'll be executed. Good thing you managed to warn me; he's a dangerous one. I see he stabbed the girl and transformed you, but you managed to get away. Good thing you had the sense to come here."

Bink tried to speak again, and failed again. He danced about anxiously.

"More to say? This way." The gnomelike Magician took down a book and opened it, setting it on top of his prior volume on the table. The pages were blank. "Speak," he said.

Bink tried yet again. No sound emerged, but he saw the words forming in neat script on the pages of the book:

Chameleon is dying! We must save her.

"Oh, of course," Humfrey agreed. "A few drops of healing water will take care of that. There'll be my fee, naturally. But first we'll have to deal with the Evil Magician, which means we'll have to detour to the North Village to pick up a stunner. No magic of mine can handle Trent!"

No! Trent is trying to save her! He's not—

Humfrey's brow wrinkled. "You are saying that the Evil Magician helped you?" he asked, surprised. "That is hard to believe, Bink."

As quickly as possible, Bink explained about Trent's conversion.

"Very well," Humfrey said with resignation. "I'll take your word that he is acting in your interest in this case. But I suspect you're a bit naive, and now I don't know who's going to pay my fee. The Evil Magician is very likely to get away anyway, while we detour. But we have to try to catch him for a fair trial. He has broken the law of Xanth, and must be dealt with immediately. It would profit us nothing if we saved Chameleon while leaving Xanth in peril from the conquering lust of the transformer."

There was so much more Bink wanted to explain, but Humfrey gave him no chance. And of course he probably was being naive; once the Evil Magician had time to reconsider, he would probably revert to form. He was a serious threat to Xanth. Yet Bink knew that Trent had won the duel, and so Bink, as loser, should no longer interfere in the Magician's affairs. This was a devious but increasingly strong conviction. He hoped Trent managed to escape.

Humfrey led him down to the castle cellar, where he tapped some fluid from a barrel. He sprinkled a drop on Bink's wing, and it was instantly sound again. The rest he put in a small bottle, which he tucked into his vest pocket.

Now the Good Magician went to a closet and hauled out a plush carpet. He unrolled it, then sat cross-legged on it. "Well, get on, birdbrain!" he snapped. "You'll get lost out there by yourself, especially with Iris fooling around with the weather reports."

Bink, perplexed, stepped onto the carpet and faced the Magician. Then the rug lifted. Startled, Bink spread his wings and dug his feet deeply into the material, hanging on. It was a flying carpet.

The thing angled neatly out through a portal, then looped high up into the sky. It leveled, then accelerated. Bink, facing backward, had to furl his wings tightly and almost puncture the fabric with his claws to keep from being dislodged by the wind. He saw the castle shrink in the distance.

"Just an artifact I accepted in lieu of service some years back," Humfrey explained conversationally. He sneezed. "Never had much use for it; just collects dust. But I suppose this is an emergency." He peered at Bink, shaking his head dubiously. "You claim the Evil Magician transformed you to help you get to me quickly? Just nod your beak once for yes, twice for no."

Bink nodded once.

"But he did stab Chameleon?"

Another nod. But that was not the whole story.

"He didn't really mean to stab her? Because he was really trying to kill you, and she got in the way?"

Bink had to nod yes again. What a damning statement.

Humfrey shook his head. "It's easy to be sorry after a mistake has been made. Yet when I knew him, before his exile, he was not a man without compassion. Still, I doubt he can ever rest until he achieves his ambition—and while he remains alive and in Xanth, we can never be certain he won't. It is a difficult case. There will have to be a meticulous investigation of the facts."

Such an investigation would be the death of Trent. The old King would be determined to abolish this major threat to his declining power.

"And Trent knows what is likely to happen to him when the authorities get there, if they catch him?"

Trent surely did. Bink nodded yes again.

"And you—do you want him dead?"

Bink shook his head vehemently, no.

"Or exiled again?"

Bink had to think a moment. Then he shook his head again.

"Of course; you need him to transform you back into human form. That perhaps gives him some bargaining leverage. They might spare his life in exchange for such services. But after that, it seems likely to be exile for him—or blindness."

Blindness! But then Bink comprehended the horrible logic of it. Blind, Trent could not transform anyone; he had to see his subjects. But what a terrible fate.

"I see you don't like that notion either. Yet there are harsh realities to weigh." Humfrey pondered. "It will be difficult enough to save *your* life, since you also are an illegal immigrant. But perhaps I have a wrinkle." He frowned. "I'm really sorry to see Trent get into this scrape; he's a truly great Magician, and we've always gotten along, not interfering in each other's business. But the welfare of Xanth comes first." He smiled briefly. "After my fee, of course."

Bink didn't see much humor in it.

"Well, it will soon be out of our hands, fortunately. What will be will be."

After that he was silent. Bink watched the clouds, real ones this time; they loomed up larger and darker as the rug flew northward. Now the carpet was over the Gap, making Bink feel less secure despite his wings; it was a long way down. When the rug passed through a cloud, it dipped alarmingly; it seemed there were internal downdrafts. But Humfrey rode with seeming equanimity, eyes closed, deep in thought.

It got worse. The carpet, possessing no intelligence, zoomed straight for its preprogrammed destination, not trying to avoid the cloud banks. The clouds formed into towering mountains and awesomely deep valleys, and the drafts got worse. No illusion, this building storm; though it lacked the colors and menacing swirls of Iris's illusion-cloud, in its somber way it was just as threatening.

Then the rug dropped through the fog and came out below. There was the North Village!

The windows of the King's palace were draped in black. "I think it has happened," Humfrey remarked as they landed before the palace gate.

A village Elder came out to meet them. "Magician!" he cried. "We were about to send for you. The King is dead!"

"Well, you'd better choose his successor, then," Humfrey said acidly.

"There is no one—except you," the Elder replied.

"Lamebrain! That's no recommendation," Humfrey snapped. "What would I want with the throne? It's a big boring job that would seriously interfere with my studies."

The Elder stood his ground. "Unless you can show us another qualified Magician, the law requires that you accept."

"Well, the law can go—" Humfrey paused. "We have more pressing business. Who is caretaker during the interim?"

"Roland. He is seeing to the funeral."

Bink jumped. His father! But he knew immediately that his father would be scrupulous in avoiding any possible conflict of interest; better not even to tell him Bink was back in Xanth.

Humfrey glanced at Bink, seeming to have the same notion. "Well, I think I know just the sucker for the job," the Good Magician said. "But he has a certain technical problem to surmount first."

Bink suffered an exceedingly uncomfortable shiver of premonition. *Not me!* he tried to say, but still could not speak. *I'm no Magician, really. I know nothing of kingship. All I want to do is save Chameleon. And let Trent get away, too.*

"But first we have to settle a couple of other matters," Humfrey continued. "The Evil Magician Trent, the transformer, is back in Xanth, and a girl is dying. If we move fast, we may catch them both before it is too late."

"Trent!" The Elder was shocked. "What a time for him to show up." He ran into the palace.

Very soon they had assembled a war party. The village travel-conjurer was given the precise location, and he started popping people through.

First to go was Roland himself. With luck he would catch the Evil Magician by surprise and stun him in place, nullifying his magic. Then the others could proceed safely. Next the Good Magician went, with his vial of healing water, to save Chameleon—if she still lived.

Bink realized that if this plan was successful, Trent would never have another chance to transform anyone. If they unknowingly executed the Evil Magician before Bink was transformed, he would remain forever a phoenix. Chameleon would be alone, although well. And his father would be responsible. Was there no way out of this predicament?

Well, the plan might fail. Trent could transform Roland and Humfrey. Then Bink himself might recover his human form, but Chameleon would die. That was no good either. Maybe Trent would have escaped before Roland arrived. Then Chameleon would be cured, and Trent would survive—but Bink would remain a bird.

No matter which way it worked out, someone dear to Bink would be sacrificed. Unless Humfrey somehow managed things to make everything come out all right. Yet how could he?

One by one the Elders disappeared. Then it was Bink's turn. The conjurer gestured—

The first thing Bink saw was the body of the wolf-headed man. The creature had evidently charged, and been dispatched by Trent's singing sword. Elsewhere were a number of caterpillars that had not been here before. Trent himself stood frozen, concentrating as though in the process of casting a spell. And Chameleon—

Bink flew to her gladly. She was well! The terrible wound was gone, and she was standing, looking bewildered.

"This is Bink," Humfrey told her. "He flew to fetch help for you. Just in time, too."

"Oh, Bink!" she cried, picking him up and trying to hug him to her bare torso. Bink, as a bird with delicate plumage, did not find this as delightful as he might have in his natural form. "Change back."

"I am afraid that only the transformer can change him back," Humfrey said. "And the transformer must first stand trial."

And what would be the result of that trial? Why hadn't Trent escaped when he had the chance?

The proceedings were swift and efficient. The Elders put questions to the frozen Magician, who of course could not answer or argue his own case. Humfrey had the travel-conjurer fetch the magic mirror—no, it was Munly, the master of ceremonies at Bink's hearing, who was himself an Elder. Bink's bird-brain was letting him get confused. Munly used his talent to conjure this small object directly to his hand from the Good Magician's castle. He held it up so that all could see the images forming within it.

In the mirror were reflected scenes from the trio's travels in Xanth. Gradually the story came out, though it did not reveal Bink's talent. It showed how the three had helped one another to survive in the wilderness; how they had stayed at Castle Roogna—there was a general exclamation about that, for no one had known this old, famous, semimythical artifact remained intact. How they had fought the wiggle swarm—and that produced another reaction! How they had finally dueled. How the Sorceress Iris had mixed in. And how—Bink felt a fury of embarrassment—he had made love to Chameleon. The mirror was merciless.

The whole sequence was clearly damning to Trent, for there were no words. *But it's not really like that,* Bink tried to cry. *He's a fine man. In many ways his rationale makes sense. If he had not spared me and Chameleon, he could have conquered Xanth.*

The picture froze on the final sequence of the duel: Trent wounding Bink, making ready to strike the final blow—and halting. *See—he spared me. He is not evil. Not any more. He is not evil!*

But no one heard him. The assembled Elders looked at one another, nodding gravely. Bink's father, Roland, was among them, and the family friend Munly, saying nothing.

Then the mirror continued, showing what had happened after Bink flew away. The monsters of the wilderness, smelling fresh blood, had converged. Trent barely had time to bandage Chameleon before these threats became pressing. He had stood before her, sword in hand, bluffing the creatures back—and transforming those who attacked anyway to caterpillars. Two wolf-heads had charged together, jaws gaping wide, slavering; one became a caterpillar while the other was cut down by the sword. Trent had killed only as necessary.

He could have run, even then, Bink cried silently. *He could have let Chameleon be taken by the monsters. He could have escaped into the magic jungle. You would never have caught him—until he caught you. He is a good man now.* But he knew there was no way he could plead this good man's case. Chameleon, of course, was too stupid to do it, and Humfrey didn't know the whole story.

At last the mirror showed the arrival of Roland, as strong and handsome in his fashion as the Evil Magician, and a few years older. He had landed facing away from Trent—and directly in front of an advancing two-headed serpent, each head a yard long. Roland, searching the wilderness before him, nervous about a nearby tangle tree, had seen neither Magician nor serpent behind him.

In the mirror, Trent charged, running at the tail of the monster, grabbing it with his bare hands, causing it to whirl on him furiously. Both heads had struck —and the thing had abruptly become another caterpillar. A two-headed caterpillar.

Roland whirled. For an instant the two men looked into each other's eyes, their deadly talents equivalent at this range. They seemed very similar to each other. Then Roland squinted, and Trent froze in place. The stun had scored before the transformation.

Or had it? Trent never even tried to resist, Bink thought futilely. *He could have transformed my father instead of the serpent—or simply let the serpent strike.*

"Elders, have you seen enough?" Humfrey inquired gently.

If I could have the throne of Xanth at the expense of Trent's life, I would not take it, Bink thought savagely. The trial had been a farce; they had never let Trent speak for himself, to present his eloquent thesis of the damage magic was doing to the human population of Xanth, or of the threat of a future attack from Mundania. Were they going to dispose of him the same way they had exiled Bink? Thoughtlessly, by rote law, regardless of the meaning behind the facts?

The Elders exchanged glances gravely. Each nodded slowly, affirmatively.

At least let him talk! Bink cried mutely.

"Then it would be best to release the spell," Humfrey said. "He must be free of magic for the denouement, as is our custom."

Thank God!

Roland snapped his fingers. Trent moved. "Thank you, honorable Elders of Xanth," he said politely. "You have granted me a fair presentation, and I stand ready to accept your judgment."

Trent wasn't even defending himself. This horrendously partial, silent investigation, obviously a mere ritual to justify a decision privately arrived at—how could the Evil Magician lend credibility to that?

"We find you guilty of violating exile," Roland said. "For this the set penalty is death. But we are in a unique situation, and you have changed substantially since we knew you. You always had courage, intelligence, and strong magic; now you are also possessed of loyalty, honor, and mercy. I am not unmindful that you spared the life of my son, who had foolishly challenged you, and that you protected his chosen one from the ravages of wild beasts. You have some guilt in these matters, but you expiated it. We therefore waive the set penalty and grant you leave to remain in Xanth, under two conditions."

They were not going to kill Trent. Bink almost danced for joy. But immediately he realized that there would still be stringent restrictions, to prevent Trent from ever again aspiring to the throne. Humfrey had mentioned blinding him, so that he would be unable to perform his magic. Bink had some idea of what a life without magic would be like. Trent would be forced to assume some menial occupation, working out his days in ignobility. The Elders were generally old, but not necessarily gentle; no smart citizen ever crossed them twice.

Trent bowed his head. "I thank you sincerely, Elders. I accept your conditions. What are they?"

But there was so much more to be said! To treat this fine man as a common criminal, to force his agreement to this terrible retribution—and Trent was not even protesting.

"First," Roland said, "that you marry."

Trent looked up, startled. "I can understand a requirement that I reverse all prior transformations and desist from any future exercise of my talent—but what has marriage to do with it?"

"You are presuming," Roland said grimly. And Bink thought: *Trent hasn't caught on. They have no need to make restrictions—if they blind him. He will be helpless.*

"I apologize, Elder. I will marry. What is the other condition?"

Now it comes! Bink wished he could blot out the sounds, as if by failing to hear the words of the sentence he could alleviate it. But that was not his type of magic talent.

"That you accept the throne of Xanth."

Bink's beak fell open. So did Chameleon's mouth. Trent stood as if stun-frozen again.

Then Roland bent one knee and slowly dropped to the ground. The other Elders followed, silently.

"The King, you see, is dead," Humfrey explained. "It is essential to have a good man and strong Magician in the office, one who has the demeanor of command coupled with restraint and perspective, yet who will muster savagery when necessary in the defense of Xanth. As in the event of a wiggle invasion or similar threat. One who may also provide a potential heir, so that Xanth is not again caught in the difficult situation just past. It is not necessary to like such a monarch, but we must have him. I obviously do not qualify, for I could hardly bring myself to devote the required attention to the details of governance; the Sorceress Iris would be unsuitable even if she were not female, because of her lack of restraint; and the only other person of Magician caliber has neither personality nor talent appropriate to the needs of the crown. Therefore, Xanth needs you, Magician. You can not refuse." And Humfrey, too, bent his knee.

The Evil Magician, evil no longer, bowed his head in mute acceptance. He had conquered Xanth after all.

* * *

The ceremony of coronation was splendid. The centaur contingent marched with dazzling precision, and from all over Xanth people and intelligent beasts came to attend. Magician Trent, henceforth the Transformer King, took both crown and bride together, and both were radiant.

There were of course some sly remarks at the fringe of the spectator crowd, but most citizens agreed that the King had chosen wisely. "If she's too old to bear an heir, they can adopt a Magician-caliber boy." "After all, he's the only one who can control her, and he'll never suffer from lack of variety." "And it eliminates the last real threat to the kingdom." They were not yet aware of the other formidable external and internal threats.

Bink, restored to his natural form, stood alone, contemplating the place where Justin Tree once stood. He was glad for Trent, and certain the man would make a fine King. Yet he suffered also from a certain anticlimactic disappointment. What would he, Bink, do now?

Three youths passed, one middle-aged. Zink, Jama, and Potipher. They were chastened, their eyes downcast. They knew that the days of wild nuisance were over; with the new King in power, they would have to behave—or else be transformed.

Then two centaurs trotted up. "So glad to see you, Bink!" Cherie exclaimed. "Isn't it wonderful you weren't exiled after all!" She nudged her companion. "Isn't it, Chester?"

Chester forced his face into a tortured smile. "Yeah, sure," he mumbled.

"You must come and visit us," Cherie continued brightly. "Chester speaks so often of you."

Chester made a little throttling motion with his two powerful hands. "Yeah, sure," he repeated, more brightly.

Bink changed the subject. "Did you know, I met Herman the Hermit in the wilderness," he said. "He died a hero. He used his magic—" Bink paused, remembering that the centaurs regarded magic in a centaur as obscene. That would probably change, once Trent publicized the knowledge gained from the Castle Roogna archives. "He organized the campaign that wiped out the wiggle swarm before it infested all of Xanth. I hope Herman's name will be honored among your kind in future."

Surprisingly, Chester smiled. "Herman was my uncle," he said. "He was a great character. The colts used to kid me about his exile. Now he's a hero, you say?"

Cherie's mouth tightened. "We don't discuss obscenity in the presence of a filly," she warned him. "Come on."

Chester had to accompany her. But he looked back briefly. "Yeah, sure," he said to Bink. "You come see us real soon. Tell us all about what Uncle Herman did to save Xanth."

They were gone. Suddenly Bink felt very good. Chester was the last creature he would have expected to have something in common with, but he was glad it had happened. Bink knew all about the frustration of getting teased about some supposed failing. And he did want to tell an appreciative audience about Herman the magic Hermit centaur.

Now Sabrina approached him. She was as lovely as he had ever seen her. "Bink, I'm sorry about what happened before," she said. "But now that everything is cleared up . . ."

She was like Chameleon in her beauty stage, and she was intelligent, too. A fit bride for almost any man. But Bink knew her now, too well. His talent had stopped him from marrying her—by keeping itself secret. Smart talent.

He glanced about—and spied the new bodyguard Trent had taken, on Bink's recommendation. The man who could spot anything, including danger, before it developed. The soldier was now resplendent in his imperial uniform, and impressive of demeanor. "Crombie!" Bink called.

Crombie strode over. "Hello, Bink. I'm on duty now, so I can't stay to chat. Is something the matter?"

"I just wanted to introduce you to this lovely lady, Sabrina," Bink said. "She does a very nice holograph in air." He turned to Sabrina. "Crombie is a good man and able soldier, favored by the King, but he doesn't quite trust women. I think he's just never met the right one. I believe you two should get to know each other better."

"But I thought—" she began.

Crombie was looking at her with a certain cynical interest, and she returned the glance. He was observing her physical charms, which were excellent; she was pondering his position at the palace, which was also excellent. Bink wasn't sure whether he had just done a beautiful thing or dropped a bagful of cherry bombs into the hole of a privy. Time would tell.

"Good-bye, Sabrina," Bink said, and turned away.

King Trent summoned Bink to a royal audience. "Sorry about the delay in getting back to you," he said when they were alone. "There were some necessary preliminaries."

"The coronation. The marriage," Bink agreed.

"Those too. But mainly a certain emotional readjustment. The crown landed on my head rather suddenly, as you know."

Bink knew. "If I may ask, Your Majesty—"

"Why I did not desert Chameleon and flee into the wilderness? For you alone, Bink, I will make an answer. Setting aside the moral considerations—which I did not—I performed a calculation that in Mundania is called figuring the odds. When you took flight for the castle of the Good Magician, I judged your chances of success to be about three to one in your favor. Had you failed, I would have been safe anyway; there was no point in deserting Chameleon. I knew Xanth stood in need of a new King, for the Storm King by all accounts was failing rapidly. The chances against the Elders finding any Magician more competent for the position than I were also about three to one. And so on. Altogether, my chances of obtaining the throne by sitting tight were nine in sixteen, with only a three-in-sixteen chance of execution. These were better odds than survival alone in the wilderness, which I would rate at one chance in two. Understand?"

Bink shook his head. "Those figures—I don't see—"

"Just take my word that it was a practical decision, a calculated risk. Humfrey was my friend; I was sure he would not betray me. He knew I had figured the odds—but it didn't make any difference, because that is the kind of schemer Xanth needs in a King, and he knew it. So he went along. Not that I didn't have some serious worries at the time of the trial; Roland certainly made me sweat."

"Me too," Bink agreed.

"But had the odds been otherwise, I would still have acted as I did." Trent frowned. "And I charge you not to embarrass me by revealing that weakness to the public. They don't want a King who is unduly swayed by personal considerations."

"I won't tell," Bink said, though privately he thought it was not much of a failing. After all, it was Chameleon he had saved.

"And now to business," the King said briskly. "I shall of course grant you and Chameleon royal dispensation to remain in Xanth without penalty for your violations of exile. No, this has nothing to do with your father; I never even realized you were the son of Roland until I saw him again and recognized the family resemblance; he never said a word about you. Fine avoidance of conflict of interest there; Roland will be an important man in the new administration, I assure you. But that's beside the point. There will not be any more exiles for anyone, or restrictions on immigration from Mundania, unless there is violence connected. Of course, this means you are released from having to demonstrate your magic talent. In all Xanth, only you and I comprehend its specific nature. Chameleon was present at the discovery, but was not in condition to assimilate it. Humfrey knows only that you have Magician-class magic. So it will remain our secret."

"Oh, I don't mind—"

"You don't quite understand, Bink. It is important that the precise nature of your talent remain secret. That is its nature; it must be a private thing. To reveal it is to vitiate it. That is why it protects itself so carefully from discovery. Probably I was permitted to learn of it only to help protect it from others, and that I intend to do. No one else will know."

"Yes, but—"

"I see you still don't follow. Your talent is remarkable and subtle. It is in its totality a thing of Magician rank, equivalent to any magic in Xanth. All other citizens, whether of the spot-on-wall variety or of Magician class, are vulnerable to those types of magic they don't themselves practice. Iris can be transformed, I can be stunned, Humfrey can be harassed by illusion—you get the point. Only you are fundamentally secure from all other forms of magic. You can be fooled or shamed or grossly inconvenienced, but never actually physically hurt. That is exceedingly broad protection."

"Yes, but—"

"In fact, we may never know the ultimate limits of it. Consider the manner in which you reentered Xanth—without revealing your talent to anyone who would tell. Our entire adventure may be no more than the manifestation of one facet of your talent. Chameleon and I may merely have been tools to convey you back into Xanth safely. By yourself, you might have been trapped in Castle Roogna, or run afoul of the wiggles. So I was there to smooth your way. It may even have protected you from my Mundane sword, by bringing Chameleon in to take the killing thrust. Because, you see, I had discovered your talent in large part through my own magic. Through its effect on my magic. Because I am a full Magician, it could not balk me completely, as it might a lesser power. But still it operated to protect you; it could not completely thwart me—I was able to wound you—so it joined me, acting to alleviate my quarrel with you by making me King in a way you could accept. Maybe it was your talent that changed my mind and prevented me from killing you. Hence my reasoning that it was your talent's decision that I be allowed to ascertain its nature—for this knowledge has, as you see, profoundly affected my attitude toward you and your personal safety."

He paused, but Bink did not comment. This was quite a concept to digest in one lump. He had thought his talent was limited, not affecting those he cared for, but it seemed he had underestimated it.

"So you see," Trent continued, "my throne may merely be the most convenient agency for the promotion of your welfare. Perhaps your entire exile, and the death of the Storm King at this time, are all part of that magical scheme. Your exile brought me into Xanth—without my army, in your company. I certainly am not going to gamble that mere coincidence brought me to this pass; your talent makes most sophisticated use of coincidence. I don't want to go against you, and perhaps sicken and die the way my predecessor did, after he acted against your interest. No, Bink—I wouldn't want to be your enemy even if I weren't already your friend. So I am becoming a conscious agent for the preservation of your secret and the promotion of your welfare in the best way I am able. Knowing how you feel about Xanth, I shall try to be the best possible

King, ushering in a new Golden Age, so that you never suffer any direct or indirect threats through my mismanagement. Now do you understand?"

Bink nodded. "I guess I do, Your Majesty."

Trent stood up, clapping him heartily on the back. "Good! All had better be well!" He paused, thinking of something else. "Have you decided on an occupation yet, Bink? I can offer you anything short of the crown itself—though even that may be in your future if—"

"No!" Bink exclaimed. Then he had to backtrack, seeing Trent's broad grin. "I mean yes, I thought of a job. I—you said once—" Bink hesitated, suddenly awkward.

"You don't seem to have listened very well. What you want, you will get—if it is within my present power. But my talent is transformation, not divination. You must speak. Out with it!"

"Well, in the wilderness, when we were waiting for Chameleon to—you know, just before the wiggles. We talked about the mystery of—"

Trent raised one royal hand. "Say no more. I hereby appoint you, Bink of the North Village, Official Researcher of Xanth. Any mysteries of magic shall be your responsibility; you shall probe wherever required until they are fathomed to your satisfaction, and turn in your reports directly to me for inclusion in the royal archives. Your secret talent makes you uniquely qualified to explore the most forbidding recesses of Xanth, for the anonymous Magician needs no bodyguard. Those recesses are long overdue for discovery. Your first assignment shall be to discover the true source of the magic of Xanth."

"I—uh, thank you, Your Majesty," Bink said gratefully. "I think I like that job much better than being King."

"Perhaps you appreciate how much that gratifies me," Trent said with a smile. "Now let's go see the girls."

The travel conjurer moved them both. Abruptly they stood at the front portal of Castle Roogna.

The drawbridge had been repaired, and now gleamed in brass and polished timbers. The moat was clean and full of water, now stocked with monsters of the finest breeds. The teeth of the portcullis glittered. Bright pennants fluttered from the highest turrets. This was a castle restored to full splendor.

Bink peered at something he thought he saw around to the side. Was it a small graveyard? Something moved there, white as a bone, with a trailing bandage. *Oh, no!*

Then the ground opened up. With a final cheery wave, the zombie sank into its resting place.

"Sleep in peace," Trent murmured. "I have kept my promise."

And if he had not, would the zombies have marched out of the wilderness to compel performance? That was one mystery Bink did not intend to explore.

They entered Roogna. All six ghosts greeted them in the front hall, every one in full human shape. Milly quickly popped off to notify the Queen of the King's arrival.

Iris and Chameleon swept up together, wearing castle tunics and slippers. The Sorceress was in her natural form, but so neatly garbed and coiffed that she was not unattractive, and Chameleon was almost back to her "center" stage, average in both appearance and intellect.

The Queen made no pretense of affection for Trent; it had been a marriage of convenience, as anticipated. But her pleasure in the position and her excitement about the castle were obviously genuine.

"This place is marvelous!" Iris exclaimed. "Chameleon has been showing me around, and the ghosts instructed our toilettes. All the room and grandeur I ever wanted—and it's all real. And it wants so much to please—I know I'm going to love it here."

"That's good," Trent said gravely. "Now put on your pretty face; we are entertaining company."

The middle-aged woman was instantly replaced by a stunningly smooth and buxom young woman with a low décolletage. "I just didn't want to embarrass Chameleon—you know, in her 'average' phase."

"You cannot embarrass her in any phase. Now apologize to Bink."

Iris made a breathtaking curtsy to Bink. She was ready to do anything to remain Queen—and human. Trent could make her into a warty toad—or he could make her into the very figure she now resembled. He could probably make her young enough to bear a child, the heir to the throne. Trent was the master, and Iris seemed to lack even the inclination to question this. "I'm sorry, Bink, I really am. I just got carried away there during the duel, and after. I didn't know you were going to fetch the Elders, to make Trent King."

Bink hadn't known that either. "Forget it, Your Majesty," he said uncomfortably. He looked at Chameleon, so close now to Dee, the girl he had liked from the outset despite Crombie's dire warnings. A fit of shyness overcame him.

"Go ahead, get it over with," Trent muttered in his ear. "She's smart enough now."

Bink thought about how much of his adventure had centered around Chameleon's quest for a spell to make her normal—when she really was quite satisfactory, and even somewhat challenging, as she was. How many people similarly spent their lives searching for their own spells—some gratuitous benefit such as a silver tree or political power or undeserved acclaim—when all they really needed was to be satisfied with what they already had? Sometimes what they had was better than what they thought they wanted. Chameleon had thought she wanted to be normal; Trent had thought he wanted armed conquest; and Bink himself had thought he wanted a demonstrable magic talent. Everyone thought he wanted something. But Bink's real quest, at the end, had been to preserve Chameleon and Trent and himself as they were, and to make Xanth accept them that way.

He had not wanted to take advantage of Chameleon in her stupid phase. He wanted to be sure she understood the full implications, before he—before he—

Something tickled his nose. Embarrassingly, he sneezed.

Iris nudged Chameleon with her elbow.

"Yes, of course I'll marry you, Bink," Chameleon said.

Trent guffawed. Then Bink was kissing her—his ordinary, extraordinary girl. She had found her spell, all right; she had cast it over him. It was the same as Crombie's curse—love.

And at last Bink understood the meaning of his omen: he was the hawk who had carried away Chameleon. She would never get free.

The Source of Magic

Contents

Chapter 1

Closet Skeleton

The magic-sniffer ambled toward Bink, its long limber snout snuffling industriously. When the creature reached him it went into a frenzy of enthusiasm, snorting out flutelike notes, wagging its bushy tail, and prancing in a circle.

"Sure, I like you too, Sniffer!" Bink said, squatting to embrace it. The creature's snout kissed his nose wetly. "You were one of the first to believe in my magic, when—"

Bink paused, for the creature was acting strangely. It had stopped frisking and become subdued, almost frightened. "What's the matter, little friend?" Bink asked, concerned. "Did I say something to hurt your feelings? I apologize!"

But the sniffer curled its tail between its legs and slunk away. Bink stared after it, chagrined. It was almost as if the magic had been turned off, causing the thing to lose its function. But Bink's talent, like all others, was inherent; it could not dissipate while he lived. Something else must have frightened the sniffer.

Bink looked about, feeling uneasy. To the east was the Castle Roogna orchard, whose trees bore all manner of exotic fruit, vegetables, and sundry artifacts like cherry bombs and doorknobs. To the south was the untamed wilderness of Xanth. Bink remembered how that jungle had herded him and his companions here, seeming so menacing, way back when. Today the trees were basically friendly; they had only wanted a Magician to stay and make Castle Roogna great again. King Trent had done that. Now the considerable power of this region exerted itself for the benefit of the kingdom. Everything seemed to be in order.

Well, on with his business. There was to be a ball tonight, and his shoes were badly worn. He proceeded to the edge of the orchard where a stray shoe-tree had rooted. Shoes liked to move about, and often planted themselves in out-of-the-way places.

This one had several ripe shoes. Bink inspected individual ones without plucking them, until he was sure he had found a pair that fit him. Then he twisted them off, shook out the seeds, and put them carefully on his feet. They were quite comfortable, and looked nice because they were fresh.

He started back, walking with exaggerated motion to break in the shoes without scuffing them, his mind still nagged by the episode with the magic-sniffer. Was it an omen? Omens always came true, here in the Land of Xanth, but it was seldom possible to understand them properly until too late. Was something bad going to happen to him? That really seemed unlikely; Bink knew it was no exaggeration to assume that serious evil would have to fall on all Xanth before Bink himself was harmed. So it must be a misreading. The magic-sniffer had merely suffered a fit of indigestion, and had to scoot off.

Soon Bink was within sight of his home. It was a fine cottage cheese just off the palace grounds, which he had moved into when he married. The rind had long since hardened and lost the better part of its flavor, and the walls were fine-grained creamy-yellow petrified cheese. It was one of the most tasteful cottages extant, but since he hadn't hollowed it out himself he didn't see fit to brag about it.

Bink took a deep breath, nerved himself, and opened the front rind-door. A sweetish waft of seasoned cheese blew out, together with a raucous screech.

"That you, Bink? About time! Where did you sneak off to, right when there's work to be done? You have no consideration at all, do you!"

"I needed shoes," he said shortly.

"Shoes!" she exclaimed incredulously. "You *have* shoes, idiot!"

His wife was much smarter than he, at the moment, for Chameleon's intelligence varied with the time of the month, as did her appearance. When she was beautiful, she was stupid—in the extreme, for both. When she was smart, she was ugly. Very smart and very ugly. At the moment she was at the height of the latter phase. This was one reason she was keeping herself secluded, virtually locked in her room.

"I need good-looking ones, tonight," he said, mustering patience. But even as the words were out he realized he had phrased it badly; any reference to good looks set her off.

"The hell you do, dunce!"

He wished she wouldn't keep rubbing in his inferior intelligence. Ordinarily she was smart enough not to do that. Bink knew he was no genius, but he wasn't subnormal either; *she* was the one who was both. "I have to attend the Anniversary Ball," he explained, though of course she already knew that. "It would be an insult to the Queen if I attended sloppily dressed."

"Dolt!" she screamed from her hideaway. "You're attending in costume! No one will see your stinking shoes!"

Oops, that was right. He had made his trip for nothing.

"But that's all too typical of your selfishness," she continued with righteous ire. "Bugging off to the party to have a good time while I suffer home alone, chewing on the walls." That was literal; the cheese was old and hard, but she gnawed on it when she got angry, and she was angry most of the time now.

Still, he tried to be positive. He had only been married a year, and he loved Chameleon. He had known at the outset that there would be good times and bad times, and this was a bad time. A very bad time. "Why don't you come to the ball too, dear?"

She exploded with cynical wrath. "Me? When I'm like this? Spare me your feebleminded sarcasm!"

"But as you reminded me, it's a costume party. The Queen is cloaking every attendee in a disguise of her choosing. So no one will see—"

"You utter moronic nincompoop!" she bawled through the wall, and he had heard something crash. Now she was throwing things, in a genuine temper tantrum. "How can I go to a party in *any* guise—when I'm nine months pregnant?"

And that was what was really bothering her. Not her normal smart-ugly phase, that she had lived with all her life, but the enormous discomfort and restriction of her pregnancy. Bink had precipitated that condition during her lovely-stupid phase, only to learn when she got smarter that she had not wanted such a commitment at this time. She feared her baby would be like her—or like him. She had wanted to find some spell to ensure that the child would be positively talented, or at least normal, and now it was up to blind chance. She had accepted the situation with extremely poor grace, and had not forgiven him.

The smarter she got, and the more pregnant she got, the more intense her ire became.

Well, soon she would be over the hump, and getting prettier—just in time for the baby. It was due in a week or so. Maybe the baby would be normal, perhaps even strongly talented, and Chameleon's fears would be laid to rest. Then she would stop taking it out on him.

If, however, the baby were abnormal . . . but best not even think of that. "Sorry, I forgot," he mumbled.

"You *forgot!*" The irony in her tone cut through his sensitivities like a magic sword through the cheese of the cottage. "Imbecile! You'd like to forget, wouldn't you! Why didn't you think of that last year when you—"

"I have to go, Chameleon," he muttered, hastily retreating out the door. "The Queen gets upset when people are tardy." In fact it seemed to be the nature of women to get upset at men, and to throw tantrums. That was one of the things that distinguished them from nymphs, who looked like women but were always amenable to the idle whims of men. He supposed he should count himself lucky that his wife did not have a dangerous talent, like setting fire to people or generating thunderstorms.

"Why does the Queen have to throw her ridiculous pointless dull party now?" Chameleon demanded. "Right when she *knows* I can't attend?"

Ah, the logic of women! Why bother to try to understand it. All the intelligence in the Land of Xanth could not make sense of the senseless. Bink closed the door behind him.

Actually, Chameleon's question had been rhetorical. They both knew the answer. Queen Iris took every opportunity to flaunt her status, and this was the first anniversary of that status. Theoretically the ball was in honor of the King, but actually King Trent cared little for theatrics and would probably skip the festivities. The party was really for the Queen—and though she could not compel the King to attend, woe betide the lesser functionary who played hooky tonight! Bink was such a functionary.

And why was this so? he asked himself as he trod glumly on. He was supposed to be an important person, the Royal Researcher of Xanth, whose duty it was to probe the mysteries of magic and report directly to the King. But with Chameleon's pregnancy, and the necessary organization of his homestead, Bink had not gotten around to any real research. For that he had only himself to blame, really. He should indeed have considered the consequence of impregnating his wife. At the time, fatherhood had been the last thing on his mind. But Chameleon-lovely was a figure to cloud man's mind and excite his—never mind!

Ah, nostalgia! Back when love was new, carefree, uncomplicated, without responsibility! Chameleon-lovely was very like a nymph—

No, that was a false feeling. His life before he met Chameleon had not been all that simple, and he had encountered her three times before he recognized her. He had feared he had no magic talent—

He shimmered—and suddenly his appearance changed. The Queen's costume had arrived. Bink was the same person, mentally and physically, but now he looked like a centaur. The Queen's illusion, so he could play the game she had devised, in her infinite capacity to generate minor mischief. Each person had to guess the identities of as many others as possible before making his way to the palace ballroom, and there was a prize for the one who guessed the most correctly.

In addition, she had set up a mock-maze-hedge around Castle Roogna. Even if he did not play the people-guessing game, he would be forced to thread his way through the giant puzzle. Damn the Queen!

But he had to go through with it, as did everyone else. The King wisely did not interfere with household matters, and gave the Queen considerable play on her tether. With resignation Bink entered the maze and began the laborious chore of threading his way through the network of false paths toward the castle.

Most of the hedge was illusion, but enough of it was anchored in reality to make it safest simply to honor the maze, rather than barging through. The Queen would have her fun, especially on this important First Anniversary of the King's coronation. She could get uglier than Chameleon when not humored.

Bink whipped around a corner—and almost collided with a zombie. The thing's wormy face dripped earth and goo, and the great square eye-sockets were windows of putrefaction. The smell was appalling.

Morbidly fascinated, Bink stared into those eyes. Far within their depths there seemed to be a faint illumination, as of moonlight on a haunted plain or glow-fungus feeding on the corpse's rotting brain. It was as if he could see through twin tunnels into the very source of its foul animation, and perhaps to the root of all the magic of Xanth. Yet it was nightmare, for the zombie was one of the living dead, a horror that should be quickly buried and forgotten. Why had this one ripped free of its unquiet grave? The zombies normally roused themselves only in defense of Castle Roogna, and they had been passive since King Trent took over.

The zombie stepped toward him, opening its fossil mouth. "Vvooomm," it said, laboring to make the putrid gas that was its only breath form a word.

Bink backed away, sickened. He feared little in the Land of Xanth, for his physical prowess and magic talent made him one of the most subtly formidable people in the kingdom. But the peculiar discomfort and disgust entailed by dealing with a zombie unnerved him. He spun about and ran down a side avenue, leaving the undead thing behind. With its decayed articulation of bones and moldy flesh it could not match his speed, and did not even try.

Suddenly a gleaming sword rose up before him. Bink halted, amazed by this second apparition. He saw no person, no connections, just the weapon. What was the purpose of this illusion?

Oh—it must be another cute little trick of the Queen's. She liked to make her parties exciting and challenging. All he had to do was walk through the sword, calling the bluff of this *ad hoc* interference.

Yet he hesitated. The blade looked terribly real. Bink remembered his experience with Jama, as a youth. Jama's talent was the manifestation of flying swords, solid and sharp and dangerous for the few seconds they existed, and he tended to exert his talent arrogantly. Jama was no friend of Bink's, and if he were in the area—

Bink drew his own sword. "On guard!" he exclaimed, and struck at the other weapon, half expecting his blade to pass through it without resistance. The Queen would be pleased her bluff had worked, and this way he was taking no risk, just in case—

The other sword was solid. Steel clanged on steel. Then the other weapon twisted about to disengage from his, and thrust swiftly at his chest.

Bink parried and stepped aside. This was no temporary blade, and no mindlessly flying thing! Some invisible hand guided it, and that meant an invisible man.

The sword struck again, and again Bink parried. This thing was really trying to get him! "Who are you?" Bink demanded, but there was no answer.

Bink had been practicing with the sword for the past year, and his tutor claimed that he was an apt student. Bink had courage, speed, and ample physical power. He knew he was hardly expert yet, but he was no longer amateur. He rather enjoyed the challenge, even with an invisible opponent.

But a serious fight . . . was something else. Why was he being attacked, on this festive occasion? Who was his silent, secretive enemy? Bink was lucky that that person's spell of invisibility had not affected the sword itself, for then he would have had an awful time countering it. But every item of magic in Xanth was single; a sword could not carry its necessary charms of sharpness and hardness and also be invisible. Well, it was possible, for anything was possible with magic; but it was highly unlikely. At any rate, that weapon was all Bink needed to see.

"Halt!" he cried. "Desist, or I must counter you."

Again the enemy sword slashed at him ferociously. Bink was already aware that he faced no expert; the swordsman's style was more bold than skilled. Bink blocked the weapon off, then countered with a half-hearted thrust to his opponent's exposed midsection. There was only one place that midsection could be, visible or not, for a certain balance and position were essential in swordplay. Bink's strike was not hard enough to maim, but was sufficient to—

His blade passed right through the invisible torso without resistance. There was nothing there.

Bink, startled, lost his concentration and balance. The enemy sword thrust at his face. He ducked barely in time. His instructor, Crombie the soldier, had taught him such avoidance; but this escape was at least partly luck. Without his talent, he could have been dead.

Bink did not like to depend on his talent. That was the point in learning swordsmanship: to defend himself his own way, openly, with pride, without suffering the private snickers of those who assumed, naturally enough, that mere chance had helped him. His magic might stop or blunt an attack by having the attacker slip on a littered fruit rind; it didn't care about his pride. But when he won fairly with his sword, no one laughed. No one was laughing now, but still he did not like being attacked by a—what?

It must be one of the magic weapons of the King's private arsenal, and it was consciously directed. No way this could be the action of the King, however; King Trent never played practical jokes, and permitted no tampering with his weapons. Someone had activated this sword and sent it out to do mischief, and that person would shortly face the formidable wrath of the King.

That was little comfort to Bink at the moment, though. He didn't want to seem to hide behind the protection of the King. He wanted to fight his own battle and win. Except that he would have some problem getting at a person who wasn't there.

As he considered, Bink rejected the notion that a distant person could be wielding this weapon. It was magically possible, but as far as he knew he had no enemies; no one would want to attack him, by magical or natural means, and no one would dare do it with one of the King's own swords, in the garden of Castle Roogna.

Bink fenced with the enemy sword again, maneuvered it into a vulnerable position, and sliced through the invisible arm. No arm was there, of course. No doubt about it: the sword was wielding itself. He had never actually fought one of these before, because the King didn't trust the judgment of mindless weapons, so the experience was a novel one. But of course there was nothing inherently odd about it; why *not* do battle with a charmed sword?

Yet why should such a sword seek his life, assuming it was acting on its own? Bink had nothing but respect for bladed weapons. He took good care of his own sword, making sure the sharpness charm was in good order and never abusing the instrument. Swords of any type or creed should have no quarrel with him.

Perhaps he had inadvertently affronted this particular sword. "Sword, if I have caused you distress or wronged you, I apologize and proffer amends," he said. "I do not wish to fight you without reason."

The sword cut ferociously at his legs. No quarter there!

"At least tell me what your grievance is!" Bink exclaimed, dancing away just in time.

The sword continued its attack relentlessly.

"Then I must put you out of commission," Bink said, with mixed regret, ire, and anticipation. Here was a real challenge! For the first time he took a full offensive posture, fencing the sword with skill. He knew he was a better man than it.

But he could not strike down the wielder of that weapon, because there was none. Nobody to pierce, no hand to slice. The sword showed no sign of tiring; magic powered it. How, then, could he overcome it?

This was more of a challenge than he had supposed! Bink was not worried, because he found it hard to worry about a skill less than his own. Yet if the opposition were invulnerable—

Still, his talent would not allow the sword to hurt him. A sword wielded by a man in ordinary fashion could damage him, because that was mundane; but when magic was involved, he was safe. In Xanth, hardly anything was completely unmagical, so he was extremely well protected. The question was, was he going to prevail honestly, by his own skill and courage, or by some fantastic-seeming coincidence? If he didn't do it the first way, his talent would do it the second way.

Again he maneuvered the sword into a vulnerable position, then struck it across the flat of the blade, hoping to snap it off short. This did not work; the metal was too strong. He had not really expected such a ploy to be effective; strength was one of the basic charms built into modern swords. Well, what next?

He heard the clop-clop of someone approaching. He had to wrap this up quickly, or suffer the embarrassment of being rescued. His talent didn't care about his pride, just his body.

Bink found himself backed up against a tree—a real one. The hedge-maze had been superimposed on existing vegetation, so that everything became part of that puzzle. This was a gluebark tree: anything that penetrated the bark was magically stuck to it. Then the tree slowly grew around the object, absorbing it. Harmless, so long as the bark was intact; children could safely climb the trunk and play in its branches, as long as they did not use cleats. Woodpeckers stayed well away from it. So Bink could lean against it, but had to be careful not to—

The enemy sword slashed at his face. Bink was never sure, afterward, whether his inspiration came before or after his action. Probably after, which meant that his talent was in operation again despite his effort to avoid that. At any rate, instead of parrying this time, he ducked.

The sword passed over his head and smacked into the tree, slicing deeply into the bark. Instantly the tree's magic focused, and the blade was sealed in place. It wrenched and struggled, but could not escape. Nothing could beat the specific magic of a thing in its own bailiwick! Bink was the victor.

" 'Bye, Sword," he said, sheathing his own weapon. "Sorry we couldn't visit longer." But behind his flippancy was a certain grim disquiet: who or what had incited this magic sword to slay him? He must, after all, have an enemy somewhere, and he didn't like that. It wasn't so much any fear of attack, but a gut feeling of distress that he should be disliked to that extent by anyone, when he tried so hard to get along.

He ducked around another corner—and smacked into a needle-cactus. Not a real one, or he would have become a human pincushion; a mock one.

The cactus reached down with a prickly branch and gripped Bink by the neck. "Clumsy oaf!" it snorted. "Do you wish me to prettify your ugly face in the mud?"

Bink recognized that voice and that grip. "Chester!" he rasped past the constriction in his neck. "Chester Centaur!"

"Horseflies!" Chester swore. "You tricked me into giving myself away!" He eased his terrible grip slightly. "But now you'd better tell me who *you* are, or I might squeeze you like this." He squeezed, and Bink thought his head was going to pop off his body. Where was his talent now?

"Fink! Fink!" Bink squeaked, trying to pronounce his name when his lips would not quite close. "Hink!"

"I do *not* stink!" Chester said, becoming irritated. That made his grip tighten. "Not only are you homely as hell, you're impertinent." Then he did a double take. "Hey—you're wearing my face!"

Bink had forgotten: he was in costume. The centaur's surprise caused him to relax momentarily, and Bink snatched his opportunity. "I'm Bink! Your friend! In illusion guise!"

Chester pondered. No centaur was stupid, but this one tended to think with his muscles. "If you're trying to fool me—"

"Remember Herman the hermit? How I met him in the wilderness, and he saved Xanth from the wiggle swarm with his will-o'-the-wisp magic? The finest centaur of them all!"

Chester finally put Bink down. "Uncle Herman," he agreed, smiling. The effect was horrendous on the cactus-face. "I guess you're okay. But what are you doing in my form?"

"The same thing you're doing in cactus form," Bink said, massaging his throat. "Attending the masquerade ball." His neck did not seem to be damaged, so his talent must have let this encounter be.

"Oh, yes," Chester agreed, flexing his needles eloquently. "The mischief of Good Queen Iris, the bitch-Sorceress. Have you found a way into the palace yet?"

"No. In fact, I ran into a—" But Bink wasn't sure he wanted to talk about the sword just yet. "A zombie."

"A zombie!" Chester laughed. "Pity the poor oaf in *that* costume!"

A costume! Of course! The zombie had not been real; it had merely been another of the Queen's illusion-costumes. Bink had reacted as shortsightedly as Chester, fleeing it before discovering its identity. And thereby encountering the sword, which certainly had not been either costume or illusion. "Well, I don't much like this game anyway," he said.

"I don't go for the game either," Chester agreed. "But the prize—that is worth a year of my life."

"By definition," Bink agreed morosely. "One Question Answered by the Good Magician Humfrey—free. But everyone's competing for it; someone else will win."

"Not if we get hoofing!" Chester said. "Let's go unmask the zombie before it gets away!"

"Yes," Bink agreed, embarrassed by his previous reaction.

They passed the sword, still stuck in the tree. "Finders keepers!" Chester exclaimed happily, and put his hand to it.

"That's a gluebark; it won't let go."

But the centaur had already grasped the sword and yanked. Such was his strength there was a shower of bark and wood. But the sword did not come free.

"Hm," Chester said. "Look, tree—we have a gluebark in Centaur Village. During the drought I watered it every day, so it survived. Now all I ask in return is this sword, that you have no use for."

The sword came free. Chester tucked it into his quiver of arrows, fastening it in place with a loop of the coil of rope he also carried. Or so Bink guessed, observing the contortions of the cactus. Bink had put a hand to his own sword, half-fearing a renewal of hostilities, but the other weapon was quiescent. Whatever had animated it was gone.

Chester became aware of Bink's stare. "You just have to understand trees," he said, moving on. "It's true of course; a centaur never lies. I did water that tree. It was more convenient than the privy."

So this gluebark had given up its prize. Well, why not? Centaurs were indeed generally kind to trees, though Chester had no particular love for needle-cactuses. Which was no doubt why the Queen in her humor had imposed this costume on him.

They came to the place where Bink had encountered the zombie, but the awful thing was gone. Only a slimy chunk of dirt lay in the path. Chester nudged it with one forehoof. "Real dirt—from a fake zombie?" he inquired, puzzled. "The Queen's illusions are getting better."

Bink nodded agreement. It was a disquieting note. Obviously the Queen had extended the illusion greatly—but why should she bother? Her magic was strong, far beyond the talents of ordinary people, for she was one of the three Magician-class citizens of Xanth. But it had to be a strain on even her power to maintain every detail of every costume of every person attending the masquerade. Bink and Chester's costumes were visual only, or it would have been difficult for them to converse.

"Here is a fresh pile of dirt," Chester remarked. "Real dirt, not zombie dirt." He tapped at it with a cactus foot that nevertheless left a hoofprint. "Could the thing have gone back into the ground here?"

Curious, Bink scraped at the mound with his own foot. There was nothing inside it except more dirt. No zombie. "Well, we lost him," Bink said, upset for a reason he could not quite fathom. The zombie had seemed so real! "Let's just find our way into the palace, instead of making fools of ourselves out here."

Chester nodded, his cactus-head wobbling ludicrously. "I wasn't guessing people very well anyway," he admitted. "And the only question I could ask the Good Magician doesn't have any answer."

"No answer?" Bink asked as they turned into another channel.

"Since Cherie had the colt—mind you, he's a fine little centaur, bushy-tailed —she doesn't seem to have much time for me anymore. I'm like a fifth hoof around the stable. So what can I—?"

"You, too!" Bink exclaimed, recognizing the root of his own bad mood. "Chameleon hasn't even had ours yet, but—" He shrugged.

"Don't worry—she won't have a colt."

Bink choked, though it really wasn't funny.

"Fillies—can't run with them, can't run without them," Chester said dolefully.

Suddenly a harpy rounded a corner. There was another scramble to avoid a collision. "You blind in the beak?" Chester demanded. "Flap off, birdbrain."

"You have a vegetable head?" the harpy retorted in a fluting tone. "Clear out of my way before I sew you up in a stinking ball with your own dull needles."

"Dull needles!" Chester, somewhat belligerent even in the best of moods, swelled up visibly at this affront. Had he actually been a cactus, he would have fired off a volley of needles immediately—and none of those darts looked dull. "You want your grimy feathers crammed up your snotty snoot?"

It was the harpy's turn to swell. Most of its breed were female, but this one was male: more of the Queen's rather cutting humor. "Naturally," the birdman fluted. "Right after you have the juice squeezed out of your pulp, greenface."

"Oh, yeah?" Chester demanded, forgetting that centaurs were not common brawlers. Harpy and cactus squared off. The harpy was evidently a considerably larger creature, one that never had to take any guff off strangers. That odd, half-musical mode of speech—

"Manticora!" Bink exclaimed.

The harpy paused. "One point for you, Centaur. Your voice sounds familiar, but—"

Startled, Bink reminded himself that he was in the guise of a centaur at the moment, so that it was himself, not Chester, the creature addressed. "I'm Bink. I met you when I visited the Good Magician, way back when—"

"Oh, yes. You broke his magic mirror. Fortunately he had another. Whatever became of you?"

"I fell upon evil times. I got married."

The manticora laughed musically. "Not to this cactus, I trust?"

"Listen, thing—" Chester said warningly.

"This really is my friend, Chester Centaur," Bink said quickly. "He's the nephew of Herman the hermit, who saved Xanth from the—"

"I knew Herman!" the Manticora said. "Greatest centaur there ever was, even before he gave his noble life for his country. Only one I know who wasn't ashamed of his magic talent. His will-o'-the-wisps led me out of a dragon warren once. When I learned of his death, I was so sad I went out and stung a small tangle tree to death. He was so much better than those hoof-headed equines of the common herd who exiled him—" He broke off. "No offense, Cactus, you being his nephew and all. I may have a target to sting with you, but I would not affront the memory of that remarkable hermit."

There was no surer route to Chester's favor than praise of his hero-uncle, as perhaps the manticora knew. "No offense!" he said instantly. "Everything you said is true! My people exiled Herman because they thought magic in a centaur was obscene. Most of them still do. Even my own filly, as nice a piece of horseflesh as you'd care to—" He shook his cactus-head, becoming aware of the impropriety. "They *are* hoofheads."

"Times are changing," the manticora said. "One day all the centaurs will be flaunting their talents instead of flouting them." He made a gesture with his harpy wings. "Well, I must go identify some more people, not that I need the prize. It's merely a challenge."

He moved on. Bink marveled again at the humor of the Queen, to costume as a harpy such a formidable creature as a manticora, who possessed the head of a man with triple jaws, body of a lion, wings of a dragon, and tail of a monstrous scorpion. Certainly one of the most deadly monsters of the Land of Xanth— rendered into the likeness of one of the most disgusting. Yet the manticora was bearing up with grace, and playing the game of charades and costumes. Probably he felt secure in the knowledge that he had a soul, and so he cared little for appearances.

"I wonder if I have a magic talent?" Chester mused, sounding a trifle guilty. The transition from obscenity to pride was indeed a difficult one!

"If you won the prize, you could find out," Bink pointed out.

The cactus brightened. "That's right!" This was evidently the unanswerable question Chester had had in mind, unvoiced. Then the cactus dulled. "But Cherie would never let me have a talent, not even a little one. She's awfully prudish about that sort of thing."

Bink remembered the filly's prim attitude, and nodded. Cherie Centaur was one fine figure of a filly, and well able to handle the general magic of Xanth, but she could not abide it in any centaur. It reminded Bink of his own mother's attitude about sex in young humans. For animals it was natural, but when something like a wild-oats nymph was involved—well, Chester did have a problem.

They turned another corner—corners abounded in this infernal maze—and there was the palace gate, shining beyond the drawbridge over the moat. "Let's get over there before the maze changes!" Bink exclaimed.

They ran toward it—but even as they did, the hedge-pattern shimmered and fogged. The awful thing about this puzzle-pattern was its instability; at irregular intervals it shifted into new configurations, so that it was impossible to solve it methodically. They were going to be too late to break out.

"I'm not stopping now!" Chester cried. The sound of cactus-galloping became louder. "Get on my back!"

Bink didn't argue. He made a leap for the prickliest portion of the cactus, grimacing in half-expectation of a crotchful of needles. He landed neatly on Chester's back, which felt quite equine. Phew!

At the feel of that impact, Chester accelerated. Bink had ridden a centaur before, when Cherie had kindly given him a lift—but never a powerhouse like this! Chester was husky even by centaur standards, and now he was in a hurry. The huge muscles pulsed along his body, launching him forward with such ferocity that Bink was afraid he would be hurled off as fast as he had landed. But he clutched two handfuls of mane and hung on, confident that his talent would protect him even from this.

Few residents of Xanth were aware of Bink's talent, and he himself had been ignorant of it the first twenty-five years of his life. This was because of the way the talent clouded itself, hiding from publicity. It prevented him from being harmed by magic—but anyone who knew this could then harm him by mundane means. So Bink's talent shrouded itself in seeming coincidence. Only King Trent, besides Bink himself, knew the truth. Good Magician Humfrey probably suspected, and Chameleon had to have an idea.

A new hedge formed between them and the gate. It was probably illusion, since they had just seen the gate. Chester plunged through it—and sent branches flying. No illusion; this time it must have been the gate that was the illusion. The Sorceress Queen could make things disappear, by creating the illusion of open space; he should have remembered that before.

What drive this creature had! Invisible foliage tore at Bink like the winds of a tempest, but he clung tight. Another barrier appeared; Chester veered to follow a new channel that went his way, then smashed past another cross-hedge. Once this centaur got moving, pity the man, beast, or plant that got in his way!

Suddenly they were out of the maze and at the moat. But Chester's veer had brought him to it twenty paces to the side of the drawbridge, and there was no room to make a course correction. "Hang on!" Chester cried, and leaped.

This time the thrust was so great that Bink ripped a double handful of mane out of the centaur's hide and still slid off the rear. He tumbled end over end and splashed into the moat.

Immediately the moat-monsters converged, jaws gaping eagerly. They were ever alert; they would have been fired, otherwise. A huge serpent looped down, each glistening tooth as long as one of Bink's fingers. From the other side a purple croc opened its gnarly proboscis, showing off teeth that were even longer. And directly under Bink, rising from the swirling moat-mud, came a behemoth, its back so broad it seemed to fill the entire moat.

Bink thrashed madly in the water, trying to swim to safety, knowing that no man could escape any one of these monsters, let alone all three. The behemoth came up, lifting him half out of the water; the croc came across, its jaws parting cavernously; the serpent struck with lightning velocity from above.

And—croc and serpent collided, their teeth throwing off sparks as they clashed. Both monsters were shunted aside by the mass of the rising behemoth —and Bink slid down that lifting slope as on a greased skid, away from the teeth and safely to the stone-lined inner wall of the moat. An amazing coincidence—

Ha. That was his talent operating, saving him once again from his own folly. Trying to ride a galloping centaur that looked like a cactus—he should have picked his way out of the maze the way the others were doing. He was just lucky that both centaurs and moat-monsters were magical, so that his talent could function.

Chester had landed safely, and was on hand to haul him out of the moat. With one hand the centaur lifted Bink clear, hardly seeming to exert himself. But his voice shook. "I thought—when you fell among those monsters—I never saw anything like—"

"They weren't really hungry," Bink said, preferring to disparage the significance of the event. "They were just playing with their food, and overdid it. Let's go on inside. They must be serving the refreshments by now."

"Hey, yes!" Chester agreed. Like all powerful creatures, he had a chronic appetite.

"Hay, yes," Bink muttered. But it was not a good pun; centaurs did not eat hay, despite what detractors might imply.

They moved to the castle—and the illusions faded. The spell was off, here; they were themselves again, man and centaur. "You know, I never realized how homely my face was, until I saw it on you," Chester said musingly.

"But you have an exceedingly handsome posterior," Bink pointed out.

"True, true," the centaur agreed, mollified. "I always said Cherie didn't become my mate for my face."

Bink started to laugh, but realized his friend was serious. Also, they were at the entry now, and others were within earshot.

The guard at the palace gate frowned. "How many did you guess, Bink?" he inquired, pad poised for a note.

"One, Crombie," Bink said, indicating Chester. Then he remembered the manticora. "Two, rather."

"You're out of the running, then," Crombie said. "The leading contestant has twelve." He glanced at Chester. "You?"

"I didn't want the prize anyway," the centaur said gruffly.

"You folk haven't been trying," Crombie said. "If I'd been out there, instead of stuck here running errands for the Queen—"

"I thought you liked this palace job," Bink said. He had first encountered Crombie when the man soldiered for the prior King.

"I like it—but I like adventure better. The King's okay, but—" Crombie scowled. "Well, you know the Queen."

"All fillies are difficult," Chester said. "It's their nature; they can't help it, even if they wanted to."

"Right you are!" Crombie agreed heartily. He was the original woman-hater. "And the ones with the strongest magic—who else would have dreamed up this idiocy of a masquerade? She just wants to show off her sorcery."

"She hasn't got much else to show off," Chester said. "The King pays no attention to her."

"The King's one smart Magician!" Crombie agreed. "When she's not making mischief like this, this palace guard duty is dull as hell. I wish I were out on a man's mission, like the time when Bink and I—"

Bink smiled reminiscently. "Wasn't that Technicolor hailstorm something? We camped out under the quiescent tangle tree—"

"And the girl ran off," Crombie agreed. "Those were the days!"

Surprised, Bink found himself agreeing. The adventure had not seemed like fun at the time, but in retrospect it had a certain twilight luster. "You told me she was a threat to me."

"And she *was*," Crombie said. "She married you, didn't she?"

Bink laughed, but it was a trifle forced. "We'd better get on in before the refreshments are gone." He turned—and almost stumbled over another little mound of dirt. "You have moles around the palace?" he inquired with a certain edge.

Crombie squinted at the dirt. "That wasn't there a moment ago. Maybe a magic mole was attracted by the party. I'll notify the head grounds keeper, when I get offshift."

Bink and Chester moved on in. The palace ballroom had been decorated by Queen Iris, naturally. It was an undersea setting, with streamers of seaweed rising from the rocky deeps, and brightly colored fish swimming through, and barnacles on the walls. Here and there were subaqueous beaches of fine white sand, which shifted location magically, so that if a person stood still the scenery would come to him. A large serpentine sea monster coiled around the entire area, its pulsing, convoluted coils showing here and there in lieu of the walls.

Chester glanced around. "She's a bitch, and she shows off, but I have to admit her magic is impressive. But I'm worried about the quantity of food; if there isn't enough—"

There turned out to be no danger of a shortage. The refreshments were mountainous, and under the personal guard of Queen Iris. She had a picklepuss on a little leash. Whenever someone had the temerity to take a delicacy, the picklepuss pickled it. "No one eats until the grand prize is awarded," Iris announced, glaring about. Since she had garbed herself as a warrior-queen-mermaid, complete with spiked crown, trident, and powerful tail, and the points of the trident glistened with a coating of slime that was probably illusion too but just might possibly be genuine poison, this was an effective enough deterrent even without the picklepuss.

Bink and Chester separated, mixing with the other guests. Just about every creature of note in Xanth was present, except for Chester's filly Cherie, who was no doubt still wrapped up in the colt, and Bink's Chameleon, wrapped up in her misery. And the Good Magician Humfrey, who never socialized voluntarily.

Bink spotted his father Roland, down from the North Village. Roland was careful not to embarrass him by any overt show of affection. They shook hands "Nice shoes, son."

This was nevertheless a miscue, after the scene with Chameleon. "Fresh from the tree," Bink said awkwardly.

"What have you been doing these past few months?" Bubbles rose from Roland's mouth as he spoke, quivering spherically as they sought the surface of the ocean. When Queen Iris put on an illusion, it was some illusion! Ordinary citizens, with their motley individual magic talents, could only look upon the works of the Sorceress and despair. Which was, of course, why the Queen was putting on this show.

"Oh, practicing with the sword, tilling the garden, that sort of thing," Bink said.

"I understand Chameleon is expecting momentarily."

"That, too," Bink said, again experiencing the frustration of his situation.

"A son will help fill the house."

Provided it turned out to be a normal, talented son. Bink changed the subject. "We have a delicate young lady-slipper plant just blossoming; I think it will bear its first pair of slippers soon."

"The ladies will be pleased," Roland said gravely, exactly as if this were significant news. Suddenly Bink realized that he had very little to show for his past year. What had he accomplished? Virtually nothing. No wonder he felt out of sorts!

The illumination dimmed. It was as if dusk were falling, causing the sea to darken, too. But the diffused daylight was replaced by nocturnal fluorescence. The flotation sacs on the seaweed glowed like little lamps, and the neon-coral was brightly outlined in assorted colors. Even the puffy sponges emitted wan beams. The animal life had sharper light, with electric eels flashing searchlight beams, and assorted fish shone translucently. The overall effect was bewilderingly beautiful.

"If only her personality were as excellent as her taste," Roland murmured, referring to the Queen.

"We shall now award the door prize," Queen Iris announced. She glowed most of all: streams of light emanated from the points of her crown and trident, and her beautifully bare mermaid torso was clearly outlined. She was the mistress of illusion; she could make herself as lovely as she chose, and she chose well.

"I understand it was a marriage of convenience," Roland continued. Though no Magician himself, Roland was the King's regent north of the Gap, and did not hold royalty in awe. "It must be extremely convenient at times."

Bink nodded, slightly embarrassed by his father's evident appreciation of the well-displayed if illusory charms of the Queen. The man was bordering on fifty, after all! Yet it had to be true. The King professed no love for the Queen, and governed that temperamental woman with a subtly iron hand that amazed those who had known Iris before her marriage. Yet she thrived under that discipline. Those who knew the King well understood that not only was he a more powerful Magician than she, he was also a stronger person. In fact, it looked as if the magic Land of Xanth had its most effective King since the Fourth Wave Reign of Roogna, the builder of this castle-palace. Already formidable changes were occurring; the magic shield that had protected Xanth from intrusion had been removed, and Mundane creatures were allowed to cross the border. The first to cross had been the members of the King's former Mundane army; they had been settled in wilderness regions and were becoming productive citizens of Xanth. The requirement that each citizen demonstrate a magic talent had been abolished—and to the amazement of some conservatives, chaos had not resulted. People were becoming known and respected for their total qualities, not just the accident of their magic. Selected parties were exploring nearby Mundania, where no magic existed, and outlying guard posts were being established so that no invasion could happen by surprise. The King had not destroyed the shieldstone; he would restore the shield if it were ever needed.

At any rate, Bink was sure King Trent had an eye for all things good and useful, including the flesh of fair women, and the Queen was his to command. She could and would be anything the King wished, and he would not be human if he did not avail himself of this, at least on occasion. The question was, what did he want? This was common palace speculation, and the prevailing opinion was that the King wanted variety. The Queen seldom appeared in the same guise twice.

"Palace Guard, your report," the Queen demanded peremptorily.

Soldier Crombie came forward slowly. He was resplendent in his palace uniform, every inch the soldier in a kingdom that hardly needed soldiers. He could fight well and savagely with sword or bare hands and did not like serving as lackey to a woman—and he showed it. Therefore she enjoyed ordering him about. But she could not push him too far, for his loyalty was to the King, and the King's favor lay on him.

"The winner—" Crombie began, consulting his notes.

"No, not that way, idiot!" she exclaimed, blotting him out with a cloud of diffusing dye. More illusion, of course, but quite effective. "First you give the runner-up, *then* you give the winner. Do something right, for a change."

Crombie's scowling face emerged from the thinning dye. "Women!" he muttered with caustic freighting. The Queen smiled, enjoying his ire. "The runner-up, with nine correct identifications, is—" He scowled again. "A woman. Bianca of the North Village."

"Mother!" Bink breathed, surprised.

"She always did enjoy guessing games," Roland said with pride. "I think you inherit your intelligence as well as your looks from her."

"And my courage and strength from you," Bink said, appreciating the compliment.

Bianca walked sedately to the stage area. She was a handsome woman who in youth had been beautiful, and unlike the Queen she was genuine. Her talent was the replay, not illusion.

"So the distaff proves itself again," the Queen said, smirking at Crombie the woman-hater. "The prize is—" She paused. "Doorman, fetch the second prize. You should have had it ready."

Crombie's scowl became truly ominous, but he walked to a cabinet half concealed by seaweed and brought out a covered container.

"The prize is," the Queen repeated, then whipped off the cover. "A potted snapdragon!"

There was a murmur of well-meaning awe and envy from the ladies present as the plant's several flower-heads flexed about on their stems, snapping viciously. Snapdragons were very good for eliminating insect and animal pests, and served as useful guards for houses. Woe to the intruder who stepped in or near such a plant! But they did not take readily to potting, so that a special and rather difficult spell was necessary to confine them. Thus wild snapdragons were common enough, but potted ones rare and much prized.

Bianca showed her pleasure as she accepted the plant, turning her face away with a smile as a little dragon-head snapped at her nose. Part of the potting process included a spell to render the plant harmless to its owner, but it took a while for it to get to know that owner. "It's beautiful," she said. "Thank you, Queen Iris." Then, diplomatically: "You're beautiful too—but not the same way."

The Queen snapped her teeth in mock imitation of the snapdragon, then smiled graciously. She craved the recognition and praise of such established and reputable citizens as Bianca, for Iris had lived in semi-exile for years before assuming the crown. "*Now* the top winner, servitor," she said to Crombie. "This time give it some flair, if you have any."

"The winner, with thirteen correct identities," Crombie drawled without flair, "is Millie the ghost." And he shrugged as if to express bemusement at yet another female success. He had made the count, so he knew the contest wasn't rigged. However, it was generally understood that the men had not been trying very hard.

The pretty, young-seeming ghost floated up. She was in her fashion both the youngest and the oldest of Castle Roogna's inhabitants. She had been in her teens when she died over eight hundred years before. When Bink first saw her she had been a formless blob of vapor, but since the occupancy of the castle by mortals she had shaped up until her outline was as firm and sightly as that of any living woman. She was a very sweet ghost, well liked by all, and there was applause at her victory.

"And the grand prize is—" The Queen spread her hands dramatically. "This certificate for one free Answer by the Good Magician Humfrey!" There was background fanfare, punctuated by magically augmented applause, as she handed the paper to the ghost.

Millie hesitated. Having no physical substance, she could not carry the certificate.

"That's all right," the Queen said. "I'll just write your name on it, and Magician Humfrey will know it's yours. In fact, he's probably watching us in his magic mirror at this moment. Why don't you ask your question now?"

Millie's reply was inaudible, for she could hardly speak above a ghostly whisper.

"Don't be concerned; I'm sure everyone will be glad to help," the Queen said. "Here—we'll write it down on the magic slate, and Magician Humfrey can respond in the same way." She gestured at Crombie. "Flunky, the slate!"

Crombie paused, but his curiosity made him go along with it. He fetched the slate. The Queen conscripted the nearest centaur, who happened to be Chester (who had been trying without success to sneak a cookie from the refreshment stand without having it pickled), to transcribe the ghost's inaudible words. Centaurs were literate; many of them were teachers, so writing chores fell naturally to them.

Chester did not like the Queen's attitude much better than Crombie did, but he also played along. What possible Question could a ghost have for the Magician? He wrote in flourishing capitals: HOW CAN MILLIE LIVE AGAIN?

There was more applause. The guests liked that Question. It was a challenging one—and the Answer, given publicly, might provide insights for them all. Usually Magician Humfrey's Answers cost the asker a year's service, and were given only to the one who asked. This party was getting interesting!

The words disappeared as if erased by an invisible sponge. Then the Magician's Answer showed: THE REQUIREMENTS ARE 3REE: 1RST—YOU MUST HAVE THE TRUE WILL TO BECOME MORTAL.

It was evident that Millie did. She gestured imploringly at the slate to continue, so that she could know whether the other requirements were similarly easy—or impossible. Technically, as the common saying went, nothing was impossible with magic, but in practice some spells were prohibitively difficult. Bink yearned with her: he had once longed as ardently for a magic talent, upon which his citizenship, welfare, and self-respect then depended. To one who had died prematurely, but not expired, what a tremendous hope mortality might be! Of course, if Millie lived, she would also die, in due course. But really she would be completing the life she had started, so many centuries ago. As a ghost she was in hiatus, unable to affect her destiny materially, unable to love and fear and feel.

Well, no, Bink corrected himself. Obviously she did feel—but not in the fashion physical people did. She could not experience bodily pleasure or pain.

2COND, the slate continued, YOU MUST HAVE A SPELL DOCTOR RESTORE YOUR TALENT TO OPTIMUM POTENCY.

"Is there a spell doctor in the house?" the Queen inquired, looking about, her points flashing. "No? Very well, errand boy—point out the nearest spell doctor."

Crombie started a snarl, but again was overcome by curiosity. He closed his eyes, spun about, and extended his right arm. It came to rest pointing northeast.

"That would be the Gap Village," the Queen said. There was a spell on the Gap that rendered the giant crevice that separated Xanth into the northern and southern sections unmemorable, but a spot counterspell had been applied to the Castle so that inhabitants and visitors could remember such things. The King would have had trouble governing properly if he could not remember so critical a feature of the landscape as the Gap! "Where is our transporter?"

"On my way, Your Highness," a man said. He sighted along the line Crombie was pointing out, concentrated—and suddenly an old woman stood before them. She looked about, bewildered by the people and water, for they were still in the undersea illusion.

"You are a spell doctor?" the Queen demanded.

"Yes," the old woman agreed. "But I don't do no doctoring for foolish people sunk in the ocean. Especially when I get yanked from my laundry without a—"

"This is King Trent's Coronation Anniversary Celebration Ball," the Queen said haughtily. "Now you have a choice, old crone: doctor one spell for us, and have the run of the party and all the food and fun you want, in a costume like this—" The old woman was abruptly garbed like a matron of honor, courtesy of the Queen's illusion magic. "Or *don't* doctor the spell, and this creature will pickle you." She held up the picklepuss, who hissed eagerly.

The old woman, like Crombie and Chester, looked rebellious, but decided on the expedient course. "What spell?"

"Millie's spell," the Queen said, indicating the ghost.

The spell doctor studied Millie, then cackled. "It is done," she said, smiling broadly so that all four of her teeth showed.

"I wonder what is so funny?" Roland murmured. "Do you know what Millie's talent is?"

"Ghosts don't have talents," Bink said.

"Her spell in life. It must be something special."

"Must be. I guess we'll find out, if she can fulfill the third requirement."

3IRD, the slate continued. IMMERSE YOUR SKELETON IN HEALING ELIXIR.

"We have plenty of that," the Queen said. "Lackey—"

The soldier was already on his way. In a moment he returned with a bucket of elixir.

"Now—where is your skeleton?" the Queen demanded.

But at this point Millie balked. She seemed to be trying to speak, but was unable.

"A silence spell!" the Queen exclaimed. "You aren't permitted to tell where it is! That's why it has remained hidden all these centuries!"

Millie nodded sadly.

"This is better yet!" the Queen said. "We shall have a treasure hunt! In which closet is Millie's skeleton? A special prize to whoever finds it first!" She pondered fleetingly. "I'm out of regular prizes . . . I know! The first date with Millie the mortal!"

"But what if a woman finds it?" someone asked.

"I'll have my husband the King change her into a man for the occasion," the Queen said.

There was an uneasy laugh. Was she joking—or serious? As far as Bink knew, the King could transform anything living into any other thing living—of the same sex. But he never used his talent capriciously. So it must be humor.

"But what about the food?" Chester demanded.

"That's it!" she decided. "The women have already proved their superiority, so they'll be barred from the treasure hunt. They'll start in on the refreshments while the men go look for—" But she saw Chester swelling up, and realized she was going too far. "Oh, all right, the men can eat too, even those with appetites like horses. But don't touch the Anniversary cake. The King will serve that—when the treasure hunt is over." She looked momentarily pensive, which was unusual for her; was she sure the King would perform?

The cake was magnificent: tier on tier of scintillating icing embroidered with a huge number 1, crowned with a magically lifelike bust of King Trent. The Queen always promoted the King's glory, because her own glory was a reflection of it. Some poor chef had spent a lot of effort organizing the magic for this ornate pastry!

"Picklepuss, stand guard over that cake, and pickle anybody who durst touch it," the Queen said, fastening the end of the puss's leash to the leg of the cake's table. "Now, men—on with the treasure hunt!"

Roland shook his head. "Skeletons in closets are best left undisturbed," he remarked. "I believe I will go congratulate your mother." He glanced at Bink. "You will have to represent our family in the treasure hunt. You don't have to search too hard." He made a little gesture of parting and moved off through the glowing currents of the sea.

Bink stood in place a moment, reflecting. It was evident his father knew there was something wrong, but was not commenting directly.

And what *was* wrong? Bink knew he had a good life, now, with a fine if variable wife and the favor of the King. Why did he dream of adventures in far places, of using the sword whose art he had been studying, of danger and even death, though he knew his talent would protect him from all genuine threats? What was the matter with him? It somehow seemed he had been happier when his future was in doubt—and that was ridiculous.

Why wasn't Chameleon here? She was near term, but she could have attended the Ball if she had wanted to. There was a magic midwife on the palace staff.

He decided. On with the treasure hunt! Maybe he could prove himself by locating that skeleton in the closet!

Chapter 2

Treasure Hunt

ow he had a challenge, however superficial. He had to start with his brain. Millie was not necessarily in a closet *per se*. Her bones had to be somewhere in the palace demesnes, because her ghost was here—but that could be anywhere within the moat or even the garden. Away from the regularly traveled sections. Unless the bones were buried under a floor or between walls. That seemed unlikely; the structure of the palace was quite solid, buttressed by durability spells; it would be a major undertaking to breach any floor or wall. Presuming that Millie had died suddenly, under suspicious circumstances (otherwise she would not have become a ghost), the murderer would have had to hide her body quickly, surreptitiously. No rebuilding of walls to conceal it! Old King Roogna would not have tolerated such a thing.

Where could a body have been hidden in minutes—so well as to withstand the scrutiny of centuries? The King's renovations had covered every part of Castle Roogna, converting it to the royal palace of the present kingdom; the restorative artisans could not have missed anything like this. So the feat seemed mechanically impossible. There could be no skeletons in these closets.

Bink saw that other men were already busy rummaging in all the closets. No use to compete directly with them, even if the skeleton were there.

Mechanically impossible—ah, there was the clue! Not magically impossible! The bones must have been transformed to something else, something innocuous, misleading. The question was, *what?* There were a thousand artifacts in the palace, and any one could be it. Yet transformation was major magic, and what Magician would be fooling around with a mere chambermaid? So her bones might after all remain in their natural state, or perhaps dissolved in solvent or ground up into powder. Regardless, there should be some clue to their identity, if only it could be correctly fathomed. Yes, a most intriguing puzzle!

Bink walked up to the refreshment table. There were tarts and donuts and cookies and cakes and pies and assorted beverages. Chester was stuffing himself. Bink circled the table, searching for something interesting. As he neared the Anniversary cake, the picklepuss hissed at him warningly. It was cat-bodied, with a snout that was green and prickly like a pickle, and its eyes were moist with brine. For a moment he was tempted to advance on it, to try his magic against its magic. He could not be harmed by magic, yet surely the feline would try to pickle him. What would happen?

No—he was not a juvenile daredevil compelled to prove himself by foolish exploits. Why force his talent to labor unnecessarily?

He spotted a smiling-face cookie and picked it up. As he brought it to his mouth, the smile became an O of horror. Bink hesitated, knowing this was merely another of the Queen's illusions, but loath to bite anyway. The cookie screwed its face in anticipation of the awful end; then when the bite did not come, slowly reopened one icing-dab eye.

"Here, puss—you take it," Bink said, extending the cookie to the leashed creature. There was a faint *zoop!* and the cookie was pickled, one of its eyes opened, the other closed. Now it reeked of brine. He set it down on the floor, and the picklepuss slunk forward and took the pickle-cookie in its mouth. Bink no longer felt hungry.

"Your spell is ailing," said a woman beside him. It was the old spell doctor, enjoying her unexpected participation in the proceedings. The party was theoretically open to all, but few garden-variety citizens had the nerve to attend. "But it is too potent for me to fix. Are you a Magician?"

"No, just a strongly talented nonentity," Bink said, wishing that were as facetious as it was intended to sound.

She concentrated. "No, I am mistaken. Your spell is not sick, just balked. I think it suffers from lack of exercise. Have you used it in the last year?"

"Some," Bink said, thinking of his recent escape from the moat-monsters. "Not much."

"You have to use magic, or you lose it," she said wisely.

"But what if there is no occasion to use it?"

"There is always an occasion for magic—in Xanth."

That hardly seemed true, for him, here in the palace. His talent protected him from most harm—but so did the favor of the King. So his talent got little exercise, and might indeed be getting flabby. His fight with the animated sword had been the first real occasion for his talent to manifest in some time, and he had sought to avoid invoking his magic there. So his moat dunking was about it. He remained a little wet, but the undersea decor concealed that. Would he have to seek danger, to keep his talent healthy? That would be ironic.

The woman shrugged and moved on, sampling other delicacies. Bink looked about—and caught the ghostly eye of Millie.

He went to her. "How is it proceeding?" he inquired politely.

At close range, the ghost was audible. Perhaps the movement of her white lips helped. "It is so exciting!" she exclaimed faintly. "To be whole again!"

"Are you sure being mortal is worth it?" he asked. "Sometimes when a person achieves his dream, it sours." Was he really addressing her—or himself?

She gazed at him with sympathy. He could see the other guests milling about beyond her, for she was translucent. Milling through Millie! It was slightly hard to focus on her. Yet she was beautiful in a special way: not merely her face and figure, but her sheer niceness and concern for others. Millie had helped Chameleon a lot, showing her where things were, what fruits were edible and what were dangerous, explaining castle protocol. It was Millie who had inadvertently shown Bink himself another facet of the Magician Trent, back when Bink had believed the man to be evil. "It would be so nice if you found my bones," Millie said.

Bink laughed, embarrassed. "Millie, I'm a married man!"

"Yes," she agreed. "Married men are best. They are—broken in, experienced, gentle, durable, and they do not talk gratuitously. For my return to life, for the first experience, it would be so nice—"

"You don't understand," Bink said. "I love my wife, Chameleon."

"Yes, of course you are loyal," Millie replied. "But right now she is in her ugly phase, and in her ninth month with child, and her tongue is as sharp as the manticora's stinger. Right now is when you need relief, and if I recover my life—"

"Please, no more!" Bink exclaimed. The ghost was striking right on target.

"I love you too, you know," she continued. "You remind me of—of the one I really loved, when I lived. But he is eight hundred years dead and gone." She gazed pensively at her misty fingers. "I could not marry you, Bink, when I first met you. I could only look and long. Do you know what it is like, seeing everything and never participating? I could have been so good for you, if only—" She broke down, hiding her face, her whole head hazing before his eyes.

Bink was embarrassed and touched. "I'm sorry, Millie, I didn't know." He put his hand on her shaking shoulder, but of course passed right through it. "It never occurred to me that your life could be restored. If I had—"

"Yes, of course," she sobbed.

"But you will be a very pretty girl. I'm sure there are many other young men who—"

"True, true," she agreed, shaking harder. Now her whole body was fogging out. The other guests were beginning to stare. This was about to get awkward.

"If there is anything I can do—" Bink said.

Millie brightened instantly, and her image sharpened correspondingly. "Find my bones!"

Fortunately that was not easily accomplished. "I'll look," Bink agreed. "But I have no better chance than anyone else."

"Yes, you do. You know how to do it, if only you put your marvelous mind to it. I can't tell you where they are, but if you really try—" She looked at him with ardent urgency. "It's been so many centuries. Promise me you'll try."

"But I—what would Chameleon think if—"

Millie put her face in her hands. The stares of the other guests hardened as the ghost's outline softened. "All right, I'll try," Bink promised. Why hadn't his talent protected him from this? But he knew the answer: his magic protected him from physical, magical harm. Millie was magical but not physical—and what she intended for him when she became physical would not ordinarily be construed as harm. His talent had never concerned itself with emotional complications. Bink would have to solve this triangle by himself.

The ghost smiled. "Don't be long," she said, and drifted off, her feet not touching the floor.

Bink spotted Crombie and joined him. "I begin to comprehend your view," he said.

"Yes, I noticed her working you over," Crombie agreed. "She's had her secret eye on you for some time. A man hardly has a chance when one of those vixens starts in on him."

"She believes I can locate her bones first—and now I have to try. Really try, not just dawdle."

"Child's play," Crombie remarked. "They're that way." He closed his eyes and pointed upward at an angle.

"I didn't ask for your help!" Bink snapped.

"Oops, sorry. Forget where I pointed."

"I can't. Now I'll have to look there, and sure as hell her bones will be there. Millie must have known I'd consult you. Maybe that's her talent: knowing things ahead of time."

"Why didn't she skip out before she was murdered, then?"

Good question. "Maybe she was asleep, when—"

"Well, you're not asleep. *You* could skip out. Someone else will find her, especially if I give him the hint."

"Why don't you find the bones?" Bink demanded. "You could follow your finger and do it in an instant."

"Can't. I'm on duty." Crombie smiled smugly. "I have woman problems enough already, thanks to you."

Oh. Bink had introduced the woman-hater to his former fiancée, Sabrina, a talented and beautiful girl Bink had discovered he didn't love. Apparently that introduction had led to an involvement. Now Crombie was having his revenge.

Bink set his shoulders and followed the direction indicated. The bones had to be somewhere upstairs. But maybe they still would not be obvious. If he did his honest best but could not locate them—

Yet would it be so bad, that date with Millie? All that she had said was true; this was a very bad time for Chameleon, and she seemed fit only to be left alone. Until she phased into her beautiful, sweet aspect, and had the baby.

No, there lay ruin. He had known what Chameleon was when he married her, and that there would be good times and bad. He had only to tide through the bad time, knowing it would pass. He had done it before. When there was some difficult chore or problem, her smart phase was an invaluable asset; sometimes they saved up problems for her to work on in that phase. He could not afford to dally with Millie or any other female.

He oriented on the room that lay on the line Crombie had pointed. It was the Royal Library, where the lore of centuries was stored. The ghostly skeleton was there?

Bink entered—and there sat the King. "Oh, sorry, Your Majesty. I didn't realize—"

"Come in, Bink," King Trent said, fashioning a warm smile. He looked every bit the monarch, even when half slumped over the table, as now. "I was meditating on a personal problem, and perhaps you have been sent to provide the answer."

"I lack the answer to my own dilemma," Bink said, somewhat diffidently. "I am ill-equipped to comment on yours."

"Your problem?"

"Chameleon is difficult, and I am restless, and someone is trying to kill me, and Millie the ghost wishes to make love to me."

King Trent laughed—then stopped. "Suddenly I perceive that was not a joke," he said. "Chameleon will improve and your restlessness should abate. But the others—who seeks your life? I assure you there is no royal sanction for that."

Bink described the episode with the sword. Now the King was thoughtful. "You and I know that only a Magician could actually harm you by such means, Bink—and there are only three people of that class in Xanth, none of whom wishes you ill and none of whom possesses the talent of animating swords. So you are not really in danger. But I agree, this could be very annoying. I shall investigate. Since you made the sword captive, we should be able to trace down the root of its imperative. If someone has co-opted one of the weapons of my arsenal—"

"Uh, I think that is where it came from," Bink said. "But Chester Centaur spotted it and took it—"

"Oh. Well, let's let that aspect drop, then; the alliance of the centaurs is important to me, as it has been to every King of Xanth throughout history. Chester can keep the sword, though I believe we shall turn off its self-motivating property. But it occurs to me that there is a certain similarity here to your own magic: whatever opposes you is hidden, using other magic than its own to attack you. The sword is not your enemy; it was merely the instrument of the hostile power."

"Magic like my own . . ." Bink repeated. "I suppose that could be. It would not be identical, since magic never repeats in Xanth, but similar—" He looked at the King, alarmed. "That means I can expect trouble anywhere, from anything, all seeming coincidental!"

"From a zombie, or a sword, or moat-monsters, or a ghost," the King agreed. "There may be a pattern here." He paused, considering. "Yet how could a ghost—?"

"She is to be restored, once I find her skeleton—and that may be in this room. What bothers me most is that I find myself tempted."

"Millie is a very fetching figure of a slip of a woman," King Trent said. "I can well understand the temptation. I suffer temptation myself; that is the subject of my present meditation."

"Surely the Queen can fulfill any, uh, temptation," Bink said cautiously, unwilling to betray how freely palace speculation had dwelt on this very subject. The King's private life should be private. "She can make herself resemble any—"

"Precisely. I have not touched the Queen or any other woman, since my wife died." To King Trent, the word "wife" meant only the woman he had married in Mundania. "Yet there is pressure on me to provide an heir to the throne of Xanth, by birth or adoption, in case there should be no suitable Magician available when that time comes. I sincerely hope there *is* a Magician! I feel obliged to make the attempt, nevertheless, since this was one of the implied stipulations I agreed to when assuming the crown. Ethically this must involve the Queen. So I shall do it, though I do not love her and never shall. The question is, what form shall I have her assume for the occasion?"

This was a more personal problem than Bink felt prepared to cope with. "Any form that pleases you, I should think." One big advantage the Queen had was the ability to assume a new form instantly. If Chameleon had been able to do that—

"But I do not wish to be pleased. I want to accomplish only what is necessary."

"Why not combine them? Let the Queen assume her most provocative illusion-form, or transform her to it yourself. When there is an heir, change her back. There is no wrong in enjoying your duty, is there?"

The King shook his head. "Ordinarily, this would be true. But mine is a special case. I am not sure I would be potent with a beautiful woman, or *any* woman—other than one who closely resembled my wife."

"Then let the Queen resemble your wife," Bink said without thinking.

"My concern is that this would degrade the memory I cherish."

"Oh, I see. You mean if she was too much like your wife, she might seem to replace her, and—"

"Approximately."

That was an impasse. If the King could only be potent with his dead wife, and could not abide any other woman resembling her physically, what could he do? This was the hidden aspect of the King that Millie had shown Bink, way back when: his continuing devotion to his prior family. It had been hard, after that, to think of such a man as evil; and indeed, King Trent was not evil. He was the finest Magician and perhaps the finest man in Xanth. Bink would be the last to wish to disrupt that aspect of King Trent's being.

Yet the problem of an heir was a real one. No one wanted a repetition of the shambles resulting from lack of a well-defined royal line. There had to be an heir to serve until a suitable Magician appeared, lending continuity to the government.

"We seem to have a similar dilemma, Your Majesty," Bink said. He tried to maintain the proper attitude of respect, because of the way he had known Trent before he was King. He had to set a good example. "We each prefer to remain loyal to our original wives, yet find it difficult. My problem will pass, but yours—" He paused, struck by dubious inspiration. "Millie is to be restored by having her skeleton dipped in healing water. Suppose you were to recover your wife's bones, bring them to Xanth—"

"If that worked, I would be a bigamist," King Trent pointed out. But he looked shaken. "Still, if my wife could live again—"

"You could check how well the procedure works, as they try it on Millie," Bink said.

"Millie is a ghost—not quite dead. A special case, like that of a shade. It happens when there is pressing unfinished business for that spirit to attend to. My wife is no ghost; she never left anything unfinished, except her life. To reanimate her body without her soul—"

Bink was beginning to be sorry he had thought of the notion. What horrors might be loosed on Xanth if all bones were renovated indiscriminately? "She might be a zombie," he said.

"There are serious risks," the King decided. "Still, you have provided me food for thought. Perhaps there is hope for me yet! Meanwhile, I certainly shall not have the Queen assume the likeness of my wife. Perhaps I shall only embarrass myself by trying and failing, but—"

"Too bad you can't transform yourself," Bink said. "Then you could test your potency without anyone knowing."

"The Queen would know. And to fail with her would be to show weakness that I can hardly afford. She would feel superior to me, knowing that what she has taken to be iron control is in fact impotence. There would be much mischief in that knowledge."

Bink, knowing the Queen, could well appreciate that. Only her respect for, and fear of, the King's personality and magic power held her in check. His transforming talent would remain—but the respect she held for his personality would inevitably erode. She could become extremely difficult to manage, and that would not be good for the Land of Xanth. "Could you, er, experiment with some other woman first? That way, if you failed—"

"No," the King said firmly. "The Queen is not my love, but she is my legal spouse. I will not cheat her—or any other member of my kingdom, in this or any other respect."

And there was the essence of his nobility! Yet the Queen might cheat *him*, if she saw her opportunity, and knew him to be impotent. Bink didn't like that notion. He had seen King Trent's reign as the onset of a Golden Age; how fraught it was with liabilities, from this vantage!

Then Bink had another inspiration. "Your memory of your wife—it isn't just your memory of her you are preserving, it is your memory of yourself. Yourself when you were happy. You can't make love to another woman, or let another woman look like her. But if two other people made love—I mean, the Queen and a man who did not resemble you—no memories would be defiled. So if the Queen changed your appearance—"

"Ridiculous!" the King snapped.

"I suppose so," Bink said. "I shouldn't have mentioned it."

"I'll try it."

"Sorry I bothered you. I—" Bink broke off. "You will?"

"Objectively I know that my continuing attachment to my dead wife and son is not reasonable," the King said. "It is hampering me in the performance of my office. Perhaps an unreasonable subterfuge will compensate. I will have Iris make me into the likeness of another man, and herself another woman, and as strangers we shall make the attempt. Do you just indulge in the courtesy of maintaining the secret, Bink."

"Yes, of course, by all means," Bink said, feeling awkward. He would have preferred to have the King devoid of human fallibilities, while paradoxically respecting him *for* those weaknesses. But he knew this was a side of the King no other person saw. Bink was a confidant, uncomfortable as the position might be at times.

"I—uh, I'm supposed to locate Millie's bones. They should be somewhere in this library."

"By all means. Continue your pursuit; I shall seek out the Queen." And the King rose abruptly and departed.

Just like that! Bink was amazed again at the alacrity with which the man acted, once he had come to a decision. But that was one of the qualities that made him fit to rule, in contrast to Bink himself.

Bink looked at the books. And suddenly realized: Millie's skeleton could have been transformed into a book; that would account for its neglect over the centuries, and for Millie's frequent presence here. She hovered often by the south wall. The question was, which book?

He walked along the packed shelves, reading titles from the spines of the tomes. This was an excellent library, with hundreds of texts; how could he choose among them? And if he found the proper one, somehow, how could it be restored? It would have to be transformed first back into the skeleton—and that was Magician-class magic. He kept running into this: too much magic was involved here! No inanimate transformer was alive today, as far as he knew. So Millie's quest looked hopeless after all. Yet why, then, had the Good Magician told her to use mere healing elixir? It made no sense!

Still, he had promised to try, though it complicated his personal situation. First he had to find the book; then he could worry about the next step.

The search took some time. Some texts he could eliminate immediately, such as *The Anatomy of Purple Dragons* or *Hailstones: Magic vs. Mundane.* But others were problematical, like *The Status of Spirits in Royal Abodes* or *Tales for Ghosts.* He had to take these out and turn over the pages, looking for he knew not what.

More time passed. He was not getting anywhere. No one else came here; apparently he was the only one following this particular lead. His guess about the books must have been wrong. There was another room above this one, in a turret, and Crombie's line intersected it too. Maybe there—

Then he spotted it. *The Skeleton in the Closet.* That had to be it!

He took down the book. It was strangely heavy. The cover was of variegated leather, subtly horrible. He opened it, and a strange, unpleasant odor wafted up, as of the flesh of a zombie too long in the sun. There was no print on the first page, only a mélange of color and wash suggestive of the remains of a flattened bug.

Quickly he closed the book. He no longer had any doubt.

The bucket of elixir was downstairs in the ballroom. Bink clasped the book in both arms—it was too heavy to hold in one arm for any length of time—and started down.

He met another zombie, or perhaps the same one as before. It was hard to tell them apart! It was coming up the stairs. This one he knew was real, because the Queen had not extended the masquerade illusion inside the palace, and no illusion at all upstairs. Now Bink suspected the one in the garden had been real too. What were the zombies doing out of their earthy resting places?

"Back off!" Bink cried, protecting the book. "Get out of the palace! Return to your grave!" He advanced menacingly on the zombie, and it retreated. A healthy man could readily dismember a zombie, if he cared to make the attempt. The zombie stumbled on the stair and fell, toppling with grisly abandon down the flight. Bits of bone and goo were scattered on the steps, and dark fluid soaked into the fine old wood. The smell was such as to make Bink's stomach struggle for sudden relief, and his eyes smarted. Zombies did not have much cohesion.

Bink followed it down, pursing his lips with distaste. A number of zombies were associated with Castle Roogna, and they had been instrumental in making it the palace of the King. But now they were supposed to lie safely in their graves. What ghastly urgency brought them into the party?

Well, he would notify the King in due course. First he had to see to Millie's skeleton. He entered the ballroom—and found that the subaquatic motif was gone. The normal pillars and walls had returned. Had the Queen lost interest in her decorations?

"I've got it!" he cried, and the guests collected immediately. "What happened to the water?"

"The Queen left suddenly, and her illusion stopped," Chester said, wiping crumbs of green cake from his face. It seemed refreshments had been real enough, anyway. "Here, let me help you with that book." The centaur reached down with one hand and took it easily from Bink's tiring grasp. Oh for the power of a centaur!

"I meant the healing water, the elixir," Bink said. He knew what had happened to the Queen, now that he thought about it! The King had summoned her.

"Right here," Crombie said, bringing it out from under a table. "Didn't want crumbs to fall in it." The bucket was now on the floor beside the Anniversary Cake.

"That doesn't look like a skeleton," the manticora said.

"Transformed—or something," Bink explained. He opened the book while Chester supported it. There was a general murmur of awe. Some magic!

The spell doctor peered at it. "That's not a transformation. That's topology magic. I never saw such an extreme case before."

Neither had the others. "What is topology magic?" Crombie asked.

"Changing the form without changing it," she said.

"Old crone, you're talking nonsense," Crombie said with his customary diplomacy around the sex.

"I'm talking *magic*, young squirt," she retorted. "Take an object. Stretch it out. Squish it flat. Fold it. You have changed its shape but not its nature. It remains topologically similar. This book is a person."

"With the spirit squished out," Bink said. "Where's Millie?"

The ghost appeared, silent. She remained under the geas, unable to comment on her body. What a terrible fate she had suffered, all these centuries! Flattened and folded into a book, and prevented from telling anyone. Until the Queen's charade-contest prize had coincidentally opened the way.

Coincidentally? Bink suspected his talent was at work.

"Should the Queen supervise the restoration?" the manticora asked.

"The Queen is otherwise occupied, and must not be disturbed," Bink said. Actually it was the King he was protecting. "We'd better proceed without her."

"Right," Chester said, and dumped the book into the bucket.

"Wait!" Bink cried, knowing it was already too late. He had contemplated a gentle immersion. But perhaps this was best.

The dunked book shimmered. Millie the Ghost made an almost soundless shriek as she was drawn toward the bucket. Then the book inflated, absorbing elixir rapidly, opening and unfolding as its tissues filled out. The pages became human limbs and the heavy jacket a human head and torso, flattened horrendously but already bulging into doll-like features. Grotesquely it convulsed into a misshapen mannikin figure, swelling and firming into the semblance of a woman.

Millie the ghost, still trying to scream, floated into the mass, her outline merging with that of the forming body. Suddenly the two phased completely. She stood knee deep in the bucket, as lovely a nymph as could be desired, and an astonishing contrast to what they had just seen. "I'm whole!" she exclaimed in wonder.

"You certainly are," Chester agreed. "Someone fetch her some clothing."

There was a scramble. A form came forward bearing a decayed robe. It was a zombie. Women shrieked. Everyone scrambled to avoid it.

Crombie charged forward, scowling. "You rotters can't come in here! Out, out!"

The zombie retreated, backing toward the Anniversary Cake. "Not that way!" Bink cried, again too late. The zombie came within range of the picklepuss, who snarled.

There was a *zoop!* and the zombie was pickled. Squirting putrid juices, it fell into the cake. The picklepuss struck again, pickling the entire cake as the zombie disappeared into it. Pickled icing flew outward explosively, spattering the guests. The picklepuss broke free of its leash and bounded onto the refreshment table, pickling everything it passed. Women screamed again. It was one of the foolish, enchanting mannerisms they had.

"What is going on here?" a strange young man demanded from the main doorway.

"Stand back!" Bink snapped. "The damn Queen's damn pickler is on the loose!" Now he saw a comely young woman behind the stranger. They were evidently gate-crashers.

Crombie was dashing up. "I'll get those idiots out of the way!" he cried, drawing his sword.

The picklepuss preferred to introduce itself, and to clear its own way. It bounded directly at the strangers. There was a zap—but this time it was the puss who was pickled, in a fashion. It landed on the floor, surprised, then flapped its wings and took off. It had become a deerfly, a delicately winged miniature deer.

"My cake!" the strange young woman cried.

Then Bink caught on. "The Queen!"

"And King!" Crombie agreed, appalled. "In illusion-costume."

What had Bink called the Queen, in his distraction? And Crombie had drawn his sword against the King.

But Queen Iris was already at the cake. "Pickled—with a zombie in it! Who did this thing?" In her outrage she let her illusion slip. She appeared before the crowd in her natural form, and revealed the King in his. Both were in dishabille.

Crombie the woman-hater nevertheless suffered a seizure of gallantry. He sheathed his sword, whipped off his jacket, and put it about the Queen's shoulders, concealing her middle-aged torso. "It is cool here, Highness."

Bink hastily proffered his own jacket to the King, who accepted as if this were a quite ordinary occasion. "Thanks, Bink," he muttered.

Millie stepped out of the bucket, gloriously naked and not cold at all. "I fear I did it, Your Majesties. The zombie came to help me, and the picklepuss got loose—"

The Queen gazed for a long moment on Millie's splendor. Then she glanced down at herself. Abruptly King and Queen were clothed royally again, she rather resembling Millie, he in his natural likeness, which was handsome enough. Bink knew, as did everyone present, that both were in borrowed jackets, with embarrassing portions of their anatomy uncovered, but now there was no sign of this. And, in another moment, Millie was also clothed in illusion, garbed like the chambermaid she was, yet still very pretty.

Bink nodded to himself. It seemed his suggestion about the King changing his own image for lovemaking had been effective. Except that the commotion surrounding Millie's restoration had interrupted it.

The Queen surveyed the ruin of the refreshments. Then she glanced obliquely at the King. She decided to be gracious. "So it worked! You are no longer a ghost!" She studied Millie again, appraisingly. "But you should be dressed for the occasion; this is not a workday for you." And Millie appeared in a fetching evening gown, glassy slippers, and a sparkling tiara. "Who found your skeleton?"

Millie smiled radiantly. "Bink rescued me."

The Queen looked at Bink. "Your nose seems to be into everything," she murmured. Then, more loudly: "Then Bink gets the prize. The first date with—"

She broke off, as well she might. Behind her, the pickled zombie had risen out of the cake. Even pickling could not kill a zombie; they were half pickled by nature. Clots of briny flesh dropped along with the pickled cake. One amorphous glob had dropped on the Queen's shoulder, passing right through the illusion-dress and lodging who-knew-where. This was the cause of the interruption in her speech.

Furious, the Queen whirled on the zombie. "Get out of the palace, you hunk of decay!" She shot a look at the King. "Trent, transform this monster! It ruined my cake!"

But King Trent was thoughtful. "I think the zombie will depart of its own volition, Iris. Procure another date for Millie; I have need of Bink's services in another capacity."

"But Your Majesty—" Millie protested.

"Make the substitute look like Bink," the King murmured to the Queen. "Bink, come to the library."

In the library, King Trent spoke his mind. "Here in Xanth we have a hierarchy of magic. As the most powerful Magician, I am King, and the most powerful Sorceress is my consort. The Good Magician Humfrey is our eldest statesman. But you, Bink—you are anonymous. You have equivalent magic, but it is secret. This means you don't have the status your talent deserves. Perhaps this constitutes a threat to your welfare."

"But there is no danger—"

"Not true, Bink. Whoever sent that sword constitutes a threat to you, though probably not a great one. However, your talent is powerful, not smart. It protects you from hostile magic, but has a problem with intangible menaces. As we know, your situation at home is not ideal at the moment, and—"

Bink nodded. "But as we both also know, that will pass, Your Majesty."

"Agreed. But your talent is not so rational, perhaps. So it procured for you what it deemed to be a better woman—and I fault its ethics, not its taste. Then it balked when you realized the mischief this would cause. So it stopped you from having your date with Millie. The reanimation of the zombie was part of this. Probably the zombie was supposed to help you locate the skeleton, but then it had to reverse its initiative. There is no knowing what mischief might have resulted if Millie and the Queen had insisted on completing your date; but we do know the havoc would have seemed to be coincidental, because that is the way your talent operates. We might have had the whole palace collapse on our heads, or some unfortunate accident might have rendered Millie into a ghost again."

"No!" Bink cried, horrified.

"I know you would not wish that on so nice a creature. Neither would I. This is the reason I interceded. We must simply accept the fact that you can not date Millie, though your talent brought her back to life. I believe I have solved that problem for the nonce. It is obvious that Millie's talent is sex appeal; that accounts for her original untimely demise in ghost-generating circumstances. She shall not lack for male company—other than yours."

"Sex appeal!" Bink exclaimed. "That was why the spell doctor was so amused! She knew what sort of trouble there would be when she restored the spell! And that's why I was so tempted by her offer, despite—"

"Precisely. I felt it too—and I had just completed my liaison with the Queen, thanks to your suggestion. Here, your jacket." And the King gravely handed it back.

"It's my fault all the palace will know—"

"That I am virile as well as Kingly," Trent finished. "This is no shame. Now Iris will never know the weakness I might otherwise have shown. Obviously at such a moment, I should not have felt any attraction to another woman. I did feel it near Millie. So I knew magic was involved. But you, with a difficult home situation, and Millie's evident desire for you—Bink, I think we need to get you out of this region for the duration, at least until we get Millie settled."

"But Chameleon—I can't leave her alone—"

"Have no concern. I shall invite her to the palace, to be attended by my own staff. In fact I think Millie herself would be an excellent maid for her, until we find a better situation. All we need to do is remove you from the stress and temptation that necessarily attend your presence here. Because your talent is powerful but disruptive to palace life, I am providing it guidance. Bink, I am directing you to commence your royal mission: to locate the source of the magic of Xanth."

King Trent paused, and Bink waited. Nothing happened. "I think my talent concurs," Bink said at last.

"Good," the King said, relaxing visibly. Only he knew the peril in trying to go against Bink's talent. "I shall assign you any facilities you require. Someone to protect you, since you may have to intrude on hazardous territory and face unmagical threats, and someone to guide you—" He snapped his fingers. "Chester the Centaur! His situation is very like yours, and you are friends. You can ride him, and you could not have a finer ally in danger."

"But the centaurs are not men; he may not choose to go."

"It is true that my power becomes nominal, in the case of the centaurs. I can not order him to accompany you. But I think he will go as far as Good Magician Humfrey's castle."

"Why?" Bink asked, perplexed.

"Because only Humfrey can tell him what his magic talent may be."

The King certainly kept up on things! "But that Answer would cost him a year's service!"

The King shrugged. "No harm in talking with Humfrey, though. Chester may go along with you, just to keep you company, and incidentally chat with the Good Magician while you are there."

Slowly Bink smiled. "And Cherie Centaur would never need to know!"

"You might discuss that aspect with Chester, at any rate." The King pondered momentarily. "And Crombie—he can point the way for you."

"I don't think Crombie could keep up with Chester," Bink said. "No man can match a centaur's steady speed over ground. And Chester would not want to carry two people—"

"Easily solved! I shall transform Crombie into a form that can keep up. A dragon—"

"That would frighten people and attract attention—"

"So it would. Very well, a griffin. There are a few tame ones, so people would not be too curious. That will deprive him of speech, but give him the power of flight: a fair exchange. And there is hardly a better fighting animal than a griffin, weight for weight. With a centaur and a griffin accompanying you, there should be no mundane threat you need fear." He paused again. "Even so, I think you had better consult Humfrey for specific advice. There might be more here than we have bargained on."

Bink found himself filling with excitement. Adventure, again! "Your Majesty, I'll find the source of magic for you; when can I start?"

"Tomorrow morning," King Trent said, smiling. "Now go home and tell your wife about your preemptive mission. But don't mention Millie the ex-ghost."

"I won't!" Bink agreed, smiling too. About to go, he thought of something else. "Do you know there is a magic mole hanging around the grounds?"

The King accepted this communication gracefully. "I had not been made aware of that. I have no objection, so long as it does not disturb the zombies' graves." Then he did a double take. "That zombie—"

"There was another in the gardens, where the pile of dirt was. Maybe the same one."

"I will institute an investigation in due course." He fixed Bink with a tolerant stare. "Any other important intelligence to impart?"

"Uh, no," Bink said, abruptly embarrassed. What was he doing, telling the King of such a minor matter? He had lost all sense of proportion!

Chapter 3

Nickelpede Chase

In the morning they commenced the mission: three males with woman-problems. All professed to be glad to get away from their situations and into adventure. Crombie especially liked his new form; he spread his wings frequently and took little practice flights.

Indeed, the soldier had much to be pleased about. His lion's legs were powerfully muscled, and his eagle's head was handsome with penetrating eyes, and the feathers of his wings were glorious. The plumage of his neck was blue, and on his back it was black, and on the front red, and the wings were white. A prettier monster could hardly be found in Xanth.

But this was the wilderness: no playground. The moment they departed Castle Roogna, the hostile magic closed in. Most of the paths in this vicinity had been charmed by order of the King, so there was little danger to travelers who did not stray from them. But Good Magician Humfrey was never keen on company, so there was no direct path to his castle. All roads led *away* from it, magically. That meant no safe passage.

Fortunately Crombie's talent of location could keep them going the right way. Periodically the soldier-griffin paused, closed his eyes, extended one wing or forepaw, spun about, and came to rest pointing. Crombie's directional sense was never wrong. Unfortunately it did not take note of the inconveniences of straight-line travel.

The first thing they ran into was a clump of hell's bells. The vines of the plants reared up, their bells ringing stridently. The tintinnabulation became deafening—and disconcerting. "We have to get out of here!" Bink cried, but knew he could not be heard above the noise. Chester had his hands to his ears and he bucked about, kicking at individual bells—but for every one he smashed, a dozen clanged louder.

Crombie spread his wings and flapped violently. Bink thought he was taking off, but instead the griffin dug all four clawed feet into the massed vines and hauled them violently upward. The vines stretched and the clangor of the bells became shrill, then muted. The tension prevented them from swinging properly, so they could not ring.

Bink and Chester took the opportunity to scramble out of the clump. Then Crombie let go and flew up, out of range of the bells. They were free of the hazard, but it was a warning. They could not simply barge ahead as if treading the King's highway.

They continued on, carefully skirting the tangle trees and noose loops. Now Crombie checked often for the nearest dangers as well as for the proper direction. In some cases they had to turn aside from seemingly innocuous places, ripping through itch-weeds and sliding turf. But they trusted Crombie's talent; better itching and sliding, than some ignominious death.

Adventure did not seem quite as exciting, now that they were back in the thick of it. Or the thicket of it, Bink thought. There were many grimy little details and inconveniences that one tended to forget in the comfort of home or palace. Bink's thighs were getting sore from bouncing on the centaur's back, and he was uncomfortably sweaty.

When they got hungry, Crombie pointed out a soda tree growing in a patch of sugar sand. Chester took a sharp stone and poked a spigot-hole in the tree's trunk so that they all could drink from the spouting soda. It looked like blood, a shock at first; but it was actually strawberry-flavored. The sugar sand was too sweet, so it was possible to eat only a little. Crombie pointed out a breadfruit tree, and that was much better. The loaves were just ripe, so that they steamed warmly when opened, and were delicious.

Just when the three were feeling confident again, danger came questing for them. Crombie's talent operated only when invoked; it was not an automatic alert. In this case the threat was a hungry dragon of medium size, land-bound and fire-breathing: about the worst enemy in Xanth except for a large dragon. Such monsters were the lords of the wilderness, and were the standard against which all other viciousness was measured. Had this been the largest variety, they would have been lost. As it was, against this middle range, a man and a griffin and a centaur had a fighting chance.

Still, why had the dragon come after them? Normally dragons did not attack men or centaurs. Dragons fought them, but only when they had to. Because though the dragon was lord of the wilderness, the numbers and organization and weapons of men and centaurs made them more formidable than most dragons preferred. Some men, like the King, had magic that could finish any dragon. Normally people and dragons left each other alone.

That anonymous enemy—could he have sent the dragon? Just a little nudge in the dragon's small, hot brain—and the result would seem like a normal wilderness accident. Bink remembered the King's analysis: that his enemy's magic was very like his own. Not identical, of course. But similar. Therefore insidious.

Then his eyes spotted a little mound of dirt, seemingly freshly deposited. The magic mole here? All Xanth must be infested with the creatures!

Both Crombie and Chester had fighting hearts. But Bink ultimately depended on his secret talent. The trouble was, that protection did not necessarily extend to his two friends. Only by joining the fray directly could Bink hope to help them, for then his talent might have to save them all to save him. He felt guilty about this, knowing that his courage was false; they could die while he was charmed. Yet he could not even tell them about this. There was a lot of this kind of magic in Xanth; it was as if magic liked to clothe itself in superfluous mystery, by that means enhancing itself in the manner of a pretty woman.

At any rate, they were caught in a level clearing: the dragon's ideal hunting ground. There were no large trees to provide either shelter or escape, and no local magic they could draw on fast enough. The dragon was charging, a shaft of fire jetting from its mouth. One good scorch from that flame would be enough to roast a man entire. Dragons found roasted man very tasty, it was widely rumored.

Chester's bow was in his hands, an arrow nocked. He was well provisioned with bow, arrows, sword, and a length of pliant rope, and knew how to use them all. "Keep clear of the flame!" he yelled. "He's got to build up a bellyful between shots. When you see him start to heave, dodge sidewise!"

Good advice! Any creature the size of a dragon was likely to be a trifle slow maneuvering, and that jet of fire needed careful aiming. In fact they might be safest close to the monster, so that they could dodge around it too quickly for it to orient. Not *too* close, for the dragon's teeth and claws were devastating.

Crombie, however, also possessed claws, and his beak was as good in its fashion as teeth. He had the advantage of flight. He could maneuver faster than the dragon despite his mass, though of course his weight was only a fraction of that of the dragon. But he was not a natural griffin, so would not be able to react with the same speed and precision as a true one.

Bink himself was the weak link in the defense—or so it would naturally seem to the others. "Bink, stand back!" Chester cried as Bink charged forward. Bink had no way to explain to the centaur his seeming foolishness.

The dragon slowed as it came within a dragon's-length, its eye on its most formidable opponent: the griffin. Crombie emitted a shriek of challenge and looped toward the dragon's tail. As the monster's head turned to follow him, Chester fired an arrow into its neck. The shaft was driven with the power only a centaur could muster, but it merely bounced off the dragon's metallic scales. "Have to get a shot into its mouth—when there's no fire," Chester muttered.

Bink knew how dangerous that was. A clear shot into the mouth could be had only by standing more or less in front of the dragon while it opened its orifice—and normally it only did that to bite or fire. "Don't risk it!" he cried. "Let Crombie find us an escape!"

But Crombie was out of hearing, and busy, and in any event the ornery centaur was not in a mood to retreat. If they did not attack the dragon at their convenience, the dragon would demolish them at its convenience.

Bink moved in with his sword, seeking a vulnerable spot. The closer he got, the larger the dragon seemed. Its scales overlapped; they might be proof against most arrows, but maybe not against a blade angled up between them. If he could penetrate the armor in the vicinity of a vital organ—

Crombie dived at the dragon, screaming shrilly. The dive-bombing of a griffin was a thing not even a dragon could afford to ignore. The dragon whipped about, its whole body coiling smoothly, its head striking upward in a circle to intercept the griffin. The huge jaws gaped, but it was not quite set for fire; it intended to bite off a wing or head if it could. Its neck was bowed toward Bink, who was not regarded as a threat.

Chester shot an arrow into that mouth, but his angle was bad and the missile ricocheted from a tooth. Crombie came close, talons extended, banking to avoid those gaping jaws and score on an eye. Bink ran in close, and rammed his charmed point into the splayed scales beneath the neck.

The dragon's body was about as thick as Bink was tall, and each scale was the diameter of a spread-fingered hand, glossy blue and fringed with iridescence. Each edge was sharp as a knife. As Bink's blade sank in, those beautiful, deadly scales slid closer to his hand. Abruptly he realized that his hand could be sliced apart before his sword did critical damage to the monster. It was indeed a futile thing for a man to attempt to slay a dragon!

Bink's thrust, however, hurt, as the prick of a thorn could hurt a man. The dragon whipped about to focus on the annoyance. Its neck bent in an S-curve to bring the snout to bear on Bink. That snout seemed twice as large from this vantage. It was the height of his waist, and coppery, with two nostril-valves that hinged inward to prevent air from being expelled. The dragon breathed in through its nose and out through its mouth; probably a snootful of flames would destroy the delicate nasal passages, so the system had to be fail-safe. Below, the lips were burnished and lighter in color, as if alloyed with some sterner metal, able to tolerate the furnace heat of the dragon's breath. The teeth were stained scorch-brown, with black soot in the crevices.

The eyes were situated on the sides of the dragon's cranium, but the muzzle was channeled so that the creature could look directly forward to see where its fire struck. At the moment those eyes were on Bink, who stood there with one hand on the hilt of his sword embedded in the lower curve of the S-bend of the neck. Dragons varied in intelligence, like all creatures, but even a stupid dragon would be quick enough to connect Bink with the injury in such a circumstance. The nostril-valves closed with little pings. The mouth cracked open. Bink was about to be thoroughly scorched.

He froze. All he could think of was his sword: it was a good weapon, charmed to be always sharp and light in his hand, a gift from the King's arsenal. If he dodged out of the way, he would have to leave that faithful blade embedded in the dragon's neck, for there was not time to lever it loose. He did not want to lose it, so he hung on—and was unable to move out of the projected path of flame.

A roaring developed in the belly of the dragon. The throat opened into a round tube, ready to eject the column of fire. Bink was a standing target.

Then an arrow swished over Bink's still shoulder and down that open throat. A perfect shot by the centaur!

Too perfect. Instead of penetrating the softer lining of the deep gullet and punctuating a vital organ, the arrow disappeared into the stirring flame. Now that flame came out, a deadly shaft of golden light, destroying the arrow, hurtling toward Bink's head.

And the griffin crashed into the dragon's snout, bearing it down just as the fire emerged. The snout met the ground at Bink's feet. There was something like an explosion. The dragon's head was bathed in the backblast, and a small crater was gouged out of the earth. The griffin just missed having a wing scorched. Bink was left standing there, sword in hand, at the smoking rim, unscathed.

The griffin snatched Bink in his claws as the dragon reoriented. They were momentarily airborne as a second blast of fire passed beneath Bink's dangling feet.

Crombie could not support Bink's weight long on the ground, let alone airborne. "Find an escape!" Bink cried. "Use your talent!"

Surprised, the griffin dropped Bink in a pillow bush and performed his direction-pointing routine in midair. Meanwhile the dragon coughed out several dusty fireballs, sprayed particles of soot, cleared its pipe, and charged after them. Chester galloped beside it, trying to get in another good shot. It was evident that this dragon was too tough for the three of them together.

Crombie's right wing pointed to the side. "Squawk!" he cried.

Chester looped back and cruised by. "On my back!" he cried.

Bink leaped, and sprawled across the centaur's rump. He started to slide off, grabbed wildly, caught a handful of mane, and righted himself while the centaur galloped on, head held low. Bink almost tumbled forward, but clasped his knees tightly and held on.

He looked up—and saw the dragon charging headlong at them. The monster must have looped back too! "Chester!" Bink screamed in panic. "It's in front of us!"

"Front, hell!" the centaur yelled from behind him. "You're facing backward, dodo."

Oops. So he was. The dragon was following them, trying to catch up. Bink was holding onto Chester's handsome tail. No wonder the head had seemed low!

Well, it was a good way to watch the dragon. "The monster's gaining," Bink reported. "Where's Crombie pointing?"

"That's where I'm going!" Chester called back. "But I don't know how far it is!" His evident ire was understandable; he did not like fleeing an enemy, even so formidable a one as a dragon. If it weren't for Bink, the centaur would not have retreated at all.

Crombie had indicated the direction, but could not know whether they would be able to reach the place of safety in time. Suppose the dragon caught them first? Bink feared his talent would have to come into operation again.

"That was the bravest thing I ever saw in a man," Chester called. Obviously he felt centaurs had elevated standards of bravery. "You stood right in front of the dragon's mouth, attracting his attention, and you kept absolutely still so I could get a clear shot around you. You could have been fried."

Or skewered by the centaur's arrow. But centaurs seldom missed their targets. "That wasn't bravery," Bink replied. "I was too terrified to move a muscle."

"So? And what about when you spiked your sword into old firesnoot's neck?"

That had resembled bravery. How could Bink explain that the protection provided by his devious talent made such acts easier? Had he really believed he might get killed, he might never have had the nerve. "I only did what you two were doing: attacking. To save my hide."

Chester snorted derisively and charged on. The dragon continued to gain. Had it been a flying one, they would have been lost—except that the flying dragons were smaller, and consequently less powerful. But *any* dragon was real trouble, unless the one being attacked had nullifying magic.

Now the dragon was coming within torching range. There was dirt on its nose, but its fires remained stoked. It opened its mouth—

Chester dropped into a hole. "Hang on!" the centaur cried belatedly. "It's a crevice too broad to leap!"

Evidently so. Bink narrowly avoided doing a somersault over Chester's tail, hung on, and landed with gut-jarring impact. The walls rose up rapidly on either side. They must have approached this chasm obliquely, so that it was easy to rush down inside it. This must be the escape Crombie had indicated. Indeed, the griffin was angling down to join them.

But the dragon followed them into the crack. Its long, sinuous body was well adapted to this type of aperture. There was no crevice a centaur could hide in that would be too narrow for the dragon. That made Bink uncertain; could this be a diversion, and not the escape route?

Suddenly Chester skidded to a halt. "Don't stop!" Bink cried. "The monster's right behind us!"

"Some escape route that featherbrain picked for us," Chester muttered with disgust. "We'd better fight the dragon."

"We'll have to," Bink said, turning around to face the centaur's head. "We can't outrun it—"

Then he saw what had stopped Chester. "Nickelpedes!" he cried with new horror.

The dragon saw the nickelpedes too. It skidded to a halt and tried to turn about—but the crevice was too narrow for effective circling. It might have looped up and over its own body, but that would have meant exposing its neck again, where it had already been stung.

Crombie came to land between them. "This was your way out, birdbrain?" Chester demanded as the nickelpedes scuttled close, forming living barricades wherever there were shadows, cutting off any likely escape.

"Squawk!" the griffin replied angrily. He understood both the language and the insult perfectly, though he could not reply in kind. He stood up, wings furled so they would not bang against the close walls and get smudged. He closed his eyes, whirled awkwardly, and pointed with a forepaw. But the paw was not firm; it wavered across half a circle.

A few bold nickelpedes attacked. Each was girt with about five hundred legs and a single set of pincers, and each had a taste for fresh meat. A single nickelpede could be killed, with a certain amount of effort and unpleasantness; a hundred were insurmountable without extraordinary armor or magic. But the attempt had to be made, for if there was one thing worse than being roasted by a dragon, it was being gouged by nickelpedes.

The dragon youped. A nickelpede had clamped on its smallest front claw and was gouging out a disk of substance nearly an inch across. The dragon's claws were iron, but the nickelpede's pincers were nickel hardened by magic; they could gouge from almost anything. Chester chuckled grimly.

Then the centaur leaped high, emitting a cry like a neigh. Another nickelpede had scooped out a piece of one hoof. Chester came down, stomping the little monster hard. But the nickelpede scuttled to the side, avoiding the blow—while others attacked Chester's remaining hooves. And the dragon chuckled.

But their predicament was not funny. The crevice was deep, with a level footing below sheer vertical stone walls. It was too deep for Bink to jump out of. He might have made it by standing on Chester's back—but how would the centaur himself get out? The dragon could lift its head that high—but not its forefeet. Only the griffin might escape—except that the narrowness of the cleft prevented him from spreading his wings far enough. He had glided into a landing, but taking off required more vigorous action and lift. With Chester's help he might get high enough—but again, what about Chester? They were trapped as much by the situation as by the walls.

Very soon they would all be food for the swarm, if they didn't get out of here. Yet the bulk of the dragon blocked the exit. At this stage the dragon was fidgeting about, trying to hoist its body off the ground so that it would not get gouged in a tender place, while the nickelpedes went gleefully for its feet. Chester was performing similarly. So was Crombie, who could not fly at the moment. And Bink himself, whose extremities were the most tender of all. Where was his talent now?

"It's only the sunlight that holds them back," Chester said. "When the sun moves over, they'll all be on us."

Bink looked at the line of shadow. At the moment the sun was high, and there was only a small shadowed area. But that area was packed with the pinching monsters. Only one nickelpede in a hundred ventured forth into the light, scuttling across to the shadow of someone's body—but even so, there were a dozen or more coming.

Then Bink had an inspiration. "We must cooperate!" he cried. "All together —before we all get eaten together!"

"Of course." Chester said. "But how do we get rid of the dragon?"

"I mean cooperate *with* the dragon!"

Chester, Crombie, and the dragon looked at him, mutually startled. All of them were still dancing in place. "A dragon's too dumb to cooperate, even if it wanted to," Chester objected. "Even if there were any point. There's just a pilot light in the monster's brain. Why help it eat us?"

"There would have to be a truce," Bink said. "We help it, it doesn't eat us. The dragon can't turn about, it can't lift its body off the ground for any length of time. So it is vulnerable, just as we are. But it can fight the nickelpedes much better than we can. So if we protect its flank—"

"Flame!" Chester exclaimed. "Nickelpedes hate light—and flame has lots of light!"

"Right," Bink said. "So if we protect its dark side, and its feet—"

"And its back," Chester added, glancing at Crombie. "If it will trust us—"

"It has no choice," Bink said, moving toward the dragon.

"It doesn't *know* that! Watch out—it'll scorch you!"

But Bink, protected by his magic, knew he would not get scorched. He walked up to the nose of the dragon and stood before the copper nostrils. Wisps of smoke drifted up from them; there was a little leakage when the system was idle. "Dragon," he said, "you understand me, don't you? You can't talk, but you know we're all in trouble now, and we'll all get gouged to pieces and consumed by the nickelpedes unless we help each other fight them off?" And he jumped to avoid the onslaught of another nickelpede.

The dragon did not respond. It just looked at him. Bink hoped that was a good sign. He drew his sword, sighted at the nickelpede between his feet, and impaled it neatly on the point. The thing clicked its pincers as Bink lifted it, undead, and it strove to get at anything gougeable. From this vantage the pincers were circular; a nickelpede normally clamped onto its target with a few hundred legs and scooped inward to cut away a shallow disk of flesh. Horrible!

"I can nullify one nickelpede at a time," Bink continued, showing his captive to the dragon's right eye. "I could sit on one of your feet and protect it. My friend the centaur could defend your tail. The griffin is actually a transformed soldier, another friend; he could watch for enemies dropping on your back, and crunch them in his beak. We can help you—if you trust us."

"How can we trust *it?*" Chester demanded.

Still the dragon did not react. Was it stupid, or comprehending? As long as it listened, Bink had to assume that all was reasonably well. "Here's what we have to do," he continued hurriedly, as the shadow advanced and the nickelpedes grew bolder. Three were coming at Bink's own feet now; it would be hard to spear them all in time. "The three of us must climb over you to get to your tail and back feet. Crombie will perch on your back. So you will have to let us pass, and tolerate our weight on your body. We'll do what we can to keep your scales intact. But the main job is yours. Once we get clear, you scorch the whole mass of nickelpedes in the crevice before you. Fry them all! They don't like light, and will clear out. Then we can all back out of here. Agreed?"

The dragon merely stared at him. Had it really comprehended? Chester took a hand. "Dragon, you know centaurs are creatures of honor. Everyone knows that!

I give my word: I will not attack you if you let me past. I know Bink; even though he is a man, he is also a creature of honor. And the griffin—" He hesitated.

"Squawk!" Crombie said angrily.

"Crombie is also a creature of honor," Bink said quickly. "And we assume you are too, dragon."

Yet the dragon still stared at him. Bink realized he would have to gamble. The dragon might be too stupid to comprehend the nature of their offer, or it still might not trust them. It was possible it had no way to respond. They would have to gamble on the last alternative.

"I am going to climb over your back," Bink said. "My friends will follow me. The truce will hold until we all get out of this crevice."

Truce. He had learned to appreciate this mode of compromise over a year ago, when he and Chameleon had made truce with the Evil Magician. That arrangement had saved them all from disaster in the wilderness. It seemed no enemy was too awful to deal with in time of sufficient peril.

He addressed the silent dragon again. "If you don't believe me, scorch us now, and face the nickelpedes alone."

Bink walked boldly around the dragon's head to the base of the neck where the front legs projected. The dragon did not scorch him. He saw the wound he had made in the neck, dripping ichor that a nickelpede was greedily eating as it landed. The little monster was gouging disks out of the stone floor to get every last bit of the delicacy puddling there. The nickelpedes had to be the most rapacious monsters for their size in all the Land of Xanth!

Bink sheathed his sword after wiping off the impaled nickelpede, then stretched up his hands and jumped. His head and chest cleared the top of the leg, and he was able to scramble over the scales. Because they were lying flat, they did not cut him—so long as he did not rub them the wrong way. The dragon did not move. "Come on, Chester, Crombie!" he called back.

Prompted by his call and the encroaching nickelpedes, the two creatures followed. The dragon eyed them warily, but held its flame. Soon the three assumed their battle stations. Just in time; the nickelpedes had massed so thickly that the shadowed walls were bright with their highlights. The shadow was advancing inexorably.

"Blast out the passage ahead!" Bink yelled to the dragon. "We're protecting your flank!" And he drew his sword and speared another nickelpede on the point.

The dragon responded by belching out a tremendous wash of fire. It scorched the whole crevice, obscuring everything in flame and smoke. It was as if a bolt of lightning had struck. Nickelpedes screeched thinly as they fell from the walls, burning, some even exploding. Success!

"Very good," Bink said to the dragon, wiping his tearing eyes. There had been a fair backlash of hot gas. "Now back out." But the creature did not move.

"It can't back," Chester said, catching on. "Its legs don't work that way. A dragon never retreats."

Bink realized it was true. The dragon was limber, and normally it twined about to reverse course. Its legs and feet were structured for forward only. No wonder it had not expressed agreement to Bink's proposal; it could not perform. Without words, it could not explain; any negation would have seemed to be a refusal of the truce. Even a really intelligent creature would have been in a dilemma there, and the dragon was less than that. So it had shut up.

"But that means we can only advance deeper into the crevice!" Bink said, appalled. "Or wait until dark." Either course was disaster; in complete darkness the nickelpedes would be upon them in a mass, and gobble every part of their bodies in disk-chunks called nickels. What a horrible fate, to be nickeled to death!

The dragon's flame would not last forever; the creature had to refuel. Which was what it had been trying to do at the outset, chasing them. The moment its fires gave out, the nickelpedes would swarm back in.

"The dragon can't be saved," Chester said. "Get on my back, Bink; I'll gallop out of here, now that we're past the obstruction. Crombie can leap from its back and fly."

"No," Bink said firmly. "That would violate our truce. We agreed to see the whole party safe outside."

"We did not," the centaur said, nettled. "We agreed not to attack it. We shall not attack it. We shall merely leave it."

"And let the nickelpedes attack it instead?" Bink finished. "That was not my understanding. You go if you choose; I'm finishing my commitment, implied as well as literal."

Chester shook his head. "You're not only the bravest man I've seen, you're the man-headedest."

I.e., brave and stubborn. Bink wished it were true. Buoyed by his talent, he could take risks and honor pledges he might otherwise have reneged on. Crombie and Chester had genuine courage; they knew they could die. He felt guilty, again, knowing that he would get out of this somehow, while his friends had no such assurance. Yet he knew they would not desert him. So he was stuck: he had to place them in terrible peril—to honor his truce with an enemy who had tried to kill them all. Where was the ethical course?

"If we can't go back, we'll just have to go forward," Chester decided. "Tell your friend to get up steam."

The irony was unsubtle—but Chester was not a subtle centaur. In fact, he was an argumentative brawler. But a loyal friend. Bink's guilt remained. His only hope was that as long as they were all in this fix together, his talent might extricate them together. Might.

"Dragon, if you would—" Bink called. "Maybe there's an exit ahead."

"Maybe the moon isn't made of green cheese," Chester murmured. It was sarcasm, but it reminded Bink poignantly of the time in his childhood when there had been what the centaurs called an eclipse: the sun had banged into the moon and knocked a big chunk out of it, and a great wad of the cheese had fallen to the ground. The whole North Village had gorged on it before it spoiled. Green cheese was the best—but it only grew well in the sky. The best pies were in the sky, too.

The dragon lurched forward. Bink threw his arms about its ankle to keep from being dislodged; this was worse than riding a centaur! Crombie spread his wings partially for balance, and Chester, facing the rear, trotted backward, startled. What was a cautious pace for the dragon was a healthy clip for the others.

Bink was afraid the crevice would narrow, making progress impossible. Then he would really have a crisis of conscience! But it stabilized, extending interminably forward, curving back and forth so that no exit was visible. Periodically the dragon blasted out the path with a snort of flame. But Bink noticed the blasts were getting weaker. It took a lot of energy to shoot out fire, and the dragon was hungry and tiring. Before long it would no longer be able to brush back the nickelpedes. Did dragons like green cheese? Irrelevant thought! Even if cheese would restore the fire, there was no moon available right now, and if the moon were in the sky, how could they reach it?

Then the crevice branched. The dragon paused, perplexed. Which was the most promising route?

Crombie closed his griffin eyes and spun as well as he could on the dragon's back. But again his wing pointed erratically, sweeping past both choices and finally falling, defeated. Crombie's spell was evidently in need of the spell doctor —at a most inopportune time.

"Trust the bird-head to foul it up," Chester muttered.

Crombie, whose bird hearing evidently remained in good order, reacted angrily. He squawked and walked along the dragon toward the centaur, the feathers of his neck lifting like the hackles of a werewolf.

"Relax!" Bink cried. "We'll never get out if we quarrel among ourselves!"

Reluctantly, Crombie moved back to his station. It seemed to be up to Bink to decide on the route.

Was there a chance the two branches looped around and met each other? If so, this was a handy way to get the dragon turned about, so they all could get out of here. But that seemed unlikely. At any rate, if it were this way, either path would do. "Bear left."

The dragon marched into the left one. The nickelpedes followed. It was getting harder to drive them off; not only was the shadow advancing, the oblique angle of the new passage made a narrower shaft for the sunlight.

Bink looked up into the sky—and discovered that things were even worse than they had seemed. Clouds were forming. Soon there would be no sunlight at all. Then the nickelpedes would be bold indeed.

The passage divided again. Oh, no! This was becoming a maze—a deadly serious one. If they got lost in it—

"Left again," Bink said. This was awful; he was guessing, and it was getting them all deeper into trouble. If only Crombie's talent were operative here! Strange how it had failed. It had seemed to be in good order until they entered the crevice. In fact, it had pointed them here. Why had it sent them into a region that blanked it out? And why had Bink's own talent permitted this? Had it failed too?

Suddenly he was afraid. He had not realized how much he had come to depend on his talent. Without it he was vulnerable! He could be hurt or killed by magic.

No! He could not believe that. His magic had to remain—and Crombie's too. He just had to figure out why they were malfunctioning at the moment.

Malfunctioning? How did he know they were? Maybe those talents were trying to do their jobs, but weren't being interpreted correctly. Like the dragon, they were powerful but silent. Crombie merely had to ask the right question. If he asked "Which road leads out of the maze?" it was possible that any of them did—or none. What would his talent do then? If he demanded the specific direction of out, and the escape route curved, wouldn't his pointing appendage have to curve about, too? There was no single direction, no single choice; escape was a labyrinth. So Crombie was baffled, thinking his talent had failed, when perhaps it had only quit in disgust.

Suppose Bink's talent was aware of this. It would not worry; it would show him a way to make Crombie's talent operate, in due course. But it would be better if Bink figured that way out himself, because then he could be sure that all of them escaped. That way, both friendship and honor would be preserved.

So now the test of his mettle was upon him. How could he solve the riddle of the balked talent? Obviously straight direction was not the answer to the question of out. Yet Crombie's talent was directional. He asked where something was, and it showed the direction. If direction were not the answer in this case, what was—and how could Crombie identify it?

Maybe he could use Crombie's talent to find out. "Crombie," he called around the dragon's body. "Where is something that will get us out of here?"

The griffin obligingly went through his routine, to no avail.

"It's no good," Chester grumbled. "His talent's soured. Not that it ever was much good. Now if *I* had a talent—"

Crombie squawked, and the tone was such that it was obvious that the centaur had been treated to a rich discourse on prospective orifices available for shoving such a talent. Chester's ears reddened.

"That's what you're along to find out," Bink reminded him. "Right now, Crombie's all we have. I think there's a key, if I can only find it in time." He paused to skewer another nickelpede. The things died slowly, but they didn't attack after skewering. They couldn't; their companions gobbled them up immediately. Soon it would not be possible to concentrate on anything but nickelpedes! "Crombie, where is something that will show us how to get out of here?"

"You just asked that," Chester grumbled.

"No, I modified the language slightly. Showing is not the same as—" He stopped to watch the griffin. For a moment it seemed Crombie's talent was working, but then his wing wavered back and forth and gave up.

"Still, we must be getting warm," Bink said with false hope. "Crombie, where is there something that will stop the nickelpedes?"

Crombie's wing pointed straight up.

"Sure," Chester said, disgusted. "The sun. But it's going behind a cloud."

"At least it proves his talent is working."

They came to another fork. "Crombie, which fork will bring us fastest to something that will help us?" Bink asked.

The wing pointed firmly to the right. "Hey, it actually worked!" Chester exclaimed mockingly. "Unless he's faking it."

Crombie let out another vile-sounding squawk, almost enough in itself to scorch a few nickelpedes.

But now the cloud covered the sun, sinking the entire cleft in awful shadow. The nickelpedes moved in with a multiple clicking of satisfaction and anticipation and garden-variety greed. "Dragon, take the right fork!" Bink cried. "Blast it out ahead of you, and *run*. Use up your last reserves of fire if you have to. We're on to something good." He hoped.

The dragon responded by shooting out a searing bolt of flame that illuminated the passage far ahead. Again the nickelpedes squeeked as they died. The dragon galloped over their smoking corpses, carrying Bink and Chester and Crombie along. But it was tiring.

Something sparkled in the dim passage ahead. Bink inhaled hope—but quickly realized it was only a will-o'-the-wisp. No help there!

No help? Suddenly Bink remembered something. "That's it!" he cried. "Dragon, follow that wisp!"

The dragon obeyed, despite Chester's incredulous neigh. It snorted no more flame, for its furnace was almost exhausted, but it could still run at a respectable pace. The wisp dodged about, as wisps had always done, always just at the verge of perception. Wisps were born teases. The dragon lumbered through fork after fork, quite lost—and suddenly emerged into a dry riverbed.

"We're out!" Bink cried, hardly believing it himself. But not yet safe; the nickelpedes were boiling out of the chasm.

Bink and Chester scrambled away from the dragon and up and out of the gully, and found themselves in the ashes of an old burn. Crombie spread his wings and launched into the sky with a squawk of pure relief. The nickelpedes did not follow even the dragon; they could not scuttle well through ashes, and might get caught by returning sunlight. The party was safe.

The dragon collapsed, panting, in a cloud of ashes. Bink walked around to its snout. "Dragon, we had a good fight, and you were winning. We fled, and you pursued, and we all got caught in the cleft. We made a truce to escape, and you honored it well and so did we. By working together we saved all our lives. Now I would rather have you as a friend than an enemy. Will you accept friendship with the three of us before we part?"

The dragon looked at him. Finally, slowly, it inclined its nose slightly forward in an affirmative nod.

"Until we meet again—good hunting," Bink said. "Here, we can help you a little. Crombie, where is the nearest good dragon-prey—something even a tired dragon can nab?"

Crombie spun in the air and flung out a wing as he fell. It pointed north—and now they heard the thrashing of something large, probably caught in a noose-loop bush. Something fat and foolish, who would die a slow death in the loops if not dispatched more mercifully by the scorch of a dragon.

"Good hunting," Bink repeated, patting the dragon on its lukewarm copper nose and turning away. The dragon started north.

"What was the point in that?" Chester asked in a low tone. "We have no need of a dragon's friendship."

"I wanted it amicable, here," Bink said. "This is a very special place, where peace should exist among all creatures of Xanth."

"Are you crazy? This is a burnout!"

"I'll show you," Bink said. "We'll follow that wisp."

The will-o'-the wisp was still present, hovering not quite close enough to overtake. "Look, Bink," Chester protested. "We lucked out on that wisp—but we dare not follow it any farther. It'll lead us into destruction."

"Not this one," Bink said, following it. After a moment Chester shrugged, gave a what-can-you-do? kick with his hind hooves, and followed. Crombie glided down to join them.

Soon the wisp stopped at a glowstone marking a grave. As they approached, the stone lit up with the words HERMAN THE HERMIT.

"Uncle Herman!" Chester exclaimed. "You mean this is the place he—?"

"The place he saved Xanth from the wiggles," Bink said. "By summoning many creatures with his wisps, then setting a salamander-fire to burn the wiggles out. He gave his noble life in that effort, and died a hero. I knew the wisp would lead us here, once I recognized the burnout, because you are his kind and kin and the wisps honor his memory. Crombie's talent located the wisp, and the wisp—"

"Uncle Herman, hero," Chester said, his face twisting into an unfamiliar expression. The belligerent centaur was unused to the gentle emotions of reverence and respect. Almost, it seemed there was a forlorn melody played by a flute, enhancing the mood.

Bink and Crombie withdrew, leaving Chester to his contemplation in privacy. Bink tripped over a pile of dirt that hadn't been there a moment ago and almost fell headlong; that was the only sour note.

Chapter 4

Magician's Castle

ood Magician Humfrey's castle was the same as ever. It stood
tall and slender, with stout outer ramparts and a high inner
tower topped by embrasures and parapets and similar accouterments normal to
castles. It was smaller than Bink remembered, but he knew it had not changed.
Perhaps the problem was that his memory of the interior made it larger than his
memory of the exterior. With magic, it was possible that the inside really was
larger than the outside.

The magic access routes had been changed, however, and the hippocampus or
water-horse was gone from the moat, its time of service expired. There was
surely another creature standing guard inside, in lieu of the manticora Bink had
known: the one at the Anniversary party. Even monsters had to give a year of

their lives as fee for the Good Magician's Answers, and they normally performed as guardians of the castle. Humfrey did not appreciate casual intrusions.

As they came to the moat, the nature of the new guardian became apparent. Monster? Monsters! The water teemed with serpentine loops, some white, some black, sliding past each other interminably.

"But where are the heads, the tails?" Chester inquired, perplexed. "All I see are coils."

The three of them stood by the moat, pondering. What could a whole fleet of sea serpents have wanted to ask the Good Magician, needing his Answer so badly that all were willing to pay the fee? How had they gotten here? It seemed it was not for Bink and his friends to know.

Fortunately, this was not a hazard he had to brave. Bink was on the King's business, and would be admitted to the castle as soon as he made his presence known. "Magician Humfrey!" he called.

There was no response from the castle. Doubtless the Good Magician was buried in a good book of magic, oblivious to outside proceedings. "Magician, it is Bink, on a mission for the King!" he called again.

Still no response. "The old gnome must be hard of hearing," Chester muttered. "Let me try." He cupped his hands before his mouth and bellowed: "MA-GICIAN: COMPANY!"

The bellow echoed and re-echoed from the battlements, but the castle was silent. "He should be at home," Bink said. "He never goes anywhere. Still, we can check. Crombie, where is the Good Magician?"

The griffin went through his act and pointed—directly toward the castle. "Must be beyond it," Chester said. "If your talent's not on the blink again."

Crombie squawked, his blue hackle-feathers rising again. He stood on his hind feet and made boxing motions with his front feet, challenging the centaur to fight. Chester seemed quite ready to oblige.

"No, no!" Bink cried, diving between them. "We don't want to make a bad impression!"

"Hell, I wanted to make a good impression—on his feathery face," Chester grumbled.

Bink knew he had to separate the two combative creatures. "Go around to the other side of the castle and get another fix on the Magician," he told Crombie.

"Triangulate," Chester said.

Triangulate? Bink, accustomed to his friend's surly manner, had forgotten how educated centaurs were. Triangulation was a magical means of locating something without going there directly. Chester had a good mind and a lot of background information, when he cared to let it show.

The griffin decided that the word was not, after all, a scatological insult, and flew to one side of the castle and pointed again. Toward the castle. No question about it: the Magician was home.

"Better fly in and notify him we're here," Bink said. "We don't want to mess with those moat-monsters."

Crombie took off again. There was a small landing area between the moat and the castle, but no opening in the wall, so the griffin mounted to the high turrets. But there seemed to be no entry there for a creature of that size, so after circling the tower twice the griffin flew back.

"I remember now," Bink said. "The windows are barred. A small bird can get through, but not a griffin. We'll just have to brave the moat after all."

"We're here on the King's business!" Chester exclaimed angrily. His unhandsome face was excellent for scowling. "We don't have to run the gauntlet!"

Bink was piqued himself. But he knew he could make it through, because of his talent. "It is my responsibility. I'll see if I can navigate the castle obstacles and get his attention, then he'll let you in."

"We won't let you brave that moat alone!" Chester protested, and Crombie squawked agreement. These two might have their rivalry, but they knew their ultimate loyalty.

This was awkward. They had no magical protection. "I'd really rather do it alone," Bink said. "I am smaller than you, and more likely to slip through. If I fall in the moat, you can lasso me and haul me out, quickly. But I could never haul *you* out, if—"

"Got a point," Chester admitted grudgingly. "Crombie can fly across the water, but we already know he can't get in. Too bad he's not strong enough to fly with you."

Crombie started to bridle again, but Bink cut in quickly. "He could carry your rope to me, in an emergency. I really think it is best this way. You can help me most by figuring out what type of monsters are in that moat. Is there anything in the centaur's lexicon about headless serpents?"

"Some—but the coils don't match the pattern. They look more like pieces of a—" Chester broke off, staring. "It *is!* It's an ouroboros!"

"An ouroboros?" Bink repeated blankly. "What's that—a fleet of sea monsters?"

"It is all one monster, a water dragon, clutching its own tail between its teeth. Half of it white, half black. The symbolism is—"

"But there are a score or more segments, all over the moat! Some are in toward the castle, and some out near the edge. Look—there's three lined up parallel. They can't be pieces of the same monster!"

"Yes they can," Chester said wisely. "The ouroboros loops entirely around the castle—"

"But that would account for only a single-file line of—"

"Loops several times, and its head plunges below its own coils to catch the tail. A little like a mobius strip. So—"

"A what?"

"Never mind. That's specialized magic. Take my word: that thing in the moat is all one monster—and it can't bite because it won't let go of its tail. So if you're good at balancing, you can walk along it to the castle."

"But no segment shows above the water more than five feet! I'd fall in, if I tried to jump from segment to segment!"

"Don't jump," Chester said with unusual patience, for him. "Walk. Even coiled several times around the loop, the thing is too long for the moat, so it has to make vertical convolutions. These can never straighten out; as soon as one subsides, another must rise, and this happens in a progressive undulation. That's how the ouroboros moves, in this restricted locale. So you need never get wet; just follow one stage of the thing to the end."

"This makes no sense to me!" Bink said. "You're speaking in Centaurese. Can't you simplify?"

"Just jump aboard the nearest loop and stay there," Chester advised. "You'll understand it once you do it."

"You have more confidence in me than I do," Bink said dubiously. "I hope you know what I'm doing."

"I trusted you to get us out of the nickelpede crevice Crombie got us into," Chester said. "Now you trust me to get you across that moat. It isn't as if you've never ridden a monster before."

"Squawk!" Crombie cried, pointing a wing at the centaur. Bink smiled; he *had* been riding the centaur. Score one for the soldier.

"Just don't fall off," Chester continued evenly. "You'd get crushed by the coils."

"Um," Bink agreed, sobering. Even with his talent backing him up, he didn't like this. Walking the back of a moving sea monster? Why not walk the wings of a flying roc, while he was at it!

He cast his gaze about, as he tended to do when he sought some escape from what he knew he could not escape—and spotted another mound of earth. Angrily he marched a few paces and stepped on it, pressing it down.

But when a convenient loop offered, Bink jumped across to it, windmilling his arms in the fashion of a mill-tree to regain his balance. The segment of monster sank somewhat beneath his weight, then stabilized pneumatically. Though glistening with moisture, the white skin was not slippery. Good; maybe this walk was possible after all!

The flesh rippled. The section in front of him subsided into the water. "Turn about!" Chester called from the bank. "Stay with it!"

Bink turned, windmilling again. There, behind/before him, the loop was extending. He stepped along it, hurrying as the water lapped at his heels. This was like a magic highway, opening out ahead of him, closing behind him. Maybe that was the basic principle of such one-way paths; they were really the backs of monsters! Yet though the serpent seemed to be moving toward Bink's rear, the loop stayed in place, or drifted slightly forward. So he was walking fairly swiftly, to make rather slow progress. "I'll never get across this way," he complained. "I'm not even walking toward the castle."

"You'll get there," Chester called. "Keep your feet going."

Bink kept walking, and the centaur and griffin moved slowly around the moat to keep pace. Suddenly a loop developed between him and his friends. "Hey, I've crossed to an inner loop—and I never left this one!" Bink exclaimed.

"You are spiraling inward," Chester explained. "There is no other way to go. When you get to the inner bank, jump off."

Bink continued, rather enjoying it now that he had his sea legs and understood the mechanism. There was no way he could avoid reaching the other shore, so long as he kept his place here. Yet what an ingenious puzzle it was; could he have solved it without Chester's help?

Abruptly the segment narrowed. He was coming to the end of the tail! Then the head of the ouroboros came in sight, its teeth firmly clamped to the tail. Suddenly nervous again, Bink had no alternative but to tread on that head. Suppose it decided to let go the tail, just this once, and take him in instead? The big dragon eyes stared briefly at him, sending a chill through his body.

Then the head was past, continuing its undulation into the water, and Bink was treading the massive neck, broad as a highway after the slender tail. Apparently this dragon, serpent, or whatever was independent of air; it could keep its head submerged indefinitely. Yet how did it eat, if it never let go of its tail? It couldn't be eating itself, could it? Maybe that had been its Question for the Magician: how could it let go of its tail, so it could consume the idiots who walked along its length? No, if it had the answer to that, it would have gobbled up Bink as he passed.

"Jump, Bink!" Chester called.

Oops—had the serpent changed its mind, let go, and come to gobble? Bink looked back, but saw nothing special. Then he looked ahead—and discovered that the body was twisting down and under the adjacent leg of the spiral. No more highway! He leaped to shore as his footing ended.

Now he was at the outer rampart of the castle. He looked for the great doorway he had encountered on his first approach to this castle, back before Trent was King—and found a waterfall.

A waterfall? How had *that* gotten here? He traced it upward and saw a ledge; the water issued from somewhere out of sight, to course down over the frame of the door.

Was there an aperture behind the sheet of water? Bink did not relish getting wet here, after traversing the whole moat dry, but he would have to look. He removed his clothing and set it aside, so that it would not get soaked, then nudged cautiously into the waterfall.

The water was cool but not chill. There was a small air space behind it. Then the wood facing of the door. He explored the surface with his hands, pushing here and there, but found no looseness anywhere. There was no entrance here.

He backed out of the fall, shaking his head to clear it of drip. Where could he go from here? The ledge circled the castle, but he knew the wall was solid stone throughout. There would be no access to the interior.

Nevertheless, Bink made the circuit, verifying his suspicion. No access. What now?

He suffered a surge of anger. Here he was on the King's business; why should he have to go through all this nonsense? The old gnome-Magician thought he was so clever, putting a maze around himself! Bink had just about had it with mazes. First the Queen's, then the nickelpede crevice, now this.

But at heart Bink was a practical man. In due course the pressure of his anger ceased, like the steam of a relaxing dragon. He came to look at the waterfall again. This was no mountain, with natural drainage. The water had to be raised by mundane or magical means to an upper level, then poured out. Surely it was a circulatory system, drawn from the moat and returning to it. Could he swim in where the water was sucked up?

No. Water could go where he could not. Such as through a sieve. He could drown, if his body got stuck in the water channel. Not worth the risk.

The only other direction was up. Could he climb?

Yes he could. He now noted little handholds in the wood at the edge of the waterfall. "Here I come;" he muttered.

He climbed. As his head poked over the sill, he froze. There on the roof squatted a gargoyle. The water issued from its grotesque mouth.

Then he realized that this monster, like the ouroboros, should not be dangerous if he handled it properly. The gargoyle, assigned to water-spouting duty, would be unlikely to chase him.

Bink clambered to the surface of the small roof. He surveyed the situation from this firmer footing. The gargoyle was about his own height, but it was mostly face. The body was so foreshortened as to represent no more than a pedestal. The head was so distorted that Bink could not tell whether it was man, animal, or other. Huge eyes bulged, the nose was like that of a horse, the ears flared out enormously, and the mouth took up fully a third of the face. With the water pouring out like a prolonged regurgitation.

Behind the monster the wall of the castle resumed. There were no handholds, and even if he could scale it, he saw only barred apertures above. No particular hope there.

Bink contemplated the gargoyle. How had it gotten up here? It had no real hands or feet to use to climb the way Bink had. Was there a door behind it? That seemed reasonable.

He would have to move the monster away from that door. But how? The thing had not attacked him, but its attitude might change if he molested it. The gargoyle was more massive than he; it might shove him right off the roof. Too bad he didn't have his sword to defend himself; that was with his clothing, back beside the moat.

Should he climb back down to get it? No, he was sure that would not be wise; it would give away his intent. The gargoyle could move over and crunch his fingers as he ascended with the weapon.

Maybe he could bluff it. "Move over, foulface; I am on a mission for the King."

The gargoyle ignored him. That was another thing that was getting to Bink: being ignored. "Move, or I'll move you myself!" He stepped toward the monster.

No reaction. How could he back down now? Trusting his talent to protect him, Bink moved in beside the gargoyle, staying clear of the river of water spouting from its mouth, and applied his hands to its surface. The grotesque face felt like stone, completely hard. It was heavy, too; shove as he might, he could not budge it.

This monster was defeating him—and it hadn't even noticed him!

Then Bink had a bright idea. Sometimes creatures were vulnerable to their own specialties. The gargoyle's specialty was ugliness.

Bink stood before it, straddling the river. "Hey, homely—here's what you look like!" He put his fingers in the corners of his mouth to stretch it wide while he bugged his eyes.

The gargoyle reacted. It pursed its lips to funnel the water toward Bink. Bink jumped nimbly aside. "Nyaa!" he yelled, puffing out his cheeks to make another ludicrous face.

The monster shuddered with rage. It shot another blast of water at him. Bink was tagged by the fringe of it, and almost washed off the ledge. This was, after all, a chancy business!

He opened his mouth and stuck out his tongue. "Haa!" he cried, unable to form anything much better while holding the expression.

The gargoyle was infuriated. Its mouth opened until it took up half the face. But with the opening that large, the water emerged at low pressure, dribbling down the ugly chin.

Bink dived forward—directly into that mouth. He scrambled upstream against the slowly moving water—and emerged into a reservoir tank within the castle. In a moment he had stroked to the surface and climbed out. He was inside!

But not yet safe. A cactus cat perched at the edge of the reservoir. It was about half Bink's height, with a normal feline face, but its fur was composed of thorns. On the ears the thorns were very large and stiff, like slender spikes. But the cat's real weapons were on its front legs: knifelike blades of bone projecting from the front, scintillatingly sharp. These obviously could not be wielded endwise like daggers, but would be devastating as slicers.

The thorn-fur was horizontally striped, green and brown, and this pattern carried over into the three tails. A pretty but dangerous creature; one that no cognizant person would pat casually on the head saying "Nice kitty."

Was this another guardian of the castle, or merely a houseguest? Cactus cats normally ran wild, slicing up cactus with their blades and feeding on the fermenting sap. Needle cactuses fought back, however, shooting their needles into anything that annoyed them, so they were natural enemies to the cactus cats. Encounters between the two were said to be quite something! But there was no cactus of any kind here. Maybe this was an animal soliciting an Answer from the Good Magician.

Bink tried to skirt it, but the cat moved lithely to the only apparent exit and settled there. So it seemed he would have to force the issue, regardless.

Suddenly Bink got mad. He had had enough of these obstructions. He was no mere supplicant, he was here on the King's business! "Cat, get out of my way!" he said loudly.

The animal began to snore. But Bink knew it would come awake instantly and violently if he tried to sneak past it. Cats were ornery that way. This creature was playing cat and mouse with him—and that made him madder yet.

But what could he do? He was no needle cactus, with hundreds of sliver-thorns to launch. How could he strike at this insufferable cat?

Needles. There were other missiles than needles.

"Then pay the consequence!" Bink snapped. He leaned over the reservoir and sliced his hand across its surface, scooping out a fierce splash of water. The droplets arched across the room and splatted against the wall beside the sleeping cat.

The creature rose up with a screech of sheerest feline fury. Sparks radiated from its ears. Most cats hated water, other than small tame amounts for drinking, and desert cats were enraged by it. The thing charged Blink, its forelimb blades gleaming.

Bink scooped another volley of liquid at it. The cat leaped straight up in horror, letting the splash pass under. Oh, it was ecstatically angry now!

"We can handle this two ways, Cactus," Bink said calmly, his hand ready by the water. "Either I can soak you down thoroughly—or you can stand and let me pass. Or any combination of the two."

The cat snarled. It looked at Bink, then at the water. Finally it affected loss of interest, in the manner of balked felines, and stalked to the side, all three tails standing stiffly.

"Very good, Cactus," Bink said. "But a word to the cunning: if I were to be attacked on the way, I should simply have to grab my antagonist and plunge into the pool and drown him, whatever the mutual cost. That would be inconvenient, and I hope it does not become necessary."

The cat pretended not to hear. It settled down again to sleep.

Bink walked toward the door, affecting a nonchalance similar to that of the cactus cat, but was wary. Fortunately he had bluffed it out; the cat did not move.

Now he was past the hurdles. He explored the castle until he located the Good Magician Humfrey. The man was gnomelike, perched on top of three huge tomes so as to gain the elevation he needed to pore over a fourth. He was old, perhaps the oldest man in the Land of Xanth, with skin wrinkled and mottled. But he was a fine and honest Magician, and Bink knew him to be a kindly individual under all his gruffness.

"Magician!" Bink exclaimed, still irked by the challenge of entry. "Why don't you pay attention to who's visiting! I had to run your infernal gauntlet—and I'm not even coming as a supplicant. I'm on the King's business."

Humfrey looked up, rubbing one reddish eye with a gnarled little hand. "Oh, hello, Bink. Why haven't you visited me before this?"

"We were yelling across the moat! You never answered!"

Humfrey frowned. "Why should I answer a transformed griffin who squawks in a manner that would make a real griffin blush? Why should I acknowledge the bellow of an ornery centaur? The one has no Question, and the other doesn't want to pay for his. Both are wasting my time."

"So you were aware of us all the time!" Bink exclaimed, half-angry, half-admiring, with a little indefinable emotion left over. What a personality this was! "You let me struggle through the whole needless route—"

"Needless, Bink? You come on a mission that will cost me an inordinate amount of time, and will threaten the welfare of Xanth itself. Why should I encourage you in such folly?"

"I don't need encouragement!" Bink cried hotly. "All I need is advice—because the King thought that was best."

The Good Magician shook his head. "The King is a remarkably savvy customer. You need more than advice, Bink."

"Well, all I need from *you* is advice!"

"You shall have it, and without charge: forget this mission."

"I can't forget this mission! I'm on assignment for the—"

"So you said. I did tell you that you needed more than advice. You're as ornery as your friends. Why didn't you leave that poor dragon alone?"

"Leave the poor—" Bink started indignantly. Then he laughed. "You're some character, Magician! Now stop teasing me and tell me why, since you obviously have been well aware of my progress, you did not let us into the castle the easy way."

"Because I hate to be disturbed for minor matters. Had you been balked by my routine defenses, you could hardly have possessed the will to pursue your mission properly. But as I feared, you persevered. What started as a minor diversion with a shapely ghost has become a serious quest—and the result is opaque even to my magic. I queried Beauregard on the matter, and he got so upset I had to rebottle him before he had a nervous breakdown."

Beauregard—that was the bespectacled demon corked in a container, highly educated. Bink began to feel uncomfortable. "What could so shake up a demon?"

"The end of Xanth," Humfrey said simply.

"But all I'm looking for is the source of magic," Bink protested. "I'm not going to do anything to harm Xanth. I love Xanth!"

"You weren't going to install the Evil Magician as King, last time you were here," Humfrey reminded him. "Your minor personal quests have a way of getting out of hand."

"You mean this present mission is going to be worse than the last one?" Bink asked, feeling both excited and appalled. He had only wanted to find his own talent, before.

The Magician nodded soberly. "So it would seem. I can not fathom in what precise manner your quest will threaten Xanth, but am certain the risks are extraordinary."

Bink thought of giving up the quest and returning to Chameleon, ugly and sharp of tongue as she was at the moment, with Millie the nonghost hovering near. Suddenly he became much more interested in the source of the magic of Xanth. "Thanks for your advice. I'm going on."

"Less hasty, Bink! That was not my magic advice; that was just common sense, for which I make no charge. I knew you would ignore it."

Bink found it hard at times not to get impatient with the Good Magician. "Let's have your magic Answer, then."

"And what do you proffer for payment?"

"Payment!" Bink expostulated. "This is—"

"The King's business," the Magician finished. "Be realistic, Bink. The King is merely getting you out of his hair for a while until your home life sweetens up. He can't have you tearing up his palace every time he tries to make out with the Queen. That hardly warrants my waiver of fee."

Only a foolish man tried to argue with a Magician whose talent was information. Bink argued. "The King merely timed the mission conveniently. My job always has been to seek out the source of magic; it just took me a while to get around to it. It is important for the King to have this knowledge. Now that I'm actually on the quest, the authority of the King is behind it, and he can call on your resources if he chooses. You knew that when you helped make him King."

Humfrey shook his head. "Trent has become arrogant in his power. He draws ruthlessly on the talents of others to forward his purposes." Then he smiled. "In other words, he is exactly the kind of monarch Xanth needs. He does not plead or petition, he commands. I as a loyal citizen must support that exercise of power." He glanced at Bink. "However capriciously it happens to be exercised. Thus my fee becomes forfeit to the good of Xanth, though in this case I fear it is the bad of Xanth."

This capitulation was too sudden and too amiable. There had to be a catch. "What is your Answer, then?"

"What is your Question?"

Bink choked on a mouthful of air. "What do I need for this quest?" he spluttered.

"Your quest can not be successful unless you take a Magician along."

"Take a Magician!" Bink exclaimed. "There are only three Magician-class people in Xanth, and two of them are the King and Queen! I can't—" He broke off, realizing. *"You?"*

"I told you this was going to cost me time!" Humfrey grumbled. "All my arcane researches interrupted, my castle mothballed—because you can't wait a few days for your wife to finish her pregnancy and get sweet and pretty again."

"You old rogue!" Bink cried. "You *want* to come!"

"I hardly made that claim," the Magician said sourly. "The fact is, this quest is too important to allow it to be bungled by an amateur, as well the King understood when he sent you here. Since there is no one else of suitable expertise available, I am forced to make the sacrifice. There is no necessity, however, that I be gracious about it."

"But you could have sought the source of magic anytime! You didn't have to co-opt the quest right when I—"

"I co-opt nothing. It is your quest; I merely accompany you, as an emergency resource."

"You mean you're not taking over?"

"What do I want with leadership? I shall stick to my own business, leaving the pesky details of management and routing to you, until my resources are needed—which I trust will not be soon or often."

Now Bink was uncertain how serious Humfrey was. Surely a man who specialized in magical information would be seriously interested in the source of magic

—but certainly the Good Magician liked his convenience and privacy, as his castle and mode of operation testified. Probably Humfrey was torn between desires for isolation and knowledge, so reacted negatively while doing what he deemed to be the right thing. No sense in aggravating the situation. The man would certainly be an incalculable asset on a quest of this nature. "I am sorry to be the agent of such inconvenience to you, but glad to have your help. Your expertise is vastly greater than mine."

"Umph," Humfrey agreed, trying not to seem mollified. "Let's get on with it. Go tell the troll to let down the drawbridge for your companions."

"Uh, there is one other thing," Bink said. "Someone may be trying to kill me—"

"And you want to know who."

"Yes. And why. I don't like—"

"That is not the King's business. It will have to be covered by a separate fee."

Oh. Just when Bink had begun to suspect there was a decent streak in the Good Magician, he had this confirmation of the man's mercenary nature. One year of service for the Answer? Bink preferred to locate and deal with his enemy himself. "Forget it," he said.

"It is already forgotten," Humfrey said graciously.

Miffed, Bink trekked downstairs, found the troll, and gave it the instruction. The brute winched down the bridge. Where the drawbridge mechanism was Bink did not know, as it had not been apparent from the outside, and the troll stood in a chamber near the center of the castle. There had to be magical augmentation to connect what the troll did to what the bridge did. But it worked, and Chester and Crombie entered at last, emerging from a gate that opened from the center of the castle. How could there be an opening here, with no hole through the wall? The Magician was evidently squandering a lot of magic here! Maybe some clever technician had brought a Question, and constructed this mechanism in fee.

"I knew you'd come through, Bink!" the centaur said. "What did the old gnome say about your quest?"

"He's coming with me."

Chester shook his head. "You're in trouble."

The Magician came downstairs to meet them. "So you want to know your obscene talent," he said to the centaur. "What fee do you offer the old gnome?"

Chester was for once abashed. "I'm not sure I—centaurs aren't supposed to—"

"Aren't supposed to be wishy-washy?" Humfrey asked cuttingly.

"Chester just came along to give me a ride," Bink said. "And fight dragons."

"Bink will still need a ride," Humfrey said. "Since I am now associated with this quest, it behooves me to arrange for it. I proffer you this deal: in lieu of the customary year's service for the Answer, I will accept service for the duration of this quest."

Chester was startled. "You mean I do have a talent? A magic one?"

"Indubitably."

"And you know it already? What it is?"

"I do."

"Then—" But the centaur paused. "I might figure it out for myself, if it was so easy for you to do. Why should I pay you for it?"

"Why, indeed," the Magician agreed.

"But if I don't figure it out, and if Bink gets in trouble because he meets a dragon when I'm not there—"

"I would love to let you stew indefinitely in your dilemma," Humfrey said. "But I am in a hurry and Bink needs a ride, so I'll cut it short. Undertake the service I require, in advance of my Answer. If you fail to solve your talent yourself, I will tell you at the termination of the quest—or any prior time you so request. If you do solve it yourself, I will provide a second Answer to whatever other question you may ask. Thus you will in effect have two Answers for the price of one."

Chester considered momentarily. "Done," he agreed. "I like adventure anyway."

The Magician turned to Crombie. "Now you are directly in the King's service, so are committed for the duration. He has given you a fine form, but it lacks intelligible speech. I believe it would be better for you to be more communicative. Accordingly, meet another of my fee-servitors: Grundy the Golem." A miniature man-figure appeared, his whole height hardly the span of an ordinary man's hand. He seemed to have been formed from bits of string and clay and wood and other refuse, but he was animate.

The griffin looked at the golem with a certain surprised contempt. One bite of that eagle's beak could sever all four appendages from the figure. "Squawk!" Crombie remarked.

"Same to you, birdbeak," the golem said without special emphasis, as if he didn't really care.

"Grundy's talent is translation," the Magician explained. "I shall assign him to render the soldier's griffin-speech into human speech, so we can better understand him. He already understands us, as so many animals do, so no reverse translation is required. The golem is small enough for any of us to carry without strain, so his transportation will be no problem. Bink will ride the centaur, and I will ride the griffin. That way we shall make expeditious progress."

And so, efficiently, it was arranged. The quest for the source of the magic of Xanth had begun.

C h a p t e r   5

Golem Heights

They stood outside the castle, across the moat, watching while the Magician mothballed his residence. The ouroboros and other creatures under fee had been granted leaves of absence and were already gone. Humfrey fumbled in his clothing, showing a large heavy belt containing many pockets, and drew from this belt a closed vial or narrow bottle. He applied his thumbs to its cork until it popped free.

Smoke swirled out, looming high into the sky. Then it coalesced into the largest moth Bink had ever imagined, with a wingspan that cast the entire castle into shadow. The creature flew up over the castle and dropped a ball. As the ball fell near the highest turret it exploded. Gray-white streamers shot out in a huge sphere, drifting down to touch every part of the castle. Then they drew in tight, and suddenly the whole edifice was sheathed in a silky net, and looked like a giant tent. A cold, bitter odor emanated from it, smelling vaguely disinfectant.

"There," Humfrey said with grudging satisfaction. "That'll keep a hundred years, if it has to."

"A hundred years!" Chester exclaimed. "Is that how long you figure this mission will take?"

"Come on, come on, we're wasting time," the Good Magician grumped.

Bink, astride the centaur, looked across at the griffin. "What he means, Crombie, is that we need to know the direction of the source of magic. The mission should be accomplished in a few days, with your help."

The griffin squawked irately. "Well, why didn't the old fool say so?" the golem translated promptly. He shared the griffin's back with the Magician, as the two together massed barely half what Bink did.

"Well spoken, soldier," Chester muttered low.

Crombie whirled, almost throwing off his riders. "That way," Grundy said, pointing—around in a continuing circle, his tiny arm settling nowhere.

"Oh, no," Chester muttered. "His talent's on the blink again."

"It is not malfunctioning," Humfrey snapped. "You asked the wrong question."

Bink's brow furrowed. "We had some trouble that way before. What is the right question?"

"It's your job to pursue this quest," Humfrey said. "I must conserve my information for emergencies." And he settled down comfortably amid the feathers of the griffin's back and closed his eyes.

The Good Magician remained his taciturn self. He was out of the habit of helping anyone without his fee, even when he himself might benefit from such help. Now Bink was on the spot again; he had to figure out how to make Crombie's talent work—while the Magician snoozed.

Before, in the nickelpede cleft, Crombie had fouled up because there had been no single direction for escape. Was that the case now—no single source for magic? If so, that would be very hard to locate. But the cynosure of this group was on him; he had to perform, and in a hurry. It was evident that the Good Magician had done him no particular favor by leaving the leadership of the quest to Bink. "Where is the most direct route to the source of magic?"

This time the griffin's wing pointed down at an angle.

So that was why there was no horizontal direction; the source was not across, but down. Yet that was not much help. They couldn't dig down very far, very fast. They would have to get a person whose talent was magic-tunneling, and that would mean delay and awkwardness. This group was already larger than Bink had anticipated. Better to find a natural route.

"Where is there an access to this source, from the surface?" Bink asked.

The wing began to vibrate back and forth. "The nearest one!" Bink amended hastily. The wing stabilized, pointing roughly south.

"The heart of the unexplored wilderness," Chester said. "I should have known. Maybe I should take my Answer now and quit."

Crombie squawked. "Birdbeak says if you take your stupid Answer now, you *can't* quit, horserear."

Chester swelled up angrily. "Birdbeak said that? You tell him for me he has bird droppings for brains, and—"

"Easy," Bink cautioned the centaur. "Crombie needs no translation for your words."

"Actually he called you an ass," Grundy said helpfully. "I assume he meant your rear end, which is about as asinine as—"

The griffin squawked again. "Oops, my error," the golem said. "He referred to your *front* end."

"Listen, birdbrain!" Chester shouted. "I don't need your ignorant opinion! Why don't you take it and stuff it—"

But Crombie was squawking at the same time. The two faced off aggressively. The centaur was bigger and more muscular than the griffin, but the griffin was probably the more deadly fighter, for he had the mind of a trained human soldier in the body of a natural combat creature.

"Squawk!" Bink screamed. "I mean, stop! The golem is just making trouble. Obviously the word Crombie used was 'centaur.' Isn't that so, Crombie?"

Crombie squawked affirmatively. "Spoilsport," Grundy muttered, speaking for himself. "Just when it was getting interesting."

"Never mind that," Bink said. "Do you admit I was correct, Golem?"

"A centaur is an ass—front *and* rear," Grundy said sullenly. "It depends on whether you are defining it intellectually or physically."

"I think I will squeeze your big loud mouth into a small silent ball," Chester said, reaching for the golem.

"You can't do that, muleface!" Grundy protested. "I'm on the dwarf's business!"

Chester paused, seeing the Good Magician stir. "Whose business?"

"This midget's business!" Grundy said, gesturing back at Humfrey with a single stiffened finger.

Chester looked at Humfrey, feigning perplexity. "Sir, how is it you accept such insults from a creature who works for you?"

"Oops," the golem muttered, discovering the trap. "I thought he was asleep."

"The golem has no personal reality," Humfrey said. "Therefore his words carry no personal onus. One might as well get angry at a lump of clay."

"That's telling him, imp," Grundy agreed. But he seemed chastened.

"Let's get on with our quest," Bink suggested as the Good Magician closed his eyes again. Privately he wondered how it was that an unreal construct, the golem, could be in fee to the Magician. Grundy must have asked a Question, and had an Answer—but what could have motivated this magical entity to seek such information?

Then Bink had a minor inspiration as they trekked south. "Crombie, someone or something has been trying to eliminate me. I think that's why the dragon came after us. Can you point out where that enemy is?"

"Squawk!" Crombie agreed. He whirled, and the Good Magician wobbled on his back but did not wake up. When the wing stabilized, it pointed—the same direction as it had for the source of magic.

"It seems," Chester said gravely, "that it is your mission your enemy opposes. Does that affect your attitude?"

"Yes," Bink said. "It makes me twice as determined as before." Though he remembered that the sword had attacked him before he set out on his quest. Had his enemy anticipated him? That would be grim news indeed, implying more than ordinary strategy or magic. "Let's get on with it."

Near the Magician's castle the terrain was fairly quiet, but as they penetrated the wilderness it changed. High brush grew up, obscuring the view, and as they passed it there was a static discharge from the foliage that made hair and fur and feathers and string stand out eerily from their bodies. Overlooking this brush was an antenna, orienting unerringly on the party; Bink had never gotten close enough to one of these things to discover exactly what it was, and did not propose to start now. Why did these antennae watch so closely, yet take no action?

Sweat gnats came, making them all miserable until Humfrey woke, brought out a tiny vial, and opened it. Vapor emerged and spread, engulfing the gnats— then it suddenly sucked back into its bottle, carrying the gnats with it. "Misty was due for feeding anyway," the Good Magician explained, putting away the vial. He offered no further explanation, and no one had the nerve to inquire. Again Humfrey slept.

"Must be nice, being a Magician," Chester said. "He's got the answer to all his problems, in one bottle or another."

"Must be acquisitions from prior fees," Bink agreed.

Then they blundered into a patch of curse-burrs. The things were all over their legs, itching incessantly. There was only one way to get rid of such a burr; it had to be banished by a curse. The problem was, no particular curse could be used twice in a day; each had to be different.

Humfrey was not pleased to be awakened yet again. This time it seemed he had no solution in a vial. "By the beard of my Great-Uncle Humbug, begone!" the Good Magician said, and the burr he addressed fell off, stunned. "By the snout of a sick sea serpent, begone!" And another dropped.

Chester was more direct, for several burrs were tangled in his beautiful tail. "To the grave with you, prickleface! I'll stomp you flat as a nickelpede's nickel! Out out, damned burr!" And three burrs fell, overwhelmed.

"Leave me," Bink said, envying the imagination of the others. "Go itch a dragon!" And his burrs too started falling, though not so readily as those conked by the harder-hitting curses of the others. Bink just didn't have the touch.

Crombie, however, was in trouble. Griffins were not native to this particular region of Xanth, and the burrs evidently did not comprehend his squawks. Then the golem started translating, and they fell in droves. "By the bloody mouths of a field of wild snapdragons, drop your ugly purple posteriors into the nearest stinking privy, sidewise! If your faces were flowers, you'd poison the whole garden! Jam your peppery pink rootlets up your—" The golem paused, amazed. "Is that possible? I don't think I can translate it." But the curse burrs comprehended, and suddenly the griffin's bright feathers were free of them. No one could curse like a soldier!

Still, it was impossible to avoid all the burrs in this area, and by the time they escaped it their curses had become extremely farfetched. Sometimes two or even three curses had to be expended to make a single burr let go.

By this time they were hungry. There was nothing like a good bout of cursing to work up an appetite. "You know this area," Chester said to the Magician before he could fall asleep again. "Where is there something to eat?"

"Don't bother me with details," Humfrey snapped. "I brought my own food—as you would have done too, had you had proper foresight." He opened another vial. This time the vapor emerged to coalesce into a layered cake, complete with icing. The Magician took this from the air, broke out a perfect wedge-shaped slice, and ate that while the remainder of the cake dissolved, misted, and flowed back into its bottle.

"I realize we were remiss in not packing food for the journey," Bink said. "You don't suppose you might share some of that, this one time?"

"Why should I suppose anything like that?" Humfrey inquired curiously.

"Well, we are hungry, and it would facilitate—"

The Magician burped. "Go find your own slop, freeloader," the golem translated.

It occurred to Bink that the Good Magician was not as congenial a companion as the Evil Magician had been, the last time he had braved the wilderness of Xanth. But he well knew that appearances could be deceptive.

Crombie squawked. "Birdbeak says there should be some fruit trees around. He'll point them out." And the griffin did his thing, pointing the direction.

In a moment they spied a giant fruit cup. The plant was the shape of an open bowl, filled to overflowing with assorted fruits. The party ran joyfully up to it—and, startled, the fruits erupted upward, filling the air with color.

"Oh, no—they're winged fruits!" Bink exclaimed. "We should have sneaked up on them. Why didn't you warn us, Crombie?"

"You didn't ask, fathead," the golem retorted.

"Catch them!" Chester cried, jumping and reaching high to snatch an apple out of the air. Bink, half-dislodged, hastily dismounted.

A ripe peach hovered for a moment, getting its bearings. Bink leaped at it, catching it in one hand. The wings fluttered frantically as it tried to escape, then gave up. They were leaves, green and ordinary, adapted to this special purpose. He stripped them off ruthlessly so his food could not escape, and went after the next.

He tripped over something and fell flat, missing a bobbing pomegranate. Angrily he looked at the obstacle that had thwarted him. It was another of the ubiquitous mounds of fresh earth. This time he got up and stomped it absolutely flat. Then he dashed on after more fruit.

Soon he had a small collection of fruits: apple, peach, plum, two pears (of course), several grapes, and one banana. The last, flying on monstrous vulture-like wing-leaves, had given him a terrible struggle, but it was delicious. Bink did not feel entirely easy about consuming such fruit, because it seemed too much like living creatures, but he knew the wings were merely a magic adaptation to enable the plants to spread their seeds more widely. Fruit was supposed to be eaten; it wasn't really conscious or feeling. Or was it?

Bink put that thought from his mind and looked about. They were on the verge of a forest of standing deadwood. Humfrey came awake. "I suffer misgivings," he volunteered. "I don't want to have to waste my magic ferreting out what killed those trees. We'd better go around."

"What's the good of being a Magician if you don't use your magic?" Chester demanded testily.

"I must conserve my magic rigorously for emergency use," Humfrey said. "These are mere nuisances we have faced so far, not worthy of my talent."

"You tell 'em, twerp," the golem agreed.

Chester looked unconvinced, but retained too much respect for the Magician to make further issue of it. "It's getting on in the afternoon," he remarked. "Where's a good place to spend the night?"

Crombie stopped and whirled so vigorously he almost dislodged his riders. "Hmph!" Humfrey exclaimed, and the golem dutifully translated: "You blundering aviary feline! Get your catty feet on the ground!"

The griffin's head rotated entirely around until the deadly eyes and beak pointed back. "Squawk!" Crombie said with authority. The golem did not translate, but seemed cowed. Crombie completed his maneuver and pointed a slightly new direction.

"That's not far off the track; we'll go there," Chester decided, and no one contradicted him.

Their route skirted the dead forest, and this was fortuitous because there were few other hazards here. Whatever had killed the forest had also wiped out most of the magic associated with it, good and evil. Yet Bink developed a mounting curiosity about the huge trees they spied to the side. There were no marks upon them, and the grass beneath was luxuriant because of the new light let down. This suggested that the soil had not been poisoned by any monster. Indeed, a few new young shoots were rising, beginning the long task of restoring the forest. Something had struck and killed and departed without other trace of its presence.

To distract himself from the annoyance of the unanswerable riddle, Bink addressed the golem. "Grundy, if you care to relate it—what was your Question to the Magician?"

"Me?" the golem asked, amazed. "You have interest in *me?*"

"Of course I do," Bink said. "You're a—" He had been about to say "person" but remembered that the golem was technically not a person. "An entity," he finished somewhat lamely. "You have consciousness, feelings—"

"No, no feelings," Grundy said. "I am just a construct of string and clay and wood, animated by magic. I perform as directed, without interest or emotion."

Without interest or emotion? That hardly seemed true. "You seemed to experience a personal involvement just now, when I expressed interest in you."

"Did I? It must have been a routine emulation of human reaction. I have to perform such emulations in the course of my translation service."

Bink was not convinced, but did not challenge this. "If you have no personal interest in human affairs, why did you come to the Good Magician? What did you ask him?"

"I asked him how I could become real," the golem said.

"But you *are* real! You're here, aren't you?"

"Take away the spell that made me, and I'd be nothing but a minor pile of junk. I want to be real the way you are real. Real without magic."

Real without magic. It made sense after all. Bink remembered how he himself had suffered, as a youth, thinking he had no magic talent. This was the other face of the problem: the creature who had no reality *apart* from magic. "And what was the Answer?"

"Care."

"What?"

"Care, dumbbell."

"Care?"

"Care."

"That's all?"

"All."

"All the Answer?"

"All the Answer, stupid."

"And for that you serve a year's labor?"

"You think you have a monopoly on stupidity?"

Bink turned to the Good Magician, who seemed to have caught up on his sleep but remained blithely silent. "How can you justify charging such a fee for such an Answer?"

"I don't have to," Humfrey said. "No one is required to come to the grasping old gnome for information."

"But anyone who pays a fee is entitled to a decent Answer," Bink said, troubled.

"The golem has a decent Answer. He doesn't have a decent comprehension."

"Well, neither do I!" Bink said. "Nobody could make sense of that Answer!"

The Magician shrugged. "Maybe he asked the wrong Question."

Bink turned to Chester's human portion. "Do you call that a fair Answer?"

"Yes," the centaur said.

"I mean that one word 'care'? Nothing else, for a whole year's service?"

"Yes."

"You think it's worth it?" Bink was having trouble getting through.

"Yes."

"You'd be satisfied with that Answer for your Question?"

Chester considered. "I don't think that Answer relates."

"So you *wouldn't* be satisfied!"

"No, I'd be satisfied if that were my Answer. I just don't believe it is. I am not a golem, you see."

Bink shook his head in wonder. "I guess I'm part golem, then. I don't think it's enough."

"You're no golem," Grundy said. "You aren't smart enough."

Some diplomacy! But Bink tried again. "Chester, can you explain that Answer to us?"

"No, I don't understand it either."

"But you said—"

"I said I thought it was a fair Answer. Were I a golem, I would surely appreciate its reference. Its relevance. This is certainly more likely than the notion that the Good Magician would fail to deliver in full measure."

Bink remembered how Humfrey had told the manticora that he had a soul—in such a manner that the creature was satisfied emotionally as well as intellectually. It was a convincing argument. There must be some reason for the obscurity of the Answer for the golem.

But oh, what frustration until that reason became clear!

Near dusk they spied a house. Crombie's talent indicated that this was their residence for the night.

The only problem was the size of it. The door was ten feet tall.

"That is the domicile of a giant—or an ogre," Humfrey said, frowning.

"An ogre!" Bink repeated. "We can't stay there!"

"He'd have us all in his pot in a moment, and the fire high," Chester agreed. "Ogres consider human flesh a delicacy."

Crombie squawked. "The idiot claims his fool talent is never mistaken," Grundy reported.

"Yes, but remember what his talent doesn't cover!" Bink said. "We asked for a good place to spend the night; we didn't specify that it had to be safe."

"I daresay a big pot of hot water is as comfortable a place to relax as any," Chester agreed. "Until it becomes too hot. Then the bath becomes—"

"I suppose I'll have to expend some of my valuable magic," Humfrey complained. "It's too late to go wandering through the woods in search of alternate lodging." He brought out yet another little stoppered bottle and pulled out the cork. It was an ornery cork, as corks tended to be, and gave way only grudgingly, so that the process took some time.

"Uh, isn't that a demon container?" Bink asked, thinking he recognized the style. Some bottles were solider than others, and more carefully crafted, with magical symbols inscribed. "Shouldn't you—?"

The Magician paused. "Umph."

"He says he was just about to, nitwit," the golem said. "Believe it if you will."

The Magician scraped a pentacle in the dirt, sat the bottle in it, and uttered an indecipherable incantation. The cork popped out and the smoky demon issued, coalescing into the bespectacled entity Bink recognized as Beauregard.

The educated demon didn't even wait for the question. "You routed me out for this, old man? Of course it's safe; that ogre's a vegetarian. It's your mission that's unsafe."

"I didn't ask you about the mission!" Humfrey snapped. "I *know* it's unsafe! That's why I'm along."

"It is not like you to indulge in such foolishness, especially at the expense of your personal comfort," Beauregard continued, pushing his spectacles back along his nose with one finger. "Are you losing your marbles at last? Getting senile? Or merely attempting to go out in a blaze of ignominy?"

"Begone, infernal spirit! I will summon you when I need your useless conjectures."

Beauregard shook his head sadly, then dissipated back into the bottle.

"That's another feeling spirit," Bink said, uneasy. "Do you have to coop him up like that, in such a little bottle?"

"No one can coop a demon," the Magician said shortly. "Besides, his term of service is not yet up."

At times it was hard to follow the man's logic! "But you had him when I first met you, more than a year ago."

"He had a complex Question."

"A demon of information, who answers the questions you get paid fees for, has to pay you for Answers?"

Humfrey did not respond. Bink heard a faint booming laughter, and realized after a moment that it was coming from the demon's bottle. Something was certainly funny here, but not humorous.

"We'd better move in before it gets dark," Chester said, eyeing the ogre's door somewhat dubiously.

Bink would have liked to explore the matter of the demon further, but the centaur had a point.

They stepped up to the door. It was a massive portal formed of whole tree trunks of hewn ironwood, scraped clean of bark and bound together by several severed predator vines. Bink marveled at this; unrusted ironwood could be harvested only from freshly felled trees, and not even a magic axe could cut those very well. And what monster could blithely appropriate the deadly vines for this purpose? The vines normally used their constrictive power to crush their prey, and they were killingly strong.

Chester knocked resoundingly. There was a pause while the metallic echoes faded. Then slow thuds approached from inside. The door wrenched open with such violence that the ironwood hinges grew hot and the suction of air drew the centaur forward a pace. Light burst out blindingly, and the ogre stood there in terrible silhouette. It stood twice Bink's height, dwarfing even the monstrous door, and its body was thick in proportion. The limbs carried knots of muscles like the gnarly boles of trees. "Ungh!" it boomed.

"He says what the hell is this bad smell?" the golem translated.

"Bad smell!" Chester cried. "He's the one who smells!"

It was true. The ogre seemed not to believe in washing or in cleansing magic. Dirt was caked on his flesh, and he reeked of rotting vegetation. "But we don't want to spend the night outside," Bink cautioned.

Crombie squawked. "Birdbeak says let's get on with it, slowpokes."

"Birdbeak would," Chester grumbled.

The ogre grunted. "Stoneface says that's what he's sniffin', a putrid griffin."

The griffin stood tall and angry, half-spreading his brilliant wings as he squawked. "How'd you like that problem corrected by amputation of your schnozzle?" Grundy translated.

The ogre swelled up even more massively than before. He growled. "Me grind you head to make me bread," the golem said.

Then there was a medley of squawks and growls, with the golem happily carrying both parts of the dialogue.

"Come outside and repeat that, numbskull!"

"Come into me house, you beaked mouse. Me break you bone upon me dome."

"You'd break your dome just trying to think!" Crombie squawked.

"Do all ogres speak in rhyming couplets?" Bink asked when there was a pause to replenish the reservoirs of invective. "Or is that just the golem's invention?"

"That little twit not have wit," the golem said, then reacted angrily. "Who's a twit, you frog-faced sh—"

"Ogres vary, as do other creatures," Humfrey cut in smoothly. "This one does seem friendly."

"Friendly!" Bink exclaimed.

"For an ogre. We'd better go on in."

"Me test you mettle in me kettle!" the ogre growled via the golem. But the griffin nudged on in, and the ogre gave grudging way.

The interior was close and gloomy, as befitted the abode of a monster. The blinding light that had manifested when the door first opened was gone; evidently the proprietor had charged up a new torch for the occasion, and it had already burned out. Dank straw was matted on the floor, stocked cordwood lined the walls, and a cauldron bubbled like volcanic mud over a fire blazing in a pit in the center of the room. There seemed to be, however, no piles of bones. That, at least, was encouraging. Bink had never before heard of a vegetarian ogre, but the demon Beauregard surely knew his business.

Bink, realizing that the constant threats were mostly bluffs, found himself embarrassed to be imposing on the good-natured (for an ogre) monster. "What is your name?" he inquired.

"You lunch; me crunch."

Apparently the brute had not understood. "My name's Bink; what's your name?"

"Me have hunch you not know crunch." The ogre dipped a hairy, grimy mitt into the boiling cauldron, fished about, grabbed, withdrew a gooey fistful, plunked it into a gnarly wooden bowl which he shoved at Bink. "Drink, Bink."

"He means his name is Crunch," Chester said, catching on. "He's offering you something to eat. He doesn't distinguish between meals; all food is 'lunch.'"

"Oh. Uh—thank you, Crunch," Bink said awkwardly. *You lunch; me Crunch* —now it made sense. An offer of food, an answer to a question, rather than a threat. He accepted the glop. The ogre served the others similarly; his huge paw seemed immune to the heat.

Bink looked at his portion dubiously. The stuff was too thick to pool, too thin to pick up, and despite its bubbling heat it hardly seemed dead yet. It was a deep-purple hue, with green excrescences. It smelled rather good, actually, though there was a scalded fly floating in it.

Chester sniffed his serving appreciatively. "Why this is purple bouillon with green nutwood—a phenomenal delicacy! But it requires a magic process to extract the bouillon juice, and only a nutty green elf can procure nutwood. How did you come by this?"

The ogre smiled. The effect was horrendous, even in the gloom. "Me have elf, work for pelf," the golem translated. Then Crunch lifted a log from his stack and held it over the cauldron. He twisted one hand on each end—and the wood screwed up like a wet towel. A thin stream of purple liquid fell from it into the cauldron. When the log was dry, the ogre casually ripped it into its component cords and tossed it into the fire, where it flared up eagerly. Well, that was one way to burn cordwood.

Bink had never before witnessed such a feat of brute strength. Rather than comment, he fished out the fly, dipped a finger into his cooling pudding, brought out a creamy glob and put it gingerly to his mouth. It was delicious. "This is the best food I ever ate!" he exclaimed, amazed.

"You say that, Bink. You think it stink," Crunch growled, flattered.

Crombie squawked as he sampled his bowl. "*You* may stink, this is great," the golem translated.

Crunch, highly pleased by the double compliment, served himself a glob by dumping a bubbling fistful directly into his gaping maw. He licked off his fingers, then took another glob. As the others finished their helpings, the ogre served them more with the same hand. No one saw fit to protest; after all, what magic germs could survive that heat?

After the repast, they settled on the straw for the evening. The others seemed satisfied to sleep, but Bink was bothered by something. In a moment he identified it: "Crunch, among our kind we offer some return service for hospitality. What can we do for you to repay this fine meal and lodging?"

"Say, that's right," Chester agreed. "You need some wood chopped or something?"

"That no good. Have plenty wood," the ogre grunted. He smashed one fist down on a log, and it splintered into quivering fragments. He obviously needed no help there.

Crombie squawked. "Birdbeak says he can point out where anything is. What do you want, stoneface?"

"Want sleep, you creep," Crunch mumbled.

"Not until we do you some service," Bink insisted.

"Take heed, no need!" Crunch closed one fist on a handful of straw, squeezed, and when he let go the straw had fused into one spindly stick. The ogre used this to pick at his gross teeth.

Chester argued caution for once. "We can't force a service on him he doesn't want."

"Maybe he doesn't know he wants it," Bink said. "We must honor the code."

"You sure are a stubborn lout," Grundy said, for once speaking for himself. "Why stir up trouble?"

"It's a matter of principle," Bink said uncertainly. "Crombie, can you point out where the thing Crunch desires is?"

The griffin squawked affirmatively, spun about, stirred up the straw, and pointed. At the Good Magician Humfrey, nodding in the corner, one piece of straw straddling his head.

"Forget it," Humfrey snapped sleepily. "I am not available for consumption."

"But he's a vegetarian!" Bink reminded him. "It can't be that he wants to eat you. Maybe he wants to ask you a Question."

"Not for one measly night's lodging! He'd have to serve me for a year."

"Me have no question, no suggestion," the ogre grunted.

"It does seem we're forcing something unwanted on our host," Chester said, surprisingly diplomatic. That log-twisting and straw-squeezing and wood-splintering had evidently impressed the centaur profoundly. The ogre was clearly the strongest creature this party had encountered.

"There is something Crunch wants, even if he doesn't know it himself," Bink said. "It is our duty to locate it for him." No one argued, though he was sure they all wished he would drop the subject. "Crombie, maybe it isn't the Magician he wants, but something *on* the Magician. Exactly where did you point?"

Crombie squawked with tired resignation. He pointed again. Bink lined up his own finger, tracing the point. "There!" he said. "Something in his crotch." Then he paused, abashed. "Uh, his jacket, maybe."

But the Magician, tired, had fallen asleep. His only answer was a snore.

"Oh, come *on!*" Grundy said. "I'll check it out." And he scrambled up on the Magician, climbing inside his jacket.

"I don't think—" Bink began, startled by this audacity.

"That's your problem," the golem said from inside the jacket. "It must be—this." He emerged, clasping a vial in both arms. For him it was a heavy weight.

"That's the demon-bottle!" Chester said. "Don't fool with—"

But Grundy was already prying out the cork.

Bink dived for him, but as usual was too late. The cork was not ornery this time; it popped off cleanly as Bink grabbed the bottle.

"Now you've done it!" Chester exclaimed. "If Humfrey wakes—"

Bink was left holding the bottle as the demon coalesced, unbound by any magic inscription or incantation. "Some—some—somebody make a—a—" Bink stammered.

Beauregard firmed, standing with a huge tome tucked under one arm. He peered at Bink beneath his spectacles. "A pentacle?" the demon finished. "I think not."

"What have I done?" Bink moaned.

Beauregard waved negligently with his free hand. "You have done nothing, Bink. It was the foolish golem."

"But I set him in motion!"

"Perhaps. But do not be concerned. Rather consider yourself as the instrument of fate. Know that neither the bottle nor the pentacle constrained me; I but honored these conventions to please the Magician, to whom I owed professional courtesy. The agreement was that I should serve in this capacity of reserve-informant until circumstances should free me, by the ordinary rules of demon control. That chance has now occurred, as it was fated. A genuinely bound demon would have escaped, so I am free to go. I thank you for that accident, and now I depart." He began to fade.

"Wait!" Bink cried. "At least answer this nice ogre's Question!"

Beauregard firmed again. "He has no Question. He only wants to sleep. Ogres need plenty of rest, or they lose their meanness."

"But Crombie's talent indicated—"

"Oh, that. Technically there is something, but it is not a conscious desire."

"It will do," Bink said. He had not realized that ogres could have unconscious desires. "Tell us what it is, before you go."

"He wants to know whether he should take a wife," the demon said.

The ogre growled. "What kind of life, if me have wife?" the golem said.

"Now that's interesting," Beauregard said. "A golem, serving fee for an Answer he can not comprehend."

"Who could make sense of a one-word Answer?" Grundy demanded.

"Only a real creature," Beauregard replied.

"That's the point—he's not real," Bink said. "He wants to know how to *become* real."

Beauregard turned to the centaur. "And you want to know your talent. I could tell you, of course, but you would then be in fee to me, and neither of us would want that."

"Why don't you just answer the ogre's question and go?" Bink asked, not quite trusting this too-knowledgeable freed demon.

"I can not do that directly, Bink. I am a demon; he would not accept my answer, rational though it would be. He is of an irrational species, like yourself; you must answer him."

"Me! I—" Bink broke off, not wanting to comment on his present problem with Chameleon.

"I spoke in the plural," Beauregard said, a bit condescendingly. "You and Chester and Crombie should discuss your relations with your respective females, and the consensus will provide the ogre with the perspective he needs." He considered. "In fact, in that context, my own comment might become relevant." And he settled down on the straw with them.

There was a silence. "Uh, how did you—that is, there is a lady ogre—uh, ogress in mind?" Bink asked Crunch.

The ogre responded with a volley of growls, snorts, and gnashings of yellow teeth. It was all the golem could do to keep up the translation, but Grundy rose to the occasion and spouted at the height of his form:

"One lovely bleak morning during thunderstorm warning me wandered far out beyond hail of a shout. Me was in a good mood just looking for food. No creature stirred this far from home; no dragon, no monster, not even a gnome. Me entered a forest huge and tall; the trees were so big me seemed small. The way was so tangled no walker could pass, but it opened like magic a lovely crevasse, with nickelpedes and more delights, and stagnant water rich with blights, and me tramped up to a hidden castle with shroud for flag and scalp for tassel. The wind blew by it with lovely moans, and all the timbers were giant bones. At entrance slept little dragon called Puk, guarding what left meself awestruck: a fountain packed with purple mud, spouting gouts of bright-red blood. Me stared so long me stood in doze, and me mouth watered so hard it drooled on me toes. But me knew such enchantment would be complete the moment me yielded and started to eat. Me wanted to see what further treasure offered itself for the hero's pleasure. And in the center in a grimy sack lay a wonderful ogress stretched on a rack. She had hair like nettles, skin like mush, and she face would make a zombie blush. She breath reeked of carrion, wonderfully foul, and she stench was so strong me wanted to howl. Me thought me sick with worm in gut, but knew it was love for that splendid slut. Me smashed she in face with hairy fist, which is ogre way of making tryst. Then me picked she up by she left leg and dragged she away, me golden egg. Then whole castle come awake: goblin and troll and green mandrake. They celebrated the union of hero and cute by pelting we with rotten fruit. But on way out we tripped a spell that sounded alarm where evil fiends dwell. They had put castle to sleep for a hundred years, those fiends who hated ogres' rears. They fired a spell of such terrible might we had to flee it in a fright. Me dodged it every way me could, but it caught we good in midst of wood. As it struck me cried 'Me crunch no bone!' and it thought we ogres both had flown. It dissipated in such mighty flash the whole near forest was rendered trash. Now me crunch no bones lest fiends of lake learn they curse have make mistake. Me not want them throw another curse maybe like first and maybe worse. Me love lies stunned within the wood, sleeping away she maidenhood. But one thing now gives me pause: she never did make much applause. All me want to know is this: should me leave or fetch the miss?"

The others sat in silence for a time following this remarkable recital. At last Crombie squawked. "That was a considerable adventure and romance," Grundy said for him. "While I can appreciate the fetching qualities of your lady friend, I must say from my own experience that all females are infernal creatures whose primary purpose in life is to deceive, entrap, and make miserable the males. Therefore—"

The ogre's grunt interrupted the griffin in mid-squawk. "Hee hee hee, hee hee hee!" Grundy translated, interrupting himself. "Me fetch she instantly!"

Chester smiled. "Despite my friend's recommendation, I must offer a note of caution. No matter how badly the filly nags the stallion, and how unreasonable she normally seems, there comes a time when she births her first foal. Then the dam no longer has much interest in—"

"She no nag? That is snag," Crunch growled, disappointed.

"But in due course," Bink said, "she is bound to return to normal, often with extremely cutting wit. In any event, I should think some nagging is better than no nagging. So why not rouse your beauty and give her a proper chance? She may make your life completely miserable."

The ogre's eyes lighted like torches.

"I must concur," Beauregard said. "This conversation has been a most intriguing insight into the condition of human, animal, and ogre emotions. What is nagging to humans is applause to ogres. This will do nicely to conclude my dissertation."

"Your what?" Bink asked.

"My doctoral thesis on the fallibilities of intelligent life on the surface of Xanth," Beauregard explained. "I sought information from the human Magician Humfrey, and he assured me that a term of service in his bottle would provide me the insights I required, since a person's nature may best be gauged through the questions he considers most vital. This has indeed been the case, and I am now virtually assured of my degree. That will qualify me to form permanent liaison with my chosen demoness, who would seem to be worth the effort. This causes me to experience a certain demoniac exhilaration. Therefore I present you each with a small token gleaned from my researches."

The demon turned to Chester. "I prefer not to inform you of your magic talent directly, for the reason given above, but will provide a hint: it reflects the suppressed aspect of your character. Because you, like most centaurs, have disbelieved in magic among your kind, whole aspects of your personality have been driven as it were underground. When you are able to expiate this conditioning, your talent will manifest naturally. Do not waste a year of your life for the Answer of the Good Magician; just allow yourself more self-expression."

He turned to Crombie. "You can not escape your fate in this manner. When you return from this quest—*if* you return—Sabrina will trap you into an unhappy marriage unless you arrange for a more suitable commitment elsewhere before you see her. Therefore enjoy yourself now; have your last fling and do not be concerned for the morrow, for it will be worse than today. Yet marriage is not after all, for you, a fate worse than death; you will know that when you do face death."

He left the crestfallen griffin and oriented on the golem. "The meaning of the Magician's Answer to you is this: people care; inanimate objects do not. Only when you experience genuine feelings that pre-empt your logic will you be real. You can achieve this height only if you work at it—but beware, for the emotions of living things are in many cases extremely uncomfortable."

He turned to Crunch. "I say to you, ogre: go fetch your lady. She sounds like a worthy companion for you, in every respect a truly horrendous bitch." And Crunch was so moved he almost blushed.

Beauregard turned to Bink. "I have never been able to fathom your magic, but I feel its operation now. It is extremely strong—but that which you seek is infinitely stronger. If you persist, you run the risk of being destroyed, and of destroying those things you hold most dear. Yet you *will* persist, and so I extend my condolence. Until we meet again—" He faded out.

The members of the remaining circle exchanged glances. "Let's go to sleep," Chester said. That seemed like the best idea of the evening.

Chapter 6

Magic Dust

I n the morning they thanked the ogre and continued on their quest, while Crunch tramped eagerly into the dead forest to rouse his beautiful bride: her with the hair like nettles and skin like mush.

They had new material for thought. Now they knew the cause of the death of the trees—but what of the evil fiends who dwelt in the lake and possessed such devastating curses? Were there Magicians among them, and was the source of magic near them?

Magician Humfrey was particularly thoughtful. Either he had not been entirely asleep during the evening session, or he had drawn on his informational magic to ascertain the situation. He had to know that the demon Beauregard was gone. "What magic," he murmured, "could devastate an entire living forest by the dissipation of a single curse? Why have I not known of this before?"

"You never thought to look," Chester said undiplomatically.

"We're looking now," Bink pointed out. "Magic should be stronger near the source."

Crombie squawked. "Strong magic is one thing. Magician-class curses are another. Let me get another line on it." And he did his act once more.

They were headed in the right direction. The terrain seemed ordinary; large trees glowered at the trespassers while small ones shied away as well as they were able. Fruit flies buzzed about: berries, cherries, and grapefruits hovered as if in search of another salad bowl. Tempting paths appeared through tangled reaches, which the party avoided as a matter of course. In Xanth, the easy course was seldom best! There was a dragon run, with scorch marks on the trees to show the dragon's territorial limits. The safest place to be, when pursued by a dragon, was a few paces within another dragon's marked demesnes; any poaching would lead to a settlement between dragons.

But soon the way became more difficult. Brambles with glistening points and ugly dispositions closed off large sections, and a pride of ant lions patrolled others. A copse of stinkweeds surrounded the most direct remaining route, and they were of a particularly large and potent breed. The party tried to pass through them, but the stench became so intense that even the ogre might have hesitated. They retreated, gasping.

They contemplated the alternatives: brambles and ant lions. Bink tried to clear a path through the plants with his sword, but every time he made a cut, several more branches closed in, threatening his body. These were exceptionally alert brambles, and the sheen on their points suggested poison. Bink backed off. Once again he was up against the possibility that his talent might protect him while letting his friends die.

He approached the ant-lion section. The lion-headed ants had beaten out good highways throughout, and ruthlessly eliminated all hazards in their way. All hazards except the ant lions themselves.

Bink's sword might dispatch one lion, and Chester's arrows and hooves could handle two or three more, and as a griffin Crombie could take on as many as four—but the creatures would attack a dozen at a time without fear or mercy. Again, Bink himself would probably emerge intact, by some incredible fluke—but what of the others?

He turned back—and his eyes wandered skyward, he saw a path through the trees. The tops of the trees.

He rubbed his eyes. A path in air? Yet why not? With magic, he reminded himself for the umpteenth time, all things were possible. The question was, could men and half-men walk on it? And if they could, where did it lead?

Still, it seemed to be the most promising route. If he rode Chester, his talent would not let them get on the airy path unless it would support them both. The griffin, Magician, and golem weighed much less, so they would be safe if they followed. "I think I see a way," Bink said.

They tried it. They located a place where the magic path looped down within reach of the ground, and Crombie whirled and pointed to discover whether there was any danger along this limited-access highway. There was not. They climbed aboard and followed it up high into the trees. The strange thing about it was that the path was always level, no matter how it looped. The forest turned crazy circles about it, however. At times the sun was underfoot, and at times to one side, while the trees assumed varying angles. Bink, curious, reached out to touch the foliage of one tree whose trunk reached up into the ground above; it was solid. Of course he knew that he was the one who was upside down; the path established its own orientation. Looking back, he could see the griffin marching at a different tilt, and knew that to griffin, Magician, and golem the centaur was the tilted one. Intriguing magic, but harmless. So far.

Meanwhile, he enjoyed the convenience and the view. The path led through the forest, generally high above the ground, and this new view of things was refreshing. Slants of sunlight crossed it, and gently hued columns of mist. It was neither man's-eye nor bird's-eye, but an intermediate and unique perspective. The path passed safely above the ant-lion range, yet below the flying-predator range. Bink observed several small flying dragons, a harpy, and a distant roc, but none flew near the path.

The plants, too, were unusually passive. Constrictor tentacles dangled in the vicinity of the path, but never *on* it, and no branches reached across to block it. Obviously this path was charmed, and that was suspicious; the best paths were almost by definition the worst ones. Bink remembered how easy it had been to penetrate the forest around Castle Roogna, back when it had been derelict, and how hard it had been to escape it. What were they walking into now?

Crombie's talent said there was no danger in the direction the path went— but Crombie's talent could be too literal. To Bink, anything that might delay the completion of his quest was a threat. One simply could not afford to trust strange magic. He'd better ask the Good Magician.

"Of course it's safe, Bink," Humfrey said with irritation. "Do you suppose I would be riding it otherwise?"

Bink hadn't even asked the question yet! The Magician retained his special talent, though his grumpy refusal to use it for the convenience of the party made his company seem at times to be worth little more than that of a harpy. What point was there in having a Magician along, if he never used his magic to facilitate things? Even the Evil Magician had freely pitched in when danger threatened to—

"That is the point, Bink," Humfrey said. "There is no present danger. When the situation changes, I will expend my carefully hoarded magic. You are young, yet; you dissipate your resources heedlessly, and get into scrapes you should have avoided."

Served him right for letting his thoughts flow carelessly! Bink shut up, mentally, and rode on. In due course the path wound down to a pleasant little village, with houses thatched with hay and daubed with colored muds, and neat walkways connecting places of faint interest.

"Do you notice," Chester said, "there is no magic in the local construction? Only mundane materials."

"That's right," Bink said, surprised. "If we're approaching the source of magic, on a magic path, shouldn't there be more magic rather than less?" He turned to the griffin. "Crombie, are you sure this is—?"

Crombie squawked. "Birdbeak is sure this is the right direction," the golem said. "But the village may be a mere item on the way, not the destination itself."

A grizzled old harpy flapped out to meet the party as it reached the foot of the path. All of them braced for trouble, for harpies were notorious. But this one, though suitably hideous, was clean and unaggressive. "Welcome, travelers," she said without even bothering to insult them. A most restrained harpy!

"Uh, thanks," Bink said. "We're looking for—a place to spend the night. We don't mean any mischief." He had never heard of a harpy acting polite, so remained on guard, hand over sword.

"You shall have it," she agreed. "You are all males?"

"Yes," Bink said uneasily. "We are on a quest for the source of magic. Your village appears to lie near this. We—"

"Five males," the harpy said. "What a bonanza!"

"We're not interested in your females," Chester said with some of his normal belligerence.

Crombie squawked. "Not their minds, anyway," the golem translated.

Chester's lip curled with almost equine facility. Bink had to speak at once, before another quarrel brewed. "We shall be happy to do some chore for you, in return for food and safe lodging overnight. Then tomorrow, if you have information about magic—"

"You will have to discuss that with Trolla," the harpy said. "This way, please." And she flapped off, muttering once more: "Men!" with hideous excitement.

"Then again, you may have a point," Chester murmured to Crombie. "If we have fallen into a nest of harpies . . ."

"We may be best advised to get on that aerial path and go back the way we came," Bink finished, glancing back.

But the path was gone. They could not escape that way.

Trolla turned out to be—a female troll. She was almost as ugly as the harpy, but she too was amazingly polite. "I realize you are uneasy, you handsome male visitors," Trolla said. "And you have reason to be. But not because of any of the residents of this village. Allow me to serve you supper, while I explain our situation."

Bink exchanged glances with the others. Both centaur and griffin looked distinctly uncomfortable, but the Good Magician seemed to have no concern.

Trolla clapped her horny hands, and several wood-nymphs came in, bearing platters. Their hair was green, their skin brown, their lips and fingernails red: like flowering trees. But their outlines were human; each was a pert, lithe, full-breasted bare beauty. Each eyed Bink and Humfrey with more than casual interest. "Hunger" might be a better term.

The food was virtually mundane: vegetables and fruits harvested locally, and small dragon steaks. Milkweed pods provided the liquid; it was good milk, but in no way special.

"You may have noted we have used no magic in the preparation of this meal," Trolla said. "We use as little magic as possible here, because there is more magic here than anywhere else on the surface of Xanth. I realize that may not make much sense to you—"

"Quite sensible," Humfrey said, chomping into another steak.

Trolla focused on him. "You must be a Magician, sir."

"Umph." He seemed to be more interested in his food than in her discussion. Bink knew that was deceptive. Humfrey paid close attention to all things magic.

"If you are—if any of you have strong magic—I must caution you to be extremely careful in exerting it," she said. "Please do not misunderstand; this is no threat. We do not want you to feel at all uncomfortable here. It is simply that all magic—well, permit me to make a small demonstration." She clapped her hands, and a nymph entered, as buxom and bare as the others. "Bring a small firefly," Trolla said.

In a moment the nymph returned with the firefly. It was very small—the kind that generated hardly more than a spark, harmless. It squatted on the table, rather pretty with its folded flame-hued wings and insulated legs. "Now observe what happens when I frighten it," Trolla said.

She rapped the table with a hooflike knuckle. The firefly jumped up, startled, and generated its momentary fire. A burst of light and heat emanated from it, and a ball of smoke roiled up toward the ceiling. A spot on the table a hands-breadth in diameter was charred. The firefly itself had disappeared.

"It burned itself up!" Chester exclaimed.

"It did not mean to," Trolla said. "This was a normal Xanth firefly, not acclimatized to this region. Here near the source its magic is multiplied a hundredfold. Thus its little spark became a self-immolating fireball. Until you males become acclimatized, I urge you not to practice your magic in this village. We value your presence, and do not wish you to suffer any mishaps."

Bink looked to Humfrey, but the Good Magician continued eating. "Uh, none of us have inflammatory magic." Bink said, realizing that it was up to him to respond for their party. Yet he wondered: what would his talent do if anything threatened? What it might intend to be a mere "coincidental" amelioration might become much worse. "But it would be best if—if nothing seemed to threaten our welfare."

"There is, unfortunately, a most extreme threat to your welfare," Trolla said gravely. "Because you are males. You must have noticed we have no males in this village."

"We noticed," Bink agreed. "Your nymphs seem quite intrigued by us." Indeed, the nymphs were hovering so close that Bink's elbows tended to bump their soft midriffs as he ate.

"Our problem is this," Trolla continued. "A siren has been luring away our males. Originally we were a normal human village, except for our unique and critical task. Then the siren came and deprived us of our men. Because our job could not be neglected, we undertook at great personal risk the construction of the charmed access route you arrived on, so as to encourage immigration. But the new men, too, were soon taken away from us. We extended our search to nonhuman people; this was how I myself came here, with my husband the troll. But the awful drain continued; I was soon a widow—and not by the proper route."

Bink felt sudden alarm. Some female trolls ate their husbands. It was said that the only thing a troll was afraid of was his wife—with excellent reason. Was this predaceous female looking for another husband?

"Our village now is composed of every type of intelligent female," Trolla continued. "And a number of supporting animals. The magic access route transports only intelligent creatures, but some animals drift in through the jungle. But the siren—this is what I meant by the danger to you. Once you hear her call, you will disappear into the forest and never return. We would spare you this if we could, but we are helpless unless we resort to unconscionable measures."

"What would those be?" Bink asked nervously.

"We might deafen you so you could not hear her," Trolla explained. "Or geld you, so that you would not react to—"

"Why don't some of you females go out and slay the siren?" Chester asked. "Meaning no offense, madam, but you could probably handle it."

"The siren I would gladly tear apart and consume in bleeding chunks," Trolla said. "But I can not pass the tangle tree. The siren has made a deal with the tangler; the tree lets the males through to her, but grabs the females."

"Then you need to eliminate the tangle tree," Bink said. "With magic as strong here as you've shown, it should be a fairly simple chore. A few fireflies, or some pineapple bombs—"

"This is no ordinary tangle tree," Trolla said. "We have tried to destroy it, but though it is outside our village, it has absorbed enough extra magic to foil our efforts. We are, after all, only females—and the men will not fight it when they are in thrall to the siren."

Bink took a deep breath. "I believe this is the service we can render, in return for your hospitality. Tomorrow we shall slay the tangler."

Trolla merely shook her head sadly. "It is kind of you to think so," she said. "But the siren will not permit it."

The siren did not know about Bink's talent. Since both siren and tangle tree were magical entities, his magic would protect him against them. Somehow. But considering the possible complications of the enhanced potency of magic here, he would do best to tackle the tree alone. He didn't want his friends being hurt by the backlash. Maybe he could sneak out at night and do it, while the others slept.

Crombie squawked. "What is the village employment, crone?" the golem translated.

"We are situated atop the source-lode of magic," Trolla said. "This is the origin of the magic of Xanth. The dust is highly charged with magic, and were it allowed to accumulate, most of the rest of Xanth would slowly become mundane, while the village would develop a fatal concentration. Thus we must spread the dust about, maintaining a reasonable equilibrium." She looked about. "We seem to have completed our repast. Allow me to show you our operations."

"Umph," Humfrey agreed. Now Bink was sure the Magician was only feigning disinterest, as was his fashion; the conclusion of their quest was at hand! Yet Bink found himself disappointed; he had expected more challenge to the acquisition of this knowledge than this.

Trolla showed them to a large central building fashioned of mundane stone. Inside, it was one huge gravel pit, where small female elves, gnomes, and fairies dug and scraped out sand with their little picks and scoops. They loaded it into wheeled wagons drawn by female centaurs, a manticora, and a small sphinx. Bink's skin prickled when he approached the sand; strong magic was associated with it, no doubt of that! Yet this was the first time he had encountered indeterminate magic. That sand performed no magic of its own, and cast no spells; it merely *was* magic, waiting for direction. Bink was not quite sure he could believe that.

The sand was hauled to another structure, where three huge hephalumphs tromped it constantly into dust. The hephalumphs were animals, normally wild creatures of the wilderness, but these were evidently tame and well cared for, and seemed happy. Then a captive roc-bird blew the dust into the air, employing great sweeps of her monstrous wings. So powerful was this forced draft that small tornadoes formed in the turbulence.

"The Technicolor hailstorms!" Bink exclaimed. "Fallout from this operation!"

"Exactly," Trolla agreed. "We try to feed the dust high into the sky so that it will ride the upper currents all over Xanth before it falls, but localized storms bring it down prematurely. The region immediately downwind of us is untenable for intelligent life; the concentration of airborne dust disrupts the local ecology and leads to madness. Thus there are risks associated with our operation—but we must continue. We should be pleased if you males would remain here, encouraging our females—but we know you must flee before the siren calls. Unfortunately our access route is one-way; we have been too busy recently to construct a departure ramp. You can escape only through the Region of Madness. Yet this is preferable to the siren. We shall help you all we can, but—"

"Not until we render our service," Bink said. "We have assorted talents, and should be able to handle this." But privately he was uneasy; he found it hard to believe that they should prevail where all other men had failed. And he wondered again why the source of the magic of Xanth had remained unknown all these centuries, if the people of this village had known about it all along. Maybe the fact that no one ever seemed to leave this village and live—or maybe the magic dust fogged up other magic, so that things like magic mirrors could not focus on this area. There were probably a lot of secrets in the Land of Xanth that remained to be discovered. . . .

"We shall have a gathering this evening," Trolla said. "Some of our younger girls have never seen a male, and deserve this chance. You will meet everyone, and we shall plan how we can best help you to escape the siren. So far, no way has been found to block off her sound from the males, though we females can not hear it. We can, with your permission, confine you in cages so that you can not respond to—"

"No!" Bink and Chester said together, and Crombie squawked.

"You are true males, always ready for a challenge," Trolla said with sad approval. "In any event, we would have to let you out sometime, and then the siren would get you, so cages are no solution. We need to be rid of the siren!" Her face, for a moment, assumed the aspect of savage hate that was normal to trolls. But then she softened. "I will show you to your lodging, and call for you again at dusk. Please be courteous to our villagers; your presence here is a considerable event, and the girls are untrained in social decorum."

When they were alone, Bink addressed the Magician. "Something is funny here. Will you use your magic to fathom the true situation?"

"Do I have to do everything?" Humfrey grumped.

"Listen, you dwarfish gnome!" Chester snapped. "We've been working our tails off, while you just loaf along."

Humfrey was unruffled. "Anytime you wish to have your payment for your efforts—"

Bink decided he had better intercede, though he had considerable sympathy for the centaur's position. He had not realized there would be so many problems in leadership! "We seem to be at our objective, the source of magic. But it has been too easy, and the villagers are too accommodating. Only you can tell us whether we have in fact completed our quest, or whether we have walked into a man-consuming trap. Surely this is the occasion to employ your magic, if you would be so generous."

"Oh, all right," Humfrey said ungraciously. "You don't deserve it after the way you loosed Beauregard, but I'll take a look."

The Magician drew out a mirror. "Mirror, mirror in my hand, are you the finest in the land?"

The mirror clouded, turning deep red. "Oh, stop blushing!" Humfrey snapped. "I was only testing."

Bink remembered a mirror like this. It answered only in pictures, and somewhat circuitously; a too-direct question about a too-delicate matter could crack it up.

"Are you aware of the source of the magic of Xanth?" the Magician asked.

A picture of a baby appeared, smiling. That evidently meant "Yes."

"Can you tell me the location of that source?" Aside to the others he murmured: "This is the crucial point. At home, the mirror never could reveal this information, but here with stronger magic—"

The baby smiled again. Humfrey echoed that smile, anticipating victory. "Will you tell me that location?"

Again the cherubic smile. Bink felt his pulse pounding. He realized the Magician was approaching the subject with extreme caution. The mirror took each question literally, and did not volunteer anything; this circuitous approach insured that the mirror would not be overwhelmed by too abrupt a challenge.

"Please show that location on your screen."

The mirror went dark.

"Oops," Bink murmured. "Is it broken?"

The mirror brightened. A crying baby appeared.

"It tells you no," Humfrey snapped. "Kindly allow me to continue my investigation." He returned to the mirror. "Are you showing me a scene of underground?"

The baby smiled.

"In short, you verify that the source of magic is not in this village we are presently sitting in?"

A big question mark appeared.

"You are saying the source of magic *is* in this village?" the Good Magician asked sharply.

The question mark returned. "Hm, a problem of resolution here," Humfrey muttered. "The mirror can't choose between truths. Anybody have another approach?"

"It's a matter of perspective," Chester said. "If the magic dust is the source, there may be more than one cache of it. More likely, a channel of it, welling up from the depths. Thus the source has a multiple definition, depending on whether you are thinking of the source on the surface, or the source of the source."

"Now there is a creature with a disciplined mind," Humfrey said approvingly. "If only he would discipline it more often instead of quarreling with the soldier." He faced the mirror. "Is the centaur's analysis correct?"

The baby smiled.

"Now," the Magician continued. "Are you aware of the motivation of these villagers?" When he received the smile, he asked: "Do they mean well by us?" The smile confirmed it. Bink felt relief. "And Trolla spoke the truth about the curse of the siren?" Another smile.

Humfrey looked up. "Now it gets difficult," he said, seeming pleased. Bink realized that this man, too, enjoyed a challenge. The magic ability the Good Magician had held in reserve was now being used, and it was good magic. "So far we have merely been confirming what we already knew. Now we must venture into the unknown." He returned to the mirror. "Are you able to tell us how to deal with the villagers' problem?"

The cherub smiled. "Unusually responsive," Humfrey remarked, aside. "The local magic-enhancement is indeed multiplying the mirror's power. We have a major research tool, now, rather than a minor one." He returned once more to the mirror. "How—"

"Are you males ready?" Trolla inquired from the door.

They jumped. Bink was about to explain, then saw Humfrey's quick negative nod. The mirror had disappeared. The Good Magician did not want to reveal the secret of his magic to these villagers. Not just yet.

Well, they had gleaned a lot already, and could resume the use of the mirror when convenient. "That's a pretty dress," Bink said to Trolla. This was no lie; the dress was very pretty, though she remained a female troll. Evidently a festive occasion was in the making. They followed her out.

The center circle of the village had been transformed, nonmagically. A genuine wood bonfire blazed, sending sparks and smoke up to the sky. It was dusk, and the stars were beginning to show. It was as if the sparks went up into the sky to become those stars—and perhaps, Bink thought, the potent magic of this region made that so. The stars had to get up there somehow, didn't they?

The females of the village were lovely in their party apparel. There were many more young ones than had been evident before, and now that their work shift was over they were eager and more than eager to mingle with the strange guests. Bink was surrounded by nymphs, sprites, and human maids, while Humfrey was mobbed by fairies, lady elves, and minionettes. Three fetching centaur fillies attended Chester. A pair of griffin cows eyed Crombie, but they hardly had a chance with this transformed woman-hater. They were, after all, animals. There was even a female golem for Grundy.

Yet how sad the remaining females looked—the manticora, the sphinx, and the harpies. They had no males to cater to.

"Uh, girls—I'm a married man," Bink protested as his covey pressed in.

"She will never know," a buxom blue-maned lass informed him. "We need you more than she does." And she planted a firm kiss on his left eye—the only part of him she could reach, because of the density of other girls.

"Yes, no man leaves this village, except at the call of the singing bitch," a furry beauty added. "It is our duty to hold you here, to save your life. Wouldn't your wife rather have you used than dead?"

Awkward question! How *would* Chameleon feel about that? In her lovely, stupid phase she would be hurt, confused, and forgiving; in her ugly, smart phase she would comprehend the situation and be realistic. So she would accept what had to be accepted, and certainly not want him to die. Still, he had no wish or intent to indulge himself with any of these—

Something distracted him. It was a faint, eerie, but somehow most intriguing sound.

He tried to listen, but the clamor of the girls almost drowned it out. "Please, I want to hear—there is a melody—"

"It is the siren!" a fairy screamed. "Sing, girls, sing! Drown out the bitch!"

They sang, loudly, passionately, and tunelessly. Still, that insidious melody penetrated, the single clear theme cutting through the nearby cacophony, compelling Bink to respond. He started toward it.

Immediately the girls restrained him. They flung their arms about him, dragging him back and down, burying him in their exposed softness. Bink collapsed in a tangle of arms, legs, breasts, and assorted other aspects of distaff anatomy he didn't bother to define.

The girls meant well—but the siren's call was not to be denied. Bink fought, and caught glimpses of other thrashing mounds where his male companions fought similarly. Bink was stronger than any of the nymphs, for they were delicate, shapely things; he did not want to hurt any of them. Yet he had to free himself of their near-suffocating embrace. He heaved them off his body, cuffing their hands loose, shoving wherever his hands made contact. There were eeeks and cries and giggles, depending on the type of contact he made; then he was on his feet, charging forward.

Chester and Crombie and the Magician closed in about him, all riveted to that compelling sound. "No, no!" Trolla cried despairingly behind them. "It is death you seek! Are you civilized males or are you mindless things?"

That bothered Bink. What did he want with a magical temptress? Yet still he could not resist the siren. Her lure had an unearthly quality that caught at the very root of his masculinity, beneath the center of his intelligence. He was male, therefore he responded.

"Let them go, they are lost," Trolla said despairingly. "We tried, as we have always tried—and failed."

Though he was in thrall to the siren, Bink felt simultaneous sympathy for Trolla and the girls. They offered life and love, yet were doomed to be rejected; their positive orientation could not compete with the negative compulsion of the siren. The villagers suffered as horrible a damnation as the men! Was it because they were nice girls, making only promises they could keep, while the siren had no such limit?

Crombie squawked. "As all females always fail," Grundy translated, responding to Trolla's despair. "Though why any of us should bother with this bitch-female call—" The griffin shrugged his wings and charged on.

Did even the golem feel it? He must, for he was not protesting.

They ran down a path that opened magically before them. It was a perfect path, exactly the kind that usually led to something huge, predatory, and stationary, like a tangle tree. But of course this particular tangler would not attack them, because they were males in thrall to the siren. *She* would dispatch them, in her own fashion.

And what might that fashion be? Bink wondered. He could not quite imagine it, but the prospect was wrenchingly exciting. "What a way to go!" he breathed.

The tree came into sight. It was monstrous, even for its kind. Its dangling tentacles were as thick as the legs of a man, and extremely long and limber. Its tempting fragrance surrounded it like an evening gown, making it seem thoroughly desirable. Gentle music emanated from its foliage, no siren call, but nice: the kind of music that made a person want to lie down and listen and relax.

But no veteran of the wilderness of Xanth could be fooled for an instant. This was one of the most deadly life forms available. Even a dragon would not venture near a tangle tree!

The path passed right under it, where the curtain of tentacles parted neatly and the soft sward grew. But elsewhere around the fringe was a developing cone of bleaching bones, the remainders of the tree's past victims. Shapely female bones, Bink suspected, and felt another twinge of guilt.

Yet the siren still called, and they followed. They funneled down to single file, for the path beneath the tree was narrow. Chester galloped first, then Crombie, for their forms were fastest; Bink and the Magician followed as well as they could. There had not been occasion to mount the steeds for faster travel.

Chester paused under the awful tree, and the tentacles quivered with suppressed eagerness but did not grab. So it was true: the siren's song nullified the tangle reflex! The distant music was stronger now, and more compelling: the very essence of female allure. The nymphs of the village had been pretty and sweet, but the siren's promise was vital; it was as if the sex appeal of all womankind had been distilled and concentrated and—

Ahead of Bink, the griffin suddenly halted. "Squawk!" Crombie exclaimed. "What am I doing here?" the golem translated, coming up behind, surprisingly fleet on his feet, considering his size. "The siren is nothing but a damned conniving female out for my blood!"

Literally true, but the others ignored him. Of course the siren was a conniving female, the ultimate one! What difference did that make? The call had to be honored!

The woman-hater, however, decided to be difficult. "She's trying to trap me!" he squawked. "All women are traps! Death to them all!" And he pecked viciously at the nearest thing available—which happened to be the slender extremity of a tentacle.

In a small bird, such a peck would have been a nuisance. Crombie, however, was a griffin. His beak was sword-sharp, powerful as a vise, a weapon capable of severing a man's leg at the ankle with a single bite. The tentacle, in this case, was the diameter of an ankle, and the chomp severed it cleanly. The separated end dropped to the ground, twitching and writhing like a headless green snake.

For a moment the whole tree froze in shock. *No* one took a bite out of a tangler! The truncated upper section of the tentacle welled dark ooze as it thrashed about as if looking for its extremity. The gentle background music soured.

"I think the truce has been broken," Bink said. But he didn't really care, for the song of the siren continued, drawing him on to better things. "Move on, Crombie; you're blocking my way."

But the soldier remained unreasonable. "Squawk! Squawk! Squawk!" he exclaimed, and before Grundy could translate, he nipped off another tentacle, then a third.

The tangle tree shuddered. Then, furious, it reacted. Its music became a deafening blare of outrage, and its tentacles grabbed for the griffin—and the centaur, man, and Magician.

"Now you've done it, birdbrain!" Chester screamed over the noise. He grabbed the first tentacle that touched him and wrung it between his two hands the way the ogre had wrung out the log. Tough as the tentacles were when grabbing, they had little resistance to cutting or compression, and this one was squished into uselessness in a moment.

Suddenly the lure of the siren was drowned out by the rage of the tree, and they were in a fight for their lives. Bink drew his sword and slashed at the tentacles that swept toward him, cutting them off. Beside him Crombie pecked and scratched viciously, all four feet operating. Long cuts appeared in the tentacles he touched, and green goo welled out. But more tentacles kept coming in, from all sides, for this was the very center of the tree's power.

Chester backed up to the trunk and operated his bow. He fired arrow after arrow through the thick upper reaches of the tentacles, paralyzing them. But—

"No, Chester!" Bink cried. "Get away from—"

Too late. The tree's huge maw opened in the trunk, the bark-lips lapping forward to engulf the centaur's handsome posterior.

Bink leaped to help his friend. But a tentacle caught his ankle, tripping him. All he could do was yell: "Kick, Chester, kick!" Then he was buried in tentacles, as firm and rounded and pneumatic as the limbs of the village girls, but not nearly as nice. His sword arm was immobilized; all he could do was bite, ineffectively. That green goo tasted awful!

Chester kicked. The kick of a centaur was a potent thing. His head and shoulders went down, counter-balancing his rear, and all the power of his extraordinary body thrust through his two hind hooves. They connected inside the maw of the tree, against the wooden throat, and the ground shook with the double impact. A few old bones were dislodged from the upper foliage to rattle down to the ground. But the wooden mouth held. Sap juices flowed, commencing the digestion of the centaur's excellent flesh. Chester's instinct would have been sound for any ordinary tree, using the inert trunk as protection for his valuable but vulnerable rear, but it was disaster here.

Chester kicked again, and again, violently. Even this predator-tree could not withstand much of this punishment. Normally its prey was unconscious or helpless by the time it reached the consumption stage, not awake and kicking. Slowly, reluctantly, the bark gave way, and the centaur dragged free. His once-beautiful flank was discolored by the saliva sap, and one hoof had been chipped by the force of its contact with the wood, but at least he was alive. Now he drew his sword and strode forward to help Bink, who was not-so-slowly suffocating in the embrace of the tentacles.

Meanwhile Magician Humfrey had problems of his own. He was trying to unstopper one of his little vials, but the tentacles were wrapping about him faster than the stopper was coming loose. The tree was overwhelming them all!

Crombie had clawed and bit his way to the fringe. Suddenly he broke out. "I'm free, you vegetable monster!" he squawked exultantly. "I'll bet you're another female, too!" He was really uncorking his worst insult! The golem had gotten aboard again, so was available for instant translation. "You can't catch me!"

Indeed the tree could not, for it was rooted. Crombie spread his wings and flew up and away, escaping it.

Yet what of the others? As if enraged even further at the loss, the tree concentrated savagely on the remaining prey. Pythons of tentacles whipped about limbs and bodies, squeezing tight. Chester was trying to help Bink, but dared not slash too closely with his sword lest he slice some of Bink along with a tentacle. Bink, now closest to the trunk, found himself being dragged headfirst toward the dread orifice.

Humfrey finally got his bottle open. Smoke issued forth, expanding and coalescing into—a spiced cheesecake.

"Curses!" the Magician cried. "Wrong vial!"

Chester kicked at the cheesecake. It slid across the turf and into the slavering maw of the tree. The bark-lips closed about it. He could hardly have made a nicer shot had he been trying for it.

The tree choked. There was a paroxysm of wooden coughing, followed by a sylvan sneeze. Gross hunks of cheese flew out of the orifice.

"The spice on that one *is* a bit strong," Humfrey muttered as he scrambled for another vial.

Now Bink's head was at the maw. The bark was writhing, trying to get the taste of spiced cheese out. This monster liked fresh meat, not processed dairy products. Sap coursed down and dripped from tooth-like knots, cleaning out the maw. In a moment it would be ready for Bink.

Chester was still trying to help, but three tentacles had wrapped around his sword arm, and more looped his other extremities. Even his great strength could not avail against the massed might of the tree. "And the cowardly soldier ran out on us!" he grunted as he fought. "If I ever get my hands on him—" He wrung out another tentacle before his free arm was pinioned.

Humfrey got another vial open. The vapor emerged—and formed into a flying vampire bat. The creature took one look at its environs, squeaked in terror, swore off blood, and flapped away. A single tentacle took one casual swing at it and knocked it out of the air. The tree was really getting on top of the situation.

The last of the cheese cleared. The orifice reopened for business, and Bink was the client. He saw the rows of ingrown knots that served as the monster's teeth, and the flowing saliva sap. Fibers like miniature tentacles extended inward from the mouth-walls, ready to absorb the juices of the prey. Suddenly he realized: the tangler was related to the carnivorous grass that grew in patches in the wilderness! Add a trunk and tentacles to such a patch—

Humfrey got another vial open. This time a basilisk formed, flapping its little wings as it glared balefully about. Bink closed his eyes to avoid its direct gaze, and Chester did the same. The tree shivered and tried to draw away. There was no creature in all the Land of Xanth who cared to meet the gaze of this little lizard-cock!

Bink heard the flapping as the basilisk flew right into the tangler's mouth—and stopped. But nothing happened. Cautiously Bink opened one eye. The tree was still alive. The basilisk had not destroyed it at a glance.

"Oh—a mock basilisk," Bink said, disappointed.

"I have a good remedy for tanglers somewhere," Humfrey insisted, still sifting through his vials. Whenever a tentacle encroached too closely he stunned it with a magic gesture. Bink had not known such gestures existed—but of course he was not a Magician of Information. "They're all mixed up—"

The tentacles shoved Bink into the mouth. The odor of carrion became strong. Helpless, he stared into his doom.

"Squawk!" sounded from beyond the trees. "Charge!"

Crombie had returned! But what could he do, alone?

Now there was a sound as of the rush of many feet. The tangle tree shuddered. The odor of smoke and scorching vegetation drifted in. Bink saw, from the corner of his eye, orange light flaring up, as if a forest fire raged.

Torches! Crombie had marshaled the females of the magic-dust village, and they were attacking the tree with blazing brands, singeing the tentacles. What a brave effort!

Now the tangler had to defend itself from attack by a superior force. It dropped Bink, freeing its tentacles for other action. Bink saw a pretty nymph get grabbed, and heard her scream as she was hauled into the air, her torch dropping.

"Squawk! Squawk!" Crombie directed, and other females rushed to the captive's rescue, forming a screen of flame. More tentacles got scorched, and the nymph dropped.

Bink recovered his sword and resumed hacking, from inside the curtain of tentacles. Now that the tree was concentrating on the outside menace, it was vulnerable to the inside one. With every stroke Bink lopped off another green branch, gradually denuding the tree of its deadly limbs.

"Squawk!" Crombie cried. "Get outside!" the golem translated.

That made sense. If the tree should refocus on the interior, Bink, Chester, and Humfrey would be in trouble again. Better to get out while they could!

In a moment they stood beside the griffin. "Squawk!" Crombie exclaimed. "Let's finish off this monster!" Grundy cried for him.

The ladies went to it with a will. There were about fifty of them, ringing the tree, pushing in with their fires, scorching back every tentacle that attacked. They could have conquered the tree anytime, instead of letting it balk them all these years—had they had the masculine drive and command. Ironic that Crombie the woman-hater should be the organizing catalyst!

Yet perhaps this was fitting. Crombie's paranoia about the motives of women had caused him to resist the siren, finally breaking her spell. Now he was using these females in the manner a soldier understood: as fodder for a battle. They might not have responded as well to a "nicer" man. Maybe they needed one who held them in contempt, who was willing to brutalize them for his purpose.

The tree was shriveling, half its awful limbs amputated or paralyzed. It would take time to kill it, but the victory now seemed certain. Thanks to Crombie, and the brave, self-sacrificing villagers.

"You know, I could get to respect women like these," Crombie murmured as he paused from his exertions to watch the wrap-up proceed. Actually it was squawk-and-translation, but Bink was so used to it now that it made little difference. "They obey orders well, and fight damn near as well as a man, allowing for—" He paused in mid-squawk, listening.

Then Bink heard the siren's call again, no longer drowned out by the battle. Oh, no! He tried to resist it—and could not. The siren had recovered her thrall.

Bink started walking toward that sound. His companions joined him, silently. The villagers, intent on their successful campaign, did not see them depart.

Chapter 7

Deadly Distaffs

T he sound of the battle faded behind. The males, Crombie included, moved on down the path, lured by the siren's song. The unearthly quality was stronger now, thrilling Bink's inner fiber. He knew the siren meant death, more certainly than the tangle tree—but what a satisfying death it would be!

It was a good path; nothing interfered with their progress. Soon they arrived at the shore of a small lake. In that lake were two tiny islands, like the tips of mountains mostly hidden beneath the surface. The path led over the water to one of these islands. This was the source of the music of the siren.

They started on the path. Bink thought Crombie might balk again, and in his heart hoped he would while fearing that that hope would be fulfilled, but the griffin did not. Apparently his resistance to females had been compromised by the spirit and sacrifice of the village women, and he could no longer master sufficient suspicion. Indeed, he was the first on the water-path, the water depressing slightly under his claws but supporting his weight. The Magician was second, Bink third, and—

There was an angry bleat from the side. A small creature came charging along the small beach. It was four-legged and woolly, like a sheep, with broad curly horns that circled entirely around its head. Evidently the path crossed this creature's territory, and the animal was taking action.

Chester, in the thing's path, paused. "A battering ram," he remarked, recognizing the species. "Not subject to the siren's call because it is a mere animal. No use to reason with it."

A battering ram! Bink paused, his curiosity momentarily overriding the lure of the siren. He had heard of such creatures, and of their relatives the hydraulic rams, but never encountered one before. As he understood it, they existed only to batter, and they loved it. If there were a door to be broken down, or a castle to be breached, such a ram was invaluable. At other times, they were a nuisance, because they never stopped beating their heads against obstacles.

Chester was far larger than the ram—but it had cut him off from the siren's path. Chester dodged it once, nimbly, but the ram screeched to a halt—a neat trick in sand, even with magic—and whirled to recharge. Chester would have been battered in the rear, had he tried to ignore it—and his rear was his proudest feature, despite the recent staining from the tangler's sap—much handsomer than his face. So he whirled to face the ram, and dodged its charge again.

But there was no end to this. The ram would happily go on forever, screeching up more mounds of sand with each miss, but Chester had a siren call to answer. The ram had to be stopped, somehow.

Bink wondered: his talent could have had a part in saving him from the tangler, as it had used the motives and magic of others freely. Was the ram another device to stop him from reaching the siren? In that case, he should be rooting for the ram, not Chester.

Chester, no dummy, maneuvered between charges until he was directly in front of a large tree. He never took his eye off the ram, lest it catch him by surprise. Next charge would fire the ram right into the trunk that Chester had oriented on peripherally, with luck knocking the animal silly. Or at least starting the process, because it took a lot of knocking to knock a battering ram silly. These creatures were pretty silly to begin with.

Then Bink recognized the variety of tree. "Not that one, Chester!" he cried. "That's a—"

Too late. Why was he always too late? It was getting quite annoying! The ram charged, Chester danced aside, there was a flutelike trill of music, and the ram plowed headfirst into the tree. Such was the force of impact, all out of proportion to the animal's size, that the entire tree vibrated violently.

". . . pineapple tree," Bink finished belatedly.

Now the fruits were falling: huge golden pineapples, quite ripe. As each hit the ground, it exploded savagely. That was how this tree reproduced: the detonating fruit sent shrapnel-seeds far across the landscape, where each could generate, with luck and magic, a new pineapple tree. But it was hardly safe to stand too near this process.

One pineapple struck the battering ram on the rump. The ram bleated and spun to face it, rear-scorched and bruised, but of course that was futile. Other fruits were exploding all around. One dropped just before the ram. With a snort of challenge the animal leaped boldly forth to intercept it, catching it squarely on the horns. The resulting concussion really did knock the ram silly; it staggered off, bleating happily.

Meanwhile Chester was doing a truly intricate dance of avoidance, trying to keep his flowing tail and sleek equine haunches out of mischief. He could avoid the pineapples falling to left, right, and front, but those behind were problematical. One dropped almost on his tail; in fact it brushed the elevated top. Chester, in a remarkable maneuver, whipped his entire hind-section out of the way—but in the process brought his head into the location vacated by the tail.

The pineapple exploded. Chester caught the blast right under his chin. His head was engulfed in flame and smoke; then the refuse cleared and he stood there, dazed.

Bink found himself unable to run back along the path, despite his concern for his friend. This was partly because the continuing summons of the siren allowed him to pause but not to withdraw, and partly because the path over the water was one-way. It was firm while he proceeded forward, but was mere water when he tried to go back. The lake was small, but seemed very deep, and he hesitated to trust himself to its reaches. Bad magic tended to lurk in the depths. So he could only watch and call. "Chester! Are you all right?"

The centaur stood there, slowing shaking his head. The explosion had not done much harm to Chester's facial appearance, since that had always been homely, but Bink was concerned about the centaur's fine mind. Had the pineapple damaged his brain?

"Chester! Can you hear me?" Then, as Chester ignored him, Bink understood the problem. The blast had deafened him!

Bink waved his hands violently, and finally Chester took note. "Speak louder—I can't hear you!" Then the centaur realized it himself. "I'm deaf! I can't hear anything!"

At least he seemed to be all right, otherwise. Bink, relieved of much of his anxiety, felt himself again overwhelmed by the continuing call of the siren. He beckoned.

"The hell with the siren!" Chester called. "I can't hear her now. It's stupid to go to her. She means death."

Crombie had been briefly freed of the compulsion, back at the tangle tree, but had been recaptured by the siren. Now Chester had been freed by the intercession of the battering ram. It must be the operation of Bink's talent! But Bink himself was still hooked. He turned about and proceeded toward the island. Crombie and the Good Magician were almost there now, as they had not paused as long as Bink.

Chester galloped along the path, catching up to Bink. His powerful hands picked Bink up by the elbows. "Don't go, Bink! It's nonsense!"

But Bink would not be denied. "Put me down, horserear. I have to go!" And his feet kept walking in midair.

"I can't hear you, but I know what you're saying, and it's not worth listening to," Chester said. "Only one way to stop this before the others are lost."

He set Bink down, then unslung his great bow. The siren was still far away, but there was no archery like that of a centaur. Chester's bowstring twanged, and the deadly shaft arced across the water toward the island and the female figure there.

There was a scream of anguish, and the melody halted abruptly. Chester's arrow had scored. Suddenly they all were freed; the compulsion was gone. Bink's talent had prevailed at last, saving him from harm without revealing itself.

They ran to the island. There lay the siren—the loveliest mermaid Bink had ever seen, with hair like flowing sunshine and tail like flowing water. The cruel arrow had passed entirely through her torso, between and slightly below her spectacular bare breasts, and she was bleeding from front and back. Her torso had collapsed across her dulcimer.

Yet she was not dead. Though the arrow, with that uncanny marksmanship of the centaur, must have pierced her heart, she still breathed. In fact, she was conscious. She tilted her beautiful face weakly to look up at Chester. "Why did you shoot me, handsome male?" she whispered.

"He can't hear you; he's deaf," Bink said.

"I mean no harm—only love," she continued. "Love to all men, you—why should you oppose that?"

"What joy is there in death?" Bink demanded. "We have brought to you what you have brought to a hundred other men." He spoke gruffly, yet his heart ached to see the agony of this lovely creature. He remembered when Chameleon had been similarly wounded.

"I brought no death!" she protested as vehemently as she was able, and gasped as the effort pushed a gout of blood from her chest. Her whole body below the shoulders was soaked in bright blood, and she was weakening visibly. "Only—only love!"

Then at last she subsided, losing consciousness. Bink, moved despite what he knew, turned to the Magician. "Is—is it possible she speaks the truth?"

Humfrey brought out his magic mirror. It showed the smiling baby face. "It is possible," he said, wise to the ways of the mirror. Then he addressed it directly: "*Did* the siren speak the truth?"

The baby smiled again. "She meant no harm," the Magician said. "She is not the killer, though she lured men here."

The men exchanged glances. Then Humfrey brought out his bottle of healing elixir and sprinkled a drop on the siren's terrible wound. Instantly it healed, and she was sound again.

The Magician offered Chester a drop of elixir for his ears, but the centaur disdained it. So Humfrey sprinkled it on the centaur's rear, and suddenly it was as beautiful as ever.

"You healed me!" the siren exclaimed, passing her hands wonderingly over her front. "There is not even blood, no pain!" Then, startled; "I must sing!" She reached for her dulcimer.

Chester kicked it out of her reach. The musical instrument flew through the air, smashed, and plunked into the water. "There is the source of her magic!" he cried. "I have destroyed it!"

The source of magic . . . destroyed. Was that an omen?

Experimentally, the siren sang. Her upper torso expanded marvelously as she took her breath, and her voice was excellent—but now there was no compulsion in it. The centaur had, indeed, deprived her of her devastating magic.

She broke off. "You mean that was what summoned all the men? I thought they liked my singing." She looked unhappy.

Apparently she really was the lovely innocent, like Chameleon in her beauty-phase. "What happened to all the men?" Bink asked.

"They went across to see my sister," she said, gesturing toward the other island. She pouted. "I offered them all my love—but they always go to her."

Curious! Who could lure victims away from the siren herself? "Who is your sister?" Bink asked. "I mean, what is her magic? Is she another siren?"

"Oh, no! She is a gorgon, very pretty."

"A gorgon!" Bink exclaimed. "But that is death!"

"No, she would not harm anyone, no more than I would," the siren protested. "She cherishes men. I only wish she would send some back to me."

"Don't you know what the gaze of a gorgon does?" Bink demanded. "What happens to someone who looks upon the face of—?"

"I have looked into my sister's face many times! There is no harm in her!"

Humfrey lifted his mirror again. "It affects men only?" he asked, and the smiling baby agreed.

It seemed the siren really did not know the devastating effect her sister's face had on men. So for years she had innocently lured in males—for the gorgon to turn to stone.

"We shall have to talk with your sister," Humfrey said.

"The path continues to her island," the siren informed him. "What will I do, without my dulcimer?"

"Your voice is pretty enough without any accompaniment, and so are you," Bink said diplomatically. It was true as far as it went; had she a lower portion to match her upper portion, it would have been true all the way. "You can sing *a capella*, without accompaniment."

"I can?" she inquired, brightening. "Will it bring nice men like you?"

"No. But perhaps a nice man will find you, regardless." Bink turned to the Magician. "How can we approach the gorgon? One glance—"

"We shall have to deal with her in the morning," Humfrey decided. Bink had lost track of time. The stars had been emerging at the village, then they had charged into the night of the jungle to battle the tangle tree, thence to this island—where it seemed dusk was only now falling. Did that make sense? Bink had somehow assumed that the sun set all over Xanth at the same instant, but realized that this was not necessarily so. But he had other things to worry about at the moment, and listened to the rest of Humfrey's speech: "Siren, if you have food and bed—"

"I'm not really that kind of female," she demurred.

Bink looked at her sleek fishtail. "Obviously not. We only want a place to sleep."

"Oh." She sounded disappointed. "Actually, I could become that kind, if—" She shimmered, and her tail transposed into two fetching legs.

"Just sleep," Chester said. It seemed his hearing was returning naturally. "And food."

But her indignation had not yet run its course. "After you impaled me with your old messy arrow, and broke my dulcimer?"

"I'm sorry," Chester said shortly. "I have a headache."

As well he might, Bink thought. Why hadn't the ornery creature accepted a drop of elixir for his head as well as for his tail?

"If you were really sorry, you'd show it," she said.

Crombie squawked. "She's setting her hooks into you already, ass," the golem said.

Doubly annoyed, Chester glowered at the siren. "How?"

"By giving me a ride on your back."

Bink almost laughed. Nymphs of any type loved to ride!

"Ride, then," Chester said, disconcerted.

She walked to his side, but was unable to mount. "You're too tall," she complained.

Chester turned his front portion, wrapped one arm about her slender waist, and hauled her up easily. "Eeek!" she screamed, delighted, as her feet swished through the air. "You're so strong!"

Crombie squawked again, and his remark needed no interpretation. She was, indeed, working her wiles on the centaur, needing no siren song.

Chester, not in the best of moods after his encounter with the pineapple, was visibly mollified. "All centaurs are strong." He set her neatly on his back, and walked forward.

The siren grabbed two handfuls of his mane. "My, your shoulders are so broad! And what sleek fur you have. You must be the handsomest centaur of all!"

"From the rear, maybe," he agreed. He began to trot.

"Oooh, that's fun!" she cried, letting go just long enough to clap her hands together girlishly. "You must be the smartest centaur, and the fastest—" She paused. "Could you, maybe, make a little jump?"

Chester, now quite puffed up by her praise, made a tremendous leap. The siren screamed and flew off his back. They were at the edge of the water, since this was a small island, and she plunked into the lake.

"Uh, sorry," Chester said, mortified. "Guess I overdid it." He reached down to fish her out.

Fish her out he did: her legs had changed back into a tail. "No harm done," the mermaid said. "I am quite at home in the water." And she wriggled within his grasp, bringing her face to his and planting a wet kiss on him.

Crombie squawked. "There's no fool like a horse-reared fool," the golem said.

"That's for sure," Chester agreed, now in a good mood. "Just don't tell Cherie."

"Cherie?" the siren asked, frowning.

"My filly. The prettiest thing in Xanth. She's back home, tending our foal. His name is Chet."

She assimilated that. "How nice," she said, disgruntled. "I'd better see to your fodder now, and stall space."

Bink smiled privately. Chester wasn't such a fool after all!

They had a modest repast of fish and sea cucumber, and bedded down in a pile of soft dry sponges. Bink stretched out his feet—and banged into another pile of dirt. This time he was too tired to stomp it flat, so he ignored it.

The siren, having given up on the centaur, nestled down in the dark beside Bink. "Say," he said, remembering. "We have to give service for hospitality!"

Crombie squawked. *"You* give service, noodlebrain," Grundy said. "You're closest to her."

"Service?" the siren inquired, nudging him.

Bink found himself blushing furiously in the dark. *Damn* Crombie's innuendo! "Uh, nothing," he said, and pretended to fall suddenly asleep. Very soon it was no pretense.

In the morning they bade farewell to the siren after taking the time to break up some wood for her cooking fire—a service she appreciated, as she was not much for that sort of thing. They set about braving her sister. "The rest of you must be blindfolded," Humfrey decided. "I will use the mirror."

So he could view the gorgon indirectly, of course. That was the only way to look at such creatures; everyone knew that. Yet why did a mirror work? The image in the glass should be as horrendous as the original.

"Polarization," the Magician explained without being asked. "The magic of partial images."

That didn't clarify things much. But a more important question remained. "What do we do, to stop the—" Bink did not want to use the word "kill" in the presence of the innocent siren. Getting close to the gorgon was one thing; dispatching her while blindfolded was another.

"We shall see," Humfrey said.

They submitted to blindfolding, including the golem. Then they formed a chain to follow the Good Magician, who walked backward on the path between the islands, using the mirror to see ahead. In this case he was not utilizing its magic, but merely the ordinary reflection: the natural magic all mirrors possessed.

It was strange and uncomfortable, crossing the water sightlessly. How awful it would be, to lose forever the power of seeing! What magic was better than the natural senses of life?

Bink's feet felt hard land. "You stand here, facing out," Humfrey told them. "Just in case. I will deal with the gorgon."

Still nervous, Bink obeyed. He felt tempted to rip off the blindfold, turn about, and look at the gorgon—but not strongly tempted. Once he had stood atop a tall mountain and suffered an urge to throw himself off it, similarly; it was as if there were a death urge in him along with the life urge. Perhaps the urge to adventure was drawn from the same wellspring.

"Gorgon," Humfrey said.

Right behind Bink, she answered. "I am she. Welcome to my isle." Her voice was dulcet; she sounded even more attractive than her sister. "Why do you not look at me?"

"Your glance would turn me into stone," Humfrey said bluntly.

"Am I not beautiful? Who else has locks as serpentine as mine?" she asked plaintively, and Bink heard the faint hissing of the snakes. He wondered what it would be like to kiss the gorgon, with those snake-hairs twining around their two faces. The notion was both alarming and tempting. Yet what was the gorgon except the literal personification of the promise and threat embodied in every woman?

"You are beautiful," Humfrey agreed gravely. She must be beautiful indeed, Bink thought, for the Good Magician did not waste compliments. Oh, for a single look! "Where are the other men who came to you?"

"They went away?" she said sadly.

"Where did they go?"

"There," she said, and Bink assumed she was pointing. "Beyond those rocks."

Humfrey moved over to investigate. "These are statues," he said, unsurprised. "Statues of men, exquisitely realistic. Carved, as it were, from life."

From life . . .

"Yes," she agreed brightly. "They look just like the men who came to me."

"Does that not suggest anything to you?"

"The men left the gifts behind, pictures of themselves, sculptures. But I would rather have had the men stay with me. I have no use for stones."

She didn't realize what she had done! She thought these were mere images offered as remembrances. Maybe she refused to realize the truth, blocking it out from her consciousness, pretending she was an ordinary girl. She refused to believe in her own magic. What a fateful delusion!

Yet, Bink thought, wasn't this too typical of the thought processes of females? What one among them chose to recognize the mischief her sex worked among men!

But that was Crombie's contention, therefore probably an exaggeration. There might be a little siren and a little gorgon in every girl, but not a lot. There was hardly any in Chameleon.

"If more men come," Humfrey continued with unusual gentleness, "they will only leave more statues. This is not good."

"Yes, there are already too many statues," she agreed naively. "My island is getting crowded."

"The men must not come any more," Humfrey said. "They must stay at their homes, with their families."

"Couldn't just one man come—and stay a while?" she asked plaintively.

"I'm afraid not. Men just aren't, er, right for you."

"But I have so much love to give—if only a man would stay! Even a little one. I would cherish him forever and ever, and make him so happy—"

Bink, listening, was beginning to appreciate the depth of the gorgon's tragedy. All she wanted was to love and be loved, and instead she sowed a harvest of horrible mischief. How many families had been destroyed by her magic? What could be done with her—except execution?

"You must go into exile," Humfrey said. "The magic shield has been lowered by order of the King; you can pass freely out of Xanth. In Mundania your magic will dissipate, and you will be able to interact freely with the man or men of your choice."

"Leave Xanth?" she cried, alarmed. "Oh, no, I would rather die! I can not leave my home!"

Bink experienced a pang of sympathy. Once he himself had faced exile. . . .

"But in Mundania you would be an ordinary girl, under no curse. You are extremely lovely, and your personality is sweet. You could have your pick of men there."

"I love men," she said slowly. "But I love my home more. I can not depart. If this is my only choice, I beg of you to slay me now and end my misery."

For once the Good Magician seemed shaken. "Slay you? I would not do that! You are the most attractive creature I have ever seen, even through a mirror! In my youth I would have—"

Now a little ordinary feminine artifice manifested. "Why, you are not old, sir. You are a handsome man."

Crombie stifled a squawk. Chester coughed, and Bink choked. She had made a gross exaggeration, if not an outright distortion! Humfrey was a good man, and a talented one, but hardly a handsome one. "You flatter me," the Magician said seriously. "But I have other business."

"Of all the men who have come here, you alone have stayed to talk with me," the gorgon continued. "I am so lonely! I beg of you, stay with me, and let me serve you always."

Now Crombie squawked aloud. "Don't turn about, fool!" The golem cried. "Keep using the mirror!"

"Um, yes," Humfrey agreed. The griffin's hearing must be acute, Bink thought, to detect the sound of the Magician's incipient turning! "Gorgon, if I were to look at you directly—"

"You would feel obliged to go away, leaving only a stone memento in your likeness," she finished. "I do not understand why men are like this! But come, close your eyes if you must, kiss me, let me show you how much love I have for you. Your least word is my command, if you will only stay!"

The Magician sighed. Was the old gnome tempted? It occurred to Bink that it might not have been disinterest in women that kept Humfrey single, but lack of a suitable partner. The average woman was not interested in a wizened, dwarfish old man—or if she expressed interest, it was likely to be only because she wanted a piece of his formidable magic. Here was a woman who knew nothing of him but his appearance, and was eager to love him, asking only his presence.

"My dear, I think not," Humfrey said at last. "Such a course would have its rewards—I hardly deny it!—and I would normally be inclined to dally with you a day or three, though love be blindfolded. But it would require the resources of a Magician to associate safely with you, and I am on a quest that takes precedence, and may not—"

"Then dally a day or three!" she exclaimed. "Be blindfolded! I know no Magician would have interest in me, but even a Magician could not be more wonderful than you, sir!"

Did she suspect the magnitude of Humfrey's talent? Did it matter? The Magician sighed again. "Perhaps, after my present quest is over, if you would care to visit at my castle—"

"Yes, yes!" She cried. "Where is your castle?"

"Just ask for Humfrey. Someone will direct you. Even so, you can not show your face to man. You would have to wear a veil—no, even that would not suffice, for it is your eyes that—"

"Do not cover my eyes! I must see!"

Bink felt another surge of sympathy, for at the moment he could not see.

"Let me consult," Humfrey said. There was a rustle as he rummaged through his magic props. Then: "This is not ideal, but it will do. Hold this vial before your face and open it."

More rustling as she accepted the vial that he held out over his shoulder. There was a pop as the cork came out, the hiss of escaping vapor, a gasp, then silence. Had the Magician executed her after all, giving her poison vapor to sniff?

"Companions, you may now remove your blindfolds and turn about," Humfrey said. "The gorgon has been nullified."

Bink ripped off the cloth. "Magician! You didn't—?"

"No, I did her no harm. Observe."

Bink observed, as did the others. Before them stood a breathtakingly lovely young woman with hair formed of many small thin snakes. But her face was—absent. There simply wasn't anything there.

"I applied a spell of invisibility to her face," Humfrey explained. "She can see out well enough, but I regret that no man can look upon her face, since it is the loveliest part of her. But this way it is impossible to meet her gaze. She is safe—as are we."

It was too bad, really, Bink had to agree. She seemed like such a nice girl, burdened with such a terrible curse, but it was disconcerting to look into that vacuum in lieu of her face.

Crombie walked around the island, studying the statues. Some were of centaurs, and some of griffins. "Squawk!" "Look at the damage the bitch has done! She must have petrified hundreds of innocent males. What good is it to nullify her now? It is like closing the house door after the man has escaped." He was evidently thinking more like a griffin, now. That was a danger of prolonged transformation.

"Yes, we shall have to do something about the statues," Humfrey agreed. "But I have expended enough of my valuable magic. Too much, in fact. Crombie, point out where the solution to this problem lies."

The griffin whirled and pointed. Down.

"Hm. Now point out the source of magic, again."

Crombie did. The result was the same. "So I supposed," Humfrey said. "Our quest has more than informational significance."

Another factor fell into place for Bink. This whole escapade with the tangle tree and the devastating sisters had seemed like a diversion from the quest and a serious threat to Bink's welfare, yet his talent had permitted it. Now he saw that his experience related to the quest. Still, it should not have been necessary to expose himself to these dangers in order to reach the source of magic. Something other than his talent must be operating.

He remembered the mound of earth, last night. Did that relate? He really could not fathom how, yet he distrusted coincidental occurrences unless they derived from his talent. If an enemy were—

The Good Magician brought out his mirror again. "Get me the Queen," he said into it.

"The Queen?" Bink asked, surprised.

The mirror fogged, then showed the face of Queen Iris. "About time you called in, Humfrey," she said. "How come you're dawdling there on the gorgon's isle, instead of pursuing your fool quest?"

Crombie squawked angrily. "Don't translate that!" Humfrey snapped at the golem. Then, to the Sorceress: "It is Bink's quest, not mine. We have nullified siren and gorgon, and are proceeding toward the source of magic. Notify the King."

Iris made a minor gesture of unconcern. "When I get around to it, midget," she said.

The visage of King Trent appeared in the mirror behind her. Abruptly she assumed the aspect of a Sweet Young Thing, complete with long braids. "Which will be very soon, Good Magician," she amended hastily. Trent waved jovially and tugged on a braid as the mirror went blank.

"How can she talk on the mirror?" Bink inquired. "It shows silent pictures for everyone else."

"She is mistress of illusion," Humfrey explained.

"Mistress of the King, you mean," Crombie squawked.

"We only think we're hearing her," Humfrey continued. He put away the mirror. "And the King only thinks he can yank at an illusory braid. But illusion has its uses, in whatever capacity."

"I'd like the illusion of reality," the golem said wistfully.

Humfrey returned his attention to the gorgon. "We shall return in due course. I suggest you go comfort your sister, meanwhile. She has lost her dulcimer."

"I will, I will!" the gorgon cried. "Farewell, handsome Sorcerer!" She flung her arms around Humfrey and planted an invisible kiss on his mouth while the snakes snapped at his ears and hissed up a storm. "Hurry back! I have so much love stored up—"

"Hm. Just so," the Magician agreed, embarrassed. He brought up a finger to snap away one serpent-hair that was gnawing too vigorously on his earlobe.

The magic path ended at the gorgon's isle, so it was necessary to swim back. They used Crombie's talent to locate a safe route across, avoiding lake monsters; then Bink mounted Chester and Humfrey rode the griffin. It was now midmorning, and the return to the magic-dust village was easy and swift. Hostile magic had not yet had time to move in to replace the prior charm of the path.

The tangle tree was a charred stump. The villagers had really done the job, destroying a long-term enemy. But the village itself was now quiet, with black drapes in the windows; it was in mourning for the last party of males to be lost to the siren.

How suddenly that changed, as those males marched in! "You survived!" Trolla cried, tears of untrollish joy streaming down her horrible face. "We tried to follow you, but could not hear the siren and could not trace the path in the dark. In the morning we knew it was too late, and we had wounded to attend to—"

"We have nullified the siren—and her sister, the gorgon," Bink said. "No more men will go that way. But the men who went before—"

"They are all dead; we know."

"No. They are stone. There may be a way to reverse the spell and restore them. If we are successful in our quest—"

"Come, we must celebrate!" Trolla cried. "We shall give you such a party—"

Bink knew the answer to that. "Uh, no thanks. You are very kind, but all we want to do now is get on with our quest. We seek the ultimate source of magic—the source of your magic dust, underground."

"There is no way down there," Trolla said. "It wells up in a solid shaft—"

"Yes. So we will seek elsewhere. If any avenue of access exists, from another direction—"

Disappointed, Trolla accepted the situation with grace. "Which way do you go?"

"That way," Bink said, indicating the direction Crombie had pointed for the resumption of their quest.

"But that's into the heart of the Region of Madness!"

Bink smiled. "Perhaps our access is through madness, then."

"The route past the tangle tree is open now. You could go out that way, and loop about to avoid the madness—"

Bink shook his head in negation, knowing that had that been the best way, Crombie would have indicated it.

"You males are so unreasonable! At least wait a few days. We will stop lofting the magic dust into the air, and the effect will diminish. Then you may traverse the region less hazardously."

"No. We have decided to push on." Bink feared that a few days' relaxation in this village of eager females would be as ruinous as continued dalliance with the siren and gorgon. They had to move on.

"Then we shall provide a guide. She can warn you of the immediate traps, and it is barely possible you will survive until clear of the worst of it. You are already half mad, after all."

"Yes," Bink agreed with a wry smile. "We are males." Neither sex understood the other; that was yet another aspect of the magic of Xanth. He rather liked this tame female troll; apparently almost any monster could be worthwhile once it was possible to know it personally.

The guide turned out to be a very pretty female griffin. "Squawk!" Crombie protested. "Awk! Awk!" she replied archly. "Don't saddle us with a chick like that!" Grundy translated happily. "Who are you calling a chick? I'm a lioness!" "You're a nuisance!" "And you're a bore!" "Female!" "Male!"

"Uh, that's enough translation, Grundy," Bink said. "They're down to the ultimate insults." He turned to Trolla. "Thank you for the guide. We'll be on our way now."

All the females of the village lined up to wave good-bye. It was a sad but necessary parting.

The wilderness of Xanth soon abolished sentimentality. The trees were extremely large here, closing in to form a dense jungle. This was the downwind region of the magic dust, as Trolla had warned; magic flourished here. Monstrous pincushions grew at the lowest level, stabbing anyone who passed too near; living stalagmites projected between the cushions, their stony points glistening with moisture that fell on them from above. Oil slicks twined wherever suitable depressions were available. The oil was more slippery than anything else, and at the same time more tenacious. "Those tanker trees shouldn't flush their wastes on the surface," Chester muttered. "They should bury it, the way civilized creatures do."

Yet the higher growths were no more promising; the huge metal trunks of ironwood trees crowded against the burned-out boles of ash. Rust and ashes coated the ground around them. Here and there bull spruces snorted and flexed their branch-horns menacingly. Above, it was worse yet; caterpillar nettles crawled along, peering down with prickly anticipation, and vomit-fungus dangled in greasy festoons. Where was there safe passage?

"Awk!" the guide said, showing the way. She glided past an outcropping of hissing serpentine, between two sharp blades of slash pine, and on over the rungs of a fallen ladder-bush. The others followed, wary but swift.

It was gloomy here, almost dark, though the day was rising onto noon. The canopy overhead, not satisfied with shutting out the sun, now constricted like an elastic band until it seemed to enclose them in one tight bubble. Like elastic? Now Bink saw it *was* elastic, from a huge elastic vine that stretched between and around the other foliage. Elastic was not a serious threat to people carrying swords or knives, but it could be a considerable inconvenience.

There seemed to be few large creatures here; but many small ones. Bugs were all over. Some Bink recognized: lightning bugs zapping their charges (this must have been where the demonstration bug had come from, the one that had burned up in the village), soldier beetles marching in precise formations to their bivouac, ladybugs and damselflies hovering near in the immemorial fashion of easy-virtue females near armies. Almost under Chester's hooves a tiger beetle pounced on a stag beetle, making its kill with merciless efficiency. Bink averted his gaze, knowing that such activity was natural, but still not liking it.

Then he noticed Humfrey. The man was staring as if enchanted: a worrisome sign, here. "Are you all right, Magician?" Bink asked.

"Marvelous!" the man murmured raptly. "A treasure trove of nature!"

"You mean the bugs?"

"There's a feather-winged beetle," Humfrey said. Sure enough, a bug with two bright feathers for wings flew by. "And an owl-fly. And two net-wings!" Bink saw the large-eyed, tufted bug sitting on a branch, watching the two nets hover. How a net-wing flew was unclear, as the nets obviously could not hold air. But with magic, what did it matter? "And a picture-winged fly!" the Magician exclaimed, really excited. "That's a new species, I believe; it must have mutated. Let me get my text." He eagerly fumbled open a vial. The vapor came forth and formed a huge tome that the Magician balanced precariously on the back of the griffin, between the folded wings, as he turned over the pages. "PICTURE-WING," he read. "Pastoral, Still-Life, Naturalistic, Surrealistic, Cubist, Watercolor, Oil, Pastel Chalk, Pen-and-Ink, Charcoal—I was right! This is a Crayon-Drawing species, unlisted! Bink, verify this for the record!"

Bink leaned over to look. The bug was sitting on the griffin's right ear, its wings outspread, covered by waxy illustrations. "Looks like crayon to me," he agreed.

"Yes!" Humfrey cried. "I must record it! What a fantastic discovery!" Bink had never seen the man so excited. Suddenly he realized something important:

this was what the Good Magician lived for. Humfrey's talent was information, and the discovery and classification of living things was right in line with this. To him there was nothing more important than the acquisition of facts, and he had naturally been resentful about being distracted from this. Now chance had returned him to his type of discovery. For the first time, Bink was seeing the Magician in his animation. Humfrey was not a cold or grasping individual; he was as dynamic and feeling as anyone—when it showed.

Bink felt a tug at his sword. He clapped his hand to the hilt—and two robber flies buzzed up. They had been trying to steal his sword! Then Chester jumped, almost dislodging him. "Almost stepped on a blister beetle," the centaur explained. "I wouldn't want to pull up with a blistered hoof at this stage!"

The lady griffin glanced back, rotating her head without turning her body, in the way griffins had. "Awk!" she exclaimed impatiently. "Hurry up, shrimp," the golem translated. "We're getting near the madness zone."

"Squawk!" Crombie replied irritably. "We're doing the best we can. Why don't you show us a better path, birdbrain?"

"Listen, cattail!" she awked back. "I'm only doing this as a favor to you! If you numbskulls had stayed at the village where you belonged—"

"Stay in a village of females? You're mad already!"

Then they had to stop squawking and awking to dodge a snake-fly that wriggled through, fangs gaping. This time Chester did step on a bug—a stink bug. A horrible odor wafted up, sending them all leaping forward to escape it. The lady griffin's passage stirred up a motley swarm of deerflies, tree hoppers, tiger moths, and a fat butterfly that splattered the Magician with butter.

One lovely gold bug fluttered up under Bink's nose. "Maybe this is another new one!" he cried, getting caught up in the Magician's enthusiasm. He grabbed for it, but Chester stumbled just then so that Bink missed it. "It's headed toward you, Magician!" he cried. "Catch it!"

But Humfrey shied away. "That's a midas fly!" he exclaimed in horror. "Don't touch it!"

"A midas fly?"

"Everything it touches turns to gold." The fly was now circling the Magician, looking for a place to land.

"But that's wonderful!" Bink said. "We must capture it. We can use gold!"

"Not if we become gold ourselves!" Humfrey snapped. He ducked so low that he fell off the griffin. The midas fly settled down to land in his place.

"Crombie!" Bink screamed. "Watch out!"

Then the lady griffin crashed into Crombie, knocking him out of the way with her leonine shoulder. He escaped—but the midas fly landed instead on her.

Just like that, she was a gold statue. The fly buzzed up and away, no longer a threat—but its damage had been done.

"They're extremely rare, and they don't land often," Humfrey said from the bush he had landed in. "I'm amazed we encountered one. Perhaps it was maddened by the dust." He picked himself up.

"It may have been sent," Bink said. "It appeared near me first."

Crombie rolled to his feet with the litheness of his kind. "Squawk!" "She did it for me—to save my life," Grundy translated. "Why?"

"It must indeed be madness," Chester said dryly.

Bink contemplated the statue. "Like the handiwork of the gorgon," he murmured. "Gold instead of stone. Is it possible she can be restored?"

Crombie whirled and pointed. "Squawk!" "The answer lies in the same direction as the quest," Grundy said. "Now birdbeak has personal reason to complete it."

"First, we must pass through the madness—without a guide," Chester pointed out.

Bink looked ahead, dismayed. Things had abruptly taken a more serious turn —and they had not been unserious before. "How can we find our way safely through this jungle, even without madness?"

"Crombie will have to point out our best route—one step at a time," Humfrey said. "Look—there is a walking stick." He indicated the stick, ambling along on two tiny feet at the base, its hooked top wobbling erratically. The huge text was gone; he must have conjured it back into its bottle while Bink had been distracted. He hardly needed it. "Mahogany-handled—a very fine specimen."

Crombie pointed the way, and they went slowly on, leaving the gold lady griffin where she stood. There was nothing they could do for her—except complete their quest, hoping to find the magic that would restore her.

Crombie looked back twice, not squawking; he seemed to be having serious private thoughts. For him, the woman-hater, the female's sacrifice had to be an awful enigma, of more significance than his own near-miss with the golden doom. As a soldier he was used to danger, but not to self-sacrifice.

All too soon, dusk loomed. Glowworms appeared from their tunnels in the ground, and bedbugs were already snoring in their bunks. A confused cockroach crowed, mistaking dusk for dawn. Swallowtails consumed their hind parts and disappeared for the night. A group of sawflies sawed boards for their own nocturnal roosts.

Bink looked about. "Right now, I wouldn't mind being a bug," he said. "They're at home here."

Chester agreed soberly. "I have spent the evening in the open before, but never in the deep wilderness. We will not enjoy this night."

Bink looked at Humfrey. The Magician was still absorbed in his taxonomy. "There's a rhinoceros beetle, trying to bull-doze down houses," Humfrey said. "Those houseflies aren't going to like that!"

"Sir, it will be dangerous to sleep out here. If your magic can help us pick the best spot—"

"Now they're bringing in carpenter ants to shore up the timbers!"

"Maybe something from one of your bottles, some temporary shelter for the night—" Bink continued.

"But that rhino is too stupid to quit! He—"

"Magician!" Bink snapped, losing his patience.

Humfrey glanced up. "Oh, hello, Bink. Haven't you set up for the night yet?" He glanced down again. "Look! They've hired an assassin bug! They're going to get rid of that—"

It was useless. The Magician cared more for information than for safety. Humfrey was no leader, which explained why he had been so ready to leave that chore to Bink. So it was up to Bink, again.

"We'll have to make some sort of shelter," he decided. "And keep watch in turns." He paused, considering the problems. How could they make shelter, when every piece of wood, stone, or foliage would be fiercely protective of its rights? This was the untamed wilderness!

Then his roving gaze spied a prospect: the great curving bones of a defunct monster. He couldn't tell what kind of animal it had been in life, but it must have been larger than a dragon. The bones seemed too solid for a roc, and there was no sign of wings, so probably it had been a grown groundborne sphinx. Ten times the height of a man. The only reason sphinxes did not rule the jungle was their rarity, and disinterest in ordinary matters. Dragons were common, while sphinxes were hardly ever encountered. Bink wondered why that was so, and what could kill a sphinx in its prime. Boredom, perhaps. "Crombie, point out the direction of the closest suitable or adaptable site for our overnight camp," he said, wishing to verify his notion.

Crombie obliged. He pointed toward the bones. Bink's hunch had been right! He was gratified. "We'll gather some blanket leaves and spread them over those bones," he said. "That will make us a decent shelter, and it can serve as a fort in case of attack. Crombie, point us out the nearest blankets."

The griffin pointed—right into the quivering ropes of a predator tree. It was not a tangler, but seemed related; it would hardly be safe to go there! "Well, maybe we can stay on guard better if we can see out," Bink decided. "Chester, why don't you stand the first watch. Wake me up the moment you find yourself getting sleepy, then wake Crombie."

The centaur nodded agreement. He did not inquire about Humfrey's share of the work; obviously the Magician would not be reliable for this.

Chapter 8

Mad Constellations

ink paused for a call of nature, not of magic—and spied a chunk of wood, so dark and moss-grown that it resembled a rock. Something like that could be useful, in case a monster attacked in the night. The wood seemed to have a nice heft, good for throwing. He squatted to pick it up—and paused, in case it should be enchanted. But his talent would protect him; if the piece were dangerous, he would be unable to touch it.

He picked it up, observing the etched grain of it, brown and green and white and altogether intriguing. It was surprisingly hard and heavy, for wood; he wondered whether it would float or sink in water. He felt a tingle in his hand as he held the chunk. There was some quality about it, something magic, strange and potent. He felt his talent responding, taking nebulous hold, sizing up this thing, as it had once before when he drank from the spring of life. As before, his magic encompassed that of the other thing, and accepted it without penalty. Bink's talent was of Magician stature; he seldom felt its action directly except when it encountered strong or complex opposing magic. Yet—a chunk of wood?

He carried the chunk back to their temporary camp. "I don't know what this is, but it seems to be strongly magical. It may be useful."

Chester took it. "Wood, unusual, durable. This might have come from a very large, old tree. I don't recognize the species, which makes it remarkable. Maybe you could find some of the bark—"

Crombie squawked. "Give it here, horseface. I've seen a lot of wood in my day."

Chester stiffened only slightly. "By all means, bird-beak."

Crombie held the chunk in one foreclaw and inspected it closely. "Squawk." "Something odd about this."

"Yes," Bink agreed. "Before you get too involved, will you point out the nearest food for us? We can eat while considering."

Crombie obligingly whirled and pointed. Bink looked, and saw a large glowing fungus. "That must be it. I never ate glow before, but your talent's never wrong." He walked over and reached down to break off a section. The fungus was firm and dry, pale inside, and emitted a pleasant odor.

"Squawk!" Crombie protested to the centaur. "I'm not through with it."

"You've had it long enough, buzzard-brain," Chester said. "My turn now."

Bink had to run to break up yet another quarrel. The trouble with fighting creatures was that they tended to fight! He couldn't turn his back on them even to fetch food. "It's the Magician's turn!" he cried. "Maybe he can identify it." He took back the wood and carried it to Humfrey. "Sir, if you care to classify this rare specimen—"

He had said the magic words. The Magician's attention was attracted. He looked. He blinked. "That's Blue Agony fungus! Get rid of it!"

Oops! Bink had put the wrong hand down, and shoved the fungus under Humfrey's nose. "Sorry. I meant to show you this wood, not the—" He paused. "The fungus is poisonous?"

"Its magic will turn your whole body blue, just before you melt into a blue puddle that kills all the vegetation in the ground where it soaks in," Humfrey assured him.

"But Crombie pointed it out as safe to eat!"

"Ridiculous! It's safe to touch, but the unsafest thing anyone could eat. They used to use it for executions, back in the bad old early Waves."

Bink dropped the fungus. "Crombie, didn't you—" He broke off, reconsidering. "Crombie, would you point out the worst thing we could eat?"

The griffin shrugged and pointed. Right toward the fungus.

"You absolute idiot!" Chester exclaimed to the griffin. "Have the feathers in your brains rotted? You just a moment ago pointed it out as safe!"

Crombie squawked angrily. "Bink must have picked up the wrong item. My talent is never wrong."

Humfrey was now examining the piece of wood. "Crombie's talent is always wrong," he remarked absently. "That's why I never rely on it."

Even Chester was surprised at this. "Magician, the soldier is no prize—even I am willing to concede that—but usually his talent is sound."

Crombie squawked, outraged at this qualified endorsement.

"Maybe so. I wouldn't know." The Magician squinted at a passing sweat gnat. "What is that creature?"

"You don't recognize a common sweat gnat?" Bink asked, amazed. "A moment ago you were classifying the most obscure bugs, discovering new species!"

Humfrey's brow furrowed. "Why should I do that? I know nothing about bugs."

Man, griffin, and centaur exchanged glances. "First Crombie, then the Magician," Chester murmured. "It must be the madness."

"But wouldn't that affect all of us?" Bink asked, worried. "This is more like a misfire of talents. Crombie pointed out the worst food instead of the best, and Humfrey switched from knowledge to ignorance—"

"Right when the chunk of wood switched hands!" Chester finished. "We'd better get him away from that wood."

"Yes," Chester agreed, and stepped toward Humfrey.

"No, please—let me do it," Bink said quickly, confident that his talent could handle the situation best. He approached Humfrey. "Excuse me, sir." He lifted the chunk gently from the Magician's grasp.

"Why doesn't it affect you?" Chester asked. "Or me?"

"It affects you, centaur," Humfrey said. "But since you don't know your talent, you don't see how it is reversed. As for Bink—he is a special case."

So the Good Magician was back in form. "Then this wood . . . reverses spells?" Bink asked.

"More or less. At least it changes the thrust of active magic. I doubt it would restore the griffin cow or the stone men, if that's what you're contemplating. Those spells are now passive. Only a complete interruption of magic itself would nullify them."

"Uh, yes," Bink said uncertainly.

"What kind of special case are you?" Chester demanded of Bink. "You don't do any magic."

"You might say I'm immune," Bink said cautiously, wondering why his talent was no longer protecting itself from discovery. Then he looked down at the wood in his hand. *Was* he immune?

He dropped the wood. "Squawk!" Crombie said. "So that's why my talent missed! That wood made me . . . *pumf squawk screech—*"

The golem had wandered near the wood, and his translation had disintegrated. Bink gently lifted Grundy away from it.

". . . of what I meant to," the golem continued, blithely unaware of the change. "It's dangerous!"

"It certainly is," Bink agreed. He kicked the wood away.

Chester was not reassured. "That means this was an incidental foul-up. We have yet to face the madness."

Crombie located the nearest safe food, successfully this time. It was a lovely cookie bush growing from the rich soil beside the bones. They feasted on chocolate-chip cookies. A handy water-chestnut tree provided ample drink: all they had to do was pluck the fresh chestnuts and puncture them to extract the water.

As Bink chewed and drank, his eye fell on another earth mound. This time he scraped it away carefully with a stick, but could find nothing except loose earth. "I think these things are following me," he said. "But what is the point? They don't do anything, they just sit there."

"I'll take a look at one in the morning," the Magician said, his curiosity moderately aroused.

They set up house within the gaunt cage of bones as darkness closed in. Bink lay back on the cushion of sponge moss beneath the skeleton—he had checked this out carefully to make sure it was harmless—and watched the stars emerge. Camping out was not so terrible!

At first the stars were mere points of light peeking between the bars of the bone-enclosure. But soon Bink perceived patterns in them: the constellations. He was not conversant with the stars, because Xanth was not safe at night; he had stayed inside, and when caught outside had hurried to shelter. Thus he found the landscape of the night sky intriguing. He had somehow thought, for no good reason, that the stars were of equivalent brightness, evenly dispersed. Instead, they were highly varied in both respects, ranging from piercing-bright to look-again dim, and from solitary splendor to clustered confusion. In fact they seemed to form patterns. In his mind he could draw lines between them, fashioning pictures. There was the head of a man, and a curving line like a snake, and a blob with tentacles like a tangle tree. As he concentrated, these things became more definite. The figures assumed greater definition and conviction, seeming almost real.

"Say, there's a centaur!" Bink exclaimed.

"Naturally," Chester said. "That's one of the established constellations. Been there for centuries."

"But it looks alive! I thought I saw it move."

"No, the constellations don't move. Not that way. They—" Chester broke off.

"He *did* move!" Bink cried. "His arm, fetching an arrow from his bag—"

"His quiver," Chester corrected him. "Something strange here. Must be atmospherics."

"Or maybe the air moving," Bink said.

Chester snorted. They watched the centaur in the sky take out his arrow, fit it to his bow, and cast about for some target. There was a swan in view, but it was a very large, tame bird, not suitable for hunting. There was a fox, but it slid out of sight behind some herdsmen before the centaur could take proper aim. Then a great bear showed up. It was trying to catch a lion cub, but the adult lion was nearby, almost as large as the bear and in an ornery mood. The two big predators circled each other, while the pointing arrowhead of the centaur traced their movements; which one should be taken first?

"Take the lion, stupid," Chester muttered. "Then the bear will take the cub, and leave you alone."

Bink was fascinated, both by this animation of the constellations, and by the strength and grace of the weird beasts. The centaur was a regular creature, of course—but only in mythology relating to Mundania did animals like bears and lions and swans exist. Parts of them showed up in the form of sphinxes, chimerae, griffins, and such, but that didn't really count. A mundane lion could also be reckoned as the body of a griffin with the head of an ant lion, a composite deriving from the Xanth originals. Now with the shield down, animals could cross the boundary freely, and probably at the fringe all types mixed. Bink regretted, in retrospect, that he had not had the chance to see such creatures as bears in the flesh, when he had visited Mundania. But he had been glad enough to return to Xanth, then!

Almost under the centaur's tail, another strange Mundane creature appeared: a wolf. It resembled a one-headed dog. Bink had seen werewolves in the flesh, but that might not count. What a horror it must be in Mundania, where wolves were locked permanently in their animal form, unable to revert to men!

The sky-centaur whirled on the wolf, aiming his bow. But the wolf was already moving on, because a huge scorpion was following him. The scorpion was being chased by a man—no, it only thought the man was after it. The man, a hugely muscled brute, was actually pursuing a serpent, trying to smash in its head with a club. Yet a dragon was hot after the man, and a really strange long-necked animal followed the dragon. In fact the whole sky was alive with oddities, making it seem like a much more interesting place than the Land of Xanth.

"What is that thing with the neck?" Bink asked.

"Mythological zoology is not my specialty," Chester said. "But I believe it is a Mundane monster called a gaffe." He paused. "No, that's not quite it. A grraff.

No. A—a giraffe! That's it. The long neck is to keep it clear of hostile ground magic, or something. It's strangest feature, as I understand it, is that despite that long neck it has no voice."

"Strange magic indeed!" Bink agreed.

"Strange *unmagic*, technically. The Land of Mundania could use a good, sensible shot of magic."

The sky was now densely crowded with animals, as the remaining stars emerged. Farther along was a crab, and a wingless bull, and a genuine single-headed dog. Birds abounded—half-familiar ones like the phoenix and bird of paradise, and a host of strange ones, like the crane, toucan, eagle, peacock, dove, and crow. There were people too—men, children, and several fetching young women.

That reminded Bink again of Chameleon. The longer he was away from her, the more he missed her. So what if she had her ugly phase? She also had her lovely phase—

"Look—there is the River Eridanus," Chester cried.

Bink found it. The river flowed half across the sky, meandering from the feet of a giant all the way to—Bink couldn't see where it finished. Where could a river in the sky go? All manner of fish were associated with it, and one—"What is that?" Bink cried.

"The fabulous Mundane whale," Chester said. "I'm glad no such monster as that exists in our land!"

Bink agreed emphatically. He traced the river again, seeking its termination. It spread and thinned, becoming vague, eluding him. Then he spied a small lizard. "A chameleon!" he exclaimed.

As he spoke its name, the lizard changed, becoming the human Chameleon he knew and loved: his wife. She looked out at him from the deepest depths of the sky, and her mouth opened. *Bink, Bink,* she seemed to say. *Come to me* . . .

Bink was on his feet, nearly banging his head against a bone. "I'm coming!" he cried joyfully. Why had he ever left her?

But there was no way to reach her. He could not climb the air, or fly up there, and in any event he knew she was just a picture, not real. Just a transformed lizard, itself imaginary. Still, he wished—"

Now the constellation centaur shot his arrow. The missile blazed as it flew, forming a brilliant streak across the sky, growing brighter and yet brighter as it drew near. Suddenly it loomed frighteningly large and close, as if flying right out of the sky—and cracked into a nearby tree. It was a dogwood; it yelped with pain, then growled and bared its teethlike inner branches in canine fury, seeking its enemy. In a moment it had torn the arrow to shreds.

Bink looked across at Chester, but could not make out the centaur's expression in the dark. That constellation arrow, no more than a shooting star, had struck a real tree close by! "Was that centaur shooting at *us?*"

"If he wasn't, he was criminally careless," Chester replied grimly. "If he was, he made a damn poor shot. That's a bad example that reflects on the merits of all centaurs. I will forward him a reminder." Now visible against the sparkling night sky in silhouette, Chester stood tall and magnificent, a fine stallion of a man, and nocked one of his own arrows. He drew on the bow with all his formidable power and loosed the shaft upward.

Up, up it flew, somehow visible despite the night. Up, impossibly high, right to the verge of the nocturnal dome, right toward the centaur constellation.

Bink knew no physical arrow could strike a star or pattern of stars. After all, the constellations were merely imaginary lines drawn between those stars. Yet—

Chester's arrow plunked into the flank of the constellation centaur. The creature leaped with pain. From his mouth issued two comets and a shooting star: a powerful exclamation!

"Yeah? Same to you, vacuumhead!" Chester retorted.

The constellation reached back and yanked at Chester's arrow. A nova exploded from his mouth as he contemplated the damage. Several dim stars pulsed there, suggestive of the wound. He grabbed a handful of soft down feathers from the swan and rubbed them against the injury. Now it was the defeathered swan who cussed a bright streak of shooting stars, but the bird did not dare attack the centaur.

The sky-centaur snatched the extensible tube called the telescope and put it to his eye. The magic of this tube enabled him to see much farther than otherwise. "****!!" he exclaimed with really foul invective, looking for the originator of the objectionable arrow.

"Right here, hoofhead!" Chester bawled, and lofted another arrow into the sky. "Come down and fight like a centaur!"

"Uh, I wouldn't—" Bink cautioned.

The constellation seemed to hear the challenge. He swung his telescope around and oriented on the bone-camp. A vile ringed planet shot from his mouth.

"That's right, dope!" Chester cried. "Come prove you're worthy of the name!"

Worthy of the name "dope"? Bink didn't like this at all, but was unable to stop it.

The constellation nocked another arrow. So did Chester, For a time the two faced each other, bows drawn, as it were, daring each other to shoot first. Then, almost together, their arrows leaped forth.

Both shots were uncomfortably accurate. Bink saw the two arrows cross midway in the heavens and home in on their targets as if magically guided. Neither centaur moved: this was evidently a point of honor in such duels. The one who jumped clear would show weakness of nerve, and few centaurs were weak in that department.

Both arrows missed—but not by much. Chester's shot almost grazed the constellation's forehead while the sky-centaur's arrow thunked into the ground beside Chester's left forehoof, which happened to be quite close to the Good Magician's head.

Humfrey woke with a start. "You equine menace!" he cried grumpily. "Watch what you're doing!"

"I am watching," Chester said. "That's not my arrow. See, it has stardust on it."

Humfrey drew the arrow from the dirt. "Why, so it does." He squinted into the sky. "But stardust is not supposed to be down here. What's going on?"

Now Crombie stirred. "Squawk!" "You're the Magician," the golem said. "You're supposed to know about things."

"About stellar constellations coming to life? It's been a long time since I reviewed that particular magic." Humfrey stared up into the sky. "However, it would be a worthwhile study. Crombie, where's the most convenient access to that realm?"

Crombie pointed. Now Bink saw a pattern of stars resembling steps coming down to the horizon. They looked increasingly solid, and they seemed closer as he looked, descending almost to the rim of bones. Maybe it was possible after all to ascend!

He looked up into the stars again. They were even more brilliant than before, and the lines between them were stronger. The stick figures had assumed shadings that made them quite realistic. He saw Chameleon again, beckoning him. "I'm going up!"

"Squawk!" Crombie agreed. "I'm always ready for a good fight, and that comet-mouthed centaur needs a lesson."

Chester was already on his way to the steps, but at this he paused.

"Don't be a fool," the Magician snapped, running after them. "Crombie refers to the centaur in the sky, not you. You are loudmouthed, not comet-mouthed."

"Um, of course," Chester agreed without complete enthusiasm. He made a visible effort to shake off the annoyance. "Charge!"

They charged for the steps.

"Are you fools crazy?" Grundy yelled. "There's nothing up there for you!"

Chester glanced at him; Bink saw the change in the shape of the centaur's head outlined against the massed constellations. "I didn't hear Crombie squawk."

"He didn't squawk!" the golem yelled. "I'm speaking for myself this time. Don't go into the sky! It's madness!"

"It's fascinating," Humfrey said. "Firsthand study of animated constellations! There may never be a better opportunity."

"I have to teach that centaur a lesson," Chester said.

Bink's eyes had returned to Chameleon. His need for her became as big as the sky. He continued forward.

"It's the madness," Grundy cried, yanking at the feathers of Crombie's neck. "It doesn't affect me. I see only the facts, because I'm not real. This is hostile magic. Don't go!"

"You're probably right, twerp," Humfrey agreed. "But this offering is too compelling to be denied."

"So was the siren! Don't do it!" Grundy repeated. "Where is your quest, if you let the madness take you now?"

"What do you care?" Chester demanded. "You have no feelings." He put his forehooves on the first step. It was firm, anchored at every corner by a pinpoint star. The lines were like threads, and the panels between them like glass. A translucent staircase, not quite invisible, going up into the sky.

Bink knew it was magic, and not to be trusted. But Chameleon was up there, waiting for him, and he had to go. His talent would not permit it if it were not safe, after all.

"Well, I'm not going!" Grundy screamed. He jumped from the griffin's back, fell into the foliage of a flower-bug bush, and scared up a swarm of flowerbugs. In a moment he was lost in the night.

"Good riddance," Chester muttered, mounting the steps. The surfaces bowed slightly under his weight, drawing the anchoring stars inward, but held. Crombie, impatient with this, spread his wings and flew around the centaur and came to rest higher on the stairway. Apparently the ascent was too step for comfortable flying by a creature of this size, so he preferred to mount by foot. The Good Magician was third, and Bink last.

In a line they ascended. The stairway spiraled, so that soon Crombie was climbing directly above Bink. It was an interesting effect, but Bink was more intrigued by the view below. As he climbed above the level of the trees, the nocturnal landscape of the Xanth wilderness opened out below, impressive because of its special nature. Bink had once been transformed into a bird, and once had ridden a magic carpet, and once had flown in human form; magic had given him quite a varied experience. But this slow ascent up through the levels of the forest, with firm footing beneath him—this was different from the various forms of flight, and in a certain respect unique. He was highly aware than he could fall; the steps had no railing to hold him in, no barrier at the fringes of the steps. This seemed to put him right into the situation in a way that flight did not. To be above the ground, yet tied to it . . .

The night forest was beautiful. A number of trees glowed. Some reached bone-white tentacles up; others were balls of pastel hues. Some had giant flowers that resembled eyes, and these eyes seemed to be focusing on Bink. Other treetops formed into mazes of interlocking branches. As he watched, the whole forest assumed the shape of a single human face. DON'T GO! it mouthed.

Bink paused, momentarily disgruntled. Was the wilderness really trying to speak to him? Whose interest did it represent? It could be jealous of his escape to the sky. Hungry for his body. Or just mischievous.

Crombie had balked at the tangle tree. Chester had been fortuitously deafened in time to save them from the siren's call. His talent had been operating then. Why was it quiescent now?

He looked upward. The enormous panorama of the sky awaited him—animals, monsters, and people. They were all frozen in place at the moment, awaiting the arrival of Bink's party. Up there lay adventure.

He resumed his climb. He had to hurry, because the others had continued moving, and were now several spirals ahead of him. He didn't want to be late for the action!

As he caught up to the Magician, who was lagging behind the stout four-legged entities, something buzzed in from the darkness to the side. It sounded like a very large insect, one of the exotic bugs. Not another gold bug, he hoped! He waved his arms, hoping to scare it off.

"Bink!" a small voice cried.

What now? He was getting winded from his rapid climb, and had to watch carefully to be sure he didn't make a misstep while absorbing the splendors of the immense canopy above and the broad disk below. He was in the very center of a phenomenal scene, and he wanted to experience every aspect of it with full intensity, and he didn't need any bugs distracting him. "Go away!"

The bug flew near. There was light associated with it. It was a flying fish, propelling itself by a jet of bubbles from its fuselage, so that its rigid wings could provide sufficient lift. The gills were air-intakes, and assorted little fins provided stability and spot maneuverability. Flying fish were swift, Bink knew; they had to be, or they dropped to the ground. This one carried a light on its back like a miniature lantern, and—

"Bink! It's Grundy!" And lo, it was indeed the golem, braced on the back of the fish, guiding it with little reins and a bit set in its mouth. Grundy's free hand held the lamp, which seemed to be a tiny star, captive in a little net. "I caught this fish by luring it with fish-talk; now it understands and is helping. I have the spell-reversal wood along." He tapped his saddle with his rein-hand. It was the gnarly fragment that Bink had discarded.

"But how can the fish fly?" Bink demanded. "How can you translate? The reversal—"

"It doesn't affect the fish because the fish has no talent; the fish *is* magical,"

Grundy explained with limited patience. "The wood only reverses exterior magic, not inherent magic."

"That doesn't make much sense to me," Bink said.

"The wood reversed birdbeak's talent, but did not change him back into a man," the golem continued. "It fouled up the gnome's information, but did not make him a regular man either. It didn't affect you, because—"

The golem was not aware of Bink's talent, but this remained a pertinent question: had Bink's talent conquered the wood—or been reversed by it? The answer could be a matter of life and death! "What about you?" Bink demanded. "You're still translating!"

"I'm not real," Grundy said shortly. "Take away my magic and I'm nothing but string and mud. The wood is just wood, to me."

"But the wood was affecting you before! You were speaking gibberish, until I got you away from it."

"Was I?" Grundy asked, startled. "I never realized. I guess translation *is* my talent, so . . ." He faded out, considering. "I know! I'm not translating now. I'm speaking for myself!"

And there was the answer. "Well, keep that wood away from me," Bink said. "I don't trust it."

"No. I have to bring it close to you. Put your hand on it, Bink."

"I will not!" Bink exclaimed.

Grundy jerked the reins to one side, kicked the flanks of the fish, and leaned forward. The fish swerved, reared, and accelerated right at Bink. "Hey!" he protested as it grazed his hand.

But at that moment his outlook changed. Abruptly the stars were mere stars, and the stairs—were the branches of a latticework tree. Above him the others were near its summit, about to step onto the thinning twigs that could not support their weight, Crombie was already supporting much of his mass by flapping his wings, and Chester—

Bink shook his head in amazement. A centaur climbing a tree!

Then the fish buzzed out of range, and the madness returned. Bink was on the translucent stairway again, climbing toward the glowing constellations. "It's crazy, I know!" he cried. "But I can't help myself. I have to go on up!"

The golem guided the fish in close again. "You can't throw it off even when you *know* it's doom?"

"It's mad!" Bink agreed, suffering a measure of sanity as the wood passed near again. "But true! But don't worry about me—I'll survive. Go get Chester off that branch before he kills himself!"

"Right!" Grundy agreed. He spurred his mount and buzzed upward. Bink resumed his climb, cursing himself for his foolishness.

The fish disappeared in the night. Only the caged star—that Bink now knew was nothing more than a glowberry—showed Grundy's location. That light moved up near the centaur.

"Good grief, golem!" Chester exclaimed. "What the horsefeathers am I doing in a tree?"

Bink could not hear Grundy's side of the conversation, but could guess its nature. After a moment Chester started backing down the stairway steps.

"Hey, oaf!" the Magician cried. "Get your ass's rear out of my face!"

"Go down," the centaur cried. "This is no stair, it's a tree. We're climbing to our doom."

"It's information. Let me by!"

"It's madness! Grundy, take your wood to him."

The light descended. "Great galloping gizzards!" Humfrey cried. "It *is* a tree! We've got to get down!"

But now the centaur was climbing again. "I haven't finished my business with that constellation centaur," he said.

"You equine fool!" Humfrey exclaimed. "Desist!"

The fish zoomed down toward Bink. "I can't handle them both," Grundy cried. "I've only got the single piece of wood, and there are four of you."

"The griffin can fly; he'll be all right for now," Bink said. "The stair—I mean the tree—is narrow. Give Chester the wood; no one can pass him. Then you search for more wood."

"I had already thought of that," the golem said. The fish zoomed off. In a moment Chester reversed his course again. The Good Magician cursed in most un-Magicianlike vernacular, but was forced to retreat in the face of the centaur's rear. Soon they were right above Bink—and he too cursed as his ascent was balked.

The constellations, seeing the retreat, exploded in rage. "***!!" the sky centaur cried silently. At his summons, the other monsters of the heavens gathered: the dragon, the hydra, the serpent, the winged horse, the giant, and in the river the whale.

The madness remained upon him, but Bink no longer wanted to climb the stairway. The monsters were converging, clustering about the top of the stair-spiral. The serpent was staring down, its sinuous body coiling along the spiral, while the winged ones flew down. Bink was not certain whether they were real or illusion or something in between—but remembering the arrow-strike at the dogwood tree, he was disinclined to gamble. "We've got to get under cover!" he cried.

But Crombie, highest on the stair and unaffected by the spell-wood, flew up to do battle with the winged horse. "Squawk!" he cried. "Neigh!" the horse replied.

Grundy buzzed by on his steed. "Oooh, what they said!"

Wings spread, griffin and horse faced off, claws swiping, hooves striking. Contact was made, but Bink couldn't tell from the whirling, flapping silhouettes which creature was prevailing.

Then the serpent arrived. Chester could not use his bow effectively, since no arrow would travel a spiral path, so waited with his sword. Bink wondered what the centaur saw, since he had the wood and so perceived reality—or something. Probably it was not a serpent, but an equivalent threat. Meanwhile Bink had to interpret it as he saw it.

As the huge snake-head came close, the centaur bellowed a warning and struck it across the nose. Blade met fang. The serpent's teeth were large, reflecting starlight, and they gleamed with what might be poison. There were two projecting ones, and they moved with the precision of a fencer. Chester was compelled to retreat, since he had only one sword.

Then Chester took a cue from the winged horse, and used his front hooves. He bashed the serpent on the nose, one-two, one-two, while dazzling it with the sword. His front feet did not have the power of his rear ones, but his hooves had sharp fighting edges and a cumulative impact that could splinter bark from a tree, or scales from a serpent.

What would happen, Bink wondered, if the wood were to touch the serpent? Would it give the serpent a different view of reality? Would the centaur then seem to be something else? How could anyone be sure what magic was real, and what false?

The serpent hissed and gaped its jaws so widely that its mouth became as tall as the centaur. Its sinuous tongue snaked out to wrap around Chester's sword arm, immobilizing it, but Chester shifted his weapon to his other hand, and efficiently lopped off the tongue. The serpent made a hissing howl of agony and snapped its mouth closed, the tusks clanging against each other. Chester took a moment to unwrap the segment of tongue from his arm, then resumed slashing at the nose. He was holding his own.

The dragon arrived. It zoomed in at the Good Magician. Humfrey might be captive to the madness, but he was not a fool. His hand dived into his jacket and came out with a vial. But so swift was the dragon's onslaught that there was no time to open the container. Instead, Humfrey flipped it into the opening mouth. The dragon snapped at it automatically. The vial crunched under its bite. Vapor exploded, expanding into a cloud that jetted out between the dragon's teeth and coalesced about its head. But it did not form into anything else—no demon, no smoke screen, not even a sandwich. It just clung there in hardening gobs.

"What is it?" Bink cried. "Did the vial misfire?"

"I had to grab randomly," Humfrey replied. "It's—I believe it is foaming insulation."

"Slavering what?"

"Foaming insulation. It foams up, then hardens in place to keep things warm —or cold."

Bink shook his head. The Magician was mad all right.

How could anything act to keep things hot *or* cold? It either had to be like fire, heating, or like ice, cooling. And why would anyone bother with such magic?

The dragon, however, was not taking it with equanimity. It flexed in midair, and shook its head violently from side to side, trying to rid itself of the clinging stuff. It chewed and gulped, seeking to eliminate the foam. "I wouldn't do that, if I were you," Humfrey told it.

The dragon ignored him. It roared. Then it huffed and puffed, working up a head of fire in its belly. It looped about, its flapping wings throwing off chunks of hardened foam. Then it oriented on the Magician and blasted out its terrible fire.

Only a thin jet of flame emerged. Then, surprisingly, the dragon's body began inflating. It swelled up like a balloon, until only the legs, tail, wing tips and snout projected from the ball."

"What—?" Bink asked, amazed.

"The insulation hardens in place immediately in the presence of heat," Humfrey explained. "Thus the dragon's own fire had solidified it. Unfortunately that particular type of insulation is also—"

The dragon exploded. Stars shot out in every direction, scorching the jungle foliage below, zooming by Bink to the side, and making a fine display above.

"—explosively flammable when ignited," Humfrey finished.

They watched the upward-flying stars rise to their heights, then explode in multicolored displays of sparks. The whole night sky became briefly brighter.

"I tried to warn that dragon," Humfrey said without sympathy. "One simply does not apply open flame to flammable insulation."

Bink, privately, hardly blamed the dragon for misunderstanding that caution. He would have made the same mistake as the dragon had. If his talent permitted it. But this did impress on him one thing: should he (perish the thought!) ever have a serious disagreement with the Good Magician, he would have to watch out for those magic bottles! There was no telling what might come out of them.

Now a monster found Bink. It was the hydra. It had no wings, and could not have used the stairs because they were blocked by the serpent. The hydra seemed to have descended by hanging from a thread—but no such thread was visible.

Bink swung at the monster with his sword. He was in excellent form; he caught the nearest of the seven heads cleanly, just behind the horns, and it flew off. Gore spouted out of the neck with such force that the jet separated into two channels. If this was all it took to beat this monster, Bink would have no trouble!

The two jets coagulated in midair, forming into twin lumps still attached to the neck. As more gore emerged, it splashed over these lumps, hardening, enlarging them. Excrescences developed, and the color darkened, until—

The lumps became two new heads! Each was smaller than the original, but just as vicious. Bink had only succeeded in doubling the menace he faced.

This was a problem. If each head he cut off converted into two, the longer and better he fought, the worse off he would be!! Yet if he did not fight well, he would soon be consumed in seven—no, eight chunks.

"Catch, Bink!" Chester called, throwing something. Bink didn't appreciate the interruption to his concentration, but grabbed for it anyway. In the dark his sweeping fingers merely batted it aside. In the moment it touched him, his sanity returned. He saw himself on a branch of the tree, pointing his sword at—

But then the reverse-spell wood bounced out of range, and the madness resumed its grip on him. He saw the chunk fly toward the hydra—and one of the heads reached out to gulp it down.

In that instant Bink suffered a rapid continuation of his prior line of thought. What would spell-reversal do *inside* an imaginary monster? If the hydra form were wholly a product of Bink's distorted perception—his madness, which he shared with his friends—it should be nullified—no, the wood had to be near him, to nullify the monsters he perceived. But since his friends saw the monsters too, and the wood could not be near them all at once—it had to be that the wood would *not* affect the monster, unless that monster had objective reality. Even then, the wood would not affect the form of the hydra, but only its talent —if the hydra had a talent. Most magical creatures did not have magic talents; their magic consisted of their very existence. So—nothing should happen.

The hydra screamed from all its eight mouths. Abruptly it dropped to the ground. It landed heavily and lay still, its stars fading out.

Bink watched it, openmouthed. The hydra had not changed form—it had suffered destruction. What had happened?

Then he worked it out. The hydra had a magic talent after all: that of hanging by an invisible thread. The spell-reversal wood had nullified that magic, causing the monster to plummet forcefully down to its death. Its invisible thread had not disappeared; it had acted to draw the creature *down* as powerfully as it had drawn it *up* before. Disaster!

But now the wood was gone. How were they to escape the madness?

Bink looked up. The Good Magician's foaming agent had destroyed the dragon, and Chester's hooves and sword had beaten back the serpent. Crombie's fighting spirit had proved to be too much for the winged horse. So the individual battles had been won. But the war remained unpromising.

A number of constellations had remained in the sky. The centaur, giant, and whale had not been able to descend, because they lacked wings or flying magic, and the stairway had been pre-empted by the serpent. Now, seeing the fate of their companions, these three bellowed their rage from the safety of the nocturnal welkin. Novas and ringed planets and miniature lightning bolts and curly-tailed comets radiated from their mouths in confusing profusion and wonderful foulness, with the whale spouting obscene curlicues.

"Oh, yeah?" Chester bawled. "We'll come up there and do the same to you! You're the cowards who started it all!" And Crombie and Humfrey and Bink closed in about him as well as they were able.

"No, stop!" Grundy screamed from his flying fish, zooming in a circular holding pattern. "You've all seen the nature of your madness. Don't yield to it again! Pass the wood around, restore your perspectives, get your feet on the ground again! Don't let the spooks lure you to destruction!"

"He's right, you know," Humfrey muttered.

"But I dropped the wood!" Bink cried. "I dropped our sanity!"

"Then go down and fetch it!" the golem cried. "And you, horserear—you threw it to him. You go down and help him."

"Squawk!" Crombie exclaimed. "And birdbeak says he's going up alone to grab all the glory for himself."

"Oh no he doesn't!" Chester roared.

"Right!" the golem agreed. "You have to go together, to be fair about it. You real creatures place great store by fairness, don't you? Or is honor a foreign concept to you, birdbeak? You don't want horserear's competition, because you know he'd show you up if you didn't have a head start?"

"Squawk! Squawk!" Bink almost thought he saw a comet spew from Crombie's mouth.

"Right! So you prove you can match him anywhere, anytime—by getting down there and finding that wood before he does. And take the gnome with you. Horse-rear can take the washout with him."

Washout? That was what the golem had decided to call Bink? Bink's blood pressure started building. Just because his talent wasn't visible—"

"All right, and may dung fall on you!" Chester said. "I'll fetch the stupid wood. Then on to glorious battle!"

Thus, ingloriously, they descended the glassy stair.

The monsters above exploded with derision. The sky lit up with their exclamations: exploding cherry bombs in many silent colors, glowing tornadoes, forest fires. The whale diverted the River Eridanus so that its water poured down in a scintillating cataract. The giant swung his huge club, bashing stars out of their sockets and sending them flying down. The centaur fired glowing arrows.

"Keep moving, slowpokes!" the golem yelled. "Keep walking away from their challenges. That makes them madder than anything else you can do!"

"Hey, yeah," Chester agreed. "You're pretty smart for a tangle of string and tar."

"I'm sane—because I have none of the foolish emotions of reality to interfere with my thought processes," Grundy said. "Sane—*because* I am string and tar."

"Therefore you are the only one qualified to lead us out of madness," the Magician said. "You are the only one who can perceive objective reality—because you have no subjective aspect."

"Yes, isn't it great?" But the golem hardly looked happy.

Bink understood, suddenly, that Grundy would gladly join them in madness, though he knew it led to disaster, if this could be the proof of his reality. Only the golem's unreality enabled him to hang on to what life he had. What a paradoxical fate!

An arrow struck a catnip bush right beside him. The plant yowled and spat, nipping at the shaft, then batting it back and forth with its paw-buds.

"Oh, I want to stick an arrow right up under his tail!" Chester muttered. "That centaur's a disgrace to the species."

"First find the wood," Grundy cried.

One of the giant's batted stars whizzed over Bink's head and ignited a rubber tree. The plant stretched enormously, trying to get away from its own burning substance. The smell was horrible.

"We can't find anything here in the smoke," Chester complained, coughing.

"Then follow me!" Grundy cried, showing the way on his fish.

Choking, they followed the golem. The constellations raged above them, firing volleys of missiles, but could not score directly. Madness had no power over sane leadership.

Yet the madness tried! The whale took hold of the river again and yanked it brutally from its new channel. The water spilled across the starry field in a thinning, milky wash, forming a flood. Then it found a new channel, coursed along it, ripped out several stars growing there, and poured down toward the ground.

"Look out!" Bink cried. "We're at the foot of that waterfall!"

Indeed they were. The mass of water was descending at them like a globulous avalanche. They scrambled desperately—but it caught them, drenching them instantly in its milky fluid, crashing about them with a sound like thunder and foaming waist high. Crombie hunched, bedraggled, his feathers losing their luster; Chester wrapped his arms about his human torso as if to fend the liquid off; and the Magician—

The Good Magician was wrapped in a big, bright, once-fluffy beach towel.

Soaked, it was worse than nothing. "Wrong vial," he explained sheepishly. "I wanted a raincoat."

They slogged out of the immediate waterfall and through the runoff. Bink found himself shivering; the water of the sky river was chill. The madness had been intriguing when the constellations first took on life, but now he wished he were home, warm and dry, with Chameleon.

Ah, Chameleon! He liked her especially in her "normal" stage, neither beautiful nor smart, but a pleasant middle range. It always seemed so fresh, that brief period when she was average, since she was always changing. But he loved her in any form and intellect —especially at times like now, when he was wet and cold and tired and afraid.

He swiped at a floating star, taking out some of his discomfort on it. The bright mote was probably as miserable as he, washed out of its place in the sky and become mere flotsam on earth.

The water here was too shallow for the whale, the only sky monster that might have been a real threat at this stage. The party wandered out of the slush. "In real life this must be a thunderstorm," Chester commented.

The walk became interminable. The golem kept urging them through the night. The wrath of the constellations pursued them some distance, then was lost as they plunged under the jungle canopy. The madness remained with them, however. The ground seemed to become a mass of peanut butter, roiling under their steps. The trees, dangerous in their own right, seemed to develop an alien menace: they turned purple, and hummed in chorus, and proffered sinister, oblong fruits.

Bink knew that the madness, whether it seemed benign or malign, would destroy them all in moments if they yielded to it. His sense of self-preservation encouraged him to resist it, and his resistance became stronger with practice— but still he could not penetrate all the way to reality. In a way this resembled the Queen's illusion—but this affected emotion as well as perception, so was more treacherous.

He heard the golem squawking at Crombie in griffin-talk, then saw Grundy rest his flying-fish steed on Crombie's head. Apparently the fish was tired, and had to be relieved. "It deserves a reward," Bink said. "For its timely service."

"It does? Why?" Grundy asked.

Bink started to answer, then realized the futility of it. The golem was not real; he did not *care*. Grundy did what he had to do, but human conscience and compassion were not part of his makeup. "Just take my word: the fish must be rewarded. What would it like?"

"This is a lot of trouble," Grundy muttered. But he swished and gurgled at the fish. "It wants a family."

"All he needs is a lady of his species," Bink pointed out. "Or a man, if he happens to be female. She. Whatever."

More fish-talk. "In the mad region he can't locate one," the golem explained.

"A little of that spell-reversal wood would solve that problem," Bink said. "In fact, we could all use some. We got mixed up by the madness and water and never thought of the obvious. Let's see if Crombie's talent can locate some more of that wood."

Crombie squawked with dismayed realization. He whirled and pointed—right at a quivering mound of jelly. "That's a bloodsucker tree," Grundy said. "We can't go there!"

"Why not?" Chester asked facetiously. "You don't have any blood."

"The wood must be beyond it," Bink said. "Crombie's talent is still working but we have to watch out for the incidental hazards along the way, now more than ever. In the night, and with the madness—only you can do it, Grundy."

"I've *been* doing it!" the golem said, aggrieved.

"We need light," Chester said. "Birdbe—uh, Crombie, where can we get safe light?"

The griffin pointed. There was a flock of long-legged, bubbly things with horrendously glowing eyes. Bink walked over cautiously, and discovered that these were plants, not animals; what had seemed like legs were actually stems. He picked one, and its eye emitted a beam that illuminated everything it touched. "What is it, really?" Bink asked.

"A torch-flower," Grundy said. "Watch you don't set fire to the forest."

The rain had stopped, but the foliage still dripped. "Not too much danger of that at the moment," Bink said.

Armed with their lights, they moved in the direction Crombie had pointed for the wood, meandering circuitously to avoid the hazards the golem perceived. It was obvious that they could not have survived the natural traps of the jungle without the guidance of the golem. It would have been bad enough in ordinary circumstances; the madness made it impossible.

Suddenly they arrived. A monstrous stump loomed out of the ground. It was as thick at the base as a man could span, but broke off at head-height in jagged ruin.

"What a tree that must have been!" Bink exclaimed. "I wonder how it died?"

They closed about the stump—and suddenly were sane. The glowing eyes they held were revealed as the torch-flowers the golem had said they were, and the deep jungle showed its true magic instead of its mad-magic. In fact, Bink felt clearer-headed than ever before in his life. "The madness spell—it has been reversed to make us absolutely sane!" he exclaimed. "Like the golem!"

"Look at the path we came by!" Chester said. "We skirted poison thorns, carnivorous grass, oil-barrel trees—our torches could have exploded this whole region!"

"Don't I know it," Grundy agreed. "Why do you think I kept yelling at you? If I had nerves, they'd be frayed to the bone. Every time you wandered from the course I set—"

More things were coming clear to Bink. "Grundy, why did you bother to help us, instead of riding away on your fish? You went to extraordinary trouble—"

"The fish!" Grundy exclaimed. "I have to pay him off!" He pried a sliver of wood from the massive stump and affixed it to the fish's dorsal fin with a bit of his own string. "There you go, bubble-eye," he said with something that sounded suspiciously like affection. "As long as you carry that, you'll see everything as it is, in the madness region. So you can spot your lady fish. Once you have succeeded, ditch the wood; I understand it is not good to see a female too realistically."

Crombie made an emphatic squawk of agreement that needed no translation.

The fish took off, zooming into the sky with a powerful thrust of bubbles, banking neatly around branches. Relieved of the golem's weight, and spurred by the hope of mad romance, it was a speedy creature.

"Why did you do that?" Bink asked the golem.

"You short of memory? You told me to, nitnoggin!"

"I mean, why did you do it with such grace? You showed genuine feeling for that fish."

"I couldn't have," Grundy snapped.

"And why did you guide us all around the hazards? If we had perished, your service to the good Magician would have been finished."

"What use would that have been to me?" Grundy demanded, kicking angrily at a tuft of grass with one motley foot.

"It would have freed you," Bink said. "Instead, you went to a great deal of trouble to herd us off that stair and to safety. You really didn't have to; your job is translation, not leadership."

"Listen, washout—I don't have to take this crap from you!"

"Think about it," Bink said evenly. "Why help a washout?"

Grundy thought about it. "I must have been mad after all," he admitted.

"How could you be mad—when you weren't affected by the madness?"

"What are you up to?" Chester demanded. "Why hassle the golem? He did good work."

"Because the golem is a hypocrite," Bink said. "There was only one reason he helped us."

"Because I *cared*, you nitwit!" Grundy yelled. "Why do I have to justify saving your life?"

Bink was silent. Crombie and Chester and the Good Magician turned mutely to face the golem.

"What did I say?" Grundy demanded angrily. "Why are you freeloaders staring at me?"

Crombie squawked. "Birdbeak says—" The golem paused. "He says—I can't make out what he says! What's the matter with me?"

"The wood of this tree reverses spells," Humfrey said. "It has canceled out your talent."

"I'm not touching that wood!"

"Neither are we," Bink said. "But we are all quite sane at the moment, because the ambience of the stump is stronger than that of a single chip. That is why we are now able to perceive you as you are. Do you realize what you said?"

"So the wood messes up my talent, same as it does yours. We knew that already!"

"Because it changes our magic without changing *us*," Bink continued. "Because what is *us* is real."

"But that would mean *I'm* halfway real!"

"And you halfway care," Chester said.

"That was just a figure of speech! I have no emotion!"

"Move away from the tree," Bink said. "Get out of the range of the stump. Tell us what you see out there."

Grundy paced away and looked about. "The jungle!" he cried. "It's changed! It's mad!"

"Care," Bink said. "The Good Magician's Answer. In your effort to save us, you brought yourself halfway to your own destination. You have begun to assume the liabilities of being real. You feel compassion, you feel anger, you suffer pleasure and frustration and uncertainty. You did what you did because conscience extends beyond logic. Is it worth it?"

Grundy looked at the distortions beyond the stump. "It's madness!" he exclaimed, and they all laughed.

Chapter 9

Vortex Fiends

At dawn they emerged from the madness region, each holding a piece of spell-reversal wood. They had traveled tediously, separating Crombie at intervals from his piece of wood, getting his indication of the best immediate route, then returning his chunk to him so that he could perceive threats accurately until the next orientation.

Once they were out, they located a reasonably secure roost in a stork-leg tree, setting their pieces of wood in a circle about its spindly trunks so that no hostile magic could approach them without getting reversed. That was not a perfect defense, but they were so tired they had to make do.

Several hours later Bink woke, stretched, and descended. The centaur remained lodged on a broad branch, his four hooves dangling down on either side; it seemed the tree experience during the madness had added a nonmagical talent to his repertoire. The Magician lay curled in a ball within a large nest he had conjured from one of his vials. Crombie, ever the good soldier, was already up, scouting the area, and the golem was with him.

"One thing I want to know . . ." Bink started, as he munched on slices of raisin bread from a loaf Crombie had plucked from a local breadfruit tree. It was a trifle overripe, but otherwise excellent.

Crombie squawked. ". . . is who destroyed that reverse-spell tree," Grundy finished.

"You're translating again!"

"I'm not touching any wood at the moment." The golem fidgeted. "But I don't think I'm as real as I was last night, during the madness.

"Still, there must be some feeling remaining," Bink said. "It can be like that, approaching a goal. Two steps forward, one back—but you must never give up."

Grundy showed more animation. "Say, that's a positive way of looking at it, mushmind!"

Bink was glad to have given encouragement, though the golem's unendearing little mannerisms remained evident. "How did you know what I was about to ask? About the destruction of—"

"You always come up with questions, Bink," the golem said. "So we pointed out the location of the subject of your next question, and it matched up with the tree stump. So we researched it. It was a challenge."

That was an intriguing ramification of Crombie's talent! Anticipating the answers to future questions! Magic kept coming up with surprises. "Only a real creature likes challenges," Bink said.

"I guess so. It's sort of fun, the challenge of becoming real. Now that I know that maybe it's possible. But I still have this ragtag body; no amount of caring can change that. It just means that now I fear the death that will surely come." He shrugged, dismissing it. "Anyway, the tree was blasted by a curse from that direction." He pointed.

Bink looked. "All I see is a lake." Then, startled: "Didn't the ogre say something about—?"

"Fiends of the lake, who hurled a curse that blasted the whole forest," Grundy said. "We checked: that is the lake."

Humfrey descended from the tree. "I'd better bottle some of this wood, if I can get my magic to work on it," he said. "Never can tell when it might be useful."

"Cast a spell hurling it away from your bottle," Chester suggested from the tree. He, too, dropped to the ground, after some awkward maneuvering that put his handsome posterior in jeopardy. Centaurs really did not belong in trees.

The Magician set up his vial and wood and uttered an incantation. There was a flash, a puff of smoke, and a gradual clearing of the air.

There sat the vial, corked. There sat the wood. The Good Magician was gone. "Where did he go?" Bink demanded.

Crombie whirled and pointed his wing. Directly toward the bottle.

"Oh, *no!*" Bink cried, horrified. "His spell reversed, all right! It banished *him* to the bottle!" He dashed over and picked it up, jerking out the cork. Vapor issued forth, expanding and swirling and coalescing and forming in due course into the Good Magician. There was a fried egg perched on his head. "I forgot I was keeping breakfast in that one," he said ruefully.

Grundy could hold back his newfound emotion no longer. He burst out laughing. He fell to the ground and rolled about, guffawing. "Oh, nobody gnomes the trouble he's seen!" the golem gasped, going into a further paroxysm.

"A sense of humor is part of being real," Chester said solemnly.

"Just so," Humfrey agreed somewhat shortly. "Good thing an enemy did not get hold of the bottle. The holder has power over the content."

The Magician tried again—and again. Eventually he found the proper aspect of reversal and managed to conjure the wood into the vial. Bink hoped the effort was worth it. At least he knew, now, how the Good Magician had assembled such an assortment of items. He simply bottled anything he thought he might need.

Then Bink encountered another pile of earth. "Hey, Magician!" he cried. "Time to investigate this thing. What is making these mounds? Are they all over Xanth, or just where we happen to be?"

Humfrey came over to contemplate the pile. "I suppose I'd better," he grumped. "There was one on the siren's isle, and another at our bone-camp." He brought out his magic mirror. "What thing is this?" he snapped at it.

The mirror clouded thoughtfully, then cleared. It produced the image of a wormlike creature.

"That's a wiggle!" Bink exclaimed, horrified. "Are the wiggles swarming again?"

"That's not a wiggle," Chester said. "Look at the scale. It's ten times too large." And in the mirror a measuring stick appeared beside the worm, showing it to be ten times the length of a wiggle. "Don't you know your taxonomy? That's a squiggle."

"A squiggle?" Bink asked blankly. He did not want to admit that he had never heard of that species. "It looks like an overgrown wiggle to me."

"They are cousins," Chester explained. "The squiggles are larger, slower, and do not swarm. They are solitary creatures, traveling under the ground. They are harmless."

"But the piles of dirt—"

"I had forgotten about that," Chester said. "I should have recognized the castings before. They eject the dirt from their tunnels behind them, and where they touch the surface it forms into a pile. As they tunnel on, the further castings plug up the hole, so there is nothing left except the pile."

"But what do they *do?*"

"They move about, make piles of earth. That's all."

"But why are they following me? I have nothing to do with squiggles."

"Could be coincidence," Humfrey said. He addressed the mirror. "Is it?"

The mirror's unhappy baby face showed.

"Someone or something is setting the squiggle to spy on us, then," Humfrey said, and the mirror smiled. "The question is, who?"

The mirror turned dark. "The same as the source of magic?" Humfrey demanded. The mirror denied it. "Bink's enemy, then?" And the smiling baby returned.

"Not the same as the fiends of the lake?" Bink asked.

The baby smiled.

"You mean it *is* the same?"

"Don't confuse the mirror with your illogic," the Magician snapped. "It agreed it was *not* the same!"

"Uh, yes," Bink said. "Still, if our route takes us past the fiends, we have a problem. With the enemy spying on us all the way, and throwing obstacles in our way, he's sure to excite the fiends into something dire."

"I believe you are correct," Humfrey said. "It may be time for me to expend some more of my magic."

"Glory be!" Chester exclaimed ironically.

"Quiet, horserear!" Humfrey snapped. "Now let me see. *Do* we have to pass the fiends of the lake to reach our destination?"

The mirror smiled.

"And the fiends have curse-magic sufficient to blast forests?"

The mirror agreed.

"What's the most convenient way to pass without trouble?"

The mirror showed a picture of Bink watching a play.

Humfrey looked up. "Can any of you make sense of this?"

Crombie squawked. "Where am I?" Grundy translated.

"Let me rephrase that question," Humfrey said quickly. "Where is Crombie while Bink is watching the play?"

The mirror showed one of the Magician's vials.

The griffin went into an angry medley of squawks. "Oh come off it, beakbrain!" the golem said. "You know I can't repeat words like that in public. Not if I want to become real."

"Beakbrain's concern is understandable," Chester said. "Why should he be banished to a bottle? He might never get out."

"*I'm* supposed to do the translations!" Grundy complained, forgetting his prior reluctance.

Humfrey put away the mirror. "If you won't pay attention to my advice," he informed Crombie, "then do it your own way."

"You temperamental real people are at it again," Grundy said. "The rational thing to do is listen to the advice, consider the alternatives, discuss them, and form a consensus."

"The little imp is making uncommon sense," Chester said.

"*Which* little imp?" Grundy demanded.

"I suspect," the Magician said grimly, "that the garrulous golem would be best off in a bottle."

"We're fighting again," Bink said. "If the mirror says we can pass the fiends most conveniently by traveling in bottles, I'd rather gamble on that than on the sort of thing we've just been through."

"You don't have to gamble," Grundy pointed out. "You have to go watch a dumb play."

"I have faith in my mirror," Humfrey said, and the mirror blushed so brightly there was a faint glow through his jacket. "To prove it, I will submit to bottling myself. I believe the one Beauregard used is pleasantly upholstered and large enough for two. Suppose Crombie and Grundy and I enter that bottle and give it to Bink to carry? Then he can ride Chester to the play."

"I'm willing," Bink said. He wondered privately whether the Good Magician would take all his other bottles with him into the bottle. That seemed a bit paradoxical, but no doubt was possible. "But I don't know exactly where the fiends are, and I'd rather not barge in on them unexpectedly. If we approach carefully, circumspectly, they may be less fiendish."

Crombie pointed to the lake.

"Yes, I know. But *where* at the lake? At the edge? On an island? I mean, before I innocently walk into a tree-blasting curse—"

Crombie squawked and spread his wings. His proud colors flashed as he flew up and made for the lake.

"Wait, featherbrain!" Chester cried. "They'll see you by air! That will give us all away!" But the griffin ignored him.

They watched Crombie wing handsomely out over the water, his plumage flexing red, blue, and white. "I have to admit the ornery cuss is a beautiful animal," Chester murmured.

Then the griffin folded his wings and plummeted toward the surface of the lake, spinning in the air. "A curse!" Bink cried. "They shot him down with a curse!"

But then the figure straightened out, regained altitude, and winged back. Crombie seemed to be all right.

"What happened?" Bink demanded as the griffin landed. "Was it a curse?"

"Squawk!" Crombie replied. Grundy translated: "What curse? I merely did my turnabout to get a closer fix on the fiends. They reside under the water."

"Under the water!" Bink cried. "How can we go there?"

Humfrey brought out another vial and handed it to Bink. "These pills will do the trick. Take one every two hours while submerged. It will—"

"There's a mound starting!" Chester cried. "A spy!"

Humfrey whipped out yet another vial, uncorked it, and aimed it at the upwelling dirt. A jet of vapor shot out, striking the mound. Crystals of ice formed. The mound froze.

"Fire extinguisher," the Magician explained. "Very cold. That squiggle is frozen stiff in its tunnel."

"Let me kill it while I can catch it!" Chester said eagerly.

"Wait!" Bink said. "How long will the freeze last?"

"Only a couple of minutes," Humfrey said. "Then the squiggle will resume activity with no impairment."

"And no memory of the missing minutes?" Bink asked.

"It should not be aware of the lapse. Squiggles aren't very smart."

"Then don't kill it! Get out of its observation. It will be convinced this was a false alarm, that we were never here. It will so report to its master, throwing the enemy off the track."

The Magician's brow lifted. "Very intelligent, Bink. You are thinking more like a leader now. We shall hide in the bottle, and you and Chester can carry it with you. Quickly, before the freeze abates."

The griffin remained uncertain, but acquiesced. The Magician set the vial, performed his incantation, and man, griffin, and Golem vanished.

"Grab the bottle, get on my back, hang on!" Chester cried. "Time's almost up!"

Bink snatched up the lone vial remaining, jumped on Chester's back, and hung on. The centaur took off. In a moment his hooves were splashing through the shallow water. "Gimme a pill!" Chester cried.

Bink fumbled out a pill from the bottle, praying he would not spill the works as he bounced around. He popped one into his mouth and handed the other forward to Chester's raised hand. "I hope these work!" he cried.

"That's all we need—another wrong bottle!" Chester exclaimed. "Gobble a foaming insulation pill . . ."

Bink wished the centaur hadn't thought of that. Insulation, or freezing extinguisher—ouch!

He glanced back. Was it his imagination, or was the dirt mound growing again? Had they gotten away in time? Suppose the squiggle saw their footprints?

Then Chester hit a dropoff, and they plunged underwater. Bink choked involuntarily as the liquid covered his mouth—but the water was just like air to his breathing. In fact, it was like air to his whole body, except for its color. They could breathe!

This experience reminded him of something. In a moment he had it: the Queen's anniversary party! That had been illusory underwater scenery, while this was genuine. Unfortunately, the Queen's version had been prettier. Here things were murky and dull.

Chester plodded on, picking his way carefully through the unfamiliar aquatic environment. Dusky clouds of sediment stirred up around his legs. Curious fish looked the pair over. Chester now held his bow in his hands, in case they should encounter a sea monster. Apart from the tension, it was soon rather dull going.

Bink drew out the bottle that held the Magician and put his eye to the side. Vaguely he made out the shapes of a tiny griffin and tinier man. They were in a carpeted room like that of a palace, and were looking at moving pictures in the magic mirror. It seemed very comfortable. Much nicer, in fact, than forging through the murk toward fiends.

Another ugly thought came. Suppose he had grabbed the wrong bottle himself, and popped the Magician into his mouth in lieu of a water-breathing pill? Such things were very scary right now.

Bink put the vial in his pocket, reassured that his friends were secure. He wondered what would happen if he shook the bottle violently, but resisted the urge to experiment. "Let's go visit the fiends," he said with false cheer.

Shortly they approached a splendid marine castle. It was formed from seashells—which meant it was probably magical, since few seashells formed in lakes without the aid of magic. Little whirlpools ascended from its turrets, apparently bringing air down to the inhabitants. Instead of a moat, the castle had a thick wall of seaweed, patrolled by vigilant swordfish.

"Well, let's hope the fiends are kind to travelers," Bink said. There were no bubbles as he spoke; the pill had fully acclimatized him.

"Let's hope the Magician's mirror knew its business," the centaur responded grimly. "And that the fiends don't connect the fool griffin with us, if they saw him."

They marched up to the main gate. A behemoth rose out of the muck, mostly mouth.

"Hooold!" the behemoth bellowed. "Whoo goooes there?" It was very proficient and resonant on the long O's; the sound reverberated across the reaches of the cavernous maw.

"Chester and Bink, travelers," Bink said with some trepidation. "We'd like lodging for the night."

"Soooo?" the monster inquired. "Then goooo!" It's mouth gaped even more horrendously.

"Go?" the centaur repeated aggressively. "We just came!"

"Soo gooo!" the behemoth reverberated, its orifice gaping so widely that the centaur could have ridden right into it without ducking his head.

Chester reached for his sword. "Uh, hooold—I mean hold," Bink murmured. "I remember—the gargoyle—I think it means to go inside. Inside the mouth."

The centaur peered into the monster's tunnel-like throat. "Dammed if I'll cooperate in my own consumption!"

"But that's the entrance to the castle!" Bink explained. "The behemoth itself."

Chester stared. "Well I'll be gelded!" And without further hesitation he galloped in.

Sure enough, the throat continued on into the castle. Lights appeared at the end of the tunnel, and soon they emerged into a partial receiving hall. Intricately woven tapestries covered the walls, and the floor was done in fancy wooden squares.

A handsome, almost pretty young man walked up to greet them. He had ornate curls about his ears and a neat mustache. His costume was a princely robe embroidered with brightly colored threads, and he wore soft slippers with pointed toes. "Welcome to Gateway Castle," he said. "May I inquire your identities and the purpose of this visit?"

"You may," Chester said.

There was a pause. "Well?" the man said, a bit nettled.

"Well, why don't you inquire?" Chester said. "I gave you permission."

Small muscles quirked about the man's mouth, making him less pretty. "I so inquire."

"I am Chester Centaur, and this is my companion Bink. He's human."

"So I noted. And your purpose?"

"We seek the source of magic," Bink said.

"You have lost your way. It is at the amazon village, some distance north. But the direct route is hazardous to your sanity."

"We have been there," Bink said. "That is not the ultimate source, but merely the upwelling of magic dust. What we seek lies below. According to our information, a more convenient route passes through this castle."

The man almost smiled. "Oh, you would not care for that route!"

"Try us and see."

"This is beyond my cognizance. You will have to talk with the lord of the manor."

"Good enough," Bink said. He wondered what sort of a fiend this lord would be, who had such a docile human servant.

"If you would be good enough to come this way."

"We're good enough," Chester said.

"But first we must do something about your hooves. The floor is teak parquet; we do not wish it scratched or dented."

"Why put it on the floor, then?" Chester demanded.

"We do not apply it to the floor of our stable," the man said. He produced several disks of furry material. "Apply these to your hooves; they will adhere, and muffle the impact."

"How about wearing one of these on your mouth?" Chester demanded.

"It's a small concession," Bink murmured. Chester's hooves were sound, since the healing elixir had eliminated all damage to the centaur's hind end, but they were hard enough to leave an imprint. "Humor the poor man. The fiends are probably very strict about such things, and punish their servants for violations."

With imperfect grace, Chester pressed his hooves one at a time into the felt disks. The material clung to them, and it made the centaur's footfalls silent.

They moved through an elegant hall, descended carpeted steps, and entered a small chamber. There was barely room for Chester to stand. "If this is your main hall—" he began.

The man touched a button. The door slid closed. Then, abruptly, the room moved.

Bink flung out his hands, startled, and Chester kicked a hole in the rear wall.

"Easy, visitors," the man said with a small frown. "Haven't you ridden an elevator before? It is inanimate magic, a chamber that rises or sinks when occupied. Saves wear on stairs."

"Oh," Bink said, abashed. He preferred more conventional magic.

The magic lift stopped. The door slid open. They stepped out into another hall, and in due course came to the chambers of the lord of the manor.

He was, to Bink's surprise, a man, garbed richly in silver cloth and diamonds, but with the same foolish slippers his servant wore. "So you proffer service for a night's lodging," he said briskly.

"This is our custom," Bink said.

"And ours too!" the lord agreed heartily. "Have you any special talents?"

Bink couldn't tell his own, and didn't know Chester's. "Uh, not exactly. But we're strong, and can do work."

"Work? Oh my heavens no!" the lord exclaimed. "People do not work here!" Oh? "How do you live, then?" Bink asked.

"We organize, we direct—and we entertain," the lord said. "Have you any entertainment abilities?"

Bink spread his hands. "I'm afraid not."

"Excellent! You will make an ideal audience."

"Audience?" Bink knew that Chester was as perplexed as he. The mirror had shown him watching a play—yet that could hardly be a service!

"We send our troupes out to entertain the masses, accepting payment in materials and services. It is a rewarding profession, esthetically and practically. But it is necessary to obtain advance audience ratings, so that we can gauge our reception precisely."

This innocuous employment hardly jibed with the local reputation! "To be an audience—to watch your shows—that's all you require? It hardly seems equitable! I'm afraid we would not be able to present an informed critical report—"

"No necessity! Our magic monitors will gauge your reactions, and point up our rough edges. You will have nothing to do but react, honestly."

"I suppose we could do that," Bink said dubiously. "If you really are satisfied."

"Something funny here," Chester said. "How come you have a reputation as fiends?"

"Uh, that's not diplomatic," Bink murmured, embarrassed.

"Fiends? Who called us fiends?" the lord demanded.

"The ogre," Chester replied. "He said you blasted a whole forest with a curse."

The lord stroked his goatee. "The ogre survives?"

"Chester, shut up!" Bink hissed.

But the centaur's unruly nature had taken control. "All he was doing was rescuing his lady ogre, and you couldn't stand to have him happy, so—"

"Ah, yes, that ogre. I suppose to an ogre's way of thinking, we would be fiends. To us, crunching human bones is fiendish. It is all in one's perspective."

Apparently the centaur had not antagonized the lord, though Bink judged that to be sheer luck. Unless the lord, like his troupe, was an actor—in which case there could be serious and subtle trouble. "This one is now a vegetarian," Bink said. "But I'm curious: do you really have such devastating curses, and why should you care what an ogre does? You really don't have cause to worry about ogres, here under the lake; they can't swim."

"We do really have such curses," the lord said. "They constitute group effort, the massing of all our magic. We have no individual talents, only individual contributions toward the whole."

Bink was amazed. Here was a whole society with duplicating talents! Magic *did* repeat itself!

"We do not employ our curses haphazardly, however. We went after the ogre as a professional matter. He was interfering with our monopoly."

Both Bink and Chester were blank. "Your what?"

"We handle all formal entertainments in southern Xanth. That bad actor blundered into one of our sets and kidnapped our leading lady. We do not tolerate such interference or competition."

"You used an ogress for a leading lady?" Bink asked.

"We used a transformed nymph—a consummate actress. *All* our players are consummate, as you shall see. In that role she resembled the most ogrelike ogress imaginable, absolutely horrible." He paused, considering. "In fact, with her artistic temperament, she was getting pretty ogrelike in life. Prima donna . . ."

"Then the ogre's error was understandable."

"Perhaps. But not tolerable. He had no business on that set. We had to scrub the whole production. It ruined our season."

Bink wondered what reception the ogre would encounter, as he rescued his ideal female. An actress in ogress guise, actually from the castle of the fiends!

"What about the reverse-spell tree?" Chester asked.

"People were taking its fruit and being entertained by the reversal effects. We did not appreciate the competition. So we eliminated it."

Chester glanced at Bink, but did not speak. Perhaps these people really were somewhat fiendish. To abolish all rival forms of entertainment—

"And where did you say you were traveling to?" the lord inquired.

"To the source of magic," Bink said. "We understand it is underground, and that the best route leads through this castle."

"I do not appreciate humor at my expense," the lord said, frowning. "If you do not wish to inform me of your mission, that is certainly your privilege. But do not taunt me with an obvious fabrication." Bink had the impression that obviousness was a worse affront than fabrication, to this person.

"Listen, fiend!" Chester said, bridling in most obvious fashion. "Centaurs do not lie!"

"Uh, let me handle this," Bink said quickly. "There is surely some misunderstanding. We are on a quest for the source of magic—but perhaps we have been misinformed as to its access."

The lord mellowed. "That must be the case. Below this castle lies only the vortex. Nothing that goes that route ever returns. We are the Gateway; we straddle the vortex, protecting innocent creatures from being drawn unwittingly into that horrible fate. Who informed you that the object of your quest lay in such a direction?"

"Well, a Magician—"

"Never trust a Magician! They are all up to mischief!"

"Uh, maybe so," Bink said uneasily, and Chester nodded thoughtfully. "He was very convincing."

"They tend to be," the lord said darkly. Abruptly he shifted the subject. "I will show you the vortex. This way, if you please." He led the way to an interior panel. It slid at his touch. There was a glistening wall of glassy substance. No, not glass; it was moving. Fleeting irregularities showed horizontally. Now Bink could see through it somewhat vaguely, making out the three-dimensional shape. It was a column, perhaps twice his armspan in diameter, with a hollow center. In fact it was water, coursing around in circles at high speed. Or in spirals, going down—

"A whirlpool!" Chester exclaimed. "We are looking at the nether column of a whirlpool!"

"Correct," the lord said with pride. "We have constructed our castle around it, containing it by magic. Substances may pass into it, but not out of it. Criminals and other untoward persons are fed into its maw, to disappear forever. This is a most salutary deterrent."

Surely so! The mass of moving fluid was awesome in its smooth power, and frightening. Yet it was also in its fashion luring, like the song of the siren, or the madness.

Bink yanked his gaze away. "But where does it go?"

"Who would presume to know?" the lord inquired in return, quirking an eyebrow expressively. He slid the panel across and the vision of the vortex was gone.

"Enough of this," the lord decided. "We shall wine and dine you fittingly, and then you will audience our play."

The meal was excellent, served by fetching young women in scant green outfits who paid flattering attention to the travelers, especially Chester. They seemed to admire both his muscular man-portion and his handsome equine portion. Bink wondered, as he had before, what it was girls saw in horses. The siren had been so eager to ride!

At last, stuffed, Bink and Chester were ushered to the theater. The stage was several times the size of the chamber for the audience. Apparently these people did not like to watch as much as they liked to perform.

The curtain lifted and it was on: a gaudily costumed affair replete with bold swordsmen and buxom women and funny jokes. The staged duels were impressive, but Bink wondered how proficient those men would be with their weapons in a real battle. There was a considerable difference between technical skill and combat nerve. The women were marvelously seductive—but would they be as shapely without the support of their special clothes, or as wittily suggestive minus the memorized lines?

"You do not find our production entertaining?" the lord inquired.

"I prefer life," Bink replied.

The lord made a note on his pad: MORE REALISM.

Then the play shifted to a scene of music. The heroine sang a lovely song of loss and longing, meditating on her faithless lover, and it was difficult to imagine how any lout, no matter how louty, could be faithless to such a desirable creature. Bink thought of Chameleon again, and longed for her again. Chester was standing raptly beside him, probably thinking of horsing around with Cherie Centaur, who was indeed a fetching filly.

Then the song was augmented by a hauntingly lovely accompaniment. A flute was playing, its notes of such absolute quality and clarity that the lady's voice was shamed. Bink looked toward that sound—and there it was, a gleaming silver flute hanging in the air beside the heroine, playing by itself. A magic flute!

The lady ceased singing, surprised, but the flute played on. Indeed, freed of the limitations of her voice, it trilled on into an aria of phenomenal expertise and beauty. Now the entire cast of players stood listening, seeming to find it as novel as Bink did.

The lord jumped to his feet. "Who is performing that magic?" he demanded.

No one answered. All were absorbed in the presentation.

"Clear the set!" the lord cried, red-faced. "Everybody out. Out, out!"

Slowly they cleared, fading into the wings, looking back at the solo instrument. The stage was empty—but still the flute played, performing a medley of melodies, each more lovely than the one preceding.

The lord grabbed Bink by the shoulders. "Are you doing it?" he demanded, seeming about ready to choke.

Bink tore his attention from the flute. "I have no magic like that!" he said.

The lord hauled on Chester's muscular arm. "You—it must be yours, then!"

Chester's head turned to face him. "What?" he asked, as if coming out of a reverie. In that instant, flute and music faded.

"Chester!" Bink exclaimed. "Your talent! All the beauty in your nature, suppressed because it was linked to your magic, and as a centaur you couldn't—"

"My talent!" Chester repeated, amazed. "It must be me! I never did dare to—who would have believed—"

"Play it again!" Bink urged. "Make beautiful music! Prove you have magic, just as your hero-uncle Herman the Hermit did!"

"Yes," Chester agreed. He concentrated. The flute reappeared. It began to play, haltingly at first, then with greater conviction and beauty. And strangely, the centaur's rather homely face began to seem less so. Not so strange, Bink realized: much of Chester's brutality of expression stemmed from his habitual snarl. That snarl had abated; he had no need of it any more.

"Now you don't owe the Magician any service," Bink pointed out. "You found your talent yourself."

"What abominable mischief!" the lord cried. "You accepted our hospitality on the agreement that you would render service as an audience. You are not an audience—you are a performer. You have reneged on your agreement with us!"

Now a portion of Chester's familiar arrogance reasserted itself. The flute blew a flat note. "Manfeathers!" the centaur snapped. "I was only playing along with your heroine's song. Bring your play back; I'll watch it, and accompany it."

"Hardly," the lord said grimly. "We tolerate no non-guild performance in our midst. We maintain a monopoly."

"What are you going to do?" Chester demanded. "Throw a fit? I mean, a curse?"

"Uh, I wouldn't—" Bink cautioned his friend.

"I'll not tolerate such arrogance from a mere half-man!" the lord said.

"Oh, yeah?" Chester retorted. With an easy and insulting gesture he caught the man's shirtfront with one hand and lifted him off the floor.

"Chester, we're their guests!" Bink protested.

"Not any more!" the lord gasped. "Get out of this castle before we destroy you for your insolence!"

"My insolence—for playing a magic flute?" Chester demanded incredulously. "How would you like that flute up your—"

"Chester!" Bink cried warningly, though he had considerable sympathy for the centaur's position. He invoked the one name that had power to restrain Chester's wrath: "Cherie wouldn't like it if you—"

"Oh, I wouldn't do it to *her!*" Chester said. Then he reconsidered. "Not with a flute—"

All this time the centaur had been holding the lord suspended in air. Suddenly the man's shirt ripped, and he fell ignominiously to the floor. More than ignominiously: he landed in a fresh pile of dirt.

Actually, this cushioned his impact, saving him from possible injury. But it multiplied his rage. "Dirt!" the lord cried. "This animal dumped me in dirt!"

"Well, that's where you belong," Chester said. "I really wouldn't want to dirty my clean silver flute on you." He glanced at Bink. "I'm glad it's silver, and not some cheap metal. Shows quality, that flute."

"Yes," Bink agreed hastily. "Now if we can leave—"

"What's dirt doing on my teak parquet?" the lord demanded. There was now a crowd of actors and servants about him, helping him up, brushing him off, fawning.

"The squiggle," Bink said, dismayed. "It found us again."

"Oh, so it's a friend of yours!" the lord cried, proceeding dramatically from rage to rage. "I should have known! It shall be the first to be cursed!" And he pointed one finger, shaking with emotion, at the pile. "All together now. A-one, a-two, a-three!"

Everyone linked hands and concentrated. At the count of three the curse came forth, like a bolt of lightning from the lord's finger. Ball lightning: it formed into a glowing mass the size of a fist, and drifted down to touch the dirt. At contact it exploded—or imploded. There was a flash of darkness and a momentary acrid odor; then the air cleared and there was nothing. No dirt, no squiggle, no flooring, in that region.

The lord glanced at the hole with satisfaction. "That's one squiggle that will never bother us again," he said. "Now for you, half-man." He raised his terrible finger to point at Chester. "A-one, a-two—"

Bink dived across, knocking the man's arm aside. The curse spun off and smashed into a column. There was another implosion of darkness, and a chunk of the column dissolved into nothingness.

"Now see what you've done!" the lord cried, becoming if possible even more angry than before. Bink could not protest; probably his talent had been responsible for the seemingly random shot. The curse had to destroy something, after all.

Bink himself would be immune—but not Chester. "Let's get out of here!" Bink said. "Give me a ride out of range of those curses!"

Chester, about to draw his sword, reconsidered in mid-motion. "That's right —I can take care of myself, but you're just a man. Come on!"

Bink scrambled to straddle the centaur's back, and they leaped away just as the lord was leveling another curse. Chester galloped down the hall, his feet oddly silent because of the hoofpads. The fiends set up a howl of pursuit.

"Which way is out?" Bink cried.

"How should I know? That's birdbeak's department. I'm only a former guest of the fiends."

Good old Chester! All prickle and performance.

"We're somewhere upstairs. We could break out a window and swim—" He reached into his pocket, feeling the bottle that contained Crombie, Grundy, and the Magician. He fumbled until he found the one containing the water-breathing-spell pills; couldn't afford a mistake now! "We'd better take new pills; it's been over two hours."

They gulped their pills on the run. Now they were ready for the water—if they could find it. They had left the pursuit behind for the moment; no man on foot could match the speed of a centaur.

Bink had a second thought. "We don't want to go out—we want to go down. Into the nether region, to the source of magic."

"Where they tried to scare us away from," Chester agreed. He spun about as neatly as he had when dodging exploding pineapples, his two front feet down so that fore and hind sections rotated about the axis. Then he cantered back the way they had come.

"Hold up!" Bink screamed. "This is suicidal! We don't even know where the entrance to the vortex is!"

"The vortex has to be in the center of the castle; matter of architectural stability," Chester said. "Besides which, I have a fair directional sense of my own; I know roughly where it is from here. I am prepared to make my own entrance." Bink tended to forget that behind the brutal façade lay a fine centaur mind. Chester knew what he was doing.

They rounded a corner—and plowed into the charging fiends. People went tumbling every which way—but a massive curse rose up from the jumble and sailed after Chester.

Bink, glancing nervously back, spied it. "Chester—run!" he cried. "There's a curse on your tail!"

"On my tail!" Chester cried indignantly, and leapt forward. He didn't mind threats to his homely face, but his beautiful behind was sacred.

The curse, oriented on its target, pursued with determination. "This one we can't avoid," Bink said. "It's locked onto us, as the other was locked onto the ogre."

"Should we swear off crunching bones?"

"I never was much for human bones anyway!"

"I think the vortex is ahead," Chester said. "Hang on—I'm going in!"

He leaped—directly at a blank wooden panel. The wood shattered under the impact of his forehooves, and the two of them crashed directly into the vortex.

Bink's last thought as the awful swirl engulfed him, hauling him brutally around and around and down and down, providing one terrifying glimpse of its dark center shaft, was: what would happen to the curse that followed them? Then he spiraled into oblivion.

Chapter 10

Precious Nymph

ink woke naked and battered, but not cold. He lay strewn on the edge of a warm, glowing lake. Hastily he dragged his feet out of the water, fearful of predators.

He heard a groan. A little farther along lay the centaur, limbs projecting in six directions. It had been an extremely violent descent; had they not had that water-breathing magic, they would surely have drowned. Bink scrambled to his feet and lumbered toward his friend. "Chester! Are you—?"

He paused. Midway between them he spied the sparkle of a star or jewel. Foolishly he paused to pick it up; he had no use for such a bauble. But it turned out to be only a shard of glass.

Chester groaned again, and lifted his head. "Takes more than a mere vortex to put away a centaur," he said. "But maybe not *much* more . . ."

Bink completed the distance between them, and tried to help his friend rise. "Hey, are you trying to cut me?" Chester demanded.

"Oops, sorry. I picked up this fragment of—" Bink paused again, looking at it. "There's something in it! That is—"

Chester got to his feet. "Let me see that." He reached down to take the fragment. His eyes rounded in surprise. "That's Humfrey!"

"What?" Bink thought he had misheard.

"It's hard to see in this dim glow, but it's him, all right. This must be a piece of the magic mirror, thrown ashore by coincidence. What happened to the Good Magician?"

"I lost the bottle!" Bink exclaimed with horror. "It was in my pocket—" His hand slapped his flesh where his pocket had been.

"He had the mirror with him. How did even one fragment of it get out of the bottle, unless—"

"Unless the bottle was smashed," Bink finished. "In which case—"

"In which case they were released. But where—and in what condition? They didn't have the water-breathing pills."

"If they got out just when that curse caught up—"

Chester looked closely at the fragment of glass. "Humfrey seems to be well— and I see the griffin behind him. I think they're still inside the bottle, though."

Bink looked. "They are! I see the curving glass walls, and the upholstery. It has been shaken up some, but the bottle never broke." He was relieved. A broken bottle might well have meant the end of his friends. "And they have another fragment of glass!" He raised his hand in a wave. "Hi, folks!"

Silently, Humfrey waved back. "He sees us in his fragment!" Chester exclaimed. "But that's impossible, because the broken mirror is out here."

"Anything is possible, with magic," Bink said. It was a cliché truism, but right now he had his doubts.

"Look at the shambles in there," Chester said. "That bottle must have been bounced against a wall."

"And the mirror broke, and a piece of it flew out here," Bink said uncertainly. "Right where we could find it. That's quite a coincidence, even if we can believe the possibility."

"What else can we believe?" Chester demanded.

Bink could not argue. His talent operated through seeming coincidence; it must have had a part in this. But wouldn't it have been easier to have the Magician's bottle itself float to shore here, instead of one piece of glass? "We can see them, but not hear them. Maybe if we print a message—" But they had nothing to do that with.

"If we can find the bottle, we can let them out," Chester pointed out. He seemed to be feeling better, physically.

"Yes." Bink held the fragment close to his face and mouth elaborately. *"Where are you?"*

Humfrey spread his hands. He pointed to the bottle wall. Outside it, turbulent water swirled, its phosphorescence making streaky line-patterns. The bottle was somewhere in a river, being carried along by the current—where?

"I guess that mirror isn't much use," Chester said. "Crombie could locate us—but can't get to us. We might get to the bottle—but can't find it."

"We'll have to follow the river down," Bink said. "It must start at the vortex pool here in this lake, and dribble on to wherever it goes. Yet if we follow it—"

"We delay our quest for the source of magic," Chester finished.

That made Bink pause. "The quest will have to wait," he decided. "We have to save our friends."

"I suppose so," the centaur agreed. "Even that arrogant griffin."

"Do you really dislike Crombie?"

"Well . . . he's a scrapper, like me. Can't blame him for that, I suppose. But I'd like to try his strength, once, just for the record."

Male competition. Well, Bink understood that, for he experienced it himself at times.

But there were more important matters now. "I'm thirsty," Bink said. He walked back to the lake shore.

"Have you noticed," Chester remarked, "that there is no life in this lake? No fish, no monsters, no plants, no beach creatures . . ."

"No life," Bink repeated. "But we're all right, so—"

"We haven't drunk from it yet. Or if we did, it was from the fresh water of the vortex, when we were on the pill."

"That's true," Bink said uncomfortably.

"I wonder whether the cork loosened in Humfrey's bottle, and he got a sample of this water, and hauled the cork back in place right after the mirror broke."

"Could be," Bink agreed. "We'd best not gamble. We'll need food soon, too. We'd better check around. We can't rescue the Magician if we don't take care of ourselves."

"Right," Chester agreed. "And the first thing to do is—"

"Is to find my clothes," Bink finished.

They were farther along the shore, complete with Bink's sword, as luck would have it. Chester had retained his weapons and rope, so was in good shape.

They moved on through the cavern passages, leaving the suspicious river behind, their eyes acclimatizing to the dimming subterranean reaches. Bink hoped they would not encounter nickelpedes here, but was careful not to voice this wish. No sense alarming Chester. They tried to mark their way by scratching X's in the floor every so often, but Bink wasn't sure how effective this would be. Time passed, and the way was interminable—especially since they did not know where they were going.

Bink's thirst had been casual, at first, but now that he knew there was no water it became more pressing. How long could they go on, before—?

Abruptly they saw light—real light, not the mere passage glow. They hurried cautiously up to it—and discovered a magic lantern suspended from a jag of stone. Its soft effulgence was a welcome sight—but there was nothing else.

"People—or goblins?" Bink asked, nervous and hopeful.

Chester took it down and studied it. "Looks like fairy-work to me," he said. "Goblins don't really need light, and in any event this is too delicately wrought."

"Even fairies aren't necessarily friendly," Bink said. "Still, it seems a better risk than starving here alone."

They took the lamp and went on with slightly improved prospects. But nothing further developed. Apparently someone or something had lit a lamp, left it, and departed. Strange.

Weary, dirty, hungry, and unpleasantly thirsty, they parked at last on a boulder. "We have to find food, or at least water," Bink said, trying to make it seem casual. "There doesn't seem to be any on this main passage, but—" He paused, listening. "Is that—?"

Chester cocked his head. "Yes, I think it is. Water dripping. You know, I haven't wanted to say anything, but my tongue has been drying up in my mouth. If we could—"

"Behind this wall, I think. Maybe if we—"

"Stand clear." The centaur faced about so that his better half addressed the wall in question. Then he kicked.

A section of the wall collapsed. Now the sound was louder: water flowing over stone. "Let me climb in there," Bink said. "If I can collect a cupful—"

"Just in case," Chester said, taking his coil of rope and looping it about Bink's waist. "We don't know what to expect in these dark chambers. If you fall in a hole, I'll haul you out."

"Yes," Bink agreed. "Let me take the magic lantern."

He scrambled into the hole. Once he got by the rubble, he found himself in a larger, irregular cavern whose floor slanted down into darkness. The sound of water was coming from that darkness.

He moved forward, careful of his footing, trailing the line behind him. The water sound became temptingly loud. Bink traced it to a crevice in the floor. He held his lantern over it. Now at last he saw the glint of a streamlet. He reached down with his fingers, and just as his shoulder nudged the crevice lip his fingers touched the water.

How could he draw any up? After a moment's thought he ripped a piece of cloth from his already tattered sleeve, and dangled that down into the water. He let it soak up what liquid it cared to, then brought it to the surface.

While he was doing this, he heard a distant singing. He stiffened with alarm. Were the lake fiends coming here? No, that seemed highly unlikely; they were water dwellers, not rock dwellers, and by the lord of the manor's own admission they knew nothing of this nether region. This had to be some creature of the caves. Perhaps the owner of the magic lantern.

By the time he brought the dripping rag to his mouth, the singing was quite close. There was the scent of fresh flowers. Bink put the dangling end of the rag in his mouth and squeezed. Cool, clear liquid dripped down. It was the best water he had ever tasted!

Then something strange happened. Bink experienced a surge of dizziness—not sickening, but wonderfully pleasant. He felt alive, vibrant, and full of the warmth of human spirit. That was good water indeed!

He dipped his rag into the crevice again, soaking it for Chester. This was an inefficient way to drink, but a great deal better than nothing. While he lay there he heard the singing again. It was a nymph, of imperfect voice but sounding young and sweet and joyful. A pleasant shiver went through him.

Bink brought up the rag and laid it on the cave floor. He took up the light and moved toward the voice. It came from a section beyond the water, and soon Bink came to the end of his tether. He untied the rope, let it drop from his waist, and went on.

Now he spied a beam of light emanating from another crack. The singer was in the chamber beyond. Bink knelt and put his eye to the crack, silently.

She was sitting on a stool fashioned of silver, sorting through a barrel filled with precious stones. Their colors reflected brilliantly, decorating all the walls of the room. She was a typical nymph, long and bare of leg with a tiny skirt just about covering a pert derrière, slender of waist, full of bosom, and innocent and large-eyed of face. Her hair sparkled like the keg of jewels. He had seen nymphs like this many times; each had her association with tree or rock or stream or lake or mountain, yet they were all so uniform in face and feature that their beauty became commonplace. It was as if some Magician had established the ideal female-human aspect and scattered it about the Land of Xanth for decoration, attaching individual units to particular locales so that the distribution would be uniform. So she was nothing special. The precious stones, in contrast, were a phenomenal treasure.

Yet Bink glanced only passingly at the stones. His gaze became fixed on the nymph. She—he felt—it was rapt adoration.

What am I doing? he demanded of himself. With Chester waiting for a drink, Bink had no business here! And for answer, he only sighed longingly.

The nymph overheard. She glanced up alertly, breaking off her innocent melody, but could not see him. Perplexed, she shook her maiden tresses and returned to her work, evidently deciding that she had imagined it.

"No, I am here!" Bink cried, surprising himself. "Behind the wall!"

She screamed a cute little scream, jumped up, and fled. The keg overturned, dumping jewels across the floor.

"Wait! Don't run!" Bink cried. He smashed his fist into the wall with such force the stones cracked. He wrenched out more fragments, widening the hole, then jumped down into the room. He almost slipped on some pearls, but did a little dance and got his balance.

Now he stood still and listened. There was a strange smell, reminiscent of the breath of an attacking dragon, one just behind a person and gaining. Bink looked about nervously, but there was no dragon. All was silent. Why didn't he hear her still running?

In a moment he had it figured. She might flee in alarm, but she would hardly leave her treasure unguarded. Obviously she had dodged around a corner and now was watching him from hiding.

"Please, miss," Bink called. "I mean no harm to you. I only want to—"

To hug you, to kiss you, to—

Shocked, he halted his thoughts in mid-train. He was a married man! What was he doing chasing a strange nymph? He should get back to Chester, take the centaur his ragful of water—

Again he paused in his thoughts. *Oh, no!*

Yet he could hardly doubt his sudden emotion. He had imbibed from a spring, and become enamored of the first maiden he had seen thereafter. It must have been a love spring!

But why had his talent let him drink it?

The answer was distressingly obvious. He wished he hadn't thought of the question. His talent had no regard for his feelings, or those of others. It protected only his physical, personal welfare. It must have decided that his wife Chameleon represented some kind of threat to his welfare, so it was finding him another love. It had not been satisfied with separating him from Chameleon temporarily; now it intended to make that separation permanent.

"I will not have it!" he cried aloud. "I love Chameleon!"

And that was true. Love potions did not undo existing relations. But now he also loved this nymph—and she was a great deal more accessible.

Was he at war with his own talent? He had ethics it evidently did not; he was civilized while it was primitive. Who was to be the master, here?

He fought, but could not undo the effect of the love spring. Had he anticipated what his talent was leading him into, he might have balked it before he drank, but now he was the victim of a *fait accompli*. Well, he would settle with his talent when he found a better occasion.

All was fair in magic. "Nymph, come here and tell me your name, or I'll steal all your treasure!" he yelled.

When she did not respond, he righted the keg and began scooping up gems. There was an amazing assortment: diamonds, pearls, opals, emeralds, sapphires, and too many others to classify. How had the nymph come by such a fortune?

Now the nymph appeared, peeking around a curve in the tunnel. Coincidentally, Bink smelled the fleeting scent of woodland flowers. "But I *need* that treasure!" she protested.

Bink continued his work. The stones sailed into the barrel. "What is your name?" he demanded.

"What's yours?" There was an odor like that of a hesitant deerfly at the edge of a glade.

"I asked you first." All he wanted to do was keep her in conversation until he could catch her.

"But you're the stranger," she pointed out with female logic.

Ah, well. He liked her logic. He knew it was the effect of the potion, but he was captive to her mannerisms. "My name is Bink."

"I am Jewel," she said. "The Nymph of Jewels, if you insist on the whole definition. Now give me back my stones."

"I'll be glad to, Jewel. For a kiss."

"What kind of a nymph do you think I am?" she protested in typical nymphly fashion. Now there was the odor of pine-oil disinfectant.

"I hope to find out. Tell me about yourself."

She edged farther into the room, distrusting him. "I'm just a rock nymph. I see that all the precious stones get properly planted in the ground, so that goblins, dragons, men and other voracious creatures can mine them." Bink smelled the mixed fumes of hard-laboring men and goblins. "It's all very important, because otherwise those creatures would be even wilder than they are. The mining gives them something to do."

So that was how the jewels got planted. Bink had always wondered about that, or would have wondered had he thought about it. "But where do you get them to start with?"

"Oh, they just appear by magic, of course. The keg never empties."

"It doesn't?"

"See, it is already overflowing with the gems you are trying to put back. You aren't supposed to put them back."

Bink looked, surprised. It was so. He had assumed the keg was empty without really checking it, because his main attention had been on the nymph.

"How am I ever going to process all those extra stones?" she demanded with cute petulance. "Usually it takes an hour to place each one, and you have spilled hundreds." She stamped her sweet little foot, not knowing how to express her annoyance effectively. Nymphs had been designed for appearance, not emotion.

"Me? *You* spilled them when you ran!" Bink retorted. "I'm trying to pick them up."

"Well, it's your fault because you scared me. What were you doing behind the wall? No one's supposed to go there. That's why it's walled off. The water—" She paused with new alarm. "You didn't—?"

"I did," Bink said. "I was thirsty, and—"

She screamed again, and fled again. Nymphs by nature were flighty. Bink continued his gathering, arranging the surplus jewels in a pile beside the keg, knowing she would be back. He hated himself somewhat, knowing he should leave her alone, but found himself unable to stop himself. And he did owe it to her to clean up this mess as well as he could, though the pile was getting unwieldy.

Jewel peeked back around the corner. "If you'd just go away and let me catch up—"

"Not until I've finished cleaning up this overflow," Bink said. "As you pointed out, it is my fault." He placed a huge egg-shaped opal on top of his mound—and watched the whole thing subside, squirting out diamonds and things. He was getting nowhere.

She edged in closer. "No, you're right. I spilled it. I'll catch up somehow. You just—just leave. Please." The sneezy tang of dust tickled his nose, as if a herd of centaurs had just charged along a dry road in mid-summer.

"Your magic talent!" Bink exclaimed. "Smells!"

"Well, I never," she said, modestly affronted. Now the dust-odor was tinged by the fumes of burning oil.

"I mean you can make—you smell like what you feel."

"Oh, that." The oil merged into perfume. "Yes. What's your talent?"

"I can't tell you."

"But I just told you mine! It's only fair—"

She edged within range. Bink grabbed her. She screamed again most fetchingly, and struggled without much strength. That, too, was the way nymphs were: delightfully and ineffectively difficult. He drew her in for a firm kiss on the lips. She was a most pleasant armful, and her lips tasted like honey. At least they smelled like it.

"That wasn't very nice," she rebuked him when he ended the kiss, but she didn't seem very angry. Her odor was of freshly overturned earth.

"I love you," Bink said. "Come with me—"

"I can't go with you," she said, smelling of freshly cut grass. "I have my job to do."

"And I have mine," Bink said.

"What's your job?"

"I'm on a quest for the source of magic."

"But that's way down in the center of the world, or somewhere," she said. "You can't travel that way. There are dragons and goblins and rats—"

"We're used to them," Bink said.

"I'm not used to them! I'm afraid of the dark! I couldn't go there, even if—" Even if she wanted to. Because of course she did not love him. She had not drunk the love-water.

Bink had a naughty idea. "Come and take a drink with me! Then we can—"

She struggled to disengage, and he let her go. The last thing he wanted to do was hurt her! "No, I couldn't afford love. I must plant all these jewels."

"But what am I to do? From the moment I saw you—"

"You'll just have to take the antidote," she said, smelling of a newly lit candle. Bink recognized the connection: the candle symbolized her bright idea.

"There is an antidote?" He hadn't thought of that.

"There must be. For every spell there's an equal and opposite counterspell. Somewhere. All you have to do is find it."

"I know who can find it," Bink said. "My friend Crombie."

"You have friends?" she asked, surprised, smelling of startled birds.

"Of course I have friends!"

"Down here, I meant. I thought you were alone."

"No. I was looking for water for me and Chester. We—"

"Chester? I thought your friend was Crombie."

"Chester Centaur. Crombie is a griffin. And there's Magician Humfrey, and—"

"A Magician!" she exclaimed, impressed. "All to look for the source of magic?"

"Yes. The King wants to know."

"There's a King along too?"

"No," Bink said, momentarily exasperated. "The King assigned me to make the quest. But we had some trouble, and got separated, and—"

"I suppose I'd better show you where there's water," she decided. "And food —you must be hungry too."

"Yes," he said, reaching for her. "We'll be glad to do some service in return—"

"Oh, no!" she cried, skipping away with an enticing bounce of anatomy and the scent of hickory smoke. "Not until you drink the antidote!"

Just so. "I really must get back to Chester," Bink said. "He'll be worried."

She considered for a moment. "Bink, I'm sorry about what happened. Fetch your friends, and I'll see they get fed. Then you really must go."

"Yes." Bink walked slowly to the hole in the wall.

"Not that way!" she cried. "Go round by the regular passages!"

"But I don't know the way! I have no light. I have to follow the rope back."

"Definitely not!" She took her own magic lantern, a twin of the one Bink had found before, from the wall and grasped Bink's arm firmly. "I know all the halls around here. I'll find him for you."

Bink willingly suffered himself to be led. Even apart from the potion, he was discerning commendable traits in her. She was not one of the empty-headed nymphs like those associated with ocean foam or wild oats; she had a sense of purpose and fitness and decency. No doubt her responsible job of jewel-placing had matured her. Still, potion or not, he had no business with this creature! Once his friends were fed, he would have to leave her. He wondered how long it would take the potion to wear off. Some spells were temporary, but others were lifelong.

They circled through intersecting passages. In a moment they came upon Chester, still waiting by the hole. "Here we are!" Bink called.

Chester jumped so that all four hooves were off the floor. "Bink!" he exclaimed as he landed. "What happened? Who is that nymph?"

"Chester, this is Jewel. Jewel—Chester," Bink introduced. "I—" He hesitated.

"He drank a love potion," Jewel said brightly.

The centaur made a motion as of tearing out two fistfulls of mane. "The secret enemy strikes again!"

Bink hadn't thought of that. Of course that was the most reasonable explanation! His talent hadn't betrayed him, but it hadn't protected him from this non-physical threat either. Thus his enemy had scored. How could he pursue the source of magic, when his heart was tied up here?

But his heart was also tied up back home, with Chameleon. That was part of the reason he was on this quest. So—he had better just get on with it. "If we can get back together with Crombie and the Magician, maybe Crombie can point out the location of the antidote," Bink said.

"Where are your friends?" Jewel asked.

"They're in a bottle," Bink explained. "But we can communicate with them through a fragment of magic mirror. Here, I'll introduce you to them." He fumbled in his pocket for the bit of glass.

His fingers found nothing. "Oh, no—I've lost the fragment!" He turned the pocket inside out. There was a hole in it, where the sharp edge of glass had sawed its way out.

"Well, we'll find them somehow," Bink said numbly. "We won't give up until we do."

"That would seem best," Chester agreed gravely. "However, we'll have to take the nymph along with us."

"Why?" Bink had mixed emotions.

"The object of the counterspell has to be present; that's the way these things work. You loved the first female you encountered after imbibing the potion; you must *un*love her in the same fashion."

"I can't come with you!" Jewel protested, though she looked at Chester as if wishing for a ride on his back. "I have a lot of work to do!"

"How much will you get done if Bink stays here?" Chester inquired.

She threw up her hands in feminine exasperation. "Come to my apartment, both of you. We'll discuss it later."

Jewel's apartment was as attractive as herself. She had a cluster of caves completely carpeted; the carpet-moss ran across the floor, up over the walls, and across the ceiling without a break except for the round doors. It was extremely cosy. She had no chairs, table, or bed; it seemed she sat or lay down anywhere, anytime, in perfect comfort.

"We'll have to do something about those clothes," she said to Bink.

Bink looked down at himself. His clothing had more or less dried on him, after its soaking in the vortex and lake; it glowed in uneven patches. "But these are all I have," he said regretfully.

"You can dry-clean them," she said. "Go into the lavatory and put them in the cleaner. It only takes a moment."

Bink entered the room she indicated and closed the curtain. He located the cleaner: an ovenlike alcove through which a warm current of air passed his tunic and shorts. He set them within this, then moved over to the basin where a rivulet of water ran through. Above it was a polished rock surface: a mirror. The vanity of the distaff always required a mirror!

Seeing himself reflected was a shock: he was more bedraggled than his clothes. His hair was tangled and plastered over his forehead, and he had a beard just at the ugly starting stage. Cave-dirt was smeared over portions of his face and body, from his crawl through the wall. No wonder the nymph had been afraid of him at first!

He used the keen blade of his sword to shave his face, since there was no magic shaving brush here to brush his whiskers away conveniently. Then he rinsed and combed his hair. He found his clothing dry and clean and pressed: obviously more than hot air was at work. His torn sleeve had been neatly hemmed so that the absence of cloth looked intentional. He wondered if some magic dust circulated in these caves, augmenting the function of such things as dry cleaners. The nymph seemed to have many magical conveniences, and quite a comfortable life-style. It would not be hard to adapt to such a style—

He shook his head. That was the love potion speaking, not his common sense! He had to be on guard against rationalization. He did not belong down here, and he would have to leave when his mission was done, though he leave part of his heart behind.

Nevertheless, he dressed himself neatly, even giving his boots a turn at the cleaner. Too bad the Magician's bottle couldn't have washed ashore instead of his footwear!

When he emerged from the lavatory, Jewel looked him over with surprised admiration. "You are a handsome man!"

Chester smiled wryly. "I suppose it was hard to tell before. Would that I could wash my face and suffer a similar transformation!" They all laughed, somewhat ill at ease.

"We must pay for your hospitality—and for your help," Chester said when the laugh subsided fitfully.

"My hospitality I give freely; pay would demean it," Jewel said. "My help you seem to be co-opting. There is no pay for slave labor."

"No, Jewel!" Bink cried, cut to the heart of his emotion. "I would not force anything on you, or cause you grief!"

She softened. "I know it, Bink. You drank of the love-water; you would not hurt me. Yet since I must help you find your friends, so they can find the counterspell, and this takes me away from my work—"

"Then we must help you do your work!" Bink said.

"You can't. You don't know the first thing about sorting precious stones, or where they should be set. And if you did, the borer would not work for you."

"The borer?"

"My steed beast. He phases through the rock to reach where I must set the stones. I alone can control him—and then only when I sing. He works for a song, nothing else."

Bink exchanged glances with Chester. "After we eat, we will show you our music," Chester said.

Jewel's meal was strange but excellent. She served an assortment of mushrooms and fungus—things that grew magically, she explained, without the need of light. Some tasted like dragon steak, and some like potato chips chipped from a hot potato tree, and desert was very like chocolate pie fresh from the brown cow, so round and soft and pungent it practically flowed off the plate. She also had a kind of chalky powder she mixed with the water to produce excellent milk.

"You know," Chester murmured aside to Bink, "you could have found a worse nymph to encounter after your draught."

Bink didn't answer. After the magic drink, he would have loved a harpy; it wouldn't have mattered how foul she was. The love potion was absolutely heedless of its consequences. Magic without conscience. Indeed, as he had learned to his horror, the history of Xanth had been influenced by just such love springs.

The original, mundane species had intermated, producing crossbreeds like the chimerae, harpies, griffins—and centaurs. Who was to say this was wrong? Where would the Land of Xanth be now, without the noble centaurs? Yet Bink's own drink of this water was supremely inconvenient in a personal way. Rationally, he had to stay with his wife, Chameleon; but emotionally—

Chester finished his repast. He concentrated, and the silver flute appeared. It played rapturously. Jewel sat frozen, listening to the silvery melody. Then she began to sing in harmony with it. Her voice could not approach the purity of the flute, but it complemented the instrument nicely. Bink was entranced—and would have been, he told himself, regardless of the potion.

Something grotesque poked into the room. Chester's flute cut off in midnote, and his sword appeared in his hand.

"Stay your hand, centaur!" Jewel cried. "That is my borer!"

Chester did not attack, but his sword remained ready. "It looks like a giant worm!"

"Yes," she agreed. "He's related to the wiggles and squiggles, but he's much larger and slower. He's a diggle—not very bright, but invaluable for my work."

Chester decided it was all right. "I thought I had seen everything in the lexicon, but I missed this one. Let's see whether we can help you work. If he likes my music, and you have any stones to place near the river—"

"Are you kidding?" Jewel asked in her nymphly idiom. "With half the keg spilled, I have dozens of stones for the river. Might as well start there."

Under her direction, they boarded the diggle. Jewel bestrode the monster worm near its front end, a basket of precious stones held before her. Bink sat next, and Chester last, his four feet somewhat awkward in this situation. He was used to being ridden, not to riding, though he had done it before with the dragon.

"Now we make music," Jewel said. "He will work as long as he likes the sound, and he doesn't require much variation. After a few hours I get tired and have to stop, but if the centaur's flute—"

The flute appeared. It played. The great worm crawled forward, carrying them along as if they were mere flies. It did not scramble or flex, as the dragon did; it elongated and contracted its body in stages, so that the sections they rode were constantly changing in diameter. It was a strange mode of travel, but an effective one. This was a very large worm, and it traveled swiftly.

A flange flexed out from the diggle's front segment, and as he tunneled into the rock, the flange extended the diameter of the phase-tunnel so that the riders could fit through also. It occurred to Bink that this was a variant of the type of magic in the Good Magician's water-breathing pills. The rock, like the water, was not being tunneled through so much as it was being temporarily changed so that they could pass through it without making a hole. Chester had to duck his head to stay within the phase, and his flute was crowded, but it kept playing its captivating melodies. Bink was sure Chester was more than happy to have this pretext to practice his newly discovered talent, after a lifetime of suppression.

"I have to admit, this is a worthwhile service," the nymph said. "I always thought centaurs had no magic."

"The centaurs thought so too," Bink said, covertly admiring her form from behind. To hell with the love potion; she had a shape to conjure with.

Then the worm lurched, striking a different type of rock, and Bink was thrown forward against the nymph. "Uh, sorry," he said, righting himself, though indeed he was not very sorry. "I, uh—"

"Yes, I know," Jewel said. "Maybe you'd better put your arms about my waist, to steady yourself. It does get bumpy on occasion."

"I . . . think I'd better not," Bink said.

"You're sort of noble, in your fashion," she observed. "A girl could get to like you."

"I—I'm married," Bink said miserably. "I—I need that antidote."

"Yes, of course," she agreed.

Suddenly the diggle emerged through a wall into a large chamber. "The river," Chester observed. When he spoke, his flute ceased its playing. The worm turned, his snout questing for the vanished music.

"Don't stop!" Jewel cried. "He quits when—"

The flute resumed. "We want to follow the river down," Bink said. "If we see a bottle floating in it—"

"First, I have to place some stones," she said firmly. She guided the worm to a projecting formation, halted him, and held out a fat diamond. "Right inside there," she said. "It'll take a million years for the water to wash that into sight."

The diggle took the stone in his orifice and carried it into the rock. His head tapered into a virtual point, with a mouth smaller than a man's, so holding the jewel was no problem. When his snout emerged, the diamond was gone and the formation was whole. Bink was startled, then realized he shouldn't be; they had not left any tunnel behind them, either.

"One down," Jewel said briskly. "Nine hundred and ninety-nine to go."

But Bink's eyes were on the glowing river, looking for the bottle. Such was the power of the potion, he half-hoped he wouldn't find it. Once they found the magician, and then located the antidote, he would be out of love with Jewel—and that was difficult to contemplate. He knew what was right, but his heart wasn't in it.

Time passed. Jewel placed diamonds, opals, emeralds, sapphires, amethysts, jades, and many garnets in the rocks along the river, and sprinkled pearls in the water for the oysters to find. "Oysters just love pearls," she explained. "They just gobble them up." She sang as she worked, alternating with Chester's flute, while

Bink's attention roved from her to the water and back again. He could, indeed, have encountered a worse subject for the potion to fix on!

Then the river opened out into another lake. "This is the abode of the demons, who are able to drink and use the tainted water," Jewel cautioned them. "The demons know me, but the two of you will have to obtain a permit to pass through their territory. They don't like trespassers."

Bink felt Chester's motion behind him, as of hand touching bow and sword. They had had trouble with fiends; they didn't need trouble with demons!

The cavern walls became carved to resemble stone buildings, with squared-off corners and alleys between: very like a city. Bink had never actually seen a city, except in pictures; the early settlers of Xanth had made cities, but with the decline in population these had disappeared.

Bink and Chester dismounted and walked beside the worm, here on the street. Soon a magic wagon rolled up. It resembled a monster-drawn coach, but lacked the monster. The wheels were fat bouncy donuts of rubber, and the body seemed to be metal. A purring emanated from the interior. There was probably a little monster inside, pedaling the wheels.

"Where's the fire?" the demon demanded from the coach. He was blue, and the top of his head was round and flat like a saucer.

"Right here, Blue Steel," Jewel said, clapping one hand to her bosom. "Will you issue a ticket for my friends? They're looking for the source of magic."

"The source of magic!" another voice exclaimed. There were, Bink now saw, two demons in the vehicle; the second was of coppery hue. "That's a matter for the Chief!"

"All right, Copper," Jewel agreed. She evidently knew these demons well enough to banter with them. Bink suffered a sharp green pang of jealousy.

Jewel guided them to a building marked PRECINCT STATION and parked the worm. "I must remain with the diggle to sing him a song," she said. "You go in and see the Chief; I will wait."

Now Bink was afraid she would not wait, that she would take this opportunity to leave them, to betray them to the demons. That way she would be safe from pursuit, either vengeful or romantic. But he had to trust her. After all, he loved her.

The demon inside sat at a broad desk, poring over a book. He glanced up as they entered. "Ah, yes—we were fated to meet again," he said.

"Beauregard!" Bink exclaimed, amazed.

"I'll issue the permits, of course," the demon said. "You were the specific instrument of my release, according to the rules of the game, and I feel an undemonly obligation. But allow me to entertain you properly, as you entertained me at the ogre's domicile. There is much you must be advised of before you pursue your quest further."

"Uh, there's a nymph waiting outside—" Bink said.

Beauregard shook his head. "You do seem to be jinxed, Bink. First you lose the bottle, then your heart. But never fear; we'll include the nymph in the party. We shall entertain the diggle at our motor pool; he will enjoy the swim. We know Jewel well; in fact, you could hardly have been more fortunate in your misfortune."

In due course Jewel joined them for supper. It was hard to believe that dawn had been at the fringe of the Region of Madness, in a tree, and breakfast had been at the lake castle of the fiends, lunch with the nymph, and supper here— all in the same day. Down here under the ground day had less meaning; still, it had been an eventful period.

The demon's meal was similar to the nymph's, only it was fashioned from minute magic creatures called yeast and bacteria. Bink wondered whether there were front-teria too, but didn't ask. Some of the food was like squash, which had been squashed only minutes before; some resembled roast haunch of medium-long pig. Dessert was the frozen eye of a scream bird. Genuine eye scream was a rare delicacy, and so was this yellow flavored imitation.

"I sampled the eye of a smilk once," Chester said. "But it was not as good as this."

"You have good taste," Beauregard said.

"Oh, no! Centaur eyes have inferior flavor," Chester said quickly.

"You are too modest." But the demon smiled reassuringly. "Screams have more fat than smilks, so their eyes provide more flavor, as you recognized."

After the repast they retired to Beauregard's den, where a tame firedrake blazed merrily. "Now we shall provide you excellent accommodations for the night," the demon said. "We shall not interfere in any way with your quest. However—"

"What is it you know, that we don't?" Bink asked anxiously.

"I know the nature of demons," Beauregard said.

"Oh, we don't plan to bother you here! We're going on to—"

"Bear with me, Bink." Beauregard brought out a fancy little bottle, uttered an obscure word, and made a mystic gesture. The cork popped out, vapor issued forth, and formed into—Good Magician Humfrey.

Amazed, Bink could only ask: "But where is Crombie?"

"Back in the bottle," Humfrey said shortly. "It would help if you recovered your fumble promptly."

"But if Beauregard can rescue you—"

"I have not rescued him," the demon said. "I have conjured him. He must now do my bidding."

"Just as you once did *his* bidding!" Bink said.

"Correct. It all depends on who is confined, and who possesses the controlling magic. The Magician has dabbled in demonology; he is now subject to our humanology."

"But does that mean—"

"No, I shall not abuse the situation. My interest is in research, not ironies. I merely make this demonstration to convince you that there is more to magic than you may have supposed, and that the possible consequences of your quest may be more extensive than you would care to risk."

"I already know something is trying to stop me," Bink said.

"Yes. It is some kind of demon—and that is the problem. Most demons have no more magic than most humans do, but the demons of the depths are something else. They are to ordinary demons like me as Magicians are to ordinary people like you. It is not wise to venture into their demesnes."

"You're a demon," Chester said suspiciously. "Why are you telling us this?"

"Because he's a good demon," Jewel said. "He helps people."

"Because I care about the welfare of Xanth," Beauregard said. "If I were convinced Xanth would be better off without people, I would work toward that end. But though I have had doubt on occasion, so far I believe the species of man is a net benefit." He looked at the Magician. "Even gnomes like him."

Humfrey merely stood there. "Why don't you set him free, then?" Bink asked, not wholly trusting the demon.

"I can not free him. Only the holder of his container can do that."

"But here he is! You summoned him from your bottle!"

"My magic has granted me a temporary lease on his service. I can only evoke him briefly, and can not keep him. If I had *his* bottle, then I could control him, since he was so foolish as to confine himself in that manner. That is why you must recover that bottle, before—"

"Before it breaks!" Bink said.

"It will never break. It is an enchanted bottle; I know, for I occupied it, and made sure it was secure. No, the danger is that your enemy will recover it first."

Bink was appalled. "The enemy!"

"For then that enemy would control the Magician and all Humfrey's power would be at the enemy's service. In that event, Humfrey's chances of surviving would be poor—almost as poor as yours."

"I must get that bottle!" Bink cried. "If only I knew where it is!"

"That is the service I require," Beauregard said. "Magician, inform Bink of your precise location, so he can rescue you."

"Latitude twenty-eight degrees northwest, longitude one hundred and—"

"Not that way, simpleton!" Beauregard interrupted. "Tell it so he can use it!"

"Er, yes," Humfrey agreed. "Perhaps we'd better put Crombie on."

"Do it," the demon snapped.

The griffin appeared beside the Magician. "Say, yes," Bink said eagerly. "If we have him point out your direction from here, I mean our direction from there, we can reverse it to reach you."

"Won't work," Beauregard said. But Crombie was already whirling. His wing came to rest pointing directly at Bink.

"Fine," Bink said. "We'll go that way."

"Try walking across the den," Beauregard said. "Griffin, hold that point."

Perplexed, Bink walked. Crombie didn't move, but his pointing wing continued aiming at Bink. "It's just a picture!" Bink explained. "No matter how you look at it, it looks right at you."

"Precisely," the demon agreed. "This conjuration is in a certain respect an image. The same aspect appears regardless of the orientation of the viewer. To orient on the conjuration is useless; it is the original we require."

"Easily solved, demon," Humfrey snapped. "Crombie, point out the direction of our bottle as viewed from the locale of the conjuration."

How simple! The conjuration was *here*, so this would give the proper direction to *there*. But would it work?

The griffin whirled and pointed again. This time the wing aimed away from Bink, and downward.

"That is the way you must go," Beauregard said gravely. "Now before I banish the image, have you any other questions?"

"I do," Chester said. "About my talent—"

Beauregard smiled. "Very clever, centaur. I think you have the mind of a demon! It is indeed possible, in this situation, for you to obtain the information you seek without incurring the Magician's normal fee, if your ethics permit such exploitation."

"No," Chester said. "I'm not trying to cheat! Magician, I know my talent now. But I've already served part of the fee, and am stuck for the rest."

Humfrey smiled. "I never specified the Question I would Answer. Pick another Question for the fee. That was part of the agreement."

"Say, good," Chester said, like a colt with sudden access to the farthest and greenest pasture. He pondered briefly. "Cherie—I'd sure like to know *her* talent, if she has one. A magical one, I mean. Her and her less-magical-than-thou attitude—"

"She has a talent," Humfrey said. "Do you wish the Answer now?"

"No. I might figure it out myself, again."

The Magician spread his hands. "As you prefer. However, we are not insured against accidents of fate. If you don't solve it, and Bink doesn't find my bottle before the enemy does, I may be forced to renege. Do you care to take that risk?"

"What do you mean, before the enemy does?" Bink demanded. "How close is the enemy to—"

"That is what we were discussing before," Beauregard said. "It seems the

Magician can not be protected from his own information-talent. He is correct: that bottle has been carried very close to the region your enemy inhabits, and it is very likely that the enemy is aware of that. Thus this is not a routine search for a bottle, but a race against active opposition."

"But what is the nature of the enemy?" Bink demanded.

"Begone, Magician," Beauregard said. Humfrey and Crombie converted into smoke and swirled into the bottle. "I can not answer that Question directly, other than to remind you that the enemy must be some sort of demon. Therefore I spare myself the embarrassment of confessing my ignorance in the presence of my human counterpart in research. Professional rivalry, you might say."

"I don't care about professional rivalry!" Bink retorted. "The Good Magician and Crombie are my friends. I've got to save them!"

"You're loyal," Jewel said admiringly.

"The thing you must understand," Beauregard continued, "is that as you approach the source of magic, the magic of the immediate environment becomes stronger, in a function resembling a logarithmic progression. Therefore—"

"I don't understand that," Bink said. "What have logs to do with it? Is the enemy a tree?"

"He means the magic gets stronger faster as you get closer," Chester explained. Centaurs had excellent mathematical comprehension.

"Precisely," the demon agreed. "Thus we demons, being more proximate to the source, tend to be more magical than you creatures at the fringe. But in the immediate vicinity of the source, the magic is far stronger than we can fathom. Therefore I can not identify your specific enemy or describe his magic—but it is likely that it is stronger magic than you have encountered before."

"I've met pretty strong magic," Bink said dubiously.

"Yes, I know. And you have extremely strong magic yourself. But this—well, though I have never been able to fathom the precise nature of your talent, therefore my prior remark about you being an ordinary individual, empirical data suggest that it relates to your personal welfare. But at the source—"

"Suddenly I understand," Bink said. "Where I'm going, the magic is stronger than mine."

"Just so. Thus you will be vulnerable in a manner you have not been before. Your own magic suffers enhancement as you proceed, but only in a geometric ratio. Therefore it can not—"

"He means the enemy magic gets stronger faster than our magic," Chester said. "So we're losing power proportionately."

"Precisely," the demon agreed. "The nature of the curves suggests that the differential will not become gross until you are extremely close to the source, so you may not be much inconvenienced by it, or even aware of it. Still—"

"So if I continue," Bink said slowly, "I'll come up against an enemy who is stronger than I am."

"Correct. Because the strength of the magic field of Xanth varies inversely with distance, on both an individual and environmental basis—"

"What about the magic dust?" Chester demanded.

"That does indeed enhance magic in its vicinity," Beauregard agreed. "But it is not the major avenue for the distribution of magic. The dust is basically convective, while most magic is conductive. Were that village to close down its operations, the magic of Xanth would continue on slightly abated."

"So they might as well relax," Bink said.

"To continue: because of the inverse ratio, the enemy was not able to harm you on the surface, though he tried with demonic persistence and cunning. (I distinguish between the terms 'demonic' and 'demoniac'; the latter has a pejorative connotation that is unwarranted.) Which is why I am convinced it is in fact a demon you face. But here in the nether region, the enemy can and will bring to bear overwhelming magic. Therefore it is foolish to pursue your quest further."

"I'm human," Bink said.

"Yes, unfortunately. A demon would be more rational. Since you *are* a foolish human of exactly the type my research paper describes, you will continue inevitably to your doom—for the sake of your ideals and friendships."

"I must be more human than demon," Jewel said. "I think he's noble."

"Don't flatter me," Bink warned her. "It only exaggerates the effect of the potion."

She looked startled, then prettily resolute. "I'm sorry the potion had to—I mean, you're such a nice, handsome, courageous, decent man, I—I can't say I'm sorry it happened. When we get back maybe I *will* take a drink myself."

"But one reason I need the Magician is to find the antidote," Bink pointed out. "Apart from my friendship for him, I mean. In fact, we should have asked Crombie to point out the locale of the antidote, so—"

"I could summon them again," Beauregard said. "But I would not advise it."

"Why not?" Bink asked.

"Because in the event the enemy is not yet aware of the precise location of their bottle, we do not wish to call further attention to it. We do not know what mechanisms the enemy has to observe you, now that its squiggle is gone, but we can not afford to assume they are negligible. It would be better to rescue your friends first, then attend to your more personal business."

"Yes, that is true," Bink said. He turned to the nymph. "Jewel, I regret having to inconvenience you further, but my loyalty to my friends comes first. I promise, as soon as we rescue them—"

"That's all right," she said, seeming not at all displeased.

"She could wait here," Chester said. "Or go about her normal business. Once we obtain the antidote, we can bring it back and—"

"No, only the diggle can take you there fast enough," Jewel said. "And only I can guide the diggle. There's lots of bad magic in the river channel, and very little in the solid rock. I'm coming along."

"I hoped you would say that," Bink said. "Of course my feeling doesn't count, since—"

Jewel stepped up and kissed him on the mouth. "I like your honesty, too," she said. "Let's get going."

Bink, momentarily stunned by the potency of his first voluntary kiss, forced his mind to focus on the mission. "Yes—we must hurry."

"The goblins are very bad in the deeper reaches," Beauregard said. "In recent years they have lost their savagery on the surface, but below they retain it. You have not encountered goblins like these."

"It is not a matter of choice," Bink said. "We have to go there."

"Then stay on well-lighted routes, when you're not phasing through actual rock. Like nickelpedes, they don't like light. They will face it if they have to, but generally they avoid it."

Bink turned to the nymph. "Is that why you're afraid of the dark? Can you keep us in the light?"

She nodded. "Yes . . . yes," she agreed to each question. Bink somehow had the impression that he could have asked somewhat more personal questions and had the same response. Or was that a flight of romantic fancy spawned by the potion?

"At least get a good night's rest," Beauregard urged. "We demons don't need sleep, as such, but you humans can get very irritable if—"

"No, we'd better move right along," Bink said. "A few hours could make the difference."

"So could fatigue," Beauregard pointed out. "You will need all your faculties about you, when you face the big magic."

"Seems to me one demon's stalling," Chester said.

Beauregard spread his hands. "Perhaps I am, centaur. There is one thing I have not told you."

"If you plan to tell it, tell it now," Bink said. "Because we're leaving now."

"It is this," the demon said reluctantly. "I am not at all certain that your quest is proper."

"Not proper!" Bink exploded. "To rescue my friend?"

"To seek the source of the magic of Xanth."

"All I want is information! You, of all demons, should understand that!"

"Too well," Beauregard said. "Information can be the most dangerous thing there is. Consider the power of your Magician, who specializes in information.

Suppose he were armed with full knowledge about the ultimate power of magic? Where would be the limits of his power then?"

"Humfrey wouldn't hurt Xanth," Bink protested. "He's a *good* Magician!"

"But once knowledge of the nature of the source of magic were known, what would stop an evil Magician from obtaining it? With the strongest magic of all, he could rule Xanth—or destroy it."

Bink considered. He remembered how an Evil Magician *had* taken over the crown of Xanth—and had turned out not to be evil at all. But that had been a special situation. Suppose a truly evil man—or woman—obtained unconscionable power? "I see your point. I'll think about it. Maybe I won't go all the way to the source. But I must rescue the Magician, regardless."

"Yes of course," Beauregard agreed, seeming ill at ease for a demon.

They boarded the diggle and moved out, following the direction Crombie had indicated. "I don't know the deeper depths so well," Jewel said. "But there's a whole lot of solid rock here, since we're not following so close to the river. I'll tell the diggle to stay within the rock until we get there, and only to come out where there is light. I think you could sleep some while we travel, while I sing the worm along."

"You are beautiful," Bink said gratefully. He leaned his head against her back and was lulled to sleep by her singing, amplified and sweetened by his contact with her. And the worm ground on.

Chapter 11

Brain Coral

ink woke with a start as the diggle halted. "I think we're here," Jewel murmured. Her voice was hoarse from hours of singing.

"You should have waked me before!" Bink said. "To take my turn singing the worm along. You've sung yourself out."

"Your head was so nice on my shoulder, I couldn't disturb you," she rasped. "Besides, you'll need all your strength. I can feel the magic intensifying as we move along."

Bink felt it too: a subtle prickle on his skin like that of the magic dust. For all he knew, the rock through which they traveled might be the magic-dust rock, before it welled to the surface. But the mystery remained: what was it that imbued the rock with magic? "Uh, thanks," he said awkwardly. "You're a sweet nymph."

"Well—" She turned her head, making it easy to kiss. She smelled of especially fine roses: this magic, too, was enhanced by the environment. Bink leaned forward, inhaling the delicious fragrance, bringing his lips close to—

They were interrupted by the sight of the bottle. It bobbled on the glowing surface of another lake. Something was attached to it, a bit of string or tar—

"Grundy!" Bink cried.

The golem looked up. "About time you got here! Fetch in this bottle, before—"

"Is it safe to swim in this lake?" Bink asked, wary of the glow. It might keep the goblins away, but that didn't make it safe for people.

"No," Jewel said. "The water is slowly poisonous to most forms of life. One drink won't hurt much, if you get out of it soon, up at the headwaters where it is diluted by the fresh flow from the surface. But down here, where it has absorbed much more horrible magic—"

"Right. No swimming," Bink said. "Chester, can you lasso it?"

"Out of range," the centaur said. "If the eddy currents carry it closer to the shore I can snag it readily enough."

"Better hurry," Grundy called. "There's something under the lake, and it—"

"The fiends live under a lake," Chester said. "Do you think the enemy—?"

Bink started stripping off his clothing. "I think I'd better swim out and get that bottle right now. If the lake harms me, the Magician can give me a drop of his healing elixir. That should be more potent, too, here."

"Don't do that!" Jewel cried. "That lake—I don't think you'd ever reach the bottle. Here, I'll have the diggle phase through the water. Nothing hurts him when he's in phase."

At her direction, and hoarse singing, the worm slid into the water, erecting its circular flange to form a temporary tunnel through the liquid, as through rock. He moved very slowly, until Chester's flute appeared and played a brisk, beautiful marching tune. The flute seemed larger and brighter than it had before, and its sound was louder: more magical enchantment. The diggle speeded up, expanding and contracting in time to the music. He advanced purposefully toward the bottle. "Oh, thank you, centaur," Jewel whispered.

"Hurry! Hurry!" the golem called. "The coral is aware of the—is trying to—is —HELP! IT'S COMING UP TO GET ME!"

Then Grundy screamed horribly, as if in human pain. "I'm not real enough, yet," he gasped after the scream had torn its way out of his system. "I'm still just a golem, just a thing, string and gum. I can be controlled. I—"

He broke off, then screamed again, then resumed more quietly. "I'm gone."

Bink understood none of this, yet had the sinking feeling that he should somehow have tried to help the golem to fight off—what? Some encouragement, some reminder of the feelings Grundy evidently did have. Maybe the golem could have fought off his private personal horror, if—

Now the worm was almost at the bottle. Quickly Grundy wrapped his string-arms about the cork, braced his feet against the neck of the bottle, and heaved. "By the power of the brain coral, emerge!" he gasped.

The cork flew out. Smoke poured from the bottle, swirled into a whirlwind, ballooned, then coalesced into the figures of the Good Magician and the griffin. "Grundy rescued them!" Chester exclaimed as his flute faded out.

"Fly to shore!" Bink cried. "Don't touch the water!"

Humfrey caught hold of Crombie, who spread his wings and bore them both up. For a moment they tilted unsteadily, then righted and moved smoothly forward.

Bink ran up as they landed at the shore. "We were so worried about you, afraid the enemy would get you first!"

"The enemy did," Humfrey said, reaching for a vial as he let go of the griffin. "Turn about, Bink; desist your quest, and you will not be harmed."

"Desist my quest!" Bink cried, amazed. "Right when I'm so close to accomplishing it? You know I won't do that!"

"I serve a new master, but my scruples remain," Humfrey said. There was something sinister about him now; he remained a small, gnomish man, but now there was no humor in that characterization. His gaze was more like that of a basilisk than that of a man: a cold, deadly stare. "It is necessary that you understand. The bottle was opened by the agency of the entity that lies beneath this lake, a creature of tremendous intelligence and magic and conscience, but lacking the ability to move. This is the brain coral, who has to operate through other agencies to accomplish its noble purpose."

"The—enemy?" Bink asked, dismayed. "The one who sent the magic sword, and the dragon, and the squiggle—"

"And countless other obstructions, most of which your own magic foiled before they manifested. The coral can not control a conscious, intelligent, living entity; it must operate through thought suggestions that seem like the creature's own notions. That was why the dragon chased you, and the squiggle spied on you, and why the other seemingly coincidental complications occurred. But your talent brought you through almost unscathed. The siren lured you, but the gorgon did not enchant you into stone; the midas fly was diverted to another target, the curse of the fiends missed you. Now, at the heart of the coral's magic, you are finally balked. You must turn back, because—"

"But it can not control *you!*" Bink protested. "You are a man, an intelligent man, a Magician!"

"It assumed control of the golem, possible only because Grundy's reality was not complete and this is the region of the coral's greatest power. It caused the golem to open the bottle. Crombie and I are subject to the holder of the bottle. It does not matter that the bottle is now floating on the surface of the coral lake; the conjuration was done in the name of the brain coral, and it is binding."

"But—" Bink protested, unable to continue because he could not formulate his thought.

"That was the most savage engagement of this campaign," Humfrey continued. "The struggle for possession of the bottle. The coral managed to dislodge it from your clothing, but your magic caused the cork to work loose, and we started to emerge. That was the impact of the fiends' curse, aiding you by what seemed like an incredible coincidence. It shook the bottle within the vortex. But the coral used a strong eddy current to jam the stopper back, trapping Grundy outside. But your magic made the magic mirror get caught halfway, shattering it, with fragments inside and out, enabling us to establish communication of a sort. Then the coral's magic caused you to lose your fragment of glass. But your magic guided you to Beauregard, who re-established communication. You very nearly reached the bottle in time, by turning the liability of your infatuation for the nymph into an asset—your talent outmaneuvered the coral neatly there!—but here the coral's magic is stronger than yours, and so it got the bottle first. Barely. In effect, your two talents have canceled out. But now the coral, through the power of the bottle, controls Crombie and me. All our powers are at its service, and you have lost."

Chester stood beside Bink. "So you have become the enemy," he said slowly.

"Not really. Now that we have access to the coral's perspective, we know that it is on the side of reason. Bink, your quest is dangerous, not merely for you, but for all the land of Xanth. You *must* desist, believe me!"

"I do not believe you," Bink said grimly. "Not now. Not now that you've changed sides."

"Same here," Chester said. "Conjure yourself back into the bottle, and let us rescue the bottle and release you in our power. Then if you can repeat that statement, I'll listen."

"No."

"That is what I thought," Chester said. "I undertook this mission as a service to you, Magician, but I have never collected my Answer from you. I can quit your service anytime I want. But I shall not renounce this quest merely because some hidden monster has scared you into changing your mind."

"Your position is comprehensible," Humfrey said with surprising mildness. "I do not, as you point out, have any present call on your service. But I am obliged to advise you both that if we can not prevail upon your reason, we must oppose you materially."

"You mean you would actually fight us?" Bink asked incredulously.

"We do not wish to resort to force," Humfrey said. "But it is imperative that you desist. Go now, give up your quest, and all will be well."

"And if we don't quit?" Chester demanded, belligerently, eyeing Crombie. Obviously the centaur would not be entirely loath to match his prowess against that of the griffin. There had been a kind of rivalry between them all along.

"In that case we should have to nullify you," Humfrey said gravely. Small he was, but he remained a Magician, and his statement sent an ugly chill through Bink. Nobody could afford to take lightly the threat of a Magician.

Bink was torn between unkind alternatives. How could he fight his friends, the very ones he had struggled so hard to rescue? Yet if they were under the spell of the enemy, how could he afford to yield to their demand? If only he could get at the brain coral, the enemy, and destroy it, then his friends would be freed from its baleful influence. But the coral was deep under the poison water, unreachable. Unless—"

"Jewel!" he cried. "Send the diggle down to make holes through the coral!"

"I can't Bink," she said sadly. "The diggle never came back after we sent it after the bottle. I'm stuck here with my bucket of gems." She flipped a diamond angrily into the water. "I can't even plant them properly, now."

"The worm has been sent away," Humfrey said. "Only the completion of your quest can destroy the coral—along with all the Land of Xanth. Depart now, or suffer the consequence."

Bink glanced at Chester. "I don't want to hurt him. Maybe if I can knock him out, get him out of range of the coral—"

"While I take care of birdbeak," Chester said, nominally regretful.

"I don't want bloodshed!" Bink cried. "These are our friends, whom we must rescue."

"I suppose so," Chester agreed reluctantly. "I'll try to immobilize the griffin without hurting him too much. Maybe I'll just pull out a few of his feathers."

Bink realized that this was as much of a compromise as Chester was prepared to make. "Very well. But stop the moment he yields."

Now he faced Humfrey again. "I intend to pursue my quest. I ask you to depart, and to refrain from trying to interfere. It grieves me even to contemplate strife between us, but—"

Humfrey rummaged in his belt of vials. He brought one out. "Huh-*uh!*" Bink cried, striding across. Yet his horror at practicing any kind of violence against his friends held him back, and he got there too late. The cork came out and the vapor issued. It formed into . . . . a green poncho, which flapped about in the air before settling to the floor.

"Wrong bottle," the Magician muttered, and uncorked another.

Bink, momentarily frozen, realized that he could not subdue the Magician until he separated the man from his arsenal of vials. Bink's talent might have helped Humfrey to confuse the bottles, but that sort of error could not be counted on after the first time. Bink drew his sword, intending to slice the belt from the Good Magician's waist—but realized that this seemed like a murderous attack. Again he hesitated—and was brought up short by the coalescing vapor. Suddenly thirteen black cats faced him, spitting viciously.

Bink had never seen a pure cat before, in the flesh. He regarded the cat as an extinct species. He just stood there and stared at this abrupt de-extinction, unable to formulate a durable opinion. If he killed these animals, would he be re-extincting the species?

Meanwhile, the centaur joined the battle with the griffin. The encounter was savage from the outset, despite Chester's promises. His bow was in his hands, and an arrow sizzled through the air. But Crombie, an experienced soldier, did not wait for it to arrive. He leaped and spread his wings, then closed them with a great backblast of air. He shot upward at an angle, the arrow passing beneath his tail feathers. Then he banked near the cavern ceiling and plummeted toward the centaur, screaming, claws outstretched.

Chester's bow was instantly replaced by his rope. He swung up a loop that closed about the griffin's torso, drawing the wings closed. He jerked, and Crombie was swung about in a quarter-circle. The centaur was about three times as massive as his opponent, so was able to control him this way.

A black cat leaped at Bink's face, forcing him to pay attention to his own battle. Reflexively he brought his sword around—and sliced the animal cleanly in half.

Bink froze again in horror. He had not meant to kill it! A rare creature like this—maybe these cats were all that remained in the whole Land of Xanth, being preserved only by the Magician's magic.

Then two things changed his attitude. First, the severed halves of the cat he had struck did not die; they metamorphosed into smaller cats. This was not a real cat, but a pseudo-cat, shaped from life-clay and given a feline imperative. Any part of it became another cat. Had a dog been shaped from the same material, it would have fractured into more dogs. So Bink hardly needed to worry about preservation of that species. Second, another cat was biting him on the ankle.

In a sudden fury of relief and ire, Bink laid about him with his blade. He sliced cats in halves, quarters, and eighths—and every segment became a smaller feline, attacking him with renewed ferocity. This was like fighting the hydra—only this time he had no spell-reversal wood to feed it, and there was no thread to make it drop. Soon he had a hundred tiny cats pouncing on him like rats, and then a thousand attacking like nickelpedes. The more he fought, the worse it got.

Was this magic related to that of the hydra? That monster had been typified by seven, while the cats were thirteen, but each doubled with each strike against a member. If there were some key, some counterspell to abolish doubling magic—

"Get smart, Bink!" Chester called, stomping on several cats that had wandered into his territory. "Sweep them all into the drink."

Of course! Bink stooped low and swung the flat of his sword sidewise, sweeping dozens of thumbnail sized cats into the lake. They hissed as they splashed, like so many hot pebbles, and then thrashed to the bottom. Whether they were drowning or being poisoned he could not tell, but none emerged.

While he swept his way to victory, Bink absorbed the continuing centaur-griffin engagement. He could not observe everything, but was able to bridge the gaps well enough. He had to keep track, because if anything happened to Chester, Bink would have another enemy to face.

Crombie, initially incapacitated by the rope, bent his head down and sheared his bond cleanly with one crunch of his sharp beak. He spread his wings explosively, made a defiant squawk, and launched a three-point charge at Chester's head: beak, claw, and talon.

The centaur, thrown off balance by the abrupt slackening of the rope, staggered. He had better stability than a man, but he had been hauling hard. His equine shoulder thudded against a stalagmite and broke it off as the griffin made contact. Bink winced—but as it turned out, the stalagmite was more of a problem to Crombie than to Chester. The pointed top fell across the griffin's left wing, weighing it down, forcing Crombie to flap his other wing vigorously to right himself.

Chester rose up, one talon slash down the side of his face where the griffin's strike had missed his eye. But his two great hands now grasped the griffin's two front legs. "Got you now, birdie!" he cried. But in this position he could not use his sword, so he tried to bash the griffin against the broken base of the stalagmite.

Crombie squawked and brought his hind legs up for a double slash that would have disemboweled the centaur's human portion had it scored. Chester hastily let go, throwing Crombie violently away from him. Then he grabbed for his bow and arrow again. The griffin, however, spread his wings to brake his flight, looped about, and closed in again before the arrow could be brought to bear. Now it was hand-to-claw.

Bink had cleared his area of little cats—but the Good Magician had had time to organize his vials and open the next. This coalesced into a mound of bright-red cherry bombs. Oh, no! Bink had experience with these violent little fruits before, as there was a tree of them on the palace grounds. In fact, these were probably from that same tree. If any of them scored on him—

He dived for Humfrey, catching the Magician's arm before he could throw.

Humfrey struggled desperately against Bink's superior strength. Bink still held back, hating this violence though he saw no alternative to it. Both of them fell to the floor. The Magician's belt tore loose, and a collection of vials tumbled across the stone. Some of their corks popped out. The cherry bombs were dislodged; they rolled away and dunked into the lake, where they detonated with harmless thuds and clouds of steam. One rolled into Jewel's bucket of gems.

The explosion sent precious stones flying all over the cavern. Diamonds shot by Bink's ears; a huge pearl thunked into the Magician's chest; opals got under Chester's hooves. "Oh, no!" Jewel cried, horrified. "That's not the way it's supposed to be done. Each has to be planted in exactly the right place!"

Bink was sorry about the gems, but he had more pressing problems. The new bottles were spewing forth a bewildering variety of things.

The first was a pair of winged shoes. "So that's where I left them!" Humfrey exclaimed. But they flew out of reach before he could grab them. The second vial loosed a giant hour-glass whose hands were running out—also harmless in this instance. The next was a collection of exotic-looking seeds, some like huge flat fish eyes, others like salt-and-pepper mix, others like one-winged flies. They fluttered out and littered a wide patch, crunching underfoot, rolling like marbles, squishing and adhering like burrs. But they did not seem to be any direct threat.

Unfortunately, the other vials were also pouring out vapors. These produced a bucket of garbage (so that was how the Magician cleaned his castle: he swept it all into a vial!), a bag of supergrow fertilizer, a miniature thunderstorm, and a small nova star. Now the seeds had food, water, and light. Suddenly they were sprouting. Tendrils poked out, bodies swelled, pods popped, leaves burst forth. Roots gripped the rock and clasped items of garbage; stems shot up to form a dense and variegated carpet. Diverse species fought their own miniature battles over the best fertilizer territory. In moments Bink and the Magician were surrounded by an expanding little jungle. Vines clung to feet, branches poked at bodies, and leaves obscured vision.

Soon the plants were flowering. Now their species were identifiable. Lady slippers produced footwear of a most delicate nature, causing Jewel to exclaim in delight and snatch off a pair for herself. Knotweeds formed the most intricate specialized knots: bow, granny, lanyard, clinch, hangman, and half-hitch. Bink had to step quickly to avoid getting tied up. That would cost him the victory right there!

Meanwhile, the Magician was trying to avoid the snapping jaws of the dog-tooth violets and dandelions, while a hawkweed made little swoops at his head. Bink would have laughed—but had too many problems of his own. A goldenrod was trying to impale him on its metallic spire, and a sunflower was blinding him with its effulgence. The nova star was no longer needed; the cave was now as bright as day, and would remain so until the sunflower went to seed.

Bink ducked just in time to avoid a flight of glinting arrowheads—but his foot slipped on a buttercup, squirting butter out and making him sit down hard—ooomph—on the squishy head of a skunk cabbage. Suddenly he was steamed in the nauseating fragrance.

Well, what had he expected? He had very little protective talent now; the enemy brain coral had canceled out his magic. Bink was on his own, and had to make his own breaks. At least Humfrey was no better off; at the moment he was being given a hotfoot by a patch of fireweed. He snatched up a flower from a water lily and poured its water out to douse the fire. Meanwhile, several paintbrushes were decorating him with stripes of red, green, and blue. Stray diamonds from the nymph's collection were sticking to his clothes.

This was getting nowhere! Bink tore his way out of the miniature jungle, holding his breath and closing his eyes as a parcel of poppies popped loudly about his head. He felt something enclosing his hands, and had to look: it was a pair of foxgloves. A bluebell rang in his ear; then he was out of it. And there was the Magician's belt with the remaining vials. Suddenly he realized: if he controlled this, Humfrey would be helpless. All his magic was contained in these vials!

Bink stepped toward it—but at that moment the Magician emerged from the foliage, plastered with crowfeet. Humfrey brushed them off, and the feet scampered away. A lone primrose turned its flower away from this gaucherie. Humfrey dived for his magic belt, arriving just as Bink did.

Bink laid his hands on it. There was a tug-of-war. More vials spilled out. One puffed into a kettle of barley soup that spilled across the floor and was eagerly lapped up by the questing rootlets of the jungle. Another developed into a package of mixed nuts and bolts. Then Bink found a steaming rice pudding and heaved it at the Magician—but Humfrey scored first with a big mince pie. Minces flew out explosively, twenty-four of them, littering a yet wider area. Bink caught the brunt of it in his face. Minces were wriggling in his hair and down his neck and partially obscuring his vision. Bink fanned the air with his sword, trying to keep the magician back while he cleared his vision. Oddly, he could perceive the neighboring battle of centaur and griffin better than his own, at this moment.

Chester's human torso was now streaked with blood from the vicious raking of the griffin's talons. But one of Crombie's forelegs was broken, and one of his wings half-stripped of feathers. That hand-to-claw combat had been savage!

Now the centaur was stalking his opponent with sword in hand, and the griffin was flying in ragged circles just out of reach, seeking an opening. Despite

Bink's caution, these two were deadly serious; they were out to kill each other. Yet how could Bink stop them?

The Magician found a vial and opened it. Bink advanced alertly—but it was another miscue. A huge bowl of yogurt manifested. It had, by the look and smell of it, been in the bottle too long; it had spoiled. It floated gently toward the lake: let the brain coral try a taste of *that!* But Humfrey already had another vial. These mistakes were not the result of Bink's talent so much as sheer, honest chance; Humfrey seemed to have a hundred things in his vials (he was reputed to have a hundred spells, after all), and few were readily adaptable to combat, and now they were all mixed up. The odds were against anything really dangerous appearing from any randomly chosen vial.

Yet the odds could be beaten. The vial produced a writhing vine from a kraken, which undulated aggressively toward Bink. But he sliced it into fragments with his sword, and advanced on the Magician again. Bink knew he could control the situation now; nothing in Humfrey's bottles could match the devastating presence of a capable sword.

Desperately Humfrey opened bottles, searching for something to further his cause. Three dancing fairies materialized, hovering on translucent, pastel-hued wings, but they were harmless and soon drifted over to consult with Jewel, who put them to work picking up stray gems. A package of cough drops formed and burst—but too close to the Magician, who went into paroxysms of coughing. But then a wyvern appeared.

Wyverns were basically small dragons—but even the tiniest of dragons were dangerous. Bink leaped at it, aiming for the monster's neck. He scored—but the wyvern's tough scales deflected the blade. It opened its mouth and fired a jet of hot steam at Bink's face. Bink danced back—then abruptly rammed his point directly into the cloud of vapor with all his force. The sword plunged into the creature's open mouth, through its palate, and out the top of its head. The wyvern gave a single cry of agony and expired as Bink yanked back his weapon.

Bink knew he had been lucky—and that this was genuine luck, not his talent at work. But the problem with such luck was that it played no favorites; the next break could go against him. He had to wrap this up before such a break occurred.

But the Magician had had time to rummage among more vials. He was looking for something, having trouble locating it amid the jumble. But each failure left him fewer vials to choose from, and a correspondingly greater chance of success. As Bink turned on him again, a set of long winter underwear formed, and several tattered comic books, and a wooden stepladder, a stink bomb, and a gross of magic writing quills. Bink had to laugh.

"Bink—watch out!" Chester cried.

"It's only a lady's evening gown," Bink said, glancing at the next offering. "No harm in it."

"Behind it is an evil eye!" Chester cried.

Trouble! *That* was what Humfrey had been searching for! Bink grabbed the gown, using it as a shield against the nemesis beyond.

A beam of light shot out, passing him—and scored on the centaur. Half-stunned, Chester reeled—and the griffin dived in for the kill. His beak stabbed at Chester's blinded eyes, forcing the centaur to prance backward.

"No!" Bink screamed.

Again, too late. Bink realized that he must have leaned on his talent a long time ago, so that his reactions to chance happenings were slow. Chester's rear hooves stepped off the ledge. The centaur gave a great neighing cry of dismay and tumbled rear first into the evil water of the lake.

The water closed murkily over Chester's head. Without further sound or struggle, the centaur disappeared below. Bink's friend and ally was gone.

There was no time for remorse. Humfrey had found another vial. "I have you now, Bink! This one contains sleeping potion!" he cried, holding it up.

Bink did not dare charge him, because the evil eye still hovered between them, balked only by the evening gown Bink held as a feeble shield. He could see the eye's outline vaguely through the filmy cloth, and had to maneuver constantly to avoid any direct visual contact with it. Yet that sleeping potion would not be stopped by mere cloth!

"Yield, Bink!" Humfrey cried. "Your ally is gone, my ally hovers behind you, the eye holds you in check, and the sleeping potion can reach you where you stand. Yield, and the coral grants you your life!"

Bink hesitated—and felt the swish of air as the griffin flew at him from behind. Bink whirled, seeing the nymph standing nearby, petrified with terror, and he knew that even as the brain coral made the offer of clemency with one mouth, it was betraying that offer with action.

Until this point Bink had been fighting a necessary if undesired battle. Now, abruptly, he was angry. His friend gone, himself betrayed—what reason had he now to stay his hand? "Look, then, at the evil eye!" Bink cried at Crombie, whipping away the gown as he faced away from the menace. Instantly Crombie turned his head away, refusing to look. Bink, still in his rage, charged the griffin with his sword.

Now it was claw and beak against sword—with neither party daring to glance toward the Magician. Bink waved the bright gown as a distraction while he sliced at the griffin's head, then wrapped the material about his left arm as a protection against the claws. Crombie could attack only with his left front leg; his tattered wings did not provide sufficient leverage for close maneuvering, so he had to stand on his hind legs. Still, he had the deadly body of a griffin, and the combat-trained mind of a soldier, and he was as clever and ferocious an enemy as Bink had ever faced. Crombie knew Bink, was long familiar with his mannerisms, and was himself a more competent swordsman than Bink. In fact, Crombie had been Bink's instructor. Though as a griffin he carried no sword, there was no maneuver Bink could make that Crombie did not know and could not counter. In short, Bink found himself outmatched.

But his anger sustained him. He attacked the griffin determinedly, slicing at legs and head, stabbing at the body, forcing his opponent to face the evil eye. He swung the gown to entangle Crombie's good wing, then screamed terribly and launched his shoulder into Crombie's bright breast. Bink was as massive as the griffin; his crudely hurtling weight bore Crombie back toward the deadly water. But it was useless; just as Bink thought he had gained the advantage, Crombie slid sidewise and let Bink stumble toward the water alone.

Bink tried to brake, and almost succeeded. He teetered on the brink. And saw —the golem Grundy, astride the still-floating bottle, now quite near the shore. "Fish me out, Bink!" the golem cried. "The poison can't hurt me, but I'm beginning to dissolve. Look out!"

At the warning, Bink dropped flat, his face landing bare inches from the water. Crombie passed over him, having missed his push, spreading his wings out to sail over the dark lake. Grundy scooped one tiny hand through the water, splashing a few drops up to splatter the griffin's tail—and immediately that tail drooped. The water was deadly, all right!

Crombie made a valiant effort, flapping so vigorously that he rose up out of range of the splashing. Then he glided to the far side of the lake and crash-landed, unable to control his flight well because of the defeathered wing and stunned tail. Bink used the respite to extend his sword to the golem, who grabbed the point and let himself be towed to shore.

Then Bink remembered: Grundy had freed Humfrey and Crombie—in the name of the enemy. The golem was also a creature of the brain coral. Why was he siding with Bink, now?

Two possibilities: first, the coral might have only borrowed the golem, then released him, so that Grundy had reverted to Bink's camp. Yet in that case, the coral could take over the golem again at any time, and Grundy was not to be trusted. In the heat of battle the coral might have forgotten Grundy, but as that battle simplified, that would change. Second, Grundy might remain an agent of the enemy right now. In that case—

But why should the coral try to fool Bink this way? Why not just finish him off without respite? Bink didn't know, but it occurred to him it might be his smartest course to play along, to pretend to be fooled. The enemy might have some weakness Bink hadn't fathomed, and if he could figure it out, using the golem as a clue—

The soldier had not given up. Unable to turn in air because of his disabled guidance system, Crombie oriented himself on land, got up speed, and took off across the lake again.

"Don't touch me—I'm steeped in poison!" Grundy cried. "I'll spot the eye for you, Bink. You concentrate on—"

Glad for the little ally despite his doubts, Bink did. As the griffin sailed at him, Bink leaped up, making a two-handed strike directly overhead with his sword. Crombie, unable to swerve, took the slash on his good wing. The blade cut through the feathers and muscle and tendon and bone, half-severing the wing.

Crombie fell to the ground—but he was not defeated. He squawked and bounced to his feet, whirling and leaping at Bink, front claw extended. Surprised at the soldier's sheer tenacity, Bink fell away, tripped over an irregularity in the rock, and landed on his back. As the griffin landed on him, beak plunging for his face, Bink shoved his sword violently upward.

This time it was no wing he scored on, but the neck. Blood spurted out, soaking him, burning hot. This had to be a mortal wound—yet still the griffin fought, slashing with three feet, going for Bink's gut.

Bink rolled from under, dragging his sword with him. But it snagged on a bone and was wrenched out of his hand. Instead he threw himself on Crombie's neck from behind, wrapping both arms about the spilling neck, choking it, trying to break it. Until this moment Bink could not have imagined himself killing his friend—but the vision of Chester's demise was burning in his mind, and he had become an almost mindless killer.

Crombie gave a tremendous heave and threw him off. Bink dived in again, grabbing for the legs as Chester had, catching a hind one. Such a tactic could never have worked on the soldier in his human form, for Crombie was an expert hand-to-hand fighter; but he was in animal form, unable to use much of his highly specialized human expertise. To prevent the griffin from reorienting, Bink hauled hard on that leg, putting his head down and dragging the form across the rock.

"Don't look!" Grundy cried. "The eye is ahead of you!"

Could he trust the golem? Surely not—yet it would be foolish to risk looking where the eye might be. Bink closed his eyes, took a new grasp, and with his greatest exertion yet, heaved the griffin over his head and forward. Crombie flew through the air—and didn't land. He was flying again, or trying to! Bink had only helped launch him; no wonder the griffin had not resisted that effort!

"The eye is circling, coming in toward your face!" Grundy cried.

To believe, or not to believe? The first demonstrably false statement the golem made would betray his affiliation. So probably Grundy would stick to the truth as long as he could. Bink could trust him *because* he was an enemy agent, ironic as that seemed. He kept his eyes closed and shook out his robe. "Where?"

"Arm's length in front of you!"

Bink spread the gown, held it in both hands, and leaped. He carried the material across and down. "You got it!" the golem cried. "Wrap it up, throw it in the lake!" And Bink did. He felt the tugging within the gown, and felt the slight mass of the captive eye; the golem had spoken truly. He heard the splash, and cautiously opened one eye. The gown was floating, but it was soaked through; anything caught in it would be finished.

Now he could look about. Crombie had flown only a short distance, and had fallen into a small crevasse; he was now wedged in its base, prevented by his wounds and weakness from rising. But the Magician had remained active. "One step, and I loose the sleeping potion!" he cried.

Bink had had enough. "If you loose it, you will be the first affected!" he said, striding toward Humfrey. "I can hold my breath as long as you can!" His sword was on the floor, where it had dropped from the griffin's wounds. Bink paused to pick it up, wiping some of the blood off against his own clothing, and held it ready. "In any event I doubt it takes effect before I reach you. And if it does, the golem will not be affected. What side will he be on then? He's part real, you know; the coral can never be certain of its control."

The Magician jerked the cork out, refusing to be bluffed. The vapor issued. Bink leaped forward, swinging his sword as the substance coalesced—and struck a small bottle.

A bottle materializing from a bottle?

"Oh, no!" Humfrey cried. "That was my supply of smart-pills, lost for this past decade!"

What irony! The Magician had absentmindedly filed his smart-pills inside another bottle, and without them had been unable to figure out where he had put them. Now, by a permutation of the war of talents, they had shown up—at the wrong time.

Bink touched the Magician's chest with the point of his sword. "You don't need any smart-pill to know what will happen if you do not yield to me now."

Humfrey sighed. "It seems I underestimated you, Bink. I never supposed you could beat the griffin."

Bink hoped never to have to try it again! If Crombie hadn't already been tired and wounded—but no sense worrying about what might have been. "You serve an enemy master. I can not trust you. Yield, and I will require one service of you, then force you back into the bottle until my quest is complete. Otherwise I must slay you, so as to render your brain coral helpless." Was this a bluff? He did not want to kill the Magician, but if the battle renewed . . . "Choose!"

Humfrey paused, evidently in communion with some other mind. "Goblins can't come; too bright, and besides, they hate the coral. No other resources in range. Can't counter your check." He paused again. Bink realized the term "check" related to the Mundane game King Trent sometimes played, called chess; a check was a direct personal threat. An apt term.

"The coral is without honor," Humfrey continued. "But I am not. I thought my prior offer to you was valid; I did not know the griffin would attack you then."

"I would like to believe you," Bink said, his anger abating but not his caution. "I dare not. I can only give you my word about my intent."

"Your word is better than mine, in this circumstance. I accept your terms."

Bink lowered the sword, but did not put it away. "And what of the golem?" he demanded. "Whose side is he on?"

"He—is one of us, as you surmised. You tricked me into acknowledging that by my reaction a moment ago. You are very clever in the clutch, Bink."

"Forget the flattery! Why was Grundy helping me?"

"The coral told me to," the golem answered.

"It doesn't make sense for the coral to fight itself! If you'd fought on Crombie's side, he might have beaten me!"

"And he might still have lost," Humfrey said. "The coral, too, had seriously underestimated you, Bink. It thought that once it canceled out your talent—which remains horribly strong and devious, forcing constant attention—you could readily be overcome by physical means. Instead you fought with increasing savagery and skill as the pressure mounted. What had seemed a near-certainty became dubious. Thus the chance of the coral prevailing by force diminished, while the chance of prevailing by reason increased."

"Reason!" Bink exclaimed incredulously.

"Accordingly, the coral delegated the golem to be your friend—the coral's agent in your camp. Then if you won the physical battle, and I were dead, you would be prepared to listen to this friend."

"Well, I'm not prepared," Bink said. "I never trusted Grundy's change of sides, and would have thrown him back into the lake the moment he betrayed me. At the moment I have more important business. Find the vial containing the healing elixir. I know that has not yet been opened."

The Magician squatted, picking through the remaining vials. "This one."

"Jewel!" Bink snapped.

Timidly the nymph stepped forward. "I'm afraid of you when you're like this, Bink."

And she had been afraid during the battle. He could have used her help when the evil eye was stalking him, instead of having to rely on the extremely questionable aid of the golem. She was an all-too-typical nymph in this respect, incapable of decisive action in a crisis. Chameleon had been otherwise, even in her stupidest phase; she had acted to save him from harm, even sacrificing herself. He loved them both—but he would stay with Chameleon.

"Take this vial and sprinkle a drop on the griffin," he directed her.

She was startled. "But—"

"Crombie may be controlled by the enemy, and because of that he did a horrible thing, but he is my friend. I'm going to cure him, and have the Magician put him back in the bottle, along with himself, until this is over."

"Oh." She took the vial and headed for the broken griffin. Bink nudged the Magician forward with the point of his sword, and they followed Jewel more slowly. Humfrey had told Bink he had won, but Bink knew it was not over yet. Not until the Magician and griffin and golem were back in the bottle, and Bink had control of that bottle. And the coral would do its best to keep them out of that bottle.

Jewel paused at the brink of the crevice, looking down. Her free hand went to her mouth in a very feminine gesture that Bink found oddly touching. No, not oddly; he loved her, therefore he reacted in a special manner even to her minor mannerisms. But intellectually he knew better. "He's all blood!" she protested.

"I can't take my attention from the Magician," Bink said, and added mentally: or the golem. "If that vial does not contain the healing elixir, I shall slay him instantly." Bold words, bolstering his waning drive. "You have to apply it. We need that griffin to point out the location of the antidote to the love potion."

"I—yes, of course," she said faintly. She fumbled at the cork. "He's—there's so much gore—where do I—?"

Crombie roused himself partially. His eagle head rotated weakly on the slashed neck, causing another gout of blood to escape. "Squawk!"

"He says don't do it," Grundy translated. "He'll only have to kill you."

Bink angled his sword so that the blade reflected a glint of nova-starlight into the griffin's glazing eyes. The sunflower had been brighter, but now was fading; its harvest time was approaching. "I don't expect honor in a creature of the enemy, or gratitude for a favor rendered," he said grimly. "I have made a truce of sorts with the brain coral, and I enforce it with this sword. Crombie will obey me implicitly—or the Magician dies. Doubt me if you will."

How could they fail to doubt him, when he doubted himself? Yet if violence broke out again, he would not simply let the coral take over.

Crombie turned his tortured gaze on Humfrey. "What Bink says is true," the Magician said. "He has defeated us, and now requires service in exchange for our lives. The coral accedes. Perform his service, and suffer confinement in the bottle—or I will die and you will have to fight him again."

The griffin squawked once more, weakly. "What is the service?" Grundy translated.

"You know what it is!" Bink said. "To point out the nearest, safest love-reversal magic." Were they stalling, waiting for the sunflower to fade all the way so the goblins could come?

Another squawk. Then the noble head fell to the floor. "He agrees, but he's too weak to point," Grundy said.

"We don't really need the antidote. . . ." Jewel said.

"Get on with it," Bink grated. He had deep cuts where the griffin's claws had raked his body, and he was desperately tired, now that the violent part of the action had abated. He had to wrap this up before he collapsed. "Sprinkle him!"

Jewel finally got the bottle open. Precious fluid sprayed out, splattering her, the rocks, and the griffin. One drop struck the golem, who was suddenly cured of his partially dissolved state. But none of it landed on Bink, with what irony only the coral knew for sure.

Crombie lifted his body free of the crevice. Bright and beautiful again, he spread his wings, turning to orient on Bink. Bink's muscles tensed painfully; he held the magician hostage, but if the griffin attacked now—"

Jewel jumped between Bink and Crombie. "Don't you dare!" she cried at the griffin. There was the odor of burning paper.

For a long moment Crombie looked at her, his colorful wings partially extended, beating slowly back and forth. She was such a slip of a girl, armed only with the bottle of elixir; there was no way she could balk the magnificent animal. Indeed, her body trembled with her nervousness; one squawk and she would collapse in tears.

Yet she had made the gesture, Bink realized. This was an extraordinary act for a true nymph. She had tried to stand up for what she believed in. Could he condemn her because her courage was no greater than her strength?

Then Crombie rotated, extended one wing fully, and pointed. Toward the lake.

Bink sighed. "Conjure him into the bottle," he told the Magician. "Do it right the first time. If you try to conjure *me*, you're dead."

There was a delay while Jewel fetched the bottle from the edge of the lake, where it still floated. She had to scoop it up carefully, not letting the moisture touch her skin, then dry it off and set it within range of the Magician.

Humfrey performed his incantation. The griffin dissolved into vapor and siphoned into the bottle. Belatedly it occurred to Bink that Humfrey could have done the same to Bink, anytime during their battle—had he thought of it. The loss of those smart-pills must really have hurt! Yet it was hard to think of the obvious, when being stalked by a sword. And—the best bottle, the demon's residential one, had not been available, then.

"Now your turn," Bink told the Magician. "Into the same bottle—you and the golem."

"The coral is reconsidering," Humfrey said. "It believes that if you knew the full story, you would agree with the coral's viewpoint. Will you listen?"

"More likely the coral is stalling until more of its minions can arrive," Bink said, thinking again of the goblins. They might not get along well with the brain coral, but if some kind of deal were made . . .

"But it knows the location and nature of the source of magic!" Humfrey said. "Listen, and it will guide you there."

"Guide me there first, then I will listen!"

"Agreed."

"Agreed?"

"We trust you, Bink."

"I don't trust *you*. But all right—I'll make the deal. I hope I'm not making a fatal mistake. Show me the source of magic—and not with any one-word riddle I can't understand—then tell me why the brain coral has tried so hard to stop me from getting there."

"First, I suggest you imbibe a drop of the healing elixir yourself," the Magician said.

Startled, Jewel turned. "Oh, Bink—you should have been the first to have it!"

"No," Bink said. "It might have been the sleeping potion."

Humfrey nodded. "Had I attempted to betray you, it would have shown when the griffin was treated," he said. "You maneuvered to guard against betrayal most efficiently. I must say, even with your talent canceled out, you have managed very well. You are far removed from the stripling you once were."

"Aren't we all," Bink growled, hand still on sword.

Jewel sprinkled a drop of elixir on him. Instantly his wounds healed, and he was strong again. But his suspicion of the Good Magician did not ease.

Chapter 12

Demon Xanth

"This way," Humfrey said. Bink kept his sword drawn as he followed the Magician. Jewel walked silently behind him, carrying the golem.

"Incidentally," Humfrey said. "Crombie was not deceiving you. The antidote you seek does lie in the direction of the lake—but beyond it. The coral could enable you to obtain it—if things work out."

"I have no interest in bribes from the enemy," Bink said curtly.

"You don't?" Jewel asked. "You don't want the antidote?"

"Sorry—I didn't mean I intended to renege," Bink told her. "It's a matter of principle. I can't let the enemy subvert me, even though I do not wish to burden you with my love any longer than—"

"It's no burden, Bink," she said. "I never saw anything so brave as—"

"But since the antidote is evidently out of reach, there is no point in keeping you. I'm sorry I inconvenienced you for nothing. You are free to go, now."

She caught at his arm. Bink automatically moved his sword out of the way. "Bink, I—"

Bink yielded to his desire at last and kissed her. To his surprise, she returned the kiss emphatically. The scent of yellow roses surrounded them. Then he pushed her gently away. "Take good care of yourself, nymph. This sort of adventure is not for you. I would like to believe that you are safe and happy with your gems and your job, always."

"Bink, I can't go."

"You have to go! Here there is only horror and danger, and I have no right to subject you to it. You must depart without discovering the source of magic, so that you will have no enemy."

Now she smelled of pine trees on a hot day, all pungent and fresh and mildly intoxicating. The elixir had cured her hoarseness, too, and had erased the no-sleep shadows under her eyes. She was as lovely as she had been the moment he first saw her. "You have no right to send me away, either," she said.

Humfrey moved. Bink's sword leaped up warningly. Jewel backed off, frightened again.

"Have no concern," the Magician said. "We approach the source of magic."

Bink, wary, hardly dared believe it. "I see nothing special."

"See this rock?" Humfrey asked, pointing. "It is the magic rock, slowly moving up, leaking through to the surface after hundreds of years, squeezing through a fault in the regular strata. Above, it becomes magic dust. Part of the natural or magical conversion of the land's crust." He pointed down. "Below—is where it becomes charged. The source of magic."

"Yes—but *how* is it charged with magic?" Bink demanded. "Why has the coral so adamantly opposed my approach?"

"You will soon know." The Magician showed the way to a natural, curving tunnel-ramp that led down. "Feel the intensifying strength of magic, here? The most minor talent looms like that of a Magician—but all talents are largely nullified by the ambience. It is as if magic does not exist, paradoxically, because it can not be differentiated properly."

Bink could not make much sense of that. He continued on down, alert for further betrayal, conscious of the pressure of magic all about him. If a lightning bug made its little spark here, there would be a blast sufficient to blow the top off a mountain! They were certainly approaching the source—but was this also a trap?

The ramp debouched into an enormous cave, whose far wall was carved into the shape of a giant demon face. "The Demon Xanth, the source of magic," Humfrey said simply.

"This statue, this mere mask?" Bink asked incredulously. "What joke is this?"

"Hardly a joke, Bink. Without this Demon, our land would be just like Mundania. A land without magic."

"And this is all you have to show me? How do you expect me to believe it?"

"I don't expect that. You have to listen to the rationale. Only then can you grasp the immense significance of what you see—and appreciate the incalculable peril your presence here means to our society."

Bink shook his head with resignation. "I said I'd listen. I'll listen. But I don't guarantee to believe your story."

"You can not fail to believe," Humfrey said. "But whether you *accept*—that is the gamble. The information comes in this manner: we shall walk about this chamber, intercepting a few of the magic vortexes of the Demon's thoughts. Then we will understand."

"I don't want any more magic experience!" Bink protested. "All I want to know is the nature of the source."

"You shall, you shall!" Humfrey said. "Just walk with me, that is all. There is no other way." He stepped forward.

Still suspicious, Bink paced him, for he did not want to let the Magician get beyond the immediate reach of his sword.

Suddenly he felt giddy; it was as if he were falling, but his feet were firm. He paused, bracing himself against he knew not what. Another siege of madness? If that were the trap—

He saw stars. Not the paltry motes of the normal night sky, but monstrous and monstrously strange balls of flaming yet unburning substance, of gas more dense than rock, and tides without water. They were so far apart that a dragon could not have flown from one to another in its lifetime, and so numerous that a man could not count them all in *his* lifetime, yet all were visible at once. Between these magically huge-small, distant-close unbelievable certainties flew the omnipotent Demons, touching a small (enormous) star here to make it flicker, a large (tiny) one there to make it glow red, and upon occasion puffing one into the blinding flash of a nova. The realm of the stars was the Demons' playground.

The vision faded. Bink looked dazedly around at the cave, and the tremendous, still face of the Demon. "You stepped out of that particular thought-vortex," Humfrey explained. "Each one is extremely narrow, though deep."

"Uh, yes," Bink agreed. He took another step—and faced a lovely she-Demon, with eyes as deep as the vortex of the fiends and hair that spread out like the tail of a comet. She was not precisely female, for the Demons had no reproduction and therefore no sex unless they wanted it for entertainment; they were eternal. They had always existed, and always would exist, as long as there was any point in existence. But for variety at times they played with variations of sex and assumed the aspect of male, female, itmale, hemale, shemale, neutermale, and anonymale. At the moment she was close enough to a category to be viewed as such, and it was not a he category.

"———," she said, formulating a concept so vastly spacious as to fail to register upon Bink's comprehension. Yet her portent was so significant it moved him profoundly. He felt a sudden compelling urgency to—but such a thing would have been inexpressibly obscene in human terms, had it been possible or even conceivable. She was not, after all, closest in category to female.

Bink emerged from the thought-eddy and saw Jewel standing transfixed, meshed in a different current. Her lips were parted, her bosom heaving. What was she experiencing? Bink suffered a quadruple-level reaction: horror that she should be subjected to any thought as crudely and sophisticatedly compelling as the one he had just experienced, for she was an innocent nymph; jealousy that she should react so raptly to something other than himself, especially if it were as suggestive a notion as the one he had absorbed; guilt about feeling that way about a nymph he could not really have, though he would not have wished the concept on the one he did have; and intense curiosity. Suppose an itmale made an offer—oh, horrible! Yet so tempting, too.

But Humfrey was moving, and Bink had to move too. He stepped into an eternal memory, so long that it resembled a magic highway extending into infinity both ways. The light-of-sight—though sight was not precisely the sense employed—to the past disappeared into a far-far distant flash. The Demon universe had begun in an explosion, and ended in another, and the whole of time and matter was the mere hiatus between these bangs—which two bangs were in turn only aspects of the same one. Obviously this was a completely alien universe from Bink's own! Yet, in the throes of this flux of relevant meaninglessness, it became believable. A super-magic framework for the super-magical Demons!

Bink emerged from the Thought. "But what do the Demons have to do with the source of the magic of Xanth?" he demanded plaintively.

Then he entered a new flux—a complete one. *If we cooperate, we can enlarge our A,* the pseudo-female Demon communicated seductively. At least, this was as much as Bink could grasp of her import, that had levels and resonances and symbolisms as myriad as the stars, and as intense and diffuse and confusing. *My formula is* $E(A/R)^{th}$, *yours* $X(A/N)^{th}$. *Our A's match.*

Ah, yes. It was a good offer, considering the situation, since their remaining elements differed, making them noncompetitive.

Not on your existence! another protested. *Enlarge our E, not our A.* It was $D(E/A)^{th}$ who stood to be diminished by the enlarging A.

Enlarge both D and E, another suggested. It was $D(E/P)^{th}$. $D(E/A)^{th}$ agreed instantly, and so did $E(A/R)^{th}$, for she would benefit to a certain degree too. But this left $X(A/N)^{th}$ out.

Reduce our N, $T(E/N)^{th}$ recommended, and this appealed to $X(A/N)^{th}$. But $T(E/N)^{th}$ was also dealing with the E-raisers, and that gave $T(E/N)^{th}$ disproportionate gain for the contract. All deals fell through for no benefit.

Bink emerged, his comprehension struggling. The names were formulae? The letters were values? What was going on?

"Ah, you have seen it," Humfrey said. "The Demons have no names, only point-scores. Variable inputs are substituted, affecting the numeric values—though they are not really numbers, but degrees of concept, with gravity and charm and luminosity and other dimensions we can hardly grasp. The running score is paramount."

That explanation only furthered the mystery. "The Demon Xanth is only a score in a game?"

"The Demon whose scoring formula is $X(A/N)^{th}$—three variables and a class-exponent, as nearly as we can understand it," the Magician said. "The rules of the game are beyond our comprehension, but we do see their scores changing."

"I don't care about a score!" Bink cried. "What's the point?"

"What's the point in life?" Humfrey asked in return.

"To—to grow, to improve, to do something useful," Bink said. "Not to play games with concepts."

"You see it that way because you are a man, not a Demon. These entities are incapable of growth or improvement."

"But what about all their numbers, their enlargements of velocity, of viscosity—"

"Oh, I thought you understood," the Magician said. "Those are not expansions of Demon intellect or power, but of status. Demons don't grow; they are already all-powerful. There is nothing that any of them could conceive of, that each could not possess. Nothing any one of them could not accomplish. So they can't improve or do anything useful by our definition, for they are already absolute. Thus there is no inherent denial, no challenge."

"No challenge? Doesn't that get boring?"

"In a billion years it gets a billion times more boring," the Magician agreed.

"So the Demons play games?" Bink asked incredulously.

"What better way to pass time and recover interest in existence? Since they have no actual limitations, they accept voluntary ones. The excitement of the artificial challenge replaces the boredom of reality."

"Well, maybe," Bink said doubtfully. "But what has this to do with us?"

"The Demon $X(A/N)^{th}$ is paying a game penalty for failing to complete a formula-application within the round," Humfrey said. "He has to remain in inertia in isolation until released."

Bink stood still, so as not to intercept any more thoughts. "I don't see any chains to hold him. As for being alone—there are lots of creatures here."

"No chains could hold him, since he is omnipotent. He plays the game by its rules. And of course we don't count as company. Nothing in all the Land of Xanth does. We're vermin, not Demons."

"But—but—" Bink grabbed for meaning, and could not hold it. "You said this Demon was the source of magic!"

"I did indeed. The Demon X(A/N)th has been confined here over a thousand years. From his body has leaked a trace amount of magic, infusing the surrounding material. hardly enough for him to notice—just a natural emanation of his presence, much as our own bodies give off heat."

Bink found this as fantastic as the Demon's vortex Thoughts. "A thousand years? Leakage of magic?"

"In that time even a small leak can amount to a fair amount—at least it might seem so to vermin," the Magician assured him. "All the magic of the Land of Xanth derives from this effect—and all of it together would not make up a single letter of the Demon's formula."

"But even if all this is so—why did the brain coral try to prevent me from learning this?"

"The coral has nothing against you personally, Bink. I think it rather respects your determination. It is against *anybody* learning the truth. Because anyone who encounters the Demon X(A/N)th might be tempted to release him."

"How could a mere vermin—I mean, person release such an entity? You said the Demon only remains by choice."

Humfrey shook his head. "What is choice, to an omnipotent? He remains here at the dictate of the game. That is quite a different matter."

"But he only plays the game for entertainment! He can quit anytime!"

"The game is valid only so long as its rules are honored. After investing over a thousand years in this aspect of it, and being so close to success within the rules, why should he abridge it now?"

Bink shook his head. "This makes little sense to me! *I* would not torture myself in such fashion!" Yet a thread of doubt tugged at the corner of his mind. He was torturing himself about the nymph Jewel, honoring the human convention of his marriage to Chameleon. That, to a Demon, might seem nonsensical.

Humfrey merely looked at him, understanding some of what was passing through his mind.

"Very well," Bink said, returning to the main point. "The coral did not want me to know about the Demon, because I might release him. How could I release an all-powerful creature who does not want to be released?"

"Oh, X(A/N)th wants to be released, I am sure. It is merely necessary that protocol be followed. You could do it simply by addressing the Demon and saying 'Xanth, I free you!' Anybody can do it, except the Demon himself."

"But we don't count, on its terms! We're nothings, vermin!"

"I did not create the rules, I only interpret them, through the comprehension gleaned over the centuries by the brain coral," the Magician said, spreading his hands. "Obviously our interpretation is inadequate. But I conjecture that just as we two might make a bet on whether a given mote of dust might settle nearer me or you, the Demons bet on whether vermin will say certain words on certain occasions. It does lend a certain entertaining randomness to the proceedings."

"With all that power, why doesn't Xanth cause one of us to do it, then?"

"That would be the same thing as doing it himself. It would constitute cheating. By the rules of the game, he is bound to remain without influencing any other creature on his behalf, much as we would not permit each other to blow on that mote of dust. It is not a matter of power, but of convention. The Demon knows everything that is going on here, including this conversation between us, but the moment he interferes, he forfeits the point. So he watches and waits, doing nothing."

"Except thinking," Bink said, feeling nervous about the scrutiny of the Demon. If Xanth were reading Bink's thoughts while Bink was reading Xanth's thoughts, especially in the case of that shemale memory . . . ouch!

"Thinking is permissible. It is another inherent function, like his colossal magic. He has not sought to influence us by his Thoughts; we have intercepted them on our own initiative. The coral, being closest to the Demon for this millennium, has intercepted more of X(A/N)th's magic and Thought than any other native creature, so understands him less imperfectly than any other vermin. Thus the brain coral has become the guardian of the Demon."

"And jealously prevents anyone else from achieving similar magic or information!" Bink exclaimed.

"No. It has been a necessary and tedious chore that the coral would gladly have given up centuries ago. The coral's dearest wish is to inhabit a mortal body, to live and love and hate and reproduce and die as we do. But it can not, lest the Demon be released. The coral has the longevity of the Demon, without his power. It is an unenviable situation."

"You mean the Demon Xanth would have been freed hundreds of years ago, but for the interference of the coral?"

"True," the Magician said.

"Of all the nerve! And the Demon tolerates this?"

"The Demon tolerates this, lest he forfeit the point."

"Well, I consider this an egregious violation of the Demon's civil rights, and I'm going to correct that right now!" Bink exclaimed with righteous wrath. But he hesitated. "What does the coral gain by keeping the Demon chained?"

"I don't know for certain, but I can conjecture," Humfrey said. "It is not for itself it does this, but to maintain the status quo. Think, Bink: what would be the consequence of the Demon's release?"

Bink thought. "I suppose he would just return to his game."

"And what of us?"

"Well, the brain coral might be in trouble. I know I would be upset if someone had balked me for centuries! But the coral must have known the risk before it meddled."

"It did. The Demon lacks human emotion. He accepts the coral's interference as part of the natural hazard of the game; he will not seek revenge. Still, there could be a consequence."

"If Xanth lacks human emotion," Bink said slowly, "what would stop him from carelessly destroying us all? It would be one dispassionate, even sensible way of ensuring that he would not be trapped here again."

"Now you are beginning to comprehend the coral's concern," Humfrey said. "Our lives may hang in the balance. Even if the Demon ignores us, and merely goes his way, there will surely be a consequence."

"I should think so," Bink agreed. "If Xanth is the source of all magic in our land—" He interrupted himself, appalled. "It could mean the end of magic! We would become—"

"Exactly. Like Mundania," Humfrey concluded. "Perhaps it would not happen right away; it might take a while for the accumulated magic of a thousand years to fade. Or the loss might be instantaneous and absolute. We just don't know. But surely there would be a disaster of greater or lesser magnitude. Now at last you understand the burden the coral has borne alone. The coral has saved our land from a fate worse than destruction."

"But maybe the Demon wouldn't go," Bink said. "Maybe he likes it here—"

"Would you care to gamble your way of life on that assumption?"

"No!"

"Do you still condemn the coral for opposing you?"

"No, I suppose I would have done the same, in its place."

"Then you will depart without freeing the Demon?"

"I'm not sure," Bink said. "I agreed to listen to the coral's rationale; I have done so. But I must decide for myself what is right."

"There is a question, when the whole of our Land's welfare is at stake?"

"Yes. The Demon's welfare is also at stake."

"But all this is just a game to X(A/N)th. It is life to us."

"Yes," Bink agreed noncommittally.

The Magician saw that argument was useless. "This is the great gamble we did not wish to take—the gamble of the outcome of an individual crisis of conscience. It rests in your hands. The future of our society."

Bink knew this was true. Nothing Humfrey or the brain coral might try could affect him before he uttered the words to free the Demon. He could ponder a second or an hour or a year, as he chose, free of duress. He did not want to make a mistake.

"Grundy," Bink said, and the golem ran up to him, not affected by the Thought vortices. "Do you wish to free the Demon Xanth?"

"I can't make decisions like that," Grundy protested. "I'm only clay and string, a creature of magic."

"Like the Demon himself," Bink said. "You're nonhuman, not quite alive. You might be construed as a miniature Demon. I thought you might have an insight."

Grundy paced the cave floor seriously. "My job is translation. I may not experience the emotion you do, but I have an awful clear notion of the Demon. He *is* like me, as a dragon is to a nickelpede. I can tell you this: he is without conscience or compassion. He plays his game rigorously by its rules, but if you free him you will have no thanks from him and no reward. In fact, that would be cheating on his part, to proffer you any advantage for your service to him, for that might influence you. But even if reward were legitimate, he wouldn't do it. He'd as soon step on you as smell you."

"He is like you," Bink repeated. "As you were before you began to change. Now you are halfway real. You care—somewhat."

"I am now an imperfect golem. Xanth is a perfect Demon. For me, humanization is a step up; for him it would be a fall from grace. He is not your kind."

"Yet I am not concerned with kind or thanks, but with justice," Bink said. "Is it right that the demon be freed?"

"By his logic, you would be an utter fool to free him."

The Good Magician, standing apart, nodded agreement.

"Jewel," Bink said.

The nymph looked up, smelling of old bones. "The Demon frightens me worse than anything," she said. "His magic—with the blink of one eye, he could click us all out of existence."

"You would not free him, then?"

"Oh, Bink—I never would." She hesitated prettily. "I know you took the potion, so this is unfair—but I'm so afraid of what that Demon might do, I'd do anything for you if only you didn't free him."

Again the Good Magician nodded. Nymphs were fairly simple, direct creatures, unfettered by complex overlays of conscience or social strategy. A real woman might feel the same way Jewel did, but she would express herself with far more subtlety, proffering a superficially convincing rationale. The nymph had named her price.

So the logical and the emotional advisers both warned against releasing the Demon X(A/N)ᵗʰ. Yet Bink remained uncertain. Something about this huge, super-magical, game-playing entity—

And he had it. Honor. Within the Demon's framework, the Demon was honorable. He never breached the code of the game—not in its slightest detail, though there were none of his kind present to observe, and had not been for a thousand years. Integrity beyond human capacity. Was he to be penalized for this?

"I respect you," Bink said at last to Humfrey. "And I respect the motive of the brain coral." He turned to the golem. "I think you ought to have your chance to achieve full reality." And to the nymph: "And I love you, Jewel." He paused. "But I would have respect for nothing, and love for nothing, if I did not respect and love justice. If I let personal attachments and desires prevail over my basic integrity of purpose, I would lose my claim to distinction as a moral creature. I must do what I think is right."

The others did not respond. They only looked at him.

"The problem is," Bink continued after a moment, "I'm not certain what *is* right. The rationale of the Demon Xanth is so complex, and the consequence of the loss of magic to our world is so great—where is right and wrong?" He paused again. "I wish I had Chester here to share his emotion and reason with me."

"You can recover the centaur," Humfrey said. "The waters of the coral lake do not kill, they preserve. He is suspended in brine, unable to escape, but alive. The coral can not release him; that brine preserves it similarly. But you, if you save the magic of our land, you can draw on the phenomenal power of this region and draw him forth."

"You offer another temptation of personal attachment," Bink said. "I can not let it influence me!" For now he realized that he had not yet won the battle against the brain coral. He had prevailed physically, but intellectually the issue remained in doubt. How could he be sure the decision he made was his own?

Then he had a bright notion. "Argue the other case, Magician! Tell me why I should free the Demon."

Startled, Humfrey demurred. "You should not free the Demon!"

"So you believe. So the coral believes. I can not tell whether that belief is really yours, or merely a function of the will of your master. So now you argue the opposite case, and I'll argue the case for leaving him chained. Maybe that way the truth will emerge."

"You are something of a demon yourself," Humfrey muttered.

"Now I submit that these friends of mine are more important than an impersonal Demon," Bink said. "I don't know what's right for X(A/N)th, but I do know that my friends deserve the best. How can I justify betraying them by freeing the Demon?"

Humfrey looked as if he had swallowed the evil eye, but he came back gamely enough. "It is not a question of betrayal, Bink. None of these creatures would ever have experienced magic, if it had not been for the presence of the Demon.

Now X(A/N)th's period of incarceration has been fulfilled, and he must be released. To do otherwise would be to betray your role in the Demon's game."

"I have no obligation to the Demon's game!" Bink retorted, getting into the feel of it. "Pure chance brought me here!"

"That *is* the role. That you, as a sapient creature uninfluenced by the Demon's will, come by your own initiative or accident of chance to free him. You fought against us all to achieve this point of decision, and won; are you going to throw it all away now?"

"Yes—if that is best."

"How can you presume to know what is best for an entity like X(A/N)th? Free him and let him forge his own destiny."

"At the expense of my friends, my land, and my love?"

"Justice is absolute; you can not weigh personal factors against it."

"Justice is *not* absolute! It depends on the situation. When there is right and wrong on both sides of the scale, the preponderance—"

"You can not weigh rights and wrongs on a scale, Bink," Humfrey said, becoming passionate in his role as Demon's Advocate. Now Bink was sure it was the Good Magician speaking, not the brain coral. The enemy had had to free Humfrey, at least to this extent, to allow him to play this game of the moment. The Magician's mind and emotion had not been erased, and that was part of what Bink had needed to know. "Right and wrong are not to be found in things or histories, and can not be properly defined in either human or Demon terms. They are merely aspects of viewpoint. The question is whether the Demon should be allowed to pursue his quest in his own fashion."

"He *is* pursuing it in his own fashion," Bink said. "If I don't free him, that's according to the rules of his game, too. I have no obligation!"

"The Demon's honor compels him to obey a stricture no man would tolerate," Humfrey said. "It is not surprising that your own honor is inferior to that perfect standard."

Bink felt as if he had been smashed by a forest-blasting curse. The Magician was a devastating infighter, even in a cause he opposed! Except that this could be the Magician's real position, that the coral was forced to allow him to argue. "My honor compels me to follow the code of my kind, imperfect as that may be."

Humfrey spread his hands. "I can not debate that. The only real war between good and evil is within the soul of yourself—whoever you are. If you are a man, you must act as a man."

"Yes!" Bink agreed. "And my code says—" He paused, amazed and mortified. "It says I can not let a living, feeling creature suffer because of my inaction. It doesn't matter that the Demon would not free me, were our positions reversed; I am not a Demon, and shall not act like one. It only matters that a man does not stand by and allow a wrong he perceives to continue. Not when he can so readily correct it."

"Oh, Bink!" Jewel cried, smelling of myrrh. "Don't do it!"

He looked at her again, so lovely even in her apprehension, yet so fallible. Chameleon would have endorsed his decision, not because she wished to please him, but because she was a human being who believed, as he did, in doing the right thing. Yet though Jewel, like all nymphs, lacked an overriding social conscience, she was as good a person as her state permitted. "I love you, Jewel. I know this is just another thing the coral did to stop me, but—well, if I hadn't taken that potion, and if I weren't already married, it would have been awfully easy to love you anyway. I don't suppose it makes you feel any better to know that I am also risking my wife, and my unborn baby, and my parents, and all else I hold dear. But I must do what I must do."

"You utter fool!" Grundy exclaimed. "If I were real, I'd snatch up the nymph and to hell with the Demon. You'll get no reward from X(A/N)th!"

"I know," Bink said. "I'll get no thanks from anyone."

Then he addressed the huge demon face. "I free you, Xanth," he said.

Chapter 13

Magic Loss

nstantly the Demon burst loose. The seeping magic of X(A/N)th's immediate environment was as nothing compared to the full magic of his release. There was a blinding effulgence, a deafening noise, and an explosion that threw Bink across the cavern. He crashed jarringly into a wall. As his senses cleared he perceived the collapse of the cavern in slow-motion sight and sound. Huge stones crunched to the floor and shattered into sand. All the world seemed to be collapsing into the space left by the Demon. This was a demise Bink had not anticipated: not willful destruction by X(A/N)th, not the tedium of loss of magic, but careless extinction in the wake of the Demon's departure. It was true: the Demon didn't *care*.

Now, as the dust clouded in to choke him and the only light was from the sparks of colliding rocks, Bink wondered: what had he done? Why hadn't he heeded the brain coral's warning, and left the Demon alone? Why hadn't he yielded to his love for Jewel, and—

Even in the ongoing carnage, while expecting momentary conclusion of his life, this made him pause in surprise. Love? Not so! He was out of love with Jewel!

That meant the magic really was gone. The love potion had been nullified. His talent would no longer protect him. The Land of Xanth was now one with Mundania.

Bink closed his eyes and cried. There was a great deal of dust in the air that needed washing out of his eyes, and he was wrackingly afraid, but it was more than that. He was crying for Xanth. He had destroyed the uniqueness of the world he knew; even if he survived this cave-in, how could he live with that?

He did not know how the society he had belonged to would react. What would happen to the dragons and tangle trees and zombies? How could the people live, without magic? It was as if the entire population had abruptly been exiled to the drear realm of no-talents.

The action abated. Bink found himself grimed with rock powder, bruised, but with limbs and sword intact. Miraculously, he had survived.

Had anyone else? He peered through the rubble. Dim light descended from a hole far above, evidently the Demon's route of departure. X(A/N)th must simply have shot up and out, forging his path heedlessly through the rock. What power!

"Magician! Jewel!" Bink cried, but there was no answer. The fall of stone had been so complete that only his own section remained even partially clear. His talent must have saved him, just before it faded. He could not depend on it any more, however; it was evident that spells had been the first magic to go.

He stepped out over the rubble. More dust swirled up; it coated everything. Bink realized that though he thought he had been aware of the whole process of the Demon's departure, he could actually have been unconscious for some time. So much dust had settled! Yet he had no bruise on his head, and no headache. Yet again, the physical and magical explosion of the Demon's release could account for many incongruous effects.

"Magician!" he called again, knowing it was futile. He, Bink, had survived— but his friends had lacked his critical protection at the key moment. Somewhere beneath this slope of stone . . .

He spied a glint, a wan reflection, only a glimmer between two dusky rocks. He pried them apart, and there it was: the bottle containing Crombie. Strewn across it was a bit of rag. Bink picked up the bottle, letting the cloth fall—and saw that it was what remained of Grundy the golem. The little man-figure had owed its animation to magic; now he was just a limp wad of material.

Bink closed his eyes again, experiencing another chill seizure of grief. He had done what he had felt was right—but he had not truly reckoned the consequence. Fine points of morality were intangible; life and death were tangible. By what right had he condemned these creatures to death? Was it moral for him to slay them in the name of his morality?

He put the cloth in his pocket along with the bottle. Evidently the golem's last act had been to grab the bottle, protecting it with his body. That had been effective, and so Grundy had given up his life for that of the griffin he served. He had cared, and therefore achieved his reality—just in time to have it dashed by circumstance. Where was the morality in that?

Startled by another thought, Bink drew out the bottle again. Was Crombie still in there? In what form? With magic gone, he could be dead—unless some magic remained corked in the bottle—

Better not open it! Whatever lingering chance Crombie had, resided in that bottle. If he were loosed and the magic dissipated into the air—would Crombie emerge as a man again, or a griffin, or a bottle-sized compressed mass? Bink had just gambled enormously, freeing the Demon; he was not about to gamble similarly with the life of his friend. He repocketed the bottle.

How drear it was, this depth of the hole. Alone with a bottle, and a defunct golem and his own mortification. The ethical principle on which he had based his decision was opaque to him now. The Demon Xanth had lain prisoner for over a thousand years. He could have lain for another century or so without harm, couldn't he?

Bink discovered he was not at the bottom of the hole, after all. The rubble opened into a deeper hole, and at the bottom was dark water. The lake! But the level had lowered drastically; now the dank gray convolutions of a formerly submerged structure lay dimly revealed. The brain coral! It, too, was dead; it could not exist without the potent magic of the Demon.

"I fear you were right, Coral," Bink said sadly. "You let me through, and I destroyed you. You and our world."

He smelled smoke—not the clean fresh odor of a healthy blaze, but the smoldering foulness of incompletely burning vegetation. Evidently the Demon's departure had ignited some brush, assuming there was brush down here underground. The intense magic must have done it, leaving behind a real fire. It probably would not burn far, here deep in the ground, but it certainly was stinking up the place.

Then he heard a delicate groan. Surely not the coral! He scrambled toward the sound—and found Jewel wedged in a vertical crevice, bleeding from a gash on the head, but definitely alive. Hastily he drew her out, half-carrying her to a brighter place. He propped her up against a rock and patted her face with his fingertips, trying to bring her to consciousness.

She stirred. "Don't wake me, Bink. Let me die in peace."

"I've killed everyone else," he said sullenly. "At least you will be able to—"

"To return to my job? I can't do it without magic."

There was something strange about her. Bink concentrated and it came: "You don't smell!"

"It was magic," she said. She sighed. "If I'm alive, I'm alive, I suppose. But I really do wish you'd let me die."

"Let you die! I wouldn't do that! I—"

She glanced up at him cannily. Even through the blood-caked dust on her face, she was lovely. "The magic is gone. You don't love me any more."

"Still, I owe it to you to get you home," Bink said. He looked up, trying to decide on the most feasible route, and did not see her enigmatic reaction.

They checked through the rubble a little longer, but could not find the Magician. Bink was relieved, in a fashion; now he could hope that Humfrey had survived, and had departed before him.

Bink peered up at the Demon's exit. "We'll never make it up there," he said glumly. "Too much of it is sheer cliff."

"I know a way," Jewel said. "It will be difficult, without the diggle, but there are natural passages—oh!" She broke off suddenly.

There was a monster barring the way. It resembled a dragon, but lacked wings and fire. It was more like a very large serpent with legs.

"That's a tunnel dragon—I think," Jewel said. "But something's missing."

"The magic," Bink said. "It's changing into a mundane creature—and it doesn't understand."

"You mean I'll change into a mundane woman?" she inquired, not entirely displeased.

"I believe so. There really is not much difference between a nymph and a—"

"They usually don't bother people," she continued uneasily. Before Bink could react, she added: "They're very shy dragons."

Oh. A nymphly nonsequitur. Bink kept his hand near his sword. "This is an unusual occasion."

Sure enough, the legged serpent charged, jaws gaping wide. Though it was small for a land dragon, since it was adapted to squeeze through narrow passages, it was still a formidable creature. Its head was larger than Bink's, and its body sinuously powerful. In the conditions of this cavern, Bink could not swing his sword freely, so he held it out ahead of him.

The serpent snapped at the blade—a foolish thing to do, since the charmed blade would likely cut its jaw in two. The teeth closed on it—and the blade was yanked out of Bink's hand.

Then he remembered: without magic, the sword's charm was gone. He had to make it work by himself—completely.

The serpent flung the sword aside and opened its jaws again. There was blood on its lower lip; the blade had done some minor damage. But now Bink faced the monster barehanded.

The head struck forward. Bink danced backward. But as the strike missed, and the head dropped low, Bink struck the serpent on the top of the head with his fist. The thing hissed in furious amazement as its chinless chin bashed into the floor. But Bink's foot was already on its neck, crushing it down. The serpent's legs scraped across the stone as it tried to free itself. But Bink had it pinned.

"My sword!" he cried. Jewel hastily picked it up and extended it point-first toward him. Bink was already grabbing for it before he noticed, and then almost lost his balance and his captive as he aborted his grab. "Other way!" he snapped.

"Oh." It had not occurred to her that he would need to take hold of the handle. She was a complete innocent about weapons. She took it gingerly by the blade and poked the hilt in his direction.

But as he took it, the serpent wrenched free. Bink jumped back, his sword ready.

The thing had had enough. It backed away—an awkward maneuver when slithering—then dived into a side-hole. "You're so brave!" Jewel said.

"I was stupid to let it disarm me," he said gruffly. He was not at all proud of the encounter; it had been fraught with clumsiness, not at all elegant. Just a stupid, indecisive brawl. "Let's get on before I make a worse mistake. I brought you out of your home, and I'll get you back there safely before I leave you. It's only right."

"Only right," she repeated faintly.

"Something wrong?"

"What am I going to do without magic?" she flared. "Nothing will work!"

Bink considered. "You're right. I have wrecked your livelihood. I'd better take you to the surface with me."

She brightened, then dulled. "No, that wouldn't work."

"It's all right. I told you the potion has no effect now. I don't love you; I won't be bothering you. You can settle in one of the villages, or maybe work in the King's palace. It won't be much without magic, but it has to be better than this." He made a gesture, indicating the dismal caverns.

"I wonder," she murmured.

They continued. Jewel did know the labyrinth of the caverns fairly well, once they were out of the Demon's depths, and brought them steadily if circuitously upward. Beyond the immediate region of the Demon's vacancy there had not been much damage. But everywhere the magic was gone, and the creatures were crazed. Rats tried to zap him with their rodent magic, and failed, and resorted to teeth. They were no more used to naked teeth as weapons than Bink was to using an uncharmed sword, so the sides were fair. He drove them back with slashing sweeps of his sword. There might be no magic in the blade, but the edge remained sharp and it could hurt and kill.

Still, it took a lot of energy to swing that sword, and his arm grew tired. There had been another charm to make the sword lighter and more responsive to direction, without making it self-willed like the one that had attacked Bink in the gardens of Castle Roogna. The rats crowded closer, staying just out of range and coming in to nip at his heels when he climbed. Jewel was no better off; she lacked even a knife of her own, and had to borrow Bink's knife to defend herself. A monster could be killed but these smaller creatures seemed inexhaustible. They weren't nickelpedes, fortunately, but they were reminiscent of them.

"The way—it will be dark in places," Jewel said. "I hadn't thought—without magic there's no glow, no magic light. I'm afraid of the dark."

There had been some residual glow, but it was fading. Bink looked at the rats, so close. "With reason," he said. "We have to see what we're fighting." He felt naked without his talent, though it only protected him against magic—a protection that was irrelevant now. For practical purposes his situation was unchanged, since no magic threatened him. Not now or ever again. "Fire—we need fire for light. Torches—if we can make torches—"

"I know where some fire stones are!" Jewel said. But she reconsidered immediately. "Only I don't think they are working, without magic."

"Do you know where there's dry grass—I mean straw—something we could twist up tight and burn? And—but I don't know how the Mundanes make fire, so—"

"I know where there's magic fire—" She broke off. "Oh, this is awful! No magic—" She looked as if about to cry. As Bink knew, real sternness of character was not to be found in nymphs. They seemed to have been fashioned by magic to accommodate man's casual dreams, not his serious ones.

Yet he had cried, too, when he first grasped the immensity of what he had done. How much of his perception of the nature of nymphs was human-chauvinistic?

"I know," Bink cried, surprising himself. "There was something burning—I smelled it before. If we went there—picked up some of whatever's burning—"

"Great!" she agreed, with a flash of nymph-enthusiasm. Or female enthusiasm, he corrected his impression mentally.

They soon found it by following their noses: the remains of a magic garden the goblins must have tended, now sere and brown. The dead foliage was smoldering, and the smoke formed layers in the upper reaches of the garden cave. The goblins, of course, were far removed from this region; they had been so afraid of the fire that they had not even tried to put it out.

Bink and Jewel gathered what seemed like the best material, forming it into an irregular rope, and lit the end. The thing guttered and flared and went out in a cloud of awful-smelling smoke. But after several tries they got it working better; it was enough to have it smolder until they needed an open flame, which they could blow up anytime. Jewel carried it; it gave her a feeling of security she sorely needed, and Bink had to have his hands free for fighting.

Now the worst of the enemies were the goblins, who evidently resented the intrusion into their garden. There had been no direct evidence of them before—but of course they had been on the diggle, with protective magic and much light. In the absence of light the goblins grew bolder. They seemed to have been bred from men and rats. Now that the magic was gone, the man-aspect was diminishing and the rat-aspect was becoming more pronounced. Bink realized that this was evident mostly in their habits; physically they still resembled brutish little men, with big soft feet and small hard heads.

The difficulty with the goblins was that they had the intelligence of men and the scruples of rodents. They slunk just out of sight, but they were not cowards. It was simply that no one, three, or six of them could stand up to Bink's sword, and there was not room for a greater number of them to approach him at one time. So they stayed clear—without giving up.

"I think they know I freed the Demon," Bink muttered. "They're out for revenge. I don't blame them."

"You did what you believed was right!" Jewel flared.

He put his arm about her slender waist. "And you are doing what you believe is right, helping me reach the surface—even though we both know I was wrong. I have destroyed the magic of Xanth."

"No, you weren't wrong," she said. "You had empathy for the Demon, and—"

He squeezed her. "Thank you for saying that. Do you mind if I—" He stopped. "I forgot! I'm not in love with you any more!"

"I don't mind anyway," she said. But he let her go, embarrassed. There was an evil cackle of laughter from a goblin. Bink stooped to pick up a stone to hurl at the creature, but of course it missed.

Bink armed himself with a number of rocks, and hurled one every time he saw a goblin. Soon he got remarkably accurate, and the goblins gave him a wider berth. Stones had a special magic that had nothing to do with real magic; they were hard and sharp and plentiful, and Bink had a much better arm than any goblin possessed. Still, they did not give up. Beauregard's warning had been accurate: Bink had not encountered goblins as brave and tenacious as these before.

Bink wanted to rest, for he was tired, but dared not. If he rested, he might sleep, and that could be disaster. Of course he could have Jewel watch while he slept—but she was after all only a nymph—rather, a young woman, and he was afraid the goblins would overwhelm her in such a situation. Her fate in goblin hands would probably be worse than his.

He glanced at her covertly. This rough trek was taking its toll. Her hair had lost its original sparkle and hung in lusterless straggles. She reminded him somewhat of Chameleon—but not in her beauty phase.

They dragged on, and made progress. Near the surface the ascent became more difficult. "There's not much communication with the topworld," Jewel gasped. "This is the best route—but how you climb it without wings or a rope I don't know."

Bink didn't know either. If this had been a convenient route, Crombie's talent would have pointed it out on the way in. The day sky was visible through a crack in the ground above—but the walls sloped in from the broader cavernspace below, and they were slick with moisture. Impossible to climb, without magic.

"We can't stay here long," Jewel said worriedly. "There's a tangle tree near the exit, and its roots can get ornery." She stopped short, startled. "I'm still doing it! Without magic—"

That was why Crombie's talent hadn't pointed this way, he realized. A tangler! But the bad magic was gone with the good. "Let's go!" he cried.

He found the tangle roots and ripped them out of the rock, and severed them where they would not come free. Quickly he knotted them into a strong if ragged rope. Tangle roots were strong; they were made for holding struggling prey fast. No question: this rope would hold his weight!

"But how can we get it up there?" Jewel asked anxiously.

"There's a major tangle root-trunk crossing at the narrowest section," Bink said. "See, right up there." He pointed.

She looked. "I never noticed! I must have been here half a dozen times before, teasing the tangler and wondering what the world above was like. I was supposed to be planting gems . . ." Her nymphly confession trailed off. "You certainly are observant."

"You certainly are complimentary. Don't worry; you will get to see the surface world this time. I won't leave you until you're safe on the surface and in good hands. Maybe at the magic-dust village."

She looked away, not answering. He glanced at her, peering through the smoke of the smoldering weed rope she held, concerned. "Did I say something wrong?"

She looked back at him with sudden decision. "Bink, you remember when we first met?"

He laughed. "How could I forget! You were so beautiful, and I was so grimy—almost as grimy as we both are now! And I had just taken the—" He shrugged, not wanting to get into the embarrassing matter of the love potion again. "You know, I'm almost sad that's over. You're an awfully nice nymph, and without your help—"

"You loved me then, and I didn't love you," she said. "You were devious, and I was simple. You lured me in close, then grabbed me and kissed me."

Bink fidgeted. "I'm sorry, Jewel. I—it won't happen again."

"That's what you think," she said, and flung her arms about him and planted a passionate kiss on his half-open mouth. Dirty as she was, it was still a remarkable experience; almost he felt the tug of the love potion again. He had loved her before without knowing her; now he knew her and understood her nymphly limitations and respected her for trying so hard to overcome them, and he liked her more than was entirely proper. A genuine affection had been developing beneath the artificial love, and that affection remained. What would Chameleon think, if she saw this embrace?

Jewel released him. "Turnabout's fair play," she said. "I am more complex than I was a few hours ago, and you are simpler. Now get on up your rope."

What did she mean by that? Bemused, Bink weighted the rope with a solid rock and lofted it up toward the root-trunk. It fell short, because of the weight of the rope. He tried again, harder, but the rope was still too heavy. It dragged steadily, its weight becoming greater as the rock got higher. Finally he made a wad out of the rope and hurled the mass of it up; this time it got there—and fell back, having failed to pass over the root. But he was making progress, and after several more tries he got it over. The rock fell down, hauling the rope after it. It snagged before the rock came down within reach, but several jerks on the other end of the rope freed it. Bink knotted the ends together, forming a complete loop of rope that could not come loose.

"I can climb this first, then you can sit in the loop and I'll haul you up," he said. He knew there was no chance of her climbing by herself; her arms were too delicate. "Blow the torch up high, so the goblins won't come too close."

She nodded. Bink took a few deep breaths, feeling his worn system revving up in anticipation of this final effort. Then he took hold and began to climb the rope.

It started out better than he had feared, but soon got worse. His arms tired quickly, since they had been none too fresh to begin with. He clamped his legs about the rope, hanging on, to give his arms a rest, but they recovered reluctantly. Oh for some healing elixir! Still, Jewel was waiting, and so were the rats and goblins; he could not afford to delay too long. Excruciatingly he dragged himself up with smaller and smaller wrenches. His breath rasped, his head felt light, and his arms seemed to turn into waterlogged wood just beyond the elbows, but he kept moving.

So suddenly it seemed a miracle, he was at the top. Maybe his mind had simply gone a bit dead too, cutting out the agony of the continuing effort, and revived when he arrived. He clung to the big root, which was somewhat furry:

the better to grip its prey, perhaps, He had never, before this adventure, antici-pated gladly embracing a tangle tree!

He flung a leg over, missed, and felt himself falling. It was almost a relief, this relaxation! But the rope was still there, and he wrapped himself about it and hung, panting. So little to go, so hard to do!

There was a knot up near the apex. Bink braced his feet against it and used his relatively fresh leg muscles to push him up, and somehow scrambled around the root. Now he perceived that rough bark underlay the fur on top, making it good for clinging to, good for scrambling. He clung and scrambled, and finally inched over to the top of it and lay there, panting weakly, too worn out even to feel proper relief.

"Bink!" Jewel cried from below. "Are you all right?"

That roused him. His labor was far from over! "I should be asking you that! Are the rats staying back? Can you get in the seat, to come up?" He didn't know how he would pull up her weight in his present state, but he couldn't tell her that.

"I'm not all right. I'm not coming up."

"Jewel! Get up the rope! The rats can't reach you there, if you pull the end up after you!"

"It's not the rats, Bink. I've lived down here all my life; I can handle the rats and even the goblins, as long as I have my light. It's you. You are a handsome man."

"Me? I don't understand!" But he was beginning to. She was not referring to his present appearance, which was homelier than Chester's face. (Oh, noble centaur—in what state was he now?) The signs had been there; he had merely refused to interpret them.

"When you took the potion, you remained an honest person," Jewel called. "You were strong, stronger than any nymph could be. You never used the potion as an excuse to betray your quest or your friends. I respected and envied that quality in you, and tried to use it as a model. The only exception was that one kiss you stole, so I stole it back. I love you, Bink, and now—"

"But you never drank that potion!" he protested. "And even if you had, now that the magic is gone—"

"I never drank that potion," she agreed. "Therefore the loss of magic could not take my love away. Growth was forced upon me, driving out my nymphly innocence. Now I can perceive reality, and I know there can be no antidote but time, for me. I can not go with you."

"But you have no life down there!" Bink cried, appalled. His love for her had been magic; hers for him was real. She loved better than he had. Her nymphhood was, indeed, behind her. "There must be some way to work it out—"

"There is, and I am utilizing it. When I saw how you sacrificed me when the spell was on you, I knew there could be no hope at all when it was off. It is ironic that my love bloomed only when you gave me up, *because* you gave me up. Because you were true to your principles and your prior commitment. Now I shall be true to mine. Farewell, Bink!"

"No!" he cried. "Come out of there! There has to be some better way—"

But the rope was sliding and bumping over the root. She had untied it at the bottom part of the loop and was drawing it free. He grabbed for it, too late. The end passed over the root and dropped into the darkness.

"Jewel!" he cried. "Don't do this! I don't love you, but I do like you. I—" But that was a dead end. She was right: even when he had loved her, he had known he could not have her. That was unchanged.

There was no answer from below. The nymph had done the honorable thing, and gone her way alone, freeing him. Exactly as he would have done, in that circumstance.

There was nothing he could do now but go home. "Farewell, Jewel!" he called, hoping she would hear. "You may not have my love, but you do have my respect. You are a woman now."

He rested, listening, but heard nothing more from her. Finally he got off the root and looked about. He was in a deep cleft that he now recognized as a section of the Gap, the great chasm that cleft the Land of Xanth in twain. The tree was anchored in the bottom, but reached up toward the top, and a branch extended over the rim. In the absence of magic, the tree was safe to climb. In fact, the terrain would hold few direct threats for him now. He could proceed directly to the King's palace, arriving there within a day.

He spied some inert bugs. They were lying in a patch of sunlight, their pincers twitching. Bink felt compassion, and nudged them gently toward the nearest shadow with one foot. Poor little things!

Then he recognized them. These were nickelpedes, shorn of their magic! What a fall they had taken!

But when he swung himself from the last tentacle of the tangler and reached the surface, he discovered it to be unfamiliar. This crevice ran north-south, not east-west, unless the loss of magic had somehow turned the sun around. It had to be a different chasm, not the Gap. He was lost after all.

Now that he thought about it, he doubted he could have come as far north as the Gap. So he was probably somewhere south of it, and south of the palace. His best bet was to travel north until he encountered the Gap, or some other familiar landmark.

The trek was more difficult than he had anticipated. There was no hostile magic, true—but there was also no beneficial magic. The nature of the landscape had changed fundamentally, becoming mundane. There were no flying fruits, no shoe-trees or jean-bushes to replace his ragged apparel, no watermelons to drink from. He had to find ordinary food and water, and hardly knew what to look for. The animals, stunned by their loss of magic, avoided him; they weren't smart enough to realize that he, too, had been shorn of magic. That was a blessing.

It was late afternoon. How many hours or days he had spent below he could not be sure, but here in the sight of the sun he would be able to keep track again. He would have to spend the night in the forest. It seemed safe enough; he could climb a tree.

He looked for a good one. Many of the trees of this forest seemed dead; perhaps they were merely dormant, in this new winter of the absence of magic. It might take months or years for the full ravages of that winter to become known. Some trees flourished; they must be the mundane varieties, freed from the competition of magic. Would he be better off in a healthy mundane tree, or a defunct magical one?

Bink shivered. It was getting chill, and he could find no blanket bushes. However, it was not merely temperature that affected him. He was tired and lonely and full of remorse for what he had done. Tomorrow he would have to face his friends at the palace and tell them—

But surely they would already have guessed his guilt. It was not confession that bothered him, but punishment. Jewel had been wise to avoid him; he had no future at home.

There seemed to be a certain vague familiarity about this region. There were trails through the brush like those of ant lions, and brambles, and regions of odoriferous plants—

"That's it!" he exclaimed. "Where we intersected the magic highway to the magic-dust village!"

He peered up through the languishing foliage. There it was—a walkway fashioned from logs and vines, suspended from the stoutest trees. It made no loops in air, but of course it wasn't magic now.

He climbed aboard the lowest loop and walked along it. The thing seemed dangerously insecure, sagging beneath his weight and swinging sidewise alarmingly, but it held. In due course it brought him to the village.

He had feared a scene of gloom. Instead, the entire village seemed to be celebrating. Another great bonfire was blazing, and men and women of all types were dancing around it.

Men? How had they gotten here? This was a village of women! Could it be another Wave of conquest from Mundania, with the brutish men reveling in this village of helpless women?

Yet there seemed to be no threat. The men were happy, of course—but so were the women. Bink walked on into the village, looking for Trolla, its leader.

A man spied him as he stepped off the hanging walk. "Hello, friend!" the man called. "Welcome home! Who's your widow?"

"Widow?" Bink asked blankly.

"Your woman—before the gorgon got you. She'll be overjoyed to have you back."

The gorgon! Suddenly Bink understood. "You're the stone men! Freed by the loss of magic!"

"And you weren't?" The man laughed. "You'd better come see the head man, then."

"Trolla," Bink said. "If she's still here—"

"Who's looking for Trolla?" someone demanded. It was a huge, ugly troll. Well, an average troll; they were all huge and ugly.

Bink's hand hovered near the hilt of his sword. "I only want to talk with her."

"Sokay," the troll said genially. He cupped his mouth with his hands. "Bitch, get over here!"

A dozen young women glanced his way, startled, thinking he meant them. Bink covered a smile. "Uh, the gorgon," he said. "What happened to her?"

"Oh, we were going to string her up, after we, you know . . ." the troll said. "She was a good-looking slut, except for those snaky tangles in her hair. But she jumped into the lake, and before we realized there weren't any more monsters in it, she was too far off to catch. Last we saw she was headed north."

North. Toward Magician Humfrey's castle. Bink was glad she had escaped, but knew she would not find Humfrey at home. That was another aspect of the tragedy Bink had wrought.

Trolla, responsive to the summons, was arriving. "Bink!" she exclaimed. "You made it!"

"I made it," he agreed gravely. "I abolished magic from the Land of Xanth. I converted it to Mundania. Now I return home to pay the penalty."

"The penalty!" the troll cried. "You freed us all! You're a hero!"

This was an aspect Bink hadn't considered. "Then you aren't angry at the loss of magic?"

"Angry?" Troll cried. "Angry that my husband is back, good enough to eat?" She hugged the troll to her in an embrace that would have cracked normal ribs. He was well able to sustain this, though he seemed momentarily uneasy about something.

A female griffin glided up. "Awk?" she inquired.

"And here's the one who guided you, released from the midas-spell," Trolla said. "Where is your handsome griffin?"

Bink thought it best not to tell about the bottle. "He is . . . confined. He was actually a transformed man. He spoke well of the lady griffin, but he . . . sends his regrets."

The griffiness turned away, disappointed. Apparently she did not have a male of her own. Perhaps she would find a male of her kind soon—though with the alteration of form that was slowly taking place in such magical creatures, Bink wondered whether that male would be more like an eagle or more like a lion. Or would the present griffins retain their shapes, while their offspring would be eagles and lions? Suppose Crombie emerged from the bottle, but retained his griffin form; would he then find this griffiness worthwhile? If so, what would *their* offspring be? The loss of magic posed as many questions as the presence of magic!

"Come, we shall fête you royally tonight, and you shall tell us the whole story!" Trolla said.

"I, uh, I'm pretty tired," Bink demurred. "I'd rather not tell the story. My friend the Good Magician—is missing, and so is the centaur, and the memories—"

"Yes, you need distraction," Trolla agreed. "We do have a few leftover females, daughters of older villagers. They are very lonely at the moment, and—"

"Uh, no thanks, please," Bink said quickly. He had broken too many hearts already! "Just some food, and a place to spend the night, if there's room—"

"We're short of room; our population has just doubled. But the girls will tend to you. It will give them something to do. They'll be glad to share their rooms."

Bink was too tired to protest further. But as it turned out, the "girls" were an assortment of fairies and lady elves who paid him flattering attention, but were not really interested in him as a man. They made a game out of feeding him odds and ends, each one putting her morsel in his mouth with her own little hands, twittering merrily. They wouldn't let him have a plate; everything had to be trotted in from another room, piecemeal. Then he lay in a bed made out of thirty small colored pillows, while the fairies flitted around, the breeze from their gossamer wings fanning him. They could no longer fly, of course, and soon their wings would fall off as they reverted to mundane forms, but at the moment they were cute. He went to sleep counting the creatures that leaped merrily over him in the course of their game of follow-the-leader.

But in the morning he had to face reality again: the bleak journey home. He was glad his quest had done at least this little bit of good; perhaps his talent had planned it this way, before being nullified by the loss of magic, so as to provide him with a good, safe place for this night. But as for the rest of Xanth—what hope remained for it?

The griffiness accompanied him for a distance, guiding him again, and in a surprisingly brief time he was up to the dead forest: halfway familiar territory. It was no longer so different from the rest of the wilderness. He thanked her, wished her well, and continued on alone, northward.

The loneliness closed in about him. The lack of magic was so pervasive and depressing! All the little amenities he was accustomed to were gone. There were no blue toads sitting on their squat vegetable stools, no Indian pipes wafting their sweet smoke aloft. No trees moved their branches out of his way, or cast avoidance-spells on him. Everything was hopelessly Mundane. He felt tired again, and not merely from the march. Was life really worthwhile, without magic?

Well, Chameleon would be locked in her "normal" phase, the one he liked best: neither pretty nor smart, but rather nice overall. Yes, he could live with that for some time before it got dull, assuming that he was allowed to—

He paused. He heard a clip-clop, as of hooves on a beaten path. An enemy? He hardly cared; it was company!

"Halloo!" he cried.

"Yes?" It was a woman's voice. He charged toward it.

There, standing on a beaten path, was a lady centaur. She was not especially pretty; her flanks were dull, her tail tangled with burrs (naturally a lady would not be able to curse them off), and her human torso and face, though obviously feminine, were not well proportioned. A colt followed her, and he was not only unhandsome, he was downright homely, except for his sleek hindquarters. In fact he resembled—

"Chester!" Bink exclaimed. "That's Chester's colt!"

"Why, you're Bink," the filly said. Now he recognized her: Cherie, Chester's mate. Yet she was in no way the beauty he had ridden before. What had happened?

But he had enough sense to express himself obliquely. "What are you doing here? I thought you were staying in the centaur village until—" But that was a trap, too, for Chester would never return.

"I'm trotting to the palace to find out what is responsible for the miracle," she said. "Do you realize that obscenity has been banished from Xanth?"

Bink remembered: Cherie considered magic obscene, at least when it manifested in centaurs. She tolerated it as a necessary evil in others, for she regarded herself as a liberal-minded filly, but preferred to discuss it only clinically.

Well, he had the detail on it! He was glad that at least one person liked the change. "I'm afraid I'm responsible."

"*You* abolished magic?" she asked, startled.

"It's a long story," Bink said. "And a painful one. I don't expect others to accept it as well as you will."

"Get on my back," she said. "You travel too slow. I'll take you in to the palace, and you can tell me the whole story. I'm dying to know!"

She might be dying literally, when she learned the truth about Chester. But he had to tell her. Bink mounted and hung on as she broke into a trot. He had anticipated a daylong march, but now this would be unnecessary; she would get them to the palace before dark.

He told her the story. He found himself going into more detail than strictly necessary, and realized this was because he dreaded the dénouement—where Chester had fought his dreadful battle and lost. True, he might have won, had the evil eye intended for Bink not stunned him—but that would be scant comfort to her. Cherie was a widow—and he had to be the one to tell her.

His narrative was interrupted by a bellow. A dragon hove into view—but it was a miserable monster. The once-bright scales had faded into mottled gray. When it snorted fire, only dust emerged. The thing was already looking gaunt and ill; it depended on magic for its hunting.

Nevertheless, the dragon charged, intent on consuming centaur, rider, and colt. Bink drew his sword, and Cherie skittered lightly on her feet, ready to kick. Even a bedraggled dragon of this size was a terror.

Then Bink saw a scar on the dragon's neck. "Say—don't I know you?" he exclaimed.

The dragon paused. Then it lifted its head in a signal of recognition.

"Chester and Crombie and I met this dragon and made a truce," Bink said. "We fought the nickelpedes together."

"The nickelpedes are harmless now," Cherie said. "Their pincers have lost their—" She pursed her lips distastefully. "Their magic. I trotted right down inside the Gap and stepped on them and they couldn't hurt me."

Bink knew. "Dragon, magic is gone from Xanth," Bink told it. "You'll have to learn to hunt and fight without your fire. In time you will change into your dominant mundane component, or your offspring will. I think that would be a large snake. I'm sorry."

The dragon stared at him in horror. Then it whipped about and half-galloped, half-slithered off.

"I'm sorry too," Cherie said. "I realize now that Xanth isn't really Xanth, without magic. Spells do have their place. Creatures like that—magic is natural to them." This was a considerable concession, for her.

Bink resumed his narrative. He could stall no longer, so nerved himself and said what he had to. "So I have Crombie here in the bottle," he concluded. And waited, aware of the awful tenseness in her body.

"But Chester and Humfrey—"

"Remain below," he said. "Because I freed the Demon."

"But you don't know they are dead," she said, her body still so tense that riding her was uncomfortable. "They can be found, brought back—"

"I don't know how," Bink said glumly. He didn't like this at all.

"Humfrey's probably just lost; that's why you couldn't find his body. Dazed by the collapse. Without his informational magic he could be confused for a goblin.

And Chester—he's too ornery to—to—he's not dead, he's just pickled. You said that was a preservative lake—"

"So I did," Bink agreed. "I—but it was drained, so that I could see the convolutions of the brain coral."

"It wasn't drained all the way! He's down there, deep below, I know it, like the griffin in the bottle. We can find him, revive him—"

Bink shook his head. "Not without magic."

She bucked him off. Bink flew through the air, saw the ground coming at his head, knew that his talent would do nothing—and landed in Cherie's arms. She had leaped to catch him at the last moment. "Sorry, Bink. It's just that obscenity bothers me. Centaurs don't . . ." She righted him and set him on his feet, never completing her statement. She might not be beautiful now, but she had the centaur strength.

Strength, not beauty. She had been a magnificently breasted creature, in the time of magic; now she remained ample, but she sagged somewhat, as most human or humanoid females of similar measurement did. Her face had been delightfully pert; now it was plain. What could account for the sudden change—except the loss of magic?

"Let me get this straight," Bink said. "You feel all magic is obscene—"

"Not *all* magic, Bink. For some of you it seems to be natural—but you're only human. For a centaur it is a different matter. We're civilized."

"Suppose centaurs had magic too?"

Her face shaped into controlled disgust. "We had better be on our way before it gets too late. There is a fair distance yet to cover."

"Like Herman the hermit, Chester's uncle," Bink persisted. "He could summon will-o'-the-wisps."

"He was exiled from our society," she said. Her expression had a surly quality that reminded him of Chester.

"Suppose other centaurs had magic—"

"Bink, why are you being so offensive? Do you want me to have to leave you here in the wilderness?" She beckoned to her colt, who came quickly to her side.

"Suppose you yourself had a magic talent?" Bink asked. "Would you still consider it obscene?"

"That does it!" she snorted. "I will not endure such obnoxious behavior, even from a human. Come, Chet." And she started off.

"Damn it, filly, listen to me!" Bink cried. "You know why Chester came on my quest? Because he wanted to discover his own magic talent. If you deny magic in centaurs, you deny him—because he does have magic, good magic, that—"

She spun about, raising her forehooves to strike him down. A filly she might be, but she could kill him with a single blow.

Bink danced back. "Good magic," he repeated. "Not anything stupid, like turning green leaves purple, or negative, like giving people hotfeet. He plays a magic flute, a silver flute, the most lovely music I ever heard. Deep inside he's an awfully pretty person, but he's suppressed it because—"

"I'm going to stomp you absolutely flat!" she neighed, smashing at him with both forefeet. "You have no right even to suggest—"

But he was cool, now, while she was half-blinded by rage. He avoided her strikes as he would those of a savage unicorn, without ever turning his back or retreating more than he had to. He could have stabbed her six times with his sword, but never drew it. This debate was all academic now, since magic was gone from Xanth, but he was perversely determined that she should admit the truth. "And you, Cherie—you have magic too. You make yourself look the way you want to look, you enhance yourself. It's a type of illusion, restricted to—"

She struck at him with both forefeet at once, in a perfect fury. He was affronting her deepest sensitivities, telling her that she herself was obscene. But he was ready, anticipating her reactions, avoiding them. His voice was his sword, and he intended to score with it. He had had too much of delusion, his own especially; he would wipe the whole slate clean. In a way, it was himself he was attacking: his shame at what he had done to Xanth when he freed the Demon. "I challenge you," he cried. "Look at yourself in a lake. See the difference. Your magic is gone!"

Even in her fury, she realized she was not getting anywhere. "All right I'll look!" she cried. "Then I'll kick you to the moon!"

As it happened, they had passed a small pond recently. They returned to it in silence, Bink already starting to be sorry for what he was doing to her, and the lady centaur looked at herself. She was certain what she would find, yet honest enough to have her certainty disrupted by the fact. "Oh, no!" she cried, shocked. "I'm homely, I'm hideous, I'm uglier than Chester!"

"No, you're beautiful—with magic," Bink insisted, wanting to make up for the revelation he had forced on her. "Because magic is natural to you, as it is to me. You have no more reason to oppose it than you do any other natural function, like eating or breeding or—"

"Get away from me!" she screamed. "You monster, you—" In another fit of fury she stamped her hoof in the pond, making a splash. But the water only settled back, as water did, and the ripples quieted, and the image returned with devastating import.

"Listen, Cherie!" Bink cried. "You pointed out that Chester can be rescued. I'm just building on that. I don't dare open Crombie's bottle because the process requires magic, and there is none. Chester must stay in the lake for the same reason, in suspended animation. We *need* magic. It doesn't matter whether we *like* it. Without it, Chester is dead. We can't get anywhere as long as you—"

With extreme reluctance, she nodded agreement. "I thought nothing would make me tolerate obscenity. But for Chester I would do anything. Even—" She gulped, and twitched her tail. "Even magic. But—"

"We need a new quest!" Bink said with sudden inspiration as he washed himself in the pond. "A quest to restore magic to the Land of Xanth! Maybe if we all work together, humans and centaurs and all Xanth's creatures, we can find another Demon—" But he petered out, realizing the futility of the notion. How could they summon X(A/N)th or E(A/R)th or any other super-magical entity? The Demons had no interest in this realm.

"Yes," Cherie agreed, finding hope as Bink lost it. "Maybe the King will know how to go about it. Get on my back; I'm going to gallop."

Bink remounted her, and she took off. She did not have the sheer power Chester had, but Bink had to cling to her slender waist to stay on as she zoomed through the forest.

"And with magic, I'll be beautiful again . . ." she murmured into the wind, wistfully.

Bink, tired, nodded sleepily as Cherie charged on through the desolate wilderness. Then he was almost pitched off as she braked.

They faced a huge shaggy pair of creatures. "Make way, you monsters!" Cherie cried without rancor. They were, after all, monsters. "This is a public easement; you can't block it!"

"We not block it, centaur lass," one monster said. "You give way to let we pass."

"Crunch the Ogre!" Bink exclaimed. "What are you doing so far from home?"

"You know this monster?" Cherie asked Bink.

"I certainly do! What's more, now I can understand him without translation!"

The ogre, who now resembled a brute of a man, peered at Bink from beneath his low skull. "You man we met, the one on quest? Me on gooeymoon with she loved best."

"Gooeymoon?" Cherie murmured.

"Oh, so that's Sleeping Beauty!" Bink said, contemplating the ogress. She was as ugly a creature as he cared to imagine. Yet beneath her hair, which resembled a mop just used to wipe up vomit, and her baggy coarse dress, she seemed to have rather more delicate contours than one might expect in an ogress. Then he remembered: she was no true ogress, but an actress, playing a part in one of the fiend's productions. She could probably look beautiful if she tried. Why, then, was she not trying? "Uh, one question—"

The female, no dummy, caught his gist before he got it out. "True, me once have other face," she told Bink. "Me glad get out of that rat race. Me find man better than any fiend; me like it best, by he be queened."

So the prima donna had found a husband worthy of her attention! After meeting the fiends, Bink found himself in agreement with her choice. She was maintaining the ogress guise, which was in any event merely a physical reflection of her normal personality, while teaching Crunch to speak more intelligibly. One savvy lady fiend, there! "Uh, congratulations," Bink said. Aside, he explained to Cherie. "They married on our advice. Humfrey and Crombie and Chester and the golem and I. Except that Humfrey was asleep. It was quite a story."

"I'm sure," Cherie agreed dubiously.

"Yes, me bash he good," the fair she-ogre said. "He head like wood."

"Ogres are very passionate," Bink murmured.

Cherie, after her initial surprise, was quick to catch on. "How do you keep his love?" she inquired with a certain female mischief. "Doesn't he like to go out adventuring?"

Bink realized she was thinking of Chester, perhaps unconsciously.

"Me let he go, me never say no," the ogress said, full of the wisdom of her sex. "When he come back, me give he crack." She struck the ogre with a horrendous backhand wallop by way of example. Just as well, for Bink had been about to misunderstand the reference. "Make he feel like beast, then give he feast."

Crunch's face contorted into a smile of agreement. He was obviously well satisfied. And probably better off, Bink thought, than he might have been with a natural ogress, who would have taken his nature for granted. Whatever faults the actress might have, she certainly knew how to handle her male.

"Does the loss of magic interfere with your lifestyle?" Bink inquired. Both ogres looked at him blankly.

"They never noticed!" Cherie exclaimed. "There's true love for you!"

The ogre couple went on its way, and Cherie resumed her run. But she was thoughtful. "Bink, just as a rhetorical example—does a male really like to feel like a beast?"

"Yes, sometimes," Bink agreed, thinking of Chameleon. When she was in her stupid-beautiful phase, she seemed to live only to please him, and he felt extremely manly. But when she was in her smart-ugly phase, she turned him off with her wit as well as her appearance. In that respect she was smarter when she was stupid than when she was smart. Of course now all that was over; she would stay always in her "normal" phase, avoiding the extremes. She would never turn him off—or on.

"And a centaur—if he felt like a real stallion at home—"

"Yes. Males need to feel wanted and needed and dominant, even when they aren't. Especially at home. That ogress knows what she's doing."

"So it seems," Cherie agreed. "She's a complete fake, a mere actress, yet he's so happy he'd do anything for her. But lady centaurs can act too, when they have reason . . ." Then she was silent as she ran.

Chapter 14

℔𝔞𝔯𝔞𝔡𝔬𝔵 𝔚𝔦𝔰𝔥

ink, nodding again, was suddenly jolted awake. Cherie was braking so hard he was being crushed against her human back. He threw his arms about her waist, hanging on, careful not to grab too high. "What—?"

"I almost forgot. I haven't nursed Chet in hours."

"Chet?" Bink repeated dazedly. Oh, the foal.

She signaled to her young one, who promptly came up to nurse. Bink hastily excused himself for another kind of call of nature. Centaurs were not sensitive about natural functions; in fact they could and did perform some of them on the run. Humans were more squeamish, at least in public. It made him realize one reason why Cherie did not seem as lovely now: her breasts were enlarged to the point of ponderosity, so that she could nurse her foal. Little centaurs required a great deal of milk, especially when they had to run as much as this one did.

After a decent interval Bink cautiously returned. The foal was still nursing, but Cherie spied Bink. "Oh, don't be so damned human," she snapped. "What do you think I'm doing—magic?"

Bink had to laugh, embarrassed. She had a point; he had no more occasion to let his squeamishness interfere with business than she did. His definitions of what might be obscene made no more sense than hers. He came forward, albeit diffidently. It occurred to him that centaurs were well adapted to their functions; had Cherie had an udder like a horse, the foal would have had a difficult time. He was an upright little chap, whose human section did not bend down like the neck of a horse.

"We're going the wrong way," Cherie exclaimed.

Oh, no! "You strayed from the path? We're lost?"

"We're on the path. But we should not be going toward Castle Roogna. Nobody there can help."

"But the King—"

"The King is just an ordinary man, now. What can he do?"

Bink sighed. He had just assumed King Trent would have some sort of answer, but Cherie was right. "What can *anyone* do without—" He was trying to spare her the use of the obscene word, though he knew this was foolish.

"Nursing Chet started me thinking," she said, giving the foal a loving pat on the head. "Here is my foal, Chester's colt, a representative of the dominant species of Xanth. What am I doing running away from Chester? Chet needs a real stud to teach him the facts of life. I could never forgive myself, if—"

"But you're not running away!" Bink protested. "We're going to the King, to find out what to do in the absence of—how we can—"

"Oh, go ahead, say it!" she exclaimed angrily. "Magic! You have shown me in your blundering human way that it is necessary and integral to our way of life, including my own private personal life, damn you. Now I'm taking the rationale further. We can't just go home and commiserate with former Magicians; we have to *do* something. Now, immediately, before it's too late."

"It's already too late," Bink said. "The Demon is gone."

"But maybe he hasn't gone far. Maybe he forgot something, and will return to fetch it, and we can trap him—"

"No, that wouldn't be right. I meant it when I freed him, even though I don't like the result of that freedom."

"You have integrity, Bink, inconvenient as it sometimes is. Maybe we can call him back, talk to him, persuade him to give us back a few spells—"

Bink shook his head. "No, nothing we can do will influence the Demon

Xanth. He doesn't care at all about our welfare. If you had met him, you'd know."

She turned her head to face him. "Maybe I'd better meet him, then."

"How can I get it through your equine brain!" Bink cried, exasperated. "I told you he's gone!"

"All the same, I want to see where he was. There might be something left. Something you missed. No offense, Bink, but you *are* only human. If there were some way we could—"

"There is *no* way!" Bink cried. Chester had been stubborn enough, but this filly—!

"Listen, Bink. You rubbed my nose in the fact of my need of magic. Now I'm rubbing yours in the fact of your need to *do* something, instead of just giving in. You may tell yourself you're going to fetch help, but actually you're just running away. The solution to our problem is at the prison of the Demon, not at the King's palace. Maybe we'll fail—but we do have to go back there and try." And she started back the way they had come. "You've been there; show me the way."

Involuntarily, he ran along beside her, very much like the foal. "To the cave of the Demon?" he asked incredulously. "There are goblins and demagicked dragons and—"

"To hell with all that obscenity!" she neighed. "Who knows what is happening to Chester now?"

There it was: her ultimate loyalty to her mate. Now that he thought of it that way, his own attitude seemed inferior. Maybe his humanity did make him imperfect. Why hadn't he stayed at least long enough to locate his friend? Because he had been afraid of what he might find. He had, indeed, been running away!

Maybe Chester could be hauled out of the brine and saved without the aid of magic. Maybe Good Magician Humfrey yet survived. A small chance, certainly —but so long as there was any chance at all, Bink was derelict in his duty to his friends by not making every possible effort to find them. He had the sick certainty that they were dead, but even that confirmation would be better than his hiding from the truth.

He climbed back aboard Cherie, and she launched herself onward. They made amazingly good progress. Soon they had passed the place where they had encountered each other, and were galloping across the terrain in the direction Bink indicated. A centaur could really move—but even so, it was almost as if there were some magic enchantment facilitating their progress. That was an illusion, of course, and not a magical one. It was just that Cherie was now goaded by her eagerness to rescue her stallion, foolish as that ambition might be. Bink directed her to the tangle-tree cleft, bypassing the magic-dust village.

As they galloped up, it seemed to Bink that the tangler quivered. That had to be a trick of the fading light, since without magic the monster was impotent.

Cherie drew up to the branch that overlapped the rim of the chasm. "Climbing down a tangle tree—I find that hard to—" She broke off. "Bink, it moved! I saw it!"

"The wind," Bink cried with abrupt illumination. "It rustles the tendrils!"

"Of course!" she agreed, relieved. "For a moment I almost thought—but I knew it wasn't so."

Bink peered down into the crevasse, and spied the crack in its base where the tree's big root crossed. He really did not want to go down there again, but didn't want to admit it. "I—uh—I can swing down on a vine. But you—"

"I can swing down too," she said. "That's why centaurs have strong arms and good chest muscles; we have greater weight to support. Come, Chet." She grasped a large tentacle and stepped off the brink.

Sure enough, she was able to let herself down, hand under hand, with her front legs acting as brakes. Her posterior swung grandly around in a descending spiral until she reached the base. The colt followed her example, though with such difficulty that she hastened to catch him at the base. Embarrassed by their examples, Bink swung down himself. He should have led the way, instead of letting fillies and foals do it!

At the base of the tree, gazing down into the looming black hole that was the aperture to the underworld, Bink had further misgivings. "This descent is worse; I don't think Chet can make it. And how could you climb up again? It nearly killed me getting to the top, and your weight—no offense—"

"Chester could climb it," Cherie said confidently. "Then he could haul the rest of us up."

Bink visualized the muscles of Chester's human torso, and remembered the colossal power of the centaur. Only a monster like the ogre had more strength of arm. Maybe, just maybe, it was possible, especially if they set up a double rope so the rest of them could haul on the other end and help Chester lift himself. But that presumed they would actually find and rescue Chester. If they failed, Cherie herself would be lost, for Bink could never haul her up. He might handle the foal, but that was the limit.

Cherie was already testing tangler tentacles for strength. She had faith that banished doubt, and Bink envied her that. He had always thought of Chester as the ornery one, but now he understood that the true strength of the family lay in Cherie. Chester was mere magic putty in her hands—oops, obscene concept!— and so also, it seemed, was Bink. *He* did not want to return to the horrors of the depths, to battle uselessly against the half-goblins and snake-dragons in the dark. But he knew he would do it, because Cherie was going to rescue her poor dead stallion, or else.

"This one's good," she announced, tugging at a particularly long, stout tentacle that dangled from the very top of the tree. "Bink, you climb up and sever it with your knife."

"Uh, yeah, sure," he said with imperfect enthusiasm. Then he was ashamed of himself. If he was going to do this thing, at least he should do it with some spirit! "Yes, of course." And he started to climb the dread trunk.

He experienced a strange uplift and exhilaration. It was as if a burden had been lifted from his body. In a moment he realized what it was: conscience. Now that he had made his decision, and knew it was right even if suicidal, he was at peace with his conscience, and it was wonderful. This was what Cherie had experienced, which had made her almost fly through the wilderness, her strength expanded. Even without magic, there was magic in a person's attitude.

He reached the point where the tentacles sprouted like grotesque hairs from the apex of the trunk, braced himself with his legs looped about it, and slashed into the base of the selected tentacle. And felt a shudder in the tree reminiscent of the one made by the tangler Crombie had attacked so long ago.

No! he reminded himself immediately. It was not magic. The tree was still alive, it had merely lost its magic and become as Mundane trees. It might feel the pain of the cut, and react, but would not be able to move its tentacles about consciously.

He severed the tentacle and watched it drop. Then he cut a second and a third, to be sure they had enough.

Yet the tree was still shuddering as he descended, and the hanging tentacles seemed to be quivering more than might reasonably be accounted for by the wind. Would it be possible for a tangler to revive without magic? No; it must be the effect of his climbing, shaking the trunk, sending ripples through the vines.

They tied the first tentacle to the root, knotting it with difficulty because of its diameter, and dangled it down. It seemed to swing freely, marvelously limber, so they hauled it back up. With some care they knotted another tentacle to its end, extending its effective length. This time they heard the thump as it struck the rock below.

"I'll go first," Bink said. "Then I'll stand guard with my sword while you lower Chet. There are goblins—uh, have we anything for a light? We need fire to scare away the—"

Cherie gave him a straight stare. "If you were a goblin, would you mess with a centaur foal?" She tapped one forefoot meaningfully.

Bink remembered how he had foiled her attack, not long ago, when he forced her to face the obscene concept. But he was twice the height of a goblin, and armed with a sword, and familiar with centaurs. Most important, he had known that whatever Cherie's rage of the moment, she was his friend, and would not really hurt him. No goblin had any such assurance—and a centaur filly protecting her young would be a terror. "I would not mess with a centaur foal even if I were a dragon," he said.

"I can see in the dark a little when I have to," she continued. "I can hear the echoes of my hooves, so I'll know the approximate contours to the caves. We'll get there."

Without another word Bink leaned down, grasped the tentacle rope, and swung himself into the hole. He handed himself into the depths rapidly, feeling much stronger than he had during the ascent. With surprising suddenness he was past the knot and at the floor. He peered up at the wan illumination above. "Okay—I'm down!"

The rope writhed up as Cherie hauled it. Centaurs had excellent balance for this sort of thing, since they could plant four feet on the ground and devote the full strength of their arms to the task. Soon Chet came swinging down, the rope looped about his middle while he held on tightly with his hands. In all this time he had spoken no word and made no demand or complaint; Bink was sure that would change drastically as Chet matured. Bink untied the little fellow at the base and gave him a pat on the back. "Chet's fine!" he called.

Now it was Cherie's turn. She had made it into the crevasse all right, but this was a narrower, darker, longer haul, with a less secure rope, and Bink was privately worried. "Stand clear, in case I should—swing," she called. Bink knew she had almost said "fall." She was well aware of the hazard, but she had courage.

She swung down without event, handing herself along until she neared the floor. Then the narrowing tentacle snapped, dropping her the last few feet. But she landed squarely, unhurt. Bink relaxed. "All right, Bink," she said immediately. "Get on my back and tell me where to go."

Silently Bink went to mount her—and in that silence he heard something. "Something's moving!" he snapped, surprised to discover how nervous he was. "Where's Chet?"

"Right here beside me," she said.

They listened—and now it was plain. A scraping, rustling sound off to the side and up. Definitely not any of them. Yet it didn't sound like goblins, either.

Then Bink saw a snakelike thing writhing between them and the hole, silhouetted by the light. "A tangler root—it's moving!" he exclaimed.

"We must have jarred it loose from the earth," she said. "It's own weight is pulling it free, and its shape makes it twist as it drops."

"Yes." But Bink was uncertain. That looked too much like conscious motion. Could the tangler be animating again? If so, there would be no escape this way!

They started along the cavern trail. Bink found he remembered it fairly well, even in the dark—and he found he could see a little. Maybe some glow remained. Actually, it seemed to get brighter as his eyes adjusted.

"The glow—it's returning," Cherie said.

"I thought it was my imagination," Bink agreed. "Maybe there is some residual magic down here."

They moved on, more rapidly. Bink couldn't help wondering: if the tangler was coming back to life, and the glow was getting brighter, could that mean that magic was returning? The implications were—

Suddenly the passage debouched into—a palace chamber so large he could not readily compass it with his gaze. Jewels sparkled on every side, hanging brilliantly in air. A fountain of scintillating water spread out upside down, its droplets falling back toward the ceiling. Streamers of colored paper formed whirls and whorls that traveled as if by their own volition, tilting sidewise or curling into spirals, only to straighten out again. On every side were fresh wonders, too many to assimilate; in all it was a display of the most phenomenal magic Bink had seen.

There had been no cave like this in this region before! Cherie looked around, as startled as he. "Is—could this be the work of your Demon Xanth?"

As she spoke the name, the Demon X(A/N)th materialized. He sat in a throne of solid diamond. His glowing eye fixed on Bink, who still bestrode Cherie, while the foal pressed closely to her side.

"You are the one I want," X(A/N)th exclaimed. "You stupid nonentity who threw yourself and your whole culture into peril, for no likely gain to either. Such idiocy deserves the penalty it brings."

Bink, awed, nevertheless tried to defend himself. "Why did you return, then? What do you want with me?"

"They have changed the nomenclature system," X(A/N)th replied. "They are into differentials now. I shall have to study that system for an eon or two, lest I apply it with gaucherie, so I am returning to this familiar place for the moment."

"An eon-moment?" Bink asked incredulously.

"Approximately. I brought you here to ensure that my privacy will be preserved. Every entity of this world that knows of me must be abolished."

"Abolished?" Bink asked, stunned.

"Nothing personal," the Demon assured him. "I really don't care about your existence one way or the other. But if my presence is known, other vermin may seek me out—and I want to be left alone. So I must abolish you and the others who are aware of me, preserving my secret. Most of you have already been eliminated; only you and the nymph remain."

"Leave Jewel out of it," Bink pleaded. "She's innocent; she only came because of me. She doesn't deserve—"

"This filly and her foal are innocent too," the Demon pointed out. "This has no relevance."

Cherie turned to face Bink. Her human torso twisted in the supple manner he remembered of old, and her beauty was back to its original splendor. Magic became her, without doubt! "You freed this thing—and this is his attitude? Why doesn't he go elsewhere, where none of us can find him?"

"He's leaked a lot of magic here," Bink said. "It is quiescent without him, but so long as magical creatures like dragons and centaurs remain, we know it hasn't departed entirely. The whole of the Land of Xanth is steeped with it, and this must be more comfortable for him. Like a well-worn shoe, instead of one fresh from the shoe-tree that chafes. The Demon is not of our kind; he has no gratitude. I knew that when I freed him."

"There will be a brief delay before I terminate you," the Demon said. "Make yourselves comfortable."

Despite his immediate peril, Bink was curious. "Why the delay?"

"The nymph has hidden herself, and I do not choose to expend magic wastefully in an effort to locate her."

"But you are omnipotent; waste should have no meaning to you!"

"True—I am omnipotent. But there is proportion in all things. It bothers my sensitivities to use more magic than a given situation warrants. Therefore I am minimizing the effort here. I have amplified your persona. She loves you—I do not pretend to know the meaning of that term—and will come to you here, believing you to be in a danger she can ameliorate. Then I can conveniently abolish you all."

So the return of magic to the Land of Xanth meant the end for Bink and his friends. Yet the rest of Xanth profited, so it was not a total loss. Still—

"I don't suppose you would be satisfied if we simply promised not to reveal your presence, or took a forget-potion?"

"No good," a voice said from Bink's pocket. It was Grundy the golem, back in form with the restoration of magic. He climbed out to perch on Bink's shoulder. "You could never keep such a promise. Magic would have the truth out of you in a moment. Even if you took a forget-potion, it would be neutralized, then the information would be exposed."

"A truth spell," Cherie agreed. "I should have trusted my original judgment. Magic is a curse."

Bink refused to give up. "Maybe we should reverse it," he told the Demon. "Spread the word to all the land that you are down here, and will destroy anyone who intrudes—"

"You'd encourage ninety-nine nuts to rise to the challenge," Cherie pointed out. "The Demon would be constantly annoyed, and have to waste his magic destroying them one by one."

The Demon looked at her approvingly. "You have an equine rear, but a sapient head," he remarked.

"Centaurs do," she agreed.

"And what do you think of me?"

"You are the absolute epitome of obscenity."

Bink froze, but the Demon laughed. The sound blasted out deafeningly. The magically ornate palace shattered about him, filling the air with debris, but none of it touched them.

"Know something?" Grundy remarked. "He's changing—like me."

"Changing—like you," Bink repeated. "Of course! While his magic was leaking out, infusing the whole Land of Xanth, some of our culture was seeping *in*, making him a little bit like us. That's why he feels comfortable here. That's why he can laugh. He *does* have some crude feelings."

Cherie was right on it. "Which means he might respond to a feeling challenge. Can you come up with one?"

"I can try," Bink said. Then, as the Demon's mirth subsided, he said: "Demon, I know a way to protect your privacy. We have a shieldstone, formerly used to protect the whole Land of Xanth from intrusion by outsiders. We valued our privacy as much as you value yours. Nothing living can pass through that shield. All I need to do is tell our King Trent about you, and he will set up the shield to prevent anyone from coming down here. The shield worked for us for over a century; it will work for you too. Then it won't matter who knows about you; every fool who tries to reach you will die, automatically."

The Demon considered. "The notion appeals. But the human mind and motivation are largely foreign to me. How can I be sure your King will honor your request?"

"I know he will," Bink said. "He's a good man, an honest one, and a savvy politician. He will immediately appreciate the need to protect your privacy, and will act on it."

"How sure of that are you?" the Demon asked.

"I'd stake my life on it."

"Your life is insignificant compared to my convenience," the Demon said without humor.

"But my talent is significant in human terms," Bink argued. "It will act in my interest by encouraging the King to—"

"Your talent is nothing to me. I could reverse it by a simple snap of my fingers." The Demon snapped his fingers with a sound like the detonation of a cherry bomb. Bink felt a horribly disquieting internal wrench. "However, your challenge intrigues me. There is a certain element of chance involved that can not occur when I myself undertake a challenge. Therefore I must indulge myself to a certain extent vicariously. You say you shall stake your life on your ability to preserve my privacy. This is really no collateral, since your life is already forfeit, but I'll accept it. Shall we gamble?"

"Yes," Bink agreed. "If that's what it takes to save my friends. I'll undertake any—"

"Bink, I don't like this," Cherie said.

"Here is the testing laboratory," the Demon said, indicating a huge pit that appeared as he gestured. Around it were spaced half a dozen doorways. The walls were vertical stone, too high and slick to climb. "And here is the intruder." A monster appeared in the center, a minotaur, with the head and tail and hooves of a bull and the body of a powerful man. "If he escapes this chamber alive, he will intrude on my privacy. You will stop him if you can."

"Done!" Bink cried. He jumped down into the arena, drawing his sword.

The minotaur surveyed him coolly. The return of magic had invigorated Bink, making him feel strong again—and he had never been a physical weakling. The muscles of his arms showed through the tattered shirt, and his body was balanced and responsive. His sword moved with smooth proficiency, buoyed by its magic, and the charmed blade gleamed. The monster decided to pass up the pleasure of this quarrel. It spun on one hoof and walked toward the exit farthest from Bink.

Bink pursued it. "Turn about and fight like a monster!" he cried, unwilling to cut it down from behind.

Instead the creature broke into a run. But Bink's momentum carried him forward faster, and he caught the minotaur before it reached the exit. He hauled on its tail, causing the thing to crash into a wall. Bink put his sword to its throat. "Yield!" he cried.

The minotaur shivered—and became a monster bug, with tremendous pincers, stinger, and mandibles. Bink, startled, stepped back. He was fighting a magic monster—one that could change its form at will! This was going to be a much more formidable challenge than he had, in his naïveté, supposed.

What a fool he had been to hold back his sword, expecting this thing to yield! Surely its life, like his own, would be forfeit if it lost. He had to kill it in a hurry, before it killed him—or got away, which amounted to the same thing.

Even while he realized this, the bug was skittering toward the exit. Bink leaped after it, his sword swinging. But the bug had eye-stalks that looked back at him—in fact, it was now a giant slug, sliding along on a trail of slime. Bink's sword swished over its head harmlessly.

He could, however, move faster than a slug, even a large one. Bink jumped over it and reached the exit first, barring the way. He took careful aim and made a two-handed strike at the slug's head, to slice it lengthwise. But his blade clanged off the shell of a snail. The monster had changed again, to the nearest variant that would protect it. Either it was hard-pressed, or it lacked imagination.

Bink gave it no chance to think. He thrust directly into the opening of the shell. This time he scored—on the substance of a big green jellyfish. His blade sliced through it and emerged from the far side, dripping, without really hurting the blob. He carried his stroke on up and out and shook the blade off, disgusted. How could he kill a mass of jelly that sealed up after his cut?

He sniffed. Now he recognized the odor of the thing: lime. Lime-flavored jelly. Was it edible? Could he destroy the monster by eating it?

But as he pondered, the monster changed into a purple vulture the size of a man. Bink leaped for it, trying to slay it before it flew up beyond his reach—and skidded on the remaining patch of lime goo. What a disastrous coincidence!

Coincidence? No—this was his talent operating—in reverse. The Demon had negligently switched it. Now seeming coincidence would always work against Bink, instead of for him. He was his own worst enemy.

Still, he had done all right for himself when his talent had been largely canceled out by the brain coral's magic. What he needed to do now was to minimize the element coincidence played in this battle. His talent never revealed itself openly, so was restricted, awaiting its chance to operate. Everything he did should be so carefully planned that it left virtually nothing to chance. That way, chance could not operate against him.

The bird did not fly. It ran toward the center of the arena. Bink scrambled to his feet and pursued, watching his step. Here was a pebble that he might have tripped over; there was another spot of grease. His prior slip in the jelly had been mainly carelessness. He could minimize that. But why didn't the bird simply fly, while Bink was being so careful of his motions?

Probably because the monster was not a Magician. Each form it assumed was about the same mass, and landbound. A good talent, but not an extraordinary one. There were definite limits. King Trent could change a fly into a hephalumph, or a worm into a flying dragon; size and function were of no account. But this monster only changed its form, not its abilities. Good!

Bink stalked the vulture, alert for any move it might make toward the exit. To flee him it would have to turn its back, and then he would strike it down. No element of chance involved there, so no way for his reversed talent to intercede. Bink's early life, when he had not known about his talent, had prepared him for operating without it. His recent adventures, when it had been either neutralized or eliminated entirely, had served as a refresher course. The monster would have to stand and fight, rather than depending on Bink to foul up.

Suddenly it was a man—a burly, tousle-haired brute in tattered clothing, carrying a gleaming sword. The man looked as if he knew his business; in fact he looked familiar.

In fact—it was a replica of Bink himself! The monster was getting smart, fighting sword with sword. "Fair enough!" Bink said, and launched his attack.

As he had guessed, the monster was no swordsman. He might look like Bink, but he couldn't *fight* the way Bink could! This battle would soon be over!

Bink made a feint, then engaged the other's sword and knocked it out of the monster's hand. He backed the monster up against the wall, ready for the finish.

"Bink!" a woman cried in despair.

Bink recognized that voice. It was Jewel! Drawn by the spell the Demon had made, she had arrived just at the wrong moment. It had to be the machination of his reversed talent, interfering just in time to save his enemy from destruction. Unless he acted immediately—

"Bink!" she cried again, jumping down into the arena and throwing herself between him and the monster. She smelled of a summer storm. "Why didn't you stay out of the caverns, where you would be safe?" Then she stopped, amazed. "You're *both* Bink!"

"No, he's the monster," the monster said before Bink spoke. "He's trying to kill an unarmed man!"

"For shame!" Jewel flashed, facing Bink. The storm had become a hurricane, with the odors of sleet and dust and crushed brick, windborne. "Begone, monster!"

"Let's get out of here," the monster said to her, taking her by the arm and walking toward an exit.

"Of all the nerve!" Cherie cried from above. "Get that fool nymph out of there!"

But Jewel stayed with the cunning monster, escorting him toward safety—and a disaster she could not imagine. Bink stood frozen, unable to bring himself to act against Jewel.

"Bink, she'll die too, if you let him go!" Cherie screamed.

That nerved him. Bink launched himself at the pair, catching them each about the waist and hauling them down. He intended to separate them, stab the monster, and explain to Jewel later.

But when he righted himself, he discovered that he had a nymph on each arm. The monster now resembled Jewel—and Bink couldn't tell them apart.

He jumped to his feet, sword ready. "Jewel, identify yourself!" he shouted. The monster could hardly have been smart enough to think of this on its own; Bink's talent had probably decreed such a fortuitous choice of appearances. Bink had not given it any opportunity to catch him in an accident, so it had acted on the monster instead. Coincidence took many forms.

"Me!" the two nymphs cried together, getting to their feet.

Oh, no! They sounded alike, too. "Jewel, I'm fighting a change-shape monster," he cried to them both. "If I don't kill him, he'll kill me. One way or another. I've got to know which one he is." Assuming the monster was male. Bink had to assume that, because he didn't want to kill a female.

"Him!" both nymphs cried, pointing at each other. The scent of skunk cabbage filled the air. Both backed away from each other, and from him.

Worse and worse! Now his talent had the bit in its teeth, determined not to let him prevail. Yet he had to kill the monster, and to spare Jewel. He could not afford to choose randomly.

The nymphs were heading for different exits. Already it was too late to catch both. Upon his choice rested the fate of himself and all his friends—and his infernal talent would surely make him choose wrongly. No matter which one he chose, it would be the wrong one. Somehow. Yet to make no choice would also spell doom.

Bink realized that the only way he could be sure of salvaging anything was to kill them both. The monster, and the nymph-woman who loved him. Appalling decision!

Unless he could somehow trick the monster into revealing itself. (Call it *it*: that would be easy to kill!)

"You are the monster!" he cried, and charged the nymph on the right, swinging his sword.

She flicked a glance over her shoulder, saw him, and screamed in mortal terror. And the smell of dragon's breath, the essence of terror, was strong.

Bink completed his swing, avoiding her as she cowered, and hurled his sword at the second nymph, who was almost at the other exit. The one he had decided was really the monster.

But the near-nymph, in her terror, threw up her hands defensively. One hand brushed Bink's sword arm, just as he threw the weapon, fouling his aim. His talent again, using his friend to balk his attack on his enemy!

Yet it was not over. The monster, seeing the approaching blade, leaped to the side—right into the misthrown sword. The blade struck the chest and plunged through, such was the force of Bink's throw and the charm of the weapon. Transfixed, the monster fell. Two bad lucks had canceled each other out!

Bink, meanwhile, crashed into Jewel, bearing her to the floor. "Sorry," he said. "I had to do it, to make sure—"

"That's quite all right," she said, struggling to get up. Bink got to his own feet and took her by the elbow, helping her. But his eyes were on the dead or dying monster. What was its natural form?

The monster didn't change. It still looked exactly like Jewel, with full bosom, slender waist, healthy hips, ideal legs, and sparkling hair—and blood washing out around the embedded sword. Strange. If the monster was mortally injured, why didn't it revert to form? If it were not, why didn't it scramble up and out the exit?

Jewel drew away from him. "Let me go clean up, Bink," she said. At the moment she smelled of nothing.

Of nothing? "Make a smell," Bink said, grabbing her arm again.

"Bink, let me go!" she cried, pulling toward the exit.

"Make a smell!" he growled, twisting her arm behind her back.

Suddenly he held a tangle tree. Its vines twisted to grab him, but they lacked the strength of a real tangler, even a dwarf species. Bink clamped both his arms about the tree, squeezing the tentacles in against the trunk, hard.

The tree became a squat sea serpent. Bink hunched his head down and continued squeezing. The serpent became a two-headed wolf whose jaws snapped at Bink's ears. He squeezed harder; he could afford to lose an ear in order to win the battle. The wolf became a giant tiger lily, snarling horrendously, but Bink was crushing its stem.

Finally it got smart. It changed into a needle cactus. The needles stabbed into Bink's arms and face—but he did not let go. The pain was terrible, but he knew that if he gave the monster any leeway at all it would change into something he couldn't catch, or his talent would arrange some coincidental break for it. Also, he was angry: because of this creature, he had cut down an innocent nymph, whose only fault was loving him. He had assumed that jinxes had canceled out when his misthrown sword cut her down, but that had not been the case. What an awful force his talent could be! His hands and face were bleeding, and a needle was poking into one eye, but Bink squeezed that cactus-torso with the passion of sheer hate until it squirted white fluid.

The thing dissolved into foul-smelling goo. Bink could no longer hold on; there was nothing to grasp. But he tore at the stuff with his hands, flinging gobs of it across the arena, and stomped the main mass flat. Could the monster survive dismemberment, even in this stage?

"Enough," the Demon said. "You have beaten it." He gestured negligently, and abruptly Bink was fit and clean again, without injury—and somehow he knew his talent was back to normal. The Demon had been testing *him*, not his talent. He had won—but at what cost?

He ran to Jewel—the real Jewel—reminded of the time Chameleon had been similarly wounded. But the Evil Magician had done that, while this time Bink himself had done it. "You desire her?" the Demon asked. "Take her along." And Jewel was whole and lovely, smelling of gardenias, just as if she had been dunked in healing elixir. "Oh, Bink!" she said—and fled the arena.

"Let her go," Cherie said wisely. "Only time can heal the wound that doesn't show."

"But I can't let her think I meant to—"

"She knows you didn't mean to hurt her, Bink. Or she *will* know, when she thinks it out at leisure. But she also knows that she has no future with you. She is a creature of the caverns; the openness of the surface world would terrify her.

Even if you weren't married, she could not leave her home for you. Now that you're safe, she has to go."

Bink stared the way Jewel had gone. "I wish there were something I could do."

"You can leave her alone," Cherie said firmly. "She must make her own life."

"Good horse sense," Grundy the golem agreed.

"I will permit you to perform the agreed task in your fashion," the Demon said to Bink. "I hold no regard for you or your welfare, but I do honor the conditions of a wager. All I want from your society is that it not intrude on my private demesnes. If it does, I might be moved to do something you would be sorry for—such as cauterizing the entire surface of the planet with a single sheet of fire. Now have I conveyed my directive in a form your puny intellect can comprehend?"

Bink did not regard his intellect as puny, compared to that of the Demon. The creature was omnipotent, not omniscient: all-powerful, not all-knowing. But it would not be politic to remark on that at the moment. Bink had no doubt that the Demon could and would obliterate all life in the Land of Xanth, if irritated. Thus it was in Bink's personal interest to keep the Demon happy, and to see that no other idiots like him intruded. So his talent would extend itself toward that end—as X(A/N)th surely was aware. "Yes."

Then Bink had a bright flash. "But it would be easier to ensure your privacy if there were no loose ends, like lost Magicians or pickled centaurs—"

Cherie perked up alertly. "Bink, you're a genius!"

"This Magician?" X(A/N)th inquired. He reached up through the ceiling and brought down a gruesome skeleton. "I can reanimate him for you—"

Bink, after his initial shock, saw that this skeleton was much larger than any Humfrey could have worn. "Uh, not that one," he said, relieved. "Smaller, like a—a gnome. And alive."

"Oh, that one," X(A/N)th said. He reached through a wall and brought back Good Magician Humfrey, disheveled but intact.

"About time you got to me," Humfrey grumped. "I was running out of air, under that rubble."

Now the Demon reached down through the floor. He brought back Chester, encased in a glistening envelope of lake water. As he set the centaur down, the envelope burst; the water evaporated, and Chester looked around.

"So you went swimming without me!" Cherie said severely. "Here I stay home tending your colt while you gad about—"

Chester scowled. "I gad about *because* you spend all your time with the colt!"

"Uh, there's no need—" Bink interposed.

"Stay out of this," she murmured to him with a wink. Then, to Chester, she flared: "Because he is just like you! I can't keep *you* from risking your fool tail on stupid, dangerous adventures, you big dumb oaf, but at least I have him to remind me of—"

"If you paid more attention to me, I'd stay home more!" he retorted.

"Well, I'll pay more attention to you now, horsehead," she said, kissing him as the arena dissolved and a more cosy room formed about them. "I need you."

"You do?" he asked, gratified. "What for?"

"For making another foal, you ass! One that looks just like me, that you can take out for runs—"

"Yeah," he agreed with sudden illumination. "How about getting started right now!" Then he looked about, remembering where he was, and actually blushed. The golem smirked. "Uh, in due course."

"And you can run some with Chet, too," she continued. "So you can help him find his talent." There was no hint of the discomfort she must have suffered getting the word out.

Chester stared at her. "His—you mean you—"

"Oh, come on, Chester," she snapped. "You're wrong ten times a day. Can't I be wrong once in my life? I can't say I like it, but since magic seems to be part of the centaur's heritage, I'll simply have to live with it. Magic does have its uses; after all, it brought you back." She paused, glancing at him sidelong. "In fact, I might even be amenable to a little flute music."

Startled, Chester looked at her, then at Bink, realizing that someone had blabbed. "Perhaps that can be arranged—in decent privacy. After all, we are centaurs."

"You're such a beast," she said, flicking her tail at him. Bink covered a smile. When Cherie learned a lesson, she learned it well!

"Which seems to cover that situation sufficiently, tedious as it has been," the Demon said. "Now if you are all quite ready to depart, never to return—"

Yet Bink was not quite satisfied. He did not trust this sudden generosity on the part of the Demon. "You're really satisfied to be forever walled off from our society?"

"You can not wall *me* off," the Demon pointed out. "I am the source of magic. You will only wall *you* off. I will watch and participate anytime I choose—which will probably be never, as your society is of little interest to me. Once you depart, I forget you."

"You ought at least to thank Bink for freeing you," Cherie said.

"I thank him by sparing his ridiculous life," X(A/N)th said, and if Bink hadn't known better he might have thought the Demon was nettled.

"He earned his life!" she retorted. "You owe him more than that!"

Bink tried to caution her. "Don't aggravate him," he murmured. "He can blink us all into nothingness—"

"Without even blinking," the Demon agreed. One eyelid twitched as if about to blink.

"Well, Bink could have left you to rot for another thousand years, without blinking himself," she cried heedlessly. "But he didn't. Because he has what you will never understand: humanity!"

"Filly, you intrigue me," X(A/N)th murmured. "It is true I am omnipotent, not omniscient—but I believe I could comprehend human motive if I concentrated on it."

"I dare you!" she cried.

Even Chester grew nervous at this. "What are you trying to do, Cherie?" he asked her. "Do you want us all extinguished?"

The Demon glanced at Grundy. "Half-thing, is there substance to her challenge?"

"What's in it for me?" the golem demanded.

The Demon lifted one finger. Light coalesced about Grundy. "That."

The light seemed to draw into the golem—and lo, Grundy was no longer a thing of clay and string. He stood on living legs, and had a living face. He was now an elf.

"I—I'm real!" he cried. Then, seeing the Demon's gaze upon him, he remembered the question. "Yes, there is substance! It's part of being a feeling creature. You have to laugh, to cry, to experience sorrow and gratitude and—and it's the most wonderful thing—"

"Then I shall cogitate on it," the Demon said. "In a century or so, when I have worked out my revised nomenclature." He returned to Cherie. "Would one gift satisfy you, feeling filly?"

"I don't need anything," she said. "I already have Chester. Bink is the one."

"Then I grant Bink one wish."

"No, that's not it! You have to show you understand by giving him something nice that he would not have thought of himself."

"Ah, another challenge," the Demon said. He pondered. Then he reached out and lifted Cherie in one hand. Bink and Chester jumped with alarm, but it was not a hostile move. "Would this suffice?" The Demon put her to his mouth. Again Bink and Chester jumped, but the Demon was only whispering, his mouth so large that the whisper shook her whole body. Yet the words were inaudible to the others.

Cherie perked up. "Why yes, that would suffice! You *do* understand!" she exclaimed.

"Merely interpolation from observed gestures of his kind." The Demon set her down, then flicked another finger. A little globe appeared in air, sailing toward Bink, who caught it. It seemed to be a solidified bubble. "That is your wish—the one you must choose for yourself," the Demon said. "Hold the sphere before you and utter your wish, and anything within the realm of magic will be yours."

Bink held up the globe. "I wish that the men who were restored from stone by the absence of magic, so they could return to the village of magic dust, will remain restored now that magic is back," he said. "And that the lady griffin will not turn back to gold. And that all the things killed by the loss of magic, like the brain coral—"

The Demon made a minor gesture of impatience. "As you see, the bubble did not burst. That means your wish does not qualify, for two reasons. First, it is not a selfish one; you gain nothing for yourself by it. Second, those stone and gold spells can only be restored by reapplication of their inputs; once interrupted, they are gone. None of those people have returned to stone or gold, and none of the similar spells in your land have been reinstated. Only magic *life* has been restored, such as that of the golem and the coral. The other spells are like fire: they burn continuously once started, but once doused remain out. Do not waste my attention on such redundancy; your wish must go for a selfish purpose."

"Oh," Bink said, taken aback. "I can't think of any wish of that kind."

"It was a generous notion, though," Cherie murmured to him.

The Demon waved his hand. "You must carry the wish until it is expended. Enough; I become bored with this trivia."

And the party stood in the forest that Bink and Cherie and the colt had left. It was as if the Demon had never been—except for the sphere. And Bink's friends, restored. And the reviving magic of the forest. Even Cherie seemed satisfied with that magic, now.

Bink shook his head and pocketed the wish-globe. All he wanted to do now was to get home to Chameleon, and he needed no special magic for that.

"I'll carry Bink, as usual," Chester said. "Cherie, you carry the Magician—" He paused. "Crombie! We forgot the loud-beaked griffin!"

Bink felt in his pocket. "No, I have him here in the bottle. I can release him now—"

"No, let him stew there a while longer," Chester decided. Evidently he had not quite forgiven the soldier for the savage fight the two had had.

"Maybe that's best," Cherie agreed. "He was in a life-and-death struggle when he was confined. He might come out fighting."

"Let him come!" Chester said belligerently.

"I think it would be better to wait," Bink said. "Just in case."

It was dusk, but they moved on rapidly. The monsters of the night seemed to hold no terror, after their adventure. Bink knew he could use his stored wish to get them out of trouble if he had to. Or he could release Crombie and let him handle it. Most of the more dangerous wilderness entities were still recovering from the shock of the temporary loss of magic, and were not aggressive.

Chester had a problem, however. "I have paid the fee for an Answer," he reminded the Good Magician. "But I found my talent by myself. Now I could ask about Cherie's talent—"

"But I already know it," Cherie said, coloring slightly at this confession of near-obscenity. "Don't waste your Question on that!"

"You know your talent?" Chester repeated, startled. "What—"

"I'll tell you another time," she said modestly.

"But that leaves me without a wish—I mean without an Answer," he said. "I paid for it with my life, but don't know what to ask."

"No problem," Humfrey said. "I could tell you what to ask."

"You could?" Then Chester saw the trap. "But that would use it up! I mean, your telling me the Question would use up the Answer—and then I wouldn't have the Answer to my Question!"

"That does seem to present a problem," Humfrey agreed. "You might elect to pay another fee—"

"Not by the hair of your handsome tail!" Cherie cried. "No more adventures away from home!"

"Already my freedom is slipping away," Chester muttered, not really displeased.

Bink listened glumly. He was glad to be getting home, but still felt guilt about what had happened to Jewel. He had a wish—but he knew he could not simply wish Jewel out of love with him. Her love was real, not magical, and could not be abolished magically. Also, how would Chameleon react to this matter? He would have to tell her. . . .

They galloped up to the palace as night became complete. The grounds were illuminated by shining luna moths whose fluttering green radiance gave the palace an unearthly beauty.

Queen Iris was evidently alert, for three moons rose to brighten the palace as they entered, and there was a fanfare from invisible trumpets. They were promptly ushered to the library, the King's favorite room.

Without ceremony, Bink told his story. King Trent listened without interrupting. As Bink concluded, he nodded. "I shall make arrangements to set the shield as you suggested," the King said at last. "I think we will not publicize the presence of the Demon, but we shall see that no one intrudes on him."

"I knew you would see it that way," Bink said, relieved. "I—I had no idea there would be such a consequence to my quest. It must have been terrible here, without magic."

"Oh, I had no trouble," the King said. "I spent twenty years in Mundania, remember. I still have a number of little unmagic mannerisms about me. But Iris was verging on a nervous breakdown, and the rest of the kingdom was not much better off. Still, I believe the net effect was beneficial; citizens really appreciate their magic, now."

"I suppose so," Bink agreed. "I never realized how important magic was, until I saw Xanth without it. But here in our group we're left with distressing magical loose ends. Chester has a surplus Answer, and I have a wish I can't use, and Crombie is confined—"

"Ah, yes," the King agreed. "We'd better reconstitute him now."

Bink uncorked the bottle, releasing Crombie. The griffin coalesced. "Squawk!" he proclaimed.

"About time," Grundy translated.

King Trent looked at the griffin—and it became a man. "Well," Crombie said, patting himself to make certain of his condition. "You didn't need to leave me bottled up. I could hear what was going on, all the time." He turned to Chester. "And you, you hoof-headed hulk—I only fought you because the coral controlled me. You didn't have to be scared of me once that was settled."

Chester swelled up. "Scared of you! You feather-brained punk—"

"Anytime you want to try it again, horsetail—"

"That will suffice," the King said gently, and both shut up, albeit with imperfect grace.

King Trent smiled, returning his attention to Bink. "Sometimes you miss the obvious, Bink. Let Chester give his Answer to you."

"To me? But it's *his*—"

"Sure, you can have it," Chester said. "I don't need it."

"But I already have a wish I can't use, and—"

"Now you use Chester's Question to ask the Good Magician what to do with your wish," the King said.

Bink turned to Humfrey. The man was snoring quietly in a comfortable chair. There was an awkward pause.

Grundy went up and jogged the Magician's ankle. "Get with it, midge."

Humfrey woke with a small start. "Give it to Crombie," the Magician said before Bink opened his mouth, and lapsed back into sleep.

"What?" Chester demanded. "The Answer I sweated for only brings a free wish to this bird?"

Bink marveled himself, but handed the wish-bubble to Crombie. "May I ask what you mean to use it for?"

Crombie fidgeted a moment, an unusual performance for him. "Uh, Bink, you remember that nymph, the one who—"

"Jewel," Bink agreed. "I dread trying to explain about her to—"

"Well, I—uh, you see, I had this fragment of the magic mirror in the bottle, and I used it to check on Sabrina, and—"

"I fear constancy was never her strong suit," the King interposed. "I don't believe you two were right for each other anyway."

"What about her?" Bink asked, perplexed.

"She was two-timing me," Crombie said, scowling. "Right when she had me on the verge—but the other guy is married, so she was going to let on the kid was mine, and—I knew I couldn't trust a woman!"

So Sabrina had deserted Crombie, as she had deserted Bink himself, before he knew Chameleon. Yet she connived to marry Crombie anyway—and it had been fated that he would have to marry her unless he married someone else first. "I'm sorry," Bink said. "But I think it would be best simply to let her go. No sense wasting a wish for vengeance."

"No, that's not what I had in mind," Crombie assured him. "I wouldn't trust *any* woman now. But I think I could love a nymph—"

"Jewel?" Bink asked, amazed.

"I don't expect you to believe this," Crombie said seriously. "I don't really believe it myself. But a soldier has to face realities. I lost the battle before it started. There I was, lying in that cleft where you had slain me, Bink. I don't blame you for that; it was a hell of a good fight, but I was really hurting. Suddenly she came, smelling of pine needles and gardenias, bringing the healing elixir. I never saw anything so sweet in my life. She was weak and hesitant, just like a nymph. No threat to any man, least of all a soldier. No competition. The kind of female I could really get along with. And the way she stood by you—" Crombie shook his head. "That's why I went back in the bottle, after pointing out the antidote for you. I wouldn't do anything to hurt that nymph, and killing you would have torn her up. And if you got the antidote, you'd get out of love with her, which was how I wanted you. She's lovely and loyal. But since she still loves you—"

"That's hopeless," Bink said. "I'll never see her again, and even if I did—" He shrugged. "There can be nothing between us."

"Right. So if you don't mind, I'll just take this wish and wish her to drink some of that love potion—and to see me next thing. Then she'll feel about me the way you felt about her. Only I'll be available, seeing as I have to marry someone anyway."

And Crombie was a dashing soldier and a handsome man. Inevitably the love the potion started would become real. The hurt Jewel felt for what Bink had done to her, striking her down with his sword, would make the transition easier. Except—

"But you like to travel about," Chester said before Bink could formulate the same objection. "She lives below, planting precious stones. That's her job; she wouldn't leave it."

"So we'll separate—and rejoin," Crombie said. "I'll be seeing her part-time, not all the time. That's the way I like it. I'm a soldier."

And that, neatly, solved Bink's problem.

"What about me?" Grundy demanded. "Without birdbeak, I have no job. I'm real, now; I can't just disappear."

"There is occasional need for translation around this court," the King said. "We shall find employment for you." He glanced about. "That about suffices for tonight. Quarters have been arranged for all of you, here at the palace." With that he ushered them out.

Bink was last to go. "I—I'm sorry I caused all this trouble," he said. "The Good Magician tried to warn me, and so did Beauregard the demon, but I wouldn't listen. Just because I wanted to know the source of magic—"

"Have no concern, Bink," the King said with a reassuring smile. "I was aware that there was an element of risk when I sent you—but I was as curious about the source of magic as you, and I felt that it was best to have the discovery made by you, protected by your talent. I knew your talent would see you through."

"But my talent was lost when the magic went, and—"

"Was it, Bink? Didn't it strike you that the Demon's return was unusually fortuitous?"

"Well, he wanted a private place to—"

"Which he could have arranged anywhere in the universe. What *really* brought him back? I submit that it was your talent, still looking out for your long-range interests. Your marriage was in trouble, so your magic indulged in an extraordinary convolution to set it straight."

"I—I can't believe my talent could operate to affect the origin of magic itself!" Bink protested.

"I have no such difficulty. The process is called feedback, and it can and does reflect profoundly on the origin. Life itself may be regarded as a feedback process. But even if that were not the case, your talent could have anticipated the chain of events, and established a course that would inevitably bring magic back to the Land of Xanth, much as an arrow shot into the air inevitably returns—"

"Uh, when we fought the constellations, Chester's arrows didn't—"

The King shook his head. "Forgive an inept analogy. I shall not bore you further with my Mundane perspective. I am satisfied with the result of your quest, and you should be satisfied too. I suspect that had any other person released the Demon, $X(A/N)^{th}$ would never have returned to our realm. At this point the matter is academic. We shall have to find another occupation for you, but there is no rush. Go home to your wife and son."

"Son?"

"Oh, did I forget to inform you? As of dusk you became the father of a Magician-class baby, my likely successor to the throne—in due course. I suggest that infant's talent is the Demon's selected gift to you, and perhaps another reason your own talent put you through this adventure."

"What talent does the baby have?" Bink asked, feeling giddy. His son—an overt Magician at birth!

"Oh, I wouldn't spoil the surprise by telling you! Go home and see for yourself!" King Trent clapped him heartily on the shoulder. "Your home life will never be dull again!"

Bink found himself on his way. Talents never repeated in the Land of Xanth, except maybe among fiends, so his son could not be a transformer like the King or a storm master like the prior King, or a magic-adapter like King Roogna who had built Castle Roogna, or an illusionist like Queen Iris. What could it be, that showed so early?

As he approached the cabin at the edge of the palace estate, and smelled the faint residual odor of cheese from the cottage, Bink's thoughts turned to Chameleon. It had been only a week since he had left her, but it seemed like a year. She would be in her normal phase now, ordinary in appearance and intelligence: his favorite. Their mutual worry about the prospects of their baby was over; the boy was not variable like her, or seemingly without talent like him. His love for her had been tested most severely, by the love potion and availability of a most desirable alternative. What a relief to have Crombie going after Jewel . . . though that could be another action of his talent. At any rate, now Bink knew how much he loved Chameleon. He might never have realized, had he not had this adventure. So the King was right; he—

Someone emerged from the cabin. She cast a triple shadow in the light of the three moons, and she was beautiful. He ran to meet her with an exclamation of joy, grabbed her and—discovered it was not Chameleon.

"Millie!" he exclaimed, turning her hastily loose. She had phenomenal sex appeal, but all he wanted was Chameleon. "Millie the ghost! What are you doing here?"

"Taking care of your wife," Millie said. "And your son. I think I'm going to like being a nursemaid again. Especially to so important a person."

"Important?" Bink asked blankly.

"He talks to things!" she blurted enthusiastically. "I mean, he goo-goos at them, and they answer back. His crib sang him a lullaby, his pillow quacked like a duck, a rock warned me not to trip over it so I wouldn't drop the Magician—"

"Communication with the inanimate!" Bink breathed, seeing the significance of it. "He'll never get lost, because every rock will give him directions. He'll never be hungry, because a lake will tell him the best place to fish, or a tree—no, not a tree, that's alive—some rock will tell him where to find fruit. He'll be able to learn more news than the Good Magician Humfrey, and without consorting with demons! Though some of my best friends are demons, like

Beauregard . . . No one will be able to betray him, because the very walls will tell him about any plots. He—"

A grim shape loomed out of the dark, dripping clods of earth. Bink gripped his sword.

"Oh, no, it's all right!" Millie cried. "That's only Jonathan!"

"That's no man—that's a zombie!" Bink protested.

"He's an old friend of mine," she said. "I knew him back when Castle Roogna was new. Now that I'm alive again, he feels responsible for my welfare."

"Oh." Bink sensed a story there—but at the moment he only wanted to see his wife and son. "Was he the zombie I met—?"

"In the garden," she agreed. "He got lost in the Queen's maze, the night of the anniversary party. Then he came to me, inside, and got pickled. It took quite a spell to undo that! Now we're looking for a spell to make him alive again, too, so we can—" She blushed delicately. Obviously the zombie had been more than a friend, in life. Millie had displayed an embarrassing interest in Bink himself, during that party, but it seemed the appearance of the zombie ended that. Another loose end Bink's talent had neatly tied up.

"When my son gets older we can have him ask about that," Bink said. "There must be some rock, somewhere, that knows where a spell to restore zombies would be."

"Oh, yes!" Millie cried ecstatically. "Oh, thank you!"

Bink faced the zombie, but did not offer to shake hands. "I think you were another omen for me, Jonathan. When I met you the first time, it signaled death with all its horrors: the death of magic. But through that death I found a kind of rebirth—and so will you."

Bink turned to the door of the cottage, ready to join his family.

Castle Roogna

Contents

Ogre

Millie the ghost was beautiful. Of course, she wasn't a ghost any more, so she was Millie the nurse. She was not especially bright, and she was hardly young. She was twenty-nine years old as she reckoned it, and about eight hundred and twenty-nine as others reckoned it: the oldest creature currently associated with Castle Roogna. She had been ensorceled as a maid of seventeen, eight centuries ago, when Castle Roogna was young, and restored to life at the time of Dor's birth. In the interim she had been a ghost, and the label had never quite worn off. And why should it? By all accounts she had been a most attractive ghost.

Indeed, she had the loveliest glowing hair, flowing like poppycorn silk to the dimpled backs of her . . . knees. The terrain those tresses covered in passing was—was—how was it that Dor had never noticed it before? Millie had been his nurse all these years, taking care of him while his parents were busy, and they tended to be busy a great deal of the time.

Oh, he understood that well enough. He told others that the King trusted his parents Bink and Chameleon, and anyone the King trusted was bound to be very busy, because the King's missions were too important to leave to nobodies. All that was true enough. But Dor knew his folks didn't have to accept all those important missions that took them all over the Land of Xanth and beyond. They simply liked to travel, to be away from home. Right now they were far away, in Mundania, and nobody went to Mundania for pleasure. It was because of him, because of his talent.

Dor remembered years ago when he had talked to the double bed Bink and Chameleon used, and asked it what had happened overnight, just from idle curiosity, and it had said—well, it had been quite interesting, especially since Chameleon had been in her beauty stage, prettier and stupider than Millie the ghost, which was going some. But his mother had overheard some of that dialogue, and told his father, and after that Dor wasn't allowed in the bedroom any more. It wasn't that his parents didn't love him, Bink had carefully explained; it was that they felt nervous about what they called "invasion of privacy." So they tended to do their most interesting things away from the house, and Dor had learned not to pry. Not when and where anyone in authority could overhear, at any rate.

Millie took care of him; she had no privacy secrets. True, she didn't like him talking to the toilet, though it was just a pot that got emptied every day into the back garden where dung beetles magicked the stuff into sweet-smelling roses. Dor couldn't talk to roses, because they were alive. He could talk to a dead rose —but then it remembered only what had happened since it was cut, and that wasn't very much. And Millie didn't like him making fun of Jonathan. Apart from that she was quite reasonable, and he liked her. But he had never really noticed her shape before.

Millie was very like a nymph, with all sorts of feminine projections and softnesses and things, and her skin was as clear as the surface of a milkweed pod just before it got milked. She usually wore a light gauzy dress that lent her an ethereal quality strongly reminiscent of her ghosthood, yet failed to conceal excitingly gentle contours beneath. Her voice was as soft as the call of a wraith. Yet she had more wit than a nymph, and more substance than a wraith. She had—

"Oh, what the fudge am I trying to figure out?" Dor demanded aloud.

"How should I know?" the kitchen table responded irritably. It had been fashioned from gnarled acorn wood, and it had a crooked temper.

Millie turned, smiling automatically. She had been washing plates at the sink; she claimed it was easier to do them by hand than to locate the proper cleaning spell, and probably for her it was. The spell was in powder form, and it came in a box the spell-caster made up at the palace, and the powder was forever running out. Few things were more annoying than chasing all over the yard after running powder. So Millie didn't take a powder; she scrubbed the dishes herself. "Are you still hungry, Dor?"

"No," he said, embarrassed. He was hungry, but not for food. If hunger was the proper term.

There was a hesitant, somewhat sodden knock on the door. Millie glanced across at it, her hair rippling down its luxuriant length. "That will be Jonathan," she said brightly.

Jonathan the zombie. Dor scowled. It wasn't that he had anything special against zombies, but he didn't like them around the house. They tended to drop putrid chunks of themselves as they walked, and they were not pretty to look at. "Oh, what do you see in that bag of bones?" Dor demanded, hunching his body and pulling his lips in around his teeth to mimic the zombie mode.

"Why, Dor, that isn't nice! Jonathan is an old friend. I've known him for centuries." No exaggeration! The zombies had haunted the environs of Castle Roogna as long as the ghosts had. Naturally the two types of freaks had gotten to know each other.

But Millie was a woman now, alive and whole and firm. Extremely firm, Dor thought as he watched her move trippingly across the kitchen to the back door. Jonathan was, in contrast, a horribly animated dead man. A living corpse. How could she pay attention to him?

"Beauty and the beast," he muttered savagely. Frustrated and angry, Dor stalked out of the kitchen and into the main room of the cottage. The floor was smooth, hard rind, polished until it had become reflective, and the walls were yellow-white. He banged his fist into one. "Hey, stop that!" the wall protested. "You'll fracture me. I'm only cheese, you know!"

Dor knew. The house was a large, hollowed-out cottage cheese, long since hardened into rigidity. When it had grown, it had been alive; but as a house it was dead, and therefore he could talk to it. Not that it had anything worth saying.

Dor stormed on out the front door. "Don't you dare slam me!" it warned, but he slammed it anyway, and heard its shaken groan behind him. That door always had been more ham than cheese.

The day outside was gloomy. He should have known; Jonathan preferred gloomy days to come calling, because they kept his chronically rotting flesh from drying up so quickly. In fact, it was about to rain. The clouds were kneading themselves into darker convolutions, getting set to clean out their systems.

"Don't you water on me!" Dor yelled into the sky in much the tone the door had used on him. The nearest cloud chuckled evilly, with a sound like thunder.

"Dor! Wait!" a little voice called. It was Grundy the golem, actually no golem any more, not that it made much difference. He was Dor's outdoor companion, and was always alert for Dor's treks into the forest. Dor's folks had really fixed it up so he would always be supervised—by people like Millie, who had no embarrassing secrets, or like Grundy, who didn't care if they did. In fact Grundy would be downright proud to have an embarrassment.

That started Dor on another chain of thought. Actually it wasn't just Bink and Chameleon; nobody in Castle Roogna cared to associate too closely with Dor. Because all sorts of things went on that the furniture saw and heard, and Dor could talk to the furniture. For him, the walls had ears and the floors had eyes. What was wrong with people? Were they ashamed of everything they did? Only King Trent seemed completely at ease with him. But the King could hardly spend all his time entertaining a mere boy.

Grundy caught up. "This is a bad day for exploring, Dor!" he warned. "That storm means business."

Dor looked dourly up at the cloud. "Go soak your empty head!" he yelled at it. "You're no thunderhead, you're a dunderhead!"

He was answered by a spate of yellow hailstones, and had to hunch over like a zombie and shield his face with his arms until they passed.

"Be halfway sensible, Dor!" Grundy urged. "Don't mess with that mean storm! It'll wash us out!"

Dor reluctantly yielded to common sense. "We'll seek cover. But not at home; the zombie's there."

"I wonder what Millie sees in him," Grundy said.

"That's what I asked." The rain was commencing. They hurried to an umbrella tree, whose great thin canopy was just spreading to meet the droplets. Umbrella trees preferred dry soil, so they shielded it against rain. When the sun shone, they folded up, so as not to obstruct the rays. There were also parasol trees, which reacted oppositely, spreading for the sun and folding for the rain. When the two happened to seed together, there was a real wilderness problem.

Two larger boys, the sons of palace guards, had already taken shelter under the same tree. "Well," one cried. "If it isn't the dope who talks to chairs!"

"Go find your own tree, twerp," the other boy ordered. He had sloping shoulders and a projecting chin.

"Look, Horsejaw!" Grundy snapped. "This tree doesn't belong to you! Everyone shares umbrellas in a storm."

"Not with chair-talkers, midget."

"He's a Magician!" Grundy said indignantly. "He talks to the inanimate. No one else can do that; no one else ever could do that in the whole history of Xanth, or ever will again!"

"Let it be, Grundy," Dor murmured. The golem had a sharp tongue that could get them both into trouble. "We'll find another tree."

"See?" Horsejaw demanded triumphantly. "Little stinker don't stand up to his betters." And he laughed.

Suddenly there was a detonation of sound right behind them. Both Dor and Grundy jumped in alarm, before remembering that this was Horsejaw's talent: projecting booms. Both older boys laughed uproariously.

Dor stepped out from under the umbrella—and his foot came down on a snake. He recoiled—but immediately the snake faded into a wisp of smoke. That was the other boy's talent: the conjuration of small, harmless reptiles. The two continued to laugh with such enthusiasm that they were collapsing against the umbrella trunk.

Dor and Grundy went to another tree, prodded by another sonic boom. Dor concealed his anger. He didn't like being treated this way, but against the superior physical power of the older boys he was helpless. His father Bink was a muscular man, well able to fight when the occasion required, but Dor took after his mother more: small and slender. How he wished he were like his father!

The rain was pelting down now, soaking Dor and Grundy. "Why do you tolerate it?" Grundy demanded. "You are a Magician!"

"A Magician of communication," Dor retorted. "That doesn't count for much, among boys."

"It counts for plenty!" Grundy cried, his little legs splashing through the forming puddles. Absentmindedly Dor reached down to pick him up; the one-time golem was only a few inches tall. "You could talk to their clothes, find out all their secrets, blackmail them—"

"No!"

"You're too damned ethical, Dor," Grundy complained. "Power goes to the unscrupulous. If your father, Bink, had been properly unscrupulous, he'd have been King."

"He didn't want to be King!"

"That's beside the point. Kingship isn't a matter of want, it's a matter of talent. Only a full male Magician can be King."

"Which King Trent is. And he's a good King. My father says the Land of Xanth has really improved since Magician Trent took over. It used to be all chaos and anarchy and bad magic except for right near the villages."

"Your father sees the best in everyone. He is entirely too nice. You take after him."

Dor smiled. "Why thank you, Grundy."

"That wasn't a compliment!"

"I know it wasn't—to you."

Grundy paused. "Sometimes I get the sinister feeling you're not as naive as you seem. Who knows, maybe little normal worms of anger and jealousy gnaw in your heart, as they do in other hearts."

"They do. Today when the zombie called on Millie—" He broke off.

"Oh, you notice Millie now! You're growing up!"

Dor whirled on him—and of course, since the golem was in his hand, Grundy whirled too. "What do you mean by that?"

"Merely that men notice things about women that boys don't. Don't you know what Millie's talent is?"

"No. What is it?"

"Sex appeal."

"I thought that was something all women had."

"Something all women *wish* they had. Millie's is magical; any man near her gets ideas."

That didn't make sense to Dor. "My father doesn't."

"Your father stays well away from her. Did you think that was coincidence?"

Dor had thought it was his own talent that kept Bink away from home so much. It was tempting to think he was mistaken. "What about the King?"

"He has iron control. But you can bet those ideas are percolating in his brain, out of sight. Ever notice how closely the Queen watches him, when Millie's around?"

Dor had always thought it was *him* the Queen was watching disapprovingly, when as a child Millie had taken him to the palace. Now he was uncertain, so he didn't argue further. The golem was always full of gossipy news that adults found hilarious even when the news was suspect. Adults could be sort of stupid at times.

They came up to a pavilion in the Castle Roogna orchard. It had a drying stone set up for just such occasions as this. As they approached it, warm radiation came out, which started the pleasant drying of their clothes. Few things felt as good as a drying stone after a chill soaking! "I really appreciate your service, drier," Dor told it.

"All part of the job," the stone replied. "My cousin, the sharpening stone, really has his work cut out for him. All those knives to hone, you know. Ha ha!"

"Ha ha," Dor agreed mildly, patting it. The trouble with talking with inanimate objects was that they weren't very bright—but thought they were.

Another figure emerged from the orchard, clasping a cluster of chocolate cherries in one hand. "Oh, no!" she exclaimed, recognizing Dor. "If it isn't dodo Dor, the lifeless snooper."

"Look who's talking," Grundy retorted. "Irate Irene, palace brat."

"Princess Irene, to you," the girl snapped. "My father is King, remember?"

"Well, you'll never be King," Grundy said.

" 'Cause women can't assume the throne, golem! But if I were a man—"

"If you were a man, you still wouldn't be King, because you don't have Magician-caliber magic."

"I do too!" she flared.

"Stinkfinger?" Grundy inquired derisively.

"That's green thumb!" she yelled, furious. "I can make any plant grow. Fast. Big. Healthy."

Dor had stayed out of the argument, but fairness required his interjection. "That's creditable magic."

"Stay out of this, dodo!" she snapped. "What do you know about it?"

Dor spread his hands. How did he get into arguments he was trying to avoid? "Nothing. I can't grow a thing."

"You will when you're a man," Grundy muttered.

Irene remained angry. "So how come they call you a Magician, while I am only—"

"A spoiled brat," Grundy finished for her.

Irene burst into tears. She was a rather pretty child, with green eyes and a greenish tinge to her hair to match her talent, but her thumbs were normal flesh color. She was a girl, and a year younger than Dor, so she could cry if she wanted to. But it bothered him. He wanted to get along with her, and somehow had never been able to. "I hate you!" she screeched at him.

Genuinely baffled, Dor could only inquire: "Why?"

"Because you're going to be K-King! And if I want to be Q-Queen, I'll have to—to—"

"To marry him," Grundy said. "You really should learn to finish your own sentences."

"Ugh!" she cried, and it sounded as if she really were about to throw up. She looked wildly about, and spotted a tiny plant at the fringe of the pavilion. "Grow!" she yelled at it, pointing.

The plant, responsive to her talent, grew. It was a shadowboxer, with little boxing gloves mounted on springy tendrils. The gloves clenched and struck at the shadows formed by distant lightning. Soon the boxer was several feet high, and the gloves were the size of human fists. They struck at the vague shadows of the pavilion's interior. Dor backed away, knowing the blows had force.

Attracted by his motion, and by the sharper shadow his body made, the plant leaned toward him. The gloves were now larger than human fists, and mounted on vines as thick as human wrists. There were a dozen of them, several striking while several more recoiled for the next strike, keeping the plant as a whole in balance. Irene watched, a small gloat playing about her mouth.

"How did I get into this?" Dor asked, disgruntled. He didn't want to flee the pavilion; the storm had intensified and yellow rain was cascading off the roof.

The booming of its fusillade was unnerving; there were too many hailstones mixed in, and it looked suspiciously like a suitable habitat for tornado wraiths.

"Well, I don't know for sure," the pavilion answered. "But once I overheard the Queen talking with a ghost, as they took shelter from a small shower, and she said Bink always had been an annoyance to her, and now Bink's son was an annoyance to her daughter. She said she'd do something about it, if it weren't for the King."

"But I never did anything to them!" Dor protested.

"Yes you did," Grundy said. "You were born a full Magician. They can't stand that."

Now the boxing gloves had him boxed in, backed to the very edge of the pavilion. "How do I get out of this?"

"Make a light," the pavilion said. "Shadowboxers can't stand light."

"I don't have a light!" One glove grazed his chest, but as he nudged away from it, water streamed down his back. This was a yellow rain; did it leave a yellow streak?

"Then you'd better run," the pavilion said.

"Yeah, dodo!" Irene agreed. The plant was not bothering her, since she had enchanted it. "Go bash your head into a giant hailstone. Some ice would be good for your brain."

Three more boxing gloves struck at him. Dor plunged into the rain. He was instantly soaked again, but fortunately the hailstones were small and light and somewhat mushy. Irene's mocking laughter pursued him.

Gusts of wind buffeted him savagely and lightning played about the sky. Dor knew he had no business being out in this storm, but he refused to return home. He ran into the jungle.

"Turn about!" Grundy yelled into his ear. The golem was clinging to his shoulder. "Get under cover!" It was excellent advice; lightning bolts could do a lot of harm if they struck too near. After they had lain for a few hours on the ground and cooled off so that they were not so bright, they could be gathered and used for bolting together walls and things. But a fresh one could spear right through a man.

Nevertheless, Dor kept running. The general frustration and confusion he felt inside exceeded that outside.

He was not so confused as to blunder into the obvious hazards of the wilderness. The immediate Castle Roogna environs were spelled to be safe for people and their friends, but the deep jungle could not be rendered safe short of annihilation. No spell would tame a tangle tree for long, or subdue a dragon. Instead, certain paths were protected, and the wise person remained on these paths.

A lightning bolt cracked past him and buried its point in the trunk of a massive acorn tree, the brilliant length of the bolt quivering. It was a small one, but it had three good sharp jags and could have wiped Dor out if it had hit him. The tree trunk was blistering with the heat of it.

That was too close a miss. Dor ran across to the nearest charmed path, one bearing south. No bolts would strike him here. He knew the path's ultimate destination was the Magic Dust village, governed by trolls, but he had never gone that far. This time—well, he kept running, though his breath was rasping past his teeth. At least the exertion kept him warm.

"Good thing I'm along," Grundy said in his ear. "That way there's at least one rational mind in the region."

Dor had to laugh, and his mood lightened. "Half a mind, anyway," he said. The storm was lightening too, as if in tandem with his mood. The way he interacted with the inanimate, that was entirely possible. He slowed to a walk, breathing hard, but continued south. How he wished he had a big, strong, muscular body that could run without panting or knock the gloves right off shadowboxers, instead of this rather small, slight frame. Of course, he didn't have his full growth yet, but he knew he would never be a giant.

"I remember a storm we suffered down this way, just before you were born," Grundy remarked. "Your daddy, Bink, and Chester Centaur, and Crombie the soldier in griffin guise—the King transformed him for the quest, you know—and the Good Magician—"

"Good Magician Humfrey?" Dor demanded. "You traveled with him? He never leaves his castle."

"It was your father's quest for the source of magic; naturally Humfrey came along. The old gnome was always keen on information. Good thing, too; he's the one who showed me how to become real. Good thing for him, too; he met the gorgon, and you should have seen the flip she did over him, the first man she could talk to who didn't turn to stone. Anyway, this storm was so bad it washed out some of the stars from the sky; they were floating in puddles."

"Stop, Grundy!" Dor cried, laughing. "I believe in magic, as any sensible person does, but I'm not a fool! Stars wouldn't float in water. They would fizzle out in seconds!"

"Maybe they did. I was riding a flying fish at the time, so I couldn't see them too well. But it was some storm!"

There was a shudder in the ground, not thunder. Dor halted, alarmed. "What is that?"

"Sounds like the tramp of a giant, to me," Grundy hazarded. His talent was translation, and he could interpret anything any creature said, but footfalls weren't language. "Or worse. It just might be—"

Suddenly it loomed from the gloom. "An ogre!" Dor finished, terrified. "Right on the path! How could the enchantment have failed? We're supposed to be safe on these—"

The ogre tramped on toward them, a towering hulk more than twice Dor's height and broad in proportion. Its great gap-toothed mouth cracked open horrendously. An awful growl blasted out like the breath of a hungry dragon.

"What say, li'l man—will you give me a han'?" Grundy said.

"What?" Dor asked, startled almost out of his fright.

"That's what the ogre says; I was translating."

Oh. Of course. "No! I need my hands! He can't eat them." Though he was uncertain how the ogre could be stopped from eating anything he wanted. Ogres were great bone-crunchers.

The ogre growled again. "Me not eat whelp; me seek for help," Grundy said. Then the golem did a double take. "Crunch!" he cried. "The vegetarian ogre!"

"Then why does he want to eat my hand?" Dor demanded.

The monster smiled. The expression most resembled the opening of a volcanic fissure. Gassy breath hissed out. "You little loudmouthed twerp, hardly bigger than a burp."

"That's me!" Grundy agreed, answering his own translation. "Good to see you again, Crunch! How's the little lady, she with hair like nettles and skin like mush, whose face would make a zombie blush?"

"She lovely as ever; me forsake she never," the ogre replied. Dor was beginning to be able to make out the words directly; the thing was speaking his language, but with a foul accent that nearly obliterated meaning. "We have good bash, make little Smash."

Dor was by this time reassured that the spell of the path had not failed. This ogre was harmless—well, *no* ogre was harmless, but at least not ravening—and therefore able to mix with men. "A *little* smash?"

"Smash baby ogre, 'bout like you; now he gone and we too few."

"You smashed your baby?" Dor asked horrified. Maybe there was something wrong with the path-spell after all.

"Dodo! Smash is the name of their baby," Grundy explained. "All the ogres have descriptive names."

"Then why is Smash gone?" Dor demanded nervously. "Troll wives eat their husbands, so maybe ogres eat—"

"Smash wandered away in drizzle; now we search for he fizzle."

This recent storm was a mere drizzle to the ogres? That made sense. No doubt Crunch used a lightning bolt for a toothpick. "We'll help you find your baby," Dor said, grasping this positive mission with enthusiasm. Nothing like a little quest to restore spirits! Crunch's search for his little one had fizzled, so he had asked for help, and few human beings ever had such a request from an ogre! "Grundy can ask living things, because he knows all their languages, and I'll ask the dead ones. We'll run him down in no time!"

Crunch heaved a grateful sigh that almost blew Dor down. Quickly they went to the spot where the tyke had last been seen. Smash had, Crunch explained, been innocently chewing up nails, getting his daily ration of iron, then must have wandered away.

"Did the little ogre pass this way?" Dor asked a nearby rock.

"Yes—and he went toward that tree," the rock replied.

"Why don't you just have the ground tell you warm or cold?" Grundy suggested.

"The ground is not an individual entity," Dor answered. "It's just part of the whole land of Xanth. I doubt I could get its specific attention. Anyway, much of it is alive—roots, bugs, germs, magic things. They mess up communication."

"There is a ridge of stone," Grundy pointed out. "You could use it."

Good idea. "Tell me warm or cold, as I walk," Dor told it, and started to walk toward the tree. Crunch followed as softly as he was able, so that the shuddering of the land did not quite drown out the rock's voice.

"Warm—warm—cool—warm," the ridge called, steering Dor on the correct course. Dor realized suddenly that he was in fact a Magician; no one else could accomplish such a search. Irene's plant-growing magic was a strong talent, a worthy one, but it lacked the versatility of this. Her green thumb could not be turned to nonbotanic uses. A King, to rule Xanth, had to be able to exert his power effectively, as Magician Trent did. Trent could transform any enemy into a toad, and everyone in Xanth knew that. But Magician Trent was also smart; he used his talent merely to back up his brains and will. What would a girl like Irene do, if she occupied the throne? Line the paths with shadowboxing plants? Dor's talent was far more effective; he could learn all the secrets anyone had except those never voiced or shown before an inanimate object. Knowledge was the root of power. Good Magician Humfrey knew that. He—

"That's a tangler!" Grundy hissed in his ear.

Dor's attention snapped back to the surface. Good thing the golem had stayed with him, instead of questioning creatures on his own; Dor had been mindlessly reacting to the ridge's directives, and now stood directly before a medium-sized tangle tree. Which was no doubt why Grundy had remained, knowing that Dor was prone to such carelessness. If little Smash had gone there—

"I could ask it," Grundy said. "But the tree would probably lie, if it didn't just ignore me. Plants don't talk much anyway."

Crunch stepped close. "Growrrh!" he roared, poking one clublike finger at the dangling tentacles. The message needed no translation.

The tangler gave a vegetable keen of fear and whipped its tentacles away.

Dor, amazed, stepped forward. "Warm," the ridge said. Dor stepped nervously into the circle normally commanded by the tangler. "Cool," the ridge said.

So the little ogre had steered just clear of the tree and gone on. A close call—

for tyke and tree! But now the trail led toward the deep cleft of a nickelpede warren. Nickelpedes would gouge disks out of the flesh of anything, even an ogre. If—but then the trail veered away.

The ridge subsided, but there were a number of individual rocks in this vicinity, and they served as well. On and on the trail went, meandering past a routine assortment of Xanth horrors: a needle-cactus, the nest of a harpy, a poison spring, a man-eating violent flower—fortunately Smash had been no man, but an ogre, so the flower had turned purple in frustration—a patch of spear-grass with its speartips glinting evilly. Plus similar threats, with which the wilderness abounded. Smash had avoided stepping into any traps, until at last the tyke had come to the lair of a flying dragon.

Dor halted, dismayed. This time there was no doubt: no one passed this close to such a lair without paying the price. Dragons were the lords of the jungle, as a class; specific monsters might prevail against specific dragons; but overall, dragons governed the wilds much as Man governed the tames.

They could hear the dragon cubs entertaining themselves with some poor prey, happily scorching each potential route of escape. Dragon cubs needed practice to get their scorching up to par. A stationary target sufficed only up to a point; after that they needed live lures, to get their reflexes and aim properly tracked.

"Smash . . . is there?" Dor asked, dreading the answer.

"Hot," the nearest stone agreed warmly.

Crunch grimaced, and this time not even an ogress would have mistaken his ire. He stomped up to the scene of the crime. The ground danced under the impact of his footfalls, but the dragon's lair seemed secure.

The lair's entrance was a narrow cleft that only the narrow torso of a small dragon could pass through. Crunch put one hand at each side of it and sent a brutal surge of power galumphing through his massively gnarly muscles. The rock split asunder, and suddenly the entrance was ogre-sized. The dragons were exposed, in their conservative nest of diamonds and other heat-resistant jewels. The thing about fire-breathing dragons was that ordinary nest material tended to burn up or melt or scorch unpleasantly, so diamonds were a dragon's best friend.

A little ogre, no larger than Dor himself, stood at bay amid three winged dragonets while the dragon lady glared benignly on. The ogreling was stoutly structured and would probably have been a match for any single dragon his size, but the three were making things hot for him. There were scorch marks all about, though the little ogre seemed as yet unhurt. Dragons did like to play with their food before roasting it.

Crunch did not even growl. He just leaned over and looked at the dragoness

—and the smoke issuing from her mouth sank like chill fog to the floor. For Crunch massed as much as she did, and it would be redundant to specify the power-to-mass ratio of ogres. She was not up to this snuff, not even with a belly full of fuel. She never moved a muscle, petrified as if she had locked gazes with a gorgon.

Now Smash advanced on one dragonet. "Me tweak you tail, you big ol' snail!" he cried gleefully. He hauled on the tail, swung the dragon around, and hurled it carelessly against the far wall.

The second little dragon opened its mouth and wafted out a small column of fire. Smash exhaled with such force that the flame rammed right back inside the dragon, who was immediately overcome by a heated fit of coughing.

The third dragonet, no coward, pounced on Smash with all four clawed feet extended. Smash raised one fist. The dragon landed squarely on it, its head and tail whipping around to smack into each other. It fell on the bed of diamonds, stunned.

Even the littlest ogre was tougher than its weight in dragons, when the odds were evened. Dor had not believed this, before; he had thought it was mere folklore.

"Now games are through, to home with you," Crunch said, reaching in to lift his son out of the lair by his tough scruff of the neck. With his other fist, Crunch struck the nest so hard that the diamonds bounced out in a cloud, scattering all over the landscape. The dragoness winced; she would have a tedious cleanup chore to do. Without a backward glance at her, they tramped away.

Except for Grundy, who couldn't resist putting in a last word: "Good thing for you you didn't hurt the tyke," he called to the dragon lady. "If you had, Crunch might have gotten angry. You wouldn't like him when he's angry."

Fortunately, Crunch was now in a good mood. "Little man help we; how pay we fee?" the ogre inquired of Dor.

Abashed, Dor demurred. "We were glad to help," he said. "We have to get home now."

Crunch considered. This took some time; he was big but not smart. He addressed Grundy: "Golem tell true: what can me do?"

"Oh, Dor doesn't really need any help," Grundy said. "He's a Magician."

Crunch swelled up ominously. "Me get mad, when truth not had."

Daunted, Grundy responded quickly. "Well, the boys around Castle Roogna do tease Dor a little. He's not as big and strong as the big boys, but he has more magic, so they sort of—"

Crunch cut him off with an impatient gesture. The ogre picked Dor up gently in one huge hand—fortunately not by the scruff of the neck—and carried him north along the path. Such was the ogre's stride, they were very soon at the edge of the Castle Roogna orchard. He set Dor down and stood silently while boy and golem proceeded forward.

"Thanks for the lift," Dor said weakly. He was certainly glad this monster was a vegetarian.

Crunch did not respond. Frozen in his hunched-over posture, he most resembled the massive stump of a burned-out gnarlbole tree.

Awkwardly, Dor went on toward his home, passing near the umbrella tree. As luck would have it, the two bullies were still there. Both jumped up when they saw Dor, and eager for sport, ran out to bar his way. "The little snooper's back!" Horsejaw cried. "What's he doing on a path meant for people?"

"I wouldn't," Grundy said warningly.

For answer, a little snake landed on his head. A sonic boom went off behind Dor. The boys laughed coarsely.

Then the ground shuddered. The bullies looked around wildly, fearing an avalanche from nowhere. There was another shudder, jarring Dor's teeth. It was the ogre tramping forward under full steam.

Horsejaw's mouth fell open as he saw that monster bearing down on him. He was too startled to move. The other boy tried to run, but the ground shook so violently that he fell on his face and lay there. Several small snakes appeared, squiggled nervously, and vanished; no help there. If there were any more sonic booms, they were drowned out by the violence of the ogre's approach.

Crunch strode up until he loomed over the small party, his thick torso dwarfing the slender metal trunk of a nearby ironwood tree. "Dor me friend," he thundered distinctly, and the umbrella tree collapsed into shambles with the vibration. "Help he lend." Small cracks opened in the hard ground of the path, and somewhere a heavy branch crashed to the forest floor. "If laugh at lad, me might get mad." And he swung one clublike fist around in a great circle, barely over Horsejaw's head, so that the wind made the bully's hair stand on end. At least, Dor thought it was the wind that did it; the boy looked terrified.

The ogre's fist smashed into the trunk of the ironwood tree. There was a nearly deafening clang. A tubular section of iron sprang out, leaving the top of the tree momentarily suspended in air; then it dropped heavily and fell over with a crash that made the ground shake once more. Ironwood was solid stuff! An acrid wisp of smoke wafted up from the stump: the top of it was glowing red with a white fringe, and part of it where the ogre's fist had touched had melted.

Crunch selected a jagged splinter of iron, picked his teeth with it, and wheeled about. His monstrous horny toes gouged a furrow from the path in the process. He tramped thunderously back south, humming a merry tune of bloodshed. In a moment he was gone, but the vibration of the terrain took a long time to quiet. Away in the palace, there was the tinkling crash of a window shattering.

Horsejaw stood looking at the iron stump. His eyes flickered momentarily to Dor, then back to the steaming metal. Then he fainted.

"I don't think the boys will tease you so much any more, Dor," Grundy remarked gravely.

Chapter 2

Tapestry

Dor was not teased much any more. No one wanted to upset his friend. But this hardly eased his unrest. The teasing had not bothered him as much as it had bothered Grundy; Dor had always known he could use his superior magic to bring others into line, if he really had to. It was his general isolation from others that weighed on him, and his new awareness of Millie the ghost. What a difference there was between a brat like Irene and a woman like Millie! Yet Irene was the one Dor was expected to get along with. It wasn't fair.

He needed to talk with someone. His parents were approachable, but Chameleon varied so much in appearance and intellect that he never could be certain how to approach her, and Bink might not be sympathetic to this particular problem. Besides which, both of them were away on a trip to Mundania, on business for the King. The Land of Xanth was busy establishing diplomatic relations with Mundania, and after the centuries of bad relations this was a touchy matter, requiring the utmost finesse. So Dor's parents were out. Grundy would chat with him anytime—but the former golem was apt to get too cute about other people's problems. Such as calling Irene's green-thumb talent "stinkfinger." Dor hardly blamed her for retaliating violently, inconvenient as it had been for him personally. Grundy cared, all right—that was how he had become a real, living person—but he didn't really understand. Anyhow, he knew Dor too well. Dor's grandfather Roland, whose talent was the stun—the ability to freeze people immobile—was a good man to talk to, but he was at his home in the North Village, a good two days' travel across the Gap.

There was only one person Dor could approach who was human, competent, mature, discreet, male, and an equivalent Magician. That was the King. He knew the King was a busy man; it seemed the trade arrangements with Mundania were constantly complex, and of course there were many local problems to be handled. But King Trent always made time for Dor. Perhaps that was one root of Irene's hostility, which had spread to the Queen and the palace personnel in insidious channels. Irene talked to her father less than Dor did. So Dor tried not to abuse his Magician's privilege. But this time he simply had to go.

He picked Grundy up and marched to the palace. The palace was actually Castle Roogna. For many years it had been a castle that was not a palace, deserted and forlorn, but King Trent had changed that. Now it was the seat of government of Xanth, as it had been in its youth.

Crombie the soldier stood guard at the drawbridge across the moat. This was mainly to remind visitors to stay clear of the water, because the moat-monsters were not tame. One would think that was evident, but every few months some fool wandered too close, or tried to swim in the murky water, or even attempted to feed some tidbit to a monster by hand. Such attempts were invariably successful; sometimes the monster got the whole person, sometimes only the hand.

Crombie was asleep on his feet. Grundy took advantage of this to generate some humor at the soldier's expense. "Hey, there, birdbeak; how's the stinking broad?"

One eye cracked open. Immediately Grundy rephrased his greeting. "Hello, handsome soldier; how's the sweet wife?"

Both eyes came open, rolling expressively. "Jewel is well and cute and smelling like a rose and too worn out to go to work today, I daresay. I had a weekend pass."

So that was why the soldier was so sleepy! Crombie's wife lived in underground caverns south of the Magic Dust village; it was a long way to travel on short notice. But that was not exactly what Crombie meant. He had the royal travel-conjurer zap him to the caverns, and back again when his pass expired. Crombie's fatigue was not from traveling.

"A soldier really knows how to make a pass," Grundy observed, with a smirk he thought Dor wouldn't understand. Dor understood, more or less; he just didn't see the humor in it.

"That's for sure!" Crombie agreed heartily. "Women—I can take 'em or leave 'em, but my wife's a Jewel of a nymph."

That had special meaning too. Nymphs were ideally shaped female creatures of little intellect, useful primarily for man's passing entertainment. It was strange that Crombie had married one. But he had been under an omen of marriage, and Jewel was said to be a very special nymph, with unusual wit for the breed, who had an important job. Dor had asked his father about Jewel once, since none of the local artifacts knew about her, but Bink had answered evasively. That was part of the reason Dor didn't want to ask his father about Millie. Millie was nymphlike at times, and evasions were disquieting. Had there been something between—? No, impossible. Anyway, this sort of information could not be elicited from inanimate objects; they did not understand living feelings at all. They were purely objective. Usually.

"Watch out for the moat-monsters," Crombie warned dutifully. "They're not tame." Slowly his eyelids sank. He was asleep again.

"I'd sure like to watch one of his passes in a magic mirror," Grundy said. "But it'd break the glass in the pattern of an X."

They went on into the palace. Suddenly a three-headed wolf stalked out before them, growling fiercely. Dor paused. "Is that real?" he murmured to the floor.

"No," the floor responded in an undertone.

Relieved, Dor walked right into the wolf—and through it. The monster was mere illusion, a construct of the Queen. She resented his presence here, and her illusions were so proficient that there was no direct way to tell them from reality except by touch—which could be dangerous if something happened *not* to be an illusion. But his magic had nullified hers, as it usually did; she could never fool him long. "Sorceresses shouldn't mess with Magicians," Grundy observed snidely, and the wolf growled in anger as it vanished.

It was replaced by an image of the Queen herself, regal in robe and crown. She always enhanced her appearance for company; she was sort of dumpy in real flesh. "My husband is occupied at the moment," she said with exaggerated formality. "Kindly wait in the upstairs drawing room." Then, under her breath, she added: "Better yet, wait in the moat."

The Queen did not conceal her dislike of him, but she would not dare misrepresent the position of the King. She would inform Dor when the King was free.

"Thank you, Your Highness," Dor replied as formally as she had addressed him, and walked to the drawing room.

Actually, the drawing room did not contain any drawings, only one huge tapestry hung on the wall. This had once been a bedroom; Dor's father mentioned sleeping in it once, back before Castle Roogna was restored. In fact Dor himself had slept in it, earlier in life; he remembered being fascinated by the great tapestry. Now the bed had been replaced by a couch, but the tapestry remained as intriguing as ever.

It was embroidered with scenes from the ancient past of Castle Roogna and its environs, eight hundred years ago. In one section was the Castle, its battlements under construction by a herd of centaurs; in other sections were the deep wilderness of Xanth, the awful Gap dragon, villages protected by stockades— such defenses were no longer used—and other castles. In fact there were more castles than there were today.

The more Dor looked at it, the more he saw—for the figures in the tapestry moved when watched. Since everything was more or less in proportion, the representations of men were tiny; the tip of his little finger could cover one of them over. But every detail seemed authentic. The whole lives of these people were shown, if one cared to watch long enough. Of course, their lives proceeded at the same rate contemporary lives did, so Dor had never seen a whole life pass; he would be an old man before that happened. And of course the process had to have some reasonable cessation, because otherwise the tapestry would long since have passed beyond the Castle Roogna stage and gotten right up to the present. So there were aspects of this magic Dor had not yet fathomed; he just had to accept what he saw. Meanwhile, the tapestry figures worked and slept and fought and loved, in miniature.

Memories flooded Dor. What adventures he had seen, years ago, riveted to this moving picture. Swordsmen and dragons and fair ladies and magic of every type, going on and on! But all in baffling silence; without words, much of the action became meaningless. Why did this swordsman battle this dragon, yet leave that other dragon alone? Why did the chambermaid kiss this courtier, and not that one, though that one was handsomer? Who was responsible for this particular enchantment? And why was that centaur so angry after a liaison with his filly? There was so much of it going on at once that it was hard to fathom any overall pattern.

He had asked Millie about it, and she had gladly told him the valiant tales of her youth—for she had been young at the time of Castle Roogna's construction. But though her tales were more cohesive than those of the moving pictures of the tapestry, they were also more selective. Millie did not enjoy healthy bloodshed or deadly peril or violent love; she preferred episodes of simple joy and family accommodation. That sort of thing could get dull after a while.

Also, she never talked about herself, after she had left her native stockade. Nothing about her own life and loves, or how she became a ghost. And she wouldn't tell how she had come to know the zombie Jonathan, though this could have happened quite naturally in the course of eight centuries of lonely association in Castle Roogna. Dor wondered whether, if he should ever happen to be a ghost for eight hundred years, zombies might begin to look good to him. He doubted it. At any rate, his thirst for knowledge had been frustrated, and he had finally given it up.

Why hadn't he simply made the tapestry itself talk to him, answering his questions? Dor didn't remember, so he asked the tapestry: "Please explain the nature of your images."

"I cannot," the tapestry replied. "They are as varied and detailed as life itself, not subject to interpretation by the likes of me." There it was: when performing its given function, the tapestry was painstakingly apt; but when speaking as a piece of rug, it lacked the mind to fathom its own images. He could learn from it whether a fly had sat on it in the past hour, but not the motive of an eight-hundred-years-gone Magician.

Now, as Dor contemplated the images, his old interest in history resurged. What a world that had been, back during the celebrated Fourth Wave of human colonization of Xanth! Then adventure had reigned supreme. Not dullness, as in the present.

A giant frog appeared. "The King will see you now, Master Do-oo-or," it croaked. It was of course another illusion of Queen Iris'; she was forever showing off her versatility.

"Thanks, frogface," Grundy said. He always knew when he could slip in a healthy insult without paying for it. "Catch any good flies in that big mouth of yours recently?" The frog swelled up angrily, but could not protest lest it step— or hop—out of character. The Queen disliked compromising her illusions. "How's your mother, the toad?" the golem continued blithely, the malice hardly showing in his tone. "Did she ever clean up those purple warts on her—"

The frog exploded. "Well, you didn't have to blow up at me," Grundy reproved the vanishing smoke. "I was only being sociable, frogbrain." Dor, with superhuman effort, kept his face straight. The Queen could still be watching, in the guise of a no-see-'em gnat or something. There were times when Grundy's caustic wit got him into trouble, but it was worth it.

The King's library was also upstairs, just a few doors down. That was where the King was always to be found when not otherwise occupied—and sometimes even when he was. It was not supposed to be generally known, but Dor had pried the news out of the furniture: sometimes the Queen made an image of the King in the library, at the King's behest, so he could interview some minor functionary when he was busy with more important things elsewhere. The King never did that with Dor, however.

Dor proceeded directly to the library, noting a ghost flitting across the dusky hall farther down. Millie had been one of half a dozen ghosts, and the only one to be restored to life; the others still hovered about their haunts. Dor rather liked them; they were friendly but rather shy, and were easily spooked. He was sure each had its story, but like Millie they were diffident about themselves.

He knocked at the library door. "Come in, Dor," the King's voice answered immediately. He always seemed to know when Dor came calling, even when the Queen was not around to inform him.

Dor entered, suddenly shy. "I—uh—if you're not too busy—"

King Trent smiled. "I am busy, Dor. But your business is important."

Suddenly it hardly seemed so. The King was a solid, graying man old enough to be Dor's grandfather, yet still handsome. He wore a comfortable robe, somewhat faded and threadbare; he depended on the Queen to garb him in illusion befitting whatever occasion occurred, so needed no real clothes. At the moment he was highly relaxed and informal, and Dor knew this was intended to make Dor himself feel the same. "I, uh, I can come back another time—"

King Trent frowned. "And leave me to pore over the next dull treaty amendment? My eyes are tired enough already!" A stray bluebottle fly buzzed him, and absentmindedly the King transformed it into a small bluebottle tree growing from a crevice in the desk. "Come, Magician—let us chat for a while. How are things with you?"

"Well, we met a big frog—" Grundy began, but silenced instantly when the King glanced his way.

"Uh, about the same," Dor said. The King was giving him an opening; why couldn't he speak his mind?

"Your cottage cheese still sound?"

"Oh, yes, the house is doing fine. Talks back quite a bit, though." Inanity!

"I understand you made friends with Crunch the ogre."

Did the King know *everything*? "Yes, I helped find his child, Smash."

"But my daughter Irene doesn't like you."

"Not much." Dor wished he had stayed at home. "But she—" Dor found himself at a loss for a polite compliment. Irene was a pretty girl; her father surely knew that already. She made plants grow—but she should have been more powerfully talented. "She—"

"She is young, yet. However, even mature women are not always explicable. They seem to change overnight into completely different creatures."

Grundy laughed. "That's for sure! Dor's sweet on Millie the ghost!"

"Shut up!" Dor cried in a fury of embarrassment.

"An exceptional woman," King Trent observed as if he had not heard Dor's outcry. "A ghost for eight centuries, abruptly restored to life in the present. Her talent makes her unsuitable for normal positions around the palace, so she has served admirably as a governess at your cottage. Now you are growing up, and must begin to train for adult responsibilities."

"Adult?" Dor asked, still bemused by his shame. It was not the Queen-frog who had the big mouth; it was Grundy!

"You are the heir apparent to the throne of Xanth. Do not be concerned about my daughter; she is not Magician level and cannot assume the office unless there is no Magician available, and then only on an interim basis until a Magician appears, preserving continuity of government. Should I be removed from the picture in the next decade, you will have to take over. It is better that you be prepared."

Suddenly the present seemed overwhelmingly real. "But I can't—I don't—"

"You have the necessary magic, Dor. You lack the experience and fortitude to use it properly. I would be remiss if I did not arrange to provide you with that experience."

"But—"

"No Magician should require the services of an ogre to enforce his authority. You have not yet been hardened to the occasional ruthlessness required."

"Uh—" Dor knew his face was crimson. He had just received a potent rebuke, and knew it was justified. For a Magician to give way to the likes of Horsejaw—

"I believe you need a mission, Dor. A man's quest. One whose completion will demonstrate your competence for the office you are coming to."

This had taken an entirely different tack than Dor had anticipated. It was as if the King had made his decision and summoned Dor for this directive, rather than merely granting an audience. "I—maybe so." Maybe so? For certain so!

"You hold Millie in respect," the King said. "But you are aware that she is not of your generation, and has one great unmet need."

"Jonathan," Dor said. "She—she loves Jonathan the zombie!" He was almost indignant.

"Then I think the nicest thing anyone could do for her would be to discover a way to restore Jonathan to full life. Then, perhaps, the reason she loves him would become apparent."

"But—" Dor had to halt. He knew that Grundy's remarks were only the least of the ridicule that would be directed at him if he ever expressed any serious ideas of his own about Millie. She was an eight-hundred-year-old woman; he was just a boy. One way to stifle all speculation would be to give her what she most wanted: Jonathan, alive. "But how—?"

The King spread his hands. "I do not know the answer, Dor. But there may be one who does."

There was only one person in the Land of Xanth who knew all the answers:

the Good Magician Humfrey. But he was a sour old man who charged a year's service for each Answer. Only a person of considerable determination and fortitude went to consult Good Magician Humfrey.

Suddenly Dor realized the nature of the challenge King Trent had laid down for him. First, he would have to leave these familiar environs and trek through the hazardous wilderness to the Good Magician's castle. Then he would have to force his way in to brace the Magician. Then serve his year for the Answer. Then use the Answer to restore Jonathan to life—knowing that in so doing, he was abolishing any chance that Millie would ever—

His mind balked. This was no quest; this was disaster!

"Ordinary citizens have only themselves to be concerned about," Trent said. "A ruler must be concerned for the welfare of others as much as for himself. He must be prepared to make sacrifices—sometimes very personal ones. He may even have to lose the woman he loves, and marry the one he doesn't love—for the good of the realm."

Give up Millie, marry Irene? Dor rebelled—then realized that the King had not been talking about Dor, but about himself. Trent had lost his wife and child in Mundania, and then married the Sorceress Iris, whom he never professed to love, and had a child by her—for the good of the realm. Trent asked nothing of any citizen he would not ask of himself.

"I will never be the man you are," Dor said humbly.

The King rose, clapping him on the back so that Grundy almost fell off his shoulder. Trent might be old, but he was still strong. "*I* was never the man I am," he said. "A man is only the man he seems to be. Inside, where no one sees, he may be a mass of gnawing worms of doubt and ire and grief." He paused reflectively as he showed Dor firmly to the doorway. "No challenge is easy. The measure of the challenge a man rises to at need is the measure of the man. I proffer you a challenge for a Magician and a King."

Dor found himself standing in the hall, still bemused. Even Grundy was silent.

Good Magician Humfrey's castle was east of Castle Roogna, not far as the dragon flew, but more than a day's journey through the treacherous wilderness for a boy on foot. There was no enchanted path to Humfrey's retreat, because the Magician abhorred company; all paths led away only. Dor could not be sent there instantly by spell, because this was his quest, his private personal challenge, to accomplish by himself.

Dor started in the morning, using his talent to solve part of the problem of travel. "Stones, give me a warning whistle whenever I approach anything dangerous to me, and let me know the best route to the Good Magician's castle."

"We can tell you what is dangerous," the rocks chorused. There were no stony silences for him! "But we don't know where the Good Magician's castle is. He has strewn little forget-spells all over."

He should have known. "I've been there," Grundy offered. "It's not far south of the Gap. Bear north toward the Gap, then east, then south to his castle."

"And if I'm off, and miss it, where will I wind up?" Dor inquired sourly.

"In the belly of a dragon, most likely."

Dor bore north, heeding the whistles. Most citizens of Xanth did not know of the Gap's existence, because it had been enchanted into anonymity, but Dor had lived all his life in this neighborhood and visited the chasm several times. Warned by his talent, he steered clear of diversions such as dragon runs, tangle trees, ant-lion prides, choke nettles, saw grass, and other threats. Only his father Bink could traverse the wilderness alone with greater equanimity, and maybe King Trent himself. Still, Grundy was nervous. "If you don't live to be King, I'll be in big trouble," he remarked, not entirely humorously.

When they got hungry, the stones directed them to the nearest breadloaf trees, soda poppies, and jelly-barrel trunks. Then on, as the day waned.

"Say!" Grundy exclaimed. "There are one-way paths from Humfrey's castle to the Gap. We're bound to cross one. The stones will know where such a path is, because they will have seen people walking along them. The forget spells are just about the location of the Magician's castle, not about stray people, so we can bypass them."

"Right!" Dor agreed. "Stones, have any of you seen such travel?"

There was a chorus of no's. But he kept checking as he progressed, and in due course found some stones that had indeed observed such travelers. After some experimentation, he managed to get aligned with the path, and took a step toward the chasm. There it was, suddenly: a clear path leading to a bridge that seemed to span the full width of the Gap. But when he faced the other way, there was only jungle. Fascinating magic, these paths!

"Maybe if you walked backward—" Grundy suggested.

"But then I'd stumble into all sorts of things!"

"Well, you walk forward, and I'll face backward and keep an eye on the path."

They tried that, and it worked. The stones gave general guidance, and Grundy warned him whenever he drifted to one side or another. They made good progress, for of course the path was charmed, with no serious hazards in its immediate vicinity. But it had taken some time to find it, and when dark closed in they were still in the wilderness. Fortunately they located a pillow bush and fashioned a bed of multicolored pillows, setting out sputtering bugbombs from a bugbomb weed to repel predatory insects. They didn't worry about rain; Dor called out to a passing cloud, and it assured him that the clouds were all resting tonight, saving up for a blowout two days hence.

In the morning they feasted on boysengirls berries, the seeds like tiny boys a bit strong, and the jelly girls a bit sweet, so that they had to be taken together for full enjoyment. They washed the berries down with the juice from punctured coffee beans and took up the march again. Dor felt somewhat stiff; he wasn't used to this amount of walking. "Funny, I feel fine," Grundy remarked. He, of course, had ridden Dor's shoulder most of the way.

Another friendly cloud advised them when the Magician's castle was in sight. Humfrey had not thought to put forget spells on the clouds, or perhaps had found it impractical, since clouds tended to drift constantly. As it was, Dor realized he was fortunate these were good-natured cumulus clouds, instead of the bad-tempered thunderheads. By midmorning they were there.

The castle was small but pretty, with round turrets stretching up beyond the battlements, and a cute blue moat. Within the moat swam a triton: a handsome man with a fish's tail, carrying a wicked triple-tipped spear. He glared at the intruders.

"I think our first hurdle is upon us," Grundy remarked. "That merman is not about to let us pass."

"How did you get past, when you came to ask a Question?" Dor asked.

"That was a dozen years ago! It's all been changed. I snuck by a carnivorous seaweed in the moat, and climbed a slippery glass wall, and outsmarted a sword swallower inside."

"A sword swallower? How could he hurt you?"

"He burped."

Dor thought about that, and smiled. But the golem was right: past experience was no aid to the present. Not while the Good Magician's defenses kept changing.

He put a foot forward to touch the surface of the water. Immediately the triton swam forward, head and arm raised, trident poised. "It is only fair to warn you, intruder, that I have five notches on my spear shaft."

Dor jerked back his foot. "How do we get past this monster?" he asked, staring into the moat.

"I'm not allowed to tell you that," the water replied apologetically. "The old gnome's got everything counterspelled."

"He would," Grundy grumbled. "You can't out-gnome a gnome in his own home."

"But there is a way," Dor said. "We just have to figure it out. That's the challenge."

"While the Magician chortles inside, waiting to see if we'll make it or get speared. He's got a sense of humor like that of a tangle tree."

Dor made as if to dive into the moat. The triton raised his trident again. The merman's arm was muscular, and as he supported his body well out of the water the points of his weapon glinted in the sun. Dor backed off again.

"Maybe there's a tunnel under the moat," Grundy suggested.

They walked around the moat. At one point there was a metallic plaque inscribed with the words TRESPASSERS WILL BE PROSECUTED.

"I don't know what that means," Dor complained.

"I'll translate," Grundy said. "It means: keep out."

"I wonder if it means more?" Dor mused. "Why should Humfrey put a sign out here, when there's no obvious way in anyway? Why say it in language only a golem understands? That doesn't seem to make sense—which means it probably makes a lot of sense, if you interpret it correctly."

"I don't know why you're fulminating about a stupid sign, when you need to be figuring out how to cross the moat."

"Now, if there were a tunnel that the Magician could use without running afoul of his own hazards, he'd need a marked place for it to emerge," Dor continued. "Naturally he wouldn't want anyone else using it without his permission. So he might cover it over and put a stay-away spell on it. Like this."

"You know, I think you've got a brain after all," Grundy admitted. "But you'd have to have a counterspell to get it open, and it's not allowed to tell you that secret."

"But it's only a stone. Not too bright. We might be able to trick it."

"I get you. Let's try a dialogue, know what I mean?" They had played this game before.

Dor nodded, smiling. They stepped up close to the plaque. "Good morning, plaque," Dor greeted it.

"Not to you, it ain't," the plaque responded. "I ain't going to tell you nothing."

"That's because you don't know nothing," Grundy said loudly, with a fine sneer in his voice.

"I do not know nothing!"

"My friend claims you have no secrets to divulge," Dor told the plaque.

"Your friend's a duh."

"The plaque says you're a duh," Dor informed Grundy.

"Yeah? Well the plaque's a dumdum."

"Plaque, my friend says you're a—"

"I am not!" the plaque retorted angrily. "He's the dumdum." What feelings objects had tended to be superficial. "He doesn't have my secret."

"What secret, dodo?" Grundy demanded, his voice even more heavily freighted with sneer than before.

"My secret chamber, that's what! He doesn't have that, does he?"

"*Nobody* has that," Grundy cried, scowling. "You're just making that up so we won't think you're the granitehead you really are!"

"Is that so? Well look at that, duh!" And the face of the plaque swung open to reveal an interior chamber. Inside was a small box.

Dor reached in and snatched out the box before the plaque caught on to its mistake. "And what have we here?" he inquired gleefully.

"Gimme that back!" the plaque cried. "It's mine, all mine!"

Dor studied the box. On the top was a button marked with the words DON'T PUSH. He pushed it.

The lid sprang up. A snakelike thing leaped out, startling Dor, who dropped the box. "HA, HA, HA, HA, HA!" it bellowed.

The snake-thing landed on the ground, its energy spent. "Jack, at your service," it said. "Jack in the box. You sure look foolish."

"A golem," Grundy said. "I should have known. Golems are insufferable."

"You oughta know, pinhead," Jack retorted. He reached into a serpentine pocket and drew out a shiny disk. "Here is an achievement button to commemorate the occasion." He held it up.

Dor reached down and took the button. It had two faces. On one side it said TRESPASSER. On the other it said PERSECUTED.

Dor had to laugh, ruefully. "I guess I fell for it! That's what I get for seeking the easy way through."

He put the button against his shirt, where it stuck magically, PERSECUTED side out. Then he picked up the Jack, put him back in the box, closed the lid, set the works back inside the plaque's chamber, and closed that. "Well played, plaque," he said.

"Yeah," the plaque agreed, mollified.

They returned their attention to the moat. "No substitute for my own ingenuity," Dor said. "But this diversion has given me a notion. If we can be tricked by a decoy—"

"I don't see what you're up to," Grundy said. "That triton knows his target."

"That triton *thinks* he knows his target. Watch this." And Dor squatted by the water and said to it: "I shall make a wager with you, water. I bet that you can't imitate my voice."

"Yeah?" the water replied, sounding just like Dor.

"Hey, that's pretty good, for a beginner. But you can't do it in more than one place at a time."

"That's what you think!" the water said in Dor's voice from two places.

"You're much better than I thought!" Dor confessed ruefully. "But the real challenge is to do it so well that a third party could not tell which is me and which is you. I'm sure you couldn't fool that triton, for example."

"That wetback?" the water demanded. "What do you want to bet, sucker?"

"That water's calling you a kind of fish," Grundy muttered.

Dor considered. "Well, I don't have anything you would value. Unless—that's it! You can't talk to other people, but you still need some way to show them your prowess. You could do that with this button." He brought up the TRESPASSER/ PERSECUTED button, showing both sides. "See, it says what you do to intruders. You can flash it from your surface in sinister warning."

"You're on!" the water said eagerly. "You hide, and if old three-point follows my voice instead of you, I win the prize."

"Right," Dor agreed. "I really hate to risk an item of this value, but then I don't think I'm going to lose it. You distract him, and I'll hide under your surface. If he can't find me before I drown, the button's yours."

"Hey, there's a flaw in that logic!" Grundy protested. "If you drown—"

"Hello, fishtail!" a voice cried from the far side of the moat. "I'm the creep from the jungle!"

The triton, who had been viewing the proceedings without interest, whirled. "Another one?"

Dor slipped into the water, took half a breath, and dived below the surface. He swam vigorously, feeling the cool flow across his skin. No trident struck him. As his lungs labored painfully against his locked throat, he found the inner wall of the moat and thrust his head up.

He gasped for breath, and so did Grundy, still clinging to his shoulder. The triton was still chasing here and there, following the shifting voices. "Over here, sharksnoot! No, here, mer-thing! Are you blind, fishface?"

Dor heaved himself out. "Safe!" he cried. "You win, moat; here's the prize. It hurts awfully to lose it, but you sure showed me up." And he flipped the button into the water.

"Anytime, sucker," the water replied smugly.

The significance of Grundy's prior comment sank in belatedly. A sucker was a kind of fish, prone to fasten to the legs of swimmers and—but he hoped there were none here.

The decoy voices subsided. The triton looked around, spotting him with surprise. "How did you do that? I chased you all over the moat!"

"You certainly did," Dor agreed. "I'm really breathless."

"You some sort of Magician or something?"

"That describes it."

"Oh." The triton swam away, affecting loss of interest.

The second challenge was now before them. There was a narrow ledge of stone between the moat and the castle wall. Dor found no obvious entry to the castle. "It's always this way," Grundy said wisely. "A blank wall. Inanimate obstacle. But the worst is always inside."

"Good to know," Dor said, feeling a chill that was not entirely from his soaking clothing. He was beginning to appreciate the depth of the challenge King Trent had made for him. At each stage he was forced to question his ability and his motive: were the risk and effort worth the prize? He had never been exposed to a sustained challenge of this magnitude before, where even his talent could help him only deviously. With the counterspells against things' giving away information, he was forced to employ his magic very cleverly, as with the moat. Maybe this was the necessary course to manhood—but he would much prefer to have a safe route home. He was, after all, only a boy. He didn't have the mass and thews of a man, and certainly not the courage. Yet here he was— and he had better go forward, because the triton would hardly let him go back.

The mass and thews of a man. The notion appealed insidiously. If by some magic he could become bigger and stronger than his father, and be skilled with the sword, so that he didn't have to have an ogre backing him up—ah, then wouldn't his problems be over! No more weaseling about, using tricks to sneak by tritons, arguing with plaques . . .

But this was foolish wishful thinking. He would never be such a man, even when full grown. "Full groan," he muttered, appreciating the morbid pun. Maybe he would have made a good zombie!

They circled the castle again. At intervals there were alcoves with plants growing in them, decorating the blank wall. But they weren't approachable plants. Stinkweeds, skunk cabbages, poison ivy—the last flipped a drop of glistening poison at him, but he avoided it. The drop struck the stone ledge and etched a smoking hole in it. Another alcove held a needle-cactus, one of the worst plant menaces of all. Dor hastened on past that one, lest the ornery vegetable elect to fire a volley of needles at him.

"You climbed a wall of glass?" Dor inquired skeptically, contemplating the blank stone. He was not a good climber, and there were no handholds, steps, or other aids.

"I was a golem then—a construct of string and gunk. It didn't matter if I fell; I wasn't real. I existed only to do translations. Today I could not climb that glass wall, or even this stone wall; I have too much reality to lose."

Too much reality to lose. That made sense. Dor's own reality became more attractive as he pondered the possible losing of it. Why was he wishing for a hero's body and power? He was a Magician, probable heir to the throne. Strong men were common; Magicians were rare. Why throw that away—for a zombie?

Then he thought of lovely Millie. To do something nice for her, make her grateful. Ah, foolishness! But it seemed he was also that kind of a fool. Maybe it came with growing up. Her talent of sex appeal—

Dor tapped at the stone. It was distressingly solid. No hollow panels there. He felt for crevices. The interstices between stones were too small for his fingers, and he already knew there were no ledges for climbing. "Got to be in one of those alcoves," he said.

They checked the alcoves, carefully. There was nothing. The noxious plants grew from stone planters sitting on the rampart; there was no secret entrance through their dirt.

But the niche of the needle-cactus seemed deeper. In fact it curved into darkness beyond the cactus. A passage!

Now all he had to do was figure out how to pass one of the deadliest of the medium-sized plants of Xanth. Needle-cactuses tended to shoot first and consider afterward. Even a tangle tree would probably give way to a needler, if they grew side by side. Chester the centaur, a friend of Dor's father, still had puncture scars marring his handsome rump where a needle had chastened him.

Dor poked his head cautiously around the corner. "I don't suppose you feel like letting a traveler pass?" he inquired without much hope.

A needle shot directly at his face. He jerked violently back, and it hissed on out to land in the moat. There was an irate protest from the triton, who didn't like having his residence littered.

"The needler says no," Grundy translated gratuitously.

"I could have guessed." How was he going to pass this hurdle? He couldn't swim under this cactus, or reason with it, or avoid it. There was barely room to squeeze by it, in the confined alcove.

"Maybe loop it with a rope, and haul it out of the way," Grundy suggested dubiously.

"We don't have a rope," Dor pointed out. "And nothing to make one with."

"I know someone whose talent is making ropes from water," Grundy said.

"So *he* could pass this menace. We can't. And if we did have rope, we'd get needled the moment we hauled the cactus out into the open."

"Unless we yanked it right into the moat."

Dor chuckled at the thought. Then he got serious. "Could we fashion a shield?"

"Nothing to fashion it from. Same problem as the rope. This ledge is barren. Now if cacti don't like water at all, maybe we can scoop—"

"They can live without it, but they like it fine," Dor said. "They get rained on all the time. Just so long as it doesn't flood too much. Splashing won't do any good, unless—" He paused, considering. "If we could send a lot of water flowing through there, flood out the cactus, wash the dirt from its pot, expose the roots—"

"How?"

Dor sighed. "No way, without a bucket. We just aren't set up to handle this cactus."

"Yeah. A firedrake could handle it. Those plants don't like fire; it burns off their needles. Then they can't fight until they grow new ones, and that takes time. But we don't have any fire." He shook a few drops from his body. "Sometimes I wish you had more physical magic, Dor. If you could point your finger and paralyze or stun or burn—"

"Then the Good Magician would have had other defenses for his castle, that those talents would be useless against. Magic is not enough; you have to use your brain."

"How can a brain stop a needler from needling?" Grundy demanded. "The thing isn't smart; you can't make a deal with it."

"The cactus isn't smart," Dor repeated, an idea forming. "So it might not grasp what would be obvious to us."

"Whatever you're talking about is not obvious to me, either," the golem said.

"Your talent is translation. Can you talk cactus language too?"

"Of course. But what has that to do with—"

"Suppose we told it we were dangerous to it? That we were salamanders, burning hot, about to burn it down?"

"Wouldn't work. It might be scared—but all it would do would be to fire off a volley of needles, to kill the salamander before the creature could get close."

"Hm, yes. But what about something that wasn't threatening, but was still sort of dangerous? A fireman, maybe, just passing through with flame on low."

Grundy considered. "That just might work. But if it failed—"

"Doom," Dor finished. "We'd be pincushions."

Both looked back at the moat. The triton was watching them alertly. "Pincushions either way," Grundy said. "I sure wish we were heroes, instead of golems and boys. We're not cut out for this sort of thing."

"The longer we stand here, the more scared I get," Dor agreed. "So let's get on with it before I start crying," he added, and wished he hadn't phrased it quite that way.

Grundy looked at the needle-cactus again. "When I was really a golem, a little thing like a needler couldn't hurt me. I wasn't real. I felt no pain. But now —I'm too scared to know what to say."

"I'll say it. It's my quest, after all; you don't have to participate. I don't know why you're risking yourself here anyway."

"Because I care, you twit!"

Which had to be true. "Okay. You just translate what I say into cactus talk." Dor nerved himself again and walked slowly toward the vegetable monster.

"Say something! Say something!" Grundy cried, as the needles oriented on them visibly, ready to fly off their handles.

"I am a fireman," Dor said uncertainly. "I—I am made of fire. Anything that touches me gets burned to a crisp. This is my firedog, Grundy the growler. I am just taking my hot dog for a walk, just passing through, chewing idly on a firecracker. I love crackers!"

Grundy made a running series of scrapes and whistles, as of wind blowing through erect cactus needles. The needler seemed to be listening; there was an alert quiver about its needles now. Could this possibly work?

"We are merely passing through," Dor continued. "We aren't looking for trouble. We don't like to burn off needles unless we really have to, because they scorch and pop and smell real bad." He saw some needles wilt as Grundy translated. The message was getting through! "We have nothing against cactuses, so long as they keep their place. Some cactuses are very nice. Some of Grundy's best friends are cactuses; he likes to—" Dor paused. What would a firedog do with a compatible cactus? Water it down, of course—with a stream of fire. That wouldn't go over very well, here. "Uh, he likes to sniff their flowers as he dogtrots by. We only get upset if any needles happen to get in our way. When we get upset, we get very hot. Very very hot. In fact we just get all burned up." He decided not to overdo it, lest he lose credibility. "But we aren't too hot right now because we know no nice cactus would try to stick us. So we won't have to burn off any inconvenient needles."

The cactus seemed to withdraw into itself, giving them room to pass without touching. His ploy was working! "My, these firecrackers are good. Would you like a cracker, cactus?" He held out one hand.

The cactus gave a little keen of apprehension, much as the tangler had when Crunch the ogre growled at it. The needles shied away. Then Dor was past it, penetrating into the alcove passage. But he was still within range of the needler, so he kept talking. After all, if the thing caught on to his ruse, it would be a very angry cactus.

"Sure was nice meeting you, cactus. You're a real sharp creature. Not like the one I encountered the other day, who tried to put a needle in my back. I fear I lost my temper. Tempering takes a lot of heat. I fired up like a wounded sala-mander, and I went back and hugged that poor cactus until all its needles burst into flame. The scorch marks are still on it, but I'm happy to say that it will probably survive. Lucky it was a wet day, raining in fact, so my heat only cooked its outer layers some instead of setting the whole thing on fire. I'm sorry I did that; I really think that needle in the back was an accident. Something that just slipped out. I just can't help myself when I get hot."

He rounded the curve in the passage, so that he was no longer in view of the needler. Then he leaned against the wall, feeling faint.

Grundy's translation came to an end. "You're the best liar I've ever seen," he said admiringly.

"I'm the scaredest liar you've ever seen!"

"Well, I guess it takes practice. But you did well; I could hardly keep up with those whoppers! But I knew if I cracked a smile, I'd really get needled."

Dor pondered the implications. He had indeed achieved his victory by lying. Was that the way it should be? He doubted it. He made a mental resolution: no more lying. Not unless absolutely necessary. If a thing could not be accomplished honestly, probably it wasn't worth accomplishing at all.

"I never realized what a coward I was," Dor said, changing the subject slightly. "I'll never grow up."

"I'm a coward too," Grundy said consolingly. "I've never been so scared since I turned real."

"One more challenge to handle—the worst one. I wish I were man-sized and man-couraged!"

"Me too," the golem agreed.

The passage terminated in a conventional door with a conventional door latch. "Here we come, ready or not," Dor muttered.

"You're not ready," the door replied.

Dor ignored it. He worked the latch and opened the door.

There was a small room paneled in bird-of-paradise feathers. A woman of extraordinary perfection stood facing them. She wore a low-cut gown, jeweled sandals, a comprehensive kerchief, and an imported pair of Mundane dark glasses. "Welcome, guests," she breathed, in such a way that Dor's gaze was attracted to the site of breathing, right where the gown was cut lowest yet fullest.

"Uh, thanks," Dor said, nonplused. This was the worst hazard of all? He needed no adult-male vision to see that it was a hazard few men would balk at.

"There's something about her—I don't like this," Grundy whispered in his ear. "I know her from somewhere—"

"Here, let me have a look at you," the woman said, lifting her hand to her glasses. Dor's glance was drawn away from her torso to her face. Her hair began to move under her kerchief, as if separately alive.

Grundy stiffened. "Close your eyes!" he cried. "I recognize her now. Those serpent locks—that's the gorgon!"

Dor's eyes snapped closed. He barged ahead, trying to get out of the room before any accident caused him to take an involuntary look. He knew what the gorgon was; her glance turned men to stone. If they met that glance with their own.

His blindly moving feet tripped over a step, and Dor fell headlong. He threw his arms up to shield his face, but did not open his eyes. He landed jarringly and lay there, eyelids still tightly screwed down.

There was the swish of long skirts coming near. "Get up, young man," the gorgon said. Her voice was deceptively soft.

"No!" Dor cried. "I don't want to turn to stone!"

"You won't turn to stone. The hurdles are over; you have won your way into the castle of the Good Magician Humfrey. No one will harm you here."

"Go away!" he said. "I won't look at you!"

She sighed, very femininely. "Golem, you look at me. Then you can reassure your friend."

"I don't want to be stone either!" Grundy protested. "I had too much trouble getting real to throw it away now. I saw what happened to all those men your sister the siren lured to your island."

"And you also saw how the Good Magician nullified me. There is no threat now."

"That's right! He—but how do I know the spell's still on? It's been a long time since—"

"Take this mirror and look at me through the reflection first," she said. "Then you will know."

"I can't handle a big mirror! I'm only inches tall, only a—oh, what's the use! Dor, I'm going to look at her. If I turn to stone, you'll know she can't be trusted."

"Grundy, don't—"

"I already have," the golem said, relieved. "It's all right, Dor, you can look."

Grundy had never deceived him. Dor clenched his teeth and cracked open an eye, seeing the lighted room and the gorgon's nearest foot. It was a very pretty foot, with fluorescently tinted toenails, topped by a shapely ankle. Funny how he had never noticed ankles before! He got to his hands and knees, his eyes traveling cautiously up her marvelously molded legs until the view was cut off by the hem of her gown. It was a shapely gown, too, slightly translucent so that the suggestion of her legs continued on up to—but enough of this stalling. He forced his reluctant eyes to travel all the way up past her contours until they approached her head.

Her hair, now unbound, consisted of a mass of writhing little snakes. They were appealingly horrible. But the face—was nothing. Just a vacuum, as if the head were a hollow ball with the front panel removed.

"But—but I saw your face before, all except the eyes—"

"You saw this mask of my face," she said, holding it up. "And the dark glasses. There was never any chance for you to look into my true face."

So it seemed. "Then why—?"

"To scare you off—if you lacked the courage to do what is necessary in order to reach the Good Magician."

"I just closed my eyes and ran," Dor said.

"But you ran forward, not back."

So he had. Even in his terror, he had not given up his quest. Or had he merely run whichever way he happened to be facing? Dor wasn't sure.

He considered the gorgon again. Once he got used to the anomaly of her missing face, he found her quite attractive. "But you—what is a gorgon doing here?"

"I am serving my year's fee, awaiting my Answer."

Dor shook his head, trying to get this straight. "You—if I may ask—what was your Question?"

"I asked the Good Magician if he would marry me."

Dor choked. "He—he made you—serve a fee, for that?"

"Oh, yes. He always charges a year's service, or the equivalent. That's why he has so much magic around the castle. He's been in this business for a century or so."

"I know all that! But yours was a different kind of—"

She seemed to smile, behind her invisibility. "No exceptions, except maybe on direct order from the King. I don't mind. I knew what to expect when I came here. Soon my year will be finished, and I will have my Answer."

Grundy shook his little head. "I thought the old gnome was nuts. But this—he's crazy!"

"By no means," the gorgon said. "I could make him a pretty good wife, once I learn the ropes. He may be old, but he's not dead, and he needs—"

"I meant, to make you work a year—why doesn't he just marry you, and have your service for life?"

"You want me to ask him a second Question, and serve another year for the Answer?" she demanded.

"Uh, no. I was just curious. I don't really understand the Good Magician."

"You and everyone else!" she agreed wryly, and Dor began to feel an affinity for this shapely, faceless female. "But slowly I'm learning his ways. It is a good question you raise; I shall have to think about it, and maybe I can figure out that answer for myself. If he wants my service, why would he settle for a year of it when he could readily have it all? If he doesn't want my service, why not send me out to guard the moat or something where he won't have to see me every day? There has got to be a reason." She scratched her head, causing several snakes to hiss warningly.

"Why do you even want to marry him?" Grundy asked. "He's such a gloomy old gnome, he's no prize for a woman, especially a pretty one."

"Who said I wanted to marry him?"

Grundy did a rare double take. "You distinctly—your Question—"

"That is for information, golem. Once I know whether he will marry me, I'll be able to decide whether I should do it. It's a difficult decision."

"Agreed," Grundy said. "King Trent must have labored similarly before marrying Queen Iris."

"Do you love him?" Dor inquired.

"Well, I think I do. You see, he's the first man who ever associated with me without . . . you know." She nodded her head toward the corner. There was the statue of a man, carved beautifully in marble.

"That's—?" Dor asked, alarmed.

"No, I really am a statue," the stone answered him. "A fine original work of sculpture."

"Humfrey won't let me do any real conversions," the gorgon said. "Not even for old times' sake. I'm just here to identify the foolish or to scare off the fainthearted. The Magician won't answer cowards."

"Then he won't answer me," Dor said sadly. "I was so scared—"

"No, that's not cowardice. Being terrified but going ahead and doing what must be done—that's courage. The one who feels no fear is a fool, and the one who lets fear rule him is a coward. You are neither. Same for you, golem. You never deserted your friend, and were willing to risk your precious flesh body to help him. I think the Magician will answer."

Dor considered that. "I sure don't feel very brave," he said at last. "All I did was hide my face."

"I admit it would have been more impressive had you closed your eyes and fenced with me blind," she said. "Or snatched up a mirror to use. We keep several handy, for those who have the wit to take that option. But you're only a boy. The standards are not as strict."

"Uh, yes," Dor agreed, still not pleased.

"You should have seen me when I came here," she said warmly. "I was so frightened, I hid my face—just as you did."

"If you didn't hide your face, you'd turn everyone to stone," Grundy pointed out.

"That too," she agreed.

"Say," Grundy demanded. "It was twelve years ago when you met the Good Gnome. I was there, remember? How come you're just now asking your Question?"

"I left my island at the Time of No Magic," she said frankly. "Suddenly no magic worked at all in the whole Land of Xanth, and the magic things were dying or turning mundane, and all the old spells were undone. I don't know why that was—"

"I know," Grundy said. "But I can't tell, except to say it won't happen again."

"All my former conquests reverted to life. There were some pretty rowdy men there, you know—trolls and things. So I got all flustered and fled. I was afraid they would hurt me."

"That was a sensible fear," Grundy said. "When they didn't catch you, they went back to the Magic Dust village where most of them had come from, and I guess they're still there. Lot of very eager women in that village, after all that time with all their men gone."

"But when the magic came back, the Magician's spell on my face was gone. It was one of the one-shot variety, that carried only until interrupted. A lot of spells are like that, mine included. So I had my face again, and I—you know."

Dor knew. She had started making statues again.

"By then, I knew what was happening," she continued. "I had been pretty naïve, there on my isolated island, but I was learning. I really didn't want to be that way. So I remembered what Humfrey had said about Mundania, where magic doesn't ever work—that certainly must be a potent counterspell laid on that land!—and I went there. And he was right. I was a normal girl. I had thought I could never stand to leave Xanth, but the Time of No Magic showed me that maybe I could stand it after all. And when I tried, I could. It was sort of strange and fun, not nearly as bad as I had feared. People accepted me, and men —do you know I'd never kissed a man in Xanth?"

Dor was ashamed to comment. He had never kissed a woman other than his mother, who of course didn't count. He thought fleetingly of Millie. If—

"But after a while I began to miss Xanth," the gorgon continued. "The magic, the special creatures—do you know I even got to miss the tangle trees? When you're born to magic you can't just set it aside; it is part of your being. So I had to come back. But that meant—you know, more statues. So I went to Humfrey's castle. By that time I knew he was the Good Magician—he never told me that when we met!—and that he wasn't all that approachable, and I got girlishly nervous. I knew that if I wanted to be with a man in Xanth, I mean man-to-woman, it would have to be one like him. Who had the power to neutralize my talent. The more I thought about it—well, here I am."

"Didn't you have trouble getting into the castle?"

"Oh, yes! It was awful. There was this foghorn guarding the moat, and I found this little boat there, but every time I tried to cross that horn blasted out such columns of fog that I couldn't see or hear anything, and the boat always turned around and came back to shore. It was a magic boat, you see; you had to steer it or it went right back to its dock. I got all covered in fog, and my hair was hissing something awful; it doesn't like that sort of thing."

Her hair, of course, consisted of myriad tiny snakes or eels. They were rather cute, now that he was getting used to the style. "How did you get across the moat, then?"

"I finally got smart. I steered the boat directly toward the foghorn, no matter how bad the fog got. It was like swimming through a waterfall! When I reached the horn—I was across. Because it was inside, not outside."

"Oops—the gnome cometh," Grundy said.

"Oh, I must get back to work!" the gorgon said, hastily tripping out of the room. "I was in the middle of the laundry when you arrived; he uses more socks!" She was gone.

"Gnomes do have big dirty feet," Grundy remarked. "Sort of like goblins, in that respect."

The Good Magician Humfrey walked in. He was, indeed, gnomelike, old and gnarled and small. His feet were big and bare and, yes, dirty. "There's not a clean pair of socks in the whole castle!" he grumped. "Girl, haven't you done that laundry yet? I asked for it an hour ago!"

"Uh, Good Magician—" Dor said, moving toward him.

"It isn't as if socks are that complicated to wash," Humfrey continued irritably. "I've shown her the cleaning spell." He looked around. "Where is that girl? Does she think the whole Land of Xanth is made of stone, merely waiting on her convenience?"

"Uh, Good Magician Humfrey," Dor said, trying again. "I have come to ask—"

"I can't stand another minute without my socks!" Humfrey said, sitting down on the step. "I'm no barefoot boy any more, and even when I was, I always wore shoes. I spilled an itching-powder formula here once, and it gets between my toes. If that fool girl doesn't—"

"Hey, old gnome!" Grundy bawled deafeningly.

Humfrey glanced at him in an offhand way. "Oh, hello, Grundy. What are you doing here? Didn't I tell you how to become real?"

"I *am* real, gnome," Grundy said. "I'm just speaking your language, as is my talent. I'm here with my friend Dor, showing him how to get a Magician's attention."

"Dor doesn't need a Magician's attention. He's a Magician himself. He needs a quest. He ought to go find the secret of making zombies human, so he can please Millie the ghost. Besides, I'm not dressed for company. My socks—"

"To hell with your socks!" Grundy exclaimed. "The boy's come all the way here to ask you how to get that secret, and you have to give him an Answer."

"To hell with my socks? Not before they're clean! I wouldn't be caught dead in dirty socks."

"All right, gnome, I'll fetch your socks," Grundy said. "You stay right here on this step and talk to Dor, okay?" He jumped down and scurried from the room.

"Uh, I'm sorry—" Dor began hesitantly.

"It did take Grundy some time to get the message, but the cranial capacity of golems is very small. Now that he has left us alone, I can convey private reflections."

"Oh, I don't mind Grundy—"

"The fact is, Dor, you are slated to be the next King of Xanth. Now I suppose I could charge you the usual fee for my Answer, but that might be impolitic if you were to become King before I died. My references suggest that will be the case. One can never be absolutely sure about the future, of course; the future-history texts misrepresent it almost as much as the past history texts do the past. But why gamble foolishly? You are a full Magician in your own right, with power as great as mine, and of a similar genre. Given time, you will know as much as I. It becomes expedient to deal with fellow Magicians on an equal basis. Besides which, a year out of your life at this stage might in some devious way pose a threat to the welfare of your father, Bink, who cares greatly for you, and that would be an unconscionable mischief. I remember when I was attempting to fathom his talent, and the invisible giant came marching by with a tread worse than an ogre's and almost shook down the castle. But that's another matter. In this case I can not provide your full Answer anyway, because there is an ambiguity in the record. It seems it is a trade secret kept by another Magician. Are you willing to make a deal?"

"I, uh—" Dor said, not overwhelmed, but verging on it. Future history? Kingship in the foreseeable future? His father's mysterious talent? Another Magician?

"Very good. What you want is the Elixir of Restoration. What I want is historical information about a critically vague but important Wave of Xanth. The elixir is similar to the Healing Elixir that is common enough today, but is of a distinct variant formula adapted to zombies. Only the Zombie Master of the Fourth Wave knows the formula. If I enable you to interview him, will you render me a complete accounting of your adventures in that realm?"

"The—the Fourth Wave? But—"

"Then it's agreed!" Humfrey said. "Sign your name to this release form, here, so I can tie my history text into the spell." He shoved a quill into Dor's flaccid hand and a printed parchment under it, and Dor almost automatically signed. "So good to do business with a reasonable Magician. Ah, here are my socks at last. High time!" For the golem had reappeared, staggering under the huge burden.

Humfrey leaned forward and began squeezing his big feet into the socks. It was no wonder, Dor thought, that they got dirty so rapidly! The Magician wasn't bothering to wash his feet before donning the socks. "The problem with the Fourth Wave of human colonization of Xanth is that it occurred circa eight centuries ago. I trust you are familiar with Xanth history? The centaur pedagogue gave you the scoop? Good. So I don't need to remind you how the people came in brutal Waves of conquest, killing and stealing and ravaging until they wasted it all, then had nothing better to do than settle down and watch their children turn magic, whereupon some new Wave of no-magic barbarians would invade and victimize them. So a Wave could be several generations in duration. The boldest of these, for reasons we won't go into now, was the Fourth Wave. The greatest of the ancient Magicians lived then: King Roogna, who built Castle Roogna; his archenemy and dinner companion, Magician Murphy; and the Zombie Master, whom you will interview. Plus lesser talents like the neo-Sorceress Vadne. How you will elicit the formula from the Zombie Master I don't know; he was something of a recluse, not sociable the way I am."

Grundy snorted derisively.

"Thank you," Humfrey said. He seemed to thrive on insult. "Sit down, Dor— right there will do." Dor, too disoriented to protest, sat down on the decorated carpet he had been standing on, Grundy beside him. The texture of it was luxuriant; he was comfortable. "But the main problem is the time frame. The Zombie Master can not come to you, so you must go to him. The only presently feasible way to do that is via the tapestry."

"The tapestry?" Dor asked, surprised by this familiar item. "The Castle Roogna tapestry?"

"The same. I shall give you a spell to enable you to enter it. You will not do so physically, of course; your body is much too big to be in scale. The spell will accommodate a reasonably close match, but you are hundreds of times too massive. So you will animate the body of one of the players already depicted there. We shall have to make an arrangement for your present body—ah, I know! The Brain Coral! I owe it a favor, or it owes me one—no difference. The Coral has always wanted to taste mortality. It can animate your body during your absence, so no one will know. The golem will have to help cover for you, of course."

"I've been doing that all along," Grundy said complacently.

"Now the carpet will take you to the Coral, then to the tapestry. Don't worry; I have preprogrammed it. Here, better take something to eat along the way. Gorgon!"

The gorgon hurried in with three vials. "You didn't wash your feet!" she cried to the Magician, appalled.

Humfrey took a white vial from her hand. "I had her fix this earlier, so if it turns your stomach to stone, blame her, not me." He almost chuckled as he handed the stoppered container to Dor. "Grundy, you better hang on to the spell. Remember, it's in two parts: the yellow puts him into the tapestry, the green puts the Coral into his body. Don't confuse them!" He gave the golem two tiny colored packets. "Or is it the other way around? Well, on with you. I don't have all day." He clapped his hands together with a sharp report—and the carpet on which Dor sat took off.

Too surprised to protest, Dor grabbed for the edges and hung on. "You *don't* have clean feet either," he heard the gorgon saying indignantly to Humfrey as the carpet looped the room, getting its bearings. "But I brought two dry-cleaning spells, one for each foot, so—"

Dor missed the rest. The carpet sailed out of the room, through several other chambers, banked around a corner, angled up an interminably coiling stair, and shot out of a high turret window whose sides almost scraped skin off Dor's tight knuckles. Suddenly the ground was far below, and getting farther; already the Magician's castle seemed small.

"Hey—I think I'm scared of heights!" Dor cried, his vision recoiling.

"Nonsense," Grundy retorted. "You made it up here okay, didn't you? What are you going to do, jump?"

"Noooo!" Dor cried, horrified. "But I might quietly fall."

"What you need is a good meal to settle your stomach during the boring flight," Grundy said. "Let's just get this white bottle open—"

"I'm not hungry! I think I'm heightsick!"

The golem hauled at the cork, and it popped out. Fine smoke issued, swirled, and coalesced into two fine sandwiches, a brimming glass of milk, and a sprig of parsley. Dor had to grab at everything before the wind whipped it away.

"We're really traveling in style!" Grundy said, crunching his little teeth on the parsley. "Drink your milk, Dor."

"You sound just like Millie." But Dor gulped his milk. It was very good, obviously fresh from the pod, and the milkweed must have been grown in chocolate soil.

"I hear that in Mundania they squeeze milk out of animals," Grundy observed. That made Dor's stomach do another roil. They really were barbarians in Mundania.

Then he started in on a sandwich, as he had either to eat it or continue holding it, and he wanted his hands free to clutch the carpet again. It was a doorjam and turnip sandwich, his favorite; obviously the Good Magician had researched his tastes and prepared for this occasion before Dor ever arrived at the castle. The second one was a red potato soup sandwich, somewhat squishy but with excellent taste. The gorgon had a very nice touch.

Dor thought about the anomaly of so formidable a creature as the gorgon reduced to being a common maid at the Magician's castle while she waited to learn whether Humfrey would marry her. Yet wasn't this the lot of the average woman? Maybe the Magician was merely showing her what she could expect if she married. That could be more important than his actual Answer. Or was that part of the Answer? The Good Magician had his peculiarities, but also a devious comprehension of the real situation. He had obviously known all about Dor himself, yet allowed him to struggle through the rigors of entry into the castle. Odd competence!

The carpet angled forward, causing Dor to suffer another spasm of vertigo. Yet his seat seemed secure. The material of the carpet seemed to hold him firmly yet comfortably, so that he did not slide off even when it tilted. Wonderful magic!

Now the carpet banked, circling for a landing—but it didn't land. It plunged at frightening speed directly toward a deep crevasse in the ground. "Where are we going?" Dor cried, alarmed.

"Into the teeth of a tangler!" Grundy replied. "A big one!" He pointed ahead, and for once he seemed less than cocksure.

"Right!" the rug agreed, still accelerating.

It was indeed a big tangle tree—one not even an ogre could cow. Its massive trunk grew from the base of the chasm, while its upper tentacles overlapped the rim. What a menace that must be to travelers seeking to cross the cleft!

The carpet banked again, accelerated again, and buzzed the crest of the tree. The tentacles reached up hungrily. "Has this rug gone crazy?" Dor demanded. "Nobody tangles with a full-sized tangler!"

"Oh, a big sphinx might get away with it," Grundy suggested. "Or the old invisible giant. Or a cockatrice."

The carpet banked yet again, sending Dor's hair flying to the side, and looped around for another nervy pass at the top of the tree. This time the tentacles were ready; they rose up in a green mass to intercept it. "Doom!" Grundy cried, covering his eyes. "Why did I ever turn real?"

But the carpet plunged directly below the tentacles, zooming right past the bared and scowling trunk of the tangler and into the ground at its base. Except that the ground opened into a small crevice transfixed by a root—and the carpet dropped into this hole.

Down, down—the horror of the heights had been abruptly replaced by the horror of the depths! Dor cowered, expecting to smash momentarily into a wall. But the carpet seemed to know its harrowing route; it never touched a wall.

There began to be a little light—a sustained glow from the walls. But this only showed how convoluted this region was. Chamber after chamber opened and closed, and passages branched at all angles. Yet the carpet sped unerringly along its programmed route, down into the very bowels of Xanth.

Bowels. Dor wished his thought hadn't phrased it that way. He still felt nervously sick. This harebrained ride—

The carpet halted abruptly beside a somber subterranean lake. In this faint illumination the water itself assumed a glow, revealing murky depths suggestive of mind-boggling secrets. The carpet settled to the cavern floor and became limp. "This must be our station," Grundy observed.

"But there's nothing here!" Nothing living, he meant.

I am here, something thought in his mind. *I am the Brain Coral—here beyond your sight beneath the lake. You bear the stigma of the Good Magician and are accompanied by his golem. Have you come to abate his debt to me?*

"I am my own golem!" Grundy protested. "And I'm not a golem any more. I'm real!"

"He said it was your debt to him," Dor answered the Brain Coral nervously. This was an uncomfortable place, and there was disquieting power in the mental voice, and an alien quality. This was a creature of Magician-class magic, but not at all human. "I think."

Same thing, the voice thought. Perhaps it was the thought voicing. *What is the offer?*

"You—if you would care to animate my body while my spirit is away—I know it's not much of a body, just a juvenile—"

Done! the Coral replied. *Go work your spells; I will be there.*

"Uh, thank you. I—"

Thank you. I have existed a thousand years, storing mortals in my preservative lake, without ever enjoying the sensations of mortality myself. Now at last I shall experience them, however fleetingly.

"Uh, yes, I guess. You do understand that I will want my body back, when—"

Naturally. Such spells are always self-limiting; there will be no more than a fortnight before it reverts. Time enough.

Self-limiting? Dor hadn't known that. What a good thing the Good Magician had set it up. Had Dor tried to work such a spell by himself, he could have been stuck forever in the tapestry. The best spells were fail-safe.

The carpet took off without warning. "Farewell, Coral!" Dor cried, but there was no answer. Either the Brain Coral's communications range was short, or it had ceased to pay attention. Or it objected to inane courtesies.

The return trip was similar to the descent, with its interminable convolutions, but now Dor felt more secure, and his stomach stayed pretty much in place. He had new confidence in the Good Magician's planning and in the carpet's competence. He hardly winced as they shot up out of the crack into the bosom of the tangle tree, though he did have a qualm as the tentacles convulsed. The carpet merely dodged the embrace, allowing the tangler to catch nothing but the qualm, and zoomed along the base of the crevasse. When well clear of the tree, it rose smoothly out of the chasm and powered into the sky. The afternoon was blindingly bright, after the gloom of the caverns.

Now they flew north. Dor looked down, trying to spot the Magic Dust village, but all he saw was jungle. One area was dark, as if burned out, but no village. Then, all too soon, Castle Roogna hove in view. The carpet circled it once, getting its bearings as was its wont, then slanted down and into a window, through a hall, and into the tapestry room.

"Here's the first spell," Grundy said, lifting the yellow package.

"No, wait!" Dor cried, abruptly afraid of the magnitude of what he contemplated. He had supposed he would only have to search out some hidden spring in the contemporary world, and now faced a far more significant undertaking. To actually enter a picture—"I need time to uncramp my legs, to—" To decide whether he was really up to this challenge. Maybe—

But Grundy had already torn open the wrapping. Yellow mist spread out, diffusing into the air, forming a little cloud.

"I don't even know what body in the tapestry to—"

Then the expanding mist encompassed him. Dor felt himself swaying, falling without falling. For a moment he saw his body standing there stupidly, tousle-haired and slack-jawed. Then the great tapestry was coming at him, expanding hugely. There was a bug on it, then this too fuzzed out. He glimpsed a section of woven jungle, with a muscular young man standing with a huge sword, at bay against—

Chapter 3

Jumper

Dor stood at bay, his trusty blade unmasked. The goblins in front of him faded back, afraid, before he could get a close look at them. He hadn't seen goblins in the flesh before. They were small, twisted, ugly creatures with disproportionately large heads and hands and feet.

Goblins? Of course he hadn't seen them before! There had been few goblins on the surface of Xanth in daylight for centuries! They hid in the caverns beneath the surface, afraid of light.

Oh—this was no longer the present! This was the tapestry, depicting the world of eight hundred years ago. So there could be goblins here—bold ones, uncowed by light.

But he, himself—what of him? What body—oh, yes, the huge-thewed, giant young man. Dor had never before experienced such ready power; the massive sword felt light in his hands, though he knew that in his real body he would barely have been able to swing it two-handed. This was the kind of body he had daydreamed about!

Something stung him on the head. Dor clapped his hand there, knocking himself momentarily dizzy, but whatever it was was gone. It had felt, however, like a louse or flea. He had no antifleas spell with him. Already the penalties of the primitive life were manifesting.

The jungle was close. Great-leaved branches formed a seemingly solid wall of green. There were fewer magic plants than he was used to; these more closely resembled Mundane trees. Which, again, made sense; the Land of Xanth was closer to Mundania in nature than it would be in Dor's day. Evolution—the pedagogue centaur had taught him about that, how magic things evolved into more magical things, to compete and survive better.

Something entered the periphery of his vision as he looked around. Dor whirled—and discovered that it had not been his sword that made the goblins retreat.

Behind him stood a spider—the height of a man.

Dor forgot all about the lurking goblins. He lifted the great sword, feeling the facility with which his body handled it. This was a trained warrior whose muscles had been augmented by experience and skill—which was fortunate, because Dor himself was no swordsman. He could have sliced himself up, if this body hadn't possessed good reflexes.

The spider reacted similarly. It carried no sword, but hardly needed to. It had eight hairy legs and two huge green eyes—no, four eyes, two large and two small —no, there were at least six, scattered about its head. Two sharp fangs projected inward from the mouth parts, and two mouth-legs fitted outside. Overall, the creature was as horrible as Dor could imagine. Now it was preparing to pounce on him.

On top of that, the thing was chittering at him, making a series of clicking sounds that could only be some sort of threat. Grundy the golem could have translated instantly—but Grundy was eight hundred years or so away, now. The spider's two larger forelegs were raised; though they had neither fingers nor claws, they looked formidable. And those mandibles behind them, and those eyes—

Dor made a feint with his sword, surprising himself; his body was bringing its own expertise into play. The monster drew back, clicking angrily. "What's that thing trying to say?" Dor asked himself nervously, not at all sure he could fend the monster off despite his own greatly enhanced size and strength.

The sword he held thought he had spoken to it. "I know battle language. The monster says he doesn't really want to fight, but he's never seen a horror like you before. He wonders whether you are good to eat."

"A horror like me!" Dor exclaimed incredulously. "Is the monster crazy?"

"I can't be the judge of that," the sword said. "I only understand battle competence. This creature seems disoriented but competent enough to me. For all I know, you could be the crazy one."

"I'm a twelve-year-old boy from eight hundred years in the future—or from outside this tapestry, whichever makes more sense."

"Now my doubt has been allayed. You are indubitably crazy."

"Hell, you're in my hand now," Dor said, nettled. "You'll do as I direct."

"By all means. Swords have ever been the best servants of crazy men."

The monster spider had not actually attacked. Its attention seemed to be diverted. It was hard to tell what was the object of its diversion, because its eyes aimed in so many directions at once. Maybe it was only trying to understand his dialogue with the sword. Dor tried to spot what it was looking at—and saw the goblins returning.

One thing about goblins: they were enemies. No one knew exactly what had happened to them, but it had been conjectured that they had been driven underground after centuries of warfare, because of their implacable hatred of man. Once, legend claimed, the goblins had gotten along with man; indeed, they were distantly related to men. But something had changed—

"This is no good," Dor said. "If I fight the monster, the goblins will attack me from behind. But if I turn my back on the spider, it will eat me. Or something."

"So slay the monster, then fight the goblins," the sword said. "Die in honorable combat. It is the warrior's way."

"I'm no warrior!" Dor cried, thoroughly frightened. It had not occurred to him that the world of the tapestry would pose an immediate threat to him. But now he was in it, this world seemed thoroughly real, and he didn't want to find out whether he could die here. Maybe his death would merely catapult him back prematurely, terminating the spell, dumping him into his own body, mission unaccomplished. Maybe it would be more final.

"You were a warrior until a few minutes ago," the sword said. "A very stupid one, to be sure, to have gotten yourself trapped by this motley band of goblins, but nevertheless a warrior. Brains never were a requirement for war anyway; in fact they tend to be a liability. Now all of a sudden you're timid as hell, and you're also talking to me. You never did that before."

"It's my talent. Talking to inanimate objects."

"That sounds like an insult," the sword said, glinting ominously.

"No, not at all," Dor said hastily. He certainly didn't need to have his own sword mad at him now! "I am the only person privileged to talk to swords. All other people must talk to other people."

"Oh," it said, mollified. "That *is* an unusual honor. How come you never did it before?"

Dor shrugged. He didn't want to go into the insanity bit again. "Maybe I just didn't feel worthy."

"Must be," the sword agreed. "Now let's slay that monster."

"No. If it hasn't attacked by this time, I believe it when it says it doesn't want to fight. My father always says it's best to be friends if you can. He even made friends with a dragon once."

"You forget I was your father's sword before you inherited me. He never said anything of the kind. He said, 'Gorge, guzzle, and wench, for tomorrow we get gutted.' Then a wench's husband caught up with him while he was gorged and guzzled, and he got gutted."

Mundanes were brutes; Dor had already known that. So this news about the family of this body was not all that shocking. Still, it was a lot more immediate than it had been. "About making friends with a dragon—the word dragon may be taken as slang for an aggressive woman."

The sword laughed. "Oh, cle-*ver!* And absolutely crazy. You're right; your old man could have said it. Friends with a dragon!"

Dor decided to gamble. Though the sword could translate some of what the monster said into human language, it could not translate what Dor said into monster-spider language, for that was not the sword's talent. It was one-way. But communication should be possible, if he tried hard enough. "I'm going to make a peace overture by gesture," he told the sword.

"A peace overture! Your father would roll over in his booze-sodden grave!"

"You just translate what the spider says to me."

"I only understand combat language, not that sissy peace stuff," the sword said with warlike dignity. "If the monster doesn't fight, I have no interest."

"Then I shall put you away." Dor looked for the scabbard. He touched his hip, but found no sheath there. "Uh, where do you go?"

The sword said something unintelligible.

"Where?" Dor repeated, frowning.

"Into my scabbard, idiot!" the sword said cuttingly.

"Where the hell is the scabbard? I can't find it."

"Don't you remember *anything?* It's across your big stupid back where it belongs!"

Dor felt his back with his left hand. There was a harness, with the scabbard angled from his right buttock to his left shoulder. He lifted the sword and maneuvered the point into the end of the sheath. Obviously there was an art to this, and he lacked that art. Had he allowed his body to do it automatically, there would have been no problem; but now he was opposing the nature of his body, putting away a sword in the face of battle. "Bro-*ther!*" the sword muttered with disgust.

But when Dor relaxed, distracted by his own chain of thought, his body took over, and the sword slid into its scabbard and was fastened into place at last.

"Then you, scabbard," Dor said. "You must understand peace, or at least truce."

"Yes," the scabbard replied. "I comprehend the language of negotiation-from-strength, of peace-with-honor."

Dor spread his arms wide before the monster spider, who had remained frozen in position all this time, while the goblins inched forward, suspecting a trap. Dor was trying to suggest peace. The monster spread its own front legs wide and chittered. Behind it the face of another goblin appeared, watching with suspicion. It seemed the goblins were not allied to the spider, and didn't understand it any better than Dor himself did.

"It says it was wondering when you would attack," the scabbard said. "It thought for a moment you intended peace, but now you are making ready to grasp it with your pincers so you can bite or crush or sting it to death."

Hastily Dor closed his arms.

The spider chittered. "Aha," the scabbard said. "Now it knows it has out-bluffed you. You are huddled in terror. It can consume you without resistance."

Dor's embarrassment turned to anger. "Now look here, monster!" he snapped, shaking his left fist in the creature's hairy green face. "I don't want to have to fight you, but if you force me—"

Another chitter. "At last!" the scabbard said. "You have elected to meet it on equal terms, it says, neither threatening nor cowering. It is a stranger here, and is willing to declare a truce."

Amazed and gratified, Dor held his pose. The spider brought its left foreleg forward. Still Dor did not move, afraid that any change might be misinterpreted. Slowly the segmented leg came up until the mittonlike tip touched Dor's fist. "Truce," the scabbard said.

"Truce," Dor agreed, relieved. The monster no longer looked so horrible; in fact its green fur was handsome in its fashion, and the eyes gleamed like flawless jewels. The top of its abdomen was variegated, so that seen from above it might resemble a smiling human face: two round black fur eyes, a white fur mouth, a broad black fur mustache, and delicate green complexion. Maybe the face-image was meant to frighten away predators, though what might predate on a spider this size Dor hesitated to conjecture. The eight legs were gray, tied neatly in to the base of the thorax. The two fangs were orange-brown, and long tufts of hair sprouted around some of the eyes. Really, quite a pretty creature, though formidable.

Suddenly the lurking goblins attacked in a swarm. Dor's body acted before he knew what it was doing. It whirled, drawing the sword from its sheath, and swung at the nearest enemy. "I thirst for your black blood, spawn of darkness!" the sword cried in a happy singsong. "Come let me taste your foul flesh!"

The goblins were hardly daunted. Two charged right at Dor. They were half Dor's height, and the outsized extremities made them look like cruel caricatures of the Good Magician Humfrey. But where the Magician was grumpy, these were evil; there was incredible malignance in their misshapen faces. Their bodies were thin, like the stalks of weeds, and bumpy. They carried crude weapons: chips of stone, splinters of wood, and small thorny branches.

"Stand back!" Dor cried, brandishing the hungry, thirsty sword. "I don't want to hurt you!" But emotionally he *did* want to hurt them; antipathy flooded through him, for no good reason he could fathom. He merely hated goblins. Maybe it was inherent in being a man, this revulsion by the caricatures of Man. Something completely alien could be tolerated, like the huge spider, but something that looked like a distorted man—

Then he jumped. A third goblin had sneaked in from the side and bitten him on the thigh. It hurt horribly. Dor punched him on the head with his left fist— and it hurt worse. The goblin's head was like a rock! Dor tried to grab an arm and haul the creature off, but it clung tenaciously, overbalancing him, still gnawing. Meanwhile, the other two were advancing, watching the gleaming blade with their beady eyes, trying to get safely around it. More goblins were crowding in behind.

Then a hairy leg swung in. It inserted itself between the goblin and Dor's leg and thrust out. The goblin was ripped away, screaming with rage.

Dor turned—and stared into the nearest eye of the monster spider. He saw his own reflection in the green depth: a large, flat, bearded man's face, wholly unlike his real face. Even after allowing for the distortion of the lens. "Uh, thanks," he said.

Then both goblins at the front dived for him. Their little gnarly legs propelled them with surprising power, perhaps because their bodies were so small and light. They sailed right at his head.

The body's mighty arm flexed. The sword swistled joyfully across in an arc, pointing outward. There was an awful double jerk, as of a stick banging through weeds—and the two goblins fell in four pieces.

Had he done that? Dor stared at the dark-red blood, seeing it turn black as it spilled out over the ground. Those goblins were thoroughly dead, and he was a killer. He felt nauseated.

The spider chittered. Dor looked—and saw four goblins clinging to four of its legs, while others tried to reach its body. The spider was stretching its legs out, lifting its roughly globular body high to keep out of their reach, but was being inevitably borne down by their weight. The underside was unprotected; even small sharp stones could puncture it quickly.

Dor took his sword, pointed it at the nearest goblin, and thrust it violently forward. The sharp point transfixed the scrawny body and plunged into the earth beside the spider's foot. Not that the spider had any foot in the usual sense; the final segment of its leg bulged slightly and rounded off toelessly.

"Don't do that!" the sword cried. "Dirt dulls my edge!"

Dor jerked it out. The transfixed goblin came up with it. "Ghaaah!" it cried, its eyes bulging, arms and legs kicking wildly. The little monster couldn't even die cleanly, but had to make it as grisly and awful as possible.

Dor lifted one of his boots—he had not realized he was wearing them, before —braced it against the goblin's contorted face, and shoved the creature off his sword. Blood squirted across the blade as the thing collapsed in a messy heap.

Then Dor transfixed a second goblin, more carefully so as not to dull the edge of the blade, removing the remains more efficiently. Something in the back of his mind was throwing up, vomiting, puking out its guts, but Dor walled that off while he methodically did his job.

The spider reached behind him with a long foreleg. A goblin screamed; it had almost reached Dor's back. Dor hardly reacted; he stabbed and cleared the third goblin, then the fourth. He was getting pretty good at this.

Abruptly the goblins were gone. A dozen of them lay dead on the ground; the rest had fled. Dor had killed six, so the spider must have matched him kill for kill. They were a good fighting team!

Now, in the aftermath, Dor suffered realization of what he had done. The back of his mind burst its retaining dam and washed forward with grisly abandon. Dor looked upon the carnage, and spewed out the potato soup sandwich he had recently consumed, eight hundred years from now. At least it looked like potato soup, more than like goblin guts. He hardly cared. To kill humanoid creatures—

The spider chittered. Dor needed no translation. "I'm not used to bloodshed," he said, suppressing another heave. "If only they hadn't attacked—I didn't want to do this!" He felt tears sting his eyes. He had heard of girls being upset about losing their virginity; now he had an inkling what it felt like. He had defended himself, he had had to do that, but in the process had lost something he knew he could never recover. He had shed humanoid blood. How could he ever get the taint from his soul?

The spider seemed to understand. It moved to a dead goblin, held it with its palps, and sank its fangs into the body. But immediately it raised its head and spat out the goblin's blood. Again, Dor needed no translation: the goblin tasted awful!

There was no way to undo what had been done, no way to reclaim his lost innocence. His body had fought in the manner it was accustomed to. As his revulsion abated, Dor realized that both he and the monster spider had had a narrow escape. Had they not been together, and made their truce, and fought together, both would have fallen prey to the savage goblins.

Why had the goblins attacked? Dor could find no reason except that he and the spider had been present and had seemed vulnerable. If goblins thought they could prevail, they attacked; it seemed to be that simple. Maybe they had been hungry, and Dor and the spider had appeared to be easier prey than whatever else offered. At any rate, it had been the goblins who started it, so Dor told himself he should not feel complete guilt. He had only done to the goblins what the goblins had tried to do to him.

Still, there remained a grim pocket of negation in him, or horror at himself, at the capacity he had discovered in himself for slaughter. His new, powerful body had been the mechanism, but the will had been his own; he could not blame that on anything else.

If this was part of growing up, he didn't like it.

He turned his attention to the spider. Was this creature native to this jungle? This seemed unlikely. The scabbard had said the spider was a stranger here, and it surely would not have fallen prey to goblins on the ground if it were familiar with this region. It would have been safe in its web, high in some tree. Dor had not seen any giant spiders illustrated in the tapestry. So yes, this could be a stranger, as he himself was. In any event, a useful ally. If he could only talk to it.

Well, he could talk with it, if he worked out a system. If he could find some object that understood spiders, not just war talk or negotiation-from-strength talk. Some pebble on the ground where spiders foraged, perhaps, or—

"That's it!" he cried.

"What's it?" his sword replied, startled. "Are you going to clean me off now, so I won't rust?"

"Uh, of course," Dor said, abashed. Swords in his own day all had antirust spells, but now he was amid primitive times. He wiped the blade carefully on the freshest grass he could find, and sheathed it. Then he walked to the nearest tree and inspected its bark carefully.

Meanwhile the monster spider was cleaning its body, wiping the blood off its legs with its mouth parts, making itself look glossy-clean again. One of its eyes—it turned out to have eight of them, not six—watched Dor. Since the eyes faced in each direction, it did not have to move its body at all to watch everything around it, but Dor was sure one of those eyes was assigned to him.

"Aha!" Dor exclaimed. He had found a cobweb.

"Are you addressing me?" the cob inquired.

"I am indeed! You're from a spider, aren't you? You understand the language of spiders?"

"I certainly do. I was fashioned by a lovely Banded Garden Spider, the prettiest arachnid you never did see, all black-and-orange-striped, with the longest legs! You should have seen her snare a mosquito! But a mean old gnat-catcher bird got her. I don't know why, it certainly wasn't out of gnats—"

"Yes, very sad," Dor agreed. "Now I'm going to take you with me—may I put you on my shoulder? I want you to translate some spider talk for me."

"Well, my schedule is—"

Dor poked a finger at it warningly. "—really quite flexible," the web concluded hastily. "In fact I'm not doing anything at the moment. Do try not to mess up my pattern when you move me. My mistress put so much effort into it—"

Dor moved it carefully to his shoulder and fixed the pattern there, only messing up a few strands. Then he returned to the monster spider. "My, he's a big one!" the web remarked. "I never realized that species grew quite so large."

"Say something to me," Dor said to the spider. "I'll signal yes or no, some way you can understand."

The spider chittered. "I wish I knew what you wanted, alien thing," the web translated. This was almost like having Grundy the golem with him! But Grundy could translate both ways. Well, on with it; he was a human being, albeit a young and inexperienced one, and he should be able to work this out.

Dor raised his fist in the spider's greeting-among-equals mode. Maybe he could let this indicate agreement, and the wide-open-arms gesture the opposite.

"You desire to renew the truce?" the spider inquired. "It doesn't really need renewal—but of course you are an alien creature, so you wouldn't know—"

Dor spread his arms. The spider drew back, alarmed. "You wish to terminate the truce? This isn't—"

Confused, Dor dropped his arms. This wasn't working! How could he hold a dialogue if the spider interpreted everything strictly on its own terms?

"I wonder if something is wrong with you," the spider chittered. "You fought well, but now you seem to be at a loss. You don't seem to be wounded. I saw you regurgitate the refuse from your last meal; are you hungry again? How long has it been since you've eaten a really juicy fly?"

Dor spread his arms in negation, causing the spider to react again. "It is almost as if you are in some fashion responding to what I am saying—"

Gladly, Dor raised his fist.

Startled, the spider surveyed him with its biggest, greenest eyes. "You *do* understand?"

Dor raised his fist again.

"Let's verify this," the spider chittered, excited. "It hadn't occurred to me that you might be sapient. Too much to expect, really, especially in a non-arachnid monster. Yet you did honor the covenant. Very well: if you comprehend what I am saying, raise your forelegs."

Dor's hands shot up over his head.

"Fascinating!" the spider chittered. "I just may have discovered non-arachnid intelligence! Now lower one appendage."

Dor dropped his left arm. It was working; the spider was establishing communication with a non-arachnid sapience!

They proceeded from there. In the course of the next hour, Dor taught the spider—or the spider evoked from his subject, depending on viewpoint—the human words for *yes-good, no-bad, danger, food,* and *rest.* And Dor learned—or the spider taught—this:

He was an adult middle-aged male of his kind. His name was Phidippus Variegatus, "Jumper" for short. He was a jumping spider of the family Salticidae, the most handsome and sophisticated of the spider clans, though not the largest or most populous. Other clans no doubt had other opinions about appearance and sophistication, it had to be conceded. His kind neither lazed in webs, waiting for prey to fly in, nor lay in ambush hoping to trap prey. His kind went out boldly by day—though he could see excellently by night too, be it understood—stalking insects and capturing them with bold jumps. That was, after all, the most ethical mode.

Jumper had been stalking a particularly luscious-looking fly perched on the tapestry wall, when something strange had happened and he had found himself —here. He had been too disoriented to jump, what with the presence of this— pardon the description, but candor becomes necessary—grotesque creature of four limbs, and the onslaught of the goblin-bugs. But now Jumper was back in possession of his faculties—and seemed to have nowhere to go. This land was strange to him; the trees had shrunk, the creatures were horribly strange, and there seemed to be no others of his kind. How could he return home?

Dor was able, now, to fathom what had happened, but lacked the means to convey it. The little spider had been walking on the tapestry when Good Magician Humfrey's yellow spell took hold, and the spell had carried him into the tapestry world along with Dor. Since the spider was peripheral, his transformation had been only partial; instead of becoming small in scale with the figures of the tapestry, and occupying the body of a tapestry spider, he had kept his original body, becoming only somewhat smaller than before. Thus, here in the tapestry, Jumper seemed like a man-sized giant. Dor, had he entered similarly, would have been the size of several mountains.

The only way Jumper could return to his own world was by being with Dor when he returned. At least, so Dor conjectured. It might be that the spell would revert everything it had put into the tapestry, when the time came. But that would be a gamble. So it was safest to stay together, returning more or less as a unit: Dor to his body and size, Jumper to the contemporary world. Dor could not make the details clear, since he hardly had them clear in his own mind, but the spider was no fool. Jumper agreed: they would stay together.

Now both of them were hungry. The black flesh of the goblins was inedible, and Dor saw none of the familiar plants of his own time. No jellybarrel trees, flying fruits, water chestnuts, or pie fungi, and certainly no giant insects for Jumper to feed on. What were they to do?

Then Dor had an idea. "Are there any buglike forms around here?" he asked the web. "You know—the big six-legged creatures, segmented, with feelers and pincers and things?"

"There are crabapple trees an hour's birdflight from here," the web said. "I have heard the birds squawking about getting pinched there."

An hour's birdflight would mean perhaps six hours' travel by land; it depended on the bird and on the terrain. "Anything closer?"

"I've seen some tree-dwelling lobsters right around here. But they have mean tempers."

"That should be just the thing; I'd feel guilty about fingering sweet-tempered ones." Dor faced Jumper. "Food," he said, pointing to the nearest tree.

Jumper brightened. It was not that his eyes glowed, but merely a heightening of posture. "I shall verify." He moved with surprising rapidity to the nearest trunk.

"Uh, is it safe?" Dor asked the web.

"Of course not. There are all manner of bug-eating birds up there, and maybe some bird-eating bugs."

Oh. Birds were deadly to spider-sized spiders. Jumper was something else. Still, best not to take chances. "Danger," Dor said.

Jumper clicked his tusks together. "All life is a danger. Hunger is a danger too. I am at home at the heights." And he continued climbing the tree with his marvelous facility, straight up the trunk. His eight legs really helped. Dor had assumed that two or four legs were best, but already he was having second or fourth thoughts. *He* could not mount a tree like that!

In a moment Jumper's worried chitter percolated down through the foliage. "Unless there are praying mantises up here?"

"What's a preying whatsit?" Dor asked the web quietly.

"That's p-r-a-y, not p-r-e-y. The mantis prays for prey."

"All *right*. What is it?"

"A bug-eating bug. Big. Bigger than almost any spider."

Just so. "None your size," Dor called up, hoping Jumper understood. Then he waited at the base, nervously. No mantises, surely—but wouldn't a steam dragon be as bad? His acquaintance with the big spider was recent, but he felt a certain responsibility for Jumper. It was Dor's fault Jumper was in this predicament, after all. And yet, if Jumper hadn't been brought along in the eddy-current of the spell, what would have happened to Dor himself, thrown innocent into the pack of goblins? The two of them together had overcome the menace, while Dor alone would have—He shuddered to think of it. He owed Jumper a considerable debt already, and his adventure in the tapestry had just begun!

Something loomed at his face. Dor ducked, alarmed, fingers scrambling at his hip for his sword—and of course not finding it there. Then he saw that the looming thing was a tree-lobster, descending on a thread. Except that lobsters didn't use threads! No, this one was tightly bound, helpless, its leaf-green claws tied close to its bark-brown body, swinging head down. A captive of the big spider!

Almost, Dor felt sympathy for the lobster, for it was still alive and struggling vainly against its webbands. But he remembered the time he had climbed a butternut tree to fetch some butter, and a lobster had nipped him. He had been nervous about them ever since; they were ornery creatures. This one's red antennae radiated malevolence at him.

Another bound lobster was lowered to hang a few feet above the ground, and then a third. Then Jumper himself floated down. "I ate the rest," he chittered. "Less juicy than flies, but nonetheless excellent. These ones I shall save for future repasts. My gratitude to you for your timely information, Dor-man."

"Yes," Dor said, using the best word he had to indicate a positive response directly. He was glad that he had been able to help, but it was not enough. His responsibility would not be through until he had returned Jumper to his own world.

Now it was Dor's turn to look for food. He asked the web, but it had seen mainly things that moved, while Dor preferred sedentary food. So he inquired of stones he saw, and sticks of wood, and soon located a hominy tree with a few ripe grits on it. This wasn't much, but it would hold him for a while. The magic vegetation did exist; it was merely sparser, more secretive than in his own day, forcing him to search it out more carefully.

By this time it was late afternoon. It would not be safe to spend the night on the ground; more goblins could come, or other threats could manifest. If this were Dor's own world, there would have been half a dozen bad threats already, as well as several nuisances and a couple of annoyances. But maybe the goblin band had cleaned out the local monsters, not liking the competition. "Rest," Dor said, pointing to the declining sun.

Jumper understood. "I can see very well in the dark, but it may be unsafe for Dor-man. The trees are not safe either; there are other things than birds up there, that I perceived a moment ago. One resembled a bird, but had a man-face and a bad odor—"

"A harpy!" Dor cried. "Face and bosom of a woman, body of a bird. They're awful!" Of course he knew Jumper couldn't follow all that, but he would pick up the tone of agreement.

"Therefore we should sleep in the air," Jumper concluded. "I will string you from a branch and you will swing safe for the night."

Dor was not sanguine about this notion either, but could neither express his objection adequately nor offer a better alternative. To be trussed up like one of those living lobsters—

With misgivings that he trusted were not evident to the spider Dor suffered himself to be looped by several strands of line. Jumper drew the material from his spinnerets, which were organs in his posterior. He cheerfully explained it in more detail than Dor cared to know, as he proceeded: "My silk is a liquid that hardens into a strong thread as it is drawn out. With my six spinnerets I shape it into strands of whatever texture, strength, and quality I happen to require. In this case I'm using single threads for the hammock and a multistrand cable for the main line. Now you wait here a moment while I make the connection."

There wasn't much else Dor could do at this stage except wait as requested. That silk was strong stuff!

Jumper climbed up through the air. Noting Dor's startled reaction, he chittered down the explanation: "My dragline. I left it in place when I finished catching the lobsters. We spiders could not survive without our draglines. They keep us from falling, ever. Sometimes my hatchmates and I would have drag races, when I was young, jumping from high places to see who could bounce closest to the ground without touching . . ." He climbed on out of sight.

"Hatchmates?" Dor inquired, mainly to keep the spider chittering so he would know where he was.

"My siblings who hatched from the egg sac," Jumper responded from above. "Several hundred of us, shedding our first skins and emerging into the great outer world to disperse and fend for ourselves. Is this not the case with your kind too?"

"No," Dor admitted. "I am the only one in my family."

"My consolations! Did some monster consume all the rest before they could escape?"

"Uh, not exactly. My parents take good care of me, when they are home."

"Your sire and siress remain together? I fear I misunderstand your expression."

"Uh, well—"

"Intriguing notion, maintaining a relationship with one's mate and offspring after procreation. Perhaps I should check with my mate, when I return, just to see how she's managing with the egg sac. Wouldn't want my spiderlings to hatch prematurely." Then, abruptly, Dor was hoisted off the ground. Jumper was hauling him into the air like a lobster!

Yet it was oddly comfortable. Jumper had not bound him, but had placed his strands competently so that Dor was well supported without being confined.

Most of the lines were invisible, unless he knew exactly where to look. The spider was really expert at this sort of thing!

It was easy to relax in this hammock, to rest—and he did feel safe. In a moment Jumper glided down to hang beside him. They dangled together as the serenity of the night closed in above them, secure from the threats of ground and tree.

Dor jumped. He scratched his head. Something scuttled away through his hair. It was that flea again, probably the same one who had bitten him when he first arrived. He thought of mentioning it to the spider, who should certainly know how to catch a flea, but then worried that he might lose an ear in the process. Those tusks of Jumper's were fierce! This was one problem he preferred to handle himself. Next time the critter bit him . . .

Dor woke as the light filtered in through the branches. He felt some discomfort, for he was not used to sleeping in a vertical position, but he knew he was better off than he might have been. His leg was sore where the goblin had bitten it, and his right arm was stiff from swinging the heavy sword, and his stomach rumbled with borderline dissatisfaction. But this was a well-conditioned body; the sensations were mere annoyances.

Jumper stirred. He dropped to the ground to make sure it was safe, then climbed back up to lower Dor. As Dor's foot touched the forest floor, the big spider moved his legs dexterously around him, and the net of web fell away. Dor was free.

Now, suddenly, he felt an urgent call of nature. He retreated to a bush to take care of it. Floating in air was nice, but was limiting in certain ways! He wondered whether real heroes were ever embarrassed by such problems; certainly the subject never came up in the heroic tales of this period.

Jumper chittered as Dor returned. Dor listened, but could make no sense of it. What had happened to his translator?

After a moment he found out: the big spider had removed it when he cut away the net-web. It was a natural error. Dor found a strand of Jumper's own left over silk and put that on his shoulder. "Translate," he ordered it.

". . . mission, while mine is merely to return to my normal world," Jumper was saying. "So it behooves me to help you complete your mission, so that we can both return."

"Yes," Dor agreed.

"Obviously magic is involved. Some spell has carried me to your world—except that you do not seem overly familiar with it yourself. So it must be a strange aspect of your world. You are here to accomplish something, after which you will be released from your enchantment. So if we stay together—"

"Yes!" Dor agreed. Jumper was one smart arachnid. He must have thought things out during the night, recognizing the seeming change in his size and Dor's ignorance of these surroundings as linked things.

"So the best thing to do is get your job done as fast as possible," Jumper concluded. "If you will indicate where you need to travel—"

"To the Zombie Master," Dor said. But of course that wasn't clear. Also, he had no idea where to find the Zombie Master. This led to a somewhat confused discussion. Finally Dor asked some of the local artifacts; they knew nothing of the Zombie Master, but had heard of King Roogna. It seemed a detachment of the King's army had passed this way.

"King Roogna! Of course!" Dor exclaimed. "He would know! He would know everything! I should talk with him first, and he will tell me how to find the Zombie Master."

Thus it was decided. Dor got general directions from the landscape, and they began their trek toward Castle Roogna. In one part of his mind Dor remained bemused by the fact that this was the tapestry world, and the entire tapestry was inside Castle Roogna. Yet they evidently faced a journey of many days to reach the Castle. It did make sense, somehow, he was sure. As much sense as magic ever did.

He was getting used to this new jungle. Rather, this old jungle. Many of the trees were giant, with voluminously proliferating foliage, but had very little magic. It was as if it took longer for magic to infuse the vegetation than the animals. Sweat gnats were present, and bluebottle flies, their bottle bodies refracting the beams of sunlight they buzzed through. But even these minor insects did not approach Jumper too closely. This was one advantage of traveling with a spider.

"No!" Dor cried suddenly. "Danger!" He pointed. "You're walking into a tangle tree!"

Jumper paused. "I gather there is some threat? All I see is the collection of vines."

In the spider's normal, small world there would be no tangle trees, Dor realized. Tanglers were there, to be sure, but they would hardly bother anything as small as a spider. Also, Jumper might have lived all his life in the tapestry room of Castle Roogna, so never encountered any of the jungle threats, regardless of relative sizes. Yet he seemed familiar with trees in general, so he must have spent some time outside.

"I'll show you," Dor said. He picked up a large stick and heaved it at the tree. The tangler's tentacles snatched it out of the air and tore it to splinters.

"I see what you mean," Jumper said appreciatively. "I believe I walked on the foliage of such a tree once in my youth, but it paid me no attention. Now that I am on its scale, it is another condition. I am glad I am keeping your company, weird though your form is."

Which was a decent compliment. Dor inspected the tangler from a safe distance. He had identified it almost too late, because it was of a different subspecies from the ones he had known. It was cruder, more like a mundane tree, with light bark on the tentacles, and it lacked the pleasant greensward and sweet perfume beneath. Tanglers had grown more sophisticated over the centuries as their prey became more wary. For a person attuned to the end product, the cruder ancestral version was hard to identify. He would have to be more careful; there was less magic in the jungle, but what there was was just as dangerous to him and Jumper.

They resumed their journey. The Land of Xanth was a peninsula connected to Mundania by a narrow, mountainous isthmus at the northwest extremity. Dor's body appeared to be that of a Mundane who had recently crossed the isthmus; maybe that was why he had been easy for the goblins to trap. It took time to appreciate all the hazards of Xanth, and even a lifetime did not suffice for some people. A Mundane would have all the wrong reflexes, and perish quickly. Which perhaps was why the Mundanes invaded in Waves; there was security in great numbers.

Now they were proceeding toward the center of Xanth, Castle Roogna, in a southerly direction. How they would cross the Gap that cut Xanth in two Dor wasn't certain. In his day the northern wilderness was not as dangerous as the southern wilderness, and since there was less magic now—or rather, less-developed magic—Dor did not anticipate too much trouble this side of the Gap. But the Land of Xanth had a way of fooling people, so he remained on guard.

Castle Roogna. He wondered whether there was a tapestry on its wall, depicting—what? The events another eight hundred years past? Or the present, including himself coming toward the Castle? Intriguing thought!

Jumper paused, raising his two frontmost forelegs, which seemed to be the most sensitive to new things. Dor had noted no ears on the spider; was it possible he heard with his legs? "Something strange," Jumper chittered.

The spider had grown accustomed to the routine strangenesses of this land, so this must be something special. Dor looked. Before them stood a creature vaguely like a small dragon, yet obviously not a dragon. Yet with dragon affinities. It had an irregularly sinuous body, small wings that did not seem functional, claws, tail, and a lizard head, but lacked the formidable teeth and fire of a true dragon. In fact, it did not look very formidable.

"I think it will be safe to circle around it," Dor said. There was a swampy region to the west with malodorous bubbles, and a thicket of glistening brambles to the east, so it was necessary to pass through this creature's territory. "We're not looking for trouble, and maybe it isn't either." Knowing Jumper could hardly understand all that discussion, he set the example by detouring right, to circle the monster at a safe distance without going too near the bubbly swamp.

But the creature extended one leg enormously, so that it stretched way out to block Dor's progress. "You may not pass," it rasped. "This is my domain, my precinct, my territory. I govern."

At least it talked! "We do not seek any quarrel with you," Dor said, remembering adult protocol for such things. "If you let us pass, we will not bother you."

"If you pass, you prevail," the monster said. "I am Gerrymander; I prevail by whatever devious configuration."

Dor knew of no such creature in his own time. This must have been an evolutionary dead end. Gerrymander—who prevailed by changing its shape to block the passage of others? A strange definition of success!

"I do not wish to damage you, Gerrymander," Dor said, placing his hand on the hilt of his sword. He feared it looked as if he were scratching his shoulder, and wished this body had a more conventional harness for the sword, but that couldn't be helped. "But we must pass."

Gerrymander's shape settled grotesquely. It contracted along its extremity and stood in its original form before Dor. "You shall not. I hold this office eternally, regardless of the need or merit of others."

The thing was meeting his challenge squarely. Dor was daunted. He was using the body of a powerful grown man, but he remained a boy at heart, and he never had been much for combat. Those goblins, the horrible way they had died—no, not that again! "Then I'll just have to go around another way." He backed off.

"You shall not!" Gerrymander repeated. "No one supersedes me by fair means!" Its neck extended in a series of odd jumps until its head came to rest behind Dor. Now he was half encircled.

Sudden fear prompted him to do what determination had not. Dor drew his sword with the practiced speed of his warrior-body and pointed it directly at the creature's heart region. "Get out of my way!"

For answer, the thing's left wing began extending with the same chunky jerks, forming a misshapen barrier around Dor's other side. "I am surrounding you, isolating your influence," Gerrymander said. "You have no power, your grass roots are shriveling, your aspirations fading away. Your strength will be mine."

And Dor did feel a sinister weakening, as if his body were being drained of some vital imperative. Terrified by this strange threat, he reacted savagely. He struck with all his power at the thing's neck. The great sword cut cleanly through Gerrymander's substance as if it were mere cocoa from a nut, cleaving the monster in twain.

But no blood flowed. "I don't have to be contiguous," Gerrymander cried, its severed head forming little legs as its ears elongated. The ears were now limbs. "I don't have to be reasonable; I have the power of accommodation. I can be any shape and any number, anytime. I am master of form and number. I cover whatever territory I need, regardless of my actual base, to hold power."

Dor struck again, separating a section of body, but the thing did not die or yield. Dor cut it into half a dozen bloodless segments, yet they maintained their formation about him. An arm coalesced into a torso, the fingers of its hands stretching into separate arms and legs; a leg sprouted legs and a tail; the original tail grew a head. "I convolute, I divide, I conquer!" the original head cried, as the segments closed in.

"Help! Jumper!" Dor cried, entirely unnerved.

"I am here, friend," the spider chittered. "Sheathe your blade, lest you injure me, and I will aid you."

Dor obeyed. His body was shaking with fear and humiliation. Whatever had given him the notion that all he needed to be a hero was a hero's body?

Jumper bounded phenomenally, passing right over Gerrymander and landing beside Dor. "I will tie this creature," the spider chittered. "I will bind it together so that it cannot move."

Jumper rapidly drew yards of silk from his versatile spinnerets. He looped his line about Gerrymander's tail section, anchoring it in several places with sticky lumps. Then he looped another segment and drew the two together, making a package. Working rapidly with his eight legs and with marvelous dexterity, he looped more segments and drew them in tight. He was forcing Gerrymander to collect back into its original volume.

As the segments came together, they merged, forming one creature. The superfluous arms, legs, heads, and tails flowed back into the main mass. Gerrymander was being put back together. But this wasn't enough.

"I surround, I select, I conquer!" the monster cried, its tail re-expanding to fill the space it had occupied as a separate segment. Jumper's strands could not prevent this; they remained in place, anchoring the creature, but could not stop its projection from growing around and between them. All the spider had accomplished was the undoing of Dor's slicing; the monster's basic talent was not affected.

"I fear that I, like you, am being overcome," Jumper chittered. "Come, friend, let us retreat and reconsider." He flung a loop around Dor, then leaped straight up thirty feet to cling to the overhanging branch of a mundane tree. Then he hauled on his line, and drew Dor slowly up after him.

Gerrymander gave a shriek of pure anguish. "Ah, they escape me!" It tried to catch Dor's rising legs.

Dor yanked his feet out of the thing's grasp. The creature extended itself, rising high to pace him, and grabbed again. Dor drew his sword and slashed at the grotesquely reaching hand-limb. Gerrymander's catching claw was cut off, and it fell to the ground, where it quickly merged with the rest of the body. The thing might not be hurt by having chunks of itself cut off, but it was unable to lift such pieces very far into the air without support. "Aaahh!" it cried despairingly. "I have been outmaneuvered!"

"We had only to jump over it!" Dor cried with realization. "Just as it blocked us, knowing no laws of motion, we could pass it without such laws. The moment we pass it, we win. *That's* how you fight Gerrymander!"

Indeed, the defeated monster was rapidly dwindling into its smaller original form. Its power existed only so long as it was matching its challenge. According to its definition.

"Strange are the ways of this world," Jumper chittered.

Dor only shook his head, agreeing.

Jumper lowered Dor down beyond Gerrymander, and the two resumed their trek. Now Dor knew how the spider got his name! He had never before seen such jumping ability. He had thought all spiders made webs, but Jumper didn't, though he certainly had facility with silk. It was, Dor realized, not safe to categorize creatures too blithely; there were enormous variations.

They were becoming wise to the ways of this region, and traveled rapidly. Most wild creatures were wary of Jumper, who looked more ferocious than he was, and seemed quite alien to this world—which he was not. He was merely large for his type.

By nightfall they had traversed most of northern Xanth, Dor judged. They might have traveled faster, but had had to stop to forage for food every so often. He remembered that there was supposed to be a grove of peace trees in this vicinity; not a good place to sleep, for the sleeper might never find the initiative to wake again. So at his behest they camped just shy of the main forest, suspended from a solitary crabapple tree in a field. A stream nearby provided water for Dor, and the crabs from the tree were a minor feast for Jumper.

Next morning they passed hastily through the peace grove, never stopping to rest. Dor felt lethargy overwhelming him, but these trees, too, had not developed their magic to its potency of later centuries, and he was able to fight it off. Jumper, unused to this effect, became sluggish, but Dor goaded him on until they were out of the grove.

At last they stood at the brink of the Gap. A thousand paces across, here, and just as deep, it was Xanth's most scenic and devastating landmark. "It doesn't appear on any maps of my day," Dor said, "because there is some kind of forget spell associated with it. But most of us at Castle Roogna have become more or less immune to the effect, so we can remember. I don't know how we can get across except by climbing down this wall and up the other. You could do that readily, I'm sure, but I'm not nearly as good a climber as you, and I get nervous about heights."

They had conversed during their trek, and Jumper was already picking up a small versatile vocabulary of Dor's words. He could now make out the general gist of Dor's speech. "I believe we can cross this, if we must," he chittered. "There is, however, a certain element of risk."

"Yes, the Gap dragon," Dor said, remembering.

"Danger?"

"Big danger, at the bottom of the chasm. Dragon—like Gerrymander, only worse. Teeth."

"We can jump over it?"

"The dragon would—the teeth—it's just not safe," Dor said, frustrated. He could not remember whether the Gap dragon was a fire-breather or a steamer, but didn't want to risk it either way. Nobody in his right mind, and not too many in their wrong minds, messed with a full-sized dragon!

"However, we do not need to descend," Jumper chittered. "I contemplate ballooning."

"Ballooning?"

"Floating across the chasm on an airborne line. There is updraft here; I believe conditions are favorable, in the height of the day when the warm air rises. But there remain risks."

"Risks," Dor repeated, stunned by the whole notion. "Flying on silk?"

"If the air current should change, or a storm arise—"

The more Dor thought about it, the less he liked it. Yet his other options did not seem better. He did not want to go down into the Gap, or to try to walk all the way around it. He had a couple of weeks here in the tapestry to complete his mission, and had used two days already; going the way around the Gap could use all the rest. He needed to get to Castle Roogna as rapidly as possible. "I guess we'd better balloon," he said reluctantly.

Jumper stood at the edge of the Gap and drew out some silk. Instead of attaching it to anything, he let the wind take it. Soon it was unreeling rapidly, the end of the silk being drawn upward like a magic kite. Dor could see only a few feet of it; beyond that the silk became invisible in the distance no matter how carefully he traced it. He did not see how this could carry anything across the chasm.

"It is almost ready," Jumper chittered. "Let me fasten it to you, friend, before it hauls me away." Indeed, the huge spider was now clinging to the ground. There was evidently quite a strong pull from that invisible thread. "Please approach."

Dor stepped close, and with deft motions of his forelegs the spider fashioned a hammock to support him. Then an extra gust of wind came, and Dor was hauled into the air and out over the Gap.

Too startled to move or scream, Dor stared down into the awesome depths. He swung down on the end of his tether as his kite achieved its special orientation. He thought he would sink right down into the chasm, but then the updraft caught hold strongly and carried him upward.

The walls of the chasm angled down on either side to form a wedgelike base. The sunlight angled down from the east, making stark shadows in the irregularities of the cliff. Even so, the depths remained gloomy. No, he didn't want to go down there!

As he rose back above the rim of the canyon the wind eased. It lifted him slowly, but also carried him westward along the chasm. He was not really getting across. Jumper remained on the rim, spinning a balloon line for himself—but this took time, and the distance between them was extending alarmingly. Suppose they got completely separated?

Dor had known Jumper only two days, but he had come to depend on the big spider. It was not merely that Jumper was company, or that he fought well, or that he had so many useful tricks with his silk—such as ballooning!—it was that Jumper was adult. Dor had the body of a man, but fell far short of the judgement or certainty of a man. He got frightened when alone, and insecure, not always for sufficient reason.

Jumper, in contrast, coolly assessed every situation and reacted with level-minded precision. He could make mistakes, but they didn't throw him. He was a stabilizing influence, and Dor needed that. He hadn't realized it until this moment—which was part of his problem. He was not good at analyzing his own motives ahead of a crisis. He needed the company of someone who understood him, someone who could prepare for Dor's mistakes without making an embarrassing issue of it. Someone like Jumper.

There was a pain in his scalp. Dor swatted at it. Damn that flea!

The wind was, if anything, picking up now. Dor sailed faster and higher. His apprehension mounted. It hardly seemed he was going to come down anywhere, certainly not the far side of the Gap. He might be blown all the way out to sea and drown or be consumed by sea monsters. Or he might float higher and higher until he starved. Worst of all, he might even land in Mundania. Why hadn't Jumper anticipated this?

The answer was, he had. The spider had warned of the risk. And Dor had decided to take that risk. Now he was paying the price of that decision.

A speck appeared among the clouds. A bug, no a bird, no a harpy, no a dragon—no, it loomed larger still. A roc—it must be a roc-bird, largest of all winged creatures. But as it came closer yet, and he gained perspective on it, he knew that it was after all too small to be a roc, though it certainly was large. It was a bird with bright but tasteless plumage; patches of red, blue, and yellow on the wings, a brown tail speckled with white, and a body streaked in shades of green. The head was black with a white patch about one eye and two purple feathers near the gray beak. In short, a hodgepodge.

The bird loomed close, cocking one eye at Dor. This was another danger he hadn't thought of: attack by a flying creature. He grabbed for his sword, but restrained himself, afraid he would cut through his silken line and plummet into the chasm. He had been lucky he didn't sever his line when he was escaping from Gerrymander—but that had been a far lesser height than this. Yet if he didn't defend himself, the bird might eat him. It did not look like a predator; the beak was wrong. More like a scavenger. But the way it peered at him—

"Hoo-rah!" the bird cried. It dived forward, extended its big handlike feet, and snatched Dor out of the air. "Hoo-rah! Hoo-rah!" and it stroked powerfully south, carrying Dor along.

This was the direction he had wanted to go, but not the manner. Prey for a monstrous, loud-beaked bird! Now he was glad Jumper wasn't with him, for the spider could not have helped him against so large a creature, and would only have fallen prey too. A big bird would be the worst possible menace to a big spider!

Now that his fate was upon him, Dor found himself much less afraid than he had thought he ought to be. Here he was going to be cruelly consumed, but most of what he felt was relief that his friend had escaped that destiny. Was this a sign he was growing up? Too bad he would never have the chance to complete the process!

Of course Jumper would be stuck in the tapestry world, without Dor's spell to release him from it, unless the spell automatically reverted whatever didn't belong here. Such as one live spider, and the digested refuse of—still, it wasn't his own body getting eaten. Maybe a compromise: his spirit halfway dead, so he would return as a zombie. He could wander about the dismal countryside swapping ghoul stories with Jonathan. Yuck!

"Hoo-rah!" the bird cried again, descending toward a hugely spreading mundane-type tree. In a moment it landed on a tremendous nest, depositing Dor in its center.

The nest was incredible. It had been fashioned from every imaginable and some unimaginable substance: string, leaves, bark, snakeskins, seaweed, human clothing, feathers, silver wire—Dor's father had mentioned a silver oak somewhere in the jungle; the bird must have found that tree—dragon's scales, a petrified peanut-butter sandwich, strands of hair from a harpy's tail—harpies had hairy feathers, or feathery hairs—a tangle-tree tentacle, pieces of broken glass, seashells strung together, an amulet fashioned from centaur mane, several dried worms, and a mishmash of less identifiable things.

But what filled the nest was even more remarkable. There were eggs, of course —but not this bird's own eggs, for they were of all colors, sizes, and shapes. Round eggs, oblong eggs, hourglass eggs; green ones, purple ones, polka-dotted ones; an egg the size of Dor's head, and another the size of his littlest fingernail.

At least one was an alabaster darning egg. There were also assorted nuts and berries and screws. There were dead fish and live wires and golden keys and brass-bound books, and pine and ice-cream cones. There was a marble statue of a winged horse, and marbles carved from unicorn horn. There was an hourglass with a quarter hour on it, and three linked rings made of ice. A soiled sunbeam and a polished werewolf dropping. Five goofballs. And Dor.

"Hoo-rah!" the bird cried exultantly, flapping its wings so that papers, leaves, and feathers flew about in a miniature windstorm within the nest. Then it took off.

It seemed this bird liked to collect things. Dor had become part of the collection. Was he the first man so collected, since he saw no other here? Or had the others been eaten? No, he saw no human bones. Not that that proved anything; the bird could digest the bones along with the flesh. Probably he had become collect-worthy because he had seemed to be a flying man: an unusual species.

Dor made his way past the bric-a-brac to the nearest rim of the nest so that he could peer over. But all he could see were layers of leaves. He was sure he was far up in the tree, however; it would be suicidal to jump. Could he climb down? The limb of the tree on which the nest perched was round, smooth-barked, and moist; only the fact that it branched at the base of the nest made it possible for anything to remain on top of it. Dor was almost certain he would fall off. He simply was not a good climber.

He knew he should make a decision soon, and take action before the Hoorah bird returned, but he found himself paralyzed with objections to any positive course. To jump was to fall and die; to climb was to fall and die; to remain here was—to be eaten? "I don't know what to do!" he cried, near tears.

"That's easy," the unicorn statue said. "Make a rope from fragments of the Hoorah's nest, and let yourself down to the ground."

"Not from *my* substance!" the nest protested.

Dor took hold of a piece of cord and yanked it out of the nest. It snapped readily. He drew on some long straw with similar result. He tried for some cloth; it, too, lacked cohesion. He took hold of the silver wire, but it was so fine it cut into his hands. "You're right, nest," he said. "Not from your substance." He looked about, however, taking some faint heart. "Any other notion, things?"

"I am a magic ring," a golden circlet said. "Put me on and make a wish, any wish, any wish at all. I am all-powerful."

Then how had it ended up here? But he couldn't afford to be too choosy. Dor put it on his little finger. "I wish I were safe on the ground."

Nothing happened. "The ring is a liar," the werewolf dropping growled.

"I am not!" the ring cried. "It just takes a little time. A little patience. Have faith in me. I'm out of practice, that's all."

Its statement was greeted by a rumble of derisive laughter from many other artifacts of the Hoorah's nest. Dor cleared junk from one area and lay down, trying to think of something. But his mind would not perform.

Then a hairy leg came up over the rim of the nest, followed by another, and a pair of huge green eyes plus a collection of smaller black eyes. "Jumper!" Dor cried, delighted. "How did you find me?"

"I never needed to search for you," the spider chittered, hauling his pretty abdomen over the brim. That variegated fur-face had never looked so good! "As a matter of routine I attached a dragline to you. When the Hoorah took you, I was carried along behind, though at a fair distance. I daresay I was virtually invisible. I did get hung up on the tree, but once I climbed the line to its end I found you."

"That's great! I was afraid I'd never see you again!"

"You forget I need your magic to escape this world." Actually their dialogue was not nearly this concise, because Jumper still did not know many human words, but it seemed like normal conversation in retrospect. "Now shall we depart?"

"Yes."

Jumper attached a new line to Dor and made ready to lower him down through the foliage. But just then they heard the beat of huge wings. The Hoorah was returning!

Jumper sprang out of the nest and disappeared below. Dor, alarmed, remembered almost immediately that no spider ever fell; his dragline protected him. Dor might have jumped similarly, but wasn't sure his own dragline was properly anchored. The Hoorah's approach had become audible just when Jumper was seeing to it, interrupting the process.

Or maybe, Dor reminded himself savagely, he was simply too scared to do what he had to, in time.

The Hoorah's mishmash plumage appeared. It covered the nest. Something dropped. "Hoo-rah!" Then the bird was off again on its insatiable mission of collection.

The thing most recently deposited stirred. It flung limbs about, and a curtain of hair. It righted itself and sat up.

Dor stared.

It was a woman. A young, pretty, girl-type maiden.

Chapter 4

Monsters

As the big bird disappeared, Jumper climbed back over the side of the nest. The girl spied him and screamed. She flung her hair about. She kicked her feet. She was a healthy young thing with a penetrating scream, marvelous blond tresses, and extremely well-formed legs.

"It's all right!" Dor cried, not certain whether he was thinking more of the situation, which was hardly all right, or of her exposed legs, which were more than all right. This body really noticed such things! "He's a friend! Don't bring back the Hoorah!"

The maiden's head snapped about to face him. She seemed almost as alarmed by Dor as by the huge spider. "Who are you? How do you know?"

"I'm Dor," he said simply. Maybe one year he would learn how to introduce himself to a lady with flair! "The spider is my companion."

Distrustfully, she watched Jumper. "Ooo, ugly! I've never seen a monster like that before. I think I'd rather be eaten by the bird. At least it's familiar."

"Jumper's not ugly! He doesn't eat people. They don't taste good."

She whirled to face him again, and once more her golden hair flung out in a spiral swirl. She looked suddenly familiar. But he was sure he had not seen her here before; he had encountered no girls here in the past. "How does he know?"

"We were attacked by a band of goblins. He tasted one."

"Goblins! They aren't real people! Of course they taste bad!"

"How do you know?" Dor countered, using her own query.

"It just stands to reason that a sweet maid like me tastes better than any old messy goblin!"

Dor found it hard to refute that logic. Certainly he would rather kiss her than a goblin.

Now what had put that thought in his mind?

"I am unable to follow your full dialogue," Jumper said. "But I gather the female of your species does not trust me."

"Right on target, monster!" she agreed.

"Uh, you do take some getting used to," Dor said. "You, uh, appear as strange to her as she does to you."

Jumper was startled. "It could not be that extreme!"

"Well, maybe I exaggerated." Diplomacy or truth?

"The thing actually talks!" the girl exclaimed. "Only it throws its voice to your shoulder."

"Well, that's hard to explain—"

"Nevertheless," Jumper cut in, "we had better vacate this nest quickly."

"Why does its voice come from your shoulder?" the girl insisted. Evidently she had a lively curiosity.

"I made a translation web," Dor explained. "Jumper's voice is the chitter. You should at least say hello to him."

"Oh." She leaned forward, giving Dor his first conscious peek down into a buxom bodice. Stunned, he stood stock-still. "Hello, Jumper-monster," she said to the web.

"Wow!" said the web. "Get a load of that—"

"You don't have to speak to the web," Dor said quickly, though he was sorry to undeceive her. Now she wouldn't be leaning at him any more. A background region of his mind wondered why a spiderweb would care to remark on the particular view offered, as it was surely not of interest to spiders.

". . . yellow silk," the web finished, even as Dor's guilty thought progressed. Oh—of course. Spiders were interested in silk, and colored silk would be a novelty.

"That's hair, not silk," he murmured. Then, more loudly to the girl: "Jumper understands you without the web."

"About vacating the nest—" Jumper chittered.

"Yes! Can you make another dragline for her?"

"Immediately." Jumper moved toward the girl.

"Eeeeek!" she screamed, flinging her silk about. "The hairy monster's going to eat me!"

"Be quiet!" Dor snapped, losing patience despite the impression her attributes had made on him. Either this body had singular appetites, or he had been missing a whole dimension of experience all his prior life! "You'll bring back the Hoorah."

She quietened reluctantly. "I won't let that thing near me."

She would talk to the spider, but not cooperate with him. She seemed almost as juvenile as Dor himself. "I can't carry you down," he told her. "I'm only—" He broke off. He was no longer a twelve-year-old boy in body, but a powerful man. "Well, maybe I can. Jumper, will the line hold two of us?"

"Indubitably. I have only to make a stronger cable," the spider chittered, his spinnerets already at work. In moments he had made a new harness for Dor, with a stronger cable.

Meanwhile the girl, with her irrepressible feminine curiosity, was exploring the nest. "Oh, jewels!" she exclaimed, clapping her cute little hands together excitedly.

"What kind?" Dor asked, wondering whether they would be useful for buying food or shelter later on. Jewels were not nearly as valuable in Xanth as in Mundania, but many people liked them.

"We are cultured pearls," several voices chorused. "Most refined and well mannered, with our lineage dating back to the emperor of all oysters. We are aristocrats among jewels."

"Oh, I'll take you!" the girl cried, seeming unsurprised at their speech. She scooped them up and filled her apron pockets.

Now they heard the Hoorah returning. Dor put his left arm around the girl's slender and supple waist and lifted her easily off her feet; what power this body had! Maybe it wasn't his muscles so much as her lack of mass; she was feather-like though firmly fleshed. There must be a special magic about girls like this, he thought, to make them full yet light.

He leaped over the edge of the nest, trusting Jumper's dragline to preserve them from a fall. The girl screamed, kicked her feet, and flung her hair in his face. "Quiet," he said around a mouthful of golden strands, holding her close so she wouldn't wriggle loose. He was feeling very heroistic at the moment.

The line went taut. It was springy, like a big rubber band from a rubber tree. They bounced back up almost to the base of the nest. The girl jiggled against him, all soft and intriguing in a fashion he would have liked to understand better. But he had no chance to explore that matter at the moment.

As they steadied, Jumper came down to join them. He did not jerk and bounce; he glided to a controlled halt beside them, for he was paying out his dragline as he went. "I have set up a pulley," he chittered. "My weight will counterbalance yours—but the two of you weigh more than I do, so I'm depending on friction to keep it slow."

Dor did not follow all of that. But if the magic called friction could safely lower them, good. They were all three descending at a fair but not frightening rate, and that was satisfactory. The branches of the huge tree were passing interminably, its layers of leaves concealing them from the nest.

A shadow fell across them. It was the Hoorah bird, circling down to spy out its lost artifacts. In a moment it would spot them, for they were in a slanting sunbeam.

Dor tried to draw his sword with his right hand, but this was difficult while he was supporting the girl with his left arm. Light she was, but she seemed to be getting heavier. Again, he worried about severing his own lifeline as the blade emerged from its scabbard.

"Hang still!" Jumper chittered. "A still target is very hard to locate."

Dor gave up on the sword. But they couldn't hang still. Dor and the girl weighed too much; they kept dropping, while the spider rose, hauled by the magic of the pulley. Jumper grabbed on to a branch with several legs, did something, and scurried along the branch toward the trunk of the tree. Dor and the girl did not fall; Dor realized that Jumper had fastened his line to the branch, halting the pulley action.

That left Dor and the terrified girl dangling like bait for the Hoorah. She was squirming, twitching her silk, and kicking her feet uselessly. His left arm, despite its mighty thews, was tiring. Pretty soon he'd be down to one thew, then none. Girls certainly were a nuisance at times.

The Hoorah spied the motion. "Hoo-rah!" it cried, and angled down.

Suddenly a green and gray-brown shape hurtled at them from the side. It seemed to have a mustached face on it. The girl screamed piercingly and flung out her arms, banging Dor's nose with her cute elbow. He almost dropped her. But the shape was now in contact with them, its momentum shoving them all to the side, swinging on the line until they came up against a leafy branch. The hurtling Hoorah missed, swerving barely in time to avoid smacking its beak into the main tree trunk.

"I will attempt to distract it," Jumper chittered—for of course he was the one who had rescued them. It was the variegated abdomen face-pattern Dor had noted. "I have tied you to this branch; the bird may not see you if you remain motionless and silent."

Fat chance! The girl inhaled and opened her pretty mouth to scream again. Dor put his big ugly right hand across it. "Quiet!"

"Mmmph mmmph, you mmmph!" she mmmphed, one eye above his hand filling with anger while the other eye retained its terror. He hoped she wasn't saying the unmaidlike thing he feared she was saying; it would be detrimental to her image.

"Well, if you'd only accepted a dragline for yourself, we wouldn't be in this picklement." Dor whispered back. But he knew that was unfair. The Hoorah had returned too soon, regardless.

"Come and get me, featherbrain," Jumper chittered from another branch. Of course the translation came from Dor's shoulder. But the spider also waved his forelegs, and that attracted the bird's attention. The Hoorah zoomed toward that branch—and the spider sprang twenty feet to another, chittering vehemently. Dor knew the big bird could not understand Jumper's actual words, but the tone was unmistakable.

Then again, why shouldn't birds comprehend spider language? The two species interacted often enough. Which illustrated the supreme courage Jumper was displaying, for the thing he most feared was birds. To save his friend and a stranger, the spider was baiting his personal nightmare menace.

"You can do better than that, squawkhead!" Jumper chittered. And jumped again, as the bird wheeled in the air. The Hoorah was remarkably agile for its size.

After several futile passes, the bird realized that Jumper was too quick for it to catch. Just as well, as the translations of the spider's insults were turning the girl's ears a delicate shell-pink. The Hoorah looked around, casting about for the other prey. Fortunately all they had to do was remain still and silent.

Dor, trying to make his fatigued left arm more comfortable, shifted his hold slightly. The girl slipped down a bit, her bosom getting squeezed. She screamed, almost without taking a breath, catching him off guard.

Oh, no! Dor, needing his right hand to help hold on to the branch, had uncovered her mouth. Foolish mistake!

The Hoorah oriented immediately on the sound. It zoomed directly toward them. Jumper was behind it, unable to distract it this time. The Hoorah knew easy prey when it found it.

With the inspiration of desperation, Dor grabbed with his right hand at the girl's clothing, questing for her pockets. Though she wore a showy dress that was cut high at the knees and low at the bodice, her apron covered much of that, and was utilitarian.

She screamed as if attacked—not unreasonably, in this case—but he continued until he found what he was looking for: the cultured pearls she had picked up from the nest. "What is your pet peeve?" he demanded as he flipped the first pearl into the air.

"I don't make pets of peeves!" the pearl retorted. "But I hate people who drop me off branches!" It dropped out of sight—and the Hoorah, tracing the sound of its voice, followed it down.

Jumper half-bounded, half-swung across to them. "Marvelous ploy!" he chittered. "Throw the next to the side, and I will lower you quietly to the ground."

"Right!" Dor agreed. He faced the girl. "And don't scream," he warned.

She inhaled to scream.

"Or I'll tickle you!" he threatened.

That got her. Meekly she let herself deflate. She even handed him a pearl from her apron breast pocket, so he wouldn't have to dig it out himself. That was almost more cooperative than he liked.

"And what is your peeve?" he inquired of the pearl, and hurled it to the side.

"I hate uncultured people who can't appreciate cultured pearls!" it cried.

They heard a "Hoo-rah!" in the distance as the bird went after it. The bird certainly appreciated cultured pearls!

By the time they reached the ground, they were out of pearls—but also out of peril. They had lost the bird. Dor picked up a few sticks of wood for emergency use in case the Hoorah came near again, and the three of them hurried away.

"You see!" the ring on Dor's finger cried. "I granted your wish! You are safe on the ground!"

"I guess I can't argue with that," Dor agreed. But he maintained a healthy private reservation.

Dor judged they were now fairly close to Castle Roogna, since the Hoorah bird had carried them in the right direction, but the day was waning and he didn't want to hurry lest they fall into another trap. So they foraged for supper, locating a few marshmallow bushes and an apple pine and some iced-tea leaves. Jumper tried a bit of pine apple, but declared he preferred crustaceans. The girl had finally come to accept the big spider as a companion, and even allowed Jumper to string her up for the night. She was, she confessed daintily, afraid of bugs and things on the ground, and at the moment was none too keen on birds in trees either.

Thus the three of them hung comfortably from silken threads, safe from the predators above and below. There were advantages to the arachnid mode, Dor decided.

Jumper fell silent, no doubt already asleep and recuperating from his formidable exertions of the day. But Dor and the girl talked for a while, in low tones so as not to attract unwanted and/or hazardous attention.

"Where do you come from?" she inquired. "Where do you go?"

Dor answered as briefly as he could, omitting the details about his age and the relation of his world to hers. He told her he was from a strange land, like this one but far removed, and he had come here looking for the Zombie Master, who might help him obtain an elixir to help a friend. He made clear that Jumper was from that same land, and was his trusted friend. "After all, without Jumper, we would never have escaped from the Hoorah's nest."

Her story was as simple. "I am a maid of just barely maybe seventeen, from the West Stockade by the lovely seashore where the gaze-gourds grow, traveling to the new capital to seek my fortune. But when I crossed a high ridge—to stay away from the tiger lilies, you know, because they have a special taste for sweet young things, those lilies of the valley—the Hoorah bird spotted me, and though I screamed and flung my hair about and kicked my feet exactly as a maid is supposed to—well, you know the rest."

"We can help you get to Castle Roogna, since we're going there too," Dor said. It probably was not much of a coincidence, since the Castle was the social and magical center of Xanth; no doubt everyone who was anyone went to Castle Roogna.

She clapped her hands in that girlishly cute way she had, and jiggled in her harness with that womanly provocation she also had. "Oh, *would* you? That's wonderful!"

Dor was pleased too. She was delightful company! "But what will you do at Castle Roogna?" he inquired.

"I hope to find employment as a chambermaid, there to encounter completely by surprise some handsome courtier who will love me madly and take me away from it all, and I shall live happily ever after in his rich house when all I ever expected was a life of chambermaiding."

Dor, even in his youth, knew this to be a simplistic ambition. Why should a courtier elect to marry a common chambermaid? But he had sense enough not to disparage her ambition. Instead he remembered a question he had overlooked before, perhaps because he had been looking at other aspects of her nature. Those aspects she kicked and bounced and flung about so freely. "What is your name?"

"Oh." She laughed musically, making a token kick and bounce and fling. "Didn't I tell you? I am Millie the maid."

Dor hung there, stunned. Of course! He should have recognized her. Twelve years younger—eight hundred twelve years younger!—herself as she was before he ever had known her, young and inexperienced and hopeful, and above all innocent. Stripped of the grim experience of eight centuries of ghosthood, a naïve cute girl hardly older than himself.

Hardly older? Five years older—and they were monstrous years. She was every resilient inch a woman, while he was but a boy of—"I wish I were a man!" he murmured.

"Done!" the ring on his finger cried. "I now pronounce you man."

"What?" Millie inquired gently.

Of course she didn't recognize him. Not only was he not in his own body, he wouldn't even exist for eight hundred years. "Uh, I was just wishing—"

"Yes?" the ring said eagerly.

Dor bopped his head. "That I could get rid of this infernal flea that keeps biting me, and get some sleep," he said.

"Now wait," the ring protested. "I can do anything, but you're asking for two things at once!"

"I'll settle for the sleep," Dor said.

Before long, the sleep came to pass. He dreamed of standing near a huge brightly bedecked gumball bush, wanting a gumball awful bad, especially a golden one close by, but restrained by the magic curse that might be protecting the fruits. It was not merely that he wasn't certain how to pluck a gumball without invoking the curse, it was that the bush was in the yard of another house, so that he really was not sure he had the right to pluck from it. It was a tall bush, with its luscious fruits dangling out of his normal reach. But he was up on magic stilts, very long and strong, so that now he stood tall enough to reach the delightful golden globe easily. If only he dared. If only he should.

More than that, he had never as a child liked gumballs that well. He had seen others liking them, but he had not understood why. Now he wanted one so badly—and was suspicious of this change in himself.

Dor woke in turmoil. Jumper was hanging near him, several eyes watching him with concern. "Are you well, friend Dor-man?" the spider chittered.

"I—just a nightmare," Dor said uncertainly.

"This is an illness?"

"There are magic horses, half illusion, who chase people at night, scaring them," Dor explained. "So when a person experiences something frightening at night, he calls it a night-stallion or a night-mare."

"Ah, figurative," Jumper agreed once he understood. "You dreamed of such a horse. A mare—a female."

"Yes. A—a horse of another color. I—I wanted to ride that mare very much, but wasn't sure I could stay on that golden mount—oh, I don't know what I'm trying to say!"

Jumper considered. "Please do not be offended, friend. I do not as yet comprehend your language well, or your nature. Are you by chance a juvenile? A young entity?"

"Yes," Dor replied tightly. The spider seemed to understand him well enough.

"One beneath the normal breeding age of your species?"

"Yes."

"And this sleeping female of your kind, her with the golden silk—she is mature?"

"I—yes."

"I believe your problem is natural. You have merely to wait until you mature, then you will suffer no further confusion."

"But suppose she—she belongs to another—?"

"There is no ownership in this sort of thing," Jumper assured him. "She will indicate whether she finds you suitable."

"Suitable for what?"

Jumper made a chitter-chuckle. "That will become apparent at the appropriate occasion."

"You sound like King Trent!" Dor said accusingly.

"Who I presume is a mature male of your species—perhaps of middle age."

On target. Despite his confusion and frustration, Dor was glad to have such a person with him. The outer form hardly mattered.

Millie stirred, and Dor suffered a sudden eagerness to halt this conversation. It was dawn, anyway; time to eat and resume the trek to Castle Roogna.

Dor got bearings from the local sticks and stones, and they set off for the Castle. But this time they encountered a large river. Dor didn't remember this from his own time—but of course the channel could have shifted in eight hundred years, and with the charmed paths he might not have noticed a river anyway. The water was quite specific in answer to Dor's question: the Castle lay beyond the far side, and there was no convenient way across the water.

"I wish I had a good way to pass this river," Dor said.

"I'll see to it," the ring on his finger said. "Just give me a little time. I got you to sleep last night, didn't I? You have to have patience, you know."

"I know," Dor said with half a smile.

"Gnome wasn't built in a day, after all."

"I could balloon us across," Jumper offered.

"Last time we ballooned, the Hoorah nabbed us," Dor pointed out. "And if it hadn't, we would probably have been blown right out of Xanth anyway. I don't want to risk that again."

"Ballooning is somewhat at the mercy of the winds," the spider agreed. "I had intended to fasten an anchor to the ground, before, so that we could not be blown too far and could always return to our starting point if necessary, but I admit I reckoned without the big bird. I had somehow thought no other creatures had been expanded in size the way I have been—in retrospect, a foolish assumption. I agree: ballooning is best saved for an emergency."

"In my stockade, we use boats to cross water," Millie offered. "With spells to ward off water monsters."

"Do you know how to make a boat?" Jumper chittered. The question was directed at Millie, but the web on Dor's shoulder translated it anyway. Inanimate objects tended to become more accommodating when they associated with him for prolonged periods.

"No," she said. "I am a maid."

And maids did not do anything useful? Maybe she simply meant she was not involved in masculine pursuits. "Do you know the anti-water-monster spells?" Dor asked her.

"No, only our stockade monster-speller can do those. That's his talent."

Dor exchanged glances with several of Jumper's eyes. The girl was nice, but she wasn't much help.

"I believe your sword would proffer some discouragement to water predators," Jumper chittered. "I could loop their extremities with silk, and render them vulnerable to your sharp edge."

Dor did not relish the prospect of battling water monsters, but recognized the feasibility of the spider's proposal. "Except the boat. We still need that," he pointed out, almost with relief.

"I think I might fashion a craft from silk," Jumper chittered. "In fact I can walk on water sometimes, when the surface is calm. I might tow the boat across."

"Why not just go across and string up one of your lines?" Millie inquired. "Then you could draw us across, as you drew us up into the tree last night."

"Excellent notion!" the spider agreed. "If I could get across without attracting attention—"

"Maybe we could set up a distraction," Dor suggested. "So they wouldn't notice you."

They discussed details, then proceeded. They gathered a number of sticks and stones for Dor to talk to, which could serve as one type of distraction, and located a few stink bugs, which they hoped would be another type of distraction. Stink bugs smelled mild enough when handled gently, but exploded with stench when abused. Jumper fashioned several stout ropes of silk, attaching one to an overhanging tree and leaving the others for the people to use as lariats.

When all was ready, Jumper set off across the water. His eight feet made dents in the surface but did not break through; actually he was quite fleet, almost skating across.

But all too soon there was a ripple behind him. A great ugly snout broke the surface: a serpentine river monster. All they could see was part of the head, but it was huge. No small boat would have been safe—and neither was Jumper. This was the type of monster much in demand for moat service.

"Hey, snoutnose!" Dor called. He saw an ear twitch on the monster's head, but its glassy eye remained fixed on the spider. More distraction was needed, and quickly!

Dor took a stick of wood, as large as he thought he could throw that distance. "Stick, I'll bet you can't insult that monster enough to make it chase you." Insults seemed to be a prime tool for making creatures react.

"Oh yeah?" the stick retorted. "Just try me, dirtface!"

Dor glanced into the surface of the water. Sure enough, he had dirt smeared across his face. But that would have to wait. "Go to it!" he said, and hurled the stick far out toward the monster.

The stick splashed just behind the great head: an almost perfect throw. Dor could never have done that in his own body! The monster whirled around, thinking it was an attack from behind. "Look at that snotty snoot!" the stick cried as it bobbled amidst its ripples. Water monsters, it was said, were quite vain about their ferocious faces. "If I had a mug like that, I'd bury it in green mud!"

The monster lifted its head high. "Honk!" it exclaimed angrily. It could not talk the human language, but evidently understood it well enough. Most monsters who hoped for moat employment made it a point to develop some acquaintance with the employers' mode of communication.

"Better blow out that tube before you choke," the stick said, warming up to its task. "I haven't heard a noise like that since a bull croak smacked into my tree and brained out its brainless brains."

The monster made a strike at the stick. The diversion was working! But already Dor saw other ripples following, the pattern of them orienting on Jumper. The spider was moving rapidly, but not fast enough to escape these creatures. Time for the next ploy.

Dor grabbed the rope strung to the tree, hauled himself up, and swung out over the water. "Hoorah!" he cried.

Heads popped out of the water, now orienting on him. Toothy, glared-eyed excrescences on sinuous necks. "You can't catch me, deadpans!" he cried. Deadpans were creatures who lurked around cooking fires, associating with slinky copperheads and similar ilk, and had the ugliest faces found in nature.

Several of the monsters were quite willing to try. White wakes appeared as the heads coursed forward.

Dor hastily swung back and jumped to shore. "How many monster *are* there?" he demanded, amazed at the number.

"Always one more than you can handle," the water replied. "That's standard operating procedure."

That made magical sense. Too bad he hadn't realized it before Jumper exposed himself on the water. But how, then, could he distract them all?

He had to try, lest Jumper be caught. It was not as if he were a garden-variety traveler; he was a Magician.

Dor picked up a stink bug, rolled it into a ball, and threw it as hard as he could toward the skating spider. Jumper was now over halfway across the river, and making good time. The bug, angered by this treatment, bounced on the water behind the spider and burst into stench. Dor could not smell it from this distance, but he heard the monsters in that vicinity choking and retreating. Dor threw three more bugs, just to be sure; then Jumper was out of range.

Millie was doing her part. She was capering beside the water and waving her hands and calling out to the monsters. Her flesh bounced in what had to be, to a monster, the tastiest manner. Even Dor felt like taking a bite. Or something. The trouble was, the monsters were responding too well. "Get back, Millie!" Dor cried. "They have long necks!"

Indeed they did. One monster shot its head forward, jaws gaping. Slaver sprayed out past the projecting tiers of teeth. Glints shot from the cruel eyes.

Millie, abruptly aware of her peril, stood frozen. What, no kicks and screams? Dor asked himself. Maybe it was because she had been kicking and screaming, in a manner, before, so that would have represented no contrast.

Dor's fingers scrambled over his shoulder for his sword as he leaped to intercept the monster. He jerked at the hilt—and it snagged, wrenching out of his hand as the sword cleared the scabbard. The blade tumbled to the ground. "Oh, no!" the sword moaned. Dor found himself striking a dramatic pose before the monster, sword hand upraised—and empty.

The monster did a double take. Then it started to chuckle. Dor somewhat sheepishly bent to retrieve his weapon—and of course the toothed snout dived down to chomp him.

Dor leaped up, legs spreading to vault the descending head, and boxed the monster on one ear with his left fist. Then he landed, whirled, and brought his sword to bear. He did not strike; he had the gleaming blade poised before one of the monster's eyeballs. The gleam of the blade bounced the eye's glints away harmlessly.

"Now I spare you, where you did not spare me," he said. "Do you take that as a signal of weakness?"

The eye stared into the swordpoint. The monster's head quivered in negation as it slid back. Dor strode forward, keeping his point near the eye. In a moment the head disappeared beneath the surface of the river.

The other monsters, noting this, did not advance. They assumed Dor had some powerful magic. And he realized this truth, which his body had known: deal with the leader, and you have dealt with the followers.

"Why, that's the bravest thing I ever saw!" Millie exclaimed, clapping her hands again. She did that often now, and it sent most interesting ripples through her torso—yet Dor had never seen her do it in his own world. What had changed?

Eight hundred years of half-life: That was what had changed her. Most of her maidenly bounce had been pressed out of her by that tragedy.

But more immediately: what had changed in him? He should never have had the nerve to face up to a full-fledged river monster, let alone cow it into retreat. Yet he had done so unthinkingly, when Millie was threatened. Maybe it was his body taking over again, reacting in a conditioned way, even to the extent of facing down a monster in such a way as to abate the whole fleet of monsters at once.

What kind of a man had this body been, before Dor arrived? Where had he gone? Would he return when Dor went back to his own world? He had thought this body was stupid, but now there seemed to be considerable compensations. Maybe the body had never needed to worry too much about danger ahead, because of its competence in handling that danger when it faced it. This body, without Dor present to mess it up, could have handled that whole goblin band alone.

The flea bit him just over the right ear. Dor almost sliced his own head off, trying to swat it with his sword hand. Here he could face down a monster, but could not get rid of a single pesky flea! One of these days he was going to find a flea-repellent plant.

"Look—the spider has made it across!" Millie cried.

So he had. Their distractions had been sufficient after all. Maybe there had been one more monster than Dor could handle—but he had not been alone.

Relieved, Dor went to the tree where the crossing cable had been anchored. Already it was tightening, lifting out of the water, as Jumper labored at the other end to draw it taut. The spider could exert a lot of force on a line, achieving special leverage with his eight legs. Soon the cable stretched from tree to tree, sagging only slightly in the middle of the river, as nearly as Dor could see. It was an extremely stout line, compared to Jumper's usual, but still it tended to disappear in the distance.

"Now we can hand-walk it across," Dor said. And asked himself: *We can?*

"Maybe you can," Millie said. "You're a big brave strong rugged man. But I am a little diffident weak soft maid. I could never—"

If only she knew Dor's true state! "Very well; I'll carry you." Dor picked her up, set her in the tree at the end of the line, then hauled himself up with a convulsive heave of his thews. He placed his boots on the cable, found his balance, and picked Millie up in his arms.

"What are you doing?" she cried, alarmed. She kicked her feet. Dor noticed again how dainty her feet were, and how cutely they kicked. There was an art to foot-kicking, and she had it; the legs had to flex at the knees, and the feet had to swing just so, not so fast that the legs could not be seen clearly. "You can't possibly keep your balance."

"That so?" he inquired. "Then I suppose we will fall into the river and have to swim after all." He walked forward, balancing.

"Are you crazy?" she demanded, horrified. And he echoed to himself: *Am I crazy?* He knew such a feat of balancing was impossible without magical assistance—yet here was this body, doing it.

What superb equilibrium this barbarian body had! No wonder Mundane Waves had conquered Xanth over and over, despite all the power of magic brought to bear against them.

Millie stopped kicking, afraid she would make him lose his balance. Dor marveled as he went; had he realized the potentialities of this body before, he would have been much less afraid of heights. He realized now that his concern about certain things, such as taking a fall, was not inherent, but more a product of his frailty of physique. When he had confidence in his abilities, fear faded. So, to that extent, the body of a man did make him more of a man in spirit too.

Then more trouble came. Big, ugly shapes flitted out of the forest to hover above the river. They were too solid for birds; their heads were man-sized.

The grotesque flock milled for a moment, then spied the figures on the cable. "Heee!" one cried, and they all wheeled and bore on Dor.

"Harpies!" Millie cried. "Oh, we are undone!"

Dor wanted to reach for his sword, but couldn't; both arms were taken with the girl. The river monsters were lurking at a discreet distance; they were cautious about approaching this formidable man while he kept his feet, but might have second thoughts if he were floundering in the water—as he soon would be if he grabbed for his sword, dropped Millie, and lost his balance. He was helpless.

The harpies closed on them, their dirty wings wafting a foul odor down. Dirty birds indeed! They were greasy avians with the heads and breasts of women. Not pretty faces and breasts like Millie's; their visages were witchlike and their dugs grotesque. Their voices were raucous. Their birdy legs had great ugly chipped talons.

"What a find, sisters!" the leader harpy screeched. "Take them, take them!"

The flock plunged down, screaming with glee. Claws closed as half a dozen foul creatures clutched at Millie, who screamed and kicked and flung her tresses about to no avail, as usual. She was torn from Dor's grasp and lifted into the sky.

Then about ten more harpies converged on Dor himself. Their talons closed on his forearms, his biceps, his calves, thighs, hair, and belt. The claws were rounded, without cutting edges, so did not hurt him so long as the points were clear; they merely clamped onto his appendages like manacles. The grimy wings beat powerfully, and he was borne upward in their putrid midst.

They carried him across the water and into the forest at treetop level, so that his sagging posterior almost brushed the highest fronds. They hoisted him on through the forest until they reached a great cleft in the ground, where they glided down. This was not the Gap; it was far smaller, more on a par with the crevasse he had entered on the magic carpet. Could it be the same one? No; the location was wrong, and the configuration different. Dug into the clifflike sides of this one were grubby holes: caves made by the harpies for their nests. They bore him down into the largest cave and dumped him unceremoniously on the filthy floor.

Dor got up, brushing dirt off his body. Millie was not here; they must have taken her to another cave. Unless there were connecting passages—which seemed unlikely, since these creatures flew better than they walked—he would be unable to reach her by foot. He retained his sword, but could not hope to slay all the harpies in this degenerate harpy city; they would overwhelm him. Either they knew this and so had contempt for his blade, or they simply hadn't recognized it in its mundane sheath across his back. The latter seemed more likely. At last he was beginning to appreciate that location! So it would be foolish to betray his possession of the weapon by making a premature move. He would have to wait and see what they wanted from him, just in case it wasn't a quick meal of his flesh, and fight only as a last resort.

One thing about being a hero: the threats were larger than life, and the glooms gloomier. In his real life he would never have gotten into a situation like this!

The harpies scuttled back, leaving one especially hideous crone before him. "My, aren't you the husky one!" she cackled, her ropy hair flying about wildly as she pecked her head forward, chickenlike. Maybe those were feathers on her pate; it was hard to tell under the muck. "Good teeth, good muscle tone, handsome—yes, you'll do just fine!"

"Just fine for what?" Dor demanded with more belligerence than he felt. He was scared.

"Just fine for my chick," the old hen clucked. "Heavenly Helen, Harpy Queen. We need a man on alternate generations, a vulture the other times."

"What have you done with—the girl?" Dor decided not to name her, lest these polluted monsters assume he was closer to her, or she to him, than he/she was and try to coerce him by torturing her. He knew monsters would do this sort of thing. That was the nature of monsters, after all.

He was quite right. "She will be cooked upon a fire of dung for supper," the canny old bird screeched gleefully. "She's such a delectable morsel! Unless you do as we demand."

"But you haven't told me what you demand."

"Haven't we now?" The dirty bird cocked her head at him cannily. "Are you trying to feign innocence? That will get you nowhere, my pretty man-type male buck! Into the nest with you!" And she partly spread her awful wings and advanced, her stink smiting him anew. Dor backed off—and stumbled into an offshoot cave.

So there were interconnecting passages. This one was not large enough for him to stand in; it was more suitable for scuttling. So he scuttled around a bend, and the tunnel opened into a fair-sized chamber whose domed ceiling did permit him to climb back to his feet.

Another harpy faced him there—but what a difference there was! This was a young bird, with metallic sheen on her feathers, shiny brass claws, the face and breasts of a lovely maiden—and she was clean. Her hair was neatly brushed, each tress luxuriant; if there were any feathers in it, they were silken ones. She was the prettiest harpy Dor had ever seen or imagined.

"So you are the man Momma found for me," Helen Harpy murmured. Her voice was sultry, no screech.

Dor looked around. The chamber was bare except for the large nest in the center, formed of fluffy down feathers so that it sprang up like a magic bubble bath. The room opened out on the canyon—a sheer drop of a couple hundred feet. Even if he were able to navigate that, how could he rescue Millie? One could hardly climb a sheer rock face while screaming and kicking one's feet.

"I think I'm going to enjoy this," Helen murmured. "I had my doubts when Momma said she'd find me a man, but I did not know how fine a man she intended. I'm so glad I wasn't in the vulture generation, the way Momma was."

"Vulture?" Dor asked, casting about for some other exit. If he could sneak through a tunnel, find Millie—

"We're half-human, half-vulture," she explained. "Since there are no males of our species, we have to alternate."

Dor had not realized there were no male harpies. Somehow he had supposed there were, in his day. But he had never looked into the matter. All he had ever actually seen were females; any males there were kept pretty much to themselves, making the females do the foraging. At any rate, this was not his present concern.

He had a bright idea. "Nest, what's the best way out of here?"

"Oblige the harpy," the nest replied, its down feathers wafting softly as it spoke. They were of pastel hues, pretty. "They hardly ever kill breeders, unless they're really hungry."

"I don't even know what the harpy wants!" Dor protested.

"Come here," the fair harpy murmured. "I'll show you what I want, you delightful hunk of man."

"I wish I were out of here," Dor muttered.

"I'm still working on the river crossing," the ring on his finger complained.

"What's that?" Helen asked, spreading her pretty wings a little. Her down feathers were as white as her breasts, and probably as soft.

"A magic ring. It grants wishes," Dor said, hoping this was not too great an exaggeration. Actually, he hadn't caught the ring failing; he just was never sure that its successes were by any agency of its own magic.

"Oh? I've always wanted one of those."

Dor pulled it off his finger. "You might as well have it; I just want to rescue Millie." Oops—he had said her name.

Helen snatched the proffered ring. Harpies were very good at snatching. "You're not a goblin spy, are you? We're at war with the goblins."

Dor hadn't known that. "I—we killed a number of goblins. A band of them attacked us."

"Good. The goblins are our mortal enemies."

Dor's curiosity was aroused. "Why? You're both monsters; I should think you'd get along together."

"We did, once, long ago. But the goblins did us the foulest of turns, so now we are at war with them."

Dor sat down on the edge of the nest. It was as soft and fluffy as it looked. "That's funny. I thought only my own kind waged wars."

"We're half your kind, you know," she said. She seemed fairly nice as he got to know her. She smelled faintly of roses. Apparently it was only the old harpies who were so awful. "A lot of creatures are, like the centaurs, mer-folk, fauns, werewolves, sphinxes, and all—and they all inherited man's warlike propensities. The worst are the pseudo-men, like the trolls, ogres, elves, giants, and goblins. They all have armies and go on rampages of destruction periodically. How much better it would be if we half-humans had inherited your intelligence, curiosity, and artistry without your barbarity."

She was making increasing sense. "Maybe if you had inherited our other halves, so you had the heads of vultures and the hindquarters of people—"

She laughed musically. "It would have made breeding easier! But I'd rather have the intelligence, despite its flaws."

"What did the goblins do to the harpies?"

She sighed, breathing deeply. She had a most impressive human portion, that way, and Dor was glad it was the upper section she had inherited. "That's a long story, handsome man. Come, rest your head against my wing, and I'll preen the dirt from your face while I tell you."

That seemed harmless. He leaned back against her wing, and found it firm and smooth and slightly resilient, with a fresh feather smell.

"Way back when Xanth was new," she said in a dulcet narrative style, "and the creatures were experiencing the first great radiation of forms, becoming all the magical combinations we know today, we half-people felt an affinity for each other." She licked his cheek delicately with her tongue; about to protest, Dor realized that this was what she meant by preening. Well, he had agreed to it, and actually the sensation was not bad at all.

"The full-men from Mundania came in savage Waves, killing and destroying," she continued, giving his ear a little nip. "We half-people had to cooperate merely to survive. The goblins lived adjacent to we harpies—or is that us harpies? I never can remember—sometimes even sharing the same caves. They slept by day and foraged by night, while we foraged by day. So our two species were able to use the same sleeping areas. But as our populations grew there was not enough room for us all." Her preening, fitted between words, had progressed to his mouth; her lips were remarkably soft and sweet as they traversed his own. If he hadn't known better, he might have thought this was a kiss.

"Some of our hens had to move out and build nests in trees," she continued, reaching the other side of his face. "They got to like that better, and still do perch in trees. But the goblins became covetous of our space, and reasoned that if there were fewer of us there would be room for more of them. So they conspired against our innocence. Their females, some of whom in those days were very comely, lured away our males, corrupting them with—with—" She paused, and her wing shuddered. This was evidently difficult for her. It was none too easy for Dor, either, because now her breast was against his cheek, as she strained to reach the far side of his neck. Somehow he found it difficult to concentrate on her words.

"With their arms and—and legs," Helen got out at last. "We had not been so long diverged from human beings that our males did not remember and lust after what they called real girls, though most human and humanoid women would not have anything to do with vulture tails. When the lady goblins became approachable—I would term them other than ladies, but I'm not supposed to know that sort of language—when these creatures beckoned our cocks—oh, males are such foolish things!"

"Right," Dor agreed, feeling pretty foolish himself, half-smothered between her neck and bosom. He knew better than to argue with the *really* foolish sex.

"And so we lost our cock-harpies, and our hens became soured. That's why we have a certain exaggerated reputation for being impolite to people. What's the use of trying, when there are no cocks to please?"

"But that was only one generation," Dor protested. "More cocks should have hatched in the next generation."

"No. There were no more eggs—no fertile ones. There had never been a great number of cocks—our kind hatched about five females for every male—and now there were none. Our hens were becoming old and bitter, unfulfilled. There's nothing so bitter as an old harpy with an empty nest."

"Yes, of course." She seemed finally to have completed the preening; he had no doubt his face was shiningly clean now. "But why didn't all the harpies die out, then?"

"We hens had to seek males of other species. We abhor the necessity—but our alternative is extinction. Since we derived originally from a cross between human and vulture—I understand that was quite a scene, there at the love spring—we have had to return to these sources to maintain our nature. There are some problems, however. The human and vulture males aren't inclined generally to mate with harpies, and we can't always get them to the love spring to make it happen—and when they do, the result is always a female chick. It seems only a harpy cock can generate males of our species. So we have become a flock of old hens."

That was some history! Dor had heard about the nefarious love springs, where diverse creatures innocently drank, then plunged into love with the next creature of the opposite sex they met. Much of the population of Xanth was the fault of such springs, producing the remarkable crossbreeds that thereafter bred true. Fortunately the love-water had to be fresh, or it lost its potency; otherwise people would be endlessly slipping it into the cups of their friends as practical jokes. But he could see how this would create a problem for the harpies, who could not always carry a potential mate to the spring, or make him drink from it.

Now Helen's whole body shook with rage, and her voice took on a little of the tone of the older hens. "And this is what the cursed goblins did to us, and why we hate them and war against them. We want to kill off all *their* males, as they did ours. We shall fight until we have our vengeance for the horrible wrong they did us. Already we are massing our armies and gathering our allies among the winged kinds, and we shall wreak a fittingly horrible vengeance by scratching the goblin nation from the fair face of Xanth!"

By this time Dor had fairly well grasped the purpose for which he had been brought here. "I, uh, I sympathize with your predicament. But I can't really help you. I'm too young; I'm not a man yet."

She drew back and twisted her head to look at him, her large eyes larger yet. "You certainly look like a man."

"I got big quite suddenly. I'm really twelve years old. That's not much for my kind. I just want to help my friend Millie."

She considered momentarily. "Twelve years old. That just might be statutory seduction. Very well. I'll accept the ring you offered, in lieu of—of the other. Maybe it can wish me a fertile egg."

"I can! I can!" the ring exclaimed eagerly.

"I didn't really want to do this anyhow," Helen said as she screwed the ring onto her largest claw. She had merely held it, up till now. "Momma insisted, that's all. You can have the girl, though at your age I really don't know what you'll do with her. She's four caves to the right."

"Uh, thank you," Dor said. "Won't your mother object—I mean, if I just walk out?"

"Not if I don't squawk. And I won't squawk if the ring works okay."

"But that ring takes time to operate, even if—"

"Oh, go ahead. Can't you see I'm trying to give you a break?"

Dor went ahead. He wasn't sure how long she would have patience with the ring, or whether she would simply change her mind. Of course it was always possible that the ring really could produce. How nice for the harpies if it could give them a male chick! But meanwhile, he didn't want to waste time.

The old harridan eyed him suspiciously, but did not challenge him. He counted four subcaves to the right and went in. Sure enough, there was Millie, disheveled but intact. "Oh, Dor!" she cried. "I knew you'd rescue me!"

"I haven't rescued you yet," he warned her. "I traded my wishing ring to get to you."

"Then we'd better get out of here in a hurry! That ring couldn't wish itself out of a dream."

Why would it want to? he wondered. He checked the cave exit. Like the other, it opened onto a formidable drop. "I don't think we can just walk out. I don't think there are any exits that don't require flying. That's why the harpies aren't worried about us escaping."

"They—they were threatening to cook me for supper. I'd rather jump, than—"

"That was just to get me to cooperate," Dor said. Yet he had the grisly fear that it had been no bluff. Why should they have told *her* the threat, when he wasn't there to hear? The harpies were not nice creatures.

"To cooperate? What did they want from you?"

"A service I couldn't perform." Though this body of his had masculine capabilities and probably could—no, that wasn't the point.

Millie looked at his face. "It's clean!" she exclaimed.

"I, uh, had it washed."

Her eyes narrowed. "About that service—are you *sure*—?"

Damn that female intuition! Dor kneeled by the exit hole, feeling around it with his fingers. "Maybe there are handholds or something."

There weren't. The face of the cliff was as hard and smooth as glass, and the drop looked horrendous. He saw harpies flitting from other caves, coming and going, always flying. No hope there!

Even if there had been handholds, they would have required both of his hands. He would have been unable to hold on to Millie with one, and she would have screamed and kicked her feet and flung her hair about and fallen to her death the moment she attempted to make such a climb by herself. She was a delectable female, but just not much use at man-business.

Not that he could make any such claim himself, after that session with Heavenly Helen Harpy.

Helen had said that the harpies had once shared quarters with the goblins.

The goblins did not fly, and he doubted they could climb well enough to handle this sheer cliff. If they had shared these caves, there had to be footpaths to them, somewhere. Maybe these had been cemented over, after the goblins had been driven out. "Walls, do any of you conceal goblin tunnels?" he asked.

"Not me!" the walls chorused.

"You mean the goblins never used these caves?" Dor demanded, disappointed. Had Helen lied to him—or had she been referring to other caves, before the harpies moved here?

"Untrue," the walls said. "Goblins originally hollowed out these caves, hollowed and hallowed, before the war started."

"Then how did the goblins get in and out?"

"Through the ceilings, of course."

Dor clapped the heel of his hand to his forehead. Of course! One problem with questioning the inanimate was that the inanimate didn't have much imagination and tended to answer literally. He had really meant to question all the artifacts in and of this chamber, but he had only actually named the walls, so only they had responded. "Ceiling, do you conceal a goblin passage?"

"I do," the ceiling replied. "You could have saved a lot of trouble if you'd asked me first, instead of talking with those stupid walls."

"Why isn't it visible?"

"The harpies sealed it over with mud plaster and droppings. Everyone knows that."

"That's why the stink!" Millie cried. "They use their dung for building."

Dor drew his sword. "Tell me where to strike to free the passage," he said.

"Right here," the ceiling said at one side.

Dor dug his swordpoint in and twisted. A chunk of brown plaster dropped to the floor. He dug harder and gouged more out. Soon the passage opened. A draft of foul air washed down from the hole.

"What's that fresh smell?" a harpy voice screeched from the cavern hall.

"Fresh smell!" Dor exclaimed, almost choking on the stench. He and Millie had become more or less acclimatized to the odor pervading the caves, but now that the air was moving, his nostrils could not so readily filter it out. Yet perhaps this breeze was offensive to the harpies.

The old hen appeared in the entrance. "They're trying to sneak out the old goblin hole!" she screeched. "Stop them!"

Dor strode across to block her advance, sword held before him. Afoot, unable to spread her wings, the harpy was at a disadvantage, and had to retreat. "Climb up into the hole!" Dor cried to Millie. "Use the goblin passage to escape!"

Millie stared up into the blackness of the hole. "I'm afraid!" she cried. "There might be nickelpedes!"

That struck him. Nickelpedes were vicious insects five times as ferocious as centipedes, with pincers made of nickel. They attacked anything that moved in darkness.

Now more harpies were pressing close. They respected Dor's bared blade, but did not retreat farther than they had to. He could not swing freely in the passage, and didn't really want to shed their blood; after all, they were half-human, and it wasn't nice to kill females.

What was he going to do? With the harpies in front, and Millie balking, and an open cliff outside—in this situation he couldn't fool anyone by making the walls talk. He was stuck. He might hold off the dirty birds indefinitely, but he couldn't escape. Actually, if they started flying in from the cliffside, he would have trouble, because he couldn't very well cover both entrances, and Millie would not be much help. And in due course he and Millie would get tired, and hungry and thirsty, and would have to sleep. They would be captive again.

"Millie, you've got to get up that goblin passage!" he cried.

"No good, no good!" the harpies outside screeched. "We know where it goes, we're covering the exit. You can't escape!"

Then why were they telling him this? Easier to nab him at the goblin-tunnel exit. So they must be bluffing.

Then Millie screamed. Dor looked—and spied a huge hairy shape dropping out of the hole. Green eyes looked back at him. "Jumper!" How glad he was to see the big spider again!

"I could not place my lines," the spider chittered. "The lady-man-birds would have spied me on the face of the cliff. So I had to come in this way."

"But the harpies are watching the exit—"

"They are. But they did not follow me inside, because of the nickelpedes."

"But you—"

"Nickelpedes are pinching bugs. I was hungry anyway. They were delicious."

Naturally a spider would be able to handle big bugs! But the harpies were more formidable. "If we can't use the goblin tunnel—" Dor began.

Jumper fastened a line to Millie, and another to Dor. "I am generating sufficient lines to lower you to the bottom, but you will have to let yourselves down. I suggest you swing and slide so the birds will not be able to catch you readily."

"I can't do that!" Millie protested. "I don't have big arm muscles and things!"

Dor glanced at her. She was half right; she did lack big arm muscles, but she certainly had things. "I'll carry you again." He flicked his swordpoint, warning back the encroaching harpies.

"You'll need both arms to lower yourself," Jumper pointed out. "I will jump across and string a guideline. That way you can swing from the center of the cleft, not banging the walls. But you will be caught in midair."

"Can't be helped. You'll have to relax the guideline, so we can drop slowly lower. Just be sure that line is tight when we start."

"Yes, that is possible, though difficult. Your two weights will make a great deal of tension."

Dor poked at the witchly face of another harpy. "Millie can watch you, and tell me when it's ready. You wave to her from the far side."

"Correct." Jumper ran to the cliff opening and disappeared. There was an outcry from the harpies outside; they had never seen a jumping spider this size before, and were amazed and frightened.

"He's waving!" Millie cried.

That had been quick! Dor made a last poke at the harpies, whirled, grabbed her with his left arm, and flung himself out over the cliff. Then he remembered: he still had the sword in his right hand. He had forgotten to hang on to the line.

They plummeted toward the bottom of the chasm. Millie screamed and kicked her feet, and her hair smacked Dor's face.

Then, with a wrench, the line drew taut. He didn't need to hold on; Jumper had attached the cable to him, and tied the other end to the center of the trans-chasm cable. Once more the spider's mature foresight had saved him. Now Dor surmised when the attachment had been made; he had been distracted by the encroaching harpies, and had not noticed.

They were swinging down and across the chasm, bouncing slightly. The harpies were milling about, screaming, but not doing anything effective. They saw his waving sword.

Across they swung, grandly, almost colliding with the far wall. Jumper had kept the line short so they would not crash, but it was so close that Dor had to put his feet out and brake against the cliff, momentarily. Then they were swinging back. And forth again, in lessening arcs. As they came to rest, they were suspended about halfway down the depth of the chasm.

The harpies were beginning to organize, trying to catch Dor and Millie in their claws, as they had before.

But Dor had his sword out this time, and that made the difference. He waved it threateningly, and the harpies stayed just clear, screaming imprecations and losing feathers to the flashing tip of his weapon. It was hard for the dirty birds to match velocities with him, because of the swinging and bouncing. They were not, however, about to give up the pursuit.

Jumper, on the far side of the chasm, levered the line in the manner only he could do, and Dor and Millie descended. The rage of the harpies increased as the range increased. "Don't let them get to the bottom!" one cried. "The enemy is there!"

That hardly reassured Dor. What good would it be, escaping one menace only to fall into the clutches of another? Well, he would have to worry about that in due course. At least the harpies hadn't thought to cut the trans-chasm cable. Or if they had thought, they had rejected the notion. They didn't want to kill Dor, for then he would certainly be useless to them. And Millie might not taste as good scraped up from the floor of the—but enough of such thoughts!

Now the base of the chasm was close. It was rocky and narrow and curvy, with holes and ridges. There seemed to be no way out, though this was uncertain since it twined out of sight in either direction.

As they swung lower, their orientation shifted, thanks to Jumper's maneuvering of the lines, so that now they were traveling along the cleft rather than across it. The harpies became more desperate. "Keep them away from ground!" the oldest and ugliest crone screeched. "Grab them! Snatch them! Lift them up. Drop the girl if you have to, we don't really need her, but save that buck!"

Dor swung his sword in increasingly desperate arcs, keeping them at bay, trying not to sever his own line. A talon lanced into his shoulder from behind, and great foul wings beat about his head. Millie screamed loudly and kicked her feet harder, and her hair formed a golden splay in a passing sunbeam. None of that helped. Dor aimed his sword up and thrust violently over his own head and down behind it. The point jammed into something. There was an ear-shattering scream that momentarily drowned out Millie's racket, and the talon released his shoulder. When he yanked the sword forward there was blood on the tip. He slashed in another circle, slicing feathers off the harpies in front. This violence sickened him, as it had when he fought the goblin band, but he kept on.

Suddenly the line dropped. Millie emitted a truly classic *Eeeeek!* as they fell— but the drop was very short. The mighty muscles and sinews of Dor's legs flexed expertly, breaking his fall, preserving his balance. He still had Millie; now he set her down gently. Her skirt and bodice had separated; Dor stared briefly, not realizing that they were different pieces, and she tucked them together self-consciously. At least she had stopped screaming.

A greenish shape dropped down beside them. "Sorry about that drop," Jumper chittered. "The harpies attacked me, and I had to move."

"Quite all right," Dor said. "You got us out of the harpy caves."

The harpies were still milling in the chasm, but no longer attacking. Jumper had plunged through them by surprise, using his dragline to brake at the last moment so he hadn't been hurt. What a marvelous thing that dragline was!

"Why are the harpies staying clear?" Millie asked.

It was a stupid question that like so many of its kind was not so stupid after all. The harpies were raucous, ugly, and evil-smelling—except for Helen—but not notably cowardly. Why were they afraid of this rocky path?

"One of them said something about the enemy down here," Dor said, remembering.

Millie screamed and pointed. Charging along the crevice-path was a contingent of goblins. No sooner feared than realized!

"I can hold them off," Dor said, striding forward with his sword leading. He didn't know whether this was his body's impulse or his own, but it was a fact that heroism was greatly facilitated by this powerful and well-coordinated physique. He *knew* it could devastate the little goblins, so he could afford to be bold. In his own twelve-year-old-sized body he would have been justifiably hesitant— and been thought a coward.

"I will lead the way out," Jumper chittered. "Perhaps there will be a slope I can enable you to climb, anchored by my lines. You can serve as rearguard."

They moved east, Dor walking backward so as to face the goblins without getting separated from his party. Obviously there would be no escape toward the goblin caves.

"It's just a small band," a harpy screeched. "We can handle them! Wipe them out, hens!"

Suddenly the harpies were plummeting toward the goblins. There was an instant melee punctuated by cries, screeches, groans, and rages. A cloud of feathers formed. Dor craned to see what was happening, but the dust stirred up to obscure it. They seemed to be fighting claw-to-nail, and it was not at all gentle.

"Trouble ahead!" Jumper chittered, and Millie screamed.

Dor glanced there—and saw more goblins charging from the west: a larger band. The spider stood to fight, though he could easily have jumped clear and clung to the cliff wall, saving himself. Except that he would not desert his friends. To no avail; the horde quickly overran him. Millie's piercing screams did not help her; a dozen goblin hands grasped her flailing arms and kicking feet and swirling tresses.

Dor whirled to help, but was already too late. Goblins grabbed him everywhere and bore him to the ground. He tried to kick his feet, but they were weighted by sheer mass of goblin. Just like that, they had been captured by the enemy.

All three of them were borne rapidly eastward, helpless. Suddenly a cave opened in the chasm wall, and the goblin band charged inside. It was dark here, and cool; Dor had the impression of descent, but couldn't be sure.

In due course they were brought to a room lit by guttering torches. This amazed Dor, for in his day goblins were desperately afraid of fire. But in his day goblins did not go abroad by day, either; in fact there were very few on the surface of Xanth at all. So this was another thing that had changed in eight centuries.

At one end of the chamber was a throne fashioned from a massive complex of stalagmites. It looked as if stone had run like hot wax, making layers and colored trails over itself until the whole had melded into this single twisted yet beautiful mass. An especially fierce-looking goblin bestrode it, his gnarled black legs almost merging with the stone.

"Well, trespassers!" the goblin chief cried angrily. "What made you suppose you could intrude on these our demesnes with impunity?"

Millie was quietly screaming and still trying to kick her feet; she didn't like the goblins' mottled hands on her legs. The goblins, however, seemed more interested than antipathetic. Jumper was chittering, but Dor knew the goblins could not comprehend that. So he stepped forward, breaking free of those who restrained him. "We did not mean to intrude, sir," he said. "We were only trying to escape the harpies." He had little hope of mercy from these monsters, but had to try.

The goblin's dusky brows lifted in astonishment. "You, a Man, call a goblin sir?"

"Well, if you'll tell me your proper title, I'll use it," Dor said nervously, though he tried to keep up a moderately bold front. Somewhere along the way his sword had been wrenched from his hand, and he felt naked without it.

"I am Subchief Craven, of the Chasm Clan of Goblins," the chief said. "However, sir will do nicely for an address."

Several goblin guards snickered. It was Craven, not Dor, who reacted to that derisive mirth. "You find the notion of sir humorous?" he demanded of them furiously.

"This is obviously no hero-man, but an impostor who knows naught of honor or combat," another goblin retorted. "His sir is so worthless as to be an insult."

"Oh yeah?" Craven cried. "We'll verify that, Crool. Will you meet him in honor challenge?"

Crool examined Dor, somewhat taken aback. But now the laughter of the clan was turning on him. "A single goblin does not meet a single human, even an impostor. The normal ratio is four or five to one."

"Then bring on your henchmen!" Craven cried. He turned to the guards at the other side of the hall. "Return to this man-warrior his sword. We shall discover whether his sir is valid."

What a devious and wonderful thing was pride, Dor thought. Now the subchief was rooting for the captive to prevail against the goblin kind.

Two goblins dashed up, carrying Dor's sword and lifting the hilt for him to take. He was glad to have it back, but did not like the prospective combat. He had not been at all pleased about the goblin-killing he had done before, and that misgiving grew as he observed how similar to his own kind these creatures were. They looked different, but their pride was similar.

The goblins gave him no choice. They cleared a disk in the center of the cavern, and the five goblins of Crool's clan came at him. They were armed with small clubs and sharp fragments of stone, and looked determined. They obviously intended to do him in if they got the chance.

Dor's body took over. He strode toward the band, his blade swinging. The goblins threw themselves to the sides. Dor turned to his right, kicking one goblin so hard the creature scooted across the smooth rock to fetch up against a wall, his stone knife fragmenting. Dor whirled on the others, swinging his blade, and they scattered again. One further foray, to clear the goblin sneaking in behind him; Dor caught the moving club on his blade and punched underneath it with his left fist. He scored on the goblin's head, the thing hard as a rock, driving the creature back, shaken.

Suddenly Dor stood alone in the circle. He had vanquished the band, thanks to the power and expertise of his body—and he hadn't killed a single goblin. That made him feel better. It could not make up for the four he had killed before, but it eased his guilt somewhat.

Craven smiled grotesquely. "Now is that a suitable sir or is it not?" he demanded rhetorically. "Keep your sword, Man; you have established your status. Come—you and your party are my guests."

Jumper chittered. "It seems goblins set great store by status," the web translated. "You were very clever to utter that mark of respect."

Dor was abashed. "I just thought that was what you said to a chief."

"It seems you were correct."

The captivity had, by this miracle of courtesy, become a visit. The goblin chief treated them to a sumptuous meal of candied cavelice, sugared slugs, and censored centipedes. Jumper pronounced it excellent. Dor and Millie weren't so sure.

"So you were fighting the horrendous harpies," Craven said, making conversation as he politely ripped several segments from a large centipede with his big yellow teeth and strained out the legs through the gap between teeth. He had seemed a bit wary of Jumper at first, but after appreciating the way the spider's chelicerae, which were the big nippers where another creature's jaws would be, crushed the food, Craven seemed quite satisfied. The crunching was even more vicious than that of the goblins, therefore better table manners. Then when the spider secreted digestive liquid that dissolved the delicacies into goo, and sucked that into his stomach, the goblins had to applaud. They had never been able to eat like that!

"Good thing we rescued you," the goblin chief said during a respite from his own attempt to emulate Jumper's mode of feasting. No matter how hard he tried, he was unable to dissolve his food with his saliva before swallowing it.

"Yes," Dor agreed. Actually, the slugs weren't bad, the flesh being spongy and juicy, and Millie was getting the hang of the lice. She chewed them and spat out the fibrous legs in approved goblin fashion, somehow making it seem dainty. The banquet table was littered with legs.

"Why were they after you?" Craven asked. "We came out because we heard the commotion, and brought you in because any enemy of the harpies may be a friend of ours."

"They wanted—" Dor was not sure how to express it. "They wanted me to do something for Heavenly Helen Harpy."

"*Heavenly* Helen?" Millie inquired, her brow furrowing suspiciously.

Craven laughed so hard he sprayed centipede legs on the cavern ceiling. The goblin courtiers applauded the marksmanship. "Heavenly Helen! So that's how they do it! Grabbing human men for studs! No wonder you fought them off! What a horrible fate!"

"Oh, I don't know—" Dor began, then caught Millie's look. He shifted the subject. "They said it was all because of you goblins. That you stole away their men."

"We were just getting even for what they did to us!" Craven cried. "Once we shared caves, but they were greedy for our space, so they wreaked a foul enchantment on us. They blighted the sight of our females so that they perceived the merits of our men in reverse. The boldest, bravest, handsomest, brightest goblins became anathema to them; they were drawn infallibly to the weakest, ugliest, stupidest cowards and thieves among us, and with those they mated. In this manner our whole species was inevitably degraded. We were once more handsome than the elves and smarter than the gnomes and stronger than the trolls and had more honor than the Men themselves—and now look at us, warped and gnarled and stupid and cowardly and given to treachery, so that five of us cannot threaten one of you. The harpies set that enchantment on us, and only they can lift it, and the vile birds refuse to do that. So we must seek whatever vengeance we can, while we yet retain some power in Xanth."

This was a side of the story the harpies hadn't told! Dor realized that peace was impossible, for there was now no way to undo the damage done to the harpies. Unless there could be an original mating between human and vulture to produce a male harpy—but he could hardly imagine any person or bird doing that! So the goblin-harpy war would continue, until—

"But we shall have the final chortle," Craven said with grim satisfaction. "Already the clans of the goblins are massing, augmented by our brothers of the deep caverns, numberless in number, and by our allies of similar species. We shall extirpate the harpies and their ilk from the face of Xanth!"

Dor remembered how the harpies were also massing their winged forces for the final battle. That would be some engagement!

The honored visitors were given a fine dark cave for the night, with healthy rats to fend off the nickelpedes, and a vent in the ceiling through which the dark air rose. They were guests—yet there was something about the firmness of their hosts that gave Dor disquieting pause. He recalled Craven's remarks about the nature of goblins, their propensity for treachery. Were they so eager to practice their low arts that, rather than kill prisoners outright, they preferred to pretend they were honored guests—who could then be betrayed? Did the goblins really intend to set them free, or were they merely fattening up fresh meat for their repasts? Craven, by his own statement, could hardly be trusted.

Dor exchanged glances with Jumper's largest eyes. No words were exchanged, for the goblins could be listening through holes in the walls, but it was evident the spider had similar misgivings.

"Make loud snoring sounds," Dor murmured to the floor where he lay in the dark. The floor obliged, and soon all other sounds were drowned out by the rasps, groans, and wheezes of supposed sleep. Under that cover, Dor held a whispered conference with his friends.

So at night—it was hard to tell the time of day down here, but Jumper had an excellent sense of time—they set about sneaking out. The goblins had not realized the potential of the giant spider, since Jumper had stood to fight instead of jumping clear. Thus Craven had not set guards in the ceiling aperture. Actually, the goblins really were rather stupid, as the subchief had said.

Jumper jumped to the ceiling, clung there, walked into the ventilator hole and explored where it led. Soon he was back to hoist Dor and Millie up. They wound their way through the darkness as silently as possible, while the raucous snores faded in the distance. At length—the length of a silken guideline—they emerged at the starlit surface.

It had been surprisingly simple. Dor knew it would have been impossibly difficult had Jumper not been with them. Jumper, with his superlative night vision, his silken lines, and his scaling ability. The spider made the impossible possible.

Chapter 5

Castle

They found a safe tree to hang from for the rest of the night, then resumed their trek in the morning. The local sticks and stones were as helpful as usual, and they located Castle Roogna without difficulty about noon. Dor was able to recognize the general lay of the land, but the vegetation was all different. There was no orchard; instead there were a number of predaceous plants. And—the Castle was only half complete.

Dor had seen Castle Roogna many times, but in this changed situation it stood out like a completely novel structure. It was large—the largest castle in all the Land of Xanth—and its outer ramparts were the tallest and most massive. It was roughly square, about a hundred feet on a side, and the walls rose thirty feet or more above the moat. It was braced by four great towers at the corners, their square outlines projecting halfway out from the main frame, enlarging it, and casting stark shadows against the recessed walls. In the center of each side of the castle was a smaller round tower, also projecting out by half its diameter, casting more subtle shadows. Solid battlements surmounted the top. There were no windows or other apertures. In Dor's day some had been cut, but this was a more adventurous period, and the defenses had to be as strong as possible. Overall, this was as powerful and impressive an edifice as Dor cared to imagine.

But the inner structure was virtually nonexistent; the beautiful palace portion had at this stage to be a mere courtyard. And the north wall lacked its upper courses; the huge stones stair-stepped down in the center, and the round support tower was incomplete.

A herd of centaurs was laboring on this section, using hoists and massive cables and sheer brute force to draw the blocks to the top. They worked with somewhat less efficiency and conviction than Dor would have expected, based on his knowledge of the centaurs of his own day. They looked rougher, too, as if the human and equine sections were imperfectly joined. Dor was reminded that not only had new species risen in eight hundred years, the old ones had suffered refinement.

Dor marched up to the centaur supervisor, who stood outside the moat, near a crude wooden scaffold supporting the next block to be hoisted. He was sweating as he trotted back and forth, calling out instructions to the pulley crew, trying to maneuver the stone up without cracking into the existing wall. Horseflies buzzed annoyingly about his hindquarters—not the big flying-horse variety, but the little horse-biting variety. They buzzed off quickly when Jumper came near, but the centaur didn't notice.

"Uh, where is King Roogna?" Dor inquired as the centaur paused to give him a harried glance.

"Go find him yourself!" the surly creature retorted brusquely. "Can't you see we're busy here?"

The centaurs of Dor's time were generally the soul of courtesy except when aroused. One notable exception was "Uncle Chester," sire of Dor's centaur playmate Chet. This centaur supervisor was reminiscent of Chester, and the other members of this herd resembled him too. Chester must have been a throwback to this original type: ugly of facial feature, handsome of posterior, powerfully constructed, surly of disposition, yet a creature of sterling qualities once his confidence was won.

Dor and his party retreated. This was obviously not the occasion to bug the centaurs. "Stone, where is King Roogna?" Dor inquired of a section of a block that had not yet been transported across the moat.

"He resides in a temporary hut south of here," the stone responded.

As Dor had suspected. There would have to be a lot more work on the Castle before it was habitable for a King, though in the event of war the inner court should be safe enough for camping. No one would choose to live there while the centaurs were hoisting massive rocks about.

They went south. Dor was tempted to make a detour to the spot where his cottage cheese existed in his own day, but resisted; there would be nothing there.

They came across a hut adapted from a large pumpkin, set in a small but neat yard. A solid, graying man in soiled shorts was contemplating a chocolate cherry tree while chewing on the fruit: evidently a gardener sampling the product. The man hailed them without waiting for an introduction: "Welcome, travelers! Come have a cherry while they are available."

The three stopped. Dor plucked a cherry and found it excellent: a delicious outer coating of sweet brown chocolate, a firm cherry interior with a liquid center. Millie liked the fruit too. "Better than candied cavelice," she opined. Jumper was too polite to demur, but evidently had another opinion.

"Pretend it is a swollen tick," Dor suggested in a low voice. The spider waved a foreleg, acquiescing.

"Well, let's try it again," the gardener said. "I'm having some difficulty with this one." He concentrated on the tree.

Nothing happened.

"Are you trying to do a spell?" Dor inquired, plucking another cherry. "To add fertilizer to it, or something?"

"Um, no. The centaurs provide plenty of fertilizer. As a matter of fact—" The man's eyes widened, startled. "Hold that cherry a moment, sir, if you please. Don't bite into it."

Dor paused, cherry near mouth. The first had been so good, he was a bit put out to have the gardener deny him the second so arbitrarily. He looked at the fruit. It lacked the chocolate covering, and its surface was bright red and hard. "I won't," he agreed. "This must be a bad one." He flipped it away."

"Don't—" the man cried, too late. "That's a—"

There was an explosion nearby. Millie screamed. The noise was deafening, and heat blasted at them. All four of them stumbled to the side, away from the blast.

The concussion subsided. Dor looked around dazedly. There was a wisp of smoke rising from the vicinity of the explosion. "What was that?" Dor asked, shaken. He discovered he had his sword in hand, and put it away self-consciously.

"The cherry bomb you threw," the gardener said. "Lucky you did not bite into it."

"The cherry—that was a chocolate cherry, from this—" Dor looked at the tree. "Why, those *are* cherry bombs, now! How—?"

"This must be King Roogna," Millie offered. "We didn't recognize him."

Nonplused, Dor worked it out. He had pictured King Roogna as a man somewhat like King Trent, polished, intelligent, commanding of demeanor, a man nobody would care to take lightly. But of course the folklore of eight hundred years would clothe the Magician in larger-than-life grandeur. It was not a person's appearance that counted in Xanth, it was his magic talent. So this pudgy, informal, gardener-type man with the gentle manner and thinning, graying hair and sweaty armpits, unprepossessing—this could indeed be the King. "This tree —he changed it from chocolate cherry to cherry bomb—Magician King Roogna's talent was adapting magic to his purpose—"

"Was?" the King inquired, raising a dust-smeared eyebrow.

Dor had been thinking of the historical figure, who was of course contemporary in the tapestry world. "I, uh, *is.* Your Majesty. I—" He started to bow, changed his mind in midmotion, started to kneel, changed his mind again, and found himself dissolving in confusion.

The King set a firm, friendly hand on his shoulder. "Be at ease, warrior. Had I desired obeisance, I would have made it known at the outset. It is my talent that sets me apart, rather than my office. In fact, my office is insecure at the moment. My troops are all on furlough because we have no quarters yet for them, and difficulties plague the construction of my Castle. So pretension would ill befit me, were I inclined toward it."

"Uh, yes, Your Majesty," Dor mumbled.

The King contemplated him. "I gather you are from Mundania, though you seem to have had some garbled account of Xanth." He glanced at Millie. "And the young lady has the aspect of the West Stockade. They do raise some pretty fruits there." He looked at Jumper. "And this person—I don't believe I have encountered a jumping spider of your magnitude before, sir. Is it an enchantment?"

"He called me sir," Jumper chittered. "Is a King supposed to do that?"

"A King," Roogna said firmly, "can do just about anything he chooses. Preferably he chooses to rule well. I note your voice is translated by a web on the warrior's shoulder." His aspect hardened, and he began to suggest the manner Dor had expected in a King. "This interests me. There appears to be unusual magic here."

"Yes, Your Majesty," Dor said quickly. "There is considerable enchantment here, but it is hard to explain."

"All magic is hard to explain," Roogna said.

"He makes things talk," Millie said helpfully. "The sticks and stones don't break his bones. They talk to him. And walls and water and things. That's how we found our way here."

"A Mundane Magician?" Roogna asked. "This is a virtual contradiction in terms!"

"I, uh, said it was hard to explain, Your Majesty," Dor said awkwardly.

A figure approached: a compact squarish man of the King's generation, with a slightly crooked smile. "Do I smell something interesting, Roogna?" he inquired.

"You do indeed, Murphy," the King replied. "Here, let's introduce ourselves more adequately. I am Magician Roogna, pro-tem King. My talent is the adaptation of living magic to my purpose." He looked meaningfully at Dor.

"I, uh, I am Dor. Er, Magician Dor. My talent is communication with the inanimate." Then, in case that wasn't clear, he added: "I talk to things."

The King prompted Millie with another glance. "I am Millie the maid, an innocent girl of the West Stockade village," she said. "My talent is—" She blushed delicately, and her talent manifested strongly. "Sex appeal."

On around the circle: "I am Phidippus Variegatus of the family of Salticidae: Jumper the spider for short," Jumper chittered. "My talent, like that of all my kind, is silk."

At last it came to the newcomer. "And I am Magician Murphy. My talent is making things go wrong. I am the chief obstacle to Roogna's power, and his rival for dominance in Xanth."

Dor's mouth dropped open. "You are the Enemy Magician? Right here with the King?"

King Roogna laughed. "What better place? It is true we oppose each other, but this is a matter of politics. Magicians, as a rule, do not practice their talents directly on each other. We prefer to manifest our powers more politely. Murphy and I are two of the three Magicians extant. The third has no interest in politics, so we two are the rivals for power in Xanth. We are trying our strength in this manner: if I can succeed in completing Castle Roogna before the year is out, Murphy will yield me uncontested title to the throne. If I fail, I will abdicate the throne, and since there is no other Magician suitable for the office, the anarchy that follows will likely foster Murphy as the dominant figure. Meanwhile we share the camaraderie of our status. It is an equitable arrangement."

"But—" Dor was appalled. "You treat the welfare of the whole Land of Xanth as if it were a game!"

The King shook his head gravely. "No game, Magician Dor. We are absolutely serious. But we also indulge ourselves in honor. If one of us can prevail in war, he can surely do it by humane rules of conduct. This is warfare of the civilized kind."

Jumper chittered. "There is warfare of the uncivilized kind approaching," the web translated. "The harpies and the goblins are massing their forces to exterminate each other."

Murphy smiled. "Ah, you betray my secret, spider!"

"If anything can go wrong, it will," Dor said. "You mean the war between monsters is your doing?"

"By no means, Magician," the Enemy demurred. "The war of monsters has roots going well back before our time, and no doubt will continue long after our time. My talent merely encourages the most violent outbreak at the least convenient time for Roogna."

"And we need hardly guess where the two armies will randomly meet," King Roogna exclaimed, his gaze turning northward toward the incomplete Castle.

"I had hoped it would be a surprise," Murphy admitted ruefully. "That would prevent you from calling back your troops in time to defend the Castle. But for the intrusion of these visitors, it might have been unforeshadowed."

"So your talent fouled *you* up, this time!" Millie said.

"Perhaps an eddy-current," Jumper chittered.

"My talent is not proof against the influence of other Magicians," Murphy said. "The ramifications of the talents of Magician caliber extend well beyond the apparent aspects. If another Magician were to oppose me, my talent would feel the impact, regardless of the specific nature of the opposing talent. And it seems another Magician has indeed entered the picture. It will take time to comprehend the significance of this new element."

That was an apt remark: Dor had entered the picture literally, for this was the tapestry, the picture-world.

Murphy studied Dor with a certain disquieting intensity. "I would like to get to know you better, sir. Would you care to accept my hospitality for the duration of your stay here, or until we all hie into the Castle to avoid the ravages of the monsters? We had thought there were no unknown Magicians in Xanth at this time."

"Sir?" Jumper chittered. He was still having a problem with this word, having seen its power.

"But you are the enemy!" Dor protested.

"Oh, go with him," Roogna said. "I lack proper facilities for three, at the moment, though soon the Castle will be in order. The maid can stay with my wife, and the spider I daresay would be happiest hanging from a tree. I assure you Murphy will not hurt you, Dor. It is his prerogative, by the rules of our contest, to be given opportunity to fathom significant new elements, particularly if they add to the strength of my position. I have a similar privilege to inspect his allies. You may both rejoin me and your companions for the evening repast."

Somewhat bemused, Dor went with Murphy. "I don't understand this business, Magician. You act as if you and King Roogna are friends!"

"We are peers. That's not the same as friends, but it will do. We have no others except the Zombie Master, and he is not one to associate with on this basis. There is of course neo-Sorceress Vadne, who would have assisted me had I agreed to marry her, but I declined and so she joined the King. But she is not a dominant figure. So if we desire the companionship of our level, we must seek it in each other. And now, it seems, in you. I am extremely curious about you, Dor."

This was awkward. "I am from a far land."

"Obviously. I had not been aware that any Magicians resided in Mundania."

"Well, I'm not really from Mundania." But could he afford to tell the whole truth?

"Don't tell me, let me guess! Not from Mundania—so it must be somewhere in Xanth. North of the Gap?"

"You remember the Gap?"

"Shouldn't I?"

"Uh, I guess it's all right. I—my people have trouble remembering the Gap, sometimes."

"Strange. The Gap is most memorable. So you're south of it?"

"Not exactly. You see, I—"

"Let's see your talent. Can you make this jewel talk?" Murphy held up a glittering emerald.

"What is your nature?" Dor asked the stone. "What are you worth? What is your secret?"

"I am glass," the jewel responded. "A fake. I am worth almost nothing. The Magician has dozens like me to give to greedy fools for their support."

Murphy raised an expressive eyebrow. "But *you* are not fake, Dor! There must be few secrets hidden from you! A remarkable informational talent!"

"Yes."

"So the mystery expands! How could a full Magician have remained concealed so long? Roogna and I once harnessed a magic sniffer and surveyed this whole region. That was how the site for the Castle was selected. There is a high concentration of useful magic here, and overall the effect is very strong. If the source of all magic is not in this vicinity, it can not be far from it. So we found enchantment aplenty, but no Magicians. Yet in our experience, no really strong magic emerges from the hinterland. How could a man of Mundane aspect, with a warrior's reflexes, turn up suddenly with such a talent? It hardly seems possible."

Dor shrugged.

"In fact, I suspect it is impossible—or rather, it must be the result of magic beyond our present comprehension. Some special enchantment—" He broke off, lifting one finger expressively. "An anachronism! That would account for it! You are from the Land of Xanth—in another time!"

"Uh, yes," Dor said. Murphy was no fool!

"Not the past, surely, for there is no record of such a talent historically. Of course many of the ancient records have been lost, owing to Waves and such.

Still, talents tend to grow more sophisticated with time, and yours is quite sophisticated. So it must be the future. How far?"

The truth could not be concealed from this clever man! "Eight hundred years," Dor admitted.

They had arrived at Murphy's tent. "Come in, have a drink of cider—a fine sweet-cider press just fruited in my yard—and tell me all about it."

"But I'm not on your side!" Dor blurted. "I want King Roogna to win!"

"Naturally you do. All right-thinking people do. Fortunately for me, there are as many wrong-thinking people as right-thinkers. But surely you must realize that ignorance serves my purpose, not his. Only the orderly categorization of facts can promote a stable kingdom."

"Then why do you want this information? Are you going to try to do something to me?" Dor's hand touched his sword.

"Magicians do not act against Magicians," Murphy reminded him. "Not directly. I mean you no personal mischief. Rather, I am trying to determine the impact and meaning of your presence here. The addition of another full Magician to the equation could change the outcome of our contest. If your force is sufficient to tip the balance in Roogna's favor, and I cannot reverse it, then I would have to concede the throne to him without further ado, and save us all much torment. Therefore it behooves both Roogna and me to ascertain your nature, early and accurately. Why do you think he sent you with me?"

"You two are the strangest enemies I ever saw! I can't follow the convolutions of your game."

"We merely abide by the rules. Without rules, there is no game." Murphy handed him a glass of cider. "Tell me the whole story, Dor, and we shall ascertain how your presence affects our situation. You will be welcome then to explain it to the King."

Dor seemed to have no choice. He wished Jumper were here to advise him, or Grundy the golem; he just didn't have confidence in his own judgment. Yet he always felt most at home with the truth. So he told the Enemy Magician as much of the story as he could organize: his quest to help restore a zombie, the inclusion of Jumper in the spell, the adventure within the tapestry.

"No problem about locating the Zombie Master," Murphy said. "The problem is, he won't help you."

"But only he knows the secret of restoring zombies! That's the whole purpose in my—"

"He may know," Murphy said. "But he won't tell. He does nothing for anyone. That is why he lives alone."

"I still have to ask him," Dor said stubbornly. "Meanwhile, what about you? Now that you know King Roogna did—I mean will—complete the Castle—"

"That is indeed a ponderous matter. Yet there are several considerations. One is that what you say may not be true."

Dor was stung. His body's hand, responsive in its fashion to his mood, reached over his shoulder for the sword.

Murphy held up a hand, unalarmed. "You sound so uncertain, yet your body reacts so aggressively! This corroborates your story, of course. Do not force me to use my magic against you. You would suffer mishap before ever you brought your weapon to bear. I did not call you a liar. I merely conjecture that you could be misinformed. History is notorious for misinformation. That castle you knew could have been built a century later and given the name of Roogna, to lend verisimilitude to the new order. How would you know?"

"Very what?" Dor asked, confused.

"Verisimilitude. Realism. To make it seem likely and true."

Dor was startled. A Castle built much later, called Roogna. He had never thought of that.

"But there are other approaches," Murphy continued. "Assume your version of history is accurate—as indeed it may be. Now you have returned. What can you do—except change your history? In which case your presence can at best be neutral, and at worst reverse the outcome of the present competition between Roogna and Murphy. So your excursion may be an auspicious omen for me. I hardly mean to interfere with you! I think it may be my talent that brought you here, to foul up Roogna."

Dor was startled again. Himself, an agent of the enemy? Yet it was suddenly all too plausible!

"But I rather suspect," Murphy continued, "that you will in fact prove unable to change history in any significant respect. I visualize it as a protean thing. Yielding to specific imperatives yet always reasserting itself when the pressure abates. I doubt anything you can do will have impact after you depart. It will be an interesting phenomenon to watch, however."

Dor was silent. This Magician had neutralized him thoroughly, expertly, without doing a thing except talk. The worst of it was, he was very much afraid that Murphy was correct. The more Dor might try to interfere, here in the tapestry world, the more likely he was to hurt King Roogna's chances. So Dor would have to remain as neutral as possible, lest even his help prove disastrous.

They finished their cider and returned to King Roogna. "This man is indeed a Magician," Murphy announced. "But I deem him no threat to my designs, though he aligns himself with you. He will explain as he chooses."

The King glanced at Dor inquiringly. "It is true," Dor said. "He has shown me that any help I may try to render you . . . can have the opposite effect. We don't know that for sure, but it is a risk. So I must remain neutral, to my regret."

Dor had surprised himself by making a very adult-sounding statement. Maybe it was Murphy's influence.

"Very well," the King said. "Murphy is many things, but his integrity is unimpeachable. Since you may not help me, may I help you?"

"Only by telling me where to find the Zombie Master."

"Oh, you can't get anything from him," the King assured Dor. "He helps no one."

"So Magician Murphy informed me. Yet it is vital that I see him, and after that I shall depart this land."

"Then wait a few days, until I complete the present phase of the Castle. Then I can spare you a guide and guard. I owe you this in deference to your Magician status. The Zombie Master lives east of here, in the heart of the wilderness; it is difficult to pass."

Dor chafed inwardly at the delay, but felt it best to accede. He and his friends had had too many narrow escapes already. A guide and guard would help.

They rejoined Millie and Jumper. "The King has given me a job!" Millie exclaimed immediately, bouncing and clapping her hands and swinging her hair in such a full circle that it lapped around her face, momentarily concealing it. "As soon as the Castle is complete."

"If we have time to wait," Jumper chittered, "I should like to recompense the King's hospitality by offering my service for the duration of our stay here."

"Uh—" Dor started to protest, realizing that what applied to himself should also apply to the spider.

"That is most courteous of you," the King said heartily. "I understand from the young lady that you are adept at hoisting and lowering objects. We have dire need of such ability at the moment. Rest tonight; tomorrow you will join my sturdy centaur crew."

Murphy glanced meaningfully at Dor. The Enemy Magician was satisfied to make this trial of the validity of his conjecture. And Dor—had to be satisfied too. Maybe Murphy was wrong, after all. They could not afford to assume he was right, if he were not. So Dor was silent, not wanting to alarm the King or Jumper unnecessarily. Silent, but not at ease.

The King served them royally enough with pies from a pie tree he had adapted for this purpose: pizza, shepherd's, mince, cheese, and pecan pies, washed down with excellent fruit punch from a punchfruit tree.

"In my land," Dor remarked, "the King is a transformer. He changes living things into other living things. He can change a man into a tree, or a dragon into a toad. How does this differ from your own talent, Your Majesty?"

"A transformer," King Roogna murmured. "That's a potent talent! I can not change a man into a tree! I only adapt forms of magic to other purposes—a sleep spell to a truth spell, a chocolate cherry to a cherry bomb. So I would say your King is a more powerful Magician than I am."

Dor was abashed. "I'm sorry, Your Majesty. I didn't mean to imply—"

"You didn't, Dor. I am not competing with your King for status. Nor am I competing with you. We Magicians have a certain camaraderie, as I mentioned; we respect each other's talents. I'd like to meet your King sometime. After I have completed the Castle."

"Which may be never," Murphy said.

"Now with *him* I am competing," the King said good-naturedly, and bit into another piece of pie. Dor said nothing, still having trouble accepting this friendly-rivalry façade.

In the morning Jumper reported to the Castle construction crew. Dor went along to help translate, since no one else could understand the spider's chittering—and because he was privately concerned about Jumper's possible influence on history. Or lack of it. If anything Dor or Jumper did could affect King Roogna's success—

Dor shook his head uneasily. King Roogna was busy today, adapting new spells to preserve the roof of the Castle—once the construction reached that stage. The magic, it seemed, had to be built right into the Castle; otherwise it would not endure. This business of adapting spells, such as the one a water dragon used to prevent the water from dousing its flame—converting that to make an unleakable roof—well, that was certainly something a transformer couldn't do! So King Roogna had no reason to be modest. It was very difficult to compare the strength of talents. But if Jumper's offer of help were only to hurt—

They approached the same centaur supervisor who had brushed them off before. It seemed he had charge of the north wall, the one still under construction. The creature was pacing and fretting about the arrival of additional blocks of stone; it seemed the quarriers had fouled up a spell or two and were running behind schedule.

"King Roogna would like to have my friend help," Dor said. "He can lift stones into place with his silken lines, or climb sheer walls to—"

"A giant bug?" the centaur demanded, swishing his tail rapidly back and forth. "We don't want his kind among us!"

"But he's here to help!"

Now the other centaur workers were dismounting from the wall and crowding in close. They loomed uncomfortably large. A centaur standing the height of a man actually had about six times the mass of a man, and these stood somewhat taller than Dor—whose present body was a giant among men. "We don't associate with no bugs!" one cried. "Get that weirdo out of here!"

Nonplused, Dor turned to Jumper. "I—they don't—"

"I understand," Jumper chittered. "I am not their kind."

Dor eyed the massed centaurs, who seemed eager for any pretext to take time off from their labors. *"I* don't understand! You can do so much—"

"We don't care if he can throw droppings at the big green moon!" one yelled. "Get him out of here before we fetch a fly swatter!"

Dor got angry. "You shouldn't talk to him like that! Jumper's not a fly; he *eats* flies! He can keep all the horseflies away—"

"Bug-lover!" the supervisor snapped. "You're as bad as he is! Now watch I don't pound you both into the ground!"

"Yeah! Yeah!" the other centaurs agreed, stomping their hooves.

Jumper chittered. "These creatures are hostile. We shall depart." He started off.

Dor followed him, but not with docility. With each step he took his anger grew. "They had no right to do that! The King needs help!" Yet at the same time he wondered whether this were not for the best. If Jumper were not allowed to participate, Murphy's curse couldn't operate, could it? They would not change history.

Soon they were back at the royal tent. The King was outdoors beside a pond, where a small water dragon was captive. The thing was snorting smoke angrily and lashing up a froth with its tail, but Roogna seemed not to be concerned. "Now climb up on this roofing material," he was telling the dragon. "Propinquity facilitates adaptation." Then he looked up and spied Dor and Jumper. "Some problem at the construction site?"

Dor tried to be civilized, but it burst out of him. "The centaurs won't let Jumper work! They say he's . . . different!"

"So I am," Jumper chittered.

King Roogna had seemed like an even-tempered, harmless sort of man. Now that changed. He stood up straight and his jaw hardened. "I will not have this attitude in my kingdom!" He snapped his fingers, and in a moment a flying dragon arrived: a beautiful creature armored in stainless steel, with burnished talons and a long snout suitable for aiming a jet of fire accurately from a distance. "Dragon, it seems my work crew is getting balky. Fetch your contingent and—"

Jumper chittered violently. "No, Your Majesty!" the web translated, almost shredding itself in its effort to transmit the force of the spider's conviction. "Do not chastise your workers. They are no more ignorant than my own kind, and they are doing necessary work. I regret I caused disruption."

"Disruption? By offering to help?" The King's brow remained stormy. "At least I must chastise them with my magic. Centaurs do not have to have such pretty tails, so useful for swishing away flies. I can adapt them to lizards' tails, useful for slinking along between rocks. That will dampen their o'erweening arrogance!"

"No!" Jumper still protested. "Do not allow the curse to distort your judgment."

Roogna's eyes widened. "Murphy! You're right, of course! This is his doing! If alienophobia could interfere, it does interfere!"

Dor too was startled. That was it, certainly! Magician Murphy had laid a curse on the construction of the Castle, and Jumper's offer had triggered it. The centaurs were not really to blame.

"You are a sensible, generous creature," the King said to Jumper. "Since you plead the cause of those who wrong you, I must abate my action. I regret the necessity, and the wrong done you, but it seems I cannot take advantage of your kind offer of assistance." He dismissed the flying dragon with a kingly offhand gesture. "The centaurs are allies, not servants; they labor on the Castle because they are most proficient at this sort of construction. I have done return favors for them. I regret that I let my temper slip. Please feel free to use my facilities until I can arrange for your escort. Meanwhile, you are welcome to watch me operate here, though I hope you will not interrupt my concentration with foolish questions."

They settled down to watch the King. Dor was quite curious about the actual mechanism for adapting a spell. Did the King just command it, as Dor commanded objects to speak, or was it a silent effort of will? But hardly had Roogna gotten the balky water dragon placed before a messenger-imp ran up. "King, sir —there's been a foul-up at the construction site! The wrong spell was on the building blocks, and they're pushing each other apart instead of pulling themselves together."

"The wrong spell!" Roogna roared indignantly. "I adapted that spell myself only last week!" There followed a brief discussion. It turned out that a full course of blocks had been laid in the wrong place, causing their spells to conflict with those of the next course instead of meshing. Someone had fouled up, and the error had not been caught in time. They were large blocks, each weighing many hundreds of pounds.

Roogna tore out a few hairs from his rapidly graying head. "The curse of Murphy again! This will cost us another week! Do I have to lay every block with my own frail hands? Tell them to rip out that course and replace it with the correct one."

The imp scurried off, and the King returned to his task. But just as he was about to work his magic, another imp arrived. "Hey, King—a goblin army is marching from the south!"

Grimly the King asked: "What is its estimated time of arrival?"

"ETA zero minus ten days."

"That's one shoe," the King muttered, and returned to his work. Naturally the water dragon had wandered out of place, and had to be coaxed laboriously back. Murphy's curse operated in small ways, too.

The King was shortly interrupted by yet another imp. "Roog, old boy—a harpy flight is massing in the north!"

"ETA?"

"Ten days."

"The other shoe," Roogna said resignedly. "The two forces will converge on this spot, courtesy of Murphy, and by the time they have destroyed each other, the landscape will be in ruins and Castle Roogna in rubble. If we had only been able to complete the breastworks in time—but now that is hopeless. My enemy has done some remarkably apt scheming. I am forced to admire it."

"He's a smart man," Dor said. "There must be some way to divert those armies, if they're not really after the Castle. I mean, if the goblins and harpies don't care about the Castle at all, but only happen to be fighting here." He was disturbed. It didn't seem that his presence had caused this problem, but he wasn't quite sure. If his encounters with the harpies and goblins had set them both off—

"Any direct attempt at diversion would cause them both to attack us," Roogna said. "They are extremely intractable creatures. We lack the inclination and means to fend off either of those brute hordes. In your world, Man may be the dominant creature, but here that has not yet been established."

"If you recruited some more creatures to help you—"

"I would have to dissipate my magic repaying them for that service—instead of working on the Castle."

"Your human army—can't you call it back from furlough?"

"Murphy's curse is especially apt at interfering with organizational messages. I doubt we could summon the full complement back before the monsters arrived. And I'm sure those men need to protect their own homesteads from the advancing monsters. I think it better to defend the Castle with what we have on hand. That's a small chance, but as good as the alternative. I fear Murphy has really checked me, this time."

Maybe another Magician could help—" Dor interrupted himself with another thought. "The Zombie Master! Would his help make the difference?"

The King considered. "Yes, it probably would. Because he represents a primary focus of magic, with all its ramifications, and because he is relatively close, with no Gap to navigate in getting here, and because his zombies could man the battlements without number or upkeep: the ideal army in this kind of situation. Just feeding my own army during siege would be a terrific problem; we have supplies only for the crews working here now. But this is useless conjecture; the Zombie Master does not participate in politics."

"I have to go see him anyway," Dor exclaimed, excited. "I could talk to him, explain what is at stake—" To hell with caution! If the King was about to lose without Dor's help, why not take the risk? He really could do no harm. "Jumper could come along; he's better than I am at lots of things. The worst I could do is fail."

The King stroked his beard. "There is that. I regard it as a long shot, but since you are willing—tell the Zombie Master I would be willing to make some reasonable exchange for his assistance." He cocked a finger, and another imp appeared. Dor wondered where those imps hid when not in use; the King was evidently well attended, though he made little show of it. Like King Trent, he masked his power except when show was necessary. "Prepare an escort and guide for an excursion to the castle of the Zombie Master. Magician Dor will depart in the morning on a mission for me."

But in the morning there was one more: Millie the maid. "With the Castle delayed, and the household staff shipping out during the emergency, I have no job yet," she explained. "Maybe I can help."

In future centuries she would be a sad ghost, and come to know the zombie Jonathan, and seek to restore him. She knew nothing of this now, but Dor did. How could he deny her her chance to assist him in this mission—since it was ultimately for her? Maybe in some way she could help.

Why did he feel so glad for her company? He knew he could never—she was not—his body appreciated aspects of her that he himself had hardly glimpsed, but she could never be his in that way. So why should he fool himself with impossible notions?

Yet how glad he was to be with her, even this brief time!

Chapter 6

Zombie Master

T

he escort was a dragon horse, with the front part of a horse and the rear of a dragon. The guide was another imp. "Well, sport, let's get on with it," the imp exclaimed impatiently. He was a good deal larger than Grundy the golem, but smaller than a goblin, and reminded Dor somewhat of each.

There were three saddles spaced along the creature's back. Dor took one, Millie another, and Jumper clung to the third, unable to sit in it. The imp perched on the equine head, whispering into the expressive ears.

Abruptly they were moving. The horse forelegs struck the ground powerfully, while the reptilian hind legs dug their claws in and shoved back. The monster half-galloped, half-slithered forward in great lurches. Millie screamed, and Dor was almost catapulted out of the saddle. The imp chuckled impishly. He had known this would happen.

Jumper bounded over Dor's head, landing just behind the girl. With deft motions the spider trussed her to the saddle with silken threads so that she could not be dislodged. Then Jumper did the same for Dor. Suddenly there was no question of being shaken loose; they did not even have to hold on. "Ah, you take all the fun out of it!" the imp complained.

The dragon moved rapidly. The lurching smoothed as the creature got up speed, and became a more or less even rising and falling. Dor closed his eyes and imagined he was on a boat, sailing the waves. Up, down, sway; up, down, sway. He began to feel seasick, and had to open his eyes again.

The foliage was rushing past. This creature was really moving! It threaded neatly through seemingly impassable tangles, avoiding tangle trees and monster warrens, hardly abating its pace even for fair-sized rifts. The imp was an obnoxious little man-thing, typical of his kind, spreading insults imp-partially—but he really knew his route and controlled the dragon expertly. Dor appreciated expertise wherever he found it.

Which was not to say the whole trip was smooth. There were hills and dales and curves. Once the dragon splashed through a boggy lake, swimming strongly but soaking their feet and lower legs in the process. Another time it ascended a steep bank, going almost vertically before crushing it. Once a griffin rose up challengingly before it, squawking; the dragon horse neighed warningly and feinted with its hooves, and the griffin decided to give way.

Soon they neared the demesnes of the Zombie Master—and Dor realized with a start that this was the same site as that of Good Magician Humfrey's castle, eight hundred years later. But maybe that was not strange; that place which seemed fit for one Magician might also appeal to another. If Dor were to build a castle someday for himself, he would look for an ideal site, and might be governed by considerations similar to those of some former Magician.

However, the Zombie Master had his own defenses, and these turned out to be as formidable in their fashion as those of Magician Humfrey. A pair of zombies rose up before the dragon horse—and the fearless creature sheered off, unwilling to suffer contact with this rotting flesh. Millie, seeing the zombies, screamed, and even the imp looked disgusted.

"This is as far as we go," the imp announced. "Nothing will bother you here —except zombies. How you get in to talk with their master I don't even care to know. Dismount and let us go home."

Dor shrugged. Zombies posed no special horror for him, since he had more or less associated with Jonathan all his life. He didn't like zombies, but he wasn't afraid of them. "Very well. Tell the King we are in conference with the Zombie Master, and will send news soon."

"Fat chance," the imp muttered. Dor pretended not to hear that.

The three dismounted. Immediately Dor felt cramps in his legs; that ride had really battered them! Millie stood bowlegged, unable even to kick her feet properly. Only Jumper was unkinked; he had perched atop his saddle throughout, being unable to sit at all.

The dragon horse neighed, wheeled on hoof and claw and tail, and shoved off. The three were showered with dirt and twigs thrown up by its feet. It was certainly glad to get away from here!

Dor worked the knots out of his legs as well as he could, and limped up to the guard-zombies. "We come on a mission from King Roogna. Take us to your Master."

The zombie opened its ponderous and marbled jaws. "Nooo nnn ffasssess!" it declared with fetid breath.

Dor concentrated, trying to make out the words. Was his talent operating here? These things were dead, yet fashioned from organic material. Wood was organic, and he could speak to it when it was dead. Did the spell that gave these monsters animation also give them sufficient pseudo-life to nullify his communication with inanimate things? Or was it partially operative? Probably the latter; he could converse, but with difficulty.

Jumper chittered. "I believe it said 'No one passes,'" the web on Dor's shoulder said.

Dor glanced at the spider, surprised. Had it come to the point where Jumper could understand Dor's language better than Dor himself could?

Jumper chittered again. "Do not be dismayed; all of your words are strange to me; this is merely another aspect of strangeness."

Dor smiled. "That makes sense! Very well; you can help me converse with the zombies." He returned his attention to the guards, who had remained as silent as the grave, as patient as time. They had no living urges to impel them. "Tell your Master he has visitors. He must see us."

"Nooo," the zombie insisted. "Nooo nnnn!"

"Then we shall just have to introduce ourselves." Dor made to pass.

The zombie raised a grisly arm to block his way. Shreds of rotten flesh festooned it, and the white bone showed through in places. Millie screamed. She certainly had no affection for any zombie at this stage of her life! But centuries of ghosthood could change a person's perspective, Dor concluded.

Dor reached for his sword, but Jumper was there before him, trussing up the zombie in silk. In a moment the other zombie was similarly incapacitated. Dor had to admit this was the better way; zombies were messy to slay, he understood, because they could not be killed. They had to be dismembered, and even the pieces fought on. Which was one reason they would make such a good army for

King Roogna, if that could only be arranged. This way, they were efficiently neutralized, and in a manner that should not offend the Zombie Master.

But they had not gone far toward the castle that stood on a mound in the forest—in Dor's day both mound and forest were gone—before a zombie serpent challenged them. It hissed and rattled in a fashion only deviously reminiscent of a live serpent, but there was no doubt it sought to bar their progress. Jumper neutralized it as he had the others. Whatever would they have done without the big spider!

Then a zombie tangle tree menaced them. This was too much even for the spider; the tree stood four times the height of a man and had perhaps a hundred moldering tentacles. Even if it were feasible to truss it up, the thing would have the strength to snap the strands. Therefore Dor menaced it with his gleaming sword while the others sidled past; even a zombie tree had some care for its extremities.

In this manner they achieved the castle. It, too, was an animated ruin. Stones had fallen from its walls to reveal fossilized inner supporting timbers, and shreds of cloth hung in the window apertures. There had once been a moat, but it had long since filled in with debris; a stench rose from what thick liquid remained. There was—yes, a zombie bog-monster languishing in the mire. Its slime-coated orbs focused on the intruders with as much glare as their sunken condition permitted them to mount.

The party crossed the broken-down drawbridge and pounded on the sagging door. Splinters and fragments were dislodged, but of course there was no answer. So Dor completed the demolition of the door with a few strokes of his sword, and the three marched in. Not without a qualm or two.

"Hallooo!" Dor called, and his voice reverberated through the tomblike halls. "Zombie Master! We are on a mission for the King!"

A zombie ogre appeared. Millie screamed and did a little skip back, her hair swinging almost straight up; she must have kicked her feet, forgetting that she was standing on them. Jumper braced her with one leg to prevent her falling backward into the moat, where the moat-monster was trying vainly to slaver. "Noo. Goo," the ogre boomed hollowly, for its chest had been eviscerated by decay. Dor remembered Crunch the ogre, and retreated; a zombie ogre was still an ogre.

"We must see the Zombie Master," Millie said, though pale with fear. In her cute way, she too, had courage.

"Soo? Ooh." The ogre shuffled down a hall, and the party followed.

They entered a chamber like a crypt. Another zombie glanced up, resting its cadaverous hands on the table before it. "On what pretext do you intrude here?" it demanded coldly.

"We want to see the Zombie Master!" Dor exclaimed. "Now get out of the way, you bundle of bones, if you're not going to help."

The zombie stared somberly at him. It was an unusually well-preserved specimen, gaunt but not yet rotten. "You have no business with me. You are not yet dead."

"Of course we're not yet—" Dor paused. That "yet" distracted him.

Jumper chittered. "This man is alive. He must be—"

"The Zombie Master himself!" Millie finished, horrified.

Dor sighed. He had done it again. When would he grow up and learn to check things out before making assumptions? First King Roogna, whom he had thought to be a gardener; now the Zombie Master. He fumbled for an apology. "Uh—"

"Why do the living seek me?" the Zombie Master demanded.

"Uh, King Roogna needs your help," Dor blurted. "And I need the elixir to restore a zombie to life."

"I do not indulge in politics," the Zombie Master said. "And I have no interest in restoring zombies to life; that would undermine my own talent." He made a chill gesture of dismissal and returned to his business—which was the corpse of an ant lion that he was evidently about to animate.

"Now see here—" Dor began angrily. But the zombie ogre stepped forward menacingly, and Dor was cowed. His present body was big and strong and swift, but in no way could it match the least of ogres. One swing of that huge fist—

Jumper chittered. "I think our mission has failed."

Dor took another look at the ogre, remembering how Crunch had snapped an ironweed tree off at the base with one careless blow. This creature was not in good condition, being dead, but could probably snap an aluminumwood tree off. Mere human flesh would be no problem at all. So his second thought was much the same as his first: he could not prevail here.

Dor turned about. He knew that they could not coerce a Magician to help; it had to be voluntary. The Zombie Master, as the others had warned, was simply not approachable.

A hero would have found some way. But Dor was just a lad of twelve, accompanied by a giant spider and a girl who screamed constantly and who would become a ghost at an early age. No heroes here! And so he accepted the gall of defeat, for both his quests. The gall of growing up, of becoming disillusioned.

Dor half-expected one of the others to protest, as Grundy the golem always did. But Millie was only a helpless maid, possessing little initiative, and Jumper was not Dor's kind; the spider comprehended human imperatives only imperfectly.

They walked out, and the zombies did not bother them. They trekked down the hill. The dragon horse was gone, of course. They might have had it wait, but they had not expected to need it this soon. Dor's lack of foresight had penalized him again. Not that delay made much difference, at this stage. So they would simply have to march back themselves.

They untied the two zombie guards Jumper had trussed in silk. "Nothing personal," Dor explained to them. "Our business with your Master is finished."

They marched. Millie made a very pretty marcher, when she wasn't screaming or kicking her feet; her hair still flung about naturally. He was getting used to her as she was now, and found her rather intriguing. In fact, he wouldn't mind— but that wouldn't be right. He had to guard against the thoughts his Mundane body put into his head; Mundanes weren't very subtle.

Abruptly they happened on a campfire. This was strange, because fire was hardly used in the Land of Xanth. Few things needed cooking, and heat was more efficiently obtained by pouring a little firewater on whatever needed warming. But this was obviously an organized fire, with sticks formed into a circular pile. The flames licked merrily up through the center. Someone had been here recently; in fact the person must have departed moments before Dor and his party arrived.

"Stand where you are, stranger," a voice called from the shadow. "I've got you covered with a bow."

Millie screamed. Dor reached for his sword, then stopped; he couldn't draw before an arrow struck him. No sense in compounding his yet-again lack of foresight by getting himself unnecessarily killed. Jumper jumped straight up and disappeared into the foliage of a tree overhanging them.

The challenger stepped forth. He was a brutish man, Mundane by the look of him, and he had not been bluffing about the bow. The string was taut, and the arrow nocked and centered on Dor's midsection. Knowing the capabilities of his own Mundane body, Dor had little reason to doubt the competence of this challenger. It seemed as if all Mundanes were born warriors. Perhaps this was in compensation for their abysmal lack of magic. Or maybe the soft, gentle, peaceful Mundanes didn't go out invading other lands.

"Who the hell are you, poking around my campfire?" the brute demanded. "What happened to that creep with you, the hairy thing with the legs?"

"I am Dor, on mission for the King," Dor said. He spoke more boldly than was his wont, fresh from the pain of failure of his missions. "The others are my companions. Who are you, to challenge me thusly?"

"So you're a Xanthie!" the man exclaimed sneeringly. "You sure could've fooled me; you look just like a man. You try a spell on me and I'll drill you!"

So this really was a Mundane. Dor had never seen one in the flesh before. "You don't have a talent?"

"Don't get smart with me, creep!" Then the man looked at him more closely. "Say, you're even dressed like one of us! You sure you're not a deserter?"

"Would you like to see my talent?" Dor asked evenly.

The man considered. "Yeah, in a moment. But no tricks." He turned his head and yelled. "Hey, Joe! Come and set guard on a pair here!"

Joe arrived. He was another brutish man, unclean and malodorous. "What's all this noise about—"

He broke off. His lips pursed in a crude whistle. "Get a load of that babe!"

Oops, Dor thought. Millie's talent was operating.

Millie made a token scream and stepped back. Joe stepped forward aggressively. "Boy, I could really use a number like this!" His hand shot out, catching her slender arm. This time Millie's scream was in earnest.

Dor's body took over. His left hand grabbed at the first Mundane's bow while his right snapped over his shoulder to whip out the sword. Suddenly the two Mundanes were standing at bay. "Leave her be!" Dor cried.

Millie turned on him, surprised and gratified. "Why Dor—I didn't know you cared!"

"I didn't know either," he muttered. And knew it was a lie. He had resolved to stop lying, but it seemed to come naturally at times like these. Was that part of growing up too: learning to lie socially? He had always cared for Millie, but had never known how to express it. Only the immediate threat to her had prompted his action.

"You won't get away with this!" Joe said angrily. "We've got troops all around here, looking for plunder."

Dor spoke to the club that dangled from the man's waist. "Is that true, club?"

"It's true," the club said. "This is the advance unit of the Mundane Fifth Wave. They marched down the coast past the Gap, then cut inland. They are completely immune to reason. All they want is wealth and women and easy living, in that order. Flee whilst you can."

The first Mundane's mouth dropped open. "Magic! He's really got magic!"

Dor backed away, Millie beside him. This was a tactical error, for the moment the two Mundanes were beyond sword-slash range they drew their own weapons. And set up a shout: "Enemy escaping! Cut him off!"

A shape dropped from above: Jumper. He landed almost on top of the two Mundanes and trussed them up before they knew what was happening. But the alarm had already been given, and there were sounds all around of men closing in.

"We had better use the upper reaches," Jumper chittered. "The Mundanes will not pursue us there."

"But they can shoot their arrows at us!" Dor protested.

"They may not see us." Jumper fastened safety lines to Dor and Millie, and they scrambled up the trunk of a tree.

The Mundanes were arriving. These alien men were worse than goblins! Dor was climbing rapidly, thanks to his body's huge muscles, but Millie was slow. She would surely be caught. "I will distract them!" Jumper chittered, and dropped low on his dragline.

Dor waited for Millie to catch up with him, then continued on up into the foliage. Just as they got to some reasonable cover, the Mundanes converged on the tree. Jumper chittered at them, swinging across to another tree.

"Get that bug!" a Mundane cried. He lunged for Jumper, but missed as the spider zipped a few feet up his line. Jumper could have escaped then, by going on up into the heights, or simply jumping over the Mundanes and running—but Dor was still struggling to haul Millie to safety. So the heroic spider dangled low, chittering in a manner that sounded challenging and insulting even without translation.

Another Mundane lunged—and missed. Mundanes just didn't think of an enemy rising suddenly up. But there were too many; now the spider had nowhere to go. One Mundane had the wit to chop at the dragline with a sword, severing the invisible silk. Jumper dropped to the ground. Instantly the men pounced on him, grabbing him one man to a leg, much as the goblins had, so that he was helpless.

Men and goblins: was there really much difference between them? The Mundanes were bigger, but . . .

Dor was about to turn back, to aid his friend, but one of Jumper's eight eyes spied him. "Don't waste my effort!" he chittered, knowing that no one besides Dor could understand him. "Return to the Zombie Master; it is the only place you can keep the girl safe."

Dor hadn't thought of that. The Zombie Master might not be friendly, but at least he was not too hostile. It was the best place to be until the Mundane horde passed.

He climbed up into the protective splay of leaves, urging Millie on. His last sight of Jumper was of the men bearing him to the ground, striking his soft body brutally with their fists. They weren't trying to kill, they were trying to hurt, to make their enemy suffer as long as possible before the end. Because Jumper had balked them from capturing the girl—and because Jumper was different. Dor winced, feeling the pain of the blows in his own gut. What would they do to his friend?

Jumper had left a network of silken lines strung through the upper foliage, guiding Dor and Millie and providing rapid transit from one great tree to another. It was amazing how much he had accomplished in the brief time he had been aloft, and with what foresight. Dor had never thought his friend was deserting him—but neither had he anticipated the sacrifice Jumper would make. He felt the unmanly tears stinging his eyes, was afraid Millie would notice them, then decided he didn't care. Jumper—to have Jumper trapped like this, perhaps badly hurt, because of Dor's own carelessness—

Suddenly there was a piercing terrible, great chittering from below. It translated into a sheer scream of agony, chilling in its implication.

"They are pulling off his legs!" Millie whispered in horror. "That's what Mundanes do to spiders. The wings off butterflies—"

Dor saw that her beautiful face was streaked with helpless tears. *She* was not ashamed to cry!

Then something congealed in Dor. "Come on!" he snapped, and swung forward at a faster pace.

"Don't you care, that—?" she demanded plaintively.

"Hurry!"

Reproachfully, she hurried. Dor felt like a heel from a No. 1 shoe-tree, knowing she thought concern for his own safety motivated him, but he wasted no effort trying to explain. Jumper had eight legs; it would take the Mundanes time to get them all, and he had to use that time well.

In moments they ran out of Jumper's lines and dropped to the ground. They were now at the base of the hill on which the Zombie Master's castle sat. A zombie rose up to challenge them, but Dor shoved it aside so roughly that it collapsed in a jumble of shredded meat and chipped bone. He dragged Millie on.

They never paused at the chopped-open castle door. Dor charged right in. The zombie ogre rose up; Dor parried it with his blade, ducked under its arm, and plunged on through the gloomy hall. At last he burst into the Zombie Master's chamber, where the zombie ant lion was now taking its first steps.

"Magician!" Dor cried. "You must save my friend the spider! The Mundanes are pulling out his legs!"

The Zombie Master shook his cadaverous head and waved with an emaciated hand. "I have no interest in—"

Dor menaced him with his sword. "If you do not help this instant, I will surely slay you!" Such was his hurt and desperation, he was not bluffing, though he feared the Magician could turn him into a zombie.

Now the Zombie Master showed some spirit. "So you, a mortal, dare to threaten a Magician?"

"I am a Magician too!" Dor cried. "But even if I weren't, I would do anything to save my friend, who sacrificed himself for me and Millie!"

Millie put a restraining hand on Dor's arm. "Please," she said. "You can not threaten a Magician. Let me handle it, Dor. I am not a Magician like you, but I do have my talent."

Dor paused, and Millie stepped close to the Zombie Master, smiling with difficulty. "Sir, I am not a forward maid, and no Sorceress, but I too would do anything to help the bold friend who preserved us. If you but knew Jumper the spider—please, now, if you have any compassion at all—"

The Magician looked at her closely for the first time. Dor remembered what her talent was, and knew how it softened men. He was just beginning to appreciate its impact on himself. The Zombie Master was after all a man, and he too had to feel the impact.

"You . . . will tarry with me?" he asked incredulously.

Dor did not like the sound of that word, *tarry*.

Millie spread her arms toward the Zombie Master. "Save my friend. What becomes of me is not important."

A kind of shudder ran through the Magician. "This becomes you not, maid," he said. "Yet—" He turned to his ogre. "Gather my forces, Egor; go with this man and do as he desires. Save the spider."

Dor took off, running through the gloomy halls and from the castle. The true horror was what lay ahead of him. The zombie ogre followed, crying out to the things of the castle: "Ssome ccome!"

Zombies erupted from the adjacent rooms, in their haste dripping stray clods, bones, and teeth. They closed in behind the ogre: men, wolves, bats, and other creatures too far gone to identify. In grisly procession they followed Dor down the hill.

His concern for his friend lent him swiftness, and somehow the zombies kept up. Yet even as he ran, Dor wondered whether he had not left Millie to as bad a fate as the one he strove to rescue Jumper from. The spider had sacrificed himself to save the two of them; Millie had sacrificed herself to save the spider. The full nature of Millie's talent had never been apparent to him, though it was coming clearer; it included holding and kissing and—

His mind balked. Kissing the Zombie Master? He ran faster yet.

They burst upon the Mundanes. The first thing Dor saw was Jumper: the brutal men had hung him up by four legs, and yanked off the other four. The spider was alive, but in terrible pain after this torture.

Dor went mad. "Kill!" he screamed, and his sword was in his hand. Almost of its own volition, the blade chopped into the neck of the Mundane nearest Jumper—the one holding the spider leg that had been torn off most recently. Dor was reminded of the centipede legs spat out at the goblin banquet. But this was his friend! The keen edge sliced through the flesh with surprising ease. It passed right through the neck, and the man's head popped off. Dor stared, momentarily numb to the implication; then he looked again at the severed leg, and whirled on the next Mundane.

Meanwhile the zombies were attacking with a will. The Mundanes panicked, becoming aware of the horror that had fallen on them. Dor had heard that Mundanes were a superstitious lot; zombies should play on that propensity. The men scattered, and in a moment there was nothing in the glade except the victors, three bodies, and Jumper.

Dor couldn't let himself relax. "Carry the spider to the castle," he ordered the ogre. "Carefully!" He turned to the other zombies. "Collect the severed legs and bring them along." Would it be possible to convert them into usable zombie legs and put them back on the spider?

The ogre picked up the mutilated body. Other zombies found the missing legs, and dragged along the dead Mundanes. The strength of the zombies was surprising—or maybe it was just willpower. They brought their prizes grimly to the castle.

Millie met them at the entrance. She looked all right. Her clothes were still on, and her hair was unmussed. Dor had trouble phrasing his question. "He— did he—?"

"The Zombie Master was a perfect gentleman," she said brightly. "We just talked. He's an educated man. I think he's lonely; no one ever visited with him before."

And no wonder! Dor's attention returned to Jumper. "He's alive, but in terrible pain. They—they pulled off four legs!"

"The brutes!" she exclaimed with feeling. She had seemed a rather innocent, helpless maid before, but now she was reacting to stress and horror with increasing personality. "How can we help him?"

Jumper revived enough to chitter weakly. "Only time will help me. Time to regrow my lost limbs. A month or so."

"But I must return to the King in mere days!" Dor cried. "And to my own land—"

"Return without me. Perhaps I can render some service to the Zombie Master in return for his hospitality."

"But I must take the Zombie Master with me, to help the King!" Yet that, too, was an impasse; the Magician had already refused to get involved in politics.

The Zombie Master was there; in his distraction Dor had not been aware of his arrival. "Why did the men torment the spider?"

"I am alien to this world," Jumper chittered. "I am a natural creature, but in my enchantment in this realm of men I become a thing of horror. Only these friends, who know me—" His chittering ceased abruptly; he was unconscious.

"A thing of horror, yet with sentience and courage," the Zombie Master murmured thoughtfully. He looked up. "I will care for this creature as long as he requires it. Egor, carry him to the guest chamber."

The ogre picked Jumper up again and tromped away.

"I wish there were some way to cure him faster," Dor said. "Some medicinal spell, like the healing elixir—" He snapped his fingers. "That's it! I know where there's a Healing Spring, within a day's journey of here!"

Now he had the Magician's attention. "I could use such elixir in my art," the Zombie Master exclaimed. "I will help you fetch it, if you will share the precious fluid with me."

"There's plenty," Dor agreed. "Only there's one catch. You can't act against the interest of the Healing Spring, or you forfeit its benefit."

"A fair stipulation." The Zombie Master showed the way to an inner courtyard. A monstrous zombie bird roosted there.

Dor stared. This was a roc! The largest of all birds, restored to pseudo-life by the talent of this Magician. The entire world of the dead was under the power of this man!

"Carry this man where he will," the Zombie Master directed the roc. "Return him safely with his burden to this spot."

"Uh, I'll need a jug or something—" Dor said.

The Magician produced two jugs: one for each of them. Dor climbed onto the stinking back of the roc, anchored himself by grasping the rotting stubs of two great feathers, and tied the jugs with a length of Jumper's silk left over from his last dragline.

The roc flapped its monstrous wings. The spread was so great, the tips touched the castle walls on either side of the courtyard. Grimy feathers flew wide, bits of meat sprayed off, and the bony substructure crackled alarmingly. But there was tremendous power remaining in this creature. A roc in its prime could carry an elephant—that was an imaginary creature the size of a small sphinx—and Dor weighed far less than that. So even this animated corpse could perform creditably enough.

They lumbered into the air, barely clearing the castle roof. There were so many holes in the great wings that Dor marveled that they did not fall apart, let alone have sufficient leverage to make flight possible. But the spell of the Zombie Master was a wondrous thing; no zombie ever quite disintegrated, though all of them seemed perpetually on the verge of doing so.

They looped above the castle. "Go east!" Dor cried. He hoped he knew the terrain well enough by air to locate the spot. He tried to visualize the tapestry to orient himself—was he actually flying above it now?—but this world was too real for that.

Dor had only been to the Healing Spring once with his father Bink, who had needed elixir for some obscure adult purpose. On that trip Bink had reminisced about his adventures there: how he had met Dor's mother Chameleon, she being then in the guise of Dee, her normal phase, at such and such a spot, and how he had found the soldier Crombie at this other spot, wounded, and used the elixir to restore him to health. Dor and Bink had visited briefly with a dryad, a wood nymph associated with a particular tree, resembling a pretty girl of about Millie's present age. She had tousled Dor's hair and wished him well. Ah, yes, it had been a fine trip! But now, high in the air, Dor could not ask the objects of the ground where the Spring was, and there were no clouds close enough to hail—hail-call, that is, not hail-stone—and his memory seemed fallible.

Then he spied a channel of especially healthy jungle, obviously benefitting from the flowing water from the Spring. "Down there," he cried. "At the head of that stream."

The zombie roc dropped like a stone, righted itself, glided in for a landing, tilted a little, and clipped a tree with one far-reaching wing tip. Immediately the wing crumpled, and the roc's whole body swerved out of control. It was a crash landing that sent Dor tumbling from his perch.

He picked himself up, bruised but intact. The roc was a wreck. Both wings had been broken; there was no way the creature could fly now. How was he to get back in time to do Jumper much good? If he walked, it would take him a day in the best of conditions; carrying two heavy jugs it would be longer. Assuming he didn't get snapped up by a tangle tree, dragon, or other monster along the way.

He reconnoitered. They had missed the Spring, but there was a handsome tree nearby on the hillside. And—he recognized it. "Dryad!" he cried, running toward it. "Remember me, Dor?"

There was no response. Suddenly he realized: this was eight hundred years earlier! The dryad would not remember him—in fact there probably was no dryad here yet, and this was probably not the same tree. Even if the time had been correct, the nymph still would hardly have recognized him in his present body. He had been boyishly foolish. Yet again.

Disconsolately he trekked down the slope. Of course this was not the same tree! The real one had been some distance from the Spring, not right beside it. And an average tree of today would be an extraordinary tree by Dor's own time; even plants aged considerably in eight centuries. His hopes had really fouled up his thinking! He would have to find his own way out of this mess, without help from any dryad.

Well, not entirely without help. "What is the best route out of here?" he asked the nearest stone.

"Ride that roc bird out," the rock replied.

"But the roc's wings are broken!"

"So sprinkle it with some elixir, idiot!"

Dor stopped dead in his tracks. So obvious! "I *am* an idiot!" he exclaimed.

"That's what I said," the stone agreed smugly.

Dor ran up to the roc, got his jugs, and ran to the Spring. "Mind if I take some of your elixir?" he inquired rhetorically.

"Yes, I mind!" the Spring replied. "All you creatures come and steal my substance, that I labor so hard to enchant, and what recompense do I get for it?"

"What recompense!" Dor retorted. "You demand the stiffest price of all!"

"What are you talking about? I never made any demands!"

Something was wrong. Then Dor caught on. Again, that eight-hundred-year factor. The Spring had not yet developed its compensatory enchantment. Well, maybe Dor could do it a favor. "Look, Spring, I intend to pay you for your substance. Give me these two jugs full of elixir, and I will tell you how to get fair recompense from all other takers."

"Done!" the Spring cried.

Dor dipped the jugs full, noting how the bruises vanished from his body as he touched the water. This was the Spring, all right! "All you need is a supplementary enchantment, requiring that anyone who benefits from your elixir cannot thereafter act against your interests. The more your water is used, the more your power will grow."

"But suppose someone calls my bluff?"

"It will be no bluff. You will take back your magic. It will be as if he never was healed by you."

"Say, yes—I could do that!" the Spring said excitedly. "It would take a while, maybe a few centuries, to build that extra spell, but since it's just a refinement of the original magic, a termination clause as it were—yes, it will work. Oh, thank you, thank you, stranger!"

"I told you I would repay you," Dor said, gratified. Then he thought of something else. "Uh—I'm only a visitor to this land, and what I do may fade out after I leave. So you'd better get right on that spell, so you don't lose it once I'm gone."

"How long do I have?"

Dor did a quick calculation. "Maybe ten days."

"I'll fix it in my mind," the Spring said. "I'll memorize it so hard that nothing can shake it loose."

"That's good," Dor said. "Farewell!"

"I'm not a well, I'm a spring!" But it was a good-natured correction.

"Maybe you're a wellspring," Dor suggested. "Because you make creatures well again."

" 'Bye," the Spring said, dismissing him.

Dor returned to the roc and sprinkled elixir from his jar on its wings. Immediately they healed; in fact, they were better than they had been. But they remained zombie wings, dead flesh. There were, after all, limits; the elixir could not restore the dead to life.

Which was why he was on this quest. Only the Zombie Master could do what needed to be done. Meanwhile, he had to get back to Jumper soon, lest the spider also require restoration from the dead.

Dor boarded, tied the jugs, and hung on. "Home, roc!" he cried.

The roc taxied about to face the channel forged by its crash landing, worked its legs to accelerate, flapped its wings, and launched violently into the air. This takeoff was far more precipitous than the first one had been; it was all Dor could do to hang on. The elixir had given the wings new power. Fortunately there were a few droplets remaining on his hands, and these healed the feathers to which he clung. Now they were great long fluffy colorful puffs of plumage suitable for ladies' hats, easy to grasp.

The roc wheeled in the sky, then stroked powerfully for the Zombie Master's castle. The landscape fairly whizzed by below. They reached their destination in half the time it had taken to make the outbound trip. No wonder the Magician wanted the elixir; his zombies would be twice as good now!

But a new problem manifested. From above, Dor could see that the Mundanes had rallied, and now were laying siege to the castle. There were many of them; their whole advance army must have gathered for this effort. They evidently were not cowards; they had been panicked by the ferocity of the zombies' attack, but now they were angry at the three deaths and sought revenge. Also, they probably thought that any castle so well guarded must conceal enormous riches, so their greed had been invoked. In helping his friend Jumper, Dor had brought serious mischief to the Zombie Master. Dor was sure his father would have had more sense than that; it was yet another reminder of his own youth and inexperience and thoughtlessness. When, oh when, would he ever grow up and be adult?

The roc dived, hawklike, banked, and plopped into place in the courtyard. The landing was heavy, for the bird's feet had not been healed; the sound carried throughout the castle.

The Zombie Master and Millie rushed up. "You got it!" Millie cried, clapping her hands.

"I got it," Dor agreed. He handed one jug to the Magician, keeping the other for himself. "Take me to Jumper."

Millie guided him to the guest room. The big spider lay there, ichor leaking from his stumps. The variegated fur face on the back of his abdomen seemed to be making a grimace of distress. His eyes, always open, were filmed with pain. He was conscious again, but so weak he could chitter only faintly. "Good to see you again, friend! I fear the injuries have been too extensive. Legs can be regrown, but internal organs have been crushed too. I cannot—"

"Yes you can, friend!" Dor cried. "Take that!" And he poured a liberal dose of elixir over Jumper's shuddering body.

Like magic—unsurprisingly—the spider was whole again. As the liquid coursed over the fur-face, the green and white and black brightened until they shone. As it touched each stump, the legs sprouted out, long and hairy and strong. As it was absorbed, the internal organs were restored, and the body firmed out. In a moment there was no sign that Jumper had ever been injured.

"It is amazing!" he chittered. "I did not even need to have my original legs returned! I have not felt so good since I was hatched! What is this medicine?"

"Healing elixir," Dor explained. "I knew where there was a Spring of it—" He broke off, overcome by emotion. "Oh, Jumper! If you had died—" And he embraced the spider as well as he could, the tears once more overflowing his eyes. To hell with being adult!

"I think it was worth the torture," Jumper chittered, one mandible moving against Dor's ear. "Watch I don't nip your antenna off."

"Go ahead! I have plenty more healing elixir to use to grow a new ear!"

"Besides which," Millie added, "human flesh tastes awful. Maybe even worse than goblin meat."

The Zombie Master had followed them. "You are human, yet you hold this alien creature in such esteem you cry for him," he remarked.

"And what's wrong with that?" Millie demanded.

"Nothing," the Magician said wanly. "Absolutely nothing. No one ever cried for me."

Even in the height of his relief, Dor perceived the meaning of the Zombie Master's words. The man had been alienated from his own kind by the nature of his magic, rendered a pariah. He identified with Jumper, another alien. That was why he had agreed to take care of Jumper. More than anything else, the Magician must want people to care for him the way Dor and Millie cared for Jumper.

"Will you help King Roogna?" Dor asked, disengaging from his friend.

"I do not indulge in politics," the Zombie Master said, the coldness returning.

Because the King was no pariah. This Magician might assist those who showed him some human compassion, but King Roogna had not done that. "Would you at least come to meet the King, to talk with him? If you helped him, he would see that you received due honor—"

"Honor by fiat? Never!"

Dor found he could not argue with that. He would not have wanted that sort of honor either. If there were such a thing as dishonorable honor, that would be it. He had made another stupid error of approach, and squelched his chances—again. Some emissary he was proving to be!

But there was another problem. "You know the Mundanes of the Fifth Wave are getting ready to attack this castle?"

"I do know," the Zombie Master agreed. "My zombie eye-flies report there are hundreds of them. Too many to overcome with my present force. I have sent the roc out to round up more bodies, to shore up my defenses. To facilitate this, the roc will not even land here at the castle; it will drop the bodies in the courtyard and proceed immediately for more."

"The Mundanes are mad at us," Dor said, "because we killed three of them. Maybe if we leave—"

"My zombies helped you," the Zombie Master pointed out. "You can gain nothing other than your own demises by departing now. The Mundanes have this castle surrounded. To them, it is a repository of unguessable riches; no reasonable demurral will change their fixed minds."

"Maybe if they saw us leave," Dor said. "The roc could carry us out. Oh—the roc's away for the duration."

"It seems we must remain, at least for a time," Jumper chittered. "Perhaps we can assist in the defense of the castle."

"Uh, yes, we'd better," Dor agreed. "Since we seem to have brought this siege down upon it." Then, for no good reason, he found himself making another appeal: "Uh, Magician—will you reconsider the matter of the zombie restorative elixir? This is not a political matter, and—"

The Zombie Master glanced at him coldly. Before the Magician could speak, Millie put her sweet little hand on his lean arm. "Please," she breathed. She was excruciatingly attractive when she breathed that way. Yet she could not know that it was as a favor to herself, of eight hundred years later, that Dor was obtaining this precious substance.

The Zombie Master's coldness faded. "Since she asks, and you are a good and loyal man, I do reconsider. I will develop the agent you require." But it was evident that most of the responsibility for his change of heart was Millie's. And her breathing.

Dor knew victory of a sort—yet it was incomplete. He was succeeding in his private personal mission, while failing in his mission for the King. Was that right? He didn't know, but had to take what he could. "Thank you, Magician," he said humbly.

Chapter 7

Siege

The siege was serious. The Mundanes were reasonably apt at this sort of thing, since they were an army. Motivated by vengeance and greed and the knowledge that at least one measurelessly pretty girl was inside the castle, they knew no decent limits. They closed in about the castle and readied their assault.

At first the Mundanes simply marched across the rickety drawbridge and up to the blasted main gate. But the zombie ogre came charging out, much of his strength restored by the healing elixir, and tossed them into the moat, where the restored bog-monster chomped them. It did not actually eat them, because zombies had no appetite, but its chomping was effective. After that the Mundanes were more cautious.

"We have to clear the junk out of that moat," Dor said. "They can just about wade across, as it is now, and the monster can't get them all. If we do it now, while they're recovering from the shock of meeting Egor Ogre—"

"You have the makings of an excellent tactician," the Zombie Master said. "By all means handle it. I am working out your zombie restorative formula, which is devious in detail."

So Dor took a squad of zombies out. "I am mortal, so should not expose myself," he told them as he eyed the bog-monster. It had been trained not to attack other zombies, but that did not help him. "Arrows cannot kill you. So I will stand watch from the ramparts and call down directions. You will go down into the moat and start hauling armfuls of garbage out." He felt less than heroic in this role, but knew it was the expedient course. The Mundanes were surely excellent archers. He was here to get the job done, after all, not to make himself look good.

The zombies marched down. They milled about uncertainly. They did not have very good minds, their brains being mostly rotten. The healing elixir worked wonders with their bodies, but could not restore the life and intellect that had once made them men and animals. Dor found his original revulsion for their condition giving way to sadness. What zombie ever knew joy?

"You with the skullhead," Dor called. "Scoop up those water weeds and dump them on the shore." The zombies started in, laboriously. "You with the scarred legs—haul that log out and bring it to the front gate. We can use it to rebuild the door." It was almost pointless to explain such things to zombies, but he couldn't help himself. It was part of his process of self-justification.

If what he did had no permanence in this tapestry world, what of this present situation? But for him, the Mundanes would not have laid siege to the castle of the Zombie Master. If the Magician were killed, would he be restored after Dor departed the scene? Or was the siege inevitable, since the Fifth Wave had already been headed this way? It was a matter of history, but Dor could not recall the details, assuming he had ever learned them. There were aspects of history the centaur pedagogues did not teach their human pupils, and Dor had not been a terrifically attentive pupil anyway. He would remedy that when he got home again.

If he got home again . . .

A few arrows came from the forest to plunk into the zombie workers, but with no effect. That evidently gave the Mundanes pause for thought. Then a party of warriors advanced with swords drawn, intending to cut the zombies into pieces too small to operate. Dor used a bow he had picked up from the castle armory, ancient and worn but serviceable. He was no expert at this, but his body had evidently been trained to this weapon too; it was very much the compleat warrior. He fired an arrow at a Mundane but struck the one beside his intended target. "Good shot!" Millie exclaimed, and Dor was ashamed to admit the truth.

No doubt if he had let the body do the whole thing itself, it would have scored properly, but he had tried to select his own target. He had better stick to swords in future.

But it sufficed to discourage the attack, since this was just an offhand Mundane gesture, not a real assault on the castle. Also, they didn't know that there was only a single archer on the wall. The Mundanes retreated, and the moat-clearing continued. Dor was pleased: he was accomplishing something useful. It would be ten times as hard to storm the castle with that moat deep and clear. Well, maybe eight times as hard.

Meanwhile, Jumper was climbing about the rafters and inner walls of the castle, routing out vermin—which he gobbled with glee—and shoring up weak spots. He lashed subsiding members with silk cords, and he patched small holes, using wood and chinks of stone fastened in place by sticky masses of silk. Then he strung alarm lines across the embrasures to alert him to any intrusions there. This was a small castle, somewhat haphazardly constructed, with a single peaked roof, so in a short time the spider was able to accomplish much.

Millie went over the living and cooking facilities. The Zombie Master, a bachelor, had a good store of provisions but evidently survived mainly on those that required least effort to prepare: cheese balls, fried eggs from the friers that nested on the rafters, hot dogs from the dogwood that grew just inside the moat, and shrimp from the shrimp plants in the courtyard. The courtyard was south of the roofed region, so that the sunlight could slant in over the south wall to reach the ground inside; a number of plants and animals existed there, since the zombies did not bother them.

Millie set about making more substantial meals. She found dried fruits in the cellar, and dehydrated vegetables, all neatly spelled to keep them from spoiling, and cooked up a genuine handmade mashed peach and potato cobblestone stew. It was amazing.

And the Zombie Master, after due experimentation in his laboratory, produced for Dor a tiny vial of life-restorative elixir, brewed from the healing water by the art of his talent. "Do not mislay this, or use it incautiously," he cautioned. "The dosage suffices only for one."

"Thank you," Dor said, feeling inadequate. "This is the whole reason I came to this—this land. I can't tell you how important this vial is to me."

"Perhaps you could offer me a hint, however," the Magician said. "Since we are about to sustain a determined siege, from which we may not emerge—I admit a certain curiosity."

Delicately put! "I'm sorry about that," Dor said. "I know you prefer living alone, and if I'd known we'd cause all this trouble—"

"I did not say I objected to either the company or the trouble," the Zombie Master said. "I find I rather enjoy both. You three are comparatively simple people, not given to duplicity, and the mere presence of a challenge to survival evokes an appreciation for life that had been lacking."

"Uh, yes," Dor said, surprised. The Magician was becoming quite sociable! "You deserve to know." Dor was feeling generous now that he had this much of his mission accomplished, and the Zombie Master's candor was nice to receive. "I am from eight hundred years in your future. There is a zombie in my time I wish to restore to full life as a favor to—to a friend." Even in this moment of confidence, he could not quite confess his real interest in Millie. This vial would make her happy, and himself desolate, but the thing had to be done. "You are the only one who knows the formula for such restoration. So, by means of enchantment, I came to you."

"A most interesting origin; I am not certain I believe it. For whom are you doing this favor?"

"A—a lady." The thought of letting Millie learn of her eight-hundred-year fate appalled him, and he resolved not to utter her name. He had not had much luck in keeping such resolutions before, but he was learning how. What horror would this knowledge wreak on so innocent a maid, who screamed and flung her hair about and kicked her feet so fetchingly at the slightest alarm? Far better that she not know!

"And who is the zombie?" the Magician prodded gently. "I do not mean to pry into what does not concern me—but zombies do concern me, for surely every zombie existing in your day is a product of my magic. I have a certain consideration for their welfare."

Dor wanted to balk, but found that, ethically, he could not deny the Zombie Master this knowledge. "She—the lady calls him Jonathan. That's all I know."

The man stiffened. "Ah, the penalty of idle curiosity!" he breathed.

"You know this zombie?"

"I—may. It becomes a lesson in philanthropy. I never suspected I would be doing such a favor for this particular individual."

"Is he one of your zombies here at the castle?" Already Dor felt a tinge of jealousy.

"Not presently. I have no doubt you will encounter him anon."

"I don't *want* to—" No, he could not say that. What was to be, was to be. "I don't know whether it would be wise to tell him—I mean, eight hundred years is a long time to wait for restoration. He might want to take the medicine now, and then he wouldn't be there for the lady—" Which was itself a fiendishly tempting notion he had to suppress. The elimination of Jonathan from his own time would not only rid him of competition for Millie's favor—it would eliminate his whole reason for coming here. How could he restore a zombie who had already been restored eight centuries ago? But if he *didn't* do it—paradox, which could be fatal magic.

"A very long time," the Zombie Master agreed. "Have no concern; I will not betray your secret to any party." He dismissed the subject with a brusque nod. "Now we must see to the castle defenses. My observerbugs inform me that the Mundanes are massing for a major effort."

The defenders girded to meet that effort. Jumper guarded the east wall and the roof, setting up a series of traplines and interferences for intruders. The Zombie Master took the south wall, which enclosed the courtyard. Dor took the west. All were augmented by contingents of zombies, and of course the ogre handled the north gate. Millie remained inside—to watch for hostile magic, conjurations and such, they told her. No one wanted to put her on the ramparts during the violence, where her cute reactions would serve as a magnet for Mundanes. She also had charge of the supply of healing elixir, so she could come to the aid of the wounded.

The zombie bugs must have made excellent use of their elixir-restored eyes, for the attack occurred right on schedule. A wave of Mundanes charged the side of the castle. Not the front gate, where Egor's reputation more than sufficed, but the weakest wall—which happened to be Dor's.

They threw down logs to form a makeshift bridge, stationed men with outsize shields on either side of it to block the moat-monster, and funneled about half their number across. They carried three scaling ladders, which they threw up against the wall. The castle had been constructed foolishly, with a ledge above the first two stories, ideal for ladders to hook to. The ledge terminated abruptly at the corner where the courtyard commenced, but led to a small door near the northern edge. Presumably this access was intended to facilitate cleaning of the gutter spouts—but it also ruined the integrity of the castle's defense. A blank wall, with no ledge and no door, would have been so much better!

Dor stationed himself before the door and waited, hoping he was ready. His stomach was restless; in fact at the moment he felt in urgent need of a toilet. But of course he couldn't leave. None of them could leave their posts until the attack was over; that had been agreed. There was no telling what tricks the Mundanes might try to draw the defenders out of position, making the castle vulnerable.

Men swarmed up the ladders. They were met at the top by zombie animals: a two-headed wolf with rotting jaws but excellently restored teeth; a serpent with gruesomely articulated coils; and a satyr with sharp horns and hooves.

The first men up were evidently braced for human zombies; these animals unnerved them, causing them to be easy prey. Then Dor ducked in with a long crowbar—he had no idea what the crows used them for—and levered off the first ladder, pushing it away from the wall so that it fell with its burden into the moat. The splashing Mundanes screamed. Dor felt a shock of remorse; he would never be acclimatized to killing! Actually, he reminded himself, the fall was not far as these things went, and the watery landing was soft. But the men were in a certain amount of armor that hampered their swimming.

Dor moved to the next ladder, but this one was really hooked on tightly. The zombie serpent was having trouble holding off the onslaught. "What's holding you on?" Dor cried in exasperation as he labored to pry it up.

"I am an enchanted ladder," it replied. "The stupid Mundanes stole me from a stockade arsenal; they don't know my properties."

"What are your properties?" Dor inquired.

"I anchor irrevocably when emplaced—until someone utters the command 'weigh anchor.' Then I kick loose violently. This facilitates disengagement."

"Way anchor?"

"That doesn't sound quite right. It's weigh as in lifting, spoken with authority."

"Weigh anchor!" Dor cried with authority.

"Oooh, now you've done it!" the ladder cried, and kicked off violently, dumping its occupants into the moat.

Dor went on to the next. The delay at the second ladder had cost him vital time, however. The top warrior had gotten over his shock of encountering the satyr, and had hacked it to pieces. Now three warriors stood on the deck, with more crowding up. Fortunately there was not room for them to stand abreast; they were in a line, and until they moved, the fourth man could not dismount from the ladder.

The first Mundane gave a loud cry and brought his sword down on Dor as if chopping wood. Dor's body parried automatically blocking the descending sword with his crowbar so that it glanced off to the side. Simultaneously he dodged forward, coming inside the Mundane's guard, striking into the man's gut with his left fist. The man doubled over, and Dor caught his leg and heaved him over the parapet into the moat. He rose to face the next Mundane in one fluid motion.

This man was smarter about his attack. He came at Dor carefully, sword extended like a spear, forcing him back. The Mundane knew he did not need to slay Dor yet; all that was required was that he widen the stretch of ledge held by his forces, so that others could get off the ladder.

Dor, on the other hand, had to keep the man penned until he could eliminate him and the next man and get at the ladder. So he met the Mundane's thrust with his own, pointing the bar, refusing to give way. In this restricted locale, the crowbar was an excellent weapon.

The Mundane's eyes widened in an expression of astonishment. "Mike!" he cried. "You survived! We thought you were lost in that damned magic jungle!"

He seemed to be addressing Dor. It might be a ruse. "Look to yourself,

Mundane," Dor said, and forced the man's sword out of the way so he could shove him outward with his arm and shoulder.

The Mundane hardly tried to resist. "They told me there was a man looked like you, but I didn't believe it! I should've known the best infighter in the troop would make it okay! Hell, with your strength and balance—"

"Balance?" Dor asked, remembering how his body had walked Jumper's line across the river.

"Sure, you could've joined a circus! But you kept pushing your luck too far. What are you doing here, Mike? Last I saw you, we got separated by goblin bands. We had to cut out to the coast, thought you'd rejoin us—and here you are! Lost your memory or something?"

Then Dor's wedging prevailed, and the Mundane, surprised, toppled into the moat. Quickly Dor charged the third, jamming the dull point of his bar into the man's middle before he got his guard up, and this one also fell. Then Dor jammed his pole into the ladder hooks and wrenched so hard that a whole section of the stone parapet gave way and the ladder lost purchase. All the men on it fell screaming. The job was done.

Now, standing victorious on the edge, looking down, Dor suffered a multiple reaction. He had killed, again, this time not in ignorance or in the agony of reaction to his friend's mutilation, but to do his job defending the castle. Murder had become a job. Was that how he proposed to forward his career? The sheer facility with which he had done it—maybe that was partly the natural prowess of his body, but he had also used his talent to gain the ladder's secret. No, it was he himself who was responsible, and he felt a great and growing guilt—after the fact.

And the Mundane—that man had recognized Dor, or rather Dor's body, calling him Mike. That must mean this body *was* that of Mundane, part of this army, a man separated from his companions in the jungle, trapped by goblins, and presumed dead. Dor had taken over that body, preventing its return to its army. What had happened to the personality of the real Mike?

Dor bashed his hand against his head. The flea had bitten him again. Infernal bug! Oops—others called Jumper a bug, and Dor didn't like that; maybe the flea didn't like being called a—oh, forget it!

Where had he been, as he pondered things and watched the Mundanes drown below? Oh, yes: the fate of the personality of the original Mike Mundane. Dor couldn't answer that. He presumed the real Mike would return when Dor left. What bothered him more was the fact that he had taken advantage of the Mundane's recognition of him, to hurl the man from the wall. The Mundane had paused, not wishing to strike a friend—and had paid for the understandable courtesy with his position, perhaps his life. How would Dor himself feel if he encountered Jumper, and welcomed him—and Jumper struck him down? That had been a cruel gesture!

Nevertheless, he had held his position. He hoped the others had held theirs. He didn't dare check directly; this was his position to defend, and another ladder crew could arrive the moment he deserted his post.

War was not nice. If Dor ever got to be King, he would see that problems were settled some other way if at all possible. No one would ever convince him that there was any glory in battle.

The sun sank slowly before him. The Mundanes scrambled out of the moat, dragging their wounded and dead. They took their ladders, too, though these were sadly broken.

At last Millie came. "You can come down, now, Dor," she said hesitantly. "The zombie bugs say the Mundanes are too busy with their wounded to mount another attack today, and they won't do it by night."

"Why not? A sneak attack—"

"Because they think this is a haunted castle, and they're afraid of the dark."

Dor burst out laughing. It was hardly that funny, but the tension in him forced itself out.

It drained from him quickly. With relief he followed her down the winding stairs to the main hall. He noted the pleasant sway of her hips as she walked. He was noticing more things like that, recently.

They organized a night-watch system. There had been no attack on the other sides; Dor had handled it all, "We would have come to your aid," Jumper chittered. "But we feared some ruse."

"Exactly," Dor agreed. "I would not have come to help you, either."

"If we don't have discipline, we have nothing," the Zombie Master said. "We living are too few."

"But tonight you rest," Millie told Dor. "You have labored hard, and have earned it."

Dor didn't argue. He was certainly tired, and somewhat sick at heart, too. That business with the Mundane who recognized him . . .

Jumper took the first watch, scrambling all about the walls and ceilings inside and out. The Zombie Master retired for half a night's sleep before relieving the spider. That left Millie—who insisted on keeping Dor company while he ate and rested.

"You fought so bravely, Dor," she said, urging a soupnut on him.

"I feel sick." Then, aware of her gentle hurt, he qualified it. "Not from your cooking, Millie. From the killing. Striking men with a weapon. Dumping them into the moat. One of them recognized me. I dumped him, too."

"Recognized you?"

How could he explain? "He thought he did. So he didn't strike me. It wasn't fair to strike him."

"But they were storming the castle! You had to fight. Or we would all have been—" She squiggled, trying to suggest something awful. It didn't come across; she was delectable.

"But I'm not a killer!" Dor protested vehemently. "I'm only a twelve-year-old—" He caught himself, but didn't know how to correct his slip.

"A twelve-year veteran of warfare!" she exclaimed. "Surely you have killed before!"

It was grossly misplaced, but her sympathy gratified him strongly. His tired body reacted; his left arm reached out to enclose her hips in its embrace, as she stood beside him. He squeezed her against his side. Oh, her posterior was resilient!

"Why, Dor!" she said, surprised and pleased. "You like me!"

Dor forced himself to drop his arm. What business did he have, touching her? Especially in the vicinity of her cushiony posterior! "More than I can say."

"I like you too, Dor." She sat down in his lap, her derriére twice as soft and bouncy as before. Again his body reacted, enfolding her in an arm. Dor had never before experienced such sensation. Suddenly he was aware that his body knew what to do, if only he let it. That she was willing. That it could be an experience like none he had imagined in his young life. He was twelve; his body was older. *It could do it.*

"Oh, Dor," she murmured, bending her head to kiss him on the mouth. Her lips were so sweet he—

The flea chomped him hard on the left ear. Dor bashed at it—and boxed his ear. The pain was brief but intense.

He stood up, dumping Millie roughly to her feet. "I have to get some rest," he said.

She made no further sound, but only stood there, eyes downcast. He knew he had hurt her terribly. She had committed the cardinal maidenly sin of being forward, and been rebuked. But what could he do? *He did not exist in her world.* He would soon depart, leaving her alone for eight hundred years, and when they rejoined he would be twelve years old again. He had no right!

But oh, what might have been, had he been more of a man.

There was no attack in the night, and none in the morning—but the siege had not been lifted. The Mundanes were preparing another onslaught, and the defenders simply had to wait for it. While precious time slipped by, and the situation worsened for King Roogna. Magician Murphy was surely smiling.

Dor found Millie and the Zombie Master having breakfast together. They were chatting merrily, but stopped as he joined them. Millie blushed and turned her face away.

The Zombie Master frowned. He was halfway handsome after one acclimatized to his gauntness. "Dor, our conversation was innocent. But it appears there is something amiss between you and the lady. Do you wish me to depart?"

"No!" Dor and Millie said together.

The Magician looked nonplused. "I have not had company in some time. Perhaps I have forgotten the social niceties. So I must inquire somewhat baldly: would you take exception, Dor, if I expressed an interest in the lady?"

A green icicle of jealousy stabbed into Dor. He fought it off. But he could not speak.

Now Millie turned her large eyes on Dor. There was a mute plea in them that he almost understood. "No!" he said. Millie's eyes dropped, hurt again. Twice he had rejected her.

The Zombie Master shrugged his bony shoulders. "I do not know what else I can say. Let us continue our meal."

Dor thought of asking him to help the King, but realized again that what the Magician might do at his behest was suspect—and had an inspiration. What Dor himself did might lack validity, and what Jumper did—but what Millie did should hold up. *She* was of this world. So if she persuaded the Zombie Master to help the King—

A zombie entered. "Ttaakk," it rattled. "Hhoourr."

"Thank you, Bruce," the Zombie Master said. He turned to the others. "The Mundanes are organizing for another attack in an hour. We had best repair to our stations."

This time the attack came on Jumper's side. The Mundanes had assembled a massive battering ram. Not a real ram; those animals did not seem to have evolved yet. A mock ram fashioned from a heavy trunk of ironwood, mounted on wheels. Dor heard the boom and shudder as it crashed over the bridge they laid down over the moat and collided with the old stone. He hoped the wall was holding, but could not go to see or help: his post was here, not to be deserted lest another ladder attack come without warning. The others had had the discipline to stay clear of his section, last time, for the same reason. This was a special kind of courage, this standing aloof and ignorant.

An arrow dropped to his ledge. It had slid over the roof of the castle and fallen, its impetus spent. "What's the news over there?" Dor asked it.

"We're trying to batter a hole in the wall," the arrow said. "But that damned huge bug keeps yanking out our moat-crossing planks with its sticky lines. We're trying to shoot that spider, but it dodges too fast. Thing runs right across a sheer brick wall! I thought I had it—" The arrow sighed. "But I didn't, quite."

"Too bad," Dor said, smiling.

"Don't patronize me!" the arrow cried sharply. "I am a first-class weapon!"

"Maybe you need a more accurate bowman."

"That's for sure. More good arrows are ruined by bad marksmanship—oh, what's the use! If arrows ruled the world, instead of stupid people—"

Life was tough all over, Dor thought. Even for the nonliving. He did not speak to the arrow again, so it could not answer. Objects had to be invoked each time, initially. Only when he gave them a continuing command, voiced or unvoiced, as with the spiderweb that translated Jumper's chittering, did they speak on their own. Or when, through constant association with him, they picked up some of his talent, as with the walls and doors of his cheese cottage, his home.

How far removed that home seemed, now!

After a while the furor subsided, and Dor knew Jumper had succeeded in balking the attack. He considered going to check, since the threat had now abated, but decided to stay at his post. His curiosity was urgent, but discipline was discipline, even when it became virtually pointless.

And, quietly, a ladder crew came to his side. They were trying to sneak in! Dor waited silently for them to work their way across the moat and lift and hook the ladder and mount it. They thought he was absent or asleep, or at least not paying attention. How close they had come to being correct!

Then, just as the first Mundane came over the parapet, Dor charged across with his lever, wedged the ladder up, and shoved it away from the wall. He hardly noticed the screams and splashes as the men landed in the moat. By his constancy he had stopped the sneak raid and helped save the castle! Had he yielded to temptation and left his post prematurely . . .

He felt somewhat more heroistic than he had before.

Finally the zombie eye-spy announced that the Mundanes had withdrawn their main attack force, and Dor rejoined the others within. It was midday. They ate, then whiled away the long afternoon working on a jigsaw puzzle that Millie had discovered while cleaning the drawing room.

It was a magic puzzle, of course, for the jigs and saws were magical creatures who delighted in their art. When assembled, it would be a beautiful picture; but now it was in myriad little pieces that had to be fitted together. No two pieces fit unless spelled by the proper plea, which was often devious, and the portions of the picture that showed kept changing. The principle seemed to be similar to that of the magic tapestry of Dor's own time, with the little figures moving as in life. In fact—

"This is it!" Dor exclaimed. "We are weaving the tapestry!"

The others looked up, except for Jumper, whose eyes were always looking up, down, and across, without moving. "What tapestry?" Millie inquired somewhat coldly. She was still sweetly angry with him for his rejection of her.

"The—I, uh, I can't exactly explain," he said lamely.

Jumper caught on. "Friend, I believe I know the tapestry you mean," he chittered. "The King mentioned it. He is looking for a suitable picture to hang upon the wall of Castle Roogna, that will entertain viewers and be representative of what he is trying to accomplish. This one should do excellently, if the Zombie Master will yield it up."

"I yield it up to you," the Magician said. "Because I respect your nature. Take it with you when you return to Castle Roogna."

"This is generous of you," Jumper chittered, placing another piece. His excellent vision made him adept at this task; he could look at several places at once, superimposing them in his brain, checking the fit without ever touching the pieces. He paused to chitter at the piece he held, and it evidently understood the invocation, because it merged seamlessly into the main mass of the forming picture. "But unless we are able to assist the King, the Castle will never be complete."

The Zombie Master did not answer, but Millie looked up, startled. She caught Dor's eye, and he nodded. She had caught on!

But she frowned. Dor knew the problem: she was interested in him, Dor, and did not want to practice her charms on the Magician. She was in no position to understand why Dor eschewed her, or why he did not continue to plead the cause of Castle Roogna himself. So she was sullen, concentrating on the puzzle. The afternoon wore on.

The puzzle was fascinating, an excellent device for whiling away the tense time. They all seemed to share its compulsion, vying together against its challenge as if it were the Mundane army.

"I have always enjoyed puzzles," the Zombie Master remarked, and indeed he was the best of the human participants. His skeletal hands became quick and sure as they fetched pieces and jerked them across to likely slots, comparing, rejecting, comparing again and matching. Thin, gaunt, but basically healthy and alert, the Magician seemed more human with each hour that he passed in Millie's company. "The excitement of discovery, without threat. When I was a child, before my talent was known, I would smash blocks of stone with a hammer, then reassemble them into the original. Of course it lacked the cohesion—"

"Was that not an aspect of your talent?" Jumper chittered. "Now you reassemble creatures, but they lack the cohesion of life."

The Magician laughed, the first time they had heard him do that. He flung back his shaggy brown hair so that his eyebrow ridges and cheekbones stood out more prominently. "A significant insight! Yes, I suppose creating zombies is not so very different from restoring stones. Yet it becomes a lonely pursuit, because others—"

"I understand," Jumper chittered. "You are a normal creature, as I am, but this world does not see it that way. I have my own world to return to, but you have only this one."

"Would that I could go to your world," the Magician said, lightly but with a certain longing beneath. "To begin fresh, unprejudged. Even among spiders, I would feel more at home."

Millie did not speak, but her demeanor softened. They worked on the puzzle. It occurred to Dor that human relations were similar to such a puzzle, meshed by the conventions of language. If only he knew where the piece that was his whole life should be fitted!

"When I was young," the Zombie Master remarked after a bit, "I dreamed idly of marrying and settling down in the normal fashion, raising a family. I had no thought of being—as you see me now. I had better appetite, was more fully fleshed, was hardly distinguishable from normal boys. Then one day I found a dead flying frog, and was sorry for it, and tried to will it back to life, and—"

"The first zombie!" Millie exclaimed.

"True. I watched that frog fly away with amazement, thinking I had wakened the dead. But it was less than that; I could only half-waken the dead. Except, perhaps, in special cases." He glanced at Dor, obviously thinking of the restorative elixir. But that was more than the Zombie Master's magic; that incorporated the magic of the healing elixir too, so was a collaboration. "From that point, my career was set. Against my preference, I achieved far greater status and isolation than any other of my time. It seemed that many others desired what I could do for them—making zombie animals to guard their homes, or fight their battles, or do their work—but none cared to associate with me on a personal level. I became disgusted; I do not like being used without respect."

Millie's softening became something more. "You poor man!" she exclaimed.

"You three are the first who have associated with me without revulsion," the Zombie Master continued. "True, you came begging favors—"

"We didn't understand!" Millie cried. "These two are from another land, far away, and I am only an innocent maid—"

"Yes," the Magician agreed, looking at her with muted intensity. "Innocent, but with a talent that causes others to react."

"Except for the three of you," she said. "Every other man has wanted to grab me. Dor dumped me on the floor." She cast a dark look at him.

"Your friend restrains himself because he is not of your world and must soon depart, and cannot take you with him," the Zombie Master said. Dor was amazed and gratified at the man's comprehension. "He can thus make you no commitments, and is too much the gentleman to take advantage on a temporary basis."

"But I would go with him!" she cried naïvely.

Jumper interjected a chitter: "It is impossible, maid. There is magic involved."

Her chin thrust forward in cute rebellion.

"Yet if you cared to remain here at my castle, Millie, you could have a life of status—" the Magician began, then reined himself. "But also of isolation. That must be confessed."

"You really have a lot of company," Millie said. "The zombies aren't so bad when you get to know them. They have different personalities. They . . . can't help it if they're not quite alive."

"They are often better company than the living creatures," the Zombie Master agreed. "They do possess muted emotions and dim memories of their prior lives. It is ignorance that makes them suspect—the ignorance of the majority of normal people. All the zombies need are set jobs to do, and a comfortable gravesite to sleep in between tasks—and acceptance."

Dor listened, noting how Millie and the Magician were coming together, forcing himself to stay out of it. His direct involvement could invalidate anything that happened—if Murphy was right. Yet it bothered him increasingly, this attempt to use the Zombie Master, who was after all a decent man.

"I don't think I'd mind living among zombies," Millie said. "I met a girl zombie in the garden; I think in life she must have been almost as pretty as I am."

"Almost," the Zombie Master agreed with a smile. "She was slain by a pneumonia spell intended for another. But when I restored her, her family would not take her back, so she remains here. I regret that I cannot undo my magic, once it has been applied; she is doomed like the others to live half-alive forever."

"I screamed when I met the first zombie. But now—"

"I realize your primary interest is elsewhere," the Magician said, glancing obliquely at Dor. "But if, accepting the fact that you cannot be with him, you would consider remaining here with me—"

"I have to help the King," she said. "We promised to—"

The Zombie bowed to the inevitable. "For you, I would even indulge in politics. Ad hoc. Employ my zombies to—"

"No!" Dor cried, surprising himself. "This is wrong!"

The Zombie Master glanced at him expressionlessly. "You are after all asserting your interest in the lady?"

"No! I can't have her. I know that. But we stay here only because we are under siege, and the moment the siege lifts we'll go back to King Roogna. It is dishonorable to let her play upon your loneliness only to gain your help for the King. The end does not justify the mean." He had heard King Trent say that, in his own time, but had not appreciated its full meaning until now. End and mean —or was it ends and means? "You have been generous to me and Jumper, because you understood our needs and respected them. How could you respect Millie if—"

For the first time, they saw Millie angry. "I wasn't trying to use him! He's a nice man! It's just that I made a promise to the King, and I can't just go off and do something else and let the whole Kingdom fall!"

Dor was chagrined. He had not really understood her innocence. "I'm sorry, Millie. I thought—"

"You think too much!" she flared.

"Yet your thought does you credit," the Zombie Master said to Dor. "And your naïveté does you credit, too," he said to Millie. "I was aware of the ramifications. I am accustomed to trading for favors. This is not an evil, when the conditions of exchange are openly negotiated. I am simply prepared to compromise, in this circumstance. If it is necessary to save the Kingdom to make the lady happy, then I am prepared to save the Kingdom. Quid pro quo. I am pleased that the damsel keeps her word to the King so stringently; I can reasonbly suppose that she would similarly keep her word to you, Dor. Or to me, were she to give it."

"I haven't given it!" Millie protested. "Not to anyone! Not that way." But she seemed subtly flattered.

"The matter may be academic," Jumper chittered. "We are under siege here, and lack the means to do more than defend ourselves within this castle, with the aid of the loyal zombies. We cannot help the King anyway."

"And even if there were no siege," the Magician said, "I have suffered attrition of zombies. They are immortal, but when physically destroyed, with the pieces lost, they become useless. I could only bring a token force to the aid of the King. Not enough to overwhelm the curse on Castle Roogna."

"You could make more zombies," Dor said. "If you had more dead bodies."

"Oh, yes, without limit. But I need intact bodies, and fresh ones are best."

"Could we but overcome the Mundanes," Jumper chittered, "we could use their bodies to fashion a mighty army."

"If we had a mighty army, we could use it to vanquish the Mundanes," Dor pointed out. "Closed circle."

"I do not wish to interfere with human concerns," Jumper chittered. "But I believe I see a course through the impasse. There is some risk entailed—"

"There is risk entailed in remaining under siege," the Zombie Master said. "Present your notion; we can consider its merit jointly." He placed another piece of puzzle, uttering the mergeance spell under his breath.

"It is an arrangement, a series of agreements utilizing all our efforts," Jumper chittered. "The Zombie Master and Millie must defend this castle for a time alone, while I convey Dor outside by night. I can swing him along a line to a near tree so that no one will notice. The Mundanes can not see as well as I can in darkness. Then Dor must use his talent to locate some of the real monsters of the wilderness—the dragons and such—and enlist their aid."

"Dragons will not help men!" Dor protested.

"They would not be helping men," Jumper chittered. "They would be fighting men."

"But—" Then Dor caught on. "Mundanes!"

"But we are people too," Millie said.

Jumper angled his head to cock eyes of three different sizes at her. He was obviously not human.

"Well, still—" she faltered.

"I will be with Dor," Jumper chittered. "They will know me for a monster, and him for a Magician. Inside the castle will be another Magician and a woman, and many zombie animals. No normal human men. We will convey this promise: any monsters who die in the battle to lift the siege will be restored as zombies. But mainly, they will have the thrill of killing men with impunity. The King will not condemn them for what they do, since it is to assist him."

"It just might work!" Dor exclaimed. "Let's go!"

"Not until dark," Jumper chittered.

"And not until you've eaten," Millie added. She bounced off to the kitchen.

Jumper placed a final puzzle-piece and retired to an upstairs rafter to rest. That left Dor and the Zombie Master with the puzzle, which was coming along nicely. They had largely completed the center, with the scene of Castle Roogna, and were working toward the Zombie Master's castle. Dor was increasingly curious to know how it would turn out. Would they be able to see themselves in it, under Mundane siege? How much of reality did these magic pictures reflect?

"Are you really going to help the King?" Dor asked. "I mean, if we break the siege here?"

"Yes. To please the lady. And to please you."

Still Dor was troubled. "There is something else I must tell you."

"You are about to risk your life in the defense of my castle. Speak without inhibition."

"The lady . . . is doomed to die young. I know this from history."

The Zombie Master's hand froze, with a translucent piece of puzzle held between gaunt fingers. The piece changed from warm red light to cold blue ice. "I know that you would not deliberately deceive me."

Maybe he had spoken too uninhibitedly! "I would be deceiving you if I failed to warn you. She—maybe death is not the right word. But she will be a ghost for centuries. So you will not be able to—" Dor found himself overcome by remorse at what he could not prevent. "I think someone will murder her, or try to. At age seventeen."

"What age is she now?"

"Seventeen."

The Magician rested his head against his hand. The puzzle-piece turned white. "I suppose I could make a zombie of her, and keep her with me. But it wouldn't be the same."

"She—if you're helping the King to please her—or to please any of us—we'll all be gone within the year. So it may not be worth it, to—"

"Your honesty becomes painful," the Zombie Master said. "Yet it seems that if I am to please any of you, I must do it promptly. There may not again in my lifetime be opportunity to please anyone worth pleasing."

Dor did not know what to say to this, so he simply put out his hand. The Magician set down the puzzlepiece, which had turned black, and shook Dor's hand gravely. They returned to the puzzle, speaking no more.

The puzzle, Dor wondered—for his mind had to get away from the grim prior subject. How could this puzzle be the tapestry, when they were all within the tapestry? Was it possible to enter this forming picture, by means of a suitable spell, and find another world within it? Or had the tapestry been merely a gateway, the entry point, not the world itself? Was it coincidence that he should be assembling this particular picture at this juncture? The Zombie Master was the key to this whole quest, the vital element—and he had the tapestry, the key to the entry to this world. Yet he had given it to Jumper. How did this relate?

Dor shook his head. Such mysteries were beyond his fathoming. All he could do was . . . what he could do.

Chapter 8

Commitment

That night Dor and Jumper departed the castle on the spider's line. It would have been possible to convey Millie out in the same manner, but they cared neither to subject her to the risk nor to desert the Zombie Master, even had circumstances been otherwise. There were Mundane sentries posted; Millie would have screamed, and that would have been disastrous. As it was, Dor trusted Jumper's night vision to thread them through the dark foliage, and they managed to pass without being detected. Soon they were deep in the jungle, beyond the Mundane ring of troops.

"We'd better start with the lord of the jungle," Dor said. "If he goes along with it, most of the rest will. That is the nature of jungles."

"And if the lord does not cooperate?"

"Then you will use your safety line to yank me out of his reach, in a hurry."

Jumper affixed a dragline to him, then carried the other end. In an emergency, the spider would be able to act quickly. Dor found himself wishing he had a silk-making gland; those lines were extremely handy.

The spider found him a rock in the dark. "Where is the local dragon king?" Dor demanded of it.

The stone directed him to a narrow hole in a rocky hillside. "This is it?" Dor inquired dubiously.

"You'd better believe it," the cave replied.

"Oh, I believe it!" Dor said, not wishing to antagonize the residen of the monster he hoped to bargain with.

"And if you care to depart uncooked, you'd better not wake the monarch," the cave said.

Jumper chittered. "That small cave has a large mouth."

"What?" the cave demanded.

Dor gulped. "I have to wake him." Then he put his hands to his mouth and called. "Dragon! I must parlay. I have news of interest to you."

There was a snort from deep within the cave. Then a plume of smoke wafted out, white in the blackness, followed by a rolling growl. The scent of scorch suffused the air.

"What does he say?" Dor asked the cave.

"He says that if you have news of interest, come into his parlor. Your life depends on the accuracy of your advance promotion."

"His parlor?" Jumper chittered. "That is an ominous phrasing. When a spider invites—"

Dor had not bargained on this. "In there? In the dragon's cave?"

"See any other caves, man-roast?" the cave demanded.

Jumper made another soft chitter. "Huge mouth!"

"I guess I'd better go down," Dor said.

"I have better night vision; let me go," Jumper chittered.

"No. You can't use objects to translate the dragon's speech, and I can't jump into trees and string a line to the castle wall. I must talk with the dragon. You must be ready to bear the news." He swallowed again. "In case my mission fails. You can communicate with Millie, now, by signals."

Jumper touched him with a foreleg, the pressure expressive. "Your logic prevails, friend Dor-man. I shall listen by this entrance, and return alone if necessary. I will draw you up by the dragline if you call, rapidly. Have courage, friend."

"I'm scared as hell." But Dor remembered what the gorgon had said about courage: that it was a matter of doing what needed to be done despite fear. He was bleakly reassured. Maybe technically he would be a dead hero, instead of a dead coward. "If—if something happens, try to salvage some piece of me, and keep it with you. I think the return spell will orient on it, and carry you home when the time is up. I wouldn't want you to be trapped in this world."

"It would not be doom," Jumper replied. "This world is a novel experience."

More of an experience than Dor had bargained for! He took a breath, then slid into the cave's big mouth. The interior was not large enough to permit him to stand, as the throat constricted, but that did not mean the dragon was small. Dragons tended to be long and sinuous.

The passage curved down and around, so black it was impossible to see. "Warn me of any drops, spikes, or other geographic hazards," Dor said.

"There are none, other than the dragon," the wall replied. "That's more than enough."

"I wish there were a little light," Dorm uttered. "Too bad I gave away my wishing ring."

The dragon growled from below. "You want light?" the wall translated. "I'll give you light!" And tongues of bright flame snaked up the passage.

"Not that much!" Dor cried, cringing from the heat.

The flames subsided. It was evident that the dragon understood human speech, and was not blasting him indiscriminately. That was both reassuring and alarming. If there was anything more dangerous than a dragon, it was an intelligent dragon. Yet of course the smartest dragon would be most likely to rise to leadership in the complex hierarchy of the wilderness. Provided it also possessed sufficient ferocity.

Dor emerged at last in the stomach of the cave. This was the dragon's lair. The light waxed and waned, here, as the monster breathed and the flames washed out of his mouth. In the waxing the whole cave glittered, for of course the nest was made of diamonds. Not paltry ones like those of the small flying dragon Crunch the ogre had cowed; huge ones, befitting the status of the lord of the jungle. They refracted the light, reflected it, focused it, and broke it up into rainbow splays. Colors cascaded across the walls and ceiling, and bathed the dragon itself in re-reflected hues. Crunch the ogre would never beard *this* monster in his den!

And the dragon himself: his scales were mirror-polished, iridescent, and as supple and overlapping as the best warrior's mail. The great front claws were burnished brass tapering to needlepoints, and its snout was gold-plated. The eyes were like full moons, their veins reminiscent of the contours of the green cheese there, and as the light changed the cheese changed flavor.

"You're beautiful!" Dor exclaimed. "I've never seen such splendor!"

"You damn me with faint praise," the dragon grumped.

"Uh, yes sir, I come to—"

"What?" the dragon demanded through a blaze of fire.

"Sir?"

"That was the word."

Dor had suspected it was. "Uh, sir, I—"

"All right already. Now what does a Man-Magician want with the likes of me, a mere monster monarch?"

"I come to, uh, make a deal. You know how it is not safe, uh, I mean expedient, for you to, uh, eat men, and—"

The dragon snorted a snort of flame uncomfortably close to Dor's boots. "I eat what I eat! I am lord of the jungle."

"Yes, sir, of course. But men are not of the jungle. When you eat too many of them, they start making, er, difficulties. They use special magic to—"

"I don't care to talk about it!" This time the snort was pungent smoke.

"Uh, yes. Sir. What I'm trying to say is that there are some men who need, er, eating. Mundane men from outside Xanth, who don't have magic. If you and your cohorts cared to, uh—"

"I begin to absorb your drift," the dragon said. "If we were to indulge in some, shall we say, sport, your Magicians would not object? Your King Whatshisname—?"

"King Roogna. No, I don't believe he would object. This time. Provided you ate only Mundanes."

"It is not always easy to tell at a glance whether a given man is native or Mundane. You all taste alike to us."

Good point. "Well—we'll wear green sashes," Dor said, thinking of some bedspreads he had seen in the Zombie Master's castle. They could be torn into sashes. "It would be only in this region; don't go near Castle Roogna."

"Castle Roogna is in the territory of my cousin, who can be touchy about infringements," the dragon said. "There is plenty to eat in this area. Those Mundanes are especially big and juicy. I understand. Is there a time limit?"

"Uh, would two days be enough?"

"More than enough. Shall we say it commences at dawn tomorrow?"

"That's fine."

"How can I be sure you speak for your King?"

"Well, I—" Dor paused, uncertain. "I suppose it would be best to verify it. Do you have a swift messenger?"

The dragon snapped his tail. It was out of sight, far down the bowels of the cave, but the report was authoritative. It was answered by a squawk, and in a moment a chickenlike bird fluttered into the main chamber. It was a woolly hen, with curly fleece instead of feathers. Dor knew little about this breed, except that it was shy, and could move quite rapidly.

"Uh, yes," he said. "Uh, have you anything to write with?" He had certainly come unprepared.

The dragon jetted smoke toward a wall. Dor looked. There was a niche. In the niche were several papershell pecans and an inkwood branch. "I have a secretary-bird," the dragon growled in explanation. "She likes to write to her cousin across the Gap. Then she carries the letter herself, because she trusts no one else to do it. Why she doesn't simply chatter out her gossip directly I don't know. But she's good at keeping track of things around here such as which monster needs a chomping and which a scorching, and when the next rainstorm is due, so I keep her on. She's across the Gap now; she'll set up an unholy squawk when she finds her stuff's been used, but go ahead and use it."

Dor unfolded a length of paper from a shell, took a splinter of inkwood, and somewhat laboriously wrote:

KING ROOGNA: PLEASE AUTHENICATE PERMISSION FOR MONSTERS TO SLAY MUNDANES FOR TWO DAYS WITHOUT PENALTY. NECESSARY TO LIFT MUNDANE SIEGE OF CASTLE OF ZOMBIE MASTER, WHO WILL COME TO YOU THEREAFTER. ALL XANTH CITIZENS IN VICINITY TO WEAR GREEN SASHES TO DISTINGUISH THEM FROM MUNDANES. SIGNED, MAGICIAN DOR.

He folded the note and gave it to the woolly hen. "Take this to the King, and return immediately with his answer."

The bird took the note and took off. She was gone in a puff of wool dust, so quickly that he never saw her move.

"I must admit this prospect pleases me," the dragon king remarked, idly stirring up a mound of diamonds with one glistening claw. "If it should fall through, I might recall how you disturbed my sleep. Don't count on your spider friend to draw you out; my flame would burn up his line instantly."

The nature of the threat was absolutely clear to Dor. He felt like screaming and kicking his feet, certain that would relieve some tension; it always seemed to work for Millie. But he wore the guise of man; he had to act like a man. "I was aware of the hazard when I committed myself to your lair."

"You do not attempt to beg, or to threaten me with vague retribution," the dragon said. "I like that. The fact is, it is impolite to toast Magicians, and I especially do not want to aggravate the Zombie Master. That roc of his has been scouring the area for bodies. I would not care to tangle with that big bird for esthetic reasons. So I do not intend to toast you—unless you attempt to do me mischief."

"I thought that might be your attitude. Sir."

The woolly hen returned in another cloud of dust, bearing another note. Dor took it and read it aloud:

PERMISSION AUTHENTICATED. GO TO IT. SIGNED, THE KING.

He showed it to the dragon.

"That would seem to be it," the dragon said, puffing out a satisfied torus of smoke. "Hen, go out to my subjects and summon them for a rampage. Tell them to get their tails swinging or I'll burn them off. I will instruct them in one hour." He angled his snout toward Dor. "It has been a pleasure doing business with you, sir."

But Dor was wary. He remembered Magician Murphy's curse on Castle Roogna: anything that could go wrong, would. This message had related to that project. Why hadn't the curse operated? This had been too easy.

"You had better depart before my cohorts arrive," the dragon said. "Until I instruct them, they will consider you and the spider fair game."

"Uh, I—" Then Dor had an idea. "Let me just check something, sir. A mere formality, but . . ." He addressed the paper he held. "Did you come from the King?"

"I did," the paper replied.

"And the message you bear really is his message?"

"It is."

"Your magic seems to endorse this message," the dragon said. "I am satisfied. Why question it?"

"I'm just . . . cautious. I fear something could have gone wrong."

The dragon considered. "Obviously you are not experienced with conspiracies and bureaucratic entanglements of the sort we encounter in the wilderness. Ask it which King."

"Which King?" Dor repeated blankly.

"The Goblin King," the paper answered.

Dor exchanged a dismayed glance with the dragon. "The Goblin King! Not King Roogna?"

"No," the paper agreed.

"That idiotic bird!" the dragon exploded, almost singeing Dor with his fiery breath. "You sent it to the King, without specifying which King, and the Goblin King must have been closer. I should have realized the response came too fast!"

"And naturally the Goblin King sought to mess us up," Dor concluded. "Murphy's curse *did* operate. A misunderstanding was possible, so—"

"Does this mean we have no deal?" the dragon inquired ominously through a ring of smoke.

"It means our deal has not been authenticated by King Roogna," Dor said. "I'm sure the King would agree to it, but if we can't get a message through—"

"Why would the Goblin King authenticate it? I have had some experience with goblins, and they are not nice creatures. They don't even taste good. Surely the goblins should be more pleased to foul up our deal than to facilitate it. The goblins have no love for men, and not much for dragons."

"That *is* strange," Dor agreed. "He should have sent a note saying 'deal denied,' so we couldn't cooperate. Or else just held it without answering, so we would be stuck waiting."

"Instead he gave exactly the response we wanted from the Human King, so we would not delay," the dragon said. He puffed some more smoke, thoughtfully. "What mischief would occur if beasts started slaying men in great numbers, without approval?"

Dor considered that. "A great deal of mischief," he decided. "It would become a matter of principle. The King can't allow unauthorized slaying; he is opposed to anarchy. Such an act could possibly lead to war between the monsters and all the King's men."

"Which could result in internecine slaughter, leaving the goblins dominant on land," the dragon concluded. "They already have considerable force. Those netherworld goblins are tough little brutes! I think your kind would have real trouble, were it not for the distraction the harpies pose to the goblins. The one thing those creatures do well is breed. There are now a great many of them."

"Well, one man can slay five goblins," Dor said.

"And one dragon can slay fifty. But there are more than that number per man or dragon."

"Um." Dor agreed pensively.

"Do you know, I would have been fooled by that note, if you had not questioned the paper," the dragon remarked. "I do not like being fooled." This time it was not smoke but a ring of fire that he puffed. The thing wafted up the tunnel entrance, rotating, glimmering like a malignant eye.

"Neither do I," Dor agreed, wishing he could puff fire.

"Would your King have any objection if a few goblins got incidentally chomped during the rampage?"

"I think not. But we'd better get another message to King Roogna."

"While we allow the goblins to think they have fooled us into an act of interspecies war."

Dor smiled grimly. "Have you another messenger—a more reliable one?"

"I have other messengers—but let us use your talent this time. We shall send a diamond from my nest to your King, along with the paper; he must return the diamond with his spoken reply. No lesser man would give up such a jewel, and no other but you could make it speak."

"Terrific!" Dor exclaimed. "It is hard to imagine any goblin faking *that* message! You are a genius!"

"You praise me with faint damns," the dragon growled.

It was almost dawn by the time Dor rejoined Jumper. Quickly they returned to the castle with their news.

Millie and the Zombie Master greeted them with joyed relief. "You must be the first to have *our* news," the Magician said. "Millie the maid has done me the honor of agreeing to become my wife."

"So the commitment has been made," Jumper chittered.

"Congratulations," Dor said, with highly mixed emotions. He was glad for the Zombie Master, who was a worthy Magician and a decent man. But what of himself?

Millie made green sashes for them all, including the spider, who settled for an envelope covering his abdomen. Then she fed them a breakfast of hominy from another plant she had discovered in the courtyard. The Zombie Master had worked all night making new zombies from the corpses the roc had found, so that the castle defenses were back to full strength.

The Zombie Master radiated a mood of restrained joy. He knew Millie would not live long, but at least he had snatched his meager share of paradise from what was available.

Mille seemed less elated, yet hardly upset. It was evident that she liked the Magician, and liked the life he offered her, and was being practical—yet there was the restraint born of Dor's presence, and of his rejection of her. They all understood the situation, except for a couple of elements. Millie did not know how soon she would perish; neither Dor nor the Zombie Master knew how she would die, for she had never spoken of that to Dor in his own world. Also, none of them were certain how the coming campaign would turn out; maybe the aid of the zombies would not be enough to bring victory to King Roogna. Yet overall, Dor felt this was the best contentment they could achieve with what they had. He tried not to look at Millie's delightful figure, because his body was too apt to respond.

I wish I were a man, he thought fiercely. As it was, how much difference was there between him and a zombie? His mind animated an otherwise largely defunct body. The Magician's magic animated the zombies. But of course zombies did not notice the figures of women. They had no interest in sex.

Then what about Jonathan Zombie, in his own time? Why did he cleave to Millie, instead of resting quietly in some nice grave? If Millie's sex appeal did not turn him on, what else motivated him? Did some zombies, after all, get lonely?

Well, if Dor got back to that world, and managed to restore Jonathan, he would inquire. There had to be something different about Jonathan, or Millie would have fled him centuries before, while she remained a ghost.

So many little mysteries, once he got on that tack! Maybe what Dor needed was not more answers, but fewer questions.

The Mundanes attacked again at dawn, this time rolling a huge wagon up to the moat. It had a projecting boom, tall enough to match the height of the outer wall and long enough to reach right across the moat. They could march their soldiers right across this to the castle! They must have worked all night, building it, and it was quite a threat.

Then the monsters struck. The lord of the jungle had really produced! He led the charge, galumphing from the deepest forest with a horrendous roar and a belch of flame that enveloped the wooden tower. Behind him came a griffin, a wyvern, a four-footed whale, several carnivorous rabbits, a pair of trolls, a thunderbird, a sliver cat, a hippogriff, a satyr, a winged horse, three hoopsnakes, a pantheon, a firedrake, a monoceros, a double-headed eagle, a cyclops, a flight of barnacle geese, a chimera, and a number of creatures of less ordinary aspect that Dor could not identify in the rush. This seemed to be the age of monsters; in Dor's own day, the dragons were more common and the others less so. Probably the fittest had survived the centuries better, and the dragons were the fittest of monsters, just as men were the fittest of humanoids and the tanglers were the fittest of predatory plants. Right now the Land of Xanth was still experimenting, producing many bizarre forms.

The Mundanes were no cowards, however, and they outnumbered the assorted monsters. They formed a new battle array to meet this onslaught, swordsmen to the fore, archers behind. Dor, Millie, Jumper and the Zombie Master watched from the ramparts with gratified amazement as the battle swirled around the castle, leaving them out of it. Now and then a flying monster buzzed them, but sheered off when it spied their green sashes. The Dragon King seemed to have excellent discipline in his army! Dor was glad once more that he had been brought up to understand the importance of cooperation; the monsters were an invaluable asset.

Yet was this not the result of his own action, rather than Millie's? Would it turn out to be invalid in the end? Millie had persuaded the Zombie Master to help King Roogna, so that was valid—but if this help could only arrive in time through Dor's agency, did it become invalid? It was so hard to know!

Right now, however, all he could do was hope Murphy was mistaken, meanwhile enjoying the battle. The Dragon King completed his charge to the burning wooden wagon tower, and chomped the boom in half with a single rearing bite. There was nothing quite like a dragon in combat! The Mundane archers rained arrows upon the polished scales, but the missiles bounced away without visible effect. The swordsmen slashed at the armored hide, but only blunted their blades. The dragon swept his great glittering tail about, knocking men off their feet and piling them in a brutal tangle of arms and legs. He swung his snout around the other way, burning another swath. Dor was glad he was not out there himself, trying to fight that dragon. There were wild stories about single men slaying large dragons in fair combat, but that was folklore. The fact was no single man was a match for even a small dragon, and no twenty men could match a large one. Anyone who doubted this had just to watch an engagement like this one, where fifty armed men in battle formation could not even wound the King of Dragons.

Meanwhile the other monsters were busy. The winged horse was rearing and stomping; the rabbits were gnawing into legs; the double-headed eagle was plucking eyeballs neatly from their sockets and swallowing them whole, the satyr was—Dor stared for a moment in amazement, then forced his gaze away. He had never imagined killing men that way. The more formidable monsters were laying about them with similar glee, reveling in an orgy of slaughter. For centuries they had restrained themselves from attacking men too freely, for men could be extremely ornery about vengeance. Now the monsters had license. Now, and perhaps never again.

The Mundanes, however, were tough. They had no magic of their own, but compensated by being extremely disciplined in combat and skilled with their weapons. Quickly realizing that they could neither prevail nor escape on the open battlefield, they fell back to natural and artificial defenses. The burning wagon made a good barricade, and next to it the moat made another. Mounds of dirt and debris had been formed by the dragon's thrashing tail, and these made excellent cover. The archers, nestled behind such shelter, were scoring on the lesser monsters, bringing down the barnacle geese and rabbits and hurting the thunderbird and sliver cat. The swordsmen were mastering the trick of sliding their blades up under the scales of the armored creatures, penetrating to their vital organs. Perhaps a quarter of the Mundanes had perished in the initial clash, but now half the monsters were dead or injured, and the tide of the battle was turning. Dor had never anticipated this. What phenomenal brutes men were!

"Now we must assist our allies," the Zombie Master said.

"Oh no you don't!" Millie protested protectively. "You'll get killed, and I haven't even married you yet."

"My life is complete, receiving such a caution from such as you," the Magician murmured.

"Don't make fun of me! I'm worried."

"There was no fun intended," he said seriously. "All my life I have longed for attention like this. Nevertheless, there is an obligation to acquit."

"No!"

"Peace, my dear. Zombies cannot die."

"Oh." Her innocence became her yet.

Dor, hearing this brief dialogue, suffered again his bit of jealousy. Yet he recognized that Millie had found in the Magician as good a man as was available. The Zombie Master loved her, but loved honor too. He knew she was to die, yet was going to marry her. He had the kind of discipline Dor was striving to master. For the Zombie Master, there was no special conflict between love and honor; they merged.

The Magician sent out a zombie contingent, wearing green sashes. Both monsters and Mundanes were startled. But the monsters let the zombies pass without hindrance. The undead charged into the Mundane positions, picking up fallen weapons along the way and hacking with unsteady but gruesome conviction.

The Mundanes had come to fight zombies. Yet they were taken aback by this sally, and repulsed by the repulsiveness of the half-dead things. The living men overreacted, hacking violently at the things in their midst—and scoring on each other.

Then the monsters rallied and bore in again. The zombies had made the difference; the defensive positions of the Mundanes were overrun, and the carnage resumed.

But the monsters were tired now, and some were pausing to glut themselves on the bodies of slain Mundanes. The monsters had been great in ferocity, not number, and some were dead. The Mundanes still outnumbered them, and after their lapse with the zombies, their excellent fighting discipline reasserted itself. The tide of battle was turning again, despite the zombies' efforts. There were too few of them to last long.

Then some wickedly smart Mundane caught on to the significance of the green sashes. He ripped one from a dismembered zombie and put it around himself. And of course the monsters did not attack him.

"Disaster!" Dor exclaimed, remembering Murphy. "In a moment they'll all be wearing green!" He started for the front gate."

"I will swing us down," Jumper chittered. "It is faster."

"But—" Millie started, appalled. Dor experienced a flush of gratitude: she was solicitious of his welfare, too.

Jumper fastened a dragline to Dor's waist. Dor jumped over the parapet. Jumper played out the line, letting him drop swiftly but carefully into the moat.

Millie made a stifled scream, but Dor was all right. The water softened the impact, and the commotion outside was such that not even the moat-monster noticed him. He sloshed to land. Jumper bounded to ground, then skated on the surface of the water to make sure Dor was all right.

No one paid attention to them. They passed the griffin, who was busy disemboweling a Mundane; the creature glanced up, saw the sashes, and returned to its business. Dor and Jumper proceeded unmolested to the nearest green-sashed Mundane. The man was laying about him with vigor, slashing at the chimera, who was backing off uncertainly. The monster didn't know whether it was legitimate to crunch this greenclad foe, however obnoxious the man became.

Dor had no scruples. He charged up, sword bared. The Mundane saw him.

"Come, friend—let's get this dumb monster!" And Dor's blade ran him through. The Mundane's only reaction as he died was surprise.

"Okay, chimera—go to it!" Dor urged the monster. The chimera, its doubt resolved, returned to the attack against unsashed Mundanes.

Dor proceeded to the next green-sashed Mundane. Now a scruple caught up to him. He felt a twinge of guilt for what he was doing, until he reminded himself that it was the same thing the Mundanes were doing: masquerading as a friend. If they hadn't started impersonating monster-exempt humans, they would not have been fooled by the real green-sashes. Dor was merely restoring the validity of the designations. So the scruple paused, then reluctantly retreated. A battlefield was not a fit home for scruples.

Jumper was an anomaly: he resembled a monster, yet wore the sash. A wyvern glanced at him, startled, then returned to the fray. Jumper looped silk around a sashed Mundane, chomped him neatly on the head with his chelicerae nippers, and went on. The spider was enjoying this; after all, these Mundanes had tortured him by pulling out four of his legs.

Thanks to Dor and Jumper's activity, the monsters swung into a slow ascendency again. The Mundanes did not stem the tide this time; they fell back toward their base camp, taking losses, pressed by monsters, zombies, and Dor and Jumper. The battle was almost over.

Then another smart Mundane popped up. Smart Mundanes were a nuisance! He ducked under Dor's swing, came in close, and ripped Dor's sash from his body. "Now fight!" he screamed.

Dor's return thrust skewered him. But the damage was done. The sash was buried under the body, and the hippogriff was bearing down on him. There was now no way Dor could distinguish himself from the Mundanes.

The hippogriff had the forepart of a griffin and the hind part of a horse. That gave it excellent fighting ability, coupled with superior running ability. The eagle's beak and claws stabbed viciously forward. Dor danced aside, then cut at a wing with his sword. He didn't strike too hard, because he did not want to hurt or kill a creature on his own side, but he had to defend himself. It was the hippogriff's turn to take evasive action. But then it closed its wings and bore in again, and Dor knew he could not survive the onslaught long. The monster was too big, too fast, too strong; it was wary of Dor's sword, but able to dodge it. The hippogriff was tired, but so was Dor.

"Jumper!" Dor cried. But then he saw that Jumper was engaged with three unsashed Mundanes, and could not extricate himself, let alone come to Dor's rescue. The four-footed whale rose up between them, opening its huge cetacean maw to engulf-gulp a Mundane; it incidentally blocked off Dor's approach to Jumper. Now he had nowhere at all to go. Oh, this was terrible!

But the Zombie Master, high in the castle, was watching out for him. Millie's faint scream came, and there was a spark of sunlight from her swirl of hair; then the Magician's faint command: "Egor!" And the zombie ogre charged out of the castle, bearing a gargantuan club. He swept aside Mundanes and monsters alike, bearing down on Dor.

Until he encountered the land whale. This monster was simply too big to move, and it was not about to give way to an ogre, even a green-sashed zombie ogre. The whale did not attack; it just hulked. It had the head and tusks of a boar, and rows of spikes on its body, with powerful lion's legs: a slow but formidable creature. The ogre had to make a detour around it—and in that critical period of delay, the hippogriff spread its wings, fanned a cloud of battle dust into Dor's face so that he was momentarily blinded, and clawed swiftly at his sword, disarming him. Dor threw up his arms in a futile defensive gesture—

And found himself lifted high, unharmed. Startled, he blinked vision back into his watering eyes, getting the dust out, and discovered himself hooked on the long tip of the Dragon King's tail. Fifty feet away, the dragon's snout growled, emitting puffs of smoke.

"What's he saying?" Dor demanded of a stone as he was being carried past.

"Better be more careful of your sash, Magician!" the stone translated.

The Dragon King had recognized Dor, and saved him. In a moment Dor was dumped beside the moat, out of the fray. The tail snaked back, to merge with Jumper. "With your concurrence," the Dragon roared, "I will personally slay a few sashed men. There are none here on your side, apart from the zombies, correct?"

"Correct!" Dor cried, thankful for the dragon's perspicacity. The regular monsters might not know the difference, but the Dragon King obviously did.

"No wonder he is King," Jumper chittered. The spider had lost a foot, but was otherwise intact. "We must get back inside the castle; the monsters will prevail."

"Right. Should we call back Egor?"

"He is having such a good time; let him rampage."

They re-entered the castle, where Millie was waiting with healing elixir. In a moment the spider's foot was whole, and Dor's many abrasions were gone.

Millie hugged Jumper briefly, turned to Dor, and refrained from making a similar gesture. After all, she was now betrothed to another man. They returned to the upper ledge to watch the conclusion of the battle.

In this installment, the monsters were mopping things up. The tough Mundanes became less tough as they perceived defeat looming, and finally they broke and fled. The monsters pursued, cutting them down without mercy. The vicinity of the castle was deserted, the ground strewn with the bodies of men and monsters, and with struggling pieces of zombies.

"Now I must work," the Zombie Master said. "Dor, if you will supervise the carrying of bodies to my laboratory, I will render them into loyal zombies. It will require a few minutes and some effort for each, so you need not hurry—but the faster we perform, the stronger the zombies will be. Also, we shall need to march within a day, to reach King Roogna's castle in time to be of service."

Dor nodded agreement. He saw how tired the Magician looked, and remembered that he had spent all the prior night making new zombies. The man needed a rest! But that would have to wait. After all, Dor himself had had no more rest.

They organized it and got to work. Millie spotted the best corpses of man and animal, now so accustomed to the gore that she worked without even token screams. Dor carried the bodies to a staging area. Jumper attached lines and hauled the objects across the moat to the castle. They concentrated first on Mundanes. When a number of these had been animated, the new zombies took over the labor of transporting corpses, and the pace accelerated. Soon there was a backlog of bodies awaiting the Magician's attention.

The Dragon King returned. He was spattered with blood, and several of his mirror-scales had been hacked off, but he was in fairly good condition. "That was some fun!" he growled. "There is not a man alive, here." There was no flame when he spoke; he had used it all up for the nonce.

"Oh, let me give you some elixir!" Millie exclaimed. She sprinkled some on him, and the dragon was instantly restored to full health. Then she went to the other monsters straggling back, and restored them similarly.

"One could almost get to like a creature like that, human though she be," the dragon said reflectively. "There is something about her—"

"The dead we shall reanimate as zombies, as promised," Dor said quickly.

"No need. The survivors will consume the dead, as is our custom. We do not care to become zombies."

"We have been taking the intact corpses. If you are satisfied to eat the dismemberd ones—"

"They will do nicely." And the monsters fell to their repast, crunching up bodies. It was a strange and grisly scene: dragon and griffin and serpent, ripping into corpses, while zombies carried other corpses around them in sepulchral silence, and the pretty maid Millie wandered amid it all sprinkling healing elixir.

"Where is Egor?" Jumper chittered.

Good question! There was no sight of the zombie ogre who had fought so valiantly to rescue them. They spread out, searching.

"You mean the ogre?" the Dragon King inquired, ripping the delicious guts out of a Mundane and smacking his long lips. "He got in a bit of trouble down by the Mundane camp, last I noted."

They ran down to the deserted camp. There, in pieces, was Egor Ogre. The last surviving Mundanes had hacked him to quivering pieces.

"Maybe we can still help," Dor said, his stomach roiling. He had become acclimatized to gore, but this was a friend! "Let's collect all we can find of him, put it together, and sprinkle some elixir."

They did this—and the ogre was restored, except for part of one hand and foot and some of his face they had not been able to locate. The zombie could no longer speak, and walked with a limp. But in his condition that was not too noticeable. They trekked back to the castle.

"Would you monsters care to join us at Castle Roogna?" Dor inquired. "I'm sure the King—the Man King—would welcome your help."

"Fighting whom?" the Dragon King inquired, slurping a tasty intestine.

"Goblins and harpies, mostly."

The dragon snorted a smoke helix. "Now I do have a gripe against the Goblin King, but let's not lose our perspective. Killing men is fun; killing other monsters is treason. We cannot join you there."

"Oh. Well, sir, we certainly thank you for—"

"Our pleasure, sir." The dragon dipped a tooth into the body and brought out a splendid liver. "I haven't eaten this well in fifty years. I'll catch my death of a stomachache." He slurped the liver down.

"Uh, yes," Dor agreed. Liver had never been his favorite food, and after this he doubted that taste would change.

"Since we monsters will not be participating, but do have a grievance against the goblins and no liking for harpies, I feel free to make a comment," the dragon said, fixing a bright eye on Dor. "This battle for the zombie castle has only been your rehearsal for the siege to come. The goblins are tougher than men. Prepare well—better then you did this time, or you are doomed."

"Tougher than Mundanes? But goblins are so small—"

"Heed my warning. 'Bye." The Dragon King moved off in quest of another succulent corpse.

Dor shook his head, ill at ease. If the dragon thought the upcoming battle would be worse . . .

They returned to the castle, where the Zombie Master was still hard at work. A new zombie army was shaping. The others helped all they could, but this was the Zombie Master's labor, and his magic alone sufficed. He worked through the day and into the night, growing even more gaunt than usual—but the zombies continued to shuffle out of the laboratory and form ranks in the courtyard. There had been a great number of Mundanes!

They ate a restive supper of poached jumping beans and bubblejuice, with the beans jumping into the juice at odd moments. Millie forced some on the Magician, who continued working. Most of the bodies were gone from the surrounding landscape now; the monsters had gorged themselves and staggered off to their lairs with toothy smiles and a final fusillade of belches. A zombie detail was burying the uneaten, unusable fragments. The night settled into morbid silence.

Finally the last corpse was done. The Zombie Master sank into a sleep like a coma, and Millie hovered near him worriedly. Dor and Jumper slept too.

Chapter 9

Journey

In the morning, early but not bright, they set off for Castle Roogna. It would have been easiest to have the roc carry them singly to the Castle, but two things argued against this. First, there was an army of about two hundred and fifty zombies to transport, and for this number marching seemed to be the only way. Second, the skies were now being patrolled by aerial sentinels, harbingers of the harpies. The roc, huge as it was, would be torn apart in midair by the vicious creatures, if they decided it was an enemy. As perhaps it was.

The Zombie Master had lived as a recluse so long that he was only vaguely familiar with the terrain, and Dor had not viewed the scenery with an eye to zombie travel when he rode in. The zombies tended to shuffle, and their feet snagged on roots and vines, tripping them or even ripping off their feet. The majority were Mundane zombies, sounder of body than the older ones; but these were as yet inexperienced and prone to accidents. So it was necessary to scout ahead for a suitable route: one more or less level, voiding dangerous magic, and reasonably direct.

Dor and Jumper did the scouting, with the man checking the lay of the ground and the spider reviewing the threats lurking in the trees. They worked together to flush out anything uncertain, to determine whether it should be ignored, eliminated, or avoided.

When they had determined a suitable portion of the route, they set magic markers along it for the zombie army to follow. All they had to do was stay well ahead, so that they had time to backtrack and change the route if necessary.

The wilderness of Xanth was not as sophisticated now as it would be in Dor's own time; the magic had not had as much time to achieve the devastating little refinements and variations that made unprotected paths so hazardous. But there was plenty of raw magic here, and no enchanted paths to follow. Overall, Dor judged the jungle to be as dangerous for him as anything he had known—if he allowed himself to get careless.

One of the first things they ran afoul of was dog fennel. The plants had evidently been taking a canine nap, noses tucked under tails, but woke ugly when Dor blundered into them. First they barked; then, gathering courage, they started nipping. Angered, Dor laid about him with his sword, clearing a circle. Then he suffered regret as the creatures yiped and whined, for they really were no threat to him. Each dog grew on a stem, rooted in the turf, and could not move beyond its tether. Its teeth were too small to do much harm.

Jumper had jumped right out of the pooch-patch, unnipped. The dogs were whimpering now, cowed by the sight of their dead packmates. It was a sad sight.

Dor strode out of the patch, bared blade held warningly before him, feeling low. Why did he always react first and think last?

"Yet an animal plant who bites strangers must suffer the consequence," Jumper chittered consolingly. "I fell among aphids once, and their ant-guardians attacked me and I was forced to kill a number of them before the rest gave over. Had they any wit, they would have realized that my presence was accidental. I had been fleeing a deadly wasp. Spiders prefer consuming flies, not aphids. Aphids are too sickly sweet."

"I guess ants aren't very bright," Dor said, comforted by the analogy.

"Correct. They have excellent inherent responses, and can function in societies far better than spiders can, but as individuals they tend to be rigid thinkers. What was good enough for their grand-ants remains sufficient for them."

Dor felt much better now. Somehow Jumper always came through, rescuing him from physical or intellectual mishap. "You know, Jumper, when this quest is over, and we return to our own worlds—"

"It will be a sad parting," Jumper chittered. "Yet you have your life to pursue, and I have mine."

"Yes, of course. But if we could somehow stay in touch—"

Dor broke off, for they had suddenly come upon the biggest fennel of them all. It was as massive as Dor himself, with a stem like a tree trunk, reaching its horned head down to graze in the nearby grass.

"That more closely resembles a herbivorous animal," Jumper chittered. "See, its teeth are grazers, not flesh renders."

"Oh, a vegetable lamb," Dor said. "A historical creature, extinct in our day. It grows wool to make blankets from. In my time we cultivate blanket trees directly."

"But what happens when it grazes everything within its tether range?" Jumper inquired.

"I don't know." Dor saw that the grass had been mowed quite low in the disk the lamb could reach; little was left. "Maybe that's why they became extinct."

They went on. The terrain was fairly even here; the zombies would have no problems. Dor set his markers as they went, certain this route would be all right. They approached a wooded section, the trees bearing large multicolored blooms whose fragrance was pleasant but not overwhelming. "Be on guard against intoxicating fumes," Dor warned.

"I doubt the same chemicals would intoxicate me," the spider chittered.

But the scents were innocent. Bees buzzed around the flowers, harvesting their pollen. Dor passed under the trees without molestation, and Jumper scrambled through them. Beyond the trees was an attractive glade.

There was a shapely young woman, brushing her hair. "Oh, pardon me," Dor said.

She smiled. "You are a man!"

"Well—"

"Are you lonely?" She stepped forward. Jumper dropped down from the trees, a little to one side.

What Dor had first taken as clothing turned out on closer inspection to be overlapping green leaves, like the scales of a dragon. She was a soft, sweet-smelling creature, with a pretty face.

"I—uh—we're just on our way to—"

"I live for lonely men," she said, opening her arms to embrace him. Dor, uncertain what to do in this case, did nothing; therefore she succeeded in enfolding him. Her body was cool and firm, her lips sweet; they resembled the petals of roses. His body began to react, as it had with Millie; it wanted to—

"Friend," Jumper chittered, standing behind the green-leafed woman. "Is this customary?"

"I—don't know," Dor admitted, as her lips reached hungrily for his.

"I refer to the shape of the female," the spider chittered. "It is very strange."

Maybe it was, to a spider! "It—seems to be—" Dor paused, for her lips had caught up to his. Oh, she was intriguing! "To be a good shape," he concluded after a moment. Those breasts, that slim waist, those fleshy thighs—

"I hesitate to interrupt your ritual of greeting. But if you would examine her backside—"

"Uh, sure." Her frontside was fully interesting enough, but he did not object to seeing the rest. His body well knew that an attractive woman was interesting from any side. Dor drew back a bit and gently turned the woman around.

From behind, she was hollow. Like a plaster cast made of some object, or a pottery bowl shaped on a rock. She was a mere solidified shell. She had no functioning internal organs at all, no guts. Cracks of light showed through the apertures where her eyes, nostrils, and mouth were in the front.

"What are you?" Dor demanded, turning her about again. From the front she remained extremely womanly.

"I am a woodwife," she replied. "I thought you knew. I comfort lonely men."

A façade covering absolute vacuity! A man who made love to such a creature—

"I—uh, guess I don't need that kind of comfort," Dor said.

"Oh." She looked disappointed. Then she dissolved into vapor, and drifted away.

"Did I do that?" Dor asked, chagrined. "Did I make her into nothing? I didn't mean to!"

"I think she existed only for whatever man she might encounter," Jumper opined. "She will no doubt re-form for the next traveler."

"That will likely be a zombie." Saying that, Dor felt humor bubbling up inside him, until it burst out his mouth in a laugh. "A zombie lover!" Then he remembered Millie's lover of his own time, Jonathan, and sobered. It wasn't funny at all!

They went on. The glade opened into a rocky valley. The rocks were irregular, some of fair mass, with cuttingly sharp edges: a disaster for zombies. But down the center was a clear path, with only a little coronet supported on four hornlike twigs in the way. All they had to do was remove that object and its supports, and the path would be clear.

Dor moved toward it—then paused. This was suspicious. "Something wants us to touch that coronet," he said.

"Allow me." Jumper fastened a small stone to a line of silk, and tossed it at the coronet.

The ground erupted violently. A snake emerged, whose head bore the four horns; it had lain buried in the ground except for those points. The reptile struck at the stone as Jumper jerked it along on the string, making it seem alive. "Lucky we checked," Dor said, shaken. "Better you than us, stone."

The stone shuddered. "Oh, the poison!" it wailed, and fragmented into gravel.

"That must have been some poison!" Dor exclaimed.

"It was," the gravel agreed, and fractured into a mound of sand.

"What would poison do to a zombie?" Jumper inquired.

"Nothing, I think. How can you kill a thing that is already dead?"

"Then we can ignore the hornworm."

Startled, Dor had to agree. "Except we must post a warning for Millie and the Zombie Master, so they know to send a zombie ahead." He walked back and emplaced a magic marker of the WARNING type. When they saw that, they would send Egor Ogre ahead to spring the trap. If the hornworm was smart, it would scoot right out of there!

The valley spread into a field of grassy growth dotted with Mundanish trees. It was pretty scenery—but all of this country was lovely, and improving as they went. If only he had watched more carefully when he rode the dragon horse! One missed a lot by riding swiftly.

Then he recognized the vegetation. "Roats!" he exclaimed happily. "If there are any mature ones—"

"What are roats?" Jumper chittered.

"A cereal. Soak old roats in water or milkweed, and they transform into excellent porridge." He shook some stems, obtaining the flat kernels. "And those are primitive mixed-nut trees."

"Nuts grow on trees?" the spider inquired dubiously.

"With magic, all things are possible." Dor went to a tree and took hold of a cluster of nuts, drawing it down. They clung to the branch. "These are tough nuts!" he said. Then the cluster let go, and he staggered back. The branch snapped up, and a small hail of nuts fell about him. One shot by his nose, and he coughed. Others came, and he coughed again. "Oh, no—some of them are cough drops!" he said, retreating.

But he had his old roats and mixed nuts. "Now all I need is water."

The field dropped down to a river, its liquid crystalline but not, fortunately, crystal. Catfish swam in it, meowing hopefully as they spied Dor, then stalking away as well as their flukes permitted when they saw there was no red meat. A pack of sea dogs sniffed up, but soon spied the cats and went baying after them. Obviously this water was wholesome.

Dor dipped his double handful of substance into a pothole, and abruptly had a doughy mass of food. He offered some to Jumper, but the spider declined, preferring to fish the river for crabs. So Dor ate his potroats himself, enjoying it immensely.

However, this seemingly excellent route was cut off by the same river they had looked for. The stream was small but deep; no trouble for Jumper and Dor to cross, but disaster for the marching zombies, who would never emerge from it intact. Wading in the quiet moat had been one thing; swimming across the current was another.

It would be possible to fell some trees to form a crude bridge across the water, but this would take time and possibly alert hostile magic. So they followed the river down a way, looking for a better fording place. It was never possible to anticipate what lay ahead; there could be some natural bridge just out of sight.

There was not. There was a hill. The river flowed merrily up over it and down the other side. Dor and Jumper contemplated this, wondering what to do. A river that flowed up as well as down was unlikely to be tractable. "I could make a silk sling to swing them across one by one," Jumper chittered.

"That would wear you out and take forever," Dor objected. "And we would have to wait here until the zombies arrive, instead of scouting out the dangers ahead. We need a bridge or a ford."

They followed the river over the hill. "I wonder whether we could divert it temporarily," Jumper chittered.

"We'd still have to get the zombies across it *some*where," Dor pointed out. "Unless we could turn it back on itself—and that hardly seems reasonable."

At the top of the hill, a cockfish crowed. "Oh, shut up," Dor told it. But it was alive, so did not obey him.

At the foot of the other side of the hill was an orc: a huge fat water monster with teeth overflowing its mouth. The water flowed over and around it; no point in trying to cross the stream here!

They returned to the top of the hill. "I'd hate to backtrack all the way and try to scout a new route," Dor said. "This is an excellent route for the zombies—up until this point. We've got to figure out a way across!"

"What makes it flow uphill?" the spider inquired.

"Magic, of course. Something in the ground here that makes it seem to fall, when actually it is rising."

"I note a different texture of stone, here. Would that be it?"

"Could be. Enchanted stone. The magic can't be in the water itself, or it would be floating right up into the sky, I think." Now Dor wondered how water did get into the sky, to make it rain. Maybe there were streams that fell upward. So much of the magic of Xanth was unexplained! "But if we moved the stone, the river would merely change channels, and then that orc would get dry and come looking for us. The only thing madder than a wet hen is a dry orc. We need to cross the river, not move it."

"Still, we might experiment." Jumper poked a leg into the water, shifting stones. The water responded by rising higher, forming a little arc in air, then dropping back into its channel.

"Say—if we could make it jump high enough, we could pass right under it!" Dor exclaimed. He plunged in, helping Jumper to move the enchanted stones.

The river rose higher and higher. At last an arch formed, leaving the riverbed clear for several feet. "If we can lift it just a little higher, so they can walk under it without ducking—" Dor said eagerly. He moved another handful of stones.

"Perhaps we should refrain from—" Jumper warned.

"Nonsense! It's working beautifully. We don't want the zombies to touch the water at all, because they would get washed out, and they're too stupid to duck properly." Dor scooped some more.

And, abruptly, the river overturned. Instead of arcing forward, it arced backward, forming a loop in the air. It splashed to the ground at the base of the hill, then continued on up and over.

"Oh, no!" Dor cried ruefully. For of course now there was no arch. The river landed beside its original channel, then flowed back into it at the top of the hill and on as before. Instead of fashioning a bridge of water, they had doubled the course of the stream. "We'll have to move it again."

"No," Jumper chittered. "We might create further difficulties. We can cross it this way." And he showed Dor how there was a narrow channel between the parallel slopes of the river as it spiraled through the air. The water was rising in the west and falling in the east, crossing overhead. It was in fact a variant of the original arch; now the passage across went north-south instead of east-west.

Dor had to agree. He place a magic marker at the loop, and they went on. What a remarkable feature of the landscape they were leaving for the zombies to find!

Just as they departed, there was a surprised "Oink!" as a seahog was carried through the loop. Dor chuckled.

The landscape beyond the river remained pleasant. It was the nicest region he had seen. He was really enjoying this trek, a complete change of pace from the violence just past, and hoped Jumper was enjoying it too. All too soon they would arrive at the Castle, completing their mission, and after that it would be time to go home. Dor really wasn't eager to return so soon.

The best path curled down into the deeper valley, where the river meandered across to form a handsome lake. Dor marveled at this; in his own day this entire section between the Good Magician's castle and Castle Roogna was deep jungle. How could it have changed so extensively? But he reminded himself yet again that there was no accounting for magic.

Beside the lake was a small mountain, its base the same size as the lake. Perhaps a thousand paces in diameter, were it possible to pace either mountain or lake. Yet the lake looked deep, and the mountain tall; though the water was clear, the depths were shrouded in gloom, while snow capped the peak. So both these features of the landscape were probably magically augmented, being much larger than they seemed.

This was another type of magic Dor didn't understand. What spell kept snow from melting from the tops of the highest mountains? Since the heights were closest to the hot sun, the heat there had to be fierce, yet they acted as if it were cold. What was the purpose in such a spell? Was it the work of some long-gone Magician whose talent was turning hot to cold, permanently? No way to know, alas. Well, he might climb up there and inquire of the features of the landscape —but that would be a lot of work, and he had other things to do. Maybe after he returned to his own time . . .

People were there, in the water and on the mountain and prancing between. Lovely nude women and delicately shaggy men. "I think we have happened on a colony of nymphs and fauns," Dor remarked. "They should be harmless but unreliable. Best to leave them alone. The problem is our best route passes right between mountain and lake—where the colony is thickest."

"Is it not feasible to march that route?" Jumper chittered.

"Well, nymphs—you know." But of course the spider didn't know, having had no experience with humanity prior to this adventure. "Nymphs, they—" Dor found himself unable to explain, since he was not certain himself. "I guess we'll find out. Maybe it will be all right."

The nymphs spied Dor and cried gleeful welcome. "Gleeful welcome!" They spied Jumper and screamed horror. "Horror!" They did little kick-foot dances and flung their hair about. The goat-footed fauns charged up aggressively.

"Settle down," Dor cried. "I am a man, and this is my friend. We mean you no harm."

"Oh—then it's all right," a nymph exclaimed. "Any friend of a man is a friend of ours." There was a shower of hand-clapping, and impromptu dances of joy that did marvelous things to the nymphly anatomy.

Good enough. "My name is Dor. My friend is Jumper. Would you like to see him jump?"

"Oh, yes!" they cried. So Jumper made a fifteen-foot jump, amazing them. It was not nearly as far as he could go when he tried. Obviously he was being cautious, so they would not know his limitations—just in case. Dor was slowly catching on to adult thinking; it was more devious than juvenile thinking. But he was glad he had thought of the jump exhibit; that made the spider a thing of harmless pleasure, for these people.

"I'm a naiad," one nymph called from the lake. She was lovely, with hair like clean seaweed and breasts that floated enticingly. "Come swim with me!"

"I, uh—" Dor demurred. Nymphs might not be hollow in quite the way woodwives were, but they were not quite the same as real women either.

"I meant Jumper!" she cried, laughing.

"I prefer to skate," Jumper chittered. He stepped carefully onto the water and slid gracefully across it.

The nymphs applauded madly, then dived into the lake and swam after the spider. Once their confidence had been won, it was complete!

"I'm a dryad," another nymph called from a tree. Her hair was leaf-green, her nails bark-brown, but her torso was as exposed and lush as that of the water nymph. "Come swing with me!"

Dor still had not learned how to handle this sort of offer, but again he remembered the hollow woodwife. "I, uh—"

"I meant Jumper!" But the spider was already on the way. If there was one thing he could do better than skating water, it was climbing trees. In a moment the other dryads were swarming after him. Soon they were squealing with glee, dangling from silken draglines attached to branches, kicking their feet.

Dor walked on toward the mountain, vaguely disgruntled. He was glad his friend was popular; still—

"I'm an oread," a nymph called from the steep side of the mountain. "Come climb with me!"

"Jumper is busy," Dor said.

"Oh," she said, disappointed.

Now a faun approached him. "I see you aren't much for the girls. Will you join us boys?"

"I'm just trying to scout a route through here for an army," Dor replied shortly.

"An army! We have no business with armies!"

"What *is* your business?"

"We dance and play our pipes, chase the nymphs, eat and sleep and laugh. I'm an orefaun, associated with the mountain, but you could join the dryfauns of the trees if you prefer, or the naifauns of the pool. There really isn't much difference between us."

So it seemed. "I don't want to join you," Dor said. "I'm just passing through."

"Come for our party, anyway," the faun urged. "Maybe you'll reconsider after you see how happy we are."

Dor started to demur, then realized that the day was getting late. This would be a better place to spend the night than the wilderness—and he was curious about the life and rationale of these nymphs and fauns. In his own day such creatures were widely scattered across Xanth, and highly specialized: a nymph for every purpose. The fauns had largely disappeared. Why? Perhaps the key was here.

"Very well. Just let me scout the terrain a little farther, then I shall return for your party." Dor had always liked parties, though he hadn't gone to many.

People had objected to his talking to the walls and furniture, learning about all the private things that went on under the cover of the formal entertainment. Too bad—because the informal entertainment was generally far more intriguing. There seemed to be something about adult people; their natures changed when they got into small groups, especially when such groups consisted of one male and one female. If what they had to do was good and wholesome, why didn't they do it in full public view? He had always been curious about that.

The fauns danced about him merrily, playing their little flutes, as he walked beyond the lake and mountain. They had horn-like tufts of hair on their heads, and their toenails had grown so heavy as to resemble hooves, but they remained human. In the following centuries the horns and hooves would become real, as the fauns took on their distinct magical identities. He had thought they were real when he first spied the fauns here, but his mind's eye had filled in more detail than was justified.

Dor realized that if he or any other man so chose, he could join them, now, and his own hair and toenails would develop similarly. It made sense; the hooves were much better for running about rocky terrain than ordinary feet were, and the horns were a natural defense, albeit as yet token, that could not be carelessly lost the way other weapons could. And as for dancing—those neat, small, hard feet were much better than Dor's own huge soft flat things. Suddenly he reminded himself of a goblin.

The subspecies of fauns were already distinguishable, as were the species of nymphs. The dryfauns of the forest had greenish hair and bark-brown fur on their legs and lower torsos, and their horns were hooked to enable them to draw down fruit. Their hoof-toes were sharp, almost spiked, so that they could climb sheer trunks, though as yet they had little difficulty walking on land. Perhaps that was the key to their eventual demise as a species, when they became so specialized they could not leave the trees, and something happened to those trees—yes.

The orefauns of the mountains had more powerful legs, their hooves merging like those of goats or deer. Even their hands were assuming a certain hooflike quality, to enable them to scamper up on all fours, and their horns curled back to enable them to butt.

The naifauns of the lake had flattened flipper-hooves and horns pointing straight up like speartips; they speared foolish fish on them when hungry. They had delicate scales on their nether portions instead of fur.

A naifaun saw Dor looking at him. "You should see my cousin the nerefaun," he called, splashing cheerily. "He lives in the sea at the foot of the river, and he has scales like those of a sea serpent, and full flipper feet. He can really swim—but he can hardly walk on land."

Scales and flippers for the sea-faun. Could this specialization eventually lead to the merfolk, the tritons and their counterparts the mermaids, who had lost their legs entirely in favor of a tail? Yet he had already encountered a triton here —no, that was at Good Magician Humfrey's castle, eight hundred years hence. There were no naifauns and nerefauns in Dor's own time because they had become sea and lake tritons, and the naiads and nereads had become mermaids. He was witnessing the first great radiation of the species of nymph and faun, experiencing firsthand the evolution of a major branch of the creatures of Xanth. It was absolutely fascinating!

And subtly horrifying, too—for this was the ongoing dehumanization of Man. There had been much killing in the land of Xanth, but even so, the population had declined over the centuries more than the bloodshed could account for. Because human beings had deserted their kind, becoming such subspecies as these: tritons and mermaids. Eventually, if this continued, there would be no true humans remaining in the Land of Xanth. That was what King Trent was trying to reverse, by establishing contact with Mundania. He wanted to infuse Xanth with new, pure human stock—without suffering another disastrous Wave of conquest. Now Dor appreciated far more clearly the importance of this project. His own parents, Bink and Chameleon, were deeply involved in this effort. "Go to it, parents!" he murmured fervently to himself. "What you are doing is more important than what I am doing."

Meanwhile, he was neglecting what he was doing: the survey of the zombie route. Dor looked about, discovering himself in a realm of increasing brush. The plants seemed harmless, but they grew larger and taller toward the west. Possibly in the heart of their range they would achieve the status of trees. Some had branches sticking up from the top, bare of leaves, with cross branches projecting at right angles. These looked vaguely familiar to Dor, but he could not quite place them. If they represented a threat, what form did it take? They weren't tangle trees, or poison brambles, or needle-cacti. What was there about them that bothered him?

He thought of questioning stray rocks, but didn't want to reveal the nature of his magic in the presence of the fauns. If he became worried enough, he would use his talent; for now he was just looking.

"What are these bushes?" he asked the orefaun, who seemed uncomfortable here on level ground, but had braved it out for the sake of companionship. "Are they dangerous?"

"We never go this far," the orefaun admitted. "We know there are dangers beyond our territory, so we never stray. What is there elsewhere to interest us anyway?"

"Why, the whole world is interesting!" Dor said, surprised.

"Not to us. We like it where we are. We have the best place in Xanth, where monsters don't come and the weather is always nice and there is plenty of food. You should taste our mountain dew!"

"But—but it is so broadening to travel," Dor protested, remembering guiltily how little he had traveled before he entered the tapestry. Yet he knew this aventure had already matured him considerably.

"Who wants to be broadened?"

Dor was taken aback. If these creatures really weren't interested—

"Suppose something happened to this place, so that you had to move? You should at least explore more widely, so you are prepared."

"Why be prepared?" the orefaun asked, perplexed.

Dor realized that the difference between him and these creatures was more than physical. Their whole mutual attitude differed. To question the need for preparedness—why, that was childlike.

Well, he was gaining increasing understanding of the roots of the faunish disappearance in Xanth. Of course the nymphs had similar shortsightedness, but there would always be a market for lovely nude girls, so their survival was more secure. *Anything* that looked like a pretty girl had its market—even hollow mockups like the woodwives. Perhaps, like the harpies, the nymphs would evolve eventually into a single-sex species, mating only with males of outside species.

Dor saw that the orefaun was in distress, so relented and turned about. "I think this is a good route; I'll explore the rest of it tomorrow, with Jumper."

The orefaun was greatly relieved. He danced back toward the mountain, and was soon joined by the less adventurous fauns. "Time for the party!" he cried, doing a caprine skip. The others picked it up as a chant: "Party! Party!"

They made a bonfire between mountain and lake, piling on dry bon-brush and igniting it with a small irritable salamander. The salamanders of Dor's day started fires that burned all substances except the ground itself, but this was a primitive ancestor who made a merely ordinary fire, fortunately. This fire would burn only wood, and could be extinguished.

They put marshmallows—from a mallow bush in the marsh at one end of the lake—on sticks and toasted them in the flames. The lake nymphs and fauns brought out fresh sea cucumbers and genuine crabs for Jumper. Hot chocolate bubbled up from one side of the lake, making an excellent beverage. The tree creatures brought fruits and nuts, and the mountain creatures rolled a huge snowball down to make cold drinks. Dor did sample the mountain dew, and it was effervescent and tasty and heady.

The nymphs and fauns sat in a great circle around the fire, feasting on the assorted delicacies. Dor and Jumper joined them, relaxing and enjoying it. After they had stuffed, the fauns brought out their flutes and piped charmingly intricate melodies while the nymphs danced. The female bodies rippled and bounced phenomenally; Dor had never before seen anything like this!

Soon the fauns responded to the anatomical signals, discarded their flutes, and joined the dance in a most unsubtle manner. Before long it was not a dance at all, but the realization of the ritual the dance had only suggested. These creatures did indeed do openly what the adults of Dor's day did in privacy!

"Is this normal procedure?" Jumper inquired. "Forgive my query; I am largely ignorant of the ways of your species."

"Yes, this is a regular festival celebrating the rites of spring," the orefaun said.

"No festivals for the other seasons?" Dor inquired.

"What other seasons? It is always spring here. Of course, the rites don't result in babies; it has something to do with our immortality. But it's fun to celebrate them anyway. You are welcome to join in."

"Thank you; I regret this is not my species," Jumper demurred.

"I, uh—I'll just wait," Dor said. His body certainly felt the temptation, but he didn't want to commit himself prematurely to this life. The mental picture of the woodwife returned.

"As you wish. No one is forced to do anything, here, ever. We all do only what we want to do." He watched the proceedings another moment. "Speaking of which—pardon me." The orefaun leaped forward to nab a passing oread. The nymph screamed fetchingly, flung her hair about, and kicked up her cute cloven feet, giving Dor a feeling of *déjà vu* and a glimpse of what clothing normally concealed. Then the faun brought her down and did what evidently delighted them both. Dor made mental notes; if he ever had occasion, he wanted to know how to proceed. He was already certain that never again would he see a nymphly girl kick her feet without thinking of this scene. A new dimension of meaning had been added to the action.

"If they are immortal, and bear no hatchlings," Jumper chitterd, "how then do they evolve?"

Dor hadn't thought of that. "Maybe they themselves just keep changing. With magic—"

"Come, join me!" a cute naiad cried, wiggling her delicately scaled hips dextrously.

"I regret—" Jumper began.

"I meant Dor!" she cried, laughing. Dor noted what these laughs and screams did to the nymphs' chest area; was that why they did such exhalations so often? "Take off those silly clothes, and—" She gave a little foot kick.

"Uh, I—" Dor said, finding himself strongly tempted despite all his private reservations. After all, if the nymph were willing—

But it would be the first step in joining this colony, and he just wasn't sure that was smart. An easy life, filled with fun—yet what was the future in it? Was fun the ultimate destiny of Man? Until he was sure, he had better wait.

"At least you should try it once," she said, as if reading his mind. Probably such mind reading was not difficult; there was only one channel a man's mind would be in, at this stage.

There was an ear-rending roar. A torrent of dark bodies burst upon the party. It was a goblin horde!

"Press gang! Press gang!" the goblin leader cried, making a gap-toothed grin of joyous malice. "Anybody we catch is hereby impressed into the goblin army!" And he grabbed a dryfaun by the arm. The faun was substantiually larger than the goblin, but, paralyzed by fear, seemed unable to defend himself.

The nymphs screamed and dived for water, trees, and mountain. So did the fauns. None thought to stand up, close ranks, and oppose the raiders. Dor saw that there were only about eight goblins, compared to a hundred or more fauns and nymphs. What was the problem? Was it that goblins inspired terror by their very appearance?

Dor's hand went for his sword. Goblins did not inspire terror in *him!* "Wait, friend," Jumper chittered. "This is not our affair."

"We can't just sit here and let them take our friends!"

"There is much we do not know about this situation," the spider chittered.

Ill at ease but respecting Jumper's judgment, Dor suffered himself to be restrained. The goblins quickly ran down five of the healthiest fauns, threw them to the ground, and bound them with vine-ropes. The goblins were capturing, not slaying; they wanted men fit for their army. So Jumper had been correct in his caution, as usual: Dor would have gained nothing by laying about him with his blade. Not anything worth gaining, anyway.

Yet still his mind was nagged: what sort of creatures were these fauns who welcomed strangers yet refused to assist each other in an emergency? If they did not fight for their own—

"That's five," the goblin sergeant said. "One more good one, we need." His darkly roving eye fell on Dor, who stood unmoving. "Kill the bug; take the man."

The goblins closed on the pair. "I think it has just become our affair." Dor said grimly.

"It seems you are correct. Perhaps you should attempt to parlay."

"Parlay!" Dor exclaimed indignantly. "They mean to kill you and impress me into their army!"

"We are more civilized than they, are we not?"

Dor sighed. He faced the goblin sergeant. "Please desist. We are not involved in your war. We do not wish to—"

"Grab him!" the goblin ordered. Evidently these goblins did not realize that

Dor was not merely a larger faun: a creature who could be expected to match five goblins in combat. The seven others dived for Dor.

Jumper bounded over their heads while Dor's sword flashed in its vicious arc. That was one thing this sword was very good at. Two goblins fell, blood oozing and turning black. Then Jumper's silk caught the sergeant, and the spider trussed him up with the efficiency of eight trained legs.

"Look to your leader!" Dor cried, smashing another goblin down.

The remaining four looked. The sergeant was virtually cocooned in silk and helpless. "Get me out of this!" he bawled.

The others rushed to him. They had not been eager to fight Dor anyway, once the ratio dropped from seven to one down to four to one. Now they knew they had a fight on their dirty little hands.

Then, from the sky, shapes dived: harpies. "Fresh meat!" the harpy sergeant screamed. Dor knew that was her rank, because the filthy grease on her wings was striped. "Haul it away!"

The dirty birds clutched the bodies available: five fauns, three wounded goblins, and the cocooned goblin sergeant. Great ugly wings beat fiercely, stirring up dust. "Not the fauns!" Dor bellowed—for one of them was the orefaun who had befriended him. He grabbed for the orefaun's dangling hooves, yanking him down to the ground. Startled at this vigorous resistance, the harpies let go.

Jumper threw up a noose, catching a dryfaun and hauling him down similarly. But the remaining three, together with the four goblins, disappeared into the sky. The other goblins ran away.

Had Jumper been right to chitter restraint? Dor wasn't sure. He didn't care about the goblins, but he was very sorry about the three lost fauns. Could he have saved them if he had attacked before? Or would he merely have gotten himself trussed up and abducted? There was no way to be sure. Certainly Jumper, once he acted, had done so most effectively; he had nullified the leader, instead of mindlessly battling the troops, as Dor had done. Jumper had taken the most sensible course, the one with the least risk. Following this course, they had taken losses, but had not lost the battle.

The nymphs and fauns returned, now that the action was over. They were chastened by the double horror of goblin and harpy raids. Three of their comrades were gone. Obviously their illusion of security had been shattered.

The party was, of course, over. They doused the bonfire and retreated to their various habitats. Dor and Jumper hung from a branch of a large tree; it belonged to no one, since these creatures were not yet at the one-creature-one-tree stage. Night sank gloomily upon them.

In the morning Dor and Jumper were sober—but they had a surprise. The first nymph to spy Jumper screamed and dived into the lake—where she almost drowned, for she was an oread, not a naiad. The fauns clustered around aggressively. Dor had to introduce himself and Jumper, for no one remembered them.

They went through the bit about the jumping again, and quickly befriended the whole community—again. They did not mention the goblin press-gang raid; those lost fauns had been forgotten, literally, and the orefaun Dor had rescued obviously was not aware of his narrow escape. The whole community knew that monsters never came *here*.

For this was part of the secret of eternal youth: the fauns and nymphs could not afford to be burdened by the harsh realities of prior experience. They were forever young, and necessarily innocent. Experience aged people. As it was aging Dor.

"At least the goblins won't do much successful recruiting here," Dor murmured as they left the colony behind and continued west. "You can't depend on troops who have to be taught again each day."

"The harpies won't have that problem," Jumper chittered.

The harpies had been foraging for fresh meat. They had found it.

"Nevertheless, the effect may wear off after a few days, when individuals are removed from the locale," Jumper continued. "Had we remained several days, we would have felt the spell's effect, and remained forever; those who are forcibly removed probably revert slowly to their original states."

"Makes sense," Dor agreed. "Stay a short time, trying it out, having a good time—" He thought of the naiad who had tempted him, and of the other naiads in the water with their floating breasts. "Then get caught by the spell, and not remember what else you have to do." He shuddered, partly from the horror of it, and partly from the appeal of it.

They continued on into the larger bushes, leaving their trail of markers. The fauns and nymphs would not tamper with the markers; they would not remember what they were for. Within a day or so the zombie army should pass this region. Dor judged that they had now marked over half the distance from the Zombie Master's castle to Castle Roogna. The worst was surely over, and by nightfall he and Jumper would be with the King with the good news.

"These plants disturb me," Jumper chittered.

"Me too. But they seem harmless, just strange."

Jumper looked about, as he could do without moving his head or eyes. The direction of his vision was merely a matter of awareness, and Dor had become sensitive to the spider's mannerisms that signaled it. "There seems to be no better channel than this. The ground is level and clear, and there are no hostile creatures. Yet I distrust it."

"The most promising paths are often the most dangerous. We should distrust this one *because* there are no hostile creatures," Dor pointed out.

"Let me survey from another vantage, while you continue as if innocent," Jumper chittered. He jumped over a bush and disappeared.

Dor walked on. He hardly had to pretend innocence! It was a good system they had. The spider was more agile and could not be caught by sudden drops, thanks to his dragline, while Dor had the solidity of his big Mundane body and the power of his sword. He would distract potential enemies while Jumper observed them from concealment. Any who attacked Dor might find themselves looped and hoisted on a line of silk.

The bushes now rose taller than his head and seemed to crowd about, though they did not move. The true walking plants seemed not to have evolved in Xanth yet. Dor checked that carefully, however, since there were other ways to move than walking. Tangle trees, for example, snatching prey that passed; predaceous vines that wrapped around anyone foolish enough to touch them, or plants that simply uprooted themselves periodically to find better locations. But these particular plants were definitely stationary; it was his forward progress into their thickening midst that made them seem to swell and crowd closer. They were all so similar that it would be easy to get lost among them—but since he was leaving magic markers, he would not mislay his way, and could always retreat. And of course Jumper was watching.

What would his venture have been like without Jumper? Dor shuddered to think of it. He was sure the big spider's presence was accidental, not planned or anticipated by Good Magician Humfrey when he arranged this quest. But without that coincidence, could Dor have survived even his first encounter with the goblins? Had he died here in the tapestry, what would have happened to his body back home? Maybe Humfrey had some way to rend the tapestry and reweave it, so that Dor's death would be eliminated and he could return safely—but even so, that would have been a humiliating failure. Far better to survive on his own—and Jumper had enabled him to do that.

So far.

Even more important was the maturity of perspective brought by the big arachnid. Dor was learning constantly from that. The juveniles of any species tended to be happy but careless, like the fauns and nymphs; it was easy to contemplate being locked into such innocence indefinitely. But the longer prospects showed this to be a nightmare. Dor was, as it were, emerging from faun to Jumper stage.

He laughed, finding the mixed image funny. He imagined himself starting with little horns and hooves, then growing four more limbs and six more eyes to resemble the spider. Before this adventure he would not have understood such imagery at all!

In the midst of his laugh, something chilling happened, causing him to choke it off. He looked around, but saw nothing. Only the plants, which were now half again as tall as he. What had happened to disturb him so? He hadn't quite caught it.

He shrugged and walked on. After a moment, to demonstrate better his unconcern, and incidentally to make sure his exact location was known to Jumper —just in case!—he began to whistle. He was not a good whistler, but he could carry a fair tune.

And the subtle thing happened again. Dor stopped in his footprints and looked again. Had he seen Jumper from the corner of his eye? No, he would have recognized his friend without even trying. How he wished for several extra eyes now! But to hell with caution; he had seen something, and he wanted to know what.

There was nothing. The tall bushes merely sat there, basically mundane, their leaves rippling periodically in the breeze. At the base they were full, their foliage so dense that their trunks could hardly be seen. At the top they thinned, their leaves sparser and smaller, until at the apex they were bare. Some had the central stem projecting straight up for several feet, with several bare cross branches. A strange design, for a plant, but not a threatening one. Maybe they were sensors for the sun or wind, conveying information to the plant's main body. Many plants liked to know what was going on, for small changes in the weather could spell great changes in vegetable welfare.

Dor gave it up. There was simply nothing here he could detect. He could ask one of the sticks that lay on the ground, of course. But again he balked at that. Something about the naïveté of the fauns and nymphs made him resist that device. The fauns and nymphs depended foolishly on their ignorance, their mountain, trees, and lake—instead of on their own intelligence, alertness, and initiative. If he depended on his magic instead of his powers of observation and reasoning, he would never become the man he should be. He recalled how little King Trent used his transforming power; now that made some sense to him. Magic was always there as a last resort; it was the other qualities of existence that needed to be strengthened. So he held off, avoiding the easy way, determined to solve this one himself.

Maybe what he sought was invisible. In his own day there were said to be invisible giants, though no one had ever seen one. How could they? He chuckled.

Again it happened, as if triggered by his noise. And this time he caught it. The top of one of the plants had moved! Not swaying in the wind; it had moved. It had turned deliberately, rotating on its trunk-axle to orient on him.

Dor considered this. He took several steps forward, whistling, watching—and the antenna swiveled to follow his progress. No doubt about it now. The thing was focusing on him.

Well, plants were also wise to keep track of mobile creatures, for the approach of monster or man could signal instant destruction—especially if it were a sala-mander in a bad mood, or a man looking for wood to build a house. What better way to keep informed than a rotary antenna! So this was probably harmless. Dor had been concerned because he had seen the movement without an object. He had been thinking in terms of animals or tangle trees, not simple wooden rota-tion.

He walked on with renewed confidence, still whistling. More of the antenna-plants were evident now; this seemed to be the mature stage of the bush. The little ones at the fringe had no antennae; the medium ones had antennae but couldn't rotate them; the grown ones were fully operative.

Just so long as they did nothing but watch . . . Assuming they could watch without eyes. Probably they could; Dor knew there were other senses than man's, some just as effective. Maybe the plants resonated to sounds, hence reacted to his laughter, which must seem strange indeed to them. Or to the heat of his body. Or the smell of his sweat. How would they react to the zombies? He smiled privately; the zombies might make quite a stir wherever they passed!

The forest—for such it had become—opened into a grassy glade. In the cen-ter there was a depression, and there was a mound in it. The mound appeared to be made of wood, yet had no branches or leaves. What was it?

The antenna-trees merely looked; they did not act. That would not protect this forest from threats unless there was something else. Something that could act, once the trees had pinpointed the threat. Could this be an action device?

Dor would ordinarily have left it alone, for it could be folly to mess with things not understood. But he was scouting a path for the zombie army, and he did not want to lead it into some devious trap. Probably this growth was harm-less, as it seemed to be immobile. But he had to be sure.

He was not so foolish as to step on it, of course. He cast about for deadwood, found an old dry branch, and used it to poke the object. He could just reach it, this way, standing on the rim of the depression. He would not have been sur-prised if water poured forth in a fountain, filling the bowl, or if the knob had sunk into an awesome hole. This whole woods could be carnivorous, luring animals to the center, dumping them into its maw.

But nothing happened. His speculations had been foolish. Why should trees go to so much trouble, when it was so much easier simply to grab passing prey, as tanglers did, or to repel intrusions by brambles or forget spells or bad odors? There had been no lure, either; he had come here only because he needed a good route through.

Well, whatever it was did seem to be inert, therefore probably harmless. The zombies could pass safely. Dor turned about and saw Jumper.

"There seems to be no threat," Jumper chittered. "Have you determined the nature of this formation?"

Dor froze. The spider had come up quietly behind him, sneaking up, intent on mischief. Only by chance had Dor turned in time. Now the sinister creature was pretending to be innocuous, until he could get close enough to bite off Dor's head with his gruesome chelicerae.

"Is there something the matter?" Jumper chittered, his ugly huge green front orbs glinting evilly. "You look unwell. May I render assistance?" And the monster took a step toward Dor with his hairy long legs.

Dor whipped out his sword. "Back, traitor!" he cried. "Come not near me!"

The spider stepped artfully back, as if confused, only far enough to remain beyond slash range. "Friend, what is the meaning of this? I seek only to help."

Goaded beyond endurance by the thing's duplicity, Dor lunged. The sword sped forward with a precision that would have been unattainable by his own body. But the hairy arachnid jumped right over his head, out of the way.

Dor whirled. Jumper had landed on the wooden knob. Even in his righteous rage, Dor had some caution; he did not wish to step into that mysterious depression. So he stood at the rim, on guard, watching the enemy spider.

Jumper's attitude had changed. He balanced neatly on six legs, his long front two legs stroking the air softly. Dor recognized this as a fighting stance. "So you attack me without provocation?" the creature demanded, and there was a harsh edge to his chitter. "I should have known better than to trust an alien thing."

The stick Dor had used to poke the knob lay at his feet. He picked it up awkwardly with his left hand, keeping his sword ready with his right. "You were the one who betrayed trust!" he cried, poking at the spider.

It was a tactical mistake. Jumper threw a line around the end of the pole and jerked it to him. Dor was almost hauled into the depression before he let go. He staggered back.

The spider seized his opening. He jumped across the depression, landing beside Dor. He threw another loop, catching Dor's sword arm, drawing him off balance. But Dor reacted with the fighting reflexes of his powerful body. He jerked the arm back. Such was the strength and weight of his body that it was the gross arachnid who was now hauled off balance. No single leg of the spider's could match Dor's arm; the muscle tissue simply wasn't there. Jumper came forward, not falling because it was just about impossible for a thing with eight legs to fall, but lurching toward Dor. Dor reversed his motion and slashed viciously with his sword.

The spider shot straight up, barely avoiding the cut. There was no overhanging branch here, so what went up had to come down. Dor stood below with his point straight up, waiting for the spider to skewer himself on it.

But he had reckoned without the creature's monstrous agility. Jumper landed on the sword—feet first, all eight of them closing about the tip of the blade, supporting him. His weight carried blade and arm down, and Dor collapsed under it. Immediately the spiders' sickening strands of web were all about him, entangling him.

Dor closed his left fist and rammed it into the spider's soft abdomen. The flesh gave way disgustingly, and strands of silk stretched and snapped. Then Dor put both hands on the sword and hauled it up, half-carrying the spider with it. He kicked with one foot to dislodge his antagonist—but this was another error. The spider looped that leg, drew his line in tight, and Dor had two hands and the leg tied together. Those spindly spider legs were savagely swift!

Dor fell on his back, fighting to free his limbs. But now the spider was all over him, throwing strand after strand around him, drawing them in tight. Dor heaved mightily, snapping more strands, but his strength was giving out. Soon he was hopelessly bound.

The monster brought his head close to Dor's head. The horrible hairy green chelicerae parted, ready to crush Dor's helpless face into a pulp. The sharp fangs were extended. The two largest green front eyes glared.

Dor screamed and kicked his bound feet and flung his head about as uselessly as Millie ever had. How had he come to this? Yet even in this moment of annihilation he retained some human perspective. "Why did you ever pretend to be my friend?" he demanded.

Jumper folded his jaws closed. "That is an excellent question," he chittered. Then he backed off, adjusted his lines, and dragged Dor over the ground toward a large tree. The antenna at the tree's top rotated to cover him, but could do nothing. The spider jumped to a stout branch, fastened a line, then hauled Dor laboriously into the air to dangle helplessly. Then he descended his own dragline to land beside Dor.

"The answer is, I did not pretend to be your friend," Jumper chittered. "I made a truce with you and treated you fairly, believing that you would honor that truce in the same fashion I did. Then, suddenly, without warning, you attacked me with your sword, and I had to defend myself. You were the one who pretended."

"I did not!" Dor cried, struggling vainly against his bonds. "You sneaked up on me!"

"I suppose it could be interpreted that way. But you attacked me, not I you."

"You jumped right at me, snagging my sword. That was an attack!"

"That was after you took your blade to me, and prodded me with the stick. Then I recognized your hostile nature, and took appropriate action." But the spider paused, considering. "I felt no hostility to you until that moment. Why should a stick provoke me when a sword did not?"

"Don't you understand your own alien nature?" Dor demanded.

"Something incomplete here. When did you become antagonistic toward me?"

"When you tried to sneak up on me and kill me of course!"

"And when did that happen?"

"What fool game are you trying to play?" Dor demanded. "You know I was looking at the wooden knob."

"The wooden knob," the spider repeated thoughtfully. "My own realization of antipathy came when I landed on that knob. Can that be coincidence?"

"Who cares!" Dor cried. "You sneaked up on me first!"

"Consider: you poked that knob; you touched it, indirectly, and became hostile to me. Then I touched it and became hostile to you. That knob must have something to do with it."

The logic began to penetrate Dor's emotion. He *had* poked the knob, just before . . . what happened. He knew the spider was his enemy, yet—

"Magic can do many things," Jumper continued. "Can it change friendship to enmity?"

"It can make strangers love each other," Dor said unwillingly. "I suppose it could do the opposite."

"The antenna-plants were tracking our approach. Had we been hostile to this forest, how would it have defended itself?"

"It would have thrown some spell, of course, since the trees aren't active the way tanglers are. Make us fall asleep, or get itchy, or something."

"Or get angry with each other?"

"Yes, that too. Anything is possible—" Dor paused. "Our fight—a spell?"

"The antennae observed us. Had we passed through without stopping, perhaps nothing would have happened. But we remained too long, poking into things—so the forest struck back. Setting us against each other. Reversing our feeling for each other. Would that not be an excellent defense?"

"Reversing emotion! That would mean the stronger the friendship, the worse the—"

"I am extremely angry with you," Jumper chittered.

"I am absolutely furious with you."

"Are we both as angry as it is possible to be? That would indicate a very strong friendship."

"Yes!" Dor cried, and it was as if a band about his heart had burst. "This spell —it could set whole armies against each other!" he exclaimed, seeing it. "The moment anyone jogs the knob, he activates it." The logic had now penetrated to his core; he had no further doubt they were the victims of a malignant spell. His hate for his friend was dissipating. It simply was not reasonable in the circumstance. Jumper's approach had not really been sneaky; the spider normally moved silently, and Dor's attention had been taken by the knob. Dor had assumed Jumper was his enemy for no good reason—except enchantment.

"May I release you now?" Jumper chittered.

"Yes. I realize what happened. It was a temporary spell, losing power with time."

"Reason abates much magic," Jumper agreed. He swung across, and with a few deft motions freed Dor. "I regret this happened," he chittered.

"So do I! Oh, I'm sorry, Jumper! I should have realized—"

"I was caught too. Emotion overcame reason—almost."

"But tell me—why didn't you bite my head off? I thought you were about to."

"The temptation was great. But one does not ordinarily kill a defenseless enemy unless one is hungry. One stores the meat alive until needed. And I do not like the taste of your type of flesh. So it was counter to logic to slay you, and that bothered me. I prefer to be governed by logic. I try to understand the complete situation, to achieve perspective at all times. To get all eight eyes on it, as we arachnids chitter."

"I didn't try to think things out," Dor admitted ruefully. "I just fought!"

"You are younger than I."

Therefore immature, and thoughtless, prone to errors of ignorance and emotion. How well he knew it! The spider's maturity had saved them again, providing the time and thought they needed to fight free of the spell. "Just how old are you, Jumper?"

"I hatched half a year ago, in the spring."

"Half a year!" Dor exclaimed. "*I* hatched—I mean was born—twelve years ago. I'm way older than you!"

"I suspect our cycles differ," Jumper said diplomatically. "In another quarter year I shall be dead of old age."

Dor was shocked. "But I've hardly had time to know you!"

"It is not how long one lives, but how well one lives that is important," Jumper chittered. "This quest with you has been generally excellent living."

"Except for the goblins and the Mudnanes," Dor said, remembering.

"You ventured in quest of the healing elixir at great peril to yourself to enable me to survive the Mundanes' torture," Jumper reminded him. "Perhaps the episode was worthwhile, showing me the extent of your loyalty. Come, let us finish our mission without regret."

Would he have been so nice about having one of his own legs pulled off, to verify the friendship of the spider? Dor doubted it. It seemed he still had some maturing to do.

They dropped to the ground and set their markers to skirt widely around the enchanting wooden knob. This forest defense seemed unnecessarily devious, but of course an obvious trap could more readily be circumvented.

Dor found himself sobered, and not merely by the hostile magic. Jumper— dead in three months!

Chapter 10

Battle

They arrived at Castle Roogna without further significant event, in the afternoon. The King was highly gratified by their tidings. "So you persuaded the Zombie Master! How did you do that?"

"Actually, Millie did it," Dor said, remembering the possible limitations of his own actions. "She is marrying the Zombie Master."

"That must have been some effort you people put forth!"

"It was." Better to omit the details.

"How soon will the zombies arrive?"

"It should be within a day of us, if nothing goes wrong." Then Dor put his hand to his mouth. "But we marked the route so that nothing *can* go wrong!"

"Let's hope so," the King said drily. "We had better establish regular communication. That will be a problem, because the goblin forces control the ground and the harpy forces control the air. I did not summon my troops home because their passage through monster-controlled territory would have been unconscionably hazardous. So I have no military couriers. Let me see." He pondered briefly, while Dor suffered a bad qualm: no troops to defend Castle Roogna! "Too bad there's not a river flowing between us. We'll have to use the ground."

"The dragon-horse!" Dor exclaimed.

"No, I let my dragons go, too, to defend their own homesites, which are more vulnerable than this tall Castle. Let's see what sort of fish we have."

"Fish?" Dor asked blankly. "But they can't—"

The King led the way to the royal fishpond, while Dor's prior qualm grew into a full-fledged funk. No troops, no dragons—and now the King planned to depend on fish?

King Roogna netted a bright goldfish. "Let me see," he said, concentrating. The fish turned blue. Ice formed on the water. "Oops—I made it into a coldfish," Roogna said. "That's no help." He concentrated again. The fish became a fiery red, and the water boiled with the thrashing of the creature's tail. "No, that's a boldfish. I am having a difficult time!"

Dor merely watched. The King was performing significant magic, his misses more potent than any lesser person's wildest successes.

The King concentrated again. The fish turned brown, its skin wormlike. "Ah! There's my groundfish!" he exclaimed, satisfied. He scribbled a note, wadded it into a ball, and inserted it in the fish's mouth. He spoke to it: "Go check on the zombie army and report back here with the Zombie Master's reply."

The fish nodded, then swam through the net and into the wall of the pond, disappearing. "Now let's see what else offers," the King said. He moved to the Royal Aviary and netted a bird shaped like a ball. Its wings were so stubby it could hardly fly, and its beak and claws projected only marginally. "This round dove really isn't much use in this form." He concentrated.

Suddenly a great ugly strap appeared, constricting the dove's body. "No, no!" the King said, annoyed. "Must Murphy's law foul me up even on minor details? Not a bound dove. I want a ground dove!" And the bird turned the color of the groundfish. "There! Now you wait here until I have a message to send; then you fly thorugh the ground and deliver it."

He returned his attention to Dor. "You are a comparative stranger to me, Magician, yet I have faith in you, and in your friend Jumper. I am extremely short of personnel at the moment. Will you accept a position in my service?"

Dor was taken aback. "Your Majesty, I am only visiting here. Soon, very soon, I must go home."

The King smiled grimly. "I would offer you transportation, as I did before. But I am short of that, too, and the goblins have closed in about the Castle. Your only egress is toward the castle of the Zombie Master, and even that is uncertain now. I would prefer that you weather the siege here at Castle Roogna, even if you choose not to participate."

"Another siege. I was just in one!"

"This one will be worse, I assure you. We have greater resources than the Zombie Master did, but the situation is more complicated. I would rather oppose Mundanes than goblins and harpies."

The Dragon King had suggested the same thing. Worse than what they had gone through at the Zombie Master's castle? Dor still could not believe that. He had fought goblins and harpies and found them revolting but not that devastating. And the enemy forces were not actually attacking Castle Roogna; they just happened to be staging their own private war here. Still, it would be pointless to try to travel through the midst of those hordes. "Well, I have a few days yet. Might as well be of what help I can."

"Excellent! I shall put you in charge of the north ramparts. You will have to keep strong rein on the centaurs there, but they'll mind you if they respect you. They must be kept working on the wall as long as possible; every stone laid in place augments our security."

"Oh, I'm not a leader!" Dor protested. "I'm only—"

"My roadrunners kept me informed of your progress, before enemy forces closed in. It is true that you are not yet an experienced leader, but you seem to have good potential. You responded excellently during the Mundane attack on the Zombie Master's castle."

"Your spies saw that? I thought you had no knowledge of what happened there!"

The King laughed. "It is wise for a King to have greater information than he allows others to be aware of. My spies could not approach near the battle itself. But there were reports of a man answering your description making a deal with monsters, and something about green sashes, and of course the message I received from the Dragon King. I inferred that you knew what you were doing. I really do not have firsthand information, however—which is why I was eager to have your report."

But the King had pretty good secondhand information! King Roogna resembled King Trent in certain fundamental ways. Perhaps all kings had an inherent similarity. There was something about them. Perhaps it was a special aspect of maturity.

"One day you will understand, Dor," Roogna said. "It is evident that your land is grooming you for the office, and in this way I can to a certain extent repay you for your services to me. You should make a creditable king, with proper experience."

Dor doubted that, but didn't argue. He didn't follow how doing another service for King Roogna constituted Roogna's repayment to him for a prior service. If this were adult logic, he certainly fell short of it.

The groundfish poked its head out of the ground at their feet. The King reached down to take the wadded paper from its mouth. "Thank you, courier," he said. "You may return to your pond for some refreshment now." He spread out the paper, frowning. "This is from the Zombie Master himself. Your marked path is good, but they are now surrounded by goblins and cannot proceed."

"How far are they?"

"Just beyond the antenna grove."

An image of himself fighting his dearest friend came to him. What a horror! "If any goblins bother the center of that grove—"

"They are too canny for that. They are waiting for the zombies to clear the grove, before taking any action."

"Why do the goblins care about the zombies? It's the harpies they're fighting, isn't it?"

"An excellent point. The zombies should be able to march on unmolested. Unless something is wrong."

"And obviously something is wrong," Dor said. "I'm beginning to get annoyed at Magician Murphy."

"I have been wrestling with this sort of thing since our contest began. Do you suppose I normally require several efforts to adapt magic to my specific purpose? Yet it is a good exercise in discipline."

"Yes," Dor agreed. "After this, I will be much more careful about everything I do, because I know things don't have to go right just by themselves."

The King looked east, though the problem was too far away to see. "Quite likely the antenna forest is annoyed by the presence of so many troops, so has put the notion into the goblins' minds that zombies are enemies."

"But if the goblins have stayed out of that forest—"

"Their army has. But their advance scouts would naturally poke into everything, exactly as you did. If a scout brought back news of an enemy force—"

"We'll have to rescue them!" Dor cried.

"We really lack the personnel," the King said regretfully. "All we have are the centaurs, who must remain at work on the wall. That is in fact why we need the zombie help. It is uncertain that we have enough force to protect the unfinished Castle, and we dare not deplete our resources further."

"But the zombies are coming to help you! Without them you may lose anyway!"

"Yes. It is a problem whose solution I have not yet fathomed. Murphy's curse is taking hold very powerfully, blocking all my efforts."

"Well, I didn't go to all this trouble only to get the Zombie Master and Millie captured by goblins!" Dor said hotly. "I'll go out myself and bring them in."

"I would prefer that you not risk yourself," Roogna said, frowning. "It is not that I am insensitive to their fate; it is that I am sensitive to the fate of the greater number. We can help them best from Castle Roogna—if we can help them at all."

Dor started a hot retort—then remembered how Jumper had controlled his reactions in the antenna forest, and saved the situation. Logic had to prevail, not emotion! "How can we do this?"

"If it were possible to bring a squadron of harpies to that vicinity—"

"Yes!" Dor cried. "Then they'll fight the goblins, and neither side will have a chance to worry about zombies. But how can we do this? The harpies will hardly honor any request we might make."

"The problem, as I see it, is the lure. We need to attract them to the region, without sacrificing any of our own personnel."

"No problem at all!" Dor said excitedly. "Do you have a catapult?"

"We do. However, harpies will not pursue flying rocks."

"They just might—after I've spelled those rocks. Let me talk to the ammunition."

"There is a unit on the north wall. Where I had thought to place you anyway."

"What, is something going right?" Dor asked, smiling.

"This is a complexly developing situation. Murphy cannot cover every detail of every contingency. His talent, like mine, is being stretched to its utmost. We shall soon know who is ultimately the more powerful Magician."

"Yes, I guess so. And we have several Magicians on our side."

"However, a single bad foul-up could foil all our efforts. In that sense, Murphy can match any number of Magicians."

"I'd better get to that catapult. Do we have the location of the harpy forces?"

"The centaurs are conversant. They have no love for harpies or for goblins, and their senses are keen." The King turned. "I will send a message to the Zombie Master, asking him to move forward as soon as the harpies appear."

Dor hurried to the north wall. Incomplete as it was, it was still far more substantial than the walls of the Zombie Master's castle. It was hard to imagine little goblins successfully storming such a massive rampart, especially when they were actually fighting harpies. Narrow stairs led around and up through the interior of the wall, until they debouched on the level upper ramp.

The centaurs were nervously pacing the rampart. They were neither the scholars of Dor's day nor the warriors of another day; they were comparatively simple workers not well equipped for war. Each carried a bow and quiver of arrows, however; centaurs always had been fine archers.

The crew was supposed to be engaged in construction, but the big stone blocks lay where they had been hauled, unplaced, while the centaurs looked out over the terrain.

"The King has put me in charge of this wall," Dor announced, attracting their attention. "We have three things to do. First, we must complete the construction of this wall as far as we can before the fighting starts. Second, we must defend it when the monsters arrive. And third, we have a special mission. I am going to—to put a spell on the shot for this catapult, and—"

"Who are you?" a centaur demanded. It was the first one Dor had met—the one who had refused to tell him where King Roogna was, and who had incited the other centaurs against Jumper. What a foul break, to have to work with this particular creature and crew!

Foul break? It was a Murphy break! That curse was getting stronger, not weaker, as the end approached. The supposedly good break of having the catapult right where Dor had been assigned anyway—was no good break at all. This was his worst possible location.

But he had to fight that curse. After all, he was a Magician too, and if that meant anything—

"Centaur, I am the Magician Dor," he said coldly. "You will address me with the respect my status requires."

"The bug lover!" the centaur exclaimed. He put his hands on his front hips. He was a large, muscular brute, taller than Dor's body. Dor was sure that his body's facility with the sword would give him a physical advantage over this creature, but he hardly wanted this to degenerate to a common bawl.

Now that the centaur had called his bluff, defying him, what was Dor to do next? This was no occasion for nicety of expression, and there was no time to win the centaur's confidence or respect slowly. Dor had to get to the heart of the matter in minutes. So—he would have to use his talent. "Come aside with me, centaur," he said. "What I have to say to you is private."

"Aside with you, bug lover?" the creature demanded incredulously. He strode forward and made as if to swing his fist—and Dor's sword pointed at his throat. Dor's body had done it after all, acting before thought. But in this case it was an appropriate response.

The centaur blinked. He had been impressively countered. That gleaming blade could have pierced his arteries before he drew back—and could still do so. He decided to accede to the private talk, at least until he could get his hooves into fighting position.

Dor sheathed his sword abruptly and turned his back, as if completely unconcerned about any action the centaur might take. And of course if the centaur struck now, it would be an act of cowardice in full view of his crew. He followed Dor to a separate place on the wall, where the catapult stood behind a battlement.

Dor turned and looked at the centaur's work harness. "What is his name?" he asked it.

"Cedric Centaur," the harness replied. The centaur jumped, startled but unspeaking.

"What is his real problem?" Dor asked.

"He's impotent," the harness responded.

"Hey, you can't—" Cedric started. But it was too late for him to conceal his secret.

This was a thing Dor did not properly understand—and he needed to, in this case. "What is impotent?"

"He is."

"I mean, what does impotent mean?"

"Impotence."

"What?"

"You should have said 'What is impotence?' " the harness said.

"Never mind!" the centaur exclaimed, agitated. "I'll work the catapult!"

"I'm not trying to tease you," Dor told him. "I'm trying to solve your problem."

"Ha!" the harness said derisively.

"No smart remarks from you!" Dor snapped at it. "Just explain what is impotence."

"This stallion can't stallion. Every time he tries to—"

"Enough!" Cedric cried. "I told you I'd work the catapult, or any other chore! And I won't call you bug lover any more! What more do you demand?"

Dor was getting a notion of the problem. It was similar to what his body felt when he stopped it from responding to Millie or to an inviting nymph. "I'm not demanding anything. I'm just—"

"Put him with a filly, he's a gelding," the harness quipped. "You never saw anything so—"

Cedric put his hands to the harness and ripped it off by brute strength, his face purple-red.

"That will do," Dor said. "I just want to have harmony among us. I won't tell anyone else about this." He addressed the broken harness. "You may be broken, but you can still talk."

"Oh, I'm hurting!" the harness groaned.

"Now you understand how Cedric feels. It is not nice to make fun of anyone's incapacities." Dor was thinking of the way the bigger boys had made fun of him, back in his own time.

"It sure isn't!" the centaur agreed.

"What is responsible for Cedric's impotence?"

"A spell, of course," the harness said, chastened.

Now the centaur was startled. "A spell?"

"What spell?" Dor asked.

"An impotence spell, dummy!"

"Don't you talk to the Magician like that!" the centaur exclaimed, giving his harness a shake.

"I mean, how does it operate?"

"It reverses the normal urges at the critical moment, so—"

"So the stronger the urge, the stronger the hang-up," Dor said, remembering his experience in the antenna forest. That was a mean sort of spell!

"So when he gets close to his sexy dapplegray filly, he—"

"I'm going to burn this harness!" Cedric cried. But he did not seem wholly displeased. He must have believed his condition was a fault of his own, and the discovery that an external spell caused it was good news.

"How may that spell be abolished?" Dor asked.

"I wouldn't know that," the harness said. "After all, I'm only an item of apparel. I only know what I have observed."

"Then how do you know about this spell?"

"This oaf was asleep when the spell was cast, but *I* wasn't. I never sleep."

"How can you sleep when you're not alive?" Cedric demanded, some of his natural belligerence returning. "Who cast that spell?" But the harness did not answer him. "Was it my rival Fancyface? I'll boot his tail through his snout!"

"Who cast it?" Dor asked.

"Celeste did it," the harness replied smugly.

"That's my filly!" Cedric cried. "Why would she—" He paused, his unhandsome face working. "Why that little bitch of an equine! No wonder she was so understanding! No wonder she always made such a point of being true to me! She *knew* why I couldn't—"

"I'm sorry I can't discover the cure," Dor said.

"Don't bother about that, Magician!" Cedric said. "Centaurs don't work magic; she had to have gotten the spell from some human witch. All I need to do is go to a shyster warlock and buy a counterspell. But I won't tell Celeste—" He smiled with grim lust. "Oh, no, I won't tell her! I'll just let her lead me on as usual, teasing me, and I'll fake it until—oh, is she going to get a surprise!"

They returned to the crew. "How's the bug lover doing?" one of the other centaurs called, neighing.

Cedric turned to fix the other with a steely stare. "I'm doing just great," he said. "So is the Magician. We're going to help him all we can, and do just exactly what he says, aren't we." It was not a question.

Dor affected not to notice the chagrin of the other centaurs. They had been brought in line, without doubt! "Where is there a harpy flight, within catapult range?" he asked.

A centaur at the parapet cocked his head. "That way," he said, pointing north.

"That way, *sir!*" Cedric corrected him, delivering a swift cuff on the flank. "You address the Magician with proper respect."

"Uh, just call me Dor," Dor said. He had made an issue of respect, but now was disinclined.

"They're coming in from the Gap, Sir Dor," the parapet centaur said.

"Can you drop a shot to the southwest of them?"

"I can drop a shot down the leader's beakface, Dor!" Cedric said. "Right in her craw."

"Well, I really want it to their southwest."

Cedric shrugged. "Colt's play." The centaurs gathered about the catapult, cranking it back and fastening its boom and lifting a hefty rock into its sling. They oriented the device toward the northeast and adjusted the elevation.

"Now repeat after me, until you strike ground," Dor said to the stone. "Harpies are birdbrained stinkers!"

"Harpies are birdbrained stinkers!" the rock repeated gleefully.

"Fire," Dor said.

Cedric fired. The arm of the catapult sprang up. The missile arced over the forest, and the rock cried out: "Harpies are birrr—" and was lost to Dor's hearing.

"Now we want to lob the next one southeast of that," Dor said. "Until we have a chain of them leading the harpies to our due east, near the antenna forest."

"I understand, Magician," Cedric said. "Then what?"

"Then they'll encounter the goblin band in that region."

The centaur smiled. "I hope they wipe each other out!"

Dor hoped so too. If there were too few harpies, the goblins would still block the zombies' route; but if there were too many harpies, *they* would block the zombies' route. And the ploy might be too late. Already reports were coming in of tremendous goblin armies advancing from the south, and the harpy flights from the north were swelling voluminously. Castle Roogna was still the focus of the war, thanks to the continuing and dire power of Murphy's curse.

"Magician," a dulcet voice said behind Dor. He turned to find a mature woman standing on the ramparts. "I am neo-Sorceress Vadne, come to assist the defense of this wall. How may I be of service?"

"Neo-Sorceress?" Dor asked with undiplomatic blankness. He remembered Murphy saying something about a Sorceress who was helping the King, but the details had fogged out.

"My talent is judged to be shy of Sorceress level," she said, her mouth quirking.

"What is your talent?" Dor realized he was being too direct, but he simply had not yet mastered the social graces of adults.

"Topology."

"What?"

"Topology. Shape-changing."

"You can change your shape? Like a werewolf?"

"Not my own shape," she said. "Other shapes."

"Like making rocks into pancakes?"

"No, my talent is limited to animate shapes. And I can't change their natures."

"I don't understand. If you changed a man into a wolf—"

"He would look like a wolf in outline, but would still be a man. No heavy fur, no keen wolf nose. Topology is not true transformation."

Dor thought of King Trent, who could change a man into a wolf—a wolf who could do everything a real wolf could, and who would produce wolf offspring. That was a superior talent, much greater than this mere shape-changing. "I guess you're right. You're not a Sorceress." For some reason he didn't know, there were no female Magicians, only Sorceresses. "Still, it sounds like good magic."

"Thank you," she said distantly.

"We won't know how you can help here until we see what side attacks, if either side does. The goblins will have to scale the wall, so we can push off their ladders as they hook them over, but the harpies will fly in. Can you top—topol —can you perform at a distance?"

"No. Only by touch," she said.

"That's not much help." He pondered, oblivious to her grimace. "Maybe you better stand at the rim and change goblins into the shape of rocks as they come over the top."

"We can use them for catapult shot!" Cedric exclaimed.

"Good idea!" Dor agreed. "Now I'll make the stone of the ramparts talk, to distract enemies, so don't any of you be fooled. The object is to make the enemy creatures attack the wrong things, breaking their weapons or their heads and giving you time to handle them. Of course we hope they won't try to storm this castle, since they really have no reason to, but you know Murphy's curse. If the goblins and harpies leave us alone, we'll leave them alone. Meanwhile, you centaurs get as many blocks placed on the wall as possible; a single one could make the difference."

The centaurs went to work with a will. Stones were emplaced and mortared rapidly. This was a good work crew, when it wanted to be.

In due course, the King summoned Dor and Vadne to a staff meeting. Jumper was there too; he had been given charge of the east-wall defense. Magician Murphy was also present, to Dor's surprise.

"The goblins have sent an envoy," King Roogna said. "I thought all of you should be present for this meeting." As he spoke, a typically gnarled goblin entered. He wore short black pants, a small black shirt, and enormous shoes. He had the usual goblin scowl.

"We require your castle for a camping base," the goblin said, showing his discolored and jagged teeth. "We give you one measly hour to clear out."

"I appreciate your courtesy," King Roogna said. "But this Castle is as yet incomplete. I doubt it would be of much use to you."

"You deaf, or just stupid?" the goblin inquired. "I said clear out."

"I regret we are not disposed to do that. However, there is some nice level ground to the east that you might use—"

"Useless against flying monsters. We need elevation, battlements, shelter—and great supplies of food. We come in one hour. If you are not gone, we shall eat you." The goblin spun awkwardly about on his ponderous feet and departed.

"Now we have the envoy from the harpy forces," the King said, half-concealing a quirky smile. The oldest and croniest of harpy hens flapped in.

"I saw that goblin!" she screeched. "You are consorting with the enemy. Your gizzards will bleed for this!"

"We declined to let the goblins use our premises," King Roogna said.

"I should think so! We will use your premises!" she screeched. "We need roosting space, cells for captives, kitchens for raw meat!"

"I regret we can not make our facilities available to you. We are not choosing sides."

That was for sure, Dor thought. Both sides were repulsive.

"We'll claw you into quivering chunks!" she screeched. "Making deals with goblins! Treason! Treason! Treason!" She flapped out.

"So much for the amenities," King Roogna said. "Are the ramparts ready?"

"As ready as possible," Jumper chittered. "The situation is not ideal."

"Agreed." The King frowned. "The rest of you may not appreciate the full gravity of the situation. Goblins and harpies are very difficult creatures to deal with. They are more numerous than humans, and have massed themselves, while our kind is dispersed all across the land of Xanth. We can not reasonably expect to withstand siege by their forces without the aid of the zombies, and even then it will be difficult. The Zombie Master has been delayed—" He glanced at Magician Murphy. "But is on the move again." He glanced at Dor. "The question is, will he arrive in time?"

"An excellent question," Murphy said. "Shall we agree that if the Zombie Master fails to arrive before the battle commences—?"

The King glanced at the others questioningly.

Dor visualized the battlements. The goblins would have to scale some thirty feet of wall buttressed by the square corner towers and round midwall towers, after fording the deep moat. He couldn't see how they could be a serious immediate threat. The harpies normally struck by picking people up and carrying them away. The centaurs were too heavy to be handled that way. Why, then, was the King so grave? Even unfinished, Castle Roogna should be proof against these threats. A long siege seemed unlikely, because the besiegers would be killing each other off, and running out of food.

"What happens if the zombies don't arrive before the battle starts?" Dor asked.

"It would be a shame to have damage done to this fine edifice, perhaps loss of human life," Murphy explained. "It is only sensible to abate the curse before the situation gets untoward."

"You mean you can call off the whole goblin-harpy battle, this whole siege, just like that?"

"Not just like that. But I can abate it, yes."

"I find that hard to believe," Dor said. "Those armies are already well on their way. They aren't just going to turn around and go home just because you—"

"The King's talent is shaping magic to his own ends. Mine is shaping circumstance to interfere with others' designs. Alternate faces of similar coins. All we have to determine is whose talent shall prevail. Destruction and bloodshed are no necessary part of it. In fact I deplore and abhor—"

"There has already been bloodshed!" Dor exclaimed angrily. "What kind of macabre game is this?"

"A game of power politics," Murphy responded, unperturbed.

"A game where my friend was tortured by Mundanes, and my life threatened, and the two of us were pitted against each other," Dor said, his anger bursting loose. "And Millie must marry the Zombie Master to—" He cut himself off, chagrined.

"So you have an interest in the maid," Vadne murmured. "And had to give her up."

"That's not the point!" But Dor knew his face was red.

"Shall we be fair?" Murphy inquired meaningfully. "Your problem with the maid is not of my making."

"No, it isn't," Dor admitted grudgingly. "I—I apologize, Magician." Adults were able to apologize with grace. "But the rest—"

"I regret these things as much as you do," Murphy said smoothly. "This contest with the Castle was intended to be a relatively harmless mode of establishing our rights. I would be happy to remove the curse and let the monsters drift as they may. All this requires is the King's acquiescence."

King Roogna was silent.

"If I may inquire," Jumper chittered, Dor's web translating for all to hear. "What would be the long-range consequence of victory by Magician Murphy?"

"A return to chaos," Vadne replied. "Monsters preying on men with impunity, men knowing no law but sword and sorcery, breakdown of communications, loss of knowledge, vulnerability to Mundane invasions, decrease of the importance of the role of the human species in Xanth."

"Is this desirable?" Jumper persisted.

"It is the natural state," Murphy said. "The fittest will survive."

"The *monsters* will survive!" Dor cried. "There will be seven or eight more Mundane Waves of conquest, each with awful bloodshed. The wilderness will become so dense and horrible that only spelled paths are safe for people to travel. Wiggles will ravage the land. There will be fewer true men in my day than there are in yours—" Oops. He had done it again.

"Magician, exactly where are you from?" Vadne demanded.

"Oh, you might as well know! Murphy knows."

"And did not tell," Murphy said.

"Murphy has honor, once you understand his ways," Vadne said, glancing at the Magician obliquely. "I once sued for his hand, but he preferred chaos to an organized household. So I am without a Magician to marry."

"You sought to marry above your station," Murphy told her.

Vadne showed her teeth in a strange crossbreed of snarl and smile. "By your definition, Magician!" Then she returned to Dor. "But I let my passion override me. Where did you say you were from, Magician?"

Dor suddenly understood her interest in him—and was glad he could prove himself ineligible. It would be as easy to deal with Helen Harpy as with this woman, and for similar reason. Vadne was no soft and sweet maid like Millie; she was a driven woman on the prowl for a marriage that would complete the status she craved. "I am from eight hundred years hence. So is Jumper."

"From the future!" King Roogna exclaimed. He had stayed out of the dialogue as much as possible, giving free rein to the expression of the others, but this forced his participation. "Exiled by a rival Magician?"

"No, there is no other Magician in my generation. I am on a quest. I—I think I'm going to be King, eventually, as you surmised before. The present King wants me to have experience." Obviously King Roogna had not discussed Dor's situation with anyone else, letting Dor present himself in his own way. More and more, Dor was coming to appreciate the nuances of adult discretion. It was as significant as much in what it did not do as in what it did do. "I'm only twelve years old, and—"

"Ah—you are in a borrowed body."

"Yes. It was the best way for me to visit here, using this Mundane body. Another creature animates my own body, back home, taking care of it during my absence. But I'm not sure that what I do here has any permanence, so I don't want to interfere too much."

"So you know the outcome of the Roogna-Murphy wager," the King said.

"No. I thought I did, but now I see I don't. Castle Roogna is complete in my day—but it stood deserted and forgotten for centuries. Some other King could have completed it. And there have been all those Waves I mentioned, and all the bad things, and the decline of the influence of Man in Xanth. So Murphy could have won."

"Or I could have won, and held off the onset of chaos for a few more decades," Roogna said.

"Yes. From my vantage, eight hundred years away, I just can't tell whether the chaos started in this year or fifty years from now. And there are other things that don't match, like the absence of goblins on the surface in my day, and the relative scarcity of harpies—I just don't know how they will fit in."

"Well, what will be, will be," Roogna said. "I suppose from that vantage of history, what we do here has little significance. I had hoped to set up a dynasty of order, to keep Xanth wholesome for centuries, but that does not seem fated to be. It is a foolish vanity, to believe that a man's influence can extend much beyond his own time, and I shall be well rid of it. Still, I hope to do what good I can within this century, and to leave Castle Roogna as a monument to my hope for a better Xanth." He looked around at the others. "We should make our decisions according to our principles."

"Then we should fight to preserve order—for as long as it can be preserved!" Dor said. "For a decade, for a year, or for a month—whatever we can do is good."

Murphy spread his hands. "We shall in due course discover whether even a month is feasible."

"I believe the consensus is clear," King Roogna said. "We shall defend the Castle. And hope the Zombie Master gets here in time."

They returned to their stations. Almost immediately the troubled arrived. From the south the dusky banners of the great goblin army came, marching in a gathering tread that shook the Castle foundations. Dor stood atop the northeast corner tower and looked over the ramparts to spy it in the distance. Drums beat, horns tooted, keeping the cadence. Like a monstrous black carpet the army spread across the field beyond the Castle. Light sparkled from the points of the goblins' small weapons, and a low half-melody carried under the clamor, like muted thunder: the goblins were chanting, "*One* two three four, *Kill* two three four, *One* two three four, *Kill* two three four," on and on endlessly. There was not much imagination to it, but plenty of feeling, and the effect expanded cumulatively, hammering into the mind.

They had allies, too. Dor spied contingents of gnomes, trolls, elves, dwarves, ghouls, and gremlins, each with its own standard and chant. Slowly a gnarly tapestry formed, a patchwork of contingents, the elves in green, dwarves in brown, gnomes in red, trolls black, marching, marching. There seemed to be so many creatures they could bury the Castle under the sheer mass of their bodies, stretching the grisly fabric of their formation across the ramparts. Yet of course they could not; mere numbers could not scale a vertical wall.

Then from the north flew the harpies and their winged minions, casting a deep shadow across land and Castle, blotting out the sun. There were contingents of ravens and vampires and winged lizards and other creatures Dor didn't recognize, in their mass resembling gross storm clouds darkening the sky in segments, the light permitted to penetrate at the perimeters only to delineate the boundaries. Thus the shadows traversed the ground in large squares, an ominous parallel advance.

The point of convergence, of course, was Castle Roogna. The two armies might indeed obliterate each other—but they would wreak havoc on the Castle in the process—if they ever got inside it. Suppose the battle took a long time? The inhabitants of the Castle could starve, waiting for it to end, even if the walls were never breached. And if the goblins had siege machinery or used the larger trolls to batter the walls, while the harpies and vampires ravaged the upper reaches—

Now Dor was coming to appreciate how unpleasant this siege could get. The Mundanes had made only sporadic assaults against the castle of the Zombie Master, but the goblins and harpies were here in such great numbers that their attack would be unremitting. There would be inevitable attrition of the Castle defenders, until no further defense was possible, and the Castle was overrun. They had to have renewable defenders. That was the key role the Zombie Master played: as long as the battle continued, there would be raw material for new zombies, who would protect the ramparts from intrusion by living creatures.

As yet there was no sign of the zombies. Even if they appeared at this moment, there would not be time for them to shuffle to the Castle before the goblins closed in about it. The Zombie Master was too late. Had Dor's ploy with the talking catapult stones failed? Or been insufficient? He should have had the King check on that with his ground-fish.

Magician Murphy walked by. He seemed to have complete freedom of the premises. "Tut. It really is too bad. Sensible people would spare themselves the awkwardness of the curse."

Cedric Centaur glowered. "Were you not a Magician, I might call you an illegitimate snot-winged dungfly."

Dor kept quiet. The centaur had put it aptly enough. Dor spied a boomerang in the arms rack on the wall of the center brace-tower. "Are you magic?" he asked it.

"Naturally. I always return to the sender's hand."

Magician Murphy shook his head, shrugged, and departed. His curse seemed to operate independently of his presence; he had just been poking around.

"Well," Dor said to the boomerang, "take a look and see if you can spy the zombie army." He hurled the boomerang out over the landscape to the northeast. He was conscious of the anomaly of calling two hundred fifty creatures an army, when the harpies evidently had thousands and the goblins tens of thousands. But the zombies were renewable; they could become an army of thousands, in due course.

The boomerang spun far out, flashing in the dwindling patch of sun remaining before the harpy force, describing a tilting circle. Soon it smacked back into Dor's hand.

"Many goblins," it reported. "No zombies."

Dor sighed. "We'll just have to hold out until they come." But he was pessimistic. Nothing in his experience had prepared him for the magnitude of this confrontation. There were so many monsters! Once the goblins closed about the Castle, how could the zombies ever get through?

First things first. There were harpy forces to deal with. They were looming much faster, like an ugly storm, already about to break over the north wall. "Cease construction. Ready bows," Dor ordered the feverishly laboring centaurs. They obeyed with alacrity. But immediately he saw that there were more flying monsters than there were arrows in all the centaurs' quivers; this would be no good.

"Do not shoot," he told them. "Let me speak first to any arrow that you fire."

A squadron of vampires bore down on them, their huge leathery wings repulsive, their glistening fangs horrifying. "Repeat after me," Dor told the first arrow Cedric had ready. "Neighbor, you couldn't puncture a rotten tomato!"

The arrow repeated it. Objects really enjoyed simple insults. "Keep saying it," Dor said, and nodded to the centaur to fire. "Over their heads," he told Cedric.

Cedric looked surprised, but didn't argue. He raised his elevation and let the shaft go.

They watched as the arrow flew high. It missed the forward rank of vampires and sailed over their heads. Dor knew the other centaurs thought this was a wasted effort. Why fire an arrow intended to miss?

Suddenly there was a disturbance in the forward ranks. "Oh yeah?" a vampire cried—at least his shriek sounded very much like that—and spun in air to sink his long fangs into his neighbor's wing tip. The victim reacted angrily, sinking his own fangs into the nearest other wing tip available, thus involving a third vampire. The formation was so tight that in a moment the whole configuration was messed up, with vampires fighting each other in an aerial free-for-all, milling about and paying little further attention to the castle or the goblins beyond it.

"That was a neat ploy, Magician," Cedric said. Dor was glad he had taken the trouble to convert the surly creature, instead of fighting him. Jumper had shown him that. If there were any way to make friends with the goblins and harpies—

Could it be done, at this late date? Suppose the goblin females could be convinced to appreciate the best of the males, instead of the worst? And the harpies—if they had males of their own species again? All it would take was some sort of mass enchantment for the goblins, and the generation of at least one original harpy male from the union of a human with a vulture. There was a love spring north of the Gap—

And no way to get to it, now. Anyway, the thought was plausible, but it revolted him. What human and what vulture would volunteer to—? In any event, it would be too late to save the Castle for it took time for any creature to be conceived and birthed and grown. Years to produce a single male harpy, even if everything were in order. They needed something to abate this battle right now—and Dor knew that no matter what he tried, Murphy's curse would foul it up, as it had the effort to parlay with the two sides. Castle Roogna would just have to weather the storm.

Now a horde of goblins charged from the east, surrounding the castle. The goblin army had advanced from the south, but spread out so far to east and west that they had been able to view the wings plainly from the corners of the north wall. At this stage it was closing in like water flowing around a rock in a stream. There was no longer any disciplined marching or measured tread or beat of drums; the army had reverted to its natural horde state. The goblin allies must be attacking the other walls; here in the north there were only pure goblins, and Dor feared they would be the most determined opponents.

The disorganized cloud of vampires was now impinging on the ramparts. Quickly Dor walked the battlement, addressing the projecting stones of the completed portions. "Repeat after me: Take that, fang-face! My arrows are trained on you! Here comes a fire arrow!" Soon he had a medley of such comments from the wall, calculated to faze the vampires as they came close. Dor hoped the vampires were too stupid to realize there were no archers there. This allowed him to concentrate his centaurs on the incomplete section of the wall, which still lacked its battlements.

The centaurs on the east wall threw cherry bombs to disrupt the onslaught. Bang! and a goblin flipped over and collapsed. Bang! and another went. But there were more goblins than cherry bombs available. Then Boom! as a pineapple blasted a crater, hurling bodies outward like straw dolls.

But the goblins did not even pause; they charged through the smoking hole, over the fresh corpses of their comrades, right up to the moat. The moat-monsters rose up to meet them, snatching goblins from the back and gulping them down whole. But still the goblins came, forging into the water.

"I didn't know goblins could swim," Dor remarked, surprised.

"They can't," Vadne said.

The goblins surrounded the moat-monsters, clawing, punching, and biting them. The monsters snapped quickly, gorging themselves. And while each could consume a dozen or so goblins, there were thousands crowding in. The monsters retreated to deeper water, but the goblins splashed after them, clinging like black ants, pinching like nickelpedes. Many were shaken loose as the moat-monsters thrashed, and these sank in the murky depths, while other came on over them.

"What point in that?" Dor asked incredulously. "Aren't they going to try to build bridges or something? They're dying pointlessly!"

"This whole war is pointless," Vadne said. "Goblins aren't builders, so they don't have bridges."

"They don't seem to have ladders, either," Dor remarked. "So they can't scale the wall. This is completely crazy!"

On and on the goblins came, sinking and drowning in droves, until at last the moat itself filled with their bodies. The water overflowed the plain. Now there was a solid mass of flesh across which the horde poured. The moat-monsters had been stifled in that mass; there was no remaining sign of them. The goblins advanced to the base of the wall.

There was no great strategy in their approach; they simply continued scrambling over each other in their effort to mount the vertical rampart. Dor watched with morbid fascination. The goblin-sea tactic had filled in the moat and gotten the survivors across—but that could not carry them straight up the stone wall!

The goblins did not stop. They hordes behind kept shoving forward, refusing to recognize the nature of the barrier. As the first ones got trampled down, the next ones got higher against the wall. Then the third layer formed, and the forth. The wall here was not complete, yet there were some thirty feet from moat to top even at this lowest point; did the foolish creatures think they could surmount that by trampling the bodies of their comrades? It would take thirty layers of crushed goblins!

Amazingly, those layers formed. Each layer required a greater number of bodies, because it sloped farther back across the moat. But the creatures kept coming. Five layers, six, seven, eight, nine, ten—already they were a third of the way up, building an earthwork of their own dead and dying.

Cedric stood beside Dor, looking down at this horror. "I never thought I'd feel sorry for goblins," he said. "We're not killing them, they're killing themselves—just to get up over a wall of a castle they don't need!"

"Maybe that's the difference between men and goblins," Dor said. "And centaurs." But he wondered. The Mundanes, who were after all true men, had stormed the castle of the Zombie Master with as much determination and little reason as this, and the centaur crew had not shown any particular enlightenment prior to Dor's private session with Cedric. When the fever of war got into a society . . .

Still the goblin tide rose. Now it was halfway up, and still progressing. It was no longer possible to tell where the moat had been; there was only a monstrous ramp of bodies slanting far out from the wall. The goblins charged in and up from their seemingly limitless supply, throwing their little lives away. There did not even seem to be any conscious self-sacrifice in this; it was plain lack of foresight, as they encountered the barrier and were ground down by those still shoving from behind. Those below chomped savagely on the feet of those above, before the increasing press of weight killed them. Maybe the goblin chiefs behind the lines knew what they were doing, but the ordinary troops were just obeying orders. Maybe there was a "charge forward" spell on them, overriding the selfish self-preservation goblins normally evinced.

With horror that mounted as the mass of goblins mounted, Dor watched. Against such a tide, what defense did they have! Arrows and cherry bombs were pointless; they would only facilitate the manufacture of bodies to use as support for the next layer. Now at last Dor understood why the King had been so concerned about this threat. Goblins *were* worse than Mundanes.

Meanwhile the harpy forces were regaining some semblance of order. Dor had prepared a number of arrows, and these had fooled the dull vampires for some time. The speaking battlements had helped considerably. But now the harpies themselves were massing for a charge. They had nearly human intelligence, and would hardly be fooled long by inanimate devices. They seemed to be progressing toward an assault timed for just about the moment the goblins would finally overflow the wall. Probably this was neither coincidence nor Murphy's curse; the dirty birds merely wished to make certain that the goblins did not capture the Castle.

Dor and the centaurs would be jammed to death the same way the moat-monsters had been. The worst of it was, there did not seem to be anything they could do about it. The enemy forces were too numerous, too mindless.

"This is where I come in," Vadne said, though she was tight about the mouth. "I can stop the goblins—I think."

Dor hoped so. He glanced nervously around at what he could see of the other walls. They were higher, and had more explosive armament, so seemed to be in less difficulty. He wondered how Jumper was doing; he could not see the spider from here. Even the arachnid's great facility with silk could hardly stop these myriad goblins.

The first goblin hand hooked over the rim of the battlement, or rather the place where the battlement had not yet been constructed. Vadne was ready. She touched the hand—and the goblin became a ball that rolled down the slope of piled bodies.

Another hand appeared. She balled the second goblin. Then a host of hands came, keeping her moving. The layers were piling up to either side of the low spot, now, so that she had to jump to one side and then to the other to catch them. Soon she would be overwhelmed. She could not hold the wall alone; no one could.

"Let the harpies come in," Dor cried to the archers, who had been selectively shooting the leaders of any potential charge, delaying that aspect somewhat.

As the arrows stopped, the harpies and vampires swarmed in. The vampires were not bright, but they had caught on that they were being manipulated, and now were bloodthirsty. But the most obvious enemy was the goblin horde. The flying creatures fell upon the goblins, literally, and plunged fangs and claws into them. The goblins fought back viciously, jabbing fists into snouts and stubby fingers into eyes, and wringing necks. They seemed to have lost what weapons they had, in the course of the scramble upward, or maybe they just preferred to meet their enemies on the most basic level of animosity.

It was a respite of sorts for the Castle defenders—but now the bodies piled up even faster, higher and higher, mounding as tall as the rampart. Soon the goblins would be able to roll down into the castle, and Vadne's magic would be largely ineffective. No sense getting buried in balls!

"Can you make them smaller—like grains of sand?" Dor yelled over the noise of battle.

"No. Their mass is the same, whatever shape I give them. I can't stop the mounding."

Too bad. King Trent could have stopped it, by changing them into gnats, so small they would never mound up over the wall. Or he would have changed a centaur into a salamander, and used it to set the bodies on fire, reducing them quickly to ashes. Vadne really was less than a Magician. Not that Dor was doing any better; he had helped hold them off for a while, but could not stop them now.

Then he had an inspiration. "Make them into blocks!" he cried.

She nodded. She got near the gap in the battlement, while Dor protected her flank with his sword. Suddenly the goblin blocks began appearing. These were much smaller than the big stone blocks used in the construction of the Castle, but larger than ordinary bricks. The centaurs shoved them into position on the wall, shaping it crudely higher. The goblin blocks were now holding back the tide of goblins!

"Now there's what I call a good goblin," Cedric exclaimed. "A blockhead!"

But even good blockheads weren't enough. They tended to wiggle and sag, though Vadne made some with interlocking edges. They were not as dense as stone, nor as hard, and squished down somewhat as the weight of other blocks went on top. As Vadne had suggested: a goblin in the shape of a block was still a goblin, not much good for anything.

Again Dor scavenged his brain for an answer. How could Castle Roogna be defended against this horrible mass of attackers? Even the corpses were enough to bury it!

A ground dove poked its head out of the floor. Dor took the message from its beak, while continuing to slash about with his sword, protecting Vadne's back. HOW GOES IT? the paper inquired.

"Repeat after me, continuously until the King hears," Dor told the paper. He could not afford to take his attention off the goblins and harpies long enough to write a note. "We can hold out only five minutes more. Situation desperate." He put the repeating paper back in the dove's beak and watched it swim, or rather fly, down out of sight through the stone. He didn't like making such a bleak report, but had to be realistic. He and Vadne and the centaurs had done everything they could, but it was not enough. If this wall fell, the castle would fall. The attack was more than ever like a savage storm, with the tide of goblins on the surface and the clouds of harpies in the air, and now there was no way they could halt the sheer avalanche of creatures. Could even the zombies have abated this menace?

Yes, they could have, Dor decided. Because the Zombie Master would change the piled-up bodies to zombies, who would then hurl the live goblins and many of the dead ones back away from the ramparts. If only the Zombie Master were here!

In moments the King himself was at the wall. "Oh my goodness!" Roogna exclaimed. "I had no idea it was this bad! The two wings of the goblin horde must have converged here on the far side of their thrust, and doubled the pileup. On the other walls it is only halfway up. You should have summoned me before."

"We were too busy fighting goblins," Dor said. Then he shoved the King, moving him out of the way as a harpy divebombed him. She missed, cursing.

"Yes, this is definitely the region of greatest crisis," the King said, as several goblin balls rolled across the wall and dropped off inside the Castle courtyard. He bent to peer at a goblin block, and it peered back, balefully cubic. "The highest tide, the lowest wall. You have done well."

"Not well enough," Dor said, skewering another diving harpy. "We are about to go down under their charge." As if that was not obvious!

"I have some emergency enchantments in the arsenal," Roogna said. "They are hazardous to health, so I have not wished to employ them, but I fear the occasion has arisen." He ducked a vampire.

"Get them!" Dor cried, growing desperate at this delay. Why hadn't the King told him there was more magic available? "Your Majesty!"

"Oh, I brought them with me, just in case." The King brought out a vial of clear fluid. "This is concentrated digestive juice of stomach of dragon. It must be dispensed upwind of the target, downwind of the user. If any drifts—" He shook his head dolefully. "Murphy's curse could cost us one King. Seek cover, please."

"Your Majesty!" Vadne protested. "You can't risk yourself!"

"Of course I can," the King reproved her. "This is my battle, for which all the rest of you are risking yourselves. If we lose it, I am lost anyway." He wet a finger and held it to the wind. "Good; it is blowing west. I can clear the wall. But don't get near until it clears." He went to the northeast corner.

"But the curse will make the wind change!" Dor protested.

"The curse is stretched to its limit," the King said. "This magic will not take long, and I don't think the wind can shift in time."

The goblins were now scrambling over the wall, being met by screaming harpies. Dor and Vadne and the centaurs drew back to the inner surface of the wall, and crowded toward the eastern end, upwind of the proposed release.

The King opened his vial. Yellowish smoke puffed out, was caught by the wind, and strewn across the rim of the wall. It sank down upon swarming goblins —and they melted into black goo. They did not even scream; they just sank into the nether mass. They dissolved off the wall, flowed across the stone, coursed in rivulets through the crannies, and dripped out of sight. Harpies snatched at dissolving goblins, got caught by the juice, and melted into juice themselves. A putrid stench rose from the fluid: the odor of hot vomit.

The wind gusted sidewise, carrying a wisp of magic smoke back across the wall. "The curse!" Dor cried in horror. The closest centaurs danced back, trying desperately to avoid it, but with the evil humor of the curse it eddied after them. One got his handsome tail melted away. "Fan it from you!" Dor cried. "We need fans!"

Vadne touched the nearest goblin. It became a huge fan. Dor grabbed it from her hands and used it to set up a counterdraft. Vadne made another, and another, and the centaurs took these. Together they set up a forced draft. The yellow smoke reared up as if trying to get around, horrible in its mindless determination.

"Where are you going?" Dor cried at it.

"I'm drifting east another six feet, then north over the wall," it replied. "The best pickings are there."

They scrambled out of its projected path. The smoke followed its course, then was gone.

"Ah, Murphy," Vadne said. "It took Magician's magic to foil you, but we foiled you."

Dor agreed weakly. King Roogna, narrowly missed by the smoke, stepped away from the parapet. "It tried to go wrong, but could not. Quite."

Dor peered over the wall. There, below, was a bubbling, frothing ocean of glop, subsiding as the effect penetrated to the bodies underneath. A sinking tide, it ebbed along the rampart and sucked down into the moat, liquefying everything organic. Before long, there was nothing on the north side except the black sea.

"More of that on the other walls will abate the whole goblin army!" Dor remarked to the King, his knees feeling weak and his stomach weaker.

"Several problems," King Roogna said. "First, the wind is wrong for the other sides; it would do as much damage to us as to the enemy. Second, it is not effective against the airborne harpy forces, since it tends to sink and they are flying above it. Third, this vial is all I had. I deemed it too dangerous to store in greater quantity."

"Those are pretty serious problems," Dor admitted. "What other magic is in your arsenal?"

"Nothing readily adaptable, I regret. There is a pied-piper flute I fashioned experimentally from a flute tree: it plays itself when blown, and creatures will follow it indefinitely. But we don't need to lead the goblins or harpies here; we want to drive them away. There is also a magic ring: anything passing through it disappears forever. But it is only two inches in diameter, so only small objects can be passed. And there is a major forget spell."

Dor considered. "Could you reverse the flute, so that it drives creatures away?"

"I might, if the curse didn't foul it up. But it would drive us away, too."

"Um. There is that. Could Vadne stretch out the ring to make it larger?"

The King searched in a pocket. "One way to find out." He brought out a golden ring and passed it to Vadne.

"I really am not skilled with inanimate things," she said. But she took it and concentrated. For a moment nothing happened; then the ring expanded. It stretched out larger and larger, but at the same time the gold that composed it was thinning. At last it was a hoop some two feet in diameter, fashioned of fine gold wire. "That's the best I can do," she said. "If I try to stretch it any farther, it will break." She looked washed out; this had evidently been a real effort.

"That should help," Dor said. He picked up the body of a goblin and shoved it through the hoop. It failed to emerge from the other side. "Yes, I think we have something useful, here." He returned it to the King, whose fingers disappeared as he took it. But they reappeared when the King changed grips, so it seemed the hoop was not dangerous to handle.

"And the forget spell," Dor continued. "Could it make the goblins and harpies forget what they are fighting about?"

"Oh, yes. It is extremely powerful. But if we detonated it here at the Castle, we would all forget why we are here, even who we are. Thus Magician Murphy would have his victory, for there would be no completion of the Castle. And the goblins and harpies might continue to fight anyway; creatures of that ilk hardly need reason to quarrel. They do it instinctively."

"But Magician Murphy himself would forget too!"

"No doubt. But the victory would still be his. He is not vying for power for himself; he is trying to prevent it from accruing to me."

Dor looked out at the barren north view, and at the battle still raging elsewhere around the Castle. A piedpiper flute, a magic ring-hoop, and a forget spell. A lot of excellent and potent magic—that by the anomaly of the situation could not seem to be used to reverse the course of this predicament.

"Murphy, I'm going to find a way," he swore under his breath. "This battle is not over yet." Or so he hoped.

Chapter 11

Disaster

"Zombies ahoy!" a centaur cried, pointing east.

There they were, at last: the zombies standing at the edge of the forest, beyond the milling goblins. The dragon-stomach smoke had obliterated the monstrous mound of goblins at the north wall, but that effect was abating now, and they were surging back from the east and west wings. Either the newly encroaching goblins would be dissolved also, in which case the region wasn't safe for zombies either, or they wouldn't, in which case the zombies couldn't pass there. So how could the Zombie Master get through?

"The Zombie Master must get to the Castle, where he can set up his magical laboratory and work undistracted," Dor said. "Now that we have him in sight, there just has to be a way."

"Yes, I believe at this stage it would tip the balance," King Roogna agreed.

"But the problem of transport still seems insuperable. It is difficult enough keeping the monsters outside the Castle; anything beyond the ramparts becomes prohibitive."

"If we believe that, so must they," Dor said. "Maybe we could surprise them. Cedric—would you join me in a dangerous mission?"

"Yes," the centaur said immediately.

The king glanced at him, mildly surprised at the change in attitude. Evidently Dor had done better with the centaurs than Roogna had expected.

"I want to take the King's flute and lure away the creatures from the vicinity of the zombies, to someplace where we can safely detonate the forget spell. That will stop the goblins from coming back here in time to interfere with the Zombie Master. Could you hold the magic hoop in such a way as to make any airborne attackers pass through it, while outrunning groundborne attacks?"

"I am a centaur!" Cedric said. Answer enough.

"Now really," the King said. "This is a highly risky venture!"

"So is doing nothing," Dor said. "The goblins are still mounding up at the other walls; before the day is out they will be coming over the top, and you have no more dragon juice to melt them down. We've got to have the zombies!"

Magician Murphy had come up again. "You are courting disaster," he said. "I respect your courage, Dor—but I must urge you not to go out so foolishly into the goblin horde."

"Listen, snotwing—" Cedric started.

Dor cut him off. "If you really cared, Magician, you would abate the curse. Is your real objection that you fear this ploy can succeed?"

The enemy Magician was silent.

"You'll need someone to lead the zombies in," Vadne said.

"Well, I thought maybe Jumper—"

"The big spider? You'd better have him with you, protecting your flank," she said. "I will guide the zombies in."

"That is very generous of you," Dor said, gratified. "You can transform any creature that gets through the zombie lines. The Zombie Master himself is the one who must be protected; get as close to him as you can and—"

"I shall. Let's get this mission going before it is too late."

The King and Magician Murphy both shook their heads with resignation, seeming strangely similar. But Roogna fetched the flute and the forget spell. They organized at the main gate. Dor mounted Cedric, Jumper joined him and bound him securely in place with silk, and Vadne mounted another centaur. The remaining centaurs of the north wall disposed themselves along the east wall, bows ready. Then the small party charged out into the melee of goblins and harpies.

There was a withering fire from the wall, as the centaurs shot fire arrows and the goblins, trolls, gnomes, and ghouls withered. It cleared a temporary path through the thickest throng. Cherry bombs and pineapples were still bombarding the allied army. This didn't seem to faze the goblins or their cohorts, but it made Dor extremely nervous. Suppose a pineapple were to land in his vicinity? He would be smithereened! And, considering Murphy's curse—

"Change course!" he screamed.

Startled, Cedric jounced to the side, through a contingent of elves. There was an explosion ahead of them. Shrapnel whizzed by Dor's nose, and the concussion hurt his ears. Eleven bodies sailed outward. Cedric veered to avoid the heavily smoking crater.

"Hey!" a centaur bellowed from the wall. "Stay on course! I almost catapulted a pineapple on you!"

Cecric got back on course with alacrity. "Centaurs have sharp eyes and quick reflexes," he remarked. "Otherwise something could have gone wrong."

Murphy's curse had tried, though, almost causing Dor to interfere with the centaur's careful marksmanship. Dor realized that he would do best to stick to his own department.

He put the flute to his lips, thankful that Jumper was there to help him, so that he had his hands and attention free. He blew experimentally into the mouthpiece. The flute played an eerie, lilting, enticing melody which floated out through the clamor of battle and brought a sudden hush. Then dwarves and gremlins, vampires and harpies, and numberless goblins swarmed after the centaurs, compelled alike by that magic music.

The winged monsters closed in faster, diving in toward Dor. Cedric twisted his human torso in that supple way centaurs had, facing back while still galloping forward. He swung the hoop through the air in an arc, intercepting the dirty birds as they came—and as each passed through the hoop, she vanished. Dor wondered where they went, but he was too busy playing the flute—if his labored blowing could be called playing—and keeping his body low so as not to get snagged by the hoop himself. He could not keep his attention on all the details!

With two of his legs, Jumper held a spear with which he prodded any goblins or similar ilk that got too close. No ilk could match the galloping pace of the centaur, but since they were forging through the whole goblin allied army, many closed in from the sides. Dor saw Vadne converting those goblins that she touched to pancake disks, and her centaur was fending off the aerial creatures with his fists.

Quickly they reached the zombie contingent. "Follow the woman in!" Dor cried. "I'll lead the monsters away! Block off your ears until I'm beyond your hearing!" Yes, that would be a fine Murphy foul-up, to lure the goblins away only to lure the Zombie Master and Millie into the same forget-spell trap! But a problem anticipated was a problem largely prevented.

Then he was off, playing the magic flute again. No matter how grossly he puffed into it, the music emerged clear and sweet and haunting. And the creatures followed.

"Where to?" Cedric inquired as they galloped.

Dor had an inspiration. "To the Gap!" he cried. "North!"

The centaur put on some speed. The air whistled by them. Experimentally Dor held the flute into the wind, and sure enough: it played. That saved him some breath. The goblins fell behind, and the elves and dwarves, but the trolls were keeping up. Cedric accelerated again, and now even the vampires lost headway. But Dor kept playing, and the creatures kept following. As they had to.

At centaur speed, the Gap was not long in drawing nigh. They had to wait for the land and air hordes to catch up.

"Now I want to get them close to the brink, then detonate the forget spell," Dor said, dropping the flute to his side for the moment. "With luck, the harpies will fly on across the Gap and get lost, and the goblins will be unable to follow them, so won't be able to fight any more."

"Commendable compassion," Jumper chittered. "But in order to gather a large number here, to obtain maximum effect from the spell, you must remain to play the flute for some time. How will *we* escape?"

"Oops! I hadn't thought of that! We're trapped by the Gap!" Dor looked down into the awesome reaches of the chasm, and felt heightsick. When would he stop being a careless child? Or was Murphy's curse catching them after all? Dor would have to sacrifice himself, to make the goblins and harpies forget?

"I can solve it." Jumper chittered. "Ballooning over the—"

"No!" Dor cried. "There is a whole hideous host of things that can and will go wrong with that. Last time we tried it—"

"Then I can drop us down over the edge, into the chasm, where the goblins cannot follow," Jumper suggested. "We can use the magic ring to protect us from descending harpies."

Dor didn't like the notion of descending into the Gap either, but the harpies and goblins and ilk were arriving in vast numbers, casting about for the missing flute music, and he had to make a quick decision."All right. Cedric, you gallop out of here; you're too heavy to lower on spider silk."

"That's for sure!" Cedric said. "But where should I go? I don't think I can make it back to the Castle. There are one or two zillion minor monsters charging from there to here, and I'd have to buck the whole tide."

"Go to Celeste," Dor suggested. "Your job is honorably finished, here, and she'll be glad to see you."

"First to the warlock!" Cedric exclaimed, grinning. He made a kind of salute, then galloped off west.

Jumper reattached the dragline to Dor, then scrambled over the cliff edge. This easy walking on a near-vertical face still amazed Dor. However, it was decidedly handy at the moment.

Dor resumed playing the flute, for the goblins were beginning to lose interest. That brought them forward with a rush. They closed on him so rapidly that they wedged against each other, blocking themselves off from him. But they were struggling so hard that Dor knew the jam would break at any moment. Yet he kept playing, waiting for Jumper's signal of readiness.

Finally his nerve broke. "Are you ready?" he called. And the goblins, loosed momentarily from their relentless press forward, eased up—and the jam did break. Dor fumbled, for his sword, knowing he could never fight off the inimical mass, yet—

But what was he thinking of? It was the magic ring he should use. Cedric had left it with him. He picked it up and held it before him. The first goblin dived right at him. Dor almost dropped the hoop, fearing the creature would smash into him—but as it passed through the ring, it vanished. Right before his face, as if it had struck an invisible wall and been shunted aside. Potent magic!

"Ready!" Jumper chittered from below. Just in time for three more goblins were charging, and Dor wasn't certain he could get them all neatly through the hoop. More likely they would snag on the rim, and their weight would have carried him back over the cliff. "Jump!"

Dor trusted his friend. He jumped. Backward off the cliff. He sailed out into the abyss, escaping the grasp of the surging goblins, swinging down and sidewise, for Jumper had providently rigged the lines so that Dor would not whomp directly into the wall. The spider always thought of these things before Dor did, anticipating what could go wrong and abating it first. Thus Murphy's curse had little power over him. That was why Jumper had taken so much time just now, despite knowing that Dor was in a desperate strait at the brink of the canyon; he had been making sure that no mistake of his would betray Dor.

And there it was, of course: the answer to the curse. Maturity. Only a careless or thoughtless person could be trapped by the curse, giving it the openings to snare him.

Now the vampires and harpies swarmed down, though the majority of them were fighting with the goblins above. "Snatch! snatch!" they screamed. A perfect characterization.

Dor found himself swinging back. He held the hoop before him, sweeping through the ugly flock—and where the ring passed, no harpies remained. But they clutched at him from the sides—

Then Jumper hauled him in against the wall, so that he could set his back to its protective solidity and hold the hoop before him. Dor saw now that the brink of the chasm was not even; the spider had skillfully utilized projections to anchor the framework of lines, so that Dor had room to swing clear of the wall. A remarkable feat of engineering that no other type of creature could have accomplished in so brief a time.

"Give me the ring!" Jumper chittered. "You play the flute!"

Right. They had to call as many creatures to this spot as possible. Dor yielded the hoop and put the flute to his lips. Jumper maneuvered deftly, using the hoop to protect them both.

Now the harpies dived in with single-minded intent, compelled by the music. They swooped through the hoop; they splatted into the wall around it, knocking themselves out and falling twistily down into the chasm, dirty feathers flying free. The vampires were no better off.

Then the goblins and trolls started dropping down from the ledge above, also summoned by the flute.

Dor broke off. "We're slaughtering them! That wasn't my intent! It's time to set off the forget spell!"

"We would be trapped by it too," Jumper reminded him. "Speak to it."

"Speak to it? Oh." Dor held out the glassy ball. "Spell, how are you detonated?"

"I detonate when a voice commands me to," the ball replied.

"Any voice?"

"That's what I said."

Dor had his answer. He set the sphere in a niche in the cliff. "Count to one thousand, then order yourself to detonate," he told it.

"Say, that's clever!" the spell said. "One, two, three-four-five—"

"Slowly!" Dor said sharply. "One number per second."

"Awww—" But the spell resumed more slowly. "Seven, eight—what a spoilsport you are!—nine, ten, a big fat hen!"

"What?" a nearby harpy screeched, taking it personally. She dived in, but Jumper snagged her with the hoop. Another potential foul-up defused.

"And don't say anything to insult the harpies," Dor told the spell.

"Ah, shucks. Eleven, twelve—"

Jumper scurried away to the side, fastened the other end of a new line he had attached to Dor, and hauled him across. This was not as fast as running on level land, but it was expedient.

They moved steadily westward, away from the spell sphere. Dor continued playing the flute intermittently, to keep the goblins massing at the brink without allowing too many to fall over. He heard the spell's counting fading in the distance, and that lent urgency to his escape. The problem was now one of management; he and Jumper had to get far enough away to be out of the forget range, without luring the goblins and harpies beyond range too. Inevitably a good many monsters would escape, but maybe the ones fazed by the forget detonation would lend sufficient confusion to the array to inhibit the others from returning to the Castle. There seemed to be no clearcut strategy; he just had to fudge through as best he could, hoping he could profit enough to give Castle Roogna the edge. It had worked well with the Mundane siege of the Zombie Master's castle, after all.

How much nicer if there were simple answers to all life's problems! But the closer Dor approached adulthood, the less satisfying such answers became. Life itself was complex, therefore life's answers were complex. But it took a mature mind to appreciate the convolutions of that complexity.

"One hundred five, one hundred six, pick up a hundred sticks!" the spell was chanting. "One hundred seven, one hundred eight, lay all hundred straight!" Now *there* was a simple mind!

Dor wondered again how wide a radius the detontion would have. Would the chasm channel it? Then the brunt would come along here, instead of out where the goblins were. Maybe he and Jumper should climb over the rim before the spell went off, and lie low there, hoping to be shielded from the direct effect. But they couldn't come up too close to the goblins, who were milling about near the brink. The harpies were still dive-bombing him, forcing Jumper to jump back with the hoop. Fortunately, the bulk of their attention was taken by the goblins, their primary enemy; Dor and Jumper were merely incidental targets, attacked because they were there. Except when Dor played the flute, as he continued to do intermittently.

"Three hundred forty-seven, three hundred forty-eight, now don't be late," the spell was saying in the fading distance. As long as he could hear it, he had to assume he was within its forget radius.

"Can we go faster?" Dor asked nervously. He had thought they were traveling well, but the numbers had jumped with seeming suddenness from the neighborhood of one hundred to the neighborhood of three hundred. Unless the spell was cheating, skipping numbers—no, the inanimate did not have the wit to cheat. Dor had just been preoccupied with his own efforts and gloomy thoughts.

"Not safely, friend," Jumper chittered.

"Let me take back the hoop," Dor suggested to the spider. "Then you can string your lines faster."

Jumper agreed, and passed back the hoop.

Another harpy made a screaming dive. Dor scooped her into the hoop, and she was gone without recall or recoil. What happened to the creatures who passed through it? Harpies could fly, goblins could climb; why couldn't either get out? Was it an inferno on the other side, killing them instantly? He didn't like that.

Jumper was ahead, setting the anchor for the next swing. Dor had a private moment. He poked a finger into the center of the hoop, from the far side, watching it disappear from his side. He saw his finger in cross section, as if severed with a sharp sword: the skin, the little blood vessels, the tendons, the bone. But there was no pain; his finger felt cool, not cold; no inferno there, and no freezing weather either. He withdrew it, and found it whole, to his relief. He poked it from the near side, and got the same effect, except that this time he could not see the cross section. It seemed that either side of the ring led to wherever it led. A different world?

Jumper tugged, and Dor swung across, feeling guilty for his surreptitious experimentation. He could have lost a finger that way. Well, maybe not; he had seen the King's fingers disappear and reappear unharmed.

"Let's check and see if the goblins are clear," Dor said. He had not played the flute for a while.

The spider scurried up the wall to peek over with two or three eyes, keeping the rest of his body low. "They are there in masses," he chittered. "I believe they are pacing the harpies—who are pacing us."

"Oh, no! Murphy strikes again! We can't get clear of the Gap, if they follow us!"

"We should be clear of the forget radius now," Jumper chittered consolingly.

"Then so are the goblins and harpies! That's no good!" Dor heard himself getting hysterical.

"Our effort should have distracted a great number of the warring creatures," Jumper pointed out reasonably. "Our purpose was to distract them so that the Zombie Master could penetrate to Castle Roogna. If he succeeded, we have succeeded."

"I suppose so," Dor agreed, calming. "So it doesn't really matter if the harpies and goblins don't get forget-spelled. Still, how are we ever going to get out of here? It is too late to turn off the spell."

"Perseverance should pay. If we continue until night—" Jumper cocked his body, lifting his two front legs so as to hear better. "What is that?"

Dor tried to fathom what direction the spider was orienting, and could not. Damn those ubiquitous eyes! "What's that?"

Then he heard it. "Nine hundred eighty-three, nine hundred eight-four, close to the hundred door; nine hundred eighty-five—"

A harpy was carrying the spell toward them—and it was about to detonate! "Oh, Murphy!" Dor wailed. "You really nabbed us now!"

"What's the big secret about this talking ball?" the harpy screeched.

"Nine hundred ninety-two, buckle the bag's shoe," the spell said.

"Stop counting!" Dor yelled at the spell.

"Countdown can't be stopped once initiated," the spell replied smugly.

"Quick," Jumper chittered. "I will fasten the draglines so we can return. We must escape through the magic hoop."

"Oh, no!" Dor cried.

"It should be safe; I saw you testing it."

"Nine hundred ninety-seven, nine hundred ninety-eight," the spell continued inexorably."Now don't be late!"

Jumper scrambled through the hoop. Dor hesitated, appalled. *Could* they return? But if he remained here—

"One thousand!" the spell cried gleefully. "Now at last I can say it!"

Dor dived through the hoop. The last thing he heard was "Deto—"

He arrived in darkness. It was pleasant, neutral. His body seemed to be suspended without feeling. There was a timelessness about him, a perpetual security. All he had to do was sleep.

You are not like the others, a thought said at him.

"Of course not," Dor thought back. Whatever he was suspended in did not permit physical talking, because there was no motion. "I am from another time. So is my friend Jumper the spider. Who are you?"

I am the Brain Coral, keeper of the source of magic.

"The Brain Coral! I know you! You're supposed to be animating my body!" *When?*

"Eight hundred years from now. Don't you remember?"

I am not in a position to know about that, being as yet a creature of my own time.

"Well, in my time you—uh, it gets complicated. But I think Jumper and I had better get out of here as soon as the forget spell dissipates."

You detonated a forget spell?

"Yes, a major one, inside the Gap. To make the goblins and harpies and cohorts and ilk stop fighting. They—"

Forget spells are permanent, until counterspelled.

"I suppose so, for the ones affected. But—"

You have just rendered the Gap itself forgotten.

"The Gap? But it's not alive! The spell only affects living things, things that remember."

Therefore all living things will forget the Gap.

Stunned, Dor realized it was true. He had caused the Gap to be forgotten by all but those people whose forgetting would be paradoxical. Such as those living adjacent to it, who would otherwise fall in and die. Their deaths would be inexplicable to their friends and relatives, leading to endless complications that would quickly neutralize the spell. Paradox was a powerful natural counterspell! But any people who had no immediate need-to-know would simply not remember the Gap. This was true in his own day—and now he knew how it had come about. He had done it, with his bumbling.

Yet if what he did here had no permanence, how could . . . ? He couldn't take time to ponder that now. "We have to get back to Castle Roogna. Or at least, we can't stay here. There would be paradox when we caught up to our own time."

So it would seem. I shall release you from my preservative fluid. The primary radiation of the spell should not affect you; the secondary may. You will not forget your personal identities and mission, but you may forget the Gap once you leave its vicinity.

"I'm pretty much immune to that anyway," Dor said. "I'm one of the near-Gap residents. Just so long as I don't forget the rest."

One question, before I release you. Through what aperture have you and all these other creatures entered my realm? I had thought the last large ring was destroyed fifty years ago.

"Oh, we have a two-inch ring that we expanded to two-foot diameter. We can change it back when we're done with it."

That will be appreciated. Perhaps we shall meet again—in eight hundred years, the Coral thought at him.

Then Dor popped out of the hoop and dangled by his dragline. Jumper followed.

"I had not anticipated immobility," the spider chittered ruefully.

"That's all right. We can't all think of everything, all the time."

Jumper was not affronted. "True."

The harpies were visible in the distance, but they paid no further attention to Dor and Jumper. They were milling about in air, trying to remember what they were doing there. Which was exactly what Dor had wanted to happen. The goblins, however, were in sadder state. They too seemed to be milling about—but they had forgotten that sharp dropoffs were hazardous to health, and were falling into the chasm at a great rate. Dor's action had decimated the goblin horde.

"It can not be helped," Jumper chittered, recognizing his disgust. "We can not anticipate or control all ramifications of any given course."

"Yeah, I guess," Dor agreed, still bothered by the slaughter he had wrought. Would he get hardened to this sort of carnage as he matured? He hoped not.

They climbed to the brim and stood on land again. The goblins ignored them, not remembering them. The forget detonation had evidently been devastating near its origin, wiping out all memories of everything.

Dor spied a glassy fragment lying on the ground. He went to pick it up. It was a shatter from the forget-spell globe. "You really did it, didn't you!" he said to it.

"That was some blast!" the fragment agreed happily. "Or was it? I forget!"

Dor dropped it and went on. "I hope Cedric got clear in time. That spell was more powerful than I expected."

"He surely did."

They hurried back toward the Castle, ignoring the wandering hordes.

The battle was not over at Castle Roogna, but it was evident that the tide had turned. As the distance from the forget-spell ground zero lengthened, the effects diminished, until here at the Castle there was little confusion—except that there were only about a third as many goblins and harpies as before, and the ramparts were manned by zombies. The Zombie Master had gotten through!

The defenders spied them, and laid down a barrage of cherry bombs to clear a path to the Castle. Even so, it was necessary to employ sword and hoop to get through, for the goblins and harpies resented strangers getting into their battle. So Dor was forced to slay again. War was hell, he thought.

King Roogna himself welcomed them at the gate. "Marvelous!" he cried. "You piped half the monsters off the field and made them forget. Vadne led the Zombie Master in while the goblins were distracted by the flute, and he has been generating new zombies from the battlefield casualties ever since. The only problem is fetching them in."

"Then there's work for me to do," Dor said shortly. He found he didn't really want to accept congratulations for doing a job of mass murder.

The King, the soul of graciousness, made no objection. "Your dedication does you credit."

Jumper helped, of course. Covered by centaur archers on the ramparts, they went out, located the best bodies, looped them with silk, and dashed back under cover. Then they hauled the corpses in on the lines. They were really old hands at this. When they had a dozen or so, they ferried them in to the Zombie Master's laboratory.

Millie was there, wan and disheveled, but she looked up with a smile when Dor entered. "Oh, you're safe, Dor! I was so worried!"

"Worry for your fiancé," he said shortly. "He's doing the work."

"He certainly is," Vadne said. She was moving the bodies into position for him by converting them to great balls that were easily rolled, then returning them to their regular shapes. As a result, he was evidently manufacturing zombies at triple the rate he had at his own castle. Time was consumed mainly in the processing, not the actual conversion. "He's making an army to defend this Castle!"

"Dor's doing a lot too!" Millie said stoutly.

Flattered despite himself, Dor realized that Millie still had feeling for him, and still might—But he had to suppress that. It was not only that his time in this world was limited, and that if he interfered with this particular aspect of history and it stayed put, he would paradoxically negate his whole original mission. It was that Millie was now betrothed to another man, and Dor had no right to—to do what he wished he could.

"We're all doing what we can, for the good of the Land of Xanth," he said, somewhat insecurely, considering his thought. How much better it would be for him, if he could find some girl more nearly his own age and status, and—

"I wish I had full Magician-caliber talent like yours," Vadne said to the Zombie Master as she shape-changed another corpse. Dor saw that she was able to handle living things, and once-living things, and inanimate things like the magic ring: a fair breadth of talent, really.

"You do have it," the Zombie Master said, surprised.

"No, I am only a neo-Sorceress."

"I would term your topological talent as Magician-caliber magic," he said, rendering the corpse into a zombie.

She almost glowed at the compliment, which carried even more impact because it was evident that he had made it matter-of-factly, unconscious of its effect. She looked at the Zombie Master with a new appraisal. What potency in a compliment, Dor thought, and filed the information in the back of his mind for future reference.

Dor went out to fetch more bodies. Jumper helped, as always. They kept working until daylight waned, and slowly the goblin and harpy forces dwindled while the zombie forces increased. Harpy zombies were now waging the defense in the air, greatly easing that situation.

Yet this left Dor unsatisfied. He had entered the tapestry for one mission, the acquisition of the elixir to restore a zombie to full life. But by the time he had that, he had been enmeshed in another mission, the conversion of the Zombie Master to King Roogna's cause. Now he had accomplished that also—and was casting about for yet another quest. What was it?

Ah, he had it now. This foolish war between the goblins and harpies—was it possible to do something about it, instead of preserving Castle Roogna by wiping out both sides? Why not simply abate the problems that had caused the war?

He had gone over this before, in his mind, and had no ansewr. But then time had been too much of a factor. Now the Caste was prevailing, now there was time, and he knew more about the magic available. The magic hoop, for example, leading into the Brain Coral's somber storage lake—

"That's it!" he exclaimed.

Jumper cocked four or five eyes at him. "There is something I missed?"

"Anchor me, so I can't fall in. I have to go through the hoop to talk with the Brain Coral."

The spider did not argue or question. He fastened a stout dragline to Dor. Dor propped the magic hoop against a wall and poked his head through.

"Brain Coral!" he thought, again finding it impossible to breathe or speak in the preservative fluid. This stuff was not mere water; it had stasis magic. "This is Dor of eight hundred years from now, again."

What is your concern? the Coral inquired patiently.

"Have you a male harpy in storage?"

Yes. An immature one, exiled three hundred years ago by a rival for the harpy throne.

"A royal male?" Dor thought, startled.

By harpy law a royal person cannot be executed like a commoner. So he was put safely away, and the access ring destroyed thereafter.

"Will you release him now? It would make a big difference to our present situation."

I will release him. Bear in mind you owe me a favor.

"Yes. I will talk to you again in eight hundred years." Dor removed his head from the Coral's realm. His head had been in stasis, but the rest of his body was responsive.

In a moment a bird-shape popped out of the hoop. "Greetings, Prince," Dor said formally.

The figure spread his wings, orienting on him. "And what ilk be ye, man-thing?"

"I am Magician Dor. I have freed you from storage."

The harpy glanced an imperial glance at him. "Show your power."

Dor picked up a fallen harpy feather. "What is the age of the Prince?" he inquired. "Exclusive of storage time."

"The Prince is twelve years old," the feather answered.

"Why, that's my age!" Dor exclaimed.

"You'll sure be a giant when you get your full growth!" the feather said.

The Prince cut in. "Very well. I accept your status, and will deal with ye. I am Prince Harold. What is it ye crave of me?"

"You are the only male harpy alive today," Dor said "You must go forth and claim your crown, to preserve your species. I charge you with two things only: do not cohabit with any but your own kind, and give to me the counterspell to the curse your people put on the goblins."

The Prince drew himself up with hauteur. "One favor ye did me, yet ye presume to impose on me for two favors! I need no stricture of cohabitation for when I come of age—not when I have the entire world of harpies to build my harem from. As to this spell, I know naught of it."

"It happened after your exile. You can discover its nature from your subjects."

"I shall do so," the harpy said "An I discover it, I shall provide the counter as your recompense."

Dor conducted the Prince to King Roogna, who did a polite double take as he observed the harpy's gender. "Rare magic indeed!" he murmured.

"We must release Prince Harold Harpy to his kind without mishap," Dor told the King. The harpies will have no need to fight, once they have him."

"I see," the King said. He glanced obliquely at Magician Murphy, standing beside him. "We shall declare an absolute cease-fire until he is free. I shall walk the ramparts myself, to be sure that nothing goes wrong."

"You may manage to free the harpy," Murphy said grimly. "But my curse will have its impact elsewhere. You have not prevailed." But he looked tired; his talent was evidently under severe strain. No single Magician, however gifted, could stand forever against the power of three. Dor was almost sorry for him.

"But we're getting there," Roogna said. He escorted the Prince to the wall, cautioning the centaurs not to fire at the harpy. Prince Harold spread his pinions and launched into the sky.

There was a screech of sheerest amazement from the nearest female. Then the harpies swarmed to the Prince. For an awful moment Dor feared they had mistaken him, and would tear him to pieces; but they had instantly recognized his nature. They lost all interest in the goblin war. In moments the entire swarm had flapped away, leaving the goblins nothing to fight except a few tired vampires.

Then a lone female harpy winged back from the flock. A centaur whistled. "Helen!" Dor cried, recognizing her.

"By order of Prince Harold," Helen said. "The counterspell." She deposited a pebble in his hand. She winked. "Too bad you didn't take your opportunity when you had it, handsome man; you will never have another. I used the ring you gave me to wish for the finest possible match, and now I am to be first concubine to the Prince." She tapped her ringed claw.

Things evidently happened fast among the harpies; it had been only a few minutes since the Prince mounted the sky. "Good for you," Dor said.

"I knew I could do it," the ring replied, thinking Dor had addressed it. "I can do anything!"

She glanced down at it. "Oh, so you're talking again!"

"It will be silent hereafter," Dor said. "Thank you for the counterspell."

"It's the least I could do for you," she said, inhaling. The centaurs goggled.

Then Heavenly Helen spread her pretty wings and was away, with all males on the parapet staring after her, and even a few of the healthier zombies were admiring her form. There were covert glances at Dor, as people wondered what he had done to attract the attention of so remarkable a creature.

Dor was satisfied. Helen had, in true harpy fashion, snatched her opportunity. And who could tell: maybe the wish ring really had had something to do with it.

Dor turned his attention to the pebble spell. "How are you invoked?" he asked it.

"I am not invoked; I am revoked," it replied. "I am not a counterspell, I am the original spell. When I am revoked, the enchantment abates."

"How are you revoked, then?"

"You just heat me to fire temperature, and my magic pours out invisibly until it is all gone."

Dor handed the pebble to the King. "That should abate the goblin complaint. With no further reason to fight, the goblins should go home. Then Murphy's curse can't make the battle continue here."

"You are phenomenal, Magician!" King Roogna said. "You have used your mind instead of your body, in a truly regal manner." He hurried away with the pebble spell.

The King cooked the goblin spell according to the directive, but no change in the goblin horde was apparent. Yet he was not dismayed. "The original spell was subtle," he explained. "It caused the goblin females to be negatively selective. The damage has been done to the goblins over the course of many generations. It will take many more generations to reverse. The females are not here on the battlefield, so the males do not even know of the change yet. So we do not see its effect immediately, or benefit from it ourselves, but still the job is worth doing. We are not trying merely to preserve Castle Roogna; we are building a better land of Xanth." He waved a hand cheerfully. "Evening is upon us; we must go to our repast and sleep, while the zombies keep watch. I believe victory is at last coming into sight."

It did look that way. Magician Murphy looked glum indeed. Dor, suddenly tired, ate perfunctorily, fell on the bed provided in the completed section of the Castle, and slept soundly. In the morning he woke to discover the Zombie Master on an adjacent bed, and Magician Murphy on another. Everyone was tired, and there was as yet very little space within the Castle.

The goblins had largely dispersed in the night, leaving their copious dead in the field. The zombies remained on guard. The centaurs had resumed their building labors, no longer needed for the defense of the Castle. Now it did seem likely that Castle Roogna would be completed on schedule.

A buffet breakfast was being served in the dining hall, amid the clods of earth, stray pieces of zombies, and discarded weapons. King Roogna was there, and Magician Murphy, and Vadne and Jumper and Dor. Murphy had little appetite; he seemed almost as gaunt as the Zombie Master.

"Frankly I think we have it in hand," the King said. "Will you not relinquish with grace, Murphy?"

"There remains yet one aspect of the curse," Murphy said. "Should it fail, then I am done, and will retire. But I must hold on until it manifests."

"Fair enough," Roogna said. "I hung on when it seemed your curse had prevailed. Indeed, had not young Dor arrived with his friend—"

"Surely nothing I did really affected the outcome," Dor said uneasily. For there, ultimately, could be Murphy's victory.

"You still feel that what you do is invalid?" the King inquired. "We can readily have the verification of that. I have a magic mirror somewhere—"

"No, I—" But the King in his gratitude was already on his way to locate the mirror.

"Perhaps it *is* time we verified this," Murphy said. "Your involvement, Dor, has become so pervasive and intricate that it becomes difficult to see how it can be undone. I may have been mistaken in my conjecture. Was my curse opposing you also?"

"I believe it was," Dor said. "Things kept going wrong—"

"Then you must have validity, for otherwise my curse would not care. In fact, if your efforts lacked validity, my curse might even have promoted them, so that they played a larger part in the false success if the King depended on you instead of on his own—"

"But how can I change my own—" Dor glanced at Vadne, then shrugged. He could not remember whether she knew about him now or did not. What did it matter, so long as Millie remained innocent? "My own past?"

"I do not know," Murphy said. "I had thought that would be a paradox, therefore invalid. Yet there are aspects of magic no man can fathom. I may have made a grievous error, and thereby cost myself the victory. Is the Gap forgotten in your day?"

"Yes."

They mulled that over for a while, chewing on waffles from the royal waffle tree. Then Murphy said: "It could be that spots of history can be rechanneled, so long as the end result is the same. If King Roogna is fated to win, it may not matter how he does it, or what agencies assist. So your own involvement may be valid, yet changes nothing. You are merely filling a role that some other party filled in your absence."

"Could be," Dor agreed. He glanced about. The others seemed interested in the discussion, except for Vadne, who was withdrawn. Something about that bothered him, but he couldn't place it.

"At any rate, we shall soon know. My power has been stretched to its limit," Murphy continued. "If I do not achieve the victory this day, I shall be helpless. I do not know exactly what form my curse will take, but it is in operation now, and I think will prove devastating. The issue remains in doubt."

The King returned with his mirror. "Let me see—how shall I phrase this?" he said to himself. "Mirror queries have to rhyme. That was built into them by the Magician who made this type of glass. Ah." He set it on the floor. "Mirror, mirror, on the floor—can we trust ourselves to Dor?"

"Corny," Murphy muttered.

The forepart of a handsome centaur appeared in the mirror. "That signifies affirmative," Roogna said. "The hind part is the negative."

"But many centaurs are far handsomer in the hind part," Dor pointed out.

"Why not simply ask it which side will prevail?" Murphy suggested wryly.

"I doubt that will work," the King said. "Because if its answer affects our actions, that would be paradox. And since we have been dealing with very strong magic, it could be beyond the mirror's limited power of resolution."

"Oh, let's discover the answer for ourselves," Murphy said. "We have fought it through this far, we might as well finish it properly."

"Agreed," Roogna said.

They ate more waffles, pouring on maple syrup from a rare maple tree. Unlike other magic beverage trees, the maple issued its syrup only a drop at a time, and it was dilute, so that a lot of the water had to be boiled off to make it thick enough for use. This made the syrup a special delicacy. In fact, maple trees no longer existed in Xanth in Dor's day. Maybe they had been overtapped, and thus this most magical species had ironically gone the way of most mundane trees.

The Zombie Master came in. Vadne perked up. "Come sit by me," she invited.

But he was not being sociable. "Where is Millie the maid, my fiancée?"

The others exchanged perplexed glances. "I assumed she was with you," Dor said.

"No. I worked late last night, and it would not be meet for such as she to keep my company unchaperoned. I sent her to bed."

"You didn't do that at your own castle," Dor pointed out.

"We were not then engaged. After the betrothal, we kept company only in company."

Dor though of asking about the journey from the zombie castle to Castle Roogna, which had had at least one night on the road. But he refrained; it seemed the Zombie Master had conservative notions about propriety, and honored them rigidly.

"She has not been to breakfast," the King said. "She must be sleeping late."

"I called at her door, but she did not answer," the Zombie Master said.

"Maybe she's sick," Dor suggested, and immediately regretted his directness, for the Zombie Master jumped as if stung.

The King interceded smoothly. "Vadne, check Millie's room."

The neo-Sorceress departed. Soon she was back. "Her room is empty."

Now the Zombie Master was really upset. "What has happened to her?"

"Do not be concerned," Vadne said consolingly. "Perhaps she became weary of Castle life and returned to her stockade. I will be happy to assist you during her absence."

But he would not be consoled. "She is my fiancée! I must find her!"

"Here, let me query the mirror," the King said. "What's a rhyme for Maid?"

"Shade," Murphy said.

"Thank you, Magician," the King said. He propped the mirror in a niche in the wall where it was in shadow. "Mirror, mirror, in the shade, tell us what happened to—"

Dor's chair thunked on the floor as he craned forward to see the picture about to form. The mirror slipped from its perch and fell. It cracked in two, and was useless.

The Zombie Master stared at it. "Murphy's curse!" he exclaimed. "Why should it prevent us from locating the maid?" He turned angrily on Murphy.

Magician Murphy spread his hands. "I do not know, sir. I assure you I have no onus against your fiancée. She strikes me as a most appealing young woman."

"She strikes everyone that way," Vadne said. "Her talent is—"

"Do not denigrate her to me!" the Zombie Master shouted. "It was only in gratitude to her that I agreed to soil my hands with politics! If anything happens to her—"

He broke off, and there was a pregnant silence. Suddenly the nature of the final curse was coming clear to them all. Without Millie, the Zombie Master had no reason to support the King, and Castle Roogna would then lose its major defensive force. Anything could happen to further interrupt its construction— and would. Murphy would win.

Yet the harpies and goblins were gone, Dor thought. Did anything remain that could really threaten the Castle? And he realized with horror that one thing did: the zombies themselves. They now controlled Castle Roogna. If they turned against the King—

"It seems your curse has struck with extreme precision," King Roogna said, evidently recognizing the implication. The issue was indeed in doubt! "We must find Millie quickly, and I fear that will not be easy."

"It was my chair that jolted the mirror," Dor said, stricken. "It's my fault!"

"Do not blame yourself," Murphy said. "The curse strikes in the readiest manner, much as water seeks the lowest channel. You have simply been used."

"Well, then, I'll find her!" Dor cried. "I'm a Magician, same as you are." He looked about. "Wall, where is she?"

"Don't ask me," the wall said. "She hasn't been here in the dining hall since last night."

Dor marched out into the hall, the others trailing after him. "Floor, when was she last here?"

"Last night after supper," the floor said. Neither wall nor floor elected to be difficult about details; they knew whom Dor meant, and recognized his mood, and gave him no trouble.

Dor traced Millie's whereabouts randomly, pacing the halls. A problem became apparent: Millie, like the others, had moved about considerably during the evening, and the walls, floors and limited furnishings were not able to distinguish all the comings and goings. It was a trail that crossed and recrossed itself, so that the point of exit could not be determined. Millie had been here at the time the Zombie Master sent her to bed—and not thereafter. She had not arrived at her own room. Where had she gone?

"The front gate—see whether she left the Castle," the King suggested.

Dor doubted Millie would depart like that—not voluntarily. But he queried the front gate. She had not exited there. He checked the ramparts. She had not gone there. In fact she had gone nowhere. It was as if she had vanished from the middle of the hall.

"Could somebody have conjured her out?" Dor wondered aloud.

"Conjuring is not a common talent," King Roogna said. "I know of no conjurers today who could accomplish this."

"The magic hoop!" Jumper chittered.

Oh, no! They fetched the hoop, still at its two-foot diameter. "Did Millie the maid pass through you last night?" Dor demanded of it.

"She did not," The hoop said acerbically. "No one has been through me since you stuck your fool head through and brought out the harpy Prince. When are you going to have me changed back to my normal size? I'm uncomfortable, stretched out like this."

"Later," Dor told it, experiencing relief. Then his relief reversed. If Millie had gone through there, at least she would be alive and safe and possibly recoverable. As it was, the mystery remained, growing more critical every moment.

"Query the flute," Jumper suggested. "If someone played it and lured her somewhere—"

Dor queried the pied-piper flute. It, too, denied any involvement. "Could it be lying?" Vadne asked.

"No," Dor answered shortly.

They crossed the Castle again, but gained nothing on their original information: Millie had left the Zombie Master in the evening, going toward her room —and never gotten there. Nothing untoward had been seen by anyone or anything.

Then Jumper had another notion. "If she is the victim of malodorous entertainment—"

"What?" Dor asked.

"Foul play," the web said, rechecking its translation. "Can't expect me to get the idiom right every time."

Dor smiled momentarily. "Continue."

Jumper chittered again. ". . . victim of smelly games, then some other person is most likely responsible. We must ascertain the whereabouts of each other living person at the time of her disappearance."

"You have an uncommonly apt perception," King Roogna told the spider. "You approach things from new directions."

"It comes from having eyes in the back of one's head," Jumper said matter-of-factly.

They checked for the others. The centaurs had remained on the ramparts, backing up the zombies. Dor and Jumper and King Roogna had slept. The Zombie Master had worked till the wee hours, then gone to the male room and thence to his sleeping cot. Magician Murphy had taken an innocent tour of the premises, also stopped at the male room, and slept. Neo-Sorceress Vadne had assisted the Zombie Master, but gone to the female room shortly before Millie was dismissed. She had returned to work late with the Zombie Master, then gone to her own room to sleep. Nothing there.

"What occurs in the female room?" Jumper inquired.

"Uh, females have functions too," Dor said.

"Excretion. I comprehend. Did Millie go there?"

"Often. Young females have great affinity for such places."

"Did she emerge on the final occasion?"

The men stared. "We never checked there!" Dor cried.

"Now don't you men go snooping into a place like that!" Vadne protested. "It's indecent!"

"We will merely ask straightforward questions," the King assured her. "No voyeurism."

Vadne looked unsatisfied, but did not protest further. They repaired to the female room, where Dor inquired somewhat diffidently of the door: "Did Millie the maid enter here late last night?"

"She did. But I won't tell you what her business was," the door replied primly.

"Did she depart thereafter?"

"Come to think of it, she never did," the door said, surprised. "That must have been some business!"

Dor looked up to find one of Jumper's green eyes bearing on him. They had located Millie! Almost.

They entered. The female room was clean, with several basins and potties and a big drainage sump for disposal of wastes. In one corner was a dumbwaiter for shipment of laundry and sundry items upstairs. Nothing else.

"She's not here," Dor said, disappointed.

"Then this is her point of departure," the King said. "Question every artifact here, if you have to, until we discover the exact mode of her demise. I mean, departure," he amended quickly, conscious of the presence of the somber Zombie Master.

Dor questioned. Millie had come in, approached a basin, looked at her pretty but tired face in a mundane mirror—and Vadne had entered the room. Vadne had doused the Magic Lantern. In the darkness Millie had screamed with surprise and dismay, and there had been a swish as of hair flinging about, and a tattoo on the floor as of feet kicking. That was all.

Vadne had departed the room alone. The light had remained doused until morning—when there was no sign of Millie.

Vadne was edging toward the door. Jumper threw a noose and snared her, preventing her escape. "So you were the one!" the Zombie Master cried. His gaunt face was twisted with incredulous rage, his eyes gleaming whitely from their sockets.

"I only did it for you," she said, bluffing it out. "She didn't love you anyway; she loved Dor. And she's just a garden-variety maid, not a Magician-caliber talent. You need a—"

"She is my betrothed!" the Zombie Master cried, his aspect wild. Dor echoed the man's passion within himself. The Zombie Master did love her—as Dor did. "What did you do with her, wretch?"

"I put her where you will never find her!" Vadne flared.

"This is murder," King Roogna said grimly.

"No it isn't!" Vadne cried. "I didn't kill her. I just—changed her."

Dor saw the strategy in that. The Zombie Master could have reanimated her dead body as a zombie; as it was, he could do nothing.

Jumper peered down the drainage sump with his largest eye. "Is it possible?" he inquired.

"We'll rip out the whole sump to find her!" the King cried.

"And if you do," Vadne said, "what will you do then? Without me you can't change her back to her stupid sex-appeal form."

"Neo-Sorceress," King Roogna said grimly. "We are mindful of your considerable assistance in the recent campaign. We do not relish showing you disfavor."

"Oh, pooh!" she said. "I only helped you because Murphy wouldn't have me, and I wanted to marry a Magician."

"You have chosen unwisely. If you do not change the maid back, we shall have to execute you."

She was taken aback, but remained defiant. "Then you'll never get her changed, because talents never repeat."

"But they do overlap," Roogna said.

"In the course of decades or centuries! The only way you can save her is to deal on my terms."

"What are your terms?" the King asked, his eyes narrow.

"Let Dor marry Millie. She likes him better anyway, the stupid slut. I'll take the Zombie Master."

"Never!" the Zombie Master cried, his hands clenching.

Vadne faced him. "Why force on her a marriage with a man she doesn't love?" she demanded.

That shook him. "In time she would—"

"How much time? Twenty years, when she's no longer so sweet and young? Two hundred? I love you *now!*"

The Zombie Master looked at Dor. His face was tight with emotional pain, but his voice was steady. "Sir, there is some truth in what she says. I was always aware that Millie—if you had—" He choked off, then forced himself to continue. "I would prefer to see Millie married to you, than locked in some hideous transformation. If you—"

Dor realized that Millie was being offered to him again. All he had to do was take her, and she would be restored and Castle Roogna would be safe. He could by his simple acquiescence nullify the last desperate aspect of Murphy's curse.

He was tempted. But he realized that this transformation was the fate that had awaited her throughout. If he took Millie now, he could offer her . . . nothing. He was soon to return to his own time. Vadne evidently didn't believe that, but it was true. If he eschewed Millie, she would remain enchanted, a ghost for eight hundred years. A dread but fated destiny.

If he interfered now, he really would change history. There was no question of that, for this was personal, his immediate knowledge. He would fashion a paradox, the forbidden type of magic—and by the devious logic of the situation, Murphy would win. The curse had at last forced Dor to nullify himself by changing too much.

Yet if he turned down Vadne's terms, King Roogna would lose anyway, as the Zombie Master turned against him. Either way, Magician Murphy prevailed.

What was he, Dor, to do? Since either choice meant disaster, he might as well do what he believed to be right, however much it hurt.

"No," Dor said, knowing he was forcing Millie to undergo the full throes of ghosthood. Eight centuries long—and what reward awaited her there? Nurse-maid to a little boy! Association with a zombie! "She goes to her betrothed—or to no one."

"But I am her betrothed!" the Zombie Master cried. "I love her—and because I love her, I yield her to you! I would do anything rather than permit her to suffer!"

"True love," King Roogna said. "It becomes you, sir."

"I'm sorry," Dor said. He understood now that his love for Millie was less, because he chose to let her suffer. He was knowingly inflicting terrible grief upon them all. Yet the alternative was the sacrifice of what they had all fought to save, deviously but certainly. He had no choice. "What's right is right, and what's wrong is wrong. I—" He spread his hands, unable to formulate his thought.

The Zombie Master gazed somberly at him. "I believe I understand." Then, surprisingly, he offered his hand.

Dor accepted it. Suddenly he felt like a man.

"If you will not restore her," the King said angrily to Vadne, "you shall be passed through the hoop."

"You're bluffing," Vadne said. "You won't throw away your Kingdom just to get at me."

But the King was not bluffing. He gave her one more chance, then had the hoop brought.

"I'll change it back to its original size," she threatened. "Then you won't be able to use it."

"You are very likely to go through it anyway," the King said, and there was something in his expression that cowed her. She stepped through the hoop and was gone.

The King turned to the Zombie Master. "It is a matter of principle," he explained. "I cannot allow any subject to commit such a crime with impunity. We shall ransack this Castle to locate Millie in whatever form she may be, and shall search out every avenue of magic that might restore her. Perhaps periodically we can recall Vadne from storage to see if she is ready to restore the maid. In time—"

"Time . . ." the Zombie Master repeated brokenly. They all knew the project could take a lifetime.

"Meanwhile, I apologize to you most abjectly for what has occurred, and will facilitate your return to your castle in whatever manner I can. I hope some year we will meet again in better circumstances."

"No, we shall not meet again."

Dor did not like the sound of that, but kept quiet.

"I understand," King Roogna said. "Again, I apologize. I would not have asked you to bring your zombies here, had I known what form the curse would take. I am sorry to see them go."

"They are not going," the Zombie Master said.

Dor felt gathering dread. What was the Zombie Master about to do, in his betrayal and grief? He could destroy everything, and there was no way to stop him except by killing him. Dor held his arms rigid, refusing to touch his sword.

"But nothing holds you here now," King Roogna said.

"I did not buy Millie with my aid, I did not bargain for her hand!" the Zombie Master cried. "I came here because I realized it would please her, and I would not wish to displease her even in death by changing that. My zombies will remain here as long as they are needed, to see Castle Roogna through this crisis and any others that arise. They are yours for eternity, if you want them."

Dor's mouth dropped open.

"Oh, I want them!" the King agreed. "I will set aside a fine graveyard for them, to rest in in comfort between crises. I will name them the honored guardians of Castle Roogna. Yet—"

"Enough," the Zombie Master said, and turned to Dor. But he did not speak. He gave Dor one enigmatic glance, then walked slowly out of the room.

"Then I have lost," Murphy said. "My curse worked, but has been overwhelmed by the Zombie Master's loyalty. I cannot overcome the zombies." He, too, walked away.

That left Dor, Jumper, and the King. "This is a sad victory," Roogna said.

Dor could only agree. "We'll stay to help you clean up the premises, Your Majesty. Then Jumper and I must return to our own land."

They made their desolate way to the dining room, but no one cared to finish breakfast. They went to work on the cleanup chore, burying unzombied bodies outside, removing refuse from inside, putting away fallen books in the library. The main palace had not yet been built, but the library stood as it would be eight hundred years hence, apart from details of decor. One large tome had somehow strayed to the dumbwaiter; Dor held the volume for a moment, struck by a nagging emotion, then filed it on the shelf in the library.

In the afternoon they found the Zombie Master hanging from a rafter. He had committed suicide. Somehow Dor had known—or should have known—that it could come to this. The man's love had been too sudden, his loss too unfair. The Zombie Master had known Millie would die, known what he would do. This was what he had meant when he told the King they would not meet again.

Yet when they cut him down, the most amazing and macabre aspect of this disaster manifested: the Zombie Master was not precisely dead. He had somehow converted himself into a zombie.

The zombie shuffled aimlessly out of the Castle, and was seen no more. Yet Dor was sure it was suffering—and would suffer eternally, for zombies never died. What awful punishment the Zombie Master had wreaked upon himself in his bereavement!

"In a way, it is fitting," King Roogna murmured. "He has become one of his own."

The lesser personnel of the Castle, whom the King had sent away for the crisis, were now returning. The maids and the cooks, the steeds and dragons. Activity resumed, yet to Dor the halls seemed empty. What a victory they had won! A victory of grief and regret and hopelessness.

Finally Dor and Jumper prepared to depart, knowing the spell that placed them here in the tapestry world would soon bring them home. They wanted to be away from Castle Roogna when it happened. "Rule well, King Roogna," Dor said as he shook the monarch's hand for the last time.

"I shall do my best, Magician Dor," Roogna replied. "I wish you every success and happiness in your own land, and I know that when your time comes to rule—"

Dor made a deprecating gesture. He had learned a lot, here—more than he cared to. He didn't want to think about being King.

"I have a present for you," Jumper said, presenting the King with a box. "It is the puzzle-tapestry the Zombie Master gave to me. I am not able to take it with me. I ask you to assemble it at your leisure and hang it from the wall of whatever room you deem fit. It should provide you with many hours of pleasure."

"It shall have a place of honor, always," the King said, accepting it.

Then Dor thought of something. "I, too, have an important object I can't take with me. But I can recover it, after eight hundred years, if you will be so kind as to spell it into the tapestry."

"No problem at all," King Roogna said. Dor gave him the vial of zombie-restorative elixir. "I shall cause it to respond to the words 'Savior of Xanth.'"

"Uh, thanks," Dor said, embarrassed.

He went up to the ramparts to bid farewell to the remaining centaurs. Cedric was not there, of course, having returned home. But Egor Ogre was present, and Dor shook his huge bony hand, cautiously.

That was it. Dor was no more adept at partings than at greetings. They walked away from the Castle, across the deserted, blasted battlefield—and into a vicious patch of saw grass at the edge. Jumper, more alert than Dor, drew him back from the swipe of the nearest saw just barely in time.

They were back in the jungle. The visible, tangible wilderness, where there was little subtlety about evil. Somehow it seemed like home.

Yet as they sloughed methodically through the forest, avoiding traps, skirting perils, and nullifying hazards in dull routine fashion, Dor found himself disturbed by more than human-related grief. He mulled it over, and finally had it.

"It is you, Jumper," he said. "We are about to return home. But there I am a boy, and you are a tiny spider. We'll never see each other again! And—" He felt the boyish tears emerging. "Oh, Jumper, you're my best friend, you've been by my side through the greatest and awfulest adventure of my life, and—and—"

"I thank you for your concern," the spider chittered. "But we need not separate completely. My home is by the tapestry. There are many fat lazy bugs trying to eat into the fabric, and now I have special reason to keep them from it. Look for me there, and you will surely find me."

"But—but in three months I'll only be an older boy—and you'll be dead!"

"It is my natural span," Jumper assured him. "I will live as much in that time as you do in the next thirty years. I will tell my offspring about you. I am thankful that chance has given me this opportunity to learn about your frame of reference. I would never otherwise have realized that the giant species have intelligence and feelings too. It has been a great and satisfying education for me."

"And for me!" Dor exclaimed. Then, spontaneously, he offered his hand. The spider solemnly lifted a forefoot and shook Dor's hand.

Chapter 12

Return

One moment Dor was swinging on spider silk across a minor chasm; the next he was standing on the floor of the Castle Roogna drawing room before the tapestry.

"Is that you, Dor?" a familiar voice inquired.

Dor looked around and spied a tiny, humanoid figure. "Of course it's me, Grundy," he told the golem. "Who else would it be?"

"The Brain Coral, of course. That's who it's been for the past two weeks."

Of course. Quickly Dor readjusted. He was no longer a great-thewed Mundane; he was a small, spindly twelve-year-old boy. His own body. Well, it would grow in due course.

He focused on the tapestry, looking for Jumper. The spider should be where they had been when the spell reverted, in the wilderness—ah, there was a speck.

Dor leaned forward and spied the tiny creature, so small he could crush it with the tip of his littlest finger. Not that he ever would do a thing like that! It raised a hairlike foreleg in a wave.

"It says you look strange in your real form," Grundy said. "It says—"

"I need no translation!" Dor snapped. Suddenly his eyes were blinded by tears, whether of joy or grief he was uncertain. "I'll—I'll see you again, Jumper. Soon. Within a few days—a few months of your time—I mean—oh, Jumper!"

"Who cares about a dumb bug?" Grundy asked.

Dor clenched his fist, for an instant tempted to smash the golem into the pulp from which he had been derived. But he controlled himself. How could Grundy know what Jumper meant to Dor? Grundy was of the old order, unenlightened.

There was nothing Dor could do. The spider had his own life to lead, and Dor had his. Their friendship was independent of size or time. But oh, he felt a choke in his heart!

Was this another aspect of becoming a man? Was it worth it?

Yet Dor had friends here, too. He must not allow his experience of the tapestry world to alienate him from his own world. He turned away from the tapestry. "Hello, Grundy. How are things in the real world?"

"Don't ask!" the golem exclaimed. "You know the Brain Coral, who took over your body? Thing was like a child—I mean even childier than you, at times —poking into everything, making *faux passes*—"

"What?"

"Cultural errors. Like belching into your soup. That thing really kept me hopping!"

"Sounds like fun," Dor said, smiling. Already he was getting used to this little body. It lacked the strength of the Mundane giant, but it wasn't a bad body. "Listen, I have to talk to that Coral. I owe it a favor."

"No you don't. You owe it a punch in the mouth, if anything. If it has a mouth. All's even—it got the fun of using your body, while you went into tapestry land for a nice vacation."

Some vacation! "I owe it from eight hundred years ago."

"Oh. Well, sure, tell the gnome."

"Who? Oh, the Good Magician Humfrey. I will. Right now I have to go see Jonathan the zombie."

"Oh, yeah. You got the stuff?"

"I got it. I think."

"This will be something! The first restored zombie to go with the first restored ghost! For centuries, she untouchable and he not worth touching. Grisly romance!"

Dor might have snapped something nasty at the golem, but recent experience had lent him discretion. So he changed the subject. "Maybe I'd better check first with King Roog—King Trent. He's the one who put me up to this."

Grundy shrugged. "Just so I don't have to exchange another word with the Coral."

"That's next." Dor couldn't help teasing the golem a little.

"Look, you know what that creature was doing with your body and Irene?"

"Who?" Dor was distracted, thinking about his upcoming interview with the Brain Coral. What kind of favor would he have to repay, after eight hundred years?

"Princess Irene, daughter of the King. Remember her?"

"Well, it has been eight centuries, in a manner of—" Dor did a double take. *"What* did my body do with Irene?"

"Coral was real curious about the distinction between male and female anatomy. Coral's asexual, or bisexual, or something, see, and—"

"Enough! Do you realize I'm about to see her father?"

"Why do you think I mentioned the matter? I tried to cover for you, but King Trent's pretty savvy and Irene's a snitch. So I'm not sure—"

"When did I—I mean, my body—?"

"Yesterday."

"Then there may still be time. She doesn't speak to her father for days at a time."

"In a case like this she might make an exception."

"She might indeed!" Dor agreed worriedly.

"Ah, what does it matter? The King knows she's a brat."

"It is my own reputation I am thinking of." Dor had been accorded the respect due a grown man, in the tapestry world, and the feeling was now important to him. But it was more than that. Other people had feelings too. He thought of how Vadne had glowed when the Zombie Master complimented her talent—and how Murphy's curse had perverted that into her doom and his. And Millie's. Feelings were important—even those of brats.

Dor addressed the floor. "Where is Irene?"

"Hasn't been here for days."

He moved into the hall, questioning as he went. Soon he located her—in her own apartment in the palace. "You go elsewhere," he told Grundy. "I have to handle this myself."

"Aw," the golem complained. "Your fights with Irene are so much fun." But he obediently departed. Dor inhaled deeply, the act reminding him fleetingly of Heavenly Helen Harpy, squared his shoulders, then knocked politely. Quickly she opened the door.

Irene was only eleven, but with his new perspective Dor saw that she was an extremely pretty child, about to blossom into a fair young woman. The lines of her face were good, and though she had not yet developed the feminine contours, the framework was present for an excellent enhancement. Give her two years, maybe three, and she might rival Millie the maid. With a different talent, of course.

"Well?" she said, with the sharpness of nervousness.

"May I come in?"

"You sure did yesterday. Want to play house again?"

"No." Dor entered and closed the door quietly behind him as she retreated. How to proceed? Obviously she had strong reactions and was wary of him without actually being frightened. She had potted plants all around the room, and one was a miniature tangler: she had no need to fear anyone! She hadn't told her father yet; he had, in the course of locating her, determined that she had not been near the library in the past day.

Irene was a palace brat whose talent fell well short of Magician caliber. No one would ever call her Sorceress. She had a sharp tongue and some obnoxious mannerisms. Yet, Dor reminded himself again, she was a person. He had always held her in a certain contempt because her talent was substantially beneath his own—but so was Millie's. Magic was important, certainly, and in some situations critical—but in other situations it hardly mattered. The Zombie Master had recognized that.

Now Dor felt ashamed, not for what his body might have done yesterday, but for what he, Dor, had done a month ago, and a year ago. Stepping on the feelings of another person. It did not matter that he had not done it maliciously; as a full Magician, in line to inherit the crown of Xanth, he should have recognized the natural resentment and frustration of those who lacked his opportunities. Like Irene, daughter of two of the three top talents in the older generation, doomed to the status of a nonentity because she had only ordinary magic. And was female. How would he feel in such a circumstance? How had his father Bink felt, as a child of no apparent magic?

"Irene, I—I guess I've come to apologize." He remembered how freely King Roogna had apologized to the Zombie Master, though the problem had only deviously been the fault of the King. Royalty had no need to be above humility! "I had no right to do what I did, and I'm sorry. It won't happen again."

She looked at him quizzically. "You're talking about yesterday?"

"I'm talking about my whole life!" he flared. "I—I have strong magic, yes. But I was born with it; it's an accident of fate, no personal credit to me. You have magic yourself, good magic, better than average. I make dead things talk; you make live things grow. There are situations in which your talent is far more useful than mine. I . . . looked down on you, and that was wrong. I can't blame you for reacting negatively; I would do the same. In fact you fought back with more spunk than I ever did. You're a person, Irene. A child, as I am, but still a human being who deserves respect. Yesterday—" He stalled, for he had no clear idea what the Coral had done. He should have gotten the specifics from Grundy. He spread his hands. "I'm sorry, and I apologize, and—"

She raised a finger in a little mannerism she had, silencing him. "You're taking back yesterday?"

Dor couldn't help thinking of his own yesterday, piping goblins and harpies after him with the magic flute, swinging on spider silk inside the Gap, detonating the forget spell that still polluted the Gap, hauling corpses from battlefield to laboratory to make zombies—unparalleled adventure, now forever past. Yesterday was eight hundred years ago. "I can't take back yesterday. It's part of my life, now. But—"

"Listen, you think I'm some naïve twit who doesn't know what's what?"

"No, Irene. I was the naïve one. I—"

"You claim you didn't know what you were doing?"

Dor sighed. How true that statement was! "I really can't make excuses. I'll take my medicine. You have a right to be angry. If you want to tell your father—"

"Father, hell!" she snapped. "I'll take care of this myself! I'll give back exactly what you gave me!"

Dor was not reassured. "As you wish. It is your right."

"Close your eyes and stand still."

She was going to hit him. Dor knew it. But it seemed he had it coming. He had let the Brain Coral use his body; he was responsible. He closed his eyes and stood still, forcing his hands to hang loose at his sides, undefensively. Maybe this was the best way to settle it.

He heard her step close, almost felt the movement of her body. She was raising her arm. He hoped she wouldn't hit him low. Better on the chest or face, though it marked him.

It was on the mouth. But strangely soft. In fact—

In fact, she was kissing him!

Totally surprised, Dor found himself putting his arms around her, partly for balance, mostly because that was what one was supposed to do when kissed by a girl. He felt her body yield to him, her hair shifting with the motion. She smelled and tasted and felt pleasant.

Then she drew back a little within his embrace and looked at him. "What do you think of that?" she asked.

"If you intended that to be punishment, it didn't work," he said. "You're sort of nice to kiss."

"So are you," she said. "You surprised me yesterday. I thought you were going to hit me or yank off my panties or something, and I was all set to scream, and it was all awkward and bumpy, noses colliding and stuff. So I practiced last night on my big doll. Was it better this time?"

A kiss? That was what they had done yesterday? Dor's knees felt weak! Trust Grundy the golem to blow it up into something gossipy! "There's no comparison!"

"Should I take off my clothes now?"

Dor froze, chagrined. "Uh—"

She laughed. "I thought that would faze you! If I wouldn't do it yesterday, what makes you think I'd do it today?"

"Nothing," Dor said, relaxing with a shuddering breath. He had seen naked nymphs galore, in the tapestry, but this was real. "Nothing at all. Nothing absolutely at all."

"You want to know what yesterday was?" she demanded. "It was the first time you really got interested in me, for anything. The first time *anybody* got interested in me who didn't want a plant grown fast, instead of calling me a palace brat who should have been a sorceress but could only grow stupid green stuff. Do you have any idea what it's like having two Magician-caliber parents and being a big disappointment to them because not only are you a girl, you have lousy talent?"

"You have good talent!" Dor protested. "And there's nothing wrong with being a girl!"

"Oh sure, sure," she countered. "You never had no talent. You never were not male. You never had people being polite to your face because of who your father was and what your mother might do to them, while they cut you down behind your back and called you skunk cabbage and garden-variety talent and weed girl and—"

"I never called you that!" Dor cried.

"Not in so many words. But you thought it, didn't you?"

Dor blushed, unable to deny it. "I . . . won't think it again," he promised lamely.

"And on top of that," she continued grimly, "you know your own parents only stand up for you because they have to, but privately they think just the same as all other people do—"

"Not the King," Dor protested. "He's not that type—"

"Shut up!" she flared, her eyes filling with angry tears. Dor did, and she composed herself. Girls of any age were good at quick composures. "So then yesterday you were different. You kept asking questions, and you paid real attention, just as if you didn't have a sexpot like Millie the ghost in your cheesy house to sneak peeks at and get the whole story, and you didn't say a word about magic, or make anything talk, or anything. It was just you and me. All you wanted to know was what it was like being a girl. It was as if something else were speaking, something awful smart and ignorant, wanting to learn from me. First I thought you were poking fun at me, teasing me—but you never smiled. Then you wanted to kiss me, and I thought, *Now he's going to bite my lip or pinch me and fall over laughing,* but you didn't laugh. So I kissed you, and it was awful, I bruised my nose, what the hell, I thought at least you'd know how but you didn't, and you just said, 'Thank you, Princess,' and left, and I lay on my bed a long time trying to figure out where the joke was, what you were telling the boys—"

"I didn't—" Dor protested.

"I know. I snooped. Some. You didn't say anything, and neither did the golem. So it seemed you really were interested in me, and—" She smiled, and she looked brilliantly sweet when she did that. "And it was the greatest experience of my whole life! You're a real Magician, and—"

"No, that has nothing to do with—"

"So I practiced kissing, just in case. Then you came in just now apologizing, as if it were something dirty. So I thought you hadn't meant it, had just been slumming, and—"

"No!" Dor cried in sudden anguish. "That wasn't it at all!"

"I know that now. Can't blame me for wondering, though." She smiled again. "Listen, Dor, I know tomorrow it'll be just like before, and I'll be a snotty palace brat to you, but—would you kiss me again?"

Dor felt deeply complimented. "Gladly, Irene." He bent to kiss her again. He was young yet, and so was she, but it was a foretaste of what they might experience when they both grew up.

"Maybe again, sometime?" she inquired wistfully. "I sort of like being a girl, now."

"Sometime," he agreed. "But we've got to fight some, too, or the others will tease us. We're still too young—" But not very much too young, he thought. He could see the road ahead rather clearly now, after his tapestry experience.

"I know." They broke, and there seemed to be nothing more to say, so Dor went to the door and opened it. He paused to look back at her, remembering what she had said about her parents being disappointed in her. She was sitting on her bed, bathed in a forlorn joy.

"Not the King," he repeated quietly. "I believe that."

Irene smiled. "No, not the King."

"And not me."

"Same thing," she said.

He stepped out and closed the door, knowing he wasn't through with her. Not today or tomorrow, or for some time to come. Not through at all.

Grundy was waiting for him. "Any black eyes? Broken teeth? Throttle marks? It was awful quiet in there."

"She's a nice girl," Dor said, walking toward the library. "Funny I never noticed that before."

"Brother!" the golem expostulated. "First he notices Millie the ghost, then Irene the brat. What's he coming to?"

Maturity, Dor thought. He was growing up, and new horizons were opening, and he was glad.

They arrived at the library. "Come in," King Trent called before Dor could knock.

Dor entered and took the seat indicated. "Remember how you sent me on a quest, Your Majesty? I have returned."

The King held up one hand, palm out. Dor thought of Jumper's mode of greeting. "Let me not deceive you, Dor. Humfrey advised me, and I could not resist watching the tapestry. I have a fair notion what you have been doing."

"You mean the tapestry showed *me*—what I was doing while I was doing it?"

"Certainly, once I knew which character to watch. You and that spider— you're lucky you didn't kill yourself in the Gap! But there was no way for me to revoke the spell before its natural span expired. I sweated to think of what I would have to say to your father, if—"

Dor laughed convulsively. "And I was worried about Irene's father!"

King Trent smiled. "Dor, I really don't like to snoop around the palace, but the Queen does. She quickly noticed the change in you, saw that you never used your talent, and found out about the Brain Coral. Her picture hangs in Irene's room; the Queen merely substituted her own illusion image for the picture and had what they call in Mundania a ringside seat. She watched everything yesterday—and today. And advised me, just now."

Dor shrugged. "I stand by what I did. Both days."

"I know you do, Dor. You're coming onto manhood nicely. Do not assume the Queen is your enemy. She wants her daughter to follow her, and knows what is required though she may resent it strongly. I am aware how ticklish the situation in the bedroom was. You handled it with the finesse I would expect in a leader."

'That wasn't finesse! I meant every word!"

"Finesse and meaning are not mutually incompatible."

"Irene's not bad at all, once you get to know her! She—" Dor stopped, embarrassed. "What am I doing, telling you this? You're her father!"

The King clapped a friendly hand on Dor's shoulder. "You have pleased me, Magician. Now through your adventure, I know the secret of the flute and the hoop in the Royal arsenal; they could be extremely useful on occasion. I shall not keep you from the completion of your quest. You must wrap it up, for there will be assignments for you in today's world, as you learn to govern Xanth." He walked to a low bookshelf and brought out a rolled rug. "We saved this for your convenience." It was the magic carpet.

"Uh, thanks, Your Majesty. I do have some traveling to do."

Dor mounted the rug. "Brain Coral," he told it, and it took off.

As the carpet ascended the sky and the landscape of modern Xanth opened out like a tapestry, Dor felt abrupt nostalgia for the tapestry world he had left. It was not that that world was superior to his own; its magic was generally cruder, its politics more violent. It was his experience of manhood and friendship, especially with Jumper. He knew he would never be able to recover the personal magic of that experience. Yet, as his session with Irene had shown, there was unexpected magic in this world too. All he had to do was appreciate it.

Down into the underworld, through the cavern passages. Goblins still reigned here, he knew, though they had almost disappeared on the surface of Xanth. What had happened to them? They had not all been slaughtered at the battle of Castle Roogna, and the forget spell would not have wiped them out. Had there been some later goblin calamity?

Then he was at the subterranean lake. Modern transport was certainly an improvement over ancient; this had hardly taken any time at all.

No Goblin calamity, the Brain Coral thought to him. *The harpy curse on the goblin populace was nullified on the surface, but lingered in the depths. Therefore the goblins above became, generation by generation, more intelligent, handsome, and noble, until they were no longer recognizable as monsters. The only true goblins today are those of the caverns.*

"Then I wiped out their species!" Dor exclaimed. "In a way I never anticipated!"

Their species, as you knew it, was a horrendous distortion, a burden to themselves as much as to others. They cared so little for themselves they were glad to die in goblin-sea tactics when storming a castle. You did well in releasing them from their curse, and in restoring the male of the species to the harpies.

"About that," Dor said. "You gave up Prince Harold Harpy as a favor to me, and now I have come to return the favor, as I said I would."

No need, Magician. When you came two weeks ago, I did not make the connection. After all, you wore a different body when I first met you, eight centuries ago. But in the past two weeks I worked it out. You returned that favor eight hundred years ago.

"No, I came back here to my own time. So—"

You brought victory to King Roogna. Therefore his rival Magician Murphy retired from politics, preferring to wait until some better situation arose. He came to me.

"Murphy was exiled?" Dor asked, startled.

It was voluntary. King Roogna would have liked to have his company, but Murphy was restless. He is in my storage now. Perhaps one century I will release him, when Xanth has need of his talent. Now, in exchange for the harpy Prince, I have Murphy and Vadne, who may one day make a fine pair. You owe me nothing.

"I, uh, guess so, if you see it that way," Dor said. "Still—"

If ever you choose to travel from your body again, keep me in mind, the Coral thought. *I learned a great deal about life, though I do not yet properly comprehend the sexual nature of Man.*

"No one does," Dor said, smiling.

I do not experience emotion. But in your body I did. I liked the little Princess.

"She is likable," Dor agreed. "Uh, look—I promised to have the access hoop shrunk back to ring size, but—"

Forgiven. Farewell, Magician.

"Farewell, Coral." The rug took off and zoomed back through the cavernly passages. When it emerged into the sky it hesitated, until Dor remembered that he had not told it where to go next. "Good Magician Humfrey's castle."

Dor was reminded again that Humfrey's castle stood where the Zombie Master's castle had once been. The two were of different designs; probably the site had been razed more than once, and rebuilt.

Humfrey was as usual poring over a massive tome, paying no attention to what went on around him—supposedly. "What, you again?" he demanded irritably.

"Listen, gnome—" Grundy began.

The Good Magician smiled—a rare thing for him. "Why listen, when I can read? Observe." And he gestured them to look at the book, over his shoulder.

"But I'm not a killer!" Dor protested vehemently. I'm only a twelve-year-old—" He caught himself, but didn't know how to correct his slip.

"A twelve-year veteran of warfare!" she exclaimed. "Surely you have killed before!"

It was grossly misplaced, but her sympathy gratified him strongly. His tired body reacted; his left arm reached out to enclose her hips in its embrace, as she stood beside him. He squeezed her against his side. Oh, her posterior was resilient!

"Why, Dor!" she said, surprised and pleased. "You like me!"

Dor forced himself to drop his arm. What business did he have, touching her? Especially in the vicinity of her cushiony posterior! "More than I can say."

"I like you too, Dor." She sat down in his lap, her derrière twice as soft and bouncy as before. Again his body reacted, enfolding her in an arm. Dor had never before experienced such sensation. Suddenly he was aware that his body knew what to do, if only he let it. That she was willing. That it could be an experience like none he had imagined in his young life. He was twelve; his body was older. *It could do it.*

"Oh, Dor," she murmured, bending her head to kiss him on the mouth. Her lips were so sweet he—

The flea chomped him hard on the left ear. Dor bashed at it—and boxed his ear. The pain was brief but intense.

He stood up, dumping Millie roughly to her feet. "I have to get some rest," he said.

She made no further sound, but only stood there, eyes downcast. He knew he had hurt her terribly. She had committed the cardinal maidenly sin of being forward, and been rebuked. But what could he do? *He did not exist in her world.* He would soon depart, leaving her alone for eight hundred years, and when they rejoined he would be twelve years old again. He had no right!

But oh, what might have been, were he more of a man.

Dor found himself blushing. "That's—you mean that book records everything, even my private feelings?" Yet obviously it did.

"We were not about to let a future King of Xanth go unmonitored," Humfrey remarked. "Especially when our own history was involved. Not that we could do anything about it, once the tapestry spell was cast. Still, as vicarious experience—"

"Was it valid?" Dor asked. "I mean, did I really change history?"

"That is a question that may never be answered to absolute satisfaction. I would say you did, and you did not."

"A typically gnomish answer," Grundy said.

"One must consider the framework of Xanth history," the Good Magician continued. "A series of Waves of Mundane conquest, with the population decimated again and again. If every person lived and reproduced without a break, any interruption in that process would eliminate many of today's residents. All the descendants of that person. But if a subsequent Wave wiped them out anyway—" He shrugged. "There could be considerable change, all nullified a generation or two later. In which case there would be no paradox relating to our own time. I would say that the original Castle Roogna engagement was real, and that you changed that reality. You rewrote the script. But you changed only the details of that particular episode, not the overall course of history. Does it matter?"

"I guess not," Dor said.

"About that page I was reading," Humfrey said. "It seems you have been concerned about manhood. Did it occur to you that you might be more of a man in the declining of the maid's offer than in the acceptance of it?"

"No," Dor admitted.

"There is somewhat more to manhood than sex."

As if on cue, the gorgon entered the room, in a splendidly sexy dress but still without a face. "That's male propaganda," she said from the vacuum. "There is certainly more to womanhood than sex, but a man is a simpler organism."

"Oooo, what you said!" Grundy exclaimed, rubbing his tiny forefingers together in a condemning gesture.

"I said organism," she said. "You authenticate my case."

"Get out of here, both of you," Humfrey snapped. "The Magician and I are trying to hold a meaningful dialogue."

"Thought you'd never ask," Grundy said. He hopped to the gorgon's shoulder, peering into the nothingness framed by her snake-ringlets. A snakelet hissed at him. "Same to you, slinky," he snapped at it, and the snake retreated. He peered down into the awesome crevice of her bodice. "Come on, honey; let's go down to the kitchen for a snack."

When they were alone, Humfrey flipped a few pages of the history tome idly. "I was surprised to learn that the Zombie Master's castle was on this very site," he remarked. "Were he alive today, I would gladly share this castle with him. He was a remarkably fine Magician, and a fine man, too."

"Yes," Dor agreed. "He was the real key to King Roogna's success. He deserved so much better than the tragedy he suffered." He felt another surge of remorse.

Humfrey sighed. "What has been, has been."

"Uh, have you given the gorgon your Answer yet?"

"Not yet. Her year is not yet complete."

"You are the most mercenary creature I know!" Dor said admiringly. "Every time I think I've seen the ultimate, you come up with a worse wrinkle. *Are* you going to marry her?"

"What do you think?"

Dor visualized the gorgon's body with historical perspective. "She's a knockout. If she wants you, you're sunk. She doesn't need a face to turn a man to stone. In a manner of speaking."

The Good Magician nodded. "You have learned a new manner of speaking! The key concept is 'she wants.' Do you really think she does?"

"Why else did she come here?" Dor demanded, perplexed.

"Her original motive was based largely on ignorance. How do you think she might feel once she knows me well?"

"Uh—" Dor searched for something diplomatic to say. The Good Magician had his points, but was no easy man to approach, or to get along with.

"Therefore the kindest thing to do is to give her sufficient opportunity to know me—well enough," the Magician concluded.

"The year!" Dor exclaimed. "That wait for her Answer! Not for you—for her! So she can change her mind, if—"

"Precisely." Humfrey looked sad. "It has been a most enticing dream, however, even for an old gnome."

Dor nodded, realizing that the Good Magician had not been proof against the attractions of the gorgon any more than the lonely Zombie Master had been proof against Millie. The two Magicians were similar in their fashion—and a similar tragedy loomed.

"Now we must conclude your case," Humfrey said briskly, refusing to dwell further on the inevitable. "You owe me no further service, of course; the history book has provided it all, and I consider the investment well worthwhile. I have now fathomed many long-standing riddles, such as the origin of the forget spell on the Gap. So I may send you on your way, your account quit."

"Thank you," Dor said. "I have brought back your magic carpet."

"Oh, yes. But I shall not leave you stranded. I believe I have a conjuration spell stashed away somewhere; have the gorgon locate it for you as you leave. It will take you home in a flash."

"Thank you." It was a relief not to have to contemplate another trek through the jungle. "Now I must go give the restorative elixir to Jonathan."

The Good Magician frowned at him. "You have had an especially difficult decision there, Dor. I believe you have acted correctly. When you become King, the discipline of emotion and action you have learned in the course of this quest will serve you in excellent stead. It may be more of an asset to you than your magic talent. King Trent's hiatus in Mundania matured him similarly. It seems there are qualities that cannot be inculcated well in a secure, familiar environment. You are already more of a man than most people ever get to be."

"Uh, thanks," Dor mumbled. He had yet to master the art of graciously receiving compliments. But the Magician had already returned to reading his tome.

Dor moved toward the door. Just as he left the room, Humfrey remarked without looking up: "You rather remind me of your father."

Suddenly Dor felt very good.

Grundy and the gorgon were sharing a scream soda in the kitchen; Dor heard the noise from several rooms away. They were using straws; hers poked into her nothing face, where the soda disappeared. She had a face, all right; it just could not be seen. Dor wondered what it would be like to kiss her. In the dark she would seem entirely normal. Except for those little snakes.

"I need the conjuration spell," Dor said. "The one that flashes."

The screams faded as she left the soda. "I know exactly where it is. I have every spell classified and properly filed. First time there's been order in this castle in a century." She reached for an upper shelf, her figure elongating enticingly. What a woman she would be, if only she had a visible face! But no, that would be ruinous; her face petrified men, literally.

"There," she said, bringing down an object that looked like a closed tube. It had a lens on one end, and a switch on the side. "You just push the switch forward, there, when you're ready."

"I'm ready now. I want to go to the tapestry room in Castle Roogna. Are you coming, Grundy?"

"One moment." The golem sucked in the last scream from the soda—no more than a whimper, actually—and crossed the room.

"Do you really want to marry the Good Magician —now that you know him?" Dor asked the gorgon curiously.

"What would he do for socks and spells, without me?" she retorted. "This castle needs a woman."

"Uh, yes. All castles do. But—"

"What kind of a man would give a pretty girl board and room for a year, never touching her, just to think it over, knowing she probably would change her mind in that period?"

"A good man. A patient one. A serious one." Then Dor nodded, understanding the thrust of her question. "One worth marrying."

"I thought I wanted him, when I came here. Now I am sure of it. Under all that grouch is a remarkably fine Magician, and a fine man, too."

Almost exactly the words Humfrey had used to describe the Zombie Master! But it seemed that tragedy was about to bypass the gnome, after all. Parallels went only so far. "I wish you every happiness."

"Would you believe there are three happiness spells on that shelf?" She winked. "And a potency spell too—but he won't need that, I suspect."

Dor eyed her once again with the memory of his erstwhile Mundane barbarian body. "Right," he agreed.

"Actually, all he needs for happiness is a good cheap historical adventure tome, like that one he's reading now, about ancient Xanth. I'm going to read it too, as soon as he finishes. I understand it has lots of sex and sorcery and a really stupid barbarian hero—"

Hastily, Dor pushed the switch. The spell flashed—and he stood before the tapestry. "Savior of Xanth," he said, feeling foolish, and his vial of restorative elixir popped out from whatever invisible place it had lain for eight hundred years. He had to catch it before it could shatter on the floor, but he lacked the muscle and reflexes his Mundane body had had, and missed. The vial plummeted—

And jerked short on an invisible thread, and swung there, undamaged. A silken dragline had been attached to it. "Not this time, Murphy!" Dor cried as he nabbed it. He looked for his friend Jumper, who had surely rescued him again in this fashion, but did not see him.

Now, with the object of his quest in hand, he wondered: how could an object be spelled into a tapestry-within-a-tapestry—how could it emerge from the main tapestry? Or were the two tapestries the same? They had to be, because—yet they couldn't be, because—He seemed to be skirting paradox here, but couldn't quite grasp it. Anyway, he had the elixir. Best not to question too deeply; he might not like the answer.

Yet he lingered, watching the tapestry. He saw Castle Roogna, with its returning personnel cleaning out the last of the debris of battle and doing preparatory work for the zombie graveyard beyond the moat—the graveyard those zombies still resided in today. They had protected the Castle well, all these centuries, but now it was in no danger, so they lay quietly out of sight. Except for Jonathan, the strange exception. It seemed there were personality differences among zombies, just as there were in people. "One in every crowd," he murmured.

His eye focused on the spot he had vacated. He and Jumper had been trying to get as close to the place they had entered the Fourth Wave world as possible. They had cut into the jungle—and the jungle had tried to cut into them, when they encountered that saw grass—navigated the Gap with the use of silk lines for descent and ascent—fortunately the Gap dragon had been elsewhere at the time, perhaps suffering from the forget spell—and forged into northern Xanth. As they drew near the spot, their presence seemed to activate the spell, and it had reverted.

There, near that place, was the Mundane giant. He had no huge spider now as companion. He had wandered to a stockaded hut, begging a place to stay the night. He faced the mistress of the hut, an attractive young woman. As Dor watched, the tiny figures animated.

"What are they saying?" Dor asked Grundy.

"I thought you said you needed no translation!"

"Grundy—"

The golem hastily translated: "I am a barbarian, recently disenchanted. I was transformed, or driven, into the body of a flea, while an alien shade governed my body."

"The flea!" Dor exclaimed. "The one that hid in my hair and kept biting me! That was the Mundane!"

"Shut up while I'm translating," Grundy said. "This lip reading is hard." He resumed: "That creature did its best to destroy me, yanking me across the Gap on a rope, throwing me among zombies, thrusting me single-handed against an army of monsters—"

"Now that's a distortion!" Dor cried indignantly.

"And that awful giant spider!" the translation continued. "I lived in daily fear it would discover my flea body and—" The barbarian shuddered. "Now at last I have fought free. But I am tired and hungry. May I stay the night?"

The woman looked him over. "For a story like that you can stay three nights! Know any more?"

"Many more," the barbarian said humbly.

"Nobody who can lie like that can be all bad."

"Right," he agreed abjectly.

She smiled. "I am a widow. My husband was roasted by a dragon. I need a man to run the farm—a strong, patient man, not too bright, willing to settle for . . ." She spread her hands and half-turned, inhaling.

The barbarian noted her inhalation. It was a good one, the kind barbarians normally paid attention to. He smiled. "Well, I'm not too patient."

"That's close enough," the woman said.

Dor turned away, satisfied. His erstwhile Mundane body would be as happy as he deserved to be.

Something about this scenelet reminded Dor of Cedric the centaur. How was he making out with Celeste, the naughty filly? But Dor restrained himself from peeking; it really was not his business, any more.

Something caught his eye. He focused on the corner of the tapestry. There was tiny Jumper, waving. There was another little spider beside him. "You've found a friend!" Dor exclaimed.

"That's no friend, that's his mate," Grundy said. "She wants to know where he was, those five years he was gone. So when the popping-out of the elixir vial alerted him to your presence, he brought her out here to meet you."

"Tell her it's true, all true," Dor said. Then: "Five *years?*"

"Two weeks, your time. It only seemed like two weeks to him, too. But back at his home—"

"Ah, I understand." Dor exchanged amenities with the skeptical Mrs. Jumper, bade his friend farewell again, promised to return next day-month or so, and strode from the room feeling better.

"You move with a new assurance," Grundy remarked. He seemed sad. "You won't be needing me much longer."

"Penalty of growing up," Dor said. "One year I'll get married, and you can bodyguard my son, exactly as you have me."

"Gee," the golem said, flattered.

They departed the Castle, going to Dor's cheese cottage. He felt increasing apprehension and nostalgia as he approached his home. His parents should still be away on their Mundane mission; only Millie would be there. Millie the maid, Millie the ghost, Millie the nurse. What had the Brain Coral animating his body said to her? What should he say to her now? Did she have any notion what he had been doing the past two weeks?

Dor steeled himself and went inside. He didn't knock; it was his own cottage, after all. He was just the lad Millie took care of; she did not know—must never know—that he had been the Magician who looked like a Mundane warrior, way back when.

"Say," Grundy inquired as they passed through the familiar-unfamiliar house toward the kitchen. "What name did you use, in the tapestry?"

"My own name, of course. My name and talent—"

Oh, no! The most certain identifiers of any person in the Land of Xanth were name and talent. He had thoughtlessly given himself away!

"Is that you, Dor?" Millie called musically from the kitchen. Too late to escape!

"Uh, yes." No help for it but to see if she recognized him. Oh, those twelve-year-old-boy mistakes! "Uh, just talking to a wall." He snapped his fingers at the nearest wall. "Say something, wall!"

"Something," the wall said obligingly.

She came to the kitchen doorway, and she was stunningly beautiful, twelve years older than she had been so recently, but almost regal in her abrupt maturity. Now she had poise, elegance, stature. She had aged, as it were overnight, more than a decade, while Dor had lost a similar amount. A gulf had opened between them, a gulf of age and time, huge as the Gap.

He loved her yet.

"Why, you haven't talked to the walls in two weeks," Millie said. Dor knew this had to be true: the Coral had animated his body, but had lacked his special magical talent.

"Is something wrong?" Millie asked. "Why are you staring at me?"

Dor forced his fixed eyes down. "I—" What could he say? "I—seem to remember you from somewhere."

She laughed with the echo of the sweetness and innocence he had known and loved in the tapestry maid. "From this morning, Dor, when I served you breakfast!"

But now he would not be put off. The thing he most feared was recognition; he had to face it now. "Millie—when you were young—before you were a ghost —did you have friends?"

She laughed again, and this time he noticed the fullness and rondure of her body as it laughed with her. "Of course I had friends!"

"Who were they? You never told me." His heart was beating hard.

She frowned. "You're serious, aren't you? But I can't tell you.. There was a forget spell detonated in the vicinity, and as a ghost I was near it a long time. I don't remember my friends."

The forget spell! It had made her forget . . . him. Yet he tried, perversely, driven by an urge he refused to define. "How—did you die?"

"Someone enchanted me. Turned me into a book—"

A book! The book he had found in the dumbwaiter leading from the female room. Vadne must have transformed her into it, then hoisted that tome to the upper floor, and no one had caught on. A stupid mistake, courtesy of Murphy's curse. He himself had placed it on the shelf in the library—where it had remained eight hundred years, unmolested.

"I couldn't even remember what my body was, or where," Millie continued. "Or maybe a spell was on that too. So much was vague, especially at first—and then I was a ghost, and it was easier not to think about it. Ghosts don't have very solid minds." She paused, studying Dor. "But sometimes there are flashes. Your father reminded me of someone—someone I think I loved—but I can't quite remember. Anyway, he's eight hundred years dead, now, and there is Jonathan. I've known Jonathan for centuries, and he's awful nice. When I was alone and lonely and confused, especially after King Roogna died and the Castle fell into oblivion—he had a long and good reign, but it had to end sometime—Jonathan came and helped me to hold on. He didn't seem to mind that I was only a ghost. If only—"

So she had loved Dor—and forgotten, in the ambience of the forget spell. His name and talent—no giveaway after all. Nothing in his birth and youth in this world had alerted her, since she had never known the origin of that bygone hero, and she could hardly be expected to make the connection.

Only Jonathan had been her comfort across the centuries. She had not forgotten Jonathan, because he had always been there. A ghost and a restless zombie, bolstering each other when the rest of the world had forgotten them. Why torture her by restoring her memory of prior heartache? Dor knew what he had to do.

"Millie, I have obtained the elixir to restore Jonathan to life." He held up the vial.

She stared at him, unbelieving. "Dor—now I remember something. Your father—he reminded me of you. Not in appearance, but in—"

"I wasn't born yet!" Dor said harshly, repenting his recent urge to have her remember exactly this. "You've got it backward. I remind you of my father—because I am growing up."

"Yes, yes of course," she agreed uncertainly. "Only somehow—your talent of —I remember talking to pearls in a big nest, or something—"

"Take the elixir," he said, presenting it to her. "Call Jonathan." *Oh, Jonathan,* he thought in momentary agony. *Do you know you fill the shoes of her lover, and of her betrothed? Be good to her, for the sake of what was never allowed to be!*

Millie was too distracted to take the vial. "I—still, there is something. A big barbarian named—"

"Jonathan!" Dor bellowed as well as his present body permitted. "Come here!"

The door opened, for Jonathan was always near Millie. The loyalty of centuries! He shuffled into the kitchen, dripping the usual clods of dirt and mold. No matter how much fell, a zombie always had more; it was part of the enchantment. His body was skeletal, his eyes rotten sockets, and the nauseating odor of putrefaction was about him.

"Yet I know now that was only passing fascination," Millie continued. "The barbarian left me, while Jonathan stayed."

Dor tore open the corked vial. "Take this!" he cried, hurling the precious drops onto the zombie.

Immediately the body began to heal. Flesh was magically restored, tissues filled out, skin formed and cleared. The figure unhunched, became fuller, taller.

"And so my true love is Jonathan," Millie concluded. Then she looked up, realizing what transformation was taking place, and her hair flung out as of old. "Jonathan!" she screamed.

Rapidly the last of the zombie attributes disappeared. The figure shaped into a gaunt but healthy living man.

"The Zombie Master!" Dor exclaimed, recognizing him at last. "I never knew your given name!"

Then he stepped back out of the way, letting true love assume its rightful place. Jonathan and Millie came together, she with a little skip-kicking of feet, and Dor knew his quest was done.

About the Author

PIERS ANTHONY, a native of Oxford, England, is one of fantasy's most popular authors. His first novel was published in 1963, and he is now the author of 119 books to date. His first Xanth novel, *A Spell for Chameleon,* won the August Derleth Fantasy Award as the best novel for 1977, and his fantasy novels began placing on the *New York Times* bestseller list with *Ogre, Ogre* and have continued since. Anthony, who's on his twenty-sixth Xanth novel, currently lives in Florida with his wife and two daughters.